THE PARASOL PROTECTORATE

THE PARASOL PROTECTORATE

SOULLESS, CHANGELESS, BLAMELESS

GAIL CARRIGER

FANTASY

SOULLESS   Copyright © 2009 by Tofa Borregaard
    Publication History: Orbit mass market, October 2009
CHANGELESS   Copyright © 2010 by Tofa Borregaard
    Publication History: Orbit mass market, April 2010
BLAMELESS   Copyright © 2010 by Tofa Borregaard
    Publication History: Orbit mass market, September 2010

First SFBC Fantasy Printing: September 2011

Published by arrangement with
Orbit
Hachette Book Group
237 Park Avenue
New York, NY 10017

Visit The SFBC online at http://www.sfbc.com

ISBN 978-1-61129-769-0

Printed in the United States of America.

An Introduction: In Which Gail Discusses Building the World of the Parasol Protectorate

The simple fact is, Gentle Reader, this was the series I wanted to read. I like steampunk but it tends to be a little too dark and riddled with technobabble for me. I enjoy urban fantasy but I am not particularly wild about a modern setting. So I thought I might just combine the two, and then shake it up with a jot more romance and a whole lot of humor.

I began by thinking about what kind of world could accommodate all these different elements: the monsters of urban fantasy, the gadgets of steampunk, the humor of comedies of manners, the romance of the Gothics. I'm familiar with the Victorian era and I find it a rich source of amusement in and of itself. It is a period of time, both in literature and fashion, that has always stolen away my heart. I used to make hoopskirts out of my hula–hoops as a child. Those ridiculous fashions and that obsession with etiquette seemed the ideal time period into which to drop vampires (dictating such things) and werewolves (chaffing against them) not to mention steampunk technology. It seemed to me that what comedy I couldn't supply with plot and character, an alternate Victorian London could provide simply by being itself.

But I had another reason. I have long been troubled by certain quirks of history that seem never adequately explained. The most confusing of these is how one tiny island with abysmal taste in food, excellent taste in beverages, and a penchant for pouffy dresses suddenly managed to take over most of the known world. How did Britain conquer an empire upon which the sun never set? I decided that the only possible answer was that England openly accepted supernatural creatures, and put them to good use, while other countries continued persecution and abhorrence of vampires, werewolves, and ghosts. This led me to postulate that King Henry's breach with the Church was over open acceptance of supernatural creatures into society (the divorce thing was just a front). This gave Great Britain a leg up dealing with messy little situations like winning major foreign battles or establishing an efficient bureaucracy or convincing the world cricket is a good idea. Vampires could sit as members of the cabinet, advising the queen on matters of state and foreign policy. Werewolves could fight in the armies, making them stronger and better and mobile at night. Ghosts could be used as spies. Suddenly, everything previously confusing about the Victorian Era made sense: the British regimental system was clearly based on werewolf pack dynamics, and pale complexions are in vogue because everyone wants to look like the trendsetting vampires.

There was one last component that cinched the Victorian setting for me. Werewolves, vampires, and ghosts are all monsters with strong ties to the literature of that age. I've read a good deal of gothic literature over the years. These three monsters in particular strike me as quintessentially Victorian. So I decided to twist it around and explore a world where such supernatural creatures were accepted as part of society. I knew werewolf culture would be based on wolf pack dynamics and I wanted a similar animal organization structure for the vampires. I also wanted something that was predatory and opposite that of wolves: female dominant instead of male, and so forth. Give those strictures, bat colonies (the obvious option) wouldn't work, nor would most birds. Bee/wasp hive structures have always fascinated me so that seemed a natural choice.

So having decided on a setting and chosen my supernatural elements, I started idly toying with the idea of how a person might become undead. After all, if vampires and werewolves are bouncing about, what's to keep them from turning everyone supernatural? There must be biological procreative controls in place. Taking into account what I knew of Victorian scientific theory, I hypothesized that an excess of soul found in only a few people might account for bite–survival rates. In other words it was too much soul, rather than too little, that would allow someone to become immortal. Very few people would have this. And like an immunity to disease, it would be impossible for Victorian scientists to predict, when face-to-face with a normal mortal human, whether that person has excess soul or not. (With one exception, creative people seem to be more likely to have excess soul, but it's still unusual. This means vampires and werewolves are more likely to become patrons of the arts.) This, in turn, led me to investigate the measuring of the soul—which an American scientist actually tried to do in the late 1800s. Combine that with the fated Counterbalance Theorem and I had the idea that if some people had too much soul, there should be others who had too little, or none at all. And these people could act as nullifiers to supernatural abilities.

Thus Alexia was born.

Alexia Tarabotti turns supernatural creatures mortal when she touches them, which can be terribly embarrassing, not to say fatal, for said creatures. It also means that on several occasions certain baser elements of society are actively trying to kill her, without proper introductions—so rude. A side effect of her soulless state is that Alexia is very practical in her approach to such trifling inconveniences as death threats. She tends to cope with most problems by either bashing them over the head with her parasol, or talking at them, with equally disastrous results. Partly as a result of her soulless state but also because she has Italian heritage (and looks it) and she reads too much, Alexia starts out the series as a spinster. She is my favorite kind of character to write—practical to a fault, capable in a crisis, frustrating to the other characters around her, and all too often getting herself into impossible situations out of sheer nerve. It can be a little annoying trying to write myself out of the corner Alexia has gotten the plot into, but she is also rich in friends, so she has aide in times of dire need.

Because the biggest side effect of being soulless is pragmatism, Alexia is both typical and wildly atypical for a female of the Victorian era. The atypical aspects come from the fact that, being soulless, she simply sees the world differently. She also has absolutely no creative skill and very little imagination. However, because of her pragmatism she recognizes these flaws in herself and tends to surround herself with friends, intentionally or subconsciously, who compensate for her own inabilities. Alexia is not one of those heroines who charges forth, one woman against the machine. She seeks out advice, travels in company, and gets things done by committee. She's peculiar in that she always acts quite the proper English gentlewoman and isn't inclined to buck the system. Yet by her very nature she is driven to unconsciously subvert it.

Alexia's first name just came to me; I've always liked the name: Alexia. Her last name, Tarabotti, is actually an ode to the deliciously named early renaissance proto-feminist Archangelica Tarabotti. Archangelica wrote a monograph arguing against the church's assertion that women had no souls. Alexia Tarabotti has Italian heritage because of her name. That is to say, when I was coming up with the character and I discovered that name and combined it with a soulless state, everything else just followed after. I've had a love affair with Italy since I excavated there over a decade ago, so it was a natural choice for me. As to the nose and the skin, I knew she had to be atypical in appearance (and attitude and thought) so I could have her a spinster. Also, I don't like to write beautiful main characters, they're boring.

So, I had myself a main character and a set of supernatural elements that I was going to inject into Victorian society, now I wanted that steampunk element. I began constructing an alternative history that would allow for the rise and dominance of steam power. I knew I wanted all key historical events to stay in place. Most major wars and battles still exist in the Parasol Protectorate universe, but it is the reasons behind them are different. I don't write so much alt-history, as re-explained history. I also knew I wanted to take the same tactic with the most ridiculous aspects of Victorian fashion as well. High cravats? Hide the bite marks. Confining bustle-skirts and healed boots? Keeps your prey from moving too fast. I wanted any new technology I injected into my world to fraternize with the frivolous as well as the dangerous and exciting. True, the Victorians discovered aluminum, but what did they do with it? They made it into jewelry. In the world of the Parasol Protectorate there are major advancements in steam power. What do they do with that? Use it to mount tea kettles on dirigibles. They've invented air travel, but they use it to run tours over Hyde Park for the aristocracy.

I then began to imagine how these steampunk elements might fit organically into a supernatural Victorian London. It seemed to me that, if vampires, werewolves, and ghosts were running around Victorian London, scientists of the day would be trying to understand them, dissect them, fight them, and avoid them. That's simply the way scientists of the day behaved. This, in turn, would lead to new and strange advancements in science and medicine. In the world of the Parasol Protectorate, simply put, urban fantasy tropes have steampunk consequences. I didn't want magic in my world, but by making 19th century science true and working along with all the wild and crazy theories and hypothesis I get to play with a technology that is almost magical.

It also seems part of the British character to ignore or quietly condone things rather than make a fuss. Very different from us Americans. It is simply more Victorian to take a stance the equivalent of, "Ah yes, vampires, jolly good chaps, excellent fashion sense, always polite, terribly charming at cards, we just won't mention that little neck biting habit. And, my, they certainly do love to invest in those silly little Babbage Engines."

That said, I do try to stay as accurate to 1873 England as possible. Changes leak in as either alternate explanations for reality, or alternate inventions to deal with the non-reality I've injected. There are still hansom cabs roaming London but dirigibles rise to prominence as an alternate mode of long distance transport because vampires and werewolves cannot use them. Alternative guns have evolved utilizing silver and wood bullets. And, of course, the supernatural creatures themselves take a keen interest in promoting new technology and have the funds to do so. The path to world building consistency, for me, lay in letting my Victorians behave like Victorians, and react to my supernatural and steampunk elements as they probably would have, by coming up with wild theories and tests and gadgets.

And so the Parasol Protectorate was born, a world where vampires, werewolves, and ghosts have too much soul, and where one soulless spinster has the ability to cancel them all out, to make them mortal. A place where the monsters are not only part of society, they have their own private Gentleman's Clubs. A time of invention and creativity; of industry and change. In Alexia's London one may walk around a street corner and find oneself face-to-face with a wolf wearing a top hat, or a ghost with an important message, or a vampire who tisks at the state of your dress shoes. What, under such circumstances as these, becomes the real monster?

—GAIL CARRIGER
April, 2011

SOULLESS

The Parasol Protectorate: Book the First

Acknowledgments

Tremendous thanks to the ladies of the WCWC and their multicolored Pens of Doom: with criticism comes wisdom and, hopefully, tea. To Mum and Dad, who had the brilliant parental idea that good behavior be rewarded with trips to the bookshop. And to G and E: purveyors of fine feelings and patrons of the scribbling beast, however fiendish she may be.

CHAPTER ONE

In Which Parasols Prove Useful

Miss Alexia Tarabotti was not enjoying her evening. Private balls were never more than middling amusements for spinsters, and Miss Tarabotti was not the kind of spinster who could garner even that much pleasure from the event. To put the pudding in the puff: she had retreated to the library, her favorite sanctuary in any house, only to happen upon an unexpected vampire.

She glared at the vampire.

For his part, the vampire seemed to feel that their encounter had improved his ball experience immeasurably. For there she sat, without escort, in a low-necked ball gown.

In this particular case, what he did not know *could* hurt him. For Miss Alexia had been born without a soul, which, as any decent vampire of good blooding knew, made her a lady to avoid most assiduously.

Yet he moved toward her, darkly shimmering out of the library shadows with feeding fangs ready. However, the moment he touched Miss Tarabotti, he was suddenly no longer darkly doing anything at all. He was simply standing there, the faint sounds of a string quartet in the background as he foolishly fished about with his tongue for fangs unaccountably mislaid.

Miss Tarabotti was not in the least surprised; soullessness always neutralized supernatural abilities. She issued the vampire a very dour look. Certainly, most daylight folk wouldn't peg her as anything less than a standard English prig, but had this man not even bothered to *read* the vampire's official abnormality roster for London and its greater environs?

The vampire recovered his equanimity quickly enough. He reared away from Alexia, knocking over a nearby tea trolley. Physical contact broken, his fangs reappeared. Clearly not the sharpest of prongs, he then darted forward from the neck like a serpent, diving in for another chomp.

"I say!" said Alexia to the vampire. "We have not even been introduced!"

Miss Tarabotti had never actually had a vampire try to bite her. She knew one or two by reputation, of course, and was friendly with Lord Akeldama. *Who was not friendly with Lord Akeldama?* But no vampire had ever actually attempted to *feed* on her before!

So Alexia, who abhorred violence, was forced to grab the miscreant by his nostrils, a delicate and therefore painful area, and shove him away. He stumbled over the fallen tea trolley, lost his balance in a manner astonishingly graceless for a vampire, and fell to the floor. He landed right on top of a plate of treacle tart.

Miss Tarabotti was most distressed by this. She was particularly fond of treacle tart and had been looking forward to consuming that precise plateful. She picked up her parasol. It was terribly tasteless for her to be carrying a parasol at an evening ball, but Miss Tarabotti rarely went anywhere without it. It was of a style entirely of her own devising: a black frilly confection with purple satin pansies sewn about, brass hardware, and buckshot in its silver tip.

She whacked the vampire right on top of the head with it as he tried to extract himself from his newly intimate relations with the tea trolley. The buckshot gave the brass parasol just enough heft to make a deliciously satisfying *thunk*.

"Manners!" instructed Miss Tarabotti.

The vampire howled in pain and sat back down on the treacle tart.

Alexia followed up her advantage with a vicious prod between the vampire's legs. His howl went quite a bit higher in pitch, and he crumpled into a fetal position. While Miss Tarabotti was a proper English young lady, aside from not having a soul and being half Italian, she did spend quite a bit more time than most other young ladies riding and walking and was therefore unexpectedly strong.

Miss Tarabotti leaped forward—as much as one could leap in full triple-layered underskirts, draped bustle, and ruffled taffeta top-skirt—and bent over the vampire. He was clutching at his indelicate bits and writhing about. The pain would not last long given his supernatural healing ability, but it hurt most decidedly in the interim.

Alexia pulled a long wooden hair stick out of her elaborate coiffure. Blushing at her own temerity, she ripped open his shirtfront, which was cheap and overly starched, and poked at his chest, right over the heart. Miss Tarabotti sported a particularly large and sharp hair stick. With her free hand, she made certain to touch his chest, as only physical contact would nullify his supernatural abilities.

"Desist that horrible noise immediately," she instructed the creature.

The vampire quit his squealing and lay perfectly still. His beautiful blue eyes watered slightly as he stared fixedly at the wooden hair stick. Or, as Alexia liked to call it, hair *stake*.

"Explain yourself!" Miss Tarabotti demanded, increasing the pressure.

"A thousand apologies." The vampire looked confused. "Who are you?" Tentatively he reached for his fangs. Gone.

To make her position perfectly clear, Alexia stopped touching him (though she kept her sharp hair stick in place). His fangs grew back.

He gasped in amazement. "*What* are you? I thought you were a lady, alone. It would be my right to feed, if you were left this carelethly unattended. Pleathe, I did not mean to prethume," he lisped around his fangs, real panic in his eyes.

Alexia, finding it hard not to laugh at the lisp, said, "There is no cause for you to be so overly dramatic. Your hive queen will have told you of my kind." She returned her hand to his chest once more. The vampire's fangs retracted.

He looked at her as though she had suddenly sprouted whiskers and hissed at him.

Miss Tarabotti was surprised. Supernatural creatures, be they vampires, werewolves, or ghosts, owed their existence to an overabundance of soul, an excess that refused to die. Most knew that others like Miss Tarabotti existed, born without any soul at all. The estimable Bureau of Unnatural Registry (BUR), a division of Her Majesty's Civil Service, called her ilk *preternatural*. Alexia thought the term nicely dignified. What vampires called her was far less complimentary. After all, preternaturals had once hunted *them*, and vampires had long memories. Natural, daylight persons were kept in the dark, so to speak, but any vampire worth his blood should know a preternatural's touch. This one's ignorance was untenable. Alexia said, as though to a very small child, "I am a *preternatural*."

The vampire looked embarrassed. "Of course you are," he agreed, obviously still not quite comprehending. "Again, my apologies, lovely one. I am overwhelmed to meet you. You are my first"—he stumbled over the word—"preternatural." He frowned. "Not supernatural, not natural, of course! How foolish of me not to see the dichotomy." His eyes narrowed into craftiness. He was now studiously ignoring the hair stick and looking tenderly up into Alexia's face.

Miss Tarabotti knew full well her own feminine appeal. The kindest compliment her face could ever hope to garner was "exotic," never " 'lovely." Not that it had ever received either. Alexia figured that vampires, like all predators, were at their most charming when cornered.

The vampire's hands shot forward, going for her neck. Apparently, he had decided if he could not suck her blood, strangulation was an acceptable alternative. Alexia jerked back, at the same time pressing her hair stick into the creature's white flesh. It slid in about half an inch. The vampire reacted with a desperate wriggle that, even without superhuman strength, unbalanced Alexia in her heeled velvet dancing shoes. She fell back. He stood, roaring in pain, with her hair stick half in and half out of his chest.

Miss Tarabotti scrabbled for her parasol, rolling about inelegantly among the tea things, hoping her new dress would miss the fallen foodstuffs. She found the parasol and came upright, swinging it in a wide arc. Purely by chance, the heavy tip struck the end of her wooden hair stick, driving it straight into the vampire's heart.

The creature stood stock-still, a look of intense surprise on his handsome face. Then he fell backward onto the much-abused plate of treacle tart, flopping in a limp-overcooked-asparagus kind of way. His alabaster face turned a yellowish gray, as though he were afflicted with the jaundice, and he went still. Alexia's books called this end of the vampire life cycle *dissanimation*. Alexia, who thought the action astoundingly similar to a soufflé going flat, decided at that moment to call it the Grand Collapse.

She intended to waltz directly out of the library without anyone the wiser to her presence there. This would have resulted in the loss of her best hair stick and her well-deserved tea, as well as a good deal of drama. Unfortunately, a small group of young dandies came traipsing in at that precise moment. What young men of such dress were doing in a *library* was anyone's guess. Alexia felt the most likely explanation was that they had become lost while looking for the card room. Regardless, their presence forced her to pretend that she, too, had just discovered the dead vampire. With a resigned shrug, she screamed and collapsed into a faint.

She stayed resolutely fainted, despite the liberal application of smelling salts, which made her eyes water most tremendously, a cramp in the back of one knee, and the fact that her new ball gown was getting most awfully wrinkled. All its many layers of green trim, picked to the height of fashion in lightening shades to complement the cuirasse bodice, were being crushed into oblivion under her weight. The expected noises ensued: a good deal of yelling, much bustling about, and several loud clatters as one of the housemaids cleared away the fallen tea.

Then came the sound she had half anticipated, half dreaded. An authoritative voice cleared the library of both young dandies and all other interested parties who had flowed into the room upon discovery of the tableau. The voice instructed everyone to "get out!" while he "gained the particulars from the young lady" in tones that brooked no refusal.

Silence descended.

"Mark my words, I will use something much, much stronger than smelling salts," came a growl in Miss Tarabotti's left ear. The voice was low and tinged with a hint of Scotland. It would have caused Alexia to shiver and think primal monkey thoughts about moons and running far and fast, if she'd had a soul. Instead it caused her to sigh in exasperation and sit up.

"And a good evening to you, too, Lord Maccon. Lovely weather we are having for this time of year, is it not?" She patted at her hair, which was threatening to fall down without the hair stick in its proper place. Surreptitiously, she looked about for Lord Conall Maccon's second in command, Professor Lyall. Lord Maccon tended to maintain a much calmer temper when his Beta was present. But, then, as Alexia had come to comprehend, that appeared to be the main role of a Beta—especially one attached to Lord Maccon.

"Ah, Professor Lyall, how nice to see you again." She smiled in relief.

Professor Lyall, the Beta in question, was a slight, sandy-haired gentleman of indeterminate age and pleasant disposition, as agreeable, in fact, as his Alpha was sour. He grinned at her and doffed his hat, which was of first-class design and sensible material. His cravat was similarly subtle, for, while it was tied expertly, the knot was a humble one.

"Miss Tarabotti, how delicious to find ourselves in your company once more." His voice was soft and mild-mannered.

"Stop humoring her, Randolph," barked Lord Maccon. The fourth Earl of Woolsey was much larger than Professor Lyall and in possession of a near-permanent frown. Or at least he always seemed to be frowning when he was in the presence of Miss Alexia Tarabotti, ever since the hedgehog incident (which really, honestly, had not been her fault). He also had unreasonably pretty tawny eyes, mahogany-colored hair, and a particularly nice nose. The eyes were currently glaring at Alexia from a shockingly intimate distance.

"Why is it, Miss Tarabotti, every time I have to clean up a mess in a library, you just happen to be in the middle of it?" the earl demanded of her.

Alexia gave him a withering look and brushed down the front of her green taffeta gown, checking for bloodstains.

Lord Maccon appreciatively watched her do it. Miss Tarabotti might examine her face in the mirror each morning with a large degree of censure, but there was nothing at all wrong with her figure. He would have to have had far less soul and a good fewer urges not to notice that appetizing fact. Of course, she always went and spoiled the appeal by opening her mouth. In his humble experience, the world had yet to produce a more vexingly verbose female.

"Lovely but unnecessary," he said, indicating her efforts to brush away nonexistent blood drops.

Alexia reminded herself that Lord Maccon and his kind were only *just* civilized. One simply could not expect too much from them, especially under delicate circumstances such as these. Of course, that failed to explain Professor Lyall, who was always utterly urbane. She glanced with appreciation in the professor's direction.

Lord Maccon's frown intensified.

Miss Tarabotti considered that the lack of civilized behavior might be the sole provenance of Lord Maccon. Rumor had it, he had only lived in London a comparatively short while—and he had relocated from Scotland of all barbaric places.

The professor coughed delicately to get his Alpha's attention. The earl's yellow gaze focused on him with such intensity it should have actually burned. "Aye?"

Professor Lyall was crouched over the vampire, examining the hair stick with interest. He was poking about the wound, a spotless white lawn handkerchief wrapped around his hand.

"Very little mess, actually. Almost complete lack of blood spatter." He leaned forward and sniffed. "Definitely Westminster," he stated.

The Earl of Woolsey seemed to understand. He turned his piercing gaze onto the dead vampire. "He must have been very hungry."

Professor Lyall turned the body over. "What happened here?" He took out a small set of wooden tweezers from the pocket of his waistcoat and picked at the back of the vampire's trousers. He paused, rummaged about in his coat pockets, and produced a diminutive leather case. He clicked it open and removed a most bizarre pair of gogglelike things. They were gold in color with multiple lenses on one side, between which there appeared to be some kind of liquid. The contraption was also riddled with small knobs and dials. Professor Lyall propped the ridiculous things onto his nose and bent back over the vampire, twiddling at the dials expertly.

"Goodness gracious me," exclaimed Alexia, "what *are* you wearing? It looks like the unfortunate progeny of an illicit union between a pair of binoculars and some opera glasses. What on earth are they called, binocticals, spectoculars?"

The earl snorted his amusement and then tried to pretend he hadn't. "How about glassicals?" he suggested, apparently unable to resist a contribution. There was a twinkle in his eye as he said it that Alexia found rather unsettling.

Professor Lyall looked up from his examination and glared at the both of them. His right eye was hideously magnified. It was quite gruesome and made Alexia start involuntarily.

"These are my monocular cross-magnification lenses with spectra-modifier attachment, and they are invaluable. I will thank you not to mock them so openly." He turned once more to the task at hand.

"Oh." Miss Tarabotti was suitably impressed. "How do they work?" she inquired.

Professor Lyall looked back up at her, suddenly animated. "Well, you see, it is really quite interesting. By turning this little knob here, you can change the distance between the two panes of glass here, allowing the liquid to—"

The earl's groan interrupted him. "Don't get him started, Miss Tarabotti, or we will be here all night."

Looking slightly crestfallen, Professor Lyall turned back to the dead vampire. "Now, what *is* this substance all over his clothing?"

His boss, preferring the direct approach, resumed his frown and looked accusingly at Alexia. "What on God's green earth is that muck?"

Miss Tarabotti said, "Ah. Sadly, treacle tart. A tragic loss, I daresay." Her stomach chose that moment to growl in agreement. She would have colored gracefully with embarrassment had she not possessed the complexion of one of those "heathen Italians," as her mother said, who never colored, gracefully or otherwise. (Convincing her mother that Christianity had, to all intents and purposes, originated with the Italians, thus making them the exact opposite of heathen, was a waste of time and breath.) Alexia refused to apologize for the boisterousness of her stomach and favored Lord Maccon with a defiant glare. Her stomach was the reason she had sneaked away in the first place. Her mama had assured her there would be food at the ball. Yet all that appeared on offer when they arrived was a bowl of punch and some sadly wilted watercress. Never one to let her stomach get the better of her, Alexia had ordered tea from the butler and retreated to the library. Since she normally spent any ball lurking on the outskirts of the dance floor trying to look as though she did not want to be asked to waltz, tea was a welcome alternative. It was rude to order refreshments from someone else's staff, but when one was promised sandwiches and there was nothing but watercress, well, one must simply take matters into one's own hands!

Professor Lyall, kindhearted soul that he was, prattled on to no one in particular, pretending not to notice the rumbling of her stomach. Though of course he heard it. He had excellent hearing. *They* all did. He looked up from his examinations, his face all catawampus from the glassicals. "Starvation would explain why the vampire was desperate enough to try for Miss Tarabotti at a ball, rather than taking to the slums like the smart ones do when they get this bad."

Alexia grimaced. "No associated hive either."

Lord Maccon arched one black eyebrow, professing not to be impressed. "How could *you* possibly know *that*?"

Professor Lyall explained for both of them. "No need to be so direct with the young lady. A hive queen would never have let one of her brood get into such a famished condition. We must have a rove on our hands, one completely without ties to the local hive."

Alexia stood up, revealing to Lord Maccon that she had arranged her faint to rest comfortably against a fallen settee pillow. He grinned and then quickly hid it behind a frown when she looked at him suspiciously.

"I have a different theory." She gestured to the vampire's clothing. "Badly tied cravat and a cheap shirt? No hive worth its salt would let a larva like that out without dressing him properly for public appearance. I am surprised he was not stopped at the front entrance. The duchess's footman really ought to have spotted a cravat like *that* prior to the reception line and forcibly ejected the wearer. I suppose good staff is hard to come by with all the best ones becoming drones these days, but such a shirt!"

The Earl of Woolsey glared at her. "Cheap clothing is no excuse for killing a man."

"Mmm, that's what you say." Alexia evaluated Lord Maccon's perfectly tailored shirtfront and exquisitely tied cravat. His dark hair was a bit too long and shaggy to be de mode, and his face was not entirely clean-shaven, but he possessed enough hauteur to carry this lower-class roughness off without seeming scruffy. She was certain that his silver and black paisley cravat must be tied under sufferance. He probably preferred to wander about bare-chested at home. The idea made her shiver oddly. It must take a lot of effort to keep a man like him tidy.

Not to mention well tailored. He was bigger than most. She had to give credit to his valet, who must be a particularly tolerant claviger.

Lord Maccon was normally quite patient. Like most of his kind, he had learned to be such in polite society. But Miss Tarabotti seemed to bring out the worst of his animal urges. "Stop trying to change the subject," he snapped, squirming under her calculated scrutiny. "Tell me what happened." He put on his BUR face and pulled out a small metal tube, stylus, and pot of clear liquid. He unrolled the tube with a small cranking device, clicked the top off the liquid, and dipped the stylus into it. It sizzled ominously.

Alexia bristled at his autocratic tone. "Do not give me instructions in that tone of voice, you . . ." she searched for a particularly insulting word, "puppy! I am jolly well not one of your pack."

Lord Conall Maccon, Earl of Woolsey, was Alpha of the local were-wolves, and as a result, he had access to a wide array of truly vicious methods of dealing with Miss Alexia Tarabotti. Instead of bridling at her insult (puppy, indeed!), he brought out his best offensive weapon, the result of decades of personal experience with more than one Alpha she-wolf. Scottish he may be by birth, but that only made him better equipped to deal with strong-willed females. "Stop playing verbal games with me, madam, or I shall go out into that ballroom, find your mother, and bring her here."

Alexia wrinkled her nose. "Well, I *like* that! That is hardly playing a fair game. How unnecessarily callous," she admonished. Her mother did not know that Alexia was preternatural. Mrs. Loontwill, as she was Loontwill since her remarriage, leaned a little too far toward the frivo-lous in any given equation. She was prone to wearing yellow and engag-ing in bouts of hysteria. Combining her mother with a dead vampire and her daughter's true identity was a recipe for disaster on all possible levels.

The fact that Alexia was preternatural had been explained to *her* at age six by a nice gentleman from the Civil Service with silver hair and a silver cane—a werewolf specialist. Along with the dark hair and prom-inent nose, preternatural was something Miss Tarabotti had to thank her dead Italian father for. What it really meant was that words like *I* and *me* were just excessively theoretical for Alexia. She certainly had an identity and a heart that felt emotions and all that; she simply had no soul. Miss Alexia, age six, had nodded politely at the nice silver-haired gentleman. Then she had made certain to read oodles of ancient Greek philosophy dealing with reason, logic, and ethics. If she had no soul, she also had no morals, so she reckoned she had best develop some kind of alternative. Her mama thought her a bluestocking, which was soulless enough as far as Mrs. Loontwill was concerned, and was terribly upset by her eldest daughter's propensity for libraries. It would be too bothersome to have to face her mama in one just now.

Lord Maccon moved purposefully toward the door with the clear intention of acquiring Mrs. Loontwill.

Alexia caved with ill grace. "Oh, very well!" She settled herself with a rustle of green skirts onto a peach brocade chesterfield near the window.

The earl was both amused and annoyed to see that she had managed to pick up her fainting pillow and place it back on the couch without his registering any swooping movement.

"I came into the library for tea. I was promised food at this ball. In case you had not noticed, no food appears to be in residence."

Lord Maccon who required a considerable amount of fuel, mostly of the protein inclination, had noticed. "The Duke of Snodgrove is notoriously reticent about any additional expenditure at his wife's balls. Victuals were probably not on the list of acceptable offerings." He sighed. "The man owns half of Berkshire and cannot even provide a decent sandwich."

Miss Tarabotti made an empathetic movement with both hands. "My point precisely! So you will understand that I had to resort to ordering my own repast. Did you expect me to starve?"

The earl gave her generous curves a rude once-over, observed that Miss Tarabotti was nicely padded in exactly the right places, and refused to be suckered into becoming sympathetic. He maintained his frown. "I suspect that is precisely what the vampire was thinking when he found you *without a chaperone.* An unmarried female alone in a room in this enlightened day and age! Why, if the moon had been full, even I would have attacked you!"

Alexia gave him the once-over and reached for her brass parasol. "My dear sir, I should like to see you try."

Being Alpha made Lord Maccon a tad unprepared for such bold rebuttals, even with his Scottish past. He blinked at her in surprise for a split second and then resumed the verbal attack. "You do realize modern social mores exist for a reason?"

"I was hungry, allowances should be made," Alexia said, as if that settled the matter, unable to understand why he persisted in harping on about it.

Professor Lyall, unobserved by the other two, was busy fishing about in his waistcoat for something. Eventually, he produced a mildly beaten-up ham and pickle sandwich wrapped in a bit of brown paper. He presented it to Miss Tarabotti, ever the gallant.

Under normal circumstances, Alexia would have been put off by the disreputable state of the sandwich, but it was meant so kindly and offered with such diffidence, she could do nothing but accept. It was actually rather tasty.

"This is delicious!" she stated, surprised.

Professor Lyall grinned. "I keep them around for when his lordship gets particularly testy. Such offerings keep the beast under control for the most part." He frowned and then added a caveat. "Excepting at full moon, of course. Would that a nice ham and pickle sandwich was all it took then."

Miss Tarabotti perked up, interested. "What do you *do* at full moon?"

Lord Maccon knew very well Miss Tarabotti was getting off the point intentionally. Driven beyond endurance, he resorted to use of her first name. "Alexia!" It was a long, polysyllabic, drawn-out growl.

She waved the sandwich at him. "Uh, do you want half of this, my lord?"

His frown became even darker, if such a thing could be conceived.

Professor Lyall pushed his glassicals up onto the brim of his top hat, where they looked like a strange second set of mechanical eyes, and stepped into the breach. "Miss Tarabotti, I do not believe you quite realize the delicacy of this situation. Unless we can establish strong grounds for self-defense by proving the vampire was behaving in a wholly irrational manner, you could be facing murder charges."

Alexia swallowed her bite of sandwich so quickly she partly choked and started to cough. "What?"

Lord Maccon turned his fierce frown on his second. "Now who is being too direct for the lady's sensibilities?"

Lord Maccon was relatively new to the London area. He had arrived a social unknown, challenged for Woolsey Castle Alpha, and won. He gave young ladies heart palpitations, even outside his wolf form, with a favorable combination of mystery, preeminence, and danger. Having acquired the BUR post, Woolsey Castle, and noble rank from the dispossessed former pack leader, he never lacked for a dinner invitation. His Beta, inherited with the pack, had a tense time of it: dancing on protocol and covering up Lord Maccon's various social gaffes. So far, bluntness had proved Professor Lyall's most consistent problem. Sometimes it even rubbed off on him. He had not meant to shock Miss Tarabotti, but she was now looking most subdued.

"I was simply sitting," Alexia explained, placing the sandwich aside, having lost her appetite. "He launched himself at me, totally unprovoked. His feeding fangs were out. I am certain if I had been a normal daylight woman, he would have bled me dry. I simply had to defend myself."

Professor Lyall nodded. A vampire in a state of extreme hunger had two socially acceptable options: to take sips from various willing drones belonging to him or his hive, or to pay for the privilege from blood-whores down dockside. This was the nineteenth century, after all, and one simply did not attack unannounced and uninvited! Even werewolves, who could not control themselves at full moon, made certain they had enough clavigers around to lock them away. He himself had three, and it took five to keep Lord Maccon under control.

"Do you think maybe he was forced into this state?" the professor wondered.

"You mean imprisoned until he was starving and no longer in possession of his faculties?" Lord Maccon considered the idea.

Professor Lyall flipped his glassicals back down off his hat and examined the dead man's wrists and neck myopically. "No signs of confinement or torture, but hard to tell with a vampire. Even in a low blood state, he would heal most superficial wounds in"—he grabbed Lord Maccon's metal roll and stylus, dipped the tip into the clear sizzling liquid, and did some quick calculations—"a little over one hour." The calculations remained etched into the metal.

"And then what? Did he escape or was he intentionally let go?"

Alexia interjected, "He seemed perfectly sane to me—aside from the attacking part, of course. He was able to carry on a decent conversation. He even tried to charm me. Must have been quite a young vampire. And"—she paused dramatically, lowered her voice, and said in sepulchral tones—"he had a fang-lisp."

Professor Lyall looked shocked and blinked largely at her through the asymmetrical lenses; among vampires, lisping was the height of vulgarity.

Miss Tarabotti continued. "It was as though he had never been trained in hive etiquette, no social class at all. He was almost a boor." It was a word she had never thought to apply to a vampire.

Lyall took the glassicals off and put them away in their little case with an air of finality. He looked gravely at his Alpha. "You know what this means, then, my lord?"

Lord Maccon was not frowning anymore. Instead he was looking grim. Alexia felt it suited him better, setting his mouth into a straight line and touching his tawny eyes with a determined glint. She wondered idly what he would look like if he smiled a real honest smile. Then she told herself quite firmly that it was probably best not to find out.

The object of her speculations said, "It means some hive queen is intentionally biting to metamorphosis outside of BUR regulations."

"Could it be just the once, do you think?" Professor Lyall removed a folded piece of white cloth from his waistcoat. He shook out the material, revealing it to be a large sheet of fine silk. Alexia was beginning to find the number of things he could stash in his waistcoat quite impressive.

Lord Maccon continued. "Or this could be the start of something more extensive. We'd better get back to BUR. The local hives will have to be interviewed. The queens are not going to be happy. Apart from everything else, this incident is awfully embarrassing for them."

Miss Tarabotti agreed. "Especially if they find out about the substandard shirt selection."

The two gentlemen wrapped the vampire's body in the silk sheet. Professor Lyall hoisted it easily over one shoulder. Even in their human form, werewolves were considerably stronger than daylight folk.

Lord Maccon rested his tawny gaze on Alexia. She was sitting primly on the chesterfield. One gloved hand rested on the ebony handle of a ridiculous-looking parasol. Her brown eyes were narrowed in consideration. He would give a hundred pounds to know what she was thinking just then. He was also certain she would tell him exactly what it was if he asked, but he refused to give her the satisfaction. Instead he issued a statement. "We'll try to keep your name out of it, Miss Tarabotti. My report will say it was simply a normal girl who got lucky and managed to escape an unwarranted attack. No need for anyone to know a preternatural was involved."

Now it was Alexia's turn to glare. "Why do you BUR types always *do* that?"

Both men paused to look at her in confusion.

"*Do* what, Miss Tarabotti?" asked the professor.

"Dismiss me as though I were a child. Do you realize I could be useful to you?"

Lord Maccon grunted. "You mean you could go around legally getting into trouble instead of just bothering us all the time?"

Alexia tried to keep from feeling hurt. "BUR employs women, and I hear you even have a preternatural on the payroll up north, for ghost control and exorcism purposes."

Lord Maccon's caramel-colored eyes instantly narrowed. "From whom, exactly, did you hear that?"

Miss Tarabotti raised her eyebrows. As if she would ever betray the source of information told to her in confidence!

The earl understood her look perfectly. "Very well, never you mind that question."

"I shall not," replied Alexia primly.

Professor Lyall, still holding the body slung over one shoulder, took pity on her. "We do have both at BUR," he admitted.

Lord Maccon elbowed him in the side, but he stepped out of range with a casual grace that bespoke much practice. "But what we do not have is any *female* preternaturals, and certainly not any gentlewomen. All women employed by BUR are good working-class stock."

"You are simply still bitter about the hedgehogs," muttered Miss Tarabotti, but she also bowed her head in acknowledgment. She'd had this conversation before, with Lord Maccon's superior at BUR, to be precise. A man her brain still referred to as that Nice Silver-Haired Gentleman. The very idea that a lady of breeding such as herself might want to *work* was simply too shocking. "My dearest girl," he had said, "what if your mother found out?"

"Isn't BUR supposed to be covert? I could be covert." Miss Tarabotti could not help trying again. Professor Lyall, at least, liked her a little bit. Perhaps he might put in a good word.

Lord Maccon actually laughed. "You are about as covert as a sledgehammer." Then he cursed himself silently, as she seemed suddenly forlorn. She hid it quickly, but she had definitely been saddened.

His Beta grabbed him by the arm with his free hand. "Really, sir, manners."

The earl cleared his throat and looked contrite. "No offense meant, Miss Tarabotti." The Scottish lilt was back in his voice.

Alexia nodded, not looking up. She plucked at one of the pansies on her parasol. "It's simply, gentlemen"—and when she raised her dark eyes they had a slight sheen in them—"I would so like something useful to do."

Lord Maccon waited until he and the professor were out in the hallway, having bid polite, on Professor Lyall's part at least, farewells to the young lady, to ask the question that really bothered him. "For goodness' sake, Randolph, why doesn't she just get married?" His voice was full of frustration.

Randolph Lyall looked at his Alpha in genuine confusion. The earl was usually a very perceptive man, for all his bluster and Scottish grumbling. "She is a bit old, sir."

"Balderdash," said Lord Maccon. "She cannot possibly have more than a quarter century or so."

"And she is very"—the professor looked for a gentlemanly way of putting it—"assertive."

"Pah." The nobleman waved one large paw dismissively. "Simply got a jot more backbone than most females this century. There must be plenty of discerning gentlemen who'd cop to her value."

Professor Lyall had a well-developed sense of self-preservation and the distinct feeling that if he said anything desultory about the young lady's appearance, he might actually get his head bitten off. He, and the rest of polite society, might believe Miss Tarabotti's skin a little too dark and her nose a little too prominent, but he did not think Lord Maccon felt the same. Lyall had been Beta to the fourth Earl of Woolsey since Conall Maccon first descended upon them all. With barely twenty years gone and the bloody memory still strong, no werewolf was yet ready to question why Conall had wanted the bother of the London territory, not even Professor Lyall. The earl was a confusing man, his taste in females equally mystifying. For all Professor Lyall knew, his Alpha might actually *like* Roman noses, tan skin, and an assertive disposition. So instead he said, "Perhaps it's the Italian last name, sir, that keeps her unwed."

"Mmm," agreed Lord Maccon, "probably so." He did not sound convinced.

The two werewolves exited the duke's town house into the black London night, one bearing the body of a dead vampire, the other, a puzzled expression.

CHAPTER TWO

An Unexpected Invitation

Miss Tarabotti generally kept her soulless state quite hush-hush, even from her own family. She was not undead, mind you; she was a living, breathing human but was simply . . . lacking. Neither her family nor the members of the social circles she frequented ever noticed she was missing anything. Miss Tarabotti seemed to them only a spinster, whose unfortunate condition was clearly the result of a combination of domineering personality, dark complexion, and overly strong facial features. Alexia thought it too much of a bother to go around explaining soullessness to the ill-informed masses. It was almost, though not quite, as embarrassing as having it known that her father was both Italian and dead.

The ill-informed masses included her own family among their ranks, a family that specialized in being both inconvenient and asinine.

"Would you look at this!" Felicity Loontwill waved a copy of the *Morning Post* at the assembled breakfast table. Her father, the Right Honorable Squire Loontwill, did not divert his concentrated attention from the consumption of an eight-minute egg and toast. But her sister, Evylin, glanced up inquiringly, and her mama said, "What is it, my dear?" pausing in midsip of her medicinal barley water.

Felicity pointed to a passage in the society section of the paper. "It says here that there was a particularly gruesome incident at the ball last night! Did you know there was *an incident*? I do not remember any incident!"

Alexia frowned at her own egg in annoyance. She had been under the impression Lord Maccon was going to keep everything respectfully quiet and out of the society papers. She refused to acknowledge the fact that the sheer number of people who had seen her with the dead vampire meant that any such endeavor was practically impossible. After all, the earl's purported specialty was accomplishing several impossible things before dawn.

Felicity elaborated, "Apparently someone died. No name has been released, but a genuine death, and I missed it entirely! A young lady discovered him in the library and fainted from the shock. Poor lamb, how horrific for her."

Evylin, the youngest, clucked her tongue sympathetically and reached for the pot of gooseberry jelly. "Does it say who the young lady is?"

Felicity rubbed her nose delicately and read on. "Unfortunately, no."

Alexia raised both eyebrows and sipped her tea in uncharacteristic silence. She winced at the flavor, looked with narrowed eyes at her cup, and then reached for the creamer.

Evylin spread jelly with great attention to applying a precisely even layer over the top of the toast. "How very tiresome! I should love to know all the relevant details. It is like something out of a gothic novel. Anything else interesting?"

"Well, the article continues on with a more extensive review of the ball. Goodness, the writer even criticizes the Duchess of Snodgrove for not providing refreshments."

"Well, really," said Evylin in heartfelt agreement, "even Almack's has those bland little sandwiches. It is not as if the duke could not see to the expense."

"Too true, my dear," agreed Mrs. Loontwill.

Felicity glanced at the byline of the article. "Written by 'anonymous.' No commentary on anyone's attire. Well, I call that a pretty poor showing. He does not even mention Evylin or me."

The Loontwill girls were quite popular in the papers, partly for their generally well-turned-out appearance and partly because of the remarkable number of beaux they had managed to garner between them. The entire family, with the exception of Alexia, enjoyed this popularity immensely and did not seem to mind if what was written was not always complimentary. So long as *something* was written.

Evylin looked annoyed. A small crease appeared between her perfectly arched brows. "I wore my new pea-green gown with the pink water lily trim simply so they'd write about it."

Alexia winced. She would prefer not to be reminded of that gown— *so many ruffles.*

The unfortunate by-product of Mrs. Loontwill's second marriage, both Felicity and Evylin were markedly different from their older half sister. No one upon meeting the three together would have thought Alexia related to the other two at all. Aside from an obvious lack of Italian blood and completely soul-ridden states, Felicity and Evylin were both quite beautiful: pale insipid blondes with wide blue eyes and small rosebud mouths. Sadly, like their dear mama, they were not much more substantive than "quite beautiful." Breakfast conversation was, therefore, not destined to be of the intellectual caliber that Alexia aspired to. Still, Alexia was pleased to hear the subject turn toward something more mundane than murder.

"Well, that's all it says about the ball." Felicity paused, switching her attention to the society announcements. "This is very interesting. That nice tearoom near Bond Street has decided to remain open until two am to accommodate and cultivate supernatural clientele. Next thing you know, they will be serving up raw meat and flutes of blood on a regular basis. Do you think we should still frequent the venue, Mama?"

Mrs. Loontwill looked up once more from her barley and lemon water. "I do not see how it can do too much harm, my dear."

Squire Loontwill added, swallowing a bite of toast, "Some of the better investors run with the nighttime crowd, my pearl. You could do worse when hunting down suitors for the girls."

"Really, Daddy," admonished Evylin, "you make Mama sound like a werewolf on the rampage."

Mrs. Loontwill gave her husband a suspicious glance. "You haven't been frequenting Claret's or Sangria these last few evenings, have you?" She sounded as though she suspected London of being suddenly overrun with werewolves, ghosts, and vampires, and her husband fraternizing with them all.

The squire hurriedly backed away from the conversation. "Of course not, my pearl, only Boodles. You know I prefer my own club to those of the supernatural set."

"Speaking of gentlemen's clubs," interrupted Felicity, still immersed in the paper, "a new one opened last week in Mayfair. It caters to intellectuals, philosophers, scientists, and their ilk—of all things. It calls itself the Hypocras Club. How absurd. Why would such a class of individual need a club? Isn't that what they have public museums for?" She frowned over the address. "Terribly fashionable location, though." She showed the printed page to her mother. "Isn't that next door to the Duke of Snodgrove's town house?"

Mrs. Loontwill nodded. "Quite right, my dear. Well, a parcel of scientists coming and going at all hours of the day and night will certainly lower the tenor of *that* neighborhood. I should think the duchess would be in a veritable fit over this occurrence. I had intended to send round a thank-you card for last night's festivities. Now I think I might pay her a call in person this afternoon. As a concerned friend, I really ought to check on her emotional state."

"How ghastly for her," said Alexia, driven beyond endurance into comment. "People actually thinking, with their brains, and right next door. Oh, the travesty of it all."

Evylin said, "I will come with you, Mama."

Mrs. Loontwill smiled at her youngest daughter and completely ignored her eldest.

Felicity read on. "The latest spring styles from Paris call for wide belts in contrasting colors. How regrettable. Of course, they will look lovely on you, Evylin, but on my figure . . ."

Unfortunately, despite invading scientists, the opportunity to gloat over a friend's misfortune, and imminent belts, Alexia's mama was still thinking about the dead man at the Snodgroves' ball. "You disappeared for quite a while at one point last night, Alexia. You would not be keeping anything important from us, would you, my dear?"

Alexia gave her a carefully bland look. "I did have a bit of a run-in with Lord Maccon." *Always throw them off the scent,* she thought.

That captured everyone's attention, even her stepfather's. Squire Loontwill rarely troubled himself to speak at length. With the Loontwill ladies, there was not much of a chance to get a word in, so he tended to let the breakfast conversation flow over him like water over tea leaves, paying only half a mind to the proceedings. But he was a man of reasonable sense and propriety, and Alexia's statement caused him to become suddenly alert. The Earl of Woolsey might be a werewolf, but he was in possession of considerable wealth and influence.

Mrs. Loontwill paled and noticeably mollified her tone. "You did not say anything disrespectful to the earl, now, did you, my dear?"

Alexia thought back over her encounter. "Not as such."

Mrs. Loontwill pushed away her glass of barley water and shakily poured herself a cup of tea. "Oh dear," she said softly.

Mrs. Loontwill had never quite managed to figure out her eldest daughter. She had thought that putting Alexia on the shelf would keep the exasperating girl out of trouble. Instead, she had inadvertently managed to give Alexia an ever-increasing degree of freedom. Thinking back on it, she really ought to have married Alexia off instead. Now they were all stuck with her outrageous behavior, which seemed to be progressively worsening as she got older.

Alexia added peevishly, "I did wake up this morning thinking of all the rude things I *could* have said but did not. I call that most aggravating."

Squire Loontwill emitted a long drawn-out sigh.

Alexia firmly put her hand on the table. "In fact, I think I shall go for a walk in the park this morning. My nerves are not quite what they should be after the encounter." She was not, as one might suppose, obliquely referring to the vampire attack. Miss Tarabotti was not one of life's milk-water misses—in fact, quite the opposite. Many a gentleman had likened his first meeting with her to downing a very strong cognac when one was expecting to imbibe fruit juice—that is to say, startling and apt to leave one with a distinct burning sensation. No, Alexia's nerves were frazzled because she was still boiling mad at the Earl of Woolsey. She had been mad when he left her in the library. She had spent a restless night fuming impotently and awoken with eyes gritty and noble feelings still on edge.

Evylin said, "But wait. What happened? Alexia, you must tell all! Why did *you* encounter Lord Maccon at the ball when we did not? He was not on the guest list. I would have known. I peeked over the footman's shoulder."

"Evy, you didn't," gasped Felicity, genuinely shocked.

Alexia ignored them and left the breakfast room to hunt down her favorite shawl. Mrs. Loontwill might have tried to stop her, but she knew such an attempt would be useless. Getting information out of Alexia when she did not want to share was akin to trying to squeeze blood from a ghost. Instead, Mrs. Loontwill reached for her husband's hand and squeezed it consolingly. "Do not worry, Herbert. I think Lord Maccon rather likes Alexia's rudeness. He's never publicly cut her for it, at least. We can be grateful for small mercies."

Squire Loontwill nodded. "I suppose a werewolf of his advanced age might find it refreshing?" he suggested hopefully.

His wife applauded such an optimistic attitude with an affectionate pat on the shoulder. She knew how very trying her second husband found her eldest daughter. Really, what *had* she been thinking, marrying an Italian? Well, she had been young and Alessandro Tarabotti so very handsome. But there was something else about Alexia, something . . . revoltingly independent, that Mrs. Loontwill could not blame entirely on her first husband. And, of course, she refused to take the blame herself. Whatever it was, Alexia had been born that way, full of logic and reason and sharp words. Not for the first time, Mrs. Loontwill lamented the fact that her eldest had not been a male child; it would have made life very much easier for them all.

Under ordinary circumstances, walks in Hyde Park were the kind of thing a single young lady of good breeding was not supposed to do without her mama and possibly an elderly female relation or two in attendance. Miss Tarabotti felt such rules did not entirely apply to her, as she was a spinster. Had been a spinster for as long as she could remember. In her more acerbic moments, she felt she had been born a spinster. Mrs. Loontwill had not even bothered with the expenditure of a come-out or a proper season for her eldest daughter. "Really, darling," Alexia's mother had said at the time in tones of the deepest condescension, "with that nose and that skin, there is simply no point in us going to the expense. I have got your sisters to think of." So Alexia, whose nose really wasn't that big and whose skin really wasn't that tan, had gone on the shelf at fifteen. Not that she had ever actually coveted the burden of a husband, but it would have been nice to know she could get one if she ever changed her mind. Alexia did enjoy dancing, so she would have liked to attend at least one ball as an available young lady rather than always ending up skulking in libraries. These days she attended balls as nothing more than her sisters' chaperone, and the libraries abounded. But spinsterhood did mean she could go for a walk in Hyde Park without her mama, and only the worst sticklers would object. Luckily, such sticklers, like the contributors to the *Morning Post,* did not know Miss Alexia Tarabotti's name.

However, with Lord Maccon's harsh remonstrations still ringing in her ears, Alexia did not feel she could go for a walk completely unchaperoned, even though it was midmorning and the antisupernatural sun shone quite brilliantly. So she took her trusty brass parasol, for the sake of the sun, and Miss Ivy Hisselpenny, for the sake of Lord Maccon's easily offended sensibilities.

Miss Ivy Hisselpenny was a dear friend of Miss Alexia Tarabotti's. They had known each other long enough to trespass on all the well-fortified territory of familiarity. So when Alexia sent round to see if Ivy wanted a walk, Ivy was very well aware of the fact that a walk was only the surface gloss to the proceedings.

Ivy Hisselpenny was the unfortunate victim of circumstances that dictated she be only-just-pretty, only-just-wealthy, and possessed of a terrible propensity for wearing extremely silly hats. This last being the facet of Ivy's character that Alexia found most difficult to bear. In general, however, she found Ivy a restful, congenial, and, most importantly, a willing partner in any excursion.

In Alexia, Ivy had found a lady of understanding and intelligence, sometimes overly blunt for her own delicate sensibilities, but loyal and kind under even the most trying of circumstances.

Ivy had learned to find Alexia's bluntness entertaining, and Alexia had learned one did not always have to look at one's friend's hats. Thus, each having discovered a means to overlook the most tiresome aspects of the other's personality early on in their relationship, the two girls developed a fixed friendship to the mutual benefit of both. Their Hyde Park conversation reflected their typical mode of communication.

"Ivy, my dear," said Miss Tarabotti as her friend bustled up, "how marvelous of you to find time to walk at such short notice! What a hideous bonnet. I do hope you did not pay too much for it."

"Alexia! How perfectly horrid of you to criticize my hat. Why should I not be able to walk this morning? You know I never have anything better to do on Thursdays. Thursdays are so tiresome, don't you find?" replied Miss Hisselpenny.

Miss Tarabotti said, "Really, I wish you would take me with you when you go shopping, Ivy. Much horror might be avoided. Why should Thursday be any different than any other weekday?"

And so on.

The day was quite a fine one, and the two ladies walked arm in arm, their full skirts swishing and the smaller, more manageable bustle, just come into fashion last season, making it comparatively easy to move around. Rumor had it that in France, certain ladies had dispensed with the bustle altogether, but that scandalous mod had yet to reach London. Ivy's and Alexia's parasols were raised against the sun, though, as Alexia was fond of saying, such an effort was wasted on her complexion. Why, oh why, did vampire-style paleness have to rule so thoroughly the fashionable world? They strolled along, presenting a fetching picture: Ivy in cream muslin with rose flowers, and Alexia in her favorite blue walking gown with velvet edging. Both outfits were trimmed with those many rows of lace, deep pleated flounces, and tucks to which only the most stylish aspired. If Miss Hisselpenny sported a slight overabundance of the above, it must be understood it was the result of too much effort rather than too little.

Partly due to the pleasant weather and partly due to the latest craze for elaborate walking dresses, Hyde Park was decidedly crowded. Many a gentleman tipped his hat in their general direction, annoying Alexia with constant interruptions and flattering Ivy with such marked attentions.

"Really," grumbled Miss Tarabotti, "what has possessed everyone this morning? One would think we were actually tempting marriage prospects."

"Alexia! You may see yourself as off the market," remonstrated her friend, smiling shyly at a respectable-looking gentleman on a handsome bay gelding, "but I refuse to accept such an injurious fate."

Miss Tarabotti sniffed.

"Speaking of which, how was the duchess's ball last night?" Ivy was always one for gossip. Her family being too nearly middle class to be invited to any but the largest of balls, she had to rely on Alexia for such detail as went unreported by the *Morning Post*. Sadly for Ivy, her dear friend was not the most reliable or loquacious source. "Was it perfectly dreadful? Who was there? What were they wearing?"

Alexia rolled her eyes. "Ivy, please, one question at a time."

"Well, was it a pleasant event?"

"Not a bit of it. Would you believe there were no comestibles on offer? Nothing but punch! I had to go to the library and order tea." Alexia spun her parasol in agitation.

Ivy was shocked. "You did not!"

Miss Tarabotti raised her black eyebrows. "I most certainly did. You wouldn't believe the fracas that resulted. As if that was not bad enough, then Lord Maccon insisted on showing up."

Miss Hisselpenny paused in her tracks to look closely into her friend's face. Alexia's expression showed nothing but annoyance, but there was something about the precise way she always spoke about the Earl of Woolsey that roused Ivy's suspicions.

Still she played the sympathy card. "Oh dear, was he utterly horrid?" Privately, Ivy felt Lord Maccon entirely respectable for a werewolf, but he was a little too, well, *much* for her particular taste. He was so very large and so very gruff that he rather terrified her, but he always behaved correctly in public, and there was a lot to be said for a man who sported such well-tailored jackets—even if he did change into a ferocious beast once a month.

Alexia actually snorted. "Pah. No more than normal. I think it must have something to do with being Alpha. He is simply too accustomed to having his orders followed all the time. It puts me completely out of humor." She paused. "A vampire attacked me last night."

Ivy pretended a faint.

Alexia kept her friend forcibly upright by stiffening her linked arm. "Stop being so squiffy," she said. "There is no one important around to catch you."

Ivy recovered herself and said vehemently, "Good heavens, Alexia. How *do* you get yourself into these situations?"

Alexia shrugged and commenced walking more briskly so that Ivy had to trot a few steps to keep up.

"What did you do?" She was not to be dissuaded.

"Hit him with my parasol, of course."

"You did not!"

"Right upside the head. I would do the same to anyone who attacked me, supernatural or not. He simply came right at me, no introduction, no nothing!" Miss Tarabotti was feeling a tad defensive on the subject.

"But, Alexia, really, it simply is not the done thing to hit a vampire, with a parasol or otherwise!"

Miss Tarabotti sighed but secretly agreed with her friend. There weren't very many vampires skulking around London society, never had been, but the few hives that were in residence included politicians, landholders, and some very important noblemen among their membership. To indiscriminately whack about with one's parasol among such luminaries was social suicide.

Miss Hisselpenny continued. "It's simply too outrageous. What's next? Charging indiscriminately about the House of Lords, throwing jam at the local supernatural set during nighttime session?"

Alexia giggled at the leaps made by Ivy's imagination.

"Oh no, now I am giving you ideas." Ivy pressed her forehead dramatically with one gloved hand. "What exactly happened?"

Alexia told her.

"You killed him?" This time Miss Hisselpenny looked like she might really faint.

"It was by accident!" insisted Miss Tarabotti, taking her friend's arm in a firmer grip.

"That was you in the *Morning Post*? The lady who found the dead man at the Duchess of Snodgrove's ball last night?" Ivy was all agog.

Alexia nodded.

"Well, Lord Maccon certainly covered things up adequately. There was no mention of your name or family." Ivy was relieved for her friend's sake.

"Or the fact that the dead man was a vampire, thank goodness. Can you imagine what my dear mother would say?" Alexia glanced heavenward.

"Or the detrimental effect on your marriage prospects, to be found unchaperoned in a library with a dead vampire!"

Alexia's expression told Ivy exactly what she felt about *that* comment.

Miss Hisselpenny moved on. "You do realize you owe Lord Maccon a tremendous debt of gratitude?"

Miss Tarabotti looked exactly as if she had swallowed a live eel. "I should think not, Ivy. It is his job to keep these things secret: Chief Minister in Charge of Supernatural-Natural Liaison for the Greater London Area, or whatever his BUR title is. I am certainly under no obligation to a man who was only doing his civic duty. Besides, knowing what I do of the Woolsey Pack's social dynamics, I would guess that Professor Lyall, not Lord Maccon, dealt with the newspapermen."

Ivy privately felt her friend did not give the earl enough credit. Simply because Alexia was immune to his charm did not mean the rest of the world felt such indifference. He was Scottish, to be sure, but he had been Alpha for what, twenty years or so? Not long by supernatural standards, but good enough for the less discriminating of daylight society. There were rumors as to how he had defeated the last Woolsey Alpha. They said it had been far too rough for modern standards, though still legal under pack protocol. However, the preceding earl was generally known to have been a depraved individual wanting in all aspects of civility and decorum. For Lord Maccon to have appeared out of nowhere and eliminated him, however draconian his methods, had left London society part shocked, part thrilled. The truth of the matter was that most Alphas and hive queens in the modern age held power by the same civilized means as everyone else: money, social standing, and politics. Lord Maccon might be new to this, but twenty years in, he was now better at it than most. Ivy was young enough to be impressed and wise enough not to dwell on his northern origin.

"I really do think you are terribly hard on the earl, Alexia," said Ivy as the two ladies turned down a side path, away from the main promenade.

"It cannot be helped," Miss Tarabotti replied. "I have never liked the man."

"So you say," agreed Miss Hisselpenny.

They circumvented a coppice of birch trees and slowed to a stop at the edge of a wide grassy area. Recently, this particular meadow, open to the sky and off the beaten track, had come into use by a dirigible company. They flew Giffard-style steam-powered airships with de Lome propellers. It was the latest and greatest in leisurely travel. The upper crust, in particular, had taken to the skies with enthusiasm. Floating had almost eclipsed hunting as the preferred pastime of the aristocracy. The ships were a sight to behold, and Alexia was particularly fond of them. She hoped one day to ride in one. The views were reportedly breathtaking, and they were rumored to serve an excellent high tea on board.

The two ladies stood watching as one of the dirigibles came in for a landing. From a distance, the airship looked like nothing so much as a prodigiously long skinny balloon, with a basket suspended from it. Closer up, however, it became clear that the balloon was partly reinforced into semirigidity, and the basket was more like an overlarge barge. The barge part was painted with the Giffard company logo in bright black and white and suspended by a thousand wires from the balloon above. It maneuvered in toward the meadow and then, as the two ladies watched, cut and cranked down its propeller before sinking softly into a landing.

"What remarkable times we live in," commented Alexia, her eyes sparkling at the spectacular sight.

Ivy was not as impressed. "It is not natural, mankind taking to the skies."

Alexia tsked at her in annoyance. "Ivy, why do you have to be such an old fuddy-duddy? This is the age of miraculous invention and extraordinary science. The working of those contraptions is really quite fascinating. Why, the calculations for liftoff alone are—"

She was interrupted by a mellow feminine voice.

Ivy let her breath out in a huff of relief—anything to keep Alexia off all that loopy intellectual mumbo jumbo.

The two ladies turned away from the dirigible and all its wonders, Alexia reluctantly and Ivy with great alacrity. They found themselves facing an entirely different kind of spectacle.

The voice had come from atop a wholly fabulous phaeton that had drawn to a stop behind them without either woman noticing. The carriage was a high flyer: a dangerous open-topped contraption, rarely driven by a woman. Yet there, behind a team of perfectly matched blacks, sat a slightly chubby lady with blond hair and a friendly smile. Everything clashed about the arrangement; from the lady, who wore an afternoon tea gown of becoming dusty rose trimmed in burgundy rather than a carriage dress, to the high-spirited mounts, who seemed far better suited to draw some dandy of the Corinthian set. She had a pleasant expression and bobbing ringlets but kept iron-steady hands on the reins. Unfamiliar with the woman, the two young ladies would have turned back to their observations, presuming the interruption an embarrassing case of mistaken identity, except that the pretty young lady spoke to them again.

"Do I have the pleasure of addressing Miss Tarabotti?"

Ivy and Alexia looked at each other. It was such a remarkable thing to happen—in the middle of the park, by the airfield, *and* without any introduction—that Alexia answered in spite of herself. "Yes. How do you do?"

"Beautiful day for it, wouldn't you say?" The lady gestured with her whip at the dirigible, which had now completed its landing and was preparing to disgorge its passengers.

"Indeed," replied Alexia crisply, a bit put off by the woman's brash and familiar tone. "Have we met?" she inquired pointedly.

The lady laughed, a mellow tinkling sound. "I am Miss Mabel Dair, and now we have."

Alexia decided she must be dealing with *an original.*

"Pleased to make your acquaintance," she replied cautiously. "Miss Dair, might I introduce Miss Ivy Hisselpenny?"

Ivy bobbed a curtsy, at the same time tugging on Alexia's velvet-trimmed sleeve. "The *actress,*" she hissed in Alexia's ear. "You know! Oh, I say, Alexia, you really must know."

Miss Tarabotti, who did not know, surmised that she ought to. "Oh," she said blankly, and then quietly to Ivy, "Should we be talking to an actress in the middle of Hyde Park?" She glanced covertly at the disembarking dirigible passengers. No one was paying them any notice.

Miss Hisselpenny hid a smile under one gloved hand. "This from the woman who last night accidentally"—she paused—"parasoled a man. I should think that talking to an actress in public would be the least of your worries."

Miss Dair's bright blue eyes followed this exchange. She laughed again. "That incident, my dears, would be the reason for this rather discourteous meeting."

Alexia and Ivy were surprised that she knew what they were whispering about.

"You must forgive my brazenness and this intrusion on your private confidences."

"Must we?" wondered Alexia under her breath.

Ivy elbowed her in the ribs.

Miss Dair explained herself at last. "You see, my mistress would like to visit with you, Miss Tarabotti."

"Your mistress?"

The actress nodded, blond ringlets bouncing. "Oh, I know they do not normally go in for the bolder artistic types. Actresses, I am under the impression, tend to become clavigers, since werewolves are far more intrigued by the performing arts."

Miss Tarabotti realized what was going on. "My goodness, you are a drone!"

Miss Dair smiled and nodded her acknowledgment. She had dimples as well as ringlets, most distressing.

Alexia was still very confused. Drones were vampire companions, servants, and caretakers who were paid with the possibility of eventually becoming immortal themselves. But vampires rarely chose drones from among those who occupied the limelight. They preferred a more behind-the-scenes approach to soul hunting: recruiting painters, poets, sculptors, and the like. The flashier side of creativity was universally acknowledged werewolf territory, who chose thespians, opera singers, and ballet dancers to become clavigers. Of course, both supernatural sets preferred the artistic element in a companion, for there was always a better chance of excess soul in a creative person and therefore a higher likelihood that he or she would survive metamorphosis. But for a vampire to choose an actress was rather unusual.

"But you are a woman!" objected Miss Hisselpenny, shocked. An even more well-known fact about drones or clavigers was that they tended to be male. Women were much less likely to survive being turned. No one knew why, though scientists suggested the female's weaker constitution.

The actress smiled. "Not all drones are after eternal life, you realize? Some of us just enjoy the patronage. I have no particular interest in becoming supernatural, but my mistress provides for me in many other ways. Speaking of which, are you free this evening, Miss Tarabotti?"

Alexia finally recovered from her surprise and frowned. She had no concrete plans, but she did not want to go into a vampire hive uninformed. So she said firmly, "Unfortunately, I am unavailable tonight." She made a quick decision to send her card round to Lord Akeldama, requesting he stop by for dinner. He might be able to fill her in on some of the local hive activities. Lord Akeldama liked perfumed handkerchiefs and pink neckties, but he also liked to *know things*.

"Tomorrow night, then?" The actress looked hopeful. This request must be particularly important to her mistress.

Alexia dipped her head in agreement. The long cascade feather on her felt hat tickled the back of her neck. "Where am I expected to go?"

Miss Dair leaned forward from her box seat, keeping a steady hand to her frisky horses, and handed Alexia a small sealed envelope. "I must ask you not to share the address with anyone. My apologies, Miss Hisselpenny. You understand the delicacy of the situation, I am sure."

Ivy held up her hands placatingly and blushed delicately. "No offense taken, Miss Dair. This entire affair is none of my concern." Even Ivy knew better than to ask questions of hive business.

"For whom do I inquire?" asked Miss Tarabotti, turning the envelope about in her hands but not opening it.

"Countess Nadasdy."

That was a name Alexia knew. Countess Nadasdy was purported to be one of the oldest living vampires, incredibly beautiful, impossibly cruel, and extremely polite. She was queen of the Westminster Hive. Lord Maccon might have learned to play the social game with aplomb, but Countess Nadasdy was its master.

Miss Tarabotti looked long and hard at the bubbly blond actress.

"You have hidden depths, Miss Dair." Alexia was not supposed to know many of the things that went on in Countess Nadasdy's circle, let alone her hive, but she read too much. Many of the books in the Loontwills' library were left over from her father's day. Alessandro Tarabotti had clearly felt a strong inclination toward literature concerning the supernatural, so Alexia had a tolerably clear concept of what occurred in a vampire hive. Miss Dair certainly must be something more than blond curls, dimples, and a perfectly-turned-out rose dress.

Miss Dair bobbed her ringlets at them. "Whatever the gossip columns may say, Countess Nadasdy is a good mistress." Her smile was slightly quirky. "If you like that sort of thing. It has been delightful to meet you ladies." She tightened the reins to her blacks and snapped them smartly. The phaeton jerked forward sharply on the uneven grass, but Miss Dair maintained a perfect seat. In mere moments, the high flyer was gone, rattling down the footpath and disappearing behind the small coppice of birch trees.

The two girls followed, the airship in all its technological glory having suddenly lost its appeal. Other more exciting events were afoot. They walked a little more slowly, conversing in a subdued manner. Alexia turned the small envelope around in her hands.

The jaunt through Hyde Park appeared to be doing the trick as far as Alexia's prickly feelings were concerned. All of her anger at Lord Maccon had dissipated to be replaced by apprehension.

Ivy looked pale. Well, paler than usual. Finally she pointed to the sealed envelope Alexia was fiddling with nervously. "You know what that is?"

Miss Tarabotti swallowed. "Of course I know." But she said it so quietly Ivy did not really hear her.

"You have been given the actual address of a hive, Alexia. They are either going to recruit you or drain you dry. No daylight humans but drones are allowed to have that kind of information."

Alexia looked uncomfortable. "I know!" She was wondering how a hive might react to a preternatural in their midst. Not very kindly, she suspected. She worried her lower lip. "I simply must speak with Lord Akeldama."

Miss Hisselpenny looked, if possible, even more worried. "Oh really, must you? He is so very outrageous." *Outrageous* was a very good way of describing Lord Akeldama. Alexia was not afraid of outrageousness any more than she was afraid of vampires, which was good because Lord Akeldama was both.

He minced into the room, teetering about on three-inch heels with ruby and gold buckles. "My darling, *darling* Alexia." Lord Akeldama had adopted use of her given name within minutes of their first meeting. He had said that he just knew they would be friends, and there was no point in prevaricating. "*Darling!*" He also seemed to speak predominantly in italics. "How perfectly, deliciously, *delightful* of you to invite *me* to dinner. *Darling.*"

Miss Tarabotti smiled at him. It was impossible not to grin at Lord Akeldama; his attire was so consistently absurd. In addition to the heels, he wore yellow checked gaiters, gold satin breeches, an orange and lemon striped waistcoat, and an evening jacket of sunny pink brocade. His cravat was a frothy flowing waterfall of orange, yellow, and pink Chinese silk, barely contained by a magnificently huge ruby pin. His ethereal face was powdered quite unnecessarily, for he was already completely pale, a predilection of his kind. He sported round spots of pink blush on each cheek like a Punch and Judy puppet. He also affected a gold monocle, although, like all vampires, he had perfect vision.

With fluid poise, he settled himself on the settee opposite Alexia, a small neatly laid supper table between them.

Miss Tarabotti had decided to host him, much to her mother's chagrin, alone in her private drawing room. Alexia tried to explain that the vampire's supposed inability to enter private residences uninvited was a myth based upon their collective obsession with proper social etiquette, but her mother refused to believe her. After some minor hysterics, Mrs. Loontwill thought better of her objections to the arrangement. Realizing that the event would occur whether she willed it or no, Alexia being assertive—Italian blood—she hastily took the two younger girls and Squire Loontwill off to an evening card party at Lady Blingchester's. Mrs. Loontwill was very good at operating on the theory that what she did not know could not hurt her, particularly regarding Alexia and the supernatural.

So Alexia had the house to herself, and Lord Akeldama's entrance was appreciated by no one more important than Floote, the Loontwills' long-suffering butler. This caused Lord Akeldama distress, for he sat so dramatically and posed with such grace, that he clearly anticipated a much larger audience.

The vampire took out a scented handkerchief and bopped Miss Tarabotti playfully on the shoulder with it. "I hear, my little sugarplum, that you were a naughty, *naughty* girl at the duchess's ball last night."

Lord Akeldama might look and act like a supercilious buffoon of the highest order, but he had one of the sharpest minds in the whole of London. The *Morning Post* would pay half its weekly income for the kind of information he seemed to have access to at any time of night. Alexia privately suspected him of having drones among the servants in every major household, not to mention ghost spies tethered to key public institutions.

Miss Tarabotti refused to give her guest the satisfaction of asking how he knew of the previous evening's episode. Instead she smiled in what she hoped was an enigmatic manner and poured the champagne.

Lord Akeldama never drank anything but champagne. Well, that is to say, except when he was drinking blood. He was reputed to have once said that the best drink in existence was a blending of the two, a mix he referred to fondly as a Pink Slurp.

"You know why I invited you over, then?" Alexia asked instead, offering him a cheese swizzle.

Lord Akeldama waved a limp wrist about dismissively before taking the swizzle and nibbling its tip. "La, my dearest *girl*, you invited me because you could not *bear* to be without my company a single *moment* longer. And I shall be cut to the very quick of my extensive soul if your reason is *anything* else."

Miss Tarabotti waved a hand at the butler. Floote issued her a look of mild disapproval and vanished in search of the first course.

"That is, naturally, exactly why I invited you. Besides which I am certain you missed me just as much, as we have not seen each other in an age. I am convinced that your visit has absolutely nothing to do with an avid curiosity as to how I managed to kill a vampire yesterday evening," she said mildly.

Lord Akeldama held up a hand. "A moment please, my dear." Then he reached into a waistcoat pocket and produced a small spiky device. It looked like two tuning forks sunk into a faceted crystal. He flicked the first fork with his thumbnail, waited a moment, and then flicked the second. The two made a dissonant, low-pitched strumming sound, like the hum of two different kinds of bee arguing, that seemed to be amplified by the crystal. He placed the device carefully in the center of the table, where it continued to hum away discordantly. It was not entirely irritating but seemed like it might grow to be.

"One gets accustomed to it after a while," explained Lord Akeldama apologetically.

"What is it?" wondered Alexia.

"That little gem is a harmonic auditory resonance disruptor. One of my boys picked it up in gay Paris recently. Charming, isn't it?"

"Yes, but what does it do?" Alexia wanted to know.

"Not much in this room, but if anyone is trying to listen in from a distance with, say, an ear trumpet or other eavesdropping device, it creates a kind of screaming sound that results in the most tremendous headache. I tested it."

"Remarkable," said Alexia, impressed despite herself. "Are we likely to be saying things people might want to overhear?"

"Well, we were discussing how you managed to kill a vampire, were we not? And while I know *exactly* how you did it, *petal,* you may not want the rest of the world to know as well."

Alexia was affronted. "Oh really, and how did I do it?"

Lord Akeldama laughed, showing off a set of particularly white and particularly sharp fangs. "Oh, princess." In one of those lightning-fast movements that only the best athletes or a supernatural person could execute, he grabbed her free hand. His deadly fangs vanished. The ethereal beauty in his face became ever so slightly too effeminate, and his strength dissipated. "*This* is how."

Alexia nodded. It had taken Lord Akeldama four meetings to deduce she was preternatural. Estranged from the hives as he was, he had never been officially informed of her existence. He considered this an embarrassing blight on his long career as a snoop. His only possible excuse for the blunder was the fact that, while preternatural men were rare, preternatural woman were practically nonexistent. He simply had not expected to find one in the form of an overly assertive spinster, enmeshed in the thick of London society, companioned by two silly sisters and a sillier mama. As a result, he took any opportunity to remind himself of what she was, grabbing her hand or arm on the merest whim.

In this particular instance, he stroked her hand fondly. There was no attraction in the movement. "*Sweetling,*" he had once said, "you are at no more risk with me in *that* regard than you are in danger of me unexpectedly biting you—both being equal impossibilities. In the one case, I do not possess the necessary equipment upon contact, in the other case you do not." Her father's library had provided Alexia with any further explanation she might require. Alessandro Tarabotti had engaged in quite an adventurous life before marriage and collected books from all around the Empire, some of them with very fascinating pictures, indeed. He had an apparent passion for explanatory studies on primitive peoples, which resulted in the kind of documentation that might encourage even Evylin to enter a library—had she been made aware of their existence. Luckily, the entirety of Alexia's family felt that if it did not originate in the gossip section of the *Morning Post,* it was probably not worth reading. Alexia, as a result, knew considerably more on the ways of the flesh than any English spinster ought to know, and certainly enough not to mind Lord Akeldama's little gestures of affection.

"You have no idea how deliciously *restful* I find the miracle of your company," he had remarked the first time he touched her. "It's like swimming in too-warm bathwater most of one's life and suddenly plunging into an icy mountain stream. Shocking but, I believe, good for the soul." He had shrugged delicately. "I enjoy feeling mortal again, if only for one moment and only in *your glorious* presence." Miss Tarabotti had granted him very unspinster-like permission to grasp her hand whenever he wished—so long as it was always done in complete privacy.

Alexia sipped her champagne. "That vampire in the library last night did not know what I was," she said. "He came charging right at me, went straight for my neck, and then lost his fangs. I thought most of your lot knew by now. BUR undoubtedly keeps close enough track of me. Lord Maccon certainly appeared last night more quickly than was to be expected. Even for him."

Lord Akeldama nodded. His hair glinted in the flickering flame from a nearby candle. The Loontwills had installed the latest in gas lighting, but Alexia preferred beeswax, unless she was reading. In the candlelight, Lord Akeldama's hair was as gold as the buckles on his shoes. One always expected vampires to be dark and slightly doomy. Lord Akeldama was the antithesis of all such expectations. He wore his blonde hair long and queued back in a manner stylish hundreds of years ago. He looked up at her, and his face was suddenly old and serious, seeming not at all as ridiculous as his attire should make him. "They *do* mostly know of you, my pearl. All four of the official hives tell their larvae directly after metamorphosis that there is a soul-sucker living in London."

Miss Tarabotti winced. Usually Lord Akeldama was sensitive to her dislike of the term. He had been the first to use it in her presence, on the night he had finally realized what she was. For once in his long life, he had lost his perfectly donned charisma in shock at discovering a preternatural in the guise of a forthright spinster. Miss Tarabotti, understandably, had not taken to the notion of being called a soul-sucker. Lord Akeldama was careful never to use it again, except to make a point. Now he had a point to make.

Floote arrived with the soup, a creamy cucumber and watercress. Lord Akeldama received no nourishment from the consumption of food, but he appreciated the taste. Unlike some of the more repulsive members of his set, he did not engage in that tradition established by

ancient Roman vampires. There was no need for Alexia to call for a
purge bucket. He merely sampled each dish politely and then left the
rest for the servants to partake of later. No sense in wasting good soup.
And it was quite good. One could say a number of impolite things
about the Loontwills, but no one had ever accused them of frugality.
Even Alexia, spinster that she was, was given an allowance large enough
to dress her to the height of fashion—although she did tend to stick to
trends a little too precisely. The poor thing could not help it. Her
choice of clothing simply lacked soul. Regardless, the Loontwills' extravagance extended to the keeping of a very fine cook.

Floote slid away softly to retrieve the next course.

Alexia removed her hand from her friend's grasp and, never one for
dissembling, got straight to the point. "Lord Akeldama, please tell me,
what is going on? Who was the vampire who attacked me last night?
How could he not know who I was? He did not even know *what* I was,
as if no one had told him preternaturals existed at all. I am well aware
that BUR keeps us secret from the general public, but packs and hives
are well informed as a rule."

Lord Akeldama reached forward and flicked the two tuning forks
on the resonator again. "My *dearest* young friend. There, I believe, you
have the *very* issue in hand. Unfortunately for you, since you eliminated the individual in question, every interested supernatural party is
beginning to believe *you* are the one who knows the answers to those
very questions. Speculation abounds, and vampires are a suspicious lot.
Some already hold that the hives are being kept *purposefully* in ignorance
by either you, or BUR, or *most likely* both." He smiled, all fangs, and
sipped his champagne.

Alexia sat back and let out a whoosh of air. "Well, that explains her
rather forceful invitation."

Lord Akeldama did not move from his relaxed position, but he
seemed to be sitting up straighter. "Her? Her *who*? Whose invitation,
my *dearest* petunia blossom?"

"Countess Nadasdy's."

Lord Akeldama actually did sit up straight at that. His waterfall of
a cravat quivered in agitation. "Queen of the Westminster hive," he
hissed, his fangs showing. "There *are* words to describe her, my *dear*,
but *one* does *not* repeat them in polite company."

Floote came in with the fish course, a simple fillet of sole with thyme
and lemon. He glanced with raised eyebrows at the humming auditory
device and then at the agitated Lord Akeldama. Alexia shook her head
slightly when he would have remained protectively in the room.

Miss Tarabotti studied Lord Akeldama's face closely. He was a rove—a hiveless vampire. Roves were rare among the bloodsucking set. It took a lot of political, psychological, and supernatural strength for a vampire to separate from his hive. And once autonomous units, roves tended to go a bit funny about the noggin and slide toward the eccentric end of societal acceptability. In deference to this status, Lord Akeldama kept all his papers in impeccable order and was fully registered with BUR. However, it did mean he was a mite prejudiced against the hives.

The vampire sampled the fish, but the delicious taste did not seem to improve his temper. He pushed the dish away peevishly and sat back, tapping one expensive shoe against the other.

"Don't you like the Westminster hive queen?" asked Alexia with wide dark eyes and a great show of assumed innocence.

Lord Akeldama seemed to remember himself. The foppishness reappeared in spades. His wrists went limp and wiggly. "La, *my dear daffodil,* the hive queen and I, we . . . have our differences. I am under the distressing impression she finds me a *tad*"—he paused as though searching for the right word—"flamboyant."

Miss Tarabotti looked at him, evaluating both his words and the meaning behind them. "And here I thought it was you who did not like Countess Nadasdy."

"Now, *sweetheart,* who has been telling you *little* stories like that?"

Alexia tucked into her fish, a clear indication that she declined to reveal her source. After she had finished, there was a moment of silence while Floote removed the plates and placed the main course before them: a delicious arrangement of braised pork chop, apple compote, and slow roasted baby potatoes. Once the butler had gone again, Miss Tarabotti decided to ask her guest the more important question she had invited him over to answer.

"What do you think she wants of me, my lord?"

Lord Akeldama's eyes narrowed. He ignored the chop and fiddled idly with his massive ruby cravat pin. "As I see it, there are two reasons. Either she knows exactly what happened last night at the ball and she wants to bribe you into silence, or she has no idea who that vampire was and what he was doing in her territory, and she thinks you do."

"In either case, it would behoove me to be better informed than I currently am," Miss Tarabotti said, eating a buttery little potato.

He nodded empathetically.

"Are you positive you do not know anything more?" she asked.

"My dearest *girl, who* do you think I am? Lord Maccon, perhaps?" He picked up his champagne glass and twirled it by the stem, gazing thoughtfully at the tiny bubbles. "Now there *is* an idea, my treasure. *Why not* go to the werewolves? They may know more of the *relevant* facts. Lord Maccon, of course, being BUR will know *most* of all."

Alexia tried to look nonchalant. "But as a minister of BUR's secrets, he is also the least likely to relay any cogent details," she countered.

Lord Akeldama laughed in a tinkling manner that indicated more artifice than real amusement. "Then there is nothing for it, *sweetest* of Alexias, but to use your plethora of feminine *wiles* upon him. Werewolves have been susceptible to the *gentler* sex for as long as I can remember, and that is a *very* long time, indeed." He wiggled his eyebrows, knowing he did not look a day over twenty-three, his original age at metamorphosis. He continued. "Favorable toward women, those *darling* beasties, even if they are a tad brutish." He shivered lasciviously. "Particularly Lord Maccon. So big and *rough.*" He made a little growling noise.

Miss Tarabotti giggled. Nothing was funnier than watching a vampire try to emulate a werewolf.

"I advise you *most* strongly to visit him tomorrow *before* you see the Westminster queen." Lord Akeldama reached forward and grasped her wrist. His fangs vanished, and his eyes suddenly looked as old as he really was. He had never told Alexia quite how old. "*La*, darling," he always said, "a vampire, like a lady, *never* reveals his true age." But he had described to her in detail the dark days before the supernatural was revealed to daylight folk. Before the hives and packs made themselves known on the British Isle. Before that prestigious revolution in philosophy and science that their emergence triggered, known to some as the Renaissance but to vampires as the Age of Enlightenment. Supernatural folk called the time before the Dark Ages, for obvious reasons. For them it had been an age spent skulking through the night. Several bottles of champagne were usually required to get Lord Akeldama to talk of it at all. Still, it meant, by Alexia's calculations, that he was at least over four hundred years old.

She looked more closely at her friend. Was that fear?

His face was honestly serious, and he said, "My dove, *I* do not know what is transpiring here. *Me*, ignorant! Please take the gravest of care in this matter."

Miss Tarabotti now knew the real source of her friend's trepidation. Lord Akeldama had no idea what was going on. For years, he had held the trump card in every major London political situation. He was accustomed to having possession of all pertinent facts before anybody else. Yet at this moment, he was as mystified as she.

"*Promise me*," he said earnestly, "you will see what information you can extract from Lord Maccon on this matter *before* you go into that hive."

Alexia smiled. "To better your understanding?"

He shook his blond head. "No, sweetheart, to better *yours*."

CHAPTER THREE

Our Heroine Heeds Some Good Advice

"B ollocks," said Lord Maccon upon seeing who stood before him. "Miss Tarabotti. What did I do to merit a visit from you first thing in the morning? I have not even had my second cup of tea yet." He loomed at the entrance to his office.

Alexia ignored his unfortunate choice of greeting and swept past him into the room. The act of sweeping, and the fact that the doorway was quite narrow while Alexia's bosoms (even corseted) were not, brought her into intimate contact with the earl. Alexia was embarrassed to note she tingled a little bit, clearly a reaction to the repulsive state of the man's office.

There were papers everywhere, piled in corners and spread out over what might have been a desk—it was difficult to tell underneath all the muddle. There were also rolls of etched metal and stacks of tubes she suspected contained more of the same. Alexia wondered why he needed metal record-keeping; from the sheer quantity, she suspected it must be a cogent one. She counted at least six used cups and saucers and a platter covered in the remains of a large joint of raw meat. Miss Tarabotti had been in Lord Maccon's office once or twice before. It had always appeared a tad masculine for her taste but never so unsightly as this.

"Good gracious me!" she said, shaking off the tingles. Then she asked the obvious question. "Where is Professor Lyall, then?"

Lord Maccon scrubbed his face with his hand, reached desperately for a nearby teapot, and drained it through the spout.

Miss Tarabotti looked away from the horrible sight. *Who was it that had said "only just civilized"?* She closed her eyes and considered, realizing it must have been she. She fluttered one hand to her throat. "Please, Lord Maccon, use one of the cups. My delicate sensibilities."

The earl actually snorted. "My dear Miss Tarabotti, if you possessed any such things, you certainly have never shown them to me." But he did put down the teapot.

Alexia looked more closely at Lord Maccon. He did not seem entirely well. Her heart moved with a funny little flipping motion in her chest. His mahogany-colored hair was standing up at the front, as though he had been running his hands through it repeatedly. Everything about his appearance seemed even more unkempt than usual. In the dim light, it also looked as though his canines were showing—a certain sign of distress. Alexia squinted to make certain. She wondered how close they were to full moon. The worry in her dark eyes, expressive even in their soullessness, softened her teapot-inspired disapproving expression.

"BUR business." Lord Maccon endeavored to explain away Professor's Lyall's absence and the state of his office in one curt phrase. He pinched the bridge of his nose between thumb and forefinger.

Alexia nodded. "I did not really expect to find you here, my lord, in the daytime. Shouldn't you be sleeping at this hour?"

The werewolf shook his head. "I can take the full sun for a few days running, especially when there's such a mystery as this. Alpha's not simply a meaningless title, you know? We can *do* things regular werewolves cannot. Besides which, Queen Victoria is curious." In addition to being BUR's supernatural liaison and Alpha of the Woolsey Castle pack, Lord Maccon was an agent of Queen Victoria's Shadow Parliament.

"Well, never mind that; you look positively ghastly," said Alexia baldly.

"Gee, thank you very much for your concern, Miss Tarabotti," replied the earl, straightening up and widening his eyes in an attempt to look more alert.

"What *have* you been doing to yourself?" asked his lady guest with all her customary bluntness.

"I have not slept since you were attacked," said Lord Maccon.

Alexia blushed slightly. "Concerned for my well-being? Why, Lord Maccon, now it is I who am touched."

"Hardly," he replied ungallantly. "Overseeing investigations, for the most part. Any concern you may note is over the idea that someone else may be attacked. You can obviously see to yourself."

Miss Tarabotti was torn between being crushed that he did not care one fig for her safety and pleased that he trusted in her competence.

She gathered up a small pile of metal slates from a side chair and sat down. Lifting one roll of thin metal, she held it open to examine with interest. She had to tilt it away from the shadows in order to make out the etched notations. "Rove vampire registration permits," she remarked. "You think the man who attacked me last night might have had a permit?"

Lord Maccon looked exasperated, marched over and snatched the stack of rolls away. They fell to the floor with a clatter and he cursed his sun-born clumsiness. But for all his sham annoyance at her presence, the earl was secretly pleased to have someone with whom to talk out his theories. Usually he used his Beta in that capacity, but with Lyall out of town, he'd been pacing about muttering to himself. "If he does have a permit, it is not in the London registry."

"Could he have come from outside the capital?" suggested Alexia.

Lord Maccon shrugged. "You know how territorial vampires are. Even without any hive ties, they tend to stay in the area of original blood metamorphosis. It is possible he traveled, but from where and why? What grave purpose would drive a vampire from his natural habitat? That is the information I've sent Lyall to hunt down."

Miss Tarabotti understood. BUR headquarters were stationed in central London, but they had offices all over England that kept tabs on the supernatural set in other parts of the country. During the Age of Enlightenment, when the supernatural became accepted instead of persecuted, what had been born out of a need to control turned into a means of understanding. BUR, a creature of that understanding, now employed werewolves and vampires, as well as mortals and even a ghost or two. Alexia also suspected there were a few sundowners still left among the ranks, though not used much anymore.

Lord Maccon continued. "He will travel by stagecoach during the day and in wolf form at night. He should be back before the full moon with a report from all six nearby cities. That is what I am hoping for, at any roads."

"Professor Lyall started in Canterbury?" Miss Tarabotti guessed.

Lord Maccon spun to stare at her intently. His eyes were more yellow than tawny gold, and particularly sharp in the dimly lit room. "I hate it when you do that," he growled.

"What, guess correctly?" Alexia's dark eyes crinkled in amusement.

"No, make me feel predictable."

Alexia smiled. "Canterbury is a port city and a center for travel. If our mystery vampire came from anywhere, it was most likely there. But you do not think he came from outside London, do you?"

Lord Maccon shook his head. "No, that does not feel right. He smelled local. All vampires get some indicative scent from their maker, particularly when they have been recently changed. Our little friend had the death odor of the Westminster hive about him."

Miss Tarabotti blinked, startled. Her father's books said nothing on this subject. *Werewolves could smell vampire bloodlines? Could vampires tell the difference between werewolf packs as well?*

"Have you spoken with the local queen?" she said.

The earl nodded. "I went straight to the hive house after leaving you that night. She completely denies any association with your attacker. If it was possible for Countess Nadasdy to be surprised, I would have said she looked shocked at my news. Of course, she would have to pretend such an appearance if she had metamorphosed a new vampire without proper paperwork. But usually the hive is proud to have made larvae. They host a ball, demand turnday presents, call in all the field drones, that kind of extravagance. BUR registry is customarily part of the ceremony. Local werewolves are even invited." His lip curled, showing several pointed teeth. "It is a sort of 'stick it in your face' to the packs. We have not gained any new members in over a decade." It was no secret how hard it was to make new supernaturals. Since it was impossible to tell beforehand how much soul a normal human had, it was a deadly gamble for humans to try and turn. Since many drones and clavigers made the attempt early on in life so their immortality might be blessed with youth, the deaths were all the more keenly felt. Of course BUR knew, and so did Miss Tarabotti, that low population numbers were part of what kept the supernatural set safe from public outcry. When they had first presented themselves to the modern world, daylight humans had overcome age-old terrors only upon realization of how few supernatural folk there really were in existence. Lord Maccon's pack numbered eleven in all, and the Westminster hive was slightly smaller—both were considered impressively large.

Miss Tarabotti cocked her head to one side. "Where does that leave you, my lord?"

"Suspecting that there is a rove queen making vampires illegally and outside of hive and BUR authority."

Alexia swallowed. "Inside Westminster territory?"

The earl nodded. "And of Countess Nadasdy's bloodline."

"The countess must be biting mad."

"You put it mildly, my dear Miss Tarabotti. As queen, of course, she insists your homicidal friend was from outside London. She has no understanding of how bloodlines smell. But Lyall identified the body as her get without doubt. He has generations of experience with the Westminster Hive and the best nose of any of us. You know Lyall's been with the Woolsey Pack far longer than I?"

Alexia nodded. Everyone knew how recently Lord Maccon had risen to the earldom. She was given to wonder idly why Professor Lyall had not tried for Alpha himself. Then she assessed Lord Maccon's un-doubtedly muscular form and imposing appearance and deduced the reason. Professor Lyall was no coward, but he was also no idiot.

The Alpha continued. "He could have been a direct metamorphic from one of Countess Nadasdy's bite-daughters. But then again, Lyall also noted that the countess has not managed to change over a female drone in his lifetime. She is understandably bitter over this fact."

Miss Tarabotti frowned. "So you have a genuine mystery on your plate. Only a female vampire, a queen, can metamorphose a new vam-pire. Yet here we find ourselves with a new vampire and no maker. Either Professor Lyall's nose or Countess Nadasdy's tongue is lying." Which explained more than anything else Lord Maccon's haggard appearance. Nothing was worse than werewolf and vampire at cross purposes, especially in this kind of investigation. "Let us hope Professor Lyall finds you some answers to these questions," she said with feeling.

Lord Maccon rang the bell for fresh tea. "Indeed. And, now, enough of my problems. Perhaps we might press on to what brought you to my doorstep at this ungodly hour."

Alexia, who was poking through another pile of rove paperwork she had scooped off the floor, waved one of the metal sheets at him. "*He* did."

Lord Maccon grabbed the metal she had gesticulated with out of her hand, looked at it, and huffed in annoyance. "Why do you persist in associating with that creature?"

Miss Tarabotti straightened her skirts, draping the pleated hem more carefully over her kid boots. She demurred. "I *like* Lord Akel-dama."

The earl abruptly looked more livid than tired. "Do you, by George! What has he been luring you in with? Little pip-squeak, I shall wallop his scrawny hide to ribbons."

"I suspect he might enjoy that," murmured Alexia, thinking of what little she knew of her vampire friend's proclivities. The werewolf did not hear her. Or perhaps he simply chose not to use his supernatu-ral auditory abilities. He paced about, looking vaguely magnificent. His teeth were now definitely showing.

Miss Tarabotti stood, marched over, and grabbed Lord Maccon's wrist. His teeth retracted instantly. The earl's yellow eyes went back to amber-brown. It was the color they must have been years ago before he yielded to the bite that made him supernatural. He also appeared slightly less shaggy, although no less large and angry. Remembering Lord Akel-dama's comment on the subject of using feminine wiles, Alexia placed a second hand pleadingly above the first on his upper arm.

What she wanted to say was, *Do not be an idiot.* What she actually said was, "I needed Lord Akeldama's advice on supernatural matters. I did not want to disturb you for anything trivial." As if she would ever willingly go to Lord Maccon for help. She was only in his office now under duress. She widened her large brown eyes, tilted her head in a way she hoped might minimize her nose, and lowered her eyelashes beseechingly. Alexia had very long eyelashes. She also had very fierce eyebrows, but Lord Maccon seemed more interested in the former than repelled by the latter. He covered her small brown hand with his massive one.

Miss Tarabotti's hand became very warm, and she was finding that her knees reacted in a decidedly wobbly way to such close proximity to the earl. *Stop it!* she instructed them fiercely. What was she supposed to say next? Right: *Do not be an idiot.* And then: *I needed help with a vampire, so I went to a vampire for help. No, that was not right. What would Ivy say? Oh yes.* "I was so upset, you see? I encountered a drone in the park yesterday, and Countess Nadasdy has requested my presence, this very night."

That distracted Lord Maccon from his homicidal thoughts of Lord Akeldama. He refused to analyze why he was so opposed to the concept of Alexia liking the vampire. Lord Akeldama was a perfectly well-behaved rove, if slightly silly, always keeping himself and his drones in flawless order. Sometimes too flawless. Alexia *should* be entirely allowed to like such a man. His lip curled once more at the very idea. He shook himself and went on to the disturbing, in quite a different manner, idea of Miss Alexia Tarabotti and Countess Nadasdy in the same room together.

He hustled Alexia over to a small couch and sat them both, with a crackle, on top of the airship transit maps scattered across it.

"Start from the beginning," he instructed.

Miss Tarabotti commenced with Felicity reading aloud the newspaper, went on to the walk with Ivy and the meeting with Miss Dair, and ended with Lord Akeldama's perspective on the situation. "You know," she added when she felt the earl tense at the vampire's name, "he was the one who suggested I see you."

"What!"

"I must know as much as possible about this situation if I am to go into a hive alone. Most supernatural battles are over information. If Countess Nadasdy wants something from me, it is far better if I know what it is and whether I am capable of providing it."

Lord Maccon stood, slightly panicked, and said exactly the wrong thing. "I forbid you to go!" He had no idea what it was about this particular woman that made him lose all sense of verbal decorum. But there it was: the unfortunate words were out.

Miss Tarabotti stood as well, instantaneously angry, her chest heaving in agitation. "You have no right!"

He circled her wrists with an iron grip. "I am BUR's chief sundowner, I'll have you know. Preternaturals fall under my jurisdiction."

"But we are allowed the same degree of freedom as members of the supernatural set, are we not? Full societal integration, among other things. The countess has asked me to attend her for one evening, nothing more."

"Alexia!" Lord Maccon groaned his frustration.

Miss Tarabotti realized that the earl's use of her given name indicated a certain degree of irritation on his part.

The werewolf took a deep breath, trying to calm himself. It did not work, because he was too close to Alexia. Vampires smelled of stale blood and family lines. His fellow werewolves smelled of fur and wet nights. And humans? Even after all this time of trapping himself away at full moon, the hunt forbidden, humans smelled like food. But Alexia's scent was something else, something . . . not meat. She smelled warm and spicy sweet, like some old-fashioned Italian pastry his body could no longer process but whose taste he remembered and craved.

He leaned into her.

Miss Tarabotti characteristically swatted him. "Lord Maccon! You forget yourself!"

Which was, Lord Maccon thought, exactly the problem. He let go of her wrists and felt the werewolf return: that strength and heightened senses a partial death had given him all those decades ago. "The hive will not trust you, Miss Tarabotti. You must understand: They believe you to be their natural enemy. Do you keep abreast of the latest scientific discoveries?" He rummaged about on his desk and produced a small weekly news pamphlet. The lead article was titled THE COUNTERBALANCE THEOREM AS APPLIED TO HORTICULTURAL PURSUITS.

Alexia blinked at it, not comprehending. She turned the paper over: *published by Hypocras Press.* That did not help either. She knew of the counterbalance theorem, of course. In fact, she found the tenets, in principle, rather appealing.

She said, "Counterbalance is the scientific idea that any given force has an innate opposite. For example, every naturally occurring poison has a naturally occurring antidote—usually located in proximity. Much in the way that the juice of crushed nettle leaves applied to the skin relieves the nettle sting. What has this to do with me?"

"Well, vampires believe that preternaturals are their counterbalance. That it is your elemental purpose to neutralize them."

Now it was Miss Tarabotti's turn to snort. "Preposterous!"

"Vampires have long memories, my dear. Longer even than us werewolves, for we fight too often among ourselves and die centuries too young. When we supernaturals hid in the night and hunted humankind, it was *your* preternatural ancestors who hunted us. It was a violent kind of balance. The vampires will always hate you and ghosts always fear you. We werewolves are not so certain. For us, metamorphosis is part curse, one that sees us imprisoned each month for everyone's safety. Some of us see preternaturals as the cure for the full moon's curse. There are stories of werewolves who turned themselves to pets, hunting their own as payment for a preternatural's touch." He looked disgusted. "All this is better understood since the Age of Reason brought about the concept of a measured soul and the Church of England broke with Rome. But new science, such as this theorem, raises old memories in the vampires. They named preternaturals *soul-suckers* for good reason. You are the only one registered in this area. And you have just killed a vampire."

Miss Tarabotti looked grave. "I already accepted Countess Nadasdy's invitation. It would be churlish to refuse now."

"Why must you always be so difficult?" wondered Lord Maccon in utter exasperation.

Alexia grinned. "No soul?" she suggested.

"No sense!" corrected the earl.

"Nevertheless"—Miss Tarabotti stood—"someone has to discover what is going on. If the hive knows anything about this dead vampire, I intend to find out what it is. Lord Akeldama said they wanted to know how much I knew because they either understood more or they understood less. It is to my advantage to figure out which is the case."

"Lord Akeldama again."

"His advice is sound, and he finds my company restful."

That surprised the werewolf. "Well, I suppose somebody must. How peculiar of him."

Miss Tarabotti, affronted, gathered up her brass parasol and made to leave.

Lord Maccon slowed her with a question. "Why *are* you so curious about this matter? Why do you insist on involving yourself?"

"Because someone is dead and it was by my own hand," she replied, looking gloomy. "Well, by my own parasol," she amended.

Lord Maccon sighed. He figured someday he might win an

argument with this extraordinary woman, but clearly today was not that day.

"Did you bring your own carriage?" he asked, admitting defeat with the question.

"I shall hire a hackney, not to worry."

The Earl of Woolsey reached for his hat and coat in a very decisive manner. "I have the Woolsey coach and four here. At least let me drive you home."

Miss Tarabotti felt she had rung enough concessions out of Lord Maccon for one morning. "If you insist, my lord," she acquiesced. "But I must ask you to drop me a little ways from the house. My mama, you see, is wholly unaware of my interest in this matter."

"Not to mention her shock at seeing you alight from my carriage without a chaperone. We would not want to compromise your reputation in any way, now, would we?" Lord Maccon actually sounded riled by the idea.

Miss Tarabotti thought she understood the reasoning behind his tone. She laughed. "My lord, you could not possibly think I have set my cap for *you*?"

"And why is that such a laughable idea?"

Alexia's eyes sparkled in merriment. "I am a spinster, long on the shelf, and you are a catch of the first water. The very notion!"

Lord Maccon marched out the door, dragging her behind him. "Don't ken why you should find it so devilish funny," he muttered under his breath. "Leastways you are nearer my age than most of those so-called incomparables the society matrons persist in hurling at me."

Miss Tarabotti let out another trill of mirth. "Oh, my lord, you are too droll. You are nearing what? Two hundred? As if my being eight or ten years older than the average marriage-market chit should matter under such circumstances. What delightful nonsense." She patted him approvingly on the arm.

Lord Maccon paused, annoyed at her belittling of herself and him. Then he realized what a ridiculous conversation they were having and how nearing dangerous it had become. Some of his hard-won London social acumen returned, and he held his tongue determinedly. But he was thinking that by "nearer his age" he had not meant nearer in years but in understanding. Then he wondered at his own recklessness in thinking any such thing. What was wrong with him today? He could not stand Alexia Tarabotti, even if her lovely brown eyes twinkled when she laughed, and she smelled good, and she had a particularly splendid figure.

He hustled his lady guest down the passageway, intent upon getting her into the carriage and out of his presence as quickly as possible.

Professor Randolph Lyall was a professor of nothing in particular and several subjects in broad detail. One of those generalities was a long running study on the typical human behavioral response when faced with werewolf transformation. His research on the subject had taught him it was best to change out of wolf shape away from polite company, preferably in a corner of a very dark alley where the only person likely to see him was equally likely to be crazy or drunk.

While the population of the greater London area, in specific, and the British Isle, in general, had learned well enough to accept werewolves on principle, to be faced with one engaging in the act of conversion was an entirely different matter. Professor Lyall considered himself rather good at the change—elegant and graceful despite the pain. Youngsters of the pack were prone to excessive writhing and spinal gyrations and sometimes a whimper or two. Professor Lyall simply melted smoothly from one form to the next. But the change was, at its root, *not natural*. Mind you, there was no glow, no mist, no magic about it. Skin, bone, and fur simply rearranged itself, but that was usually enough to give most daylight folk a large dose of the screaming heebie-jeebies. *Screaming* being the operative word.

Professor Lyall reached the Canterbury BUR offices just before dawn still in wolf shape. His animal form was nondescript but tidy, rather like his favorite waistcoat: his pelt the same sandy color as his hair but with a sheen of black about the face and neck. He was not very big, mostly because he was not a very big human, and the basic principles of conservation of mass still applied whether supernatural or not. Werewolves had to obey the laws of physics just like everyone else.

The change took only moments: his fur crawling away from his body and moving up to become hair, his bones breaking and reforming from quadruped to biped, and his eyes going from pale yellow to gentle hazel. He had carried a cloak in his mouth during his run, and he threw it on as soon as he was back to human form. He left the alleyway with no one the wiser to the arrival of a werewolf in Canterbury.

He rested against the BUR office's front doorjamb, dozing softly, until morning caused the first of the standard-issue clerks to make his appearance.

"Who are you, then?" the man wanted to know.

Professor Lyall eased himself away from the door and stepped aside so that the clerk could unlock it.

"Well?" The man barred the way when Lyall would have followed him inside.

Lyall bared his canines. It was not an easy trick in the morning sun, but he was an old enough werewolf to make it look easy. "Woolsey Castle pack Beta, BUR agent. Who is in charge of vampire registration in this office?"

The man, unperturbed by Lyall's demonstration of supernatural ability, replied without shilly-shallying. "George Greemes. He will be in around nine. Cloakroom is 'round that corner over there. Should I send the boot-boy to the butcher for you when he gets in?"

Professor Lyall moved off in the direction indicated. "Yes, do: three dozen sausages, if you would be so kind. No need to cook them."

Most BUR offices kept spare clothing in their cloakrooms, the architectural conceit of cloakrooms having spawned from generations of werewolf arrivals. He found some relatively decent garments, although not precisely to his exacting taste, and, of course, the waistcoat was significantly under par. He then gorged on several strings of sausage and settled in on a convenient ottoman for a much needed nap. He awoke just before nine, feeling much more human—or as human as was supernaturally possible.

George Greemes was an active BUR agent but not a supernatural one. He had a ghost partner who compensated for this disadvantage but who, for obvious reasons, did not work until after sunset. Greemes was therefore accustomed to quiet days full of paperwork and little excitement and was not pleased to find Professor Lyall waiting for him.

"Who did you say you were?" he asked as he came into his office to find Lyall already in residence. Greemes slapped his battered pork pie hat down over a pot full of what looked like the internal guts of several much-abused grandfather clocks.

"Professor Randolph Lyall, second in command of the Woolsey Castle pack and assistant administer of supernatural relations in London central," said Lyall, looking down his nose at Greemes.

"Aren't you a mite scrawny to be Beta to someone as substantial as Lord Maccon?" The BUR agent ran a hand distractedly down his large sideburns, as if checking to ensure they were still affixed to his face.

Lyall sighed. His slender physique engendered this reaction all too often. Lord Maccon was so large and impressive that people expected his second to be of a similar stature and nature. Few understood how much it was to a pack's advantage having one who always stood in the limelight and one who never did. Lyall preferred not to illuminate the ignorant on this subject.

So he said, "Fortunately for me, I have not yet been called upon to physically fulfill my role. Few challenge Lord Maccon, and those who do, lose. However, I did attain Beta rank by fully following all aspects of pack protocol. I may not look like much for brawn, but I have other germane qualities."

Greemes sighed. "What do you need to know? We've no local pack, so you must be here on BUR business."

Lyall nodded. "Canterbury has one official hive, correct?" He did not wait for an answer. "Has the queen reported any new additions recently? Any blood-metamorphosis parties?"

"I should say not! The Canterbury hive is old and very dignified, not given to crass displays of any kind." He actually seemed a little offended.

"Has there been anything else out of the ordinary? Vampires turning up unexpectedly without metamorphosis reports or proper registration? Anything along those lines?" Professor Lyall kept his expression mild, but those hazel eyes of his were startlingly direct.

Greemes looked annoyed. "Our local hive is very well behaved, I will have you know; no aberrations in recorded history. Vampires tend to be fairly cautious in these parts. It is not comfortable to be supernatural in a port town—too fast-paced and changeable. Our local hive tends to produce *very* careful vampires. Not to mention the fact that all those sailors in and out means a ready supply of *willing* blood-whores down dockside. The hive is very little bother so far as BUR is concerned. It is an easy job I have here, thank heavens."

"What about new unregistered roves?" Lyall refused to let the subject drop.

Greemes stood and went to crouch over a wooden wine crate filled with documents. He rifled through them, pausing periodically to read an entry. "Had one in about five years ago. The hive queen forced him to register; no problems since."

Lyall nodded. Clapping his borrowed top hat to his head, he turned to leave. He had a stagecoach to catch for Brighton.

Greemes, sorting the parchment sheaves back into the crate, continued muttering. "'Course, I have not heard from any of the registered roves in a while."

Professor Lyall stopped in the doorway. "What did you say?"

"They have been disappearing."

Lyall took his hat back off. "You made this fact clear in this year's census?"

Greemes shook his head. "I submitted a report on the matter to London last spring. Didn't you read it?"

Professor Lyall glared at the man. "Obviously not. Tell me, what does the local hive queen have to say on this particular topic?"

Greemes raised both eyebrows. "What does she care for roves in her feeding ground except that, when they are gone, things are easier for her household brood?"

The professor frowned. "How many have gone missing?"

Greemes looked up, his eyebrows arched. "Why, all of them."

Lyall gritted his teeth. Vampires were too tied to their territory to roam away from home for long. Greemes and Lyall both knew that missing roves most likely meant dead roves. It took all of his social acumen not to show his profound irritation. This might not interest the local hive, but it certainly was significant information, and BUR should have been told immediately. Most of their vampire problems involved roves. As most of their were-wolf problems involved loners. Professor Lyall decided he had better push for Greemes's reassignment. The man's behavior smacked of drone thrall, those initial stages of over-fascination with the ancient mysteries of the supernatural. It did no one any good to have someone firmly in the vampire camp in charge of vampire relations.

Despite his anger, the Beta managed to nod a neutral good-bye to the repulsive man and headed out into the hallway, thinking hard.

A strange gentleman was waiting for him in the cloakroom. A man Professor Lyall had never met before but who smelled of fur and wet nights.

The stranger held a brown bowler hat in front of his chest with both hands, like a shield. When he saw Lyall, he nodded in a way that was less greeting and more an excuse to bare the side of his neck in obeisance.

Lyall spoke first.

Pack dominance games might seem complicated to an outsider, but very few wolves in England outranked Professor Lyall, and he knew all of them by face and smell. This man was not one of them; therefore, he, Professor Lyall, was in control.

"This office has no werewolves on staff," he said harshly.

"No, sir. I am not BUR, sir. There is no pack in this city as I am certain your eminence is well aware. We are under your lord's jurisdiction."

Lyall nodded, crossing his arms. "Yet, you are not one of the Woolsey Castle pups. I would know."

"No, sir. No pack, sir."

Lyall's lip curled. "Loner." Instinctively, his hackles raised. Loners were dangerous: community-oriented animals cut off from the very social structure that kept them sane and controlled. Alpha challenges invariably came from within the pack, following official lines, with Conall Maccon's unexpected ascension to power the most recent exception to that rule. But brawling, violence, feasting on human flesh, and other such illogical carnage—that was the loner's game. They were more common than vampire roves, and far more dangerous.

The loner clutched his hat tighter at Lyall's sneer, hunching down. If he had been in wolf shape, his tail would be tucked tight between his back legs.

"Yes, sir. I set a watch to this office waiting for the Woolsey Alpha to send someone to investigate. My claviger told me you had arrived. I thought I had best come myself and ascertain if you wanted an official report, sir. I am old enough to stand daylight for a little while."

"I am here on hive, not pack, business," Lyall admitted, impatient to get to the point.

The man looked genuinely surprised. "Sir?"

Lyall did not like being confused. He did not know what was going on, and he did not appreciate being put at a disadvantage, especially not in front of a loner. "Report!" he barked.

The man straightened, trying not to cower at the irate tone in the Beta's voice. Unlike George Greemes, he had no doubt of Professor Lyall's fighting capabilities. "They have stopped, sir."

"What has stopped?" Lyall's voice took on a soft deadly timbre.

The man swallowed, twisting his hat about further. Professor Lyall began to suspect the bowler might not survive this interview. "The disappearances, sir."

Lyall was exasperated. "I know that! I just found out from Greemes."

The man looked confused. "But he is on vampires."

"Yes, and . . . ?"

"It is werewolves who have gone missing, sir. You know, the Alpha had most of us loners stashed along the coast round these parts; keeps us well out of London's way. Also ensures we stay busy fighting pirates rather than each other."

"So?"

The man cringed back. "Thought you knew, sir. Thought the Alpha had started and then stopped it. It has been going several months now."

"You thought it might be Lord Maccon doing a culling, did you?"

"Packs never take to loners, sir. He is a new Alpha, needs to establish his authority."

Professor Lyall could not argue with that reasoning. "I have got to get moving," he said. "If these disappearances start up again, you will let us know immediately."

The man cleared his throat subserviently. "Cannot do that, sir. All apologies, sir."

Lyall gave him a hard look.

The man hooked a finger in his cravat to pull it down and expose his neck defensively. "Sorry, sir, but I am the only one left."

A cold shiver caused all the hairs on Professor Lyall's body to stick up on end.

Instead of going on to Brighton, he caught the next stagecoach back to London.

CHAPTER FOUR

Our Heroine Ignores Good Advice

Alexia was embarrassed to find that she was reduced to shamefully sneaking out of her own home. It simply would not do to tell her mama she was paying a late-night call on a vampire hive. Floote, though disapproving, proved an able ally in her transgression. Floote had been Alessandro Tarabotti's valet before Alexia was even a twinkle in that outrageous gentleman's eye. As such, he knew a lot more than just how to butler, and that included a thing or two on the organization of misdemeanors. He hustled his "young miss" out of the servants' entrance at the back of the house. He had her carefully shrouded in the scullery maid's old cloak and managed to stuff her into a hired cab maintaining a stiff but capable silence all the while.

The hackney rattled through the darkened streets. Miss Tarabotti, mindful of her hat and hair, nevertheless drew down the widow sash and stuck her head out into the night. The moon, three-quarters and gaining, had not yet risen above the building tops. Above, Alexia thought she could make out a lone dirigible, taking advantage of the darkness to parade stars and city lights before one last load of passengers. For once, she did not envy them their flight. The air was cool and probably unbearably chilly so high up; this was no surprise, as London was generally a city not celebrated for its balmy evenings. She shivered and closed the window.

The carriage finally stopped at a good-enough address in one of the more fashionable ends of town, although not an end Miss Tarabotti's particular collection of acquaintances tended to frequent. Anticipating a brief engagement, she paid the hackney to wait and hurried up the front steps, holding high the skirts of her best green and gray check visiting dress.

A young maid opened the door at her approach and curtsied. She was almost too pretty, with dark blond hair and enormous violet eyes, and neat as a new penny in a black dress and white apron.

"Miz Tarabotti?" she asked in a heavy French accent.

Alexia nodded, pulling at her dress to rid it of travel wrinkles.

"Zi comtesse, she iz expecting you. Right diz way." The maid led her down a long hallway. She seemed to sway as she moved with a dancer's grace and liquid movements. Alexia felt large, dark, and clumsy next to her.

The house was typical of its kind, though perhaps a touch more luxurious than most, and outfitted with every possible modern convenience. Miss Tarabotti could not help but compare it to the Duchess of Snodgrove's palatial residence. Here there was more real affluence and grandeur, the kind that did not need to display itself openly—it simply *was*. The carpets were thick and soft, in coordinating shades of deep red, probably imported directly from the Ottoman Empire three hundred years ago. There were beautiful works of art hanging on the walls. Some were very old; some were more contemporary canvases signed with names Alexia knew from newspaper gallery announcements. Luxuriant mahogany furniture showcased beautiful statues: Roman busts in creamy marble, lapis-encrusted Egyptian gods, and modern pieces in granite and onyx. Rounding a corner, Miss Tarabotti was treated to an entire hallway of polished machinery, displayed much as the statuary had been and with the same studied care. There was the first steam engine ever built, and, after it, a silver and gold monowheel; and, Alexia gasped, *was that a model of the Babbage engine?* Everything was perfectly clean and chosen with utter precision, each object occupying the space it had been given with immense dignity. It was more impressive than any museum Alexia had ever visited—and she was fond of museums. There were drones everywhere, all attractive and perfectly dressed, efficiently going about the business of running daylight interference and nighttime entertainment for the hive. They, too, were works of art, dressed in subdued elegance to match the tenor of the house, and collected with care.

Alexia did not have the soul to truly appreciate any of it. However, she understood style well enough to know that it surrounded her. It made her very nervous. She smoothed down her dress self-consciously, worried it might be considered too simple. Then she straightened her spine. A plain tan spinster like her could never compete with such grandeur; best take advantage of what assets she did have. She puffed up her chest slightly and took a calming breath.

The French maid opened a door to a large drawing room and curtsied her inside before gliding off, her feet silent on the red carpet, her hips swaying back and forth.

"Ah, Miss Tarabotti! Welcome to the Westminster hive."

The woman who came forward to greet Alexia was not at all what she had expected. The lady was short, plump, and comfortable-looking, her cheeks rosy and her cornflower-blue eyes sparkling. She looked like a country shepherdess stepped out of a Renaissance painting. Alexia glanced about for her flock. They were there, of a kind.

"Countess Nadasdy?" she asked tentatively.

"Yes, my dear! And this is Lord Ambrose. That is Dr. Caedes. That gentlemen there is His Grace the Duke of Hematol, and you know Miss Dair." She gestured as she spoke. Her movements were simultaneously too graceful and too contrived. They looked as though they had been well studied, as carefully articulated as a linguist speaking a foreign tongue.

Aside from Miss Dair, who smiled kindly from her place on the settee, no one seemed particularly pleased to see her. Miss Dair was also the only drone present. Alexia was certain the other three were vampires. Though she knew none of them socially, she had read some of Dr. Caedes's research during her more adventurous academic pursuits.

"How do you do?" said Miss Tarabotti politely.

The party all made the requisite social murmurings.

Lord Ambrose was a large, exceedingly comely man, looking the way romantic schoolroom girls expect vampires to look—dark and broodingly arrogant with aquiline features and deep meaningful eyes. Dr. Caedes was also tall but skinny as a walking stick, with thinning hair stopped mid-retreat by metamorphosis. He had with him a doctor's bag, though Alexia knew from her readings that his Royal Society membership rested on his extensive engineering work, not a physician's license. The last hive member, the Duke of Hematol, was nondescript in a premeditated way that reminded Alexia of Professor Lyall. Consequently, she regarded him with great wariness and respect.

"If you do not mind, my dear, might I shake your hand?" The Westminster queen moved toward her with that abrupt and smooth supernatural suddenness.

Alexia was taken aback.

Up close, Countess Nadasdy looked less jolly, and it was clear her rosy cheeks were the product of artifice, not sunlight. Under layers of cream and powder, her skin was ashen white. Her eyes did not sparkle. They glittered as hard as the dark glass used by astronomers to examine the sun.

Miss Tarabotti backed away.

"We need to confirm your state," the hive queen explained, still coming at her.

She grabbed Alexia's wrist firmly. The countess's tiny hand was impossibly strong. The moment they touched, much of the hive queen's hardness vanished, and Miss Tarabotti was left wondering if once, long, long ago, Countess Nadasdy had actually *been* a shepherdess.

The vampire smiled at her. No fangs.

"I object most strenuously to this action, my queen. I want it known before the hive that I disagree with this approach to our situation," Lord Ambrose spoke curtly.

Alexia was not certain if he was angry at her preternatural state or at her physical effect on his queen.

Countess Nadasdy let go of her wrist. Her fangs reappeared. They were long and thin, almost biologically spiny, with what looked like barbed tips. Then, with a lightning-fast movement, she lashed out to the side with sharp clawlike fingernails. A long line of red appeared on Lord Ambrose's face. "You overstep your bond duties, child of my blood."

Lord Ambrose bowed his dark head, the shallow wound already closing and healing itself. "Forgive me, my queen; it is only your safety that concerns me."

"Which is why you are my *praetoriani*." In an abrupt change of mood, Countess Nadasdy reached to caress the very part of Lord Ambrose's face she had just sliced open.

"He speaks nothing but truth. You allow a soul-sucker to touch you, and once you are mortal, all it takes is one fatal injury." This time is was Dr. Caedes who spoke. His voice was slightly too high-pitched, with a fuzziness around the edges, a sound wasps make before they swarm.

To Alexia's surprise, the countess did not claw his face open. Instead she smiled, showing off the full length of her sharp barbed fangs. Alexia wondered if they had been filed into that extraordinary shape.

"And yet, this girl does nothing more threatening than stand before us. You are all too young to remember what real danger is inherent in her kind."

"We remember well enough," said the Duke of Hematol. His voice was calmer than the other two but more malicious in cadence—soft and hissing like steam escaping a boiling kettle.

The hive queen took Miss Tarabotti gently by the arm. She seemed to breathe in deeply, as though Alexia smelled of some scent she loathed but was trying desperately to identify. "We were never in any direct danger from the female preternaturals; it was only ever the males." She spoke to Alexia in a conspiratorial whisper. "Men, they do so enjoy the hunt, do they not?"

"It is not the ability to kill that worries me. Quite the opposite," said the duke softly.

"In which case it is you gentlemen who should avoid her and not I," replied the countess slyly.

Lord Ambrose laughed snidely at that remark.

Miss Tarabotti narrowed her eyes. "*You* asked me to come here. I do not wish to be an imposition, and I will not be made to feel unwelcome." She jerked her arm away, sharp enough to break the countess's grip, and turned to leave.

"Wait!" The hive queen's voice was sharp.

Miss Tarabotti continued moving toward the door. Fear made her throat tight. She comprehended what it must be like to be some trapped furry creature in a reptilian den. She stopped when she found her way barred. Lord Ambrose had moved with a vampire's characteristic swiftness to prevent her departure. He sneered at her, tall and distressingly gorgeous. Alexia found she much preferred Lord Maccon's brand of largeness: gruff and a little scruffy round the edges.

"Remove yourself from my path, sir!" hissed Miss Tarabotti, wishing she had brought her brass parasol. Why had she left it behind? What this man seemed most in need of was a good sharp prod to the nether regions.

Miss Dair stood and came over to her, all blond ringlets and troubled blue eyes. "Please, Miss Tarabotti. Do not leave just yet. It is only that their memories are longer than their tempers." She gave Lord Ambrose an evil look. Taking Alexia solicitously by the elbow, she led her firmly toward a chair.

Miss Tarabotti acquiesced, sitting with a rustle of green and gray taffeta and feeling even more at a disadvantage until the hive queen sat down across from her.

Miss Dair rang the bell rope. The pretty violet-eyed maid appeared in the doorway. "Tea, please, Angelique."

The French maid vanished and moments later reappeared pushing a fully laden tea trolley, complete with cucumber sandwiches, pickled gherkins, candied lemon peel, and Battenberg.

Countess Nadasdy served the tea. Miss Tarabotti took hers with milk, Miss Dair took hers with lemon, and the vampires took theirs with a dollop of blood, still warm and poured out of a crystal pitcher. Alexia tried not to think too hard about its origin. Then the scientific part of her wondered what would happen if that jug contained preternatural blood. Would it be toxic or just convert them to human state for a certain length of time?

Alexia and Miss Dair helped themselves to food, but no one else in the room bothered to partake. Unlike Lord Akeldama, they clearly did not appreciate the taste of food nor feel compelled by common courtesy to make a show of consuming it. Alexia felt awkward eating while her hostess touched nothing, but she was not the type to ever be put off good food, and the tea, like everything else in the hive house, was of the very highest quality. She refused to rush, sipping slowly from the exquisite blue and white bone china cup and even asking for a second helping.

Countess Nadasdy waited until Miss Tarabotti was halfway through a cucumber sandwich to reopen their conversation. They talked on safe and banal subjects: a new play down the West End, the latest art exhibit, the fact that full moon was just around the corner. Full moon was a regular holiday for working vampires, since werewolves *had* to absent themselves.

"I hear a new gentleman's club has opened near the Snodgrove town house," Miss Tarabotti offered, getting into the spirit of the small talk.

Countess Nadasdy laughed. "I understand the duchess is in high dudgeon. Apparently, it brings down the whole tenor of the neighborhood. She should count her blessings; if you ask me, it could be decidedly worse."

"It could be Boodles," giggled Miss Dair, clearly thinking how embarrassing the duchess would find country squires hanging about all day and night.

The duke added, "Or scandal of scandals, it could be Claret's." He named the gentleman's club that catered to werewolves.

The vampires all laughed uproariously at that. It was creepy in its lack of decorum.

Miss Tarabotti decided in an instant that she did not like the Duke of Hematol one jot.

"Speaking of the Duchess Snodgrove." The hive queen segued in a slithery fashion onto the subject she had really summoned Alexia in to discuss. "What was it that happened during her ball the night before last, Miss Tarabotti?"

Alexia put her teacup down carefully into its saucer, then set both onto the tea trolley with a faint clatter. "The papers described it accurately enough."

"Except that you were not named in any of them," said Lord Ambrose.

"And there was also no mention of the deceased young man being supernatural," added Dr. Caedes.

"And no reference to the fact that you had executed the killing blow." Countess Nadasdy sat back, a faint smile on her round pleasant face. The smile did not sit well there, not with the four fangs and the little dents they left in those full shepherdess lips.

Miss Tarabotti crossed her arms. "You seem well informed. Why do you need me here?"

No one said anything.

"It was an accident," grumbled Alexia, relaxing her defensive posture. She took a bite of Battenberg without really tasting it. It was an insult to the little cake, for it was usually good and worth appreciating: thick sponge with homemade marmalade and crystallized almond paste on the outside. This sponge seemed dry and the almond paste gritty.

"It was a very tidy stake to the heart," corrected Dr. Caedes.

Alexia went immediately on the defensive. "Too tidy: he barely bled. Do not blindside me with accusations, venerable ones. *I* did not drive him to starvation." No sane person would ever describe Miss Tarabotti as a shrinking violet. When attacked, she fought back with interest. It could have been the result of her preternatural state; then again, it could simply be a ridiculously stubborn disposition. She spoke decidedly, as though to a sulking child. "That vampire was suffering from serious hive neglect. He had not even been trained out of larvae stage well enough to recognize me for what I clearly am." If Alexia had been sitting close enough, she probably would have prodded the queen with a sharp finger to the sternum. *Scratch me*, Alexia thought. *I'd like to see her try!* She contented herself with frowning fiercely.

Countess Nadasdy looked taken aback, not having anticipated such a shift. "He was not one of mine!" she said defensively.

Miss Tarabotti stood, back straight, glad for once that she had an assertive figure: tall enough to tower over everyone but Lord Ambrose and Dr. Caedes. "Why do you play these games with me, venerable one? Lord Maccon said he could smell your bloodline in that dead boy. He *must* have been metamorphosed by you or one of your get. You've no right to pin *your* carelessness and inability to safeguard your own interests upon me, especially when I only acted in self-defense." She held up a hand to forestall interruption. "True, I have better defensive mechanisms than most daylight folk, but *I* am not the one being careless with hive blood."

Lord Ambrose hissed, his fangs fully extended, "You go too far, Soulless."

Miss Dair stood, one hand raised to her mouth in shock at such indelicate behavior. Her big blue eyes were wide and shifted between Alexia and Countess Nadasdy like those of a frightened rabbit.

Miss Tarabotti ignored Lord Ambrose, which was difficult, as her skin was prickling in reaction, and the prey part of her brain wanted desperately to run and hide behind the chaise lounge. She forced down the instinct. It was preternaturals who hunted vampires, not the other way around. Technically, Lord Ambrose was *her* rightful prey. He should be trembling behind the sofa! She leaned on the tea trolley, bending toward the queen. She tried to loom like Lord Maccon loomed, but suspected her green and gray check visiting dress and ample bosom mitigated any threatening aspect.

Affecting indifference, Alexia spiked a second piece of Battenberg hard with a fork. Metal clanked loudly against serving plate. Miss Dair jumped.

"You are correct in one aspect, Miss Tarabotti. This is *our* problem," said the queen, "hive business. You should not be involved. BUR should not be involved, although they *will* continue to interfere. Not until *we* know more about the situation anyway. The werewolves should certainly keep their furry noses out of it!"

Miss Tarabotti pounced on the hive queen's indiscretion. "So there *has* been more than one of these mysterious vampire appearances?"

Countess Nadasdy sneered at her.

Alexia said, "The more BUR knows, the easier it will be to figure out why and how this is happening."

"This is hive business; it is not a matter for the Registry," the queen reiterated, saying nothing more.

"Not if unregistered roves are roaming London outside hive dominion. Then it is BUR business. Do you want to go back to the Dark Ages, when humans feared you and preternaturals hunted you? Vampires must at least *appear* to be under government control; that is part of BUR's mandate. You and I both know that. Everyone in this room must know that!" Miss Tarabotti spoke firmly.

"Roves! Do not talk to me about roves—nasty, ungoverned madmen, the lot of them." Countess Nadasdy bit her lip. It was a strangely endearing gesture from one of the oldest immortals in England.

At that sign of confusion, Alexia finally realized what was really going on. The hive queen was frightened. Like Lord Akeldama, she expected to fully comprehend what occurred in her territory. Hundreds of years of experience colored every new occurrence with predictability and ennui. Yet this was something new and thus outside her comprehension. Vampires did not like surprises.

"Tell me, please." Miss Tarabotti mollified her tone. It had worked with Lord Maccon. Perhaps the trick to dealing with the supernatural set was merely to play the social submissive. "How many have there been?"

"My queen, be cautious," the Duke of Hematol advised.

Countess Nadasdy sighed. She looked from one to the next of the three male vampires. Then she said, "Three in the past two weeks. We managed to catch two of them. They know nothing of vampire etiquette, are confused and disoriented, and usually die within a few days despite our best efforts. As you say, they are ignorant of the preternatural threat, of the proper respect due to a hive queen, and even the office of the potentate. They know little of BUR and its laws of registration. It's as though they sprung, fully formed, onto the streets of London— like Athena from the mind of Zeus."

"Athena was the goddess of war," said Alexia nervously.

"In all my centuries, nothing like this has ever occurred. There were vampire hives on this tiny island before there were human governments. The feudal system was based on hive and pack dynamics. The Roman Empire took its style of organization and efficiency from our kind. The hive structure is more than just a social institution. It is supernatural instinct. No vampire is born outside the hive, because only a queen can bring about metamorphosis. It has been our greatest strength, the control this engenders, but it has also been our greatest weakness." The countess looked down at her small hands.

Miss Tarabotti sat silent throughout this speech, watching the hive queen's face. Countess Nadasdy was definitely scared, but there was an edge of hunger to her fear. To make vampires without a queen! The hive wanted to know how it was occurring so they could master the technique themselves. Such a technology was more than any vampire could wish. It was one of the reasons they invested so heavily in the modern sciences. The gadgetry in the receiving room alone was meant for more that just to amaze and delight. The hive must boast several inventor drones. There were rumors Westminster held a controlling interest in the Giffard dirigible company. But their real hope was always for just such a scientific breakthrough—supernatural birth without blood bite. Miraculous, indeed.

"What will you do next?" Miss Tarabotti asked.

"I have already done it. I have involved a preternatural in hive business."

"The potentate will not be pleased." The Duke of Hematol seemed more resigned than annoyed. It was, in the end, his duty to support his queen and her decisions.

The potentate served as advisor to Queen Victoria, acting the vampire equivalent of a prime minister. Usually a well-known rove of extensive political acumen, the potentate was elected to the position by vote from all hives in the United Kingdom and served until someone better came along. It was the only way a rove could achieve any kind of serious social standing among the vampires of the ton. The current potentate had occupied the position since Queen Elizabeth I sat on the throne of England. Queen Victoria was reported to find his advice invaluable, and there were rumors that the success of the British Empire was due in large part to his skills. Of course, they said the same thing about the dewan, Her Majesty's werewolf advisor. He was a loner who had been around almost as long as the potentate, concerned himself mostly in military matters, and stayed out of pack squabbling. The two stood head and tail above other pack and hive outsiders as invaluable political liaisons to the daylight camp. But like all outsiders in good faith with the establishment, they tended to forget their revolutionary roots and side with the establishment. The potentate would bow to the hives in the end.

"The potentate is not a queen. This is hive business, not politics," countered Countess Nadasdy sharply.

"Nevertheless, he will have to be told," insisted the duke, running a fine-boned hand through his thinning hair.

"Why?" Lord Ambrose was clearly disinclined to tell anyone. He obviously objected to Alexia being consulted, and he certainly did not like the idea of involving a politician.

Miss Dair cleared her throat delicately, interrupting them. "Gentlemen, I am quite certain this is a subject best left for later." She gestured with her head at Miss Tarabotti, who had momentarily been forgotten.

Miss Tarabotti munched down her third piece of Battenberg and tried to look cunning.

Dr. Caedes swung around and gave her a very hard look. "*You*"—his tone was excessively accusatory—"are going to be trouble. Preternaturals always are. Just you keep a careful eye on those moon howlers you keep walking out with. Werewolves also have an agenda to keep to. You do realize that?"

"And you bloodsuckers, of course, are all sweetness and light with only my best interests at heart," Alexia shot back, brushing Battenberg crumbs casually off her lap.

"Look at the plucky young thing! She is trying to make a funny," said Lord Ambrose snidely.

Miss Tarabotti stood and nodded to the assembled company. The words being bandied about were getting dangerously rude. So rude, in fact, that unless she missed her guess, actions would soon be required. She would rather cut her visit short at words. This seemed an opportune moment to vacate the premises.

"Thank you for a delightful visit," she said, smiling in a way she hoped looked predatory. "It has been most"—she paused, deliberating, choosing her words carefully—"educational."

Miss Dair looked to the hive queen. At the countess's nod, she pulled a nearby bell rope that was discreetly hidden behind a heavy velvet drape. The beautiful blond maid appeared once more in the doorway. Miss Tarabotti followed her out, feeling a bit like she had just escaped the jaws of some unpleasant beast.

She was just starting down the front steps toward her cab when she was waylaid by a fierce grip on her upper arm. The lovely Angelique was far stronger than she appeared to be. It was not supernatural strength either; she was only a drone.

"Yes?" Miss Tarabotti tried to be polite.

"You are of ze BUR?" The maid's violet eyes were wide, earnest.

Alexia did not know quite what to say to that. She did not wish to lie, for she had no official sanction. A pox on Lord Maccon and his archaic principles! "I am not quite official, but—"

"You could take zem a message, yez?"

Miss Tarabotti nodded, leaning forward. Partly to appear interested, partly to ease the viselike grip the girl persisted in maintaining on her arm. *Tomorrow,* she thought, *I will be covered in bruises.*

"Tell me."

Angelique glanced around. "Ask zem. Ask zem, please, to look for ze missing ones. My master, he iz a rove. He vanishez last week. Poof." She snapped her fingers. "Like zat. Zey brought me to ze hive because I am pretty and do good work, but ze comtesse, she only just toleratez me. Without hiz protection, I do not know how long I will last."

Miss Tarabotti had no idea what the girl was on about. Lord Akeldama once said hive politics put the workings of the British government, whether daylight or shadow, to shame. She was beginning to understand the truth of his words. "Uh, I am not sure I quite follow."

"Please try."

Well, thought Alexia, *no harm in trying.* "Try to do what, exactly?"

"To find out where ze roves are gone. Az well az why ze new onez come." Clearly, Angelique liked listening at keyholes.

Miss Tarabotti blinked, trying to follow. "Vampires are going missing, as well as appearing out of thin air? You are certain they are not the same, with, say, lots of makeup and appalling shirts to make them look like new larvae?"

"No, miz." The maid gave Alexia's weak attempt at humor a reproachful look.

"No, I suppose they would not be so unfashionable, even as a hoax."

Miss Tarabotti sighed and nodded. "Very well, I shall try." She was thinking that the world was getting even more confusing, and if the hive had no idea what was going on, and BUR even less, what could *she* possibly do to comprehend the situation?

Nevertheless, the maid seemed satisfied. Clearly, she did not share Alexia's reservations. She let go of Miss Tarabotti's arm and slipped back into the house, closing the massive door firmly behind her.

Alexia, frowning in puzzlement, marched down the stairs and into the waiting hackney. She did not notice that it was not the same hackney as the one she had originally arrived in, nor that it was driven by a different coachman.

She did, however, realize instantly that there was someone already residing inside the cab.

"Oh dear, I do beg your pardon! I thought this carriage was available," said Miss Tarabotti to the bulky individual slouched in the corner of the facing seat. "I told my driver to wait, and here you were in exactly the same spot, with the cab door open. I simply assumed. I do apologize. I . . ." She trailed off.

The man's face was in shadows, his features obscured by a wide coachman's hat. He did not seem to have anything to say. No greeting, no acceptance of her apologies. He did not even bother to move his gray-gloved hand to tip that horribly inappropriate hat to a strange lady blundering about in his rented transport.

"Well," said Miss Tarabotti, disgusted by his rudeness, "I shall just be off then."

She turned to leave, but the driver had climbed down off the box and now stood outside in the street, barring her exit. *His* features were not shadowed. A nearby gas lamp lit them silky gold and shiny. Alexia jerked backward in horror. *That face!* It was like a wax copy of something not quite human, smooth and pale with no blemish, no scar, and no hair to speak of. On the forehead four letters had been written in some sort of smudged black substance: VIXI. *And those eyes!* They were dark and curiously blank, so flat and expressionless it was as though nothing lived within the mind behind them. Here was a man who watched the world without blinking, yet somehow refrained from looking directly at anything.

Miss Tarabotti backed away from that smooth face in repugnance. The apparition reached forward and slammed the door to the cab, jerking the handle to lock it closed. Only then did his set expression change. He grinned a slow lazy grin that crept across his waxy face the way oil spreads over water. His mouth was full of straight white squares, not teeth. Alexia was certain that smile would haunt her dreams for years to come.

The wax man vanished from the door window, presumably to pull himself onto the driver's box, for, within the next moment, the carriage jerked and began to move. It rattled and creaked over the London street cobbles, heading toward a place Alexia was reasonably confident she had no desire to visit.

Miss Tarabotti grabbed the handle of the door, rattling it ineffectively. She braced one shoulder against it and pushed hard, putting her entire weight behind the shove. Nothing.

"Now, my dear," said the shadowed man, "no cause to carry on like that." His face remained obscured, although he was now leaning toward her. There was an odd smell in the air, like sweet turpentine. It was by no means a pleasant odor.

Miss Tarabotti sneezed.

"All we want to know is who you are and what you are doing visiting the Westminster hive. This will not hurt a bit." He lunged at her. He was holding a damp handkerchief in one hand—the apparent source of the unpleasant smell.

Alexia was not given to bouts of hysterics. However, she was also not one to stay quiet when circumstances warranted volume. She screamed, loud and long. It was one of those shrill, high shrieks, the kind only terrified women or very good actresses can produce. The scream exited the hackney cab as though no walls stood in the way and rent the quiet London night, cutting through the sound of horse hooves on stone. It rattled the leaded glass of the slumbering residences. It caused more than one stray cat to look about, suitably impressed.

At the same time, Miss Tarabotti braced herself back against the locked door. Without her parasol, her best defense was a good sharp-heeled kick. She was wearing her very favorite walking boots. They had lovely hourglass heels made of wood that gave her a little too much height for fashion but were pretty enough to make her feel almost elegant. They were also the pointiest pair of shoes she owned. Her mother had considered their purchase quite shockingly French. Alexia aimed one hard heel at the shadowed man's kneecap.

"No call for that!" he said, dodging the kick.

Miss Tarabotti was not certain if he was objecting to the kick or the scream, so she issued both again—with interest. He seemed to be having a difficult time negotiating Alexia's multiple layers of skirts and ruffles, which formed a particularly efficacious barrier in the tight confines of the hackney. Unfortunately, Alexia's own defensive movements were equally restricted. She leaned back stubbornly and kicked out again. Her skirts swished.

Despite Miss Tarabotti's best efforts, the shadowed man's handkerchief was coming inexorably toward her face. She twisted her head away, feeling dizzy. The sweet fumes were almost overwhelming. Her eyes began to water slightly.

Time seemed to slow. Alexia could not help wondering what she had done to offend the heavens so much they sent two attackers at her in the space of one short week.

Just when she felt there was no more hope and she was in imminent danger of succumbing to the fumes, there came an unexpected noise. One designed, Miss Tarabotti suspected, by this newfangled concept of evolution to chill the bones of mankind. It was a vast, roaring, snarling howl. It shivered the air and the blood and the flesh all up and down one's spine. It was the cry a predator made only once, when the prey was not yet dead, but the kill was assured. In this particular case, it was followed by a loud thump as something hit the front of the cab hard enough to rattle the two who struggled within.

The carriage, which had been picking up some speed, jerked to an abrupt halt. Alexia heard the screaming cry of a terrified horse. There came a snap as the animal broke free of its traces, and then the sound of galloping hooves as it took off alone through the London streets.

Another loud thump reverberated—flesh against wood. The cab shook again.

Miss Tarabotti's attacker became distracted. He left off forcing the handkerchief on her and instead pulled down the window sash and leaned out, craning his head around toward the driver's box. "What is going on out there?"

No answer was forthcoming.

Miss Tarabotti kicked the back of his knee.

He turned around, grabbed her boot, and jerked it forward.

She fell back against the door, hard enough to bruise her spine on the handle, her layers of dress and corset failing to shield her.

"You are beginning to annoy me," the shadowed man growled. He yanked her foot sharply upward. Alexia struggled valiantly to stand upright on only one leg and screamed again, this time more of a shriek of anger and frustration than distress.

As though in response, the door she leaned against opened.

With a small squeak of alarm, Miss Tarabotti fell backward out of the cab, legs and arms flailing. She landed with an "oof" on something solid but fleshy enough to comfortably break her fall.

She took a deep breath of the stale London air and then coughed.

Well, at least it was not chloroform. She had not met the chemical in person before, it being only newly circulated among the most scientifically minded of the medical profession, but she had a good idea that must be what saturated the shadowed man's ominous handkerchief.

Her landing mattress squirmed and growled. "Good God, woman! Shift off."

Miss Tarabotti was no lightweight. She made no bones about enjoying food—on a fairly regular basis and generally of the toothsome variety. She kept her figure through regular exercise, not a tightly controlled diet. But Lord Maccon, for it was he who squirmed, was very strong and ought to have shifted her easily. Instead he seemed to be having some trouble removing her from atop of him. It took an inordinate amount of time for such a big man, even if such intimate contact with a preternatural canceled out his supernatural strength.

As a general rule, Lord Maccon appreciated a voluptuous woman. He liked a bit of meat on the female form, more to grab on to—and more to chew off. His voice, annoyed as always, belied the gentleness in his big hands as he took the excuse of removing Alexia's generous curves from his person to check for injuries.

"Are you unhurt, Miss Tarabotti?"

"You mean, aside from my dignity?" Alexia suspected Lord Maccon's handling was a tad more than was strictly called for under the circumstances, but she secretly enjoyed the sensation. After all, how often did a spinster of her shelf life get manhandled by an earl of Lord Maccon's peerage? She had better take advantage of the situation. She smiled at her own daring and wondered who could be said to be taking advantage of whom!

Eventually, the earl levered her into a sitting position. He then rolled out from under her and stood, jerking her unceremoniously to her feet.

"Lord Maccon," said Miss Tarabotti, "why is it that around you I always end up in some variety of indelicate and prone position?"

The earl arched a debonair eyebrow at her. "The first time we met, I believe it was I who took a particularly undignified tumble."

"As I have informed you previously"—Alexia brushed off her dress—"I did not leave the hedgehog there intentionally. How was I to know you would sit on the poor creature?" She looked up from her ministrations and gasped in shock. "There is blood all over your face!"

Lord Maccon wiped his face hurriedly on his evening jacket sleeve, like a naughty child caught covered in marmalade, but did not explain. Instead he growled at her and pointed into the hackney. "See what you have gone and done? He got away!"

Alexia did not see, because there was nothing inside the cab to see any longer. The shadowed man had taken the opportunity her unfortunate tumble afforded to escape.

"*I* did not do anything. *You* opened the door. I simply fell out of it. A man was attacking me with a wet handkerchief. What else was I supposed to do?"

Lord Maccon could not say much in response to such an outlandish defense.

So he merely repeated, "A *wet* handkerchief?"

Miss Tarabotti crossed her arms and nodded mutinously. Then, in typical Alexia fashion, she opted to go on the attack. She had no idea what it was about Lord Maccon that always made her so inclined, but she went with the impulse, perhaps encouraged by her Italian blood. "Wait just a moment now! How did you find me here? Have you been following me?"

Lord Maccon had the good grace to look sheepish—if a werewolf can be said to look *sheepish*. "I do not trust vampire hives," he grumbled, as though that were an excuse. "I told you not to come. Didn't I tell you not to come? Well, look what happened."

"I would have you know I was perfectly safe in that hive. It was only when I left that things went all"—she waved a hand airily—"squiffy."

"Exactly!" said the earl. "You should go home and stay inside and never go out again."

He sounded so serious Alexia laughed. "You were waiting for me the entire time?" She looked curiously up at the moon. It was past three-quarters in size—an easy-change moon. She remembered the blood on his mouth and put two and two together. "It is a chilly night. I take it you were in wolf form?"

Lord Maccon crossed his arms and narrowed his eyes.

"How did you change so quickly and get dressed so fast? I heard your attack cry; you could not have been human at that point." Miss Tarabotti had a good idea how werewolves worked, though admittedly she had never seen the earl himself change shape. In fact, she had never seen anyone do it outside of the detailed sketches in some of her father's library books. Still, there the earl stood before her, top hat to tails, untidy hair and hungry yellow eyes, nothing out of place—apart from the odd bit of blood.

Lord Maccon grinned proudly, looking like a schoolboy who had just managed to translate his Latin perfectly. Instead of answering her question, he did the most appalling thing. He changed into wolf shape—but only his head—and growled at her. It was utterly bizarre: both the act itself (a weird melting of flesh and crunching of bones, most unpleasant in both appearance and sound) and the sight of a gentleman in perfect evening dress with an equally perfect wolf's head perched atop a gray silk cravat.

"That is quite revolting," said Miss Tarabotti, intrigued. She reached forward and touched his shoulder so that the earl was forced to return to fully human form. "Can all werewolves do that, or is it an Alpha thing?"

Lord Maccon was a bit insulted by the casualness with which she assumed control of his change. "Alpha," he admitted. "And age. Those of us who have been around the longest control the change best. It is called the Anubis Form, from the olden days." Brought to fully human state by Alexia's hand still resting on his shoulder, he seemed to register their surroundings with new eyes. The hackney's wild flight and sudden halt had placed them in a residential part of London, not quite so up-market as the hive neighborhood but not so bad as it could be.

"We should get you home," Lord Maccon asserted, looking around furtively. He removed her hand gently from his shoulder and curled it about his forearm, leading her at a brisk pace down the street. "Sangria is just a few blocks away. We should be able to hail a cab there at this time of night."

"And somehow you think it is a good idea for a werewolf and a preternatural to show up at the front door of the most notorious vampire club in London looking for a hackney?"

"Hush, you." Lord Maccon looked faintly offended, as though her statement were one of doubt in his ability to protect her.

"I take it you do not want to know what I found out from the vampire hive, then?" Miss Tarabotti asked.

He sighed loudly. "I take it you want to tell me?"

Alexia nodded, tugging down the sleeves of her over jacket. She shivered in the night air. She had dressed to go from carriage to house, not for an evening stroll.

"The countess seems an odd sort of queen," Miss Tarabotti began her story.

"You did not let her appearance mislead you, did you? She is very old, not very nice, and only interested in advancing her personal agenda." He removed his evening jacket and wrapped it around Alexia's shoulders.

"She is frightened. They have had three unexplainable new vampires appear inside Westminster territory in the past two weeks," said Miss Tarabotti, snuggling into the jacket. It was made from a high-end Bond Street silk blend, cut to perfection, but it smelled of open grassland. She liked that.

Lord Maccon said something very rude, and possibly true, about Countess Nadasdy's ancestry.

"I take it she did not inform BUR?" Alexia pretended artlessness.

Lord Maccon growled, low and threatening. "No, she most certainly did not!"

Miss Tarabotti nodded and looked at the earl with wide innocent eyes, imitating Ivy as best she could. It was harder than one would have thought. "The countess gave me tacit permission to involve the government at this time." Bat, bat, bat, went the eyelashes.

This statement, in conjunction with the lashes, seemed to make Lord Maccon even more annoyed. "As if it were her decision! We should have been informed at the onset."

Miss Tarabotti put a cautionary hand on his arm. "Her behavior was almost sad. She is quite frightened. Although she would never openly admit to being unable to cope with the situation. She did say the hive has managed to catch two of these mystery roves and that they died shortly thereafter."

Lord Maccon's expression said he would not put it past vampires to kill their own kind.

Alexia continued. "The mysterious newcomers seem entirely new. She said they arrive knowing nothing of customs, laws, or politics."

Lord Maccon walked along silently, processing this information for a few steps. He hated to admit it, but Miss Tarabotti had single-handedly ascertained more about what was transpiring than any of his agents. He was forced into feeling . . . What exactly was that sensation? Admiration? Surely not.

"Do you know what else these new ones do not know about?" asked Alexia nervously.

The earl suddenly had a very odd expression of confusion upon his face. He was eyeing her as though she had changed unexpectedly into something entirely non-Alexiaish.

"You seem to be far better informed than anyone else at the moment," responded the earl nervously with a sniff.

Miss Tarabotti touched her hair self-consciously under his appraising look, and then she answered her own question. "They do not know about me."

Lord Maccon nodded. "BUR, the packs, and the hives try to keep preternatural identity as secret as possible. If these vampires are being metamorphosed outside the hive, they would have no reason to know your kind even existed at all."

Miss Tarabotti was struck by something. She stopped in her tracks. "That man, he said they wanted to know *who* I was."

"What man?"

"The man with the handkerchief."

Lord Maccon groaned. "So they *were* after you specifically, blast it! I thought they might be after any drone or vampire, and you were just exiting the hive at the wrong time. You do realize they are going to try again?"

Alexia glanced up at him, pulling his jacket closer about her. "I guess I had best not give them another opportunity."

Lord Maccon was thinking exactly the same thing. He moved a little closer, curling her arm more firmly about his. He started them both moving once more toward Sangria, light, and company, and away from the empty, echoing side streets. "I'll have to set a watch on you."

Miss Tarabotti snorted. "And what happens at full moon?"

Lord Maccon winced. "BUR has daylight and vampire agents, as well as werewolves."

Alexia got on her proverbial high horse. "I will *not* have strangers dogging my every step, thank you. You, certainly, Professor Lyall if I must, but others . . ."

Lord Maccon grinned foolishly at that particular prioritization. His company had just merited a "certainly." What she said next, however, drove the smile right off his face.

"What if I arrange to be around Lord Akeldama during the full moon?"

The earl looked daggers. "I am certain he would be *extremely* helpful in a fight. He could ruthlessly flatter all your attackers into abject submission."

Miss Tarabotti grinned. "You know, your intense dislike of my dear vampire friend could almost sound like jealousy if the idea were not so patently absurd. Now, listen, my lord, if you simply let me—"

Lord Maccon let go of her arm, stopped, turned, and, to her complete surprise, kissed her full on the lips.

CHAPTER FIVE

Dinner with an American

The earl grabbed Miss Tarabotti's chin with one big hand and the small of her back with the other, pulling her toward him hard. He slanted his mouth over hers almost violently.

She jerked back. "What are you . . . ?"

"Only way to keep you quiet," he grumbled, taking her chin in a firmer grip and planting his mouth atop hers once more.

It was not the kind of kiss Alexia had ever experienced before. Not that she had been kissed all that frequently prior to this particular point in time. There were a few aberrations in her youth when some rogue or other thought a young and swarthy chaperone might be an easy mark. In such cases, the experience had been sloppy and, due to her ever-present and aptly applied parasol, brief. Lord Maccon's kiss was expertly administered. From his enthusiasm, Miss Tarabotti felt he might be trying to make up for her previous deficit in the arena of kissing. He was doing a bang-up job of it. Which was to be expected considering his years, possibly even centuries, of experience. Since she was holding his coat closed about her, Alexia's arms were effectively trapped by his sudden embrace, giving him full access without impediment. Not, Alexia thought, that she would be inclined to struggle.

The kiss itself was initially quite gentle: slow and soft. Alexia found it surprising given the violence of his embrace. She also found it faintly unsatisfying. She gave a little murmur of frustration and leaned in toward him. Then the kiss changed. It became harder, rougher, parting her lips with purpose. There was even, shockingly, tongue involved in the proceedings. Miss Tarabotti was not certain about *that*. It bordered on sloppy, but then again, the sheer heat of it . . . Her pragmatic preternatural self assessed the situation and realized that she could definitely learn to love the taste of him: like one of those expensive French soups, dark and rich. She arched her back. Her breath had gone all uneven, perhaps because her mouth was clogged with kisses. Alexia was just beginning to come to terms with the tongue concept and notice that she was now getting too warm to need the earl's jacket, when he left off kissing, pushed the coat roughly down, and started nibbling on her neck.

No need to think on that for any span of time. Miss Tarabotti knew instantly that she adored the sensation. She leaned into him even more, too lost in the gathering feelings to really register the fact that his left hand, which had been residing comfortably at the small of her back, had worked its way downward and, apparently unhindered by her bustle, was forming a newly intimate association with her posterior.

Lord Maccon moved her about, still nibbling, shoving the trailing ribbons of her perch hat aside so he could get at the back of her neck. He paused at one point to growl into her ear, sounding bewildered, "What *is* that spice you always smell like?"

Miss Tarabotti blinked. "Cinnamon and vanilla," she admitted. "I use it in my hair rinse." Not prone to flushing, even under the most trying of circumstances, her skin nevertheless felt strangely hot and full.

The earl did not reply. He simply went back to nibbling.

Alexia's head lolled, but she frowned for a second, certain there was something she was not supposed to be doing. Since engaging in a passionate embrace, with a peer of the realm, in the middle of the public street, did not occur to her as inappropriate just then, she immersed herself in the nibbles. They were becoming sharper and more insistent. Alexia found that she liked the idea of maybe a bite or two. As if in response to that thought, Lord Maccon sank his human—due to their shockingly informal embrace and the fact that she was a preternatural—teeth into the place where her neck and shoulder joined.

It sent tingling shocks through Alexia's entire body—a most delightful sensation, better than hot tea on a cold morning. She moaned and rubbed herself up against him, enjoying his big werewolf-sized body, pushing her neck against his mouth.

Someone cleared his throat delicately.

Lord Maccon bit down harder.

Miss Tarabotti lost complete control of her kneecaps, grateful for the wide hand firmly supporting her nether regions.

"Pardon me, my lord," said a polite voice.

Lord Maccon stopped biting Miss Tarabotti. He pulled away, putting about a finger's width of space between them. It felt like a yard. He shook his head, glanced at Alexia in shock, let go of her bottom, stared at his own hand as though accusing it of independent action, and then looked thoroughly ashamed of himself.

Unfortunately, Miss Tarabotti was too befuddled to truly appreciate the earl's uncharacteristic expression of chagrin.

He recovered himself soon enough and let loose a string of unsavory words Miss Tarabotti was certain no gentleman ought ever use around a lady, no matter how provoked. Then Lord Maccon turned to stand before her, shielding her decidedly mussed appearance from view.

Miss Tarabotti, knowing she should straighten her hat and probably the bodice of her dress and the fall of her bustle as well, could do nothing more than lean forward limply against Lord Maccon's back.

"Randolph, you could have chosen a better time," said the earl in exasperation.

Professor Lyall stood diffidently in front of his Alpha. "Possibly. But this is pack business, and it is important."

Alexia blinked stupidly at the Beta from around the earl's upper arm. Her heart was doing crazy things, and she still could not locate her kneecaps. She took a deep breath and put some serious attention into tracking them down.

"Miss Tarabotti, good evening," acknowledged Professor Lyall, apparently unsurprised to find her the object of his lordship's amorous attentions.

"Didn't I recently send you on circuit?" Lord Maccon, back to his customary annoyed state, seemed to have turned all his considerable aggravation on to his Beta instead of Miss Tarabotti for once.

Alexia decided, then and there, that Lord Conall Maccon clearly had only two modes of operation: annoyed and aroused. She wondered which one she would prefer to deal with on a regular basis. Her body joined in that discussion without shame, and she actually managed to shock *herself* into continued silence.

Professor Lyall did not seem to require a response to his salutation from Miss Tarabotti. He answered Lord Maccon's question instead. "I uncovered a situation in Canterbury. It was unusual enough to drive me back here to London without bothering further on circuit."

"Well?" said Lord Maccon impatiently.

Alexia came back to her senses finally and straightened her hat. She pulled up on the neckline of her dress at the shoulder and fluffed out the fall of her bustle. Then she realized she had just engaged in a protracted act of lewdness, bordering on marital relations, in a public street, with Lord Maccon! She fervently hoped that very street would open up and swallow her whole. She became even hotter than she had been moments before, this time with abject humiliation. This was, it must be admitted, a far less pleasant sensation.

While Miss Tarabotti contemplated whether spontaneous human combustion might be due to acute embarrassment, Professor Lyall continued. "You had all the loners stationed along the coast 'round Canterbury, remember? Well, all but one has gone missing. Plus a number of rove vampires have also vanished."

Lord Maccon jerked in surprise.

Alexia realized that she was still plastered against his back. She stepped away and to one side quickly. Her knees were back in working order.

With a growl of possession, Lord Maccon snaked out one long arm and yanked her back against his side.

"Funny," said Miss Tarabotti, trying to ignore the growl and the arm.

"What is funny?" asked the earl, sounding stern. Despite his gruff tone, he used his free hand to adjust his coat more securely over her shoulders and neck.

Miss Tarabotti swatted at him and his solicitousness.

"Stop that," she hissed.

Professor Lyall's bright eyes followed the interaction. His expression did not change, but Alexia had an inkling he was secretly laughing at them both.

She said, "The drone maid said exactly the same thing about the *London* roves. A good number of them have been going missing for several weeks, apparently." She paused. "What about London lone werewolves? Are they still all accounted for?"

"There are none, aside from the dewan. Although he is sort of above the packs, rather than outside of them. Woolsey Castle has always kept strict loner regulations, and we enforce them to the letter," Professor Lyall said proudly.

"The dewan has even stronger feelings on the matter than I," added Lord Maccon. "Well, you know how conservative the Shadow Council tends to be."

Miss Tarabotti, who did not, as she had very little to do with Queen Victoria's government, nodded as though she knew exactly what they were talking about. "So we have got werewolves and vampires disappearing and new vampires appearing." She mulled over the quandary.

"And someone trying to make you disappear as well," added Lord Maccon.

Professor Lyall looked upset to hear that. "What?"

Alexia was touched by his concern.

"We will discuss it later," ordered Lord Maccon. "Right now I ought to get her back home, or we will have a whole new set of problems to cope with."

"Should I come along?" asked his second.

"In that state? You will only exacerbate the situation," mocked the earl.

Alexia noted for the first time—so embarrassed was she at her inadvertent assignation—that Professor Lyall was wrapped in a large coat and wore neither hat nor shoes. She looked with greater care; he did not have any trousers on either! Scandalized, she covered her mouth with one hand.

"You had better scamper off back to the den," instructed the earl.

Professor Lyall nodded and turned away, padding silently on bare feet round the corner of a nearby building. A moment later, a small lithe sandy-colored wolf, with intelligent yellow eyes and a cloak in its mouth, trotted back into the street. He nodded at Alexia once and then took off at a flat run down the cobbled road.

The rest of the night was comparatively uneventful. Outside Sangria, Miss Tarabotti and Lord Maccon ran into a handful of young bucks, dandies of the first order with pinked collars and high-shine shoes, who offered them use of a carriage. The dandies were so inoffensively foppish and so entirely inebriated that Lord Maccon felt comfortable enough taking them up on the offer. He saw Miss Tarabotti safely to her door, the servants' entrance, of course, and into the care of a worried Floote, the family none the wiser to her evening's peregrinations. Then Lord Maccon disappeared round the edge of a building.

Miss Tarabotti peeked out her window directly after she had dressed for bed. She was not certain what it said about her lifestyle that she found it immensely comforting to see an enormous wolf, his brown coat brindled gold and gray, pacing the back alley below her room.

"Lord Maccon did *what*?" Miss Ivy Hisselpenny set her gloves and beaded reticule down with a clatter onto the hall table of the Loontwills' entranceway.

Miss Tarabotti ushered her friend into the front parlor. "Keep your voice down, my dear. And please, for goodness' sake, remove that bonnet. It's positively scorching my eyeballs."

Ivy did as requested, staring at her friend all the while. She was so surprised by what she had just heard; she did not even have the capacity to take obligatory offense at Alexia's customary hat-related abuse.

Floote appeared with a heavy-laden tray and plucked the bonnet out of Miss Hisselpenny's grasp. He held the offensive article—a purple velvet affair covered with yellow flowers and a large stuffed guinea fowl—between thumb and forefinger and retreated out of the room. Miss Tarabotti closed the door firmly behind him . . . and the bonnet.

Mrs. Loontwill and the young lady-twills were out shopping, but they were due back at any moment. It had taken Ivy eons to gather momentum that morning, and now Alexia could only hope they remained uninterrupted for sufficient time to cover all the necessary gossip.

She poured raspberry cordial.

"Well!" insisted Miss Hisselpenny, sitting down in a wicker chair and fixing one curl of her dark hair absentmindedly.

Alexia passed her a glass of cordial and said flatly, "You heard correctly. I said that Lord Maccon kissed me last night."

Miss Hisselpenny did not touch the beverage, so prodigious was her shock. Instead she set her glass down on a small side table for safety's sake and leaned forward as much as her corset would allow. "Where?" She paused. "Why? How? I thought you disliked him most intensely." She frowned, her dark brows creasing. "I thought *he* disliked *you* most intensely."

Miss Tarabotti sipped her cordial, being poised and cagey. She did so like to torture Ivy. She relished the expression of avid curiosity on her friend's face. On the other hand, she was also itching to tell all.

Miss Hisselpenny peppered her further. "What exactly happened? Spare me no detail. How did it come to pass?"

"Well, it was a cold night, but there was still one last dirigible in the sky. Floote helped me sneak out the back and—"

Ivy groaned, "Alexia!"

"You said spare no detail."

Ivy gave her a dour look.

Miss Tarabotti smiled. "After I went to see the hive queen, someone tried to abduct me."

Ivy's jaw dropped. "What!"

Alexia passed her a plate of shortbread, drawing out the suspense. Miss Hisselpenny waved it away frantically. "Alexia, this is torment!"

Miss Tarabotti ceded to her friend's nervous constitution. "Two men tried to abduct me in a fake hackney cab as I left the hive house. It was actually somewhat frightening."

Ivy remained silent and enthralled while Alexia detailed the attempted abduction. Eventually she said, "Alexia, you should report this to the constabulary!"

Miss Tarabotti poured them more raspberry cordial from the cut-glass decanter. "Lord Maccon *is* the constabulary or, more properly, BUR's form thereof. He is keeping an eye on me in case they try again."

Miss Hisselpenny was even more intrigued by this bit of news. "Is he? Really? Where?"

Alexia led her to the window. They looked out onto the road. A man stood on the street corner leaning against a gas lantern post, his eyes firmly fixed on the Loontwills' front entranceway. He was vaguely disreputable-looking, wearing a long tan duster and the most ridiculous wide-brimmed John Bull hat. It looked like something favored by American gamblers.

"And you think my hats are bad!" Ivy giggled.

"I know," agreed Miss Tarabotti fervently. "But what can one do? Werewolves lack subtlety."

"That does not look like Lord Maccon," said Miss Hisselpenny, trying to make out the features under the hat. She had met the earl only a few times, but still . . . "Much too short."

"That is because it is not. Apparently, he departed this morning before I arose. That is his Beta, Professor Lyall, all in all a superior being so far as manners are concerned. According to him, Lord Maccon's gone home to rest." Miss Tarabotti's tone said she expected the earl to have told her that himself. "Well, we had a busy night."

Ivy twitched the heavy velvet curtains back to cover the front window once more and turned to her friend. "Yes, well, so it would seem with all that kissing! Which, I must point out, you have yet to address. You simply must tell me. What was it like?" Miss Hisselpenny found most of the books in Alexia's father's library shameful to read. She covered her ears and hummed whenever Miss Tarabotti even mentioned her papa, but she never hummed so loudly she could not hear what was said. But now that her friend possessed firsthand experience, she was simply too curious to be embarrassed.

"He simply, in a manner of speaking, grabbed me. I believe I was talking too much."

Ivy made the appropriate shocked noise of disagreement over such an outlandish idea.

"And the next thing I knew . . ." Alexia fluttered her hand in the air and trailed off.

"And do go on," encouraged Miss Hisselpenny, her eyes wide with avid curiosity.

"He used his tongue. It made me feel very warm and dizzy, and I do not know quite how to articulate it." Miss Tarabotti felt odd telling

Ivy about the experience. Not because it was an indelicate topic but because she partially wished to keep the sensation to herself.

She had awoken that morning wondering if any of it had actually occurred. It was not until she noticed a large bite-shaped bruise on her lower neck that she accepted the previous night's events as reality and not some sort of torturous dream. She was forced to wear an ancient slate and navy striped walking dress as a result of the bite mark, one of the only garments in her wardrobe that boasted a high neckline. She decided it would be best not to tell Ivy about the bruise, particularly as she would then have to explain why it was impossible for Lord Maccon to ever give her a *real* werewolf bite.

Miss Hisselpenny blushed beet red but still wanted to know more. "Why would he do such a thing, do you think?"

"I am under the impression tongues are often involved in such exertions."

Ivy was not dissuaded. "You know what I mean. Why would he kiss you in the first place? And in a public thoroughfare!"

Miss Tarabotti had puzzled over that question all morning. It caused her to remain uncharacteristically silent during family breakfast. Statements from her sisters that just yesterday would have elicited cutting remarks had passed without a murmur. She had been so quiet her mother actually asked her, solicitously, if she was feeling quite the thing. She had acquiesced that she was a little out of sorts. It had given her an excuse not to go glove shopping that afternoon.

She looked at Ivy without quite seeing her. "I must conclude it was done entirely to keep me quiet. I cannot think of any other reason. As you said, we dislike each other most intensely, have done since he sat on that hedgehog and blamed me." But Miss Tarabotti's voice did not carry the same amount of conviction it once had on that subject.

Alexia was soon to discover that this did seem to be the case. That evening, at a large dinner party given by Lord Blingchester, Lord Maccon actively avoided talking to her. Miss Tarabotti was most put out. She had dressed with particular care. Given the earl's apparent partiality for her physique, she had chosen an evening dress of deep rose with a daringly low décolletage and the latest in small bustles. She had arranged her hair to fall over the side of her neck, covering the bite mark, which meant hours at the curling iron. Her mama had even commented that she looked very well for a spinster.

"Nothing we can do about the nose, of course, but otherwise quite creditable, my dear," she'd said, powdering her own tiny button specimen.

Felicity had even said the dress was a good color for Alexia's complexion, in a tone of voice that implied that *any* color found complementing Alexia's olive skin was truly a miracle of the first order.

It all went to no avail. For had Alexia looked like a vagabond, she was certain Lord Maccon would never have noticed. He greeted her with a shamefaced "Miss Tarabotti" and then seemed at a loss. He did not deliver her the cut direct, or imply anything that might affect her social standing; he simply seemed to have nothing to say to her. Nothing at all. For the entire evening. Alexia almost wished they were back at loggerheads.

She felt compelled to conclude that he was mortified to have kissed her in the first place and was hoping she would forget it ever happened. While knowing any well-bred lady would do simply that, Alexia had enjoyed the experience and did not feel like behaving properly over it. Still, she must conclude that all agreeable sensations were entirely one-sided, and now Lord Maccon felt nothing more than a palpable wish never to see her again. He would treat her with painful correctness in the meantime.

Well, Miss Tarabotti thought, what had she expected? She was nothing more than a soulless spinster, lacking both subtlety and grace. Lord Maccon was a peer of the realm, Alpha of his pack, owner of a considerable quantity of property, and, well, somewhat stunning. All her hopeful attention to appearance aside, and the fact that earlier in the evening the mirror had shown her looking, even to her critical eye, passably pretty, Alexia now felt utterly inadequate.

She must accept that Lord Maccon was providing her, to the best of his ability, with an out. He was being agonizingly polite about it. Throughout the Blingchesters' aperitifs, he arranged things so they were in each other's company, but when they were, he then had nothing to say to her. His behavior screamed acute embarrassment. He could barely stand to look in her direction.

Miss Tarabotti tolerated the ridiculous behavior for about half an hour and then went from confused and unhappy to extremely angry. It did not take much with Alexia. Italian temperament, her mother always said. She, unlike Lord Maccon, did not feel like being polite.

From that moment on, every time Lord Maccon entered a room, Miss Tarabotti arranged to leave it. When he moved purposefully across the receiving area toward her, Alexia sidled sideways and inserted herself seamlessly into a nearby conversation. It was usually something inane like the latest perfume from Paris, but it also involved various marriageable girls causing Lord Maccon to balk. When she sat, she did so between occupied chairs, and she was careful never to be alone or in any untenanted corner of a room.

When time came for supper, Lord Maccon's place card, originally near hers, had magically migrated to the other end of the table. There he spent an uncomfortable evening talking with a young Miss Wibbley on a string of utterly frivolous topics.

Miss Tarabotti, half a world away—eight whole place settings!— still managed to overhear the conversation. Her dinner partner, a scientist in some socially acceptable form, was ordinarily just the kind of personage Alexia hoped to be seated next to. In fact, her ability to converse comfortably with the intellectual set was openly acknowledged as the main reason a spinster of her shelf life continued to be invited to dinner parties. Unfortunately, she found herself uncharacteristically ill-equipped to assist the poor gentleman in his conversational inadequacies.

"Good evening. The name's MacDougall. You'd be Miss Tarabotti, correct?" was his opening gambit.

Oh dear, thought Alexia, *an American.* But she nodded politely.

The supper began with an array of petite oysters over ice with cool lemon cream. Miss Tarabotti, who thought raw oysters bore a remarkable resemblance to nasal excrement, pushed the offensive mollusks away and watched from under her eyelashes in horror as Lord Maccon consumed twelve of them.

"Is not that an Italy sort of a name?" asked the scientist timidly.

Miss Tarabotti, who always thought her Italian heritage far more embarrassing than her soulless state, considered this a weak topic— especially from an American. "My father," she admitted, "was of Italian extraction. Unfortunately, not an affliction that can be cured." She paused. "Though he did die."

Mr. MacDougall did not seem to know how to respond. He laughed nervously. "Didn't leave a ghost behind, did he?"

Alexia wrinkled her nose. "Not enough soul." *Not any soul at all,* she was thinking. Preternatural tendencies bred true. She was what she was because of her father's soullessness. The planet ought, by rights, to be overrun with her kind. But BUR, actually Lord Maccon—she winced—had said that there were simply too few of them to start with. In addition, preternaturals tended to live very short lives.

Another nervous laugh issued from her dinner companion. "Funny you should say, me boasting a bit of an academic interest in the state of the human soul."

Miss Tarabotti was only half listening. At the other end of the table,

Miss Wibbley was saying something about her third cousin who had suddenly undertaken horticultural pursuits. Her family was evidently distrustful of this development. Lord Maccon, after glancing once or twice down the table at Alexia and her scientist, was now looking down at the vacuous girl with an expression of tolerant affection and sitting far too close.

"My particular study focus," continued Mr. MacDougall desperately, "would be the weighing and measuring of the human soul."

Miss Tarabotti looked miserably into her bouillabaisse. It was tasty as these things go. The Blingchesters kept a superb French chef. "How," asked Alexia, not really interested, "would one go about measuring souls?"

The scientist looked trapped; apparently this aspect of his work did not make for civilized dinner conversation.

Miss Tarabotti became more intrigued. She put down her spoon, a mark of how unsettled her feelings that she did not finish the stew, and looked inquiringly at Mr. MacDougall. He was a plumpish young man, adorned with a pair of dented spectacles and a hairline that looked like it anticipated imminent demise. The sudden full force of her interest seemed to unnerve him.

He babbled. "Haven't quite got around to ironing out the specifics, you might say. But I've drawn up plans."

The fish course arrived. Mr. MacDougall was saved from having to elaborate by pike breaded in a rosemary-and-black-pepper crust.

Miss Tarabotti took a small bite and watched Miss Wibbley bat her eyelashes at Lord Maccon. Alexia was familiar with the maneuver; it was the one Ivy had taught her. That made her angry. She pushed the fish away peevishly.

"So how would you approach such a study?" she asked.

"I had thought to use a large Fairbanks scale, customized with supports to hold a man-sized cot," Mr. MacDougall explained.

"Then what would you do, weigh someone, kill them, and then weigh them again?"

"Please, Miss Tarabotti! No need to be crude! I've not worked out the details yet." Mr. MacDougall looked faintly ill.

Alexia, taking pity on the poor sod, switched to theoretical avenues. "Why this particular interest?"

He quoted, "The affections of soul are enmattered formulable essences. That is precisely why the study of the soul must fall within the science of nature."

Miss Tarabotti was not impressed. "Aristotle," she said.

The scientist was delighted. "You read Greek?"

"I read Greek translations," Alexia replied curtly, not wishing to encourage his obvious interest.

"Well, if we could divine the soul's substance, we might measure for its quantity. Then we would know, before the death bite, whether a person might be able to become supernatural or not. Imagine the lives that could be saved."

Alexia wondered what she would weigh on such a scale. *Nothing? Probably, that would be a novel experience.* "Is that why you have come to England? Because of our integration of vampires and were-wolves into regular society?"

The scientist shook his head. "Things are not so bad as all that across the pond these days, but, no, I'm here to present a paper. The Royal Society invited me to inaugurate the opening of their new gentlemen's club, Hypocras. Heard of it?"

Miss Tarabotti had, but she could not remember when, nor could she recall anything further about it. She simply nodded.

The fish course was taken away and the main dish set down before them: roasted beef short ribs with gravy and root vegetables.

At the far end of the table, Lord Maccon's dinner companion let out a tinkling laugh.

Miss Tarabotti asked Mr. MacDougall quite out of the blue, "Miss Wibbley is very attractive, wouldn't you say?" She tipped her rib from its upright presentation position and sawed away at the meat viciously.

The American, being an American, looked openly over at the girl in question. He blushed and said timorously into his food, "I prefer ladies with dark hair and a bit more personality."

Alexia was charmed despite herself. She decided she had wasted enough of the evening, not to mention the delicious meal, agonizing over Lord Maccon. She proceeded to give the hapless Mr. MacDougall the full force of her attention for the remainder of supper. A situation he seemed to regard with mixed terror and delight.

Miss Tarabotti, never one to pass up an opportunity to display her bluestocking tendencies, matched wits with the young scientist on a wide range of subjects. Leaving the weighing of souls for another occasion, the salad course moved them on to recent innovations in various engine designs. Over fruit and bonbons, they broached the physiological correlation between mental and behavioral phenomena and how this might affect vampire hive dynamics. By coffee, which was served in the drawing room, Mr. MacDougall had asked for and received permission to call upon Miss Tarabotti the following day. Lord Maccon was looking as black as thunderclouds, and Miss Wibbley seemed unable to distract him further. Alexia did not notice the werewolf's disgruntlement;

new techniques in the capture of evanescent reflections were just so riveting.

Miss Tarabotti departed the party still feeling rejected by the earl but secure in the knowledge she could look forward to further intellectual conversation the following day. She was also pleased with herself, convinced that while she might be upset by Lord Maccon's behavior, she had given no indication of this to him nor to anyone else who mattered.

Lord Conall Maccon, Earl of Woolsey, paced his office like a caged, well, wolf.

"I do not understand what she is playing at," he grumbled. He was looking even scruffier than usual. This contrasted sharply with the fact that he was still in evening dress, having just come from the Blingchesters' dinner party. His cravat was terribly mussed, as though someone had been pawing at it.

Professor Lyall, sitting at his own small desk in the far corner of the room, looked up from behind a mound of metal scrolls. He pushed a pile of wax rubbings to one side. He reflected sadly that his Alpha really was a hopeless case so far as fashion was concerned. He looked to be moving in that direction in the romantic arena as well.

Like most werewolves, they kept nighttime business hours. Essentially, the Blingchesters' dinner had been Lord Maccon's breakfast.

"I have had a report from the Westminster hive of yet another rove appearance," said Professor Lyall. "At least they *told* us this time. Funny that they should find out before we did; I did not think they concerned themselves so closely with rove activities."

His boss did not seem to hear this. "She completely ignored me, blasted female! Spent the entire evening flirting with a scientist. An *American* scientist, if you ken such an appalling thing!" The Alpha sounded particularly Scottish in his dudgeon.

Professor Lyall ceded to the fact that, for the moment, he was not likely to get any real work done. "Be fair, my lord. You undertook to ignore her first."

"Of course I ignored her! It is her responsibility to come to me at this juncture. I made my initial interest perfectly clear."

Silence.

"*I* kissed *her*," he explained, aggrieved.

"Mmm, yes, I had the dubious pleasure of witnessing that, ah-hem, overly public occurrence." Lyall sharpened his pen nib, using a small copper blade that ejected from the end of his glassicals.

"Well! Why hasn't she done anything about it?" the Alpha wanted to know.

"You mean like whack you upside the noggin with that deadly parasol of hers? I would be cautious in that area if I were you. I am reasonably certain she had it custom made and tipped with silver."

Lord Maccon looked petulant. "*I mean* like attempt to talk to me, or perhaps not talk at all but simply drag me off somewhere . . ." He trailed off. "Somewhere dark and soft and . . ." He shook himself like a wet dog. "But, no. Instead she utterly dismissed me, not a single word. I believe I liked it better when she was yelling at me." He paused and then nodded to himself. "I know I liked it better."

Professor Lyall sighed, put down his quill, turned his entire attention upon his boss, and attempted to explain. Ordinarily, Lord Maccon was not quite so thickheaded. "Alexia Tarabotti is not going to behave in accordance with pack dynamics. You are enacting the traditional courting ritual for Alpha females. It may be instinct for you, but this is the modern age; many things have changed."

"That woman," Lord Maccon spat, "is definitely alpha and most certainly female."

"But not a werewolf." Professor Lyall's voice was aggravatingly calm.

Lord Maccon, who had been behaving entirely on instinct, looked suddenly crestfallen. "Have I handled this situation entirely wrong?"

Professor Lyall was reminded of his Alpha's origins. He might be a relatively old werewolf, but he had spent much of that time in a barely enlightened backwater city in the Scottish Highlands. All the London ton acknowledged Scotland as a barbaric place. The packs there cared very little for the social niceties of daytime folk. Highland werewolves had a reputation for doing atrocious and highly unwarranted *things*, like wearing smoking jackets to the dinner table. Lyall shivered at the delicious horror of the very idea.

"Yes. You have behaved, I would go so far as to say, badly. I suggest a well-crafted apology and an extended session of abject groveling," said the Beta. His expression remained mild, but the look in his eyes was flinty. His Alpha would find no sympathy there.

Lord Maccon stood up very straight. He would have towered over his second even if Lyall were not sitting down. "I am *not* a groveler!"

"It is possible to learn many new and interesting skills in one lifetime," advised Professor Lyall, unimpressed by the posturing.

Lord Maccon looked mutinous.

Professor Lyall shrugged. "Well, you had best give up now, then. I never quite understood your interest in the young lady to begin with. I am convinced the dewan would have much to say on the subject of unsanctioned intimacy between a werewolf and a preternatural regardless of your mistake with Miss Tarabotti." Of course, he was baiting his Alpha, perhaps unwisely.

Lord Maccon went red and sputtered. To tell the truth, he could not quite fathom his interest in her either. There was just something about Alexia Tarabotti that made her immensely appealing. Perhaps it was the turn of her neck or the secret smile she sometimes got when they argued that said she might be yelling at him for the pure fun of it. As far as Lord Maccon was concerned, nothing was worse than a timid woman. He was often prone to lamenting the loss of all those stalwart Highland lasses of his misspent youth. Alexia, he often felt, would adapt well to rough Scottish cold, and rock, and plaid. Was that the source of the fascination? Alexia in plaid? His mind carried that image one or two steps further, taking her out of the plaid and then on top of it.

He sat down with a sigh at his desk. Silence descended for about half an hour; nothing disturbed the night's stillness but the shuffling of papers, the tink of metal slates, and an occasional sip of tea.

Finally Lord Maccon looked up. "Grovel, you say?"

Lyall did not glance away from the latest vampire report he was perusing. "Grovel, my lord."

CHAPTER SIX

Driving with Scientists,
Dabbling with Earls

Mr. MacDougall arrived promptly at eleven-thirty the next morn-ing to whisk Miss Tarabotti away for a drive. His appearance caused quite a tizzy in the Loontwill household. Alexia was, naturally, expecting the gentleman. She sat awaiting his arrival calmly in the front parlor, wearing a forest green carriage dress with gold filigree buttons down the front, an elegant new broad-brimmed straw hat, and a cagey expression. The family surmised her imminent departure from the hat and gloves, but they had no idea who might be calling to take her out. Aside from Ivy Hisselpenny, Alexia did not entertain callers often, and everyone knew the Hisselpennys owned only one carriage, and it was not of sufficient quality to merit gold filigree buttons. The Loontwills were left to assume that Alexia was awaiting a *man*. There was little in the world at that moment that any of them could find more surprising. The possible reintroduction of the crinoline would have caused less shock. They had pestered her throughout the morning's activities to reveal the gentleman's name, but to no avail. So the Loontwills had fi-nally settled into waiting with her, agog with curiosity. By the time the long-awaited knock came, they were quite frenzied with anticipation.

Mr. MacDougall smiled shyly at the four ladies who all seemed to have tried to open the front door at the same time. He issued a round of polite salutations to Mrs. Loontwill, Miss Evylin Loontwill, and Miss Felicity Loontwill. Miss Tarabotti introduced them with only minimal grace and an air of embarrassment before grabbing onto his proffered arm in a pointed manner and with an undisguised air of desperation. Without further ado, he helped her down the stairs and into his car-riage, and settled on the box next to her. Alexia deployed her trusty brass parasol and tilted it in such a way she would not have to look any more at her family.

He drove a pair of elegant chestnuts: calm and quiet beasts, but well matched for pace and color, and goers even though they lacked a certain spirited fire in the eye. The carriage was equally unassuming, not a high flyer but a tidy little buggy well appointed with all modern conveniences. The chubby scientist handled all three like he owned them, and Alexia reassessed her opinion of him. Everything about the equipage was in tip-top condition, and he had clearly spared no expense, even though he was only visiting England for a short while. The carriage included a crank-operated water-boiling canteen for tea on-the-go, a long-distance monocular optical viewing device for the better appreciation of scenery, and even a small steam engine linked to a complex hydraulic system the purpose of which Alexia could not begin to fathom. Mr. MacDougall was a scientist, certainly, and an American, no doubt, but he also seemed to possess taste and the means by which to inventively display it properly. Miss Tarabotti was suitably impressed. As far as she was concerned, it was one thing to have wealth and quite another to know how to show it off appropriately.

Behind them, Alexia's family huddled in a delighted clucking mass. Thrilled upon seeing that it was, indeed, a *man* who had come to take the eldest daughter out, they were doubly delighted to find out that he was the respectable young scientist of the evening before. New heights of euphoria had been reached (especially by Squire Loontwill) once it was deduced that he seemed to possess more capital than was to be hoped for in any standard member of the intellectual set (even an American).

"He may actually be a very good catch," said Evylin to her sister as they stood on the stoop waving Alexia off. "A little portly for my tastes, but she cannot afford to be choosey. Not with her age and appearance." Evylin tossed one of her golden ringlets carelessly behind her shoulder.

"And we all thought her marriage prospects exhausted." Felicity shook her head at the wonders of the universe.

"They are suited," said their mother. "He is clearly bookish. I did not follow a single word of their conversation at dinner last night, not one jot of it. He must be bookish."

"You know what the best of this situation is?" added Felicity, catty to the last. Her father's murmur of "All that money" going either unheard or unacknowledged, she answered her own question. "If they do marry, he will take her all the way back to the Colonies with him."

"Yes, but we will have to put up with the fact that everyone important will know we have an *American* in the family," pointed out Evylin, her eyes narrowing.

"Needs must, my darlings, needs must," said their mother, ushering them back inside and closing the door firmly behind them. She wondered how little they could get away with spending on Alexia's future wedding and retreated to the study with her husband to consult on the matter.

Of course, Miss Tarabotti's relations were getting well ahead of themselves. Alexia's intentions toward Mr. MacDougall were of an entirely platonic nature. She simply wanted to get out of the house and talk with a person, any person, in possession of an actual working brain, for a change. Mr. MacDougall's intentions might have been less pure, but he was timid enough for Miss Tarabotti to easily ignore any verbal forays in the romantic direction. She did so initially by inquiring after his scientific pursuits.

"How did you get interested in soul measuring?" she asked pleasantly, delighted to be out of doors and disposed to be kind to the facilitator of her freedom.

It was an unexpectedly beautiful day, pleasantly warm with a light and friendly little breeze. Miss Tarabotti's parasol was actually being put to its intended use, for the top was down on Mr. MacDougall's buggy, and she certainly needed no more sun than was strictly necessary. The mere whiff of daylight and her tan deepened to mocha and her mama went into hysterics. With both hat and parasol firmly in place, her mama's nerves were assured complete safety—from that quarter at least.

Mr. MacDougall tsked to his horses, and they assumed a lazy walk. A vulpine-faced sandy-haired gentleman in a long trench coat left his station beneath the lamppost outside the Loontwills' front door and followed at a discreet distance.

Mr. MacDougall looked at his driving companion. She was not one to be considered fashionably pretty, but he liked the strong tilt to her jaw and determined glint in her dark eyes. He had a particular partiality for firm-willed ladies, especially when they came coupled with a jaw that was shapely, eyes that were large and dark, and a handsome figure to boot. He decided she seemed resilient enough for the real reason he wanted to measure souls, and it made for a nicely dramatic story anyway. "It's not bad to admit here, I suppose," he said to start, "but you should understand, in my country I'd not speak of it." Mr. MacDougall had a bit of flare for the dramatic well hidden behind the receding hairline and spectacles.

Miss Tarabotti placed a sympathetic hand on his arm. "My dear sir, I did not intend to be nosy! You are of a mind to think of my question as officious?"

The gentleman blushed and pushed at his spectacles nervously. "Oh no, of course not! No such thing. It's just that my brother was turned. Vampire you see. My older brother."

Alexia's response was characteristically British. "Felicitations on a successful metamorphosis. May he make his mark on history."

The American shook his head sadly. "Here, as your comment implies, it is generally thought a good thing. In this country, I mean to say."

"Immortality is immortality." Alexia did not mean to be unsympathetic, but there it was.

"Not when it comes at the price of the soul."

"Your family keeps the old faith?" Alexia was surprised. Mr. Mac-Dougall, after all, was a scientist. Scientists were generally not given to overly religious backgrounds.

The scientist nodded. "Puritans to the very core. Not a progressive bone among them: so *supernatural* means 'undead' to them. John survived the bite, but they repudiated and disinherited him anyway. The family gave him three days' grace and then hunted him down like a rabid dog."

Miss Tarabotti shook her head in sorrow. The narrow-mindedness of it all! She knew her history. The puritans left Queen Elizabeth's England for the New World because the queen sanctioned the supernatural presence in the British Isle. The Colonies had been entirely backward ever since: religious fingers in all their dealings with vampires, werewolves, and ghosts. It made America into a deeply superstitious place. Fates only knew what they'd think of someone like her!

Curious that any man from a conservative family might opt to try for metamorphosis, she asked, "Why on earth did your brother turn in the first place?"

"It was against his will. I think the hive queen did it to prove a point. We MacDougalls have always voted against change—antiprogressive to the last breath and influential in government where it counts most."

Miss Tarabotti nodded. She had surmised his family's influence from the money he obviously possessed. She touched the fine leather of the buggy seat with one hand. Here was a scientist who needed no patronage. Strange place, that overseas land, where religion and wealth did the talking and history and age held so little sway.

Mr. MacDougall continued. "I think the hive thought that turning the eldest might make us MacDougalls all think differently."

"Did it?"

"None except me. I loved my older brother, you see? I saw him once after he'd changed. He was still the same person: stronger, paler, night-born, yes, but essentially the same. He probably still would have voted conservative, if they'd let him vote." He smiled slightly, and then his face fell back to round pudding blandness. "So I switched from banking to biology and have been studying the supernatural ever since."

Miss Tarabotti shook her head unhappily. Such a sad beginning. She contemplated the sunny day: the lovely green of Hyde Park, the bright hats and dresses of ladies walking arm in arm across the grass, the two plump dirigibles gliding sedately overhead. "BUR would never allow such behavior from any vampire—to bite without permission! Let alone for a hive queen to bite the unwilling with the intent to metamorphose! Such shocking behavior."

Mr. MacDougall sighed. "Yours is a very different world, my dear Miss Tarabotti. Very different. Mine is a land still at war with itself. The fact that the vampires sided with the Confederates still has not been forgiven."

Alexia did not wish to insult her new friend, so she refrained from criticizing his government. But what did the Americans expect if they refused to integrate the supernatural set into their society in any way? When they forced vampires and werewolves to hide and skulk about in a shoddy imitation of the European Dark Ages?

"Have you rejected your family's puritanical tenets?" Miss Tarabotti looked inquiringly at her companion. Out of the corner of her eye, she caught a flash of tan trench coat. It must be tough on Professor Lyall to be outside in all this sun, especially when full moon was soon due. She felt a moment's pity but was pleased to know that it was he who had relieved the night watch guard. It meant Lord Maccon was still thinking of her. Of course, he was thinking of her as a problem . . . but that was better than not thinking of her at all, was it not? Alexia touched her lips softly with one hand and then forcibly stopped all ruminations on the mental state of the Earl of Woolsey.

Mr. MacDougall answered her question. "You mean, have I abandoned the belief that supernatural folk have sold their souls to Satan?"

Miss Tarabotti nodded.

"Yes. But not necessarily because of my brother's misfortune. The idea was never scientific enough for me. My parents knew not what they risked, sending me to Oxford. You know, I studied for some time in this country? Several of the dons are vampires. I have come 'round to the Royal Society's way of thinking, that the soul must formulate a quantifiable entity. Some individuals have less of this soul-matter, and some have more. And those who have more can be changed into immortals, and those who have less cannot. Thus it is not lack of soul but overabundance that the puritans feared. And that very concept is heresy in my family."

Alexia agreed. She kept abreast of the Society's publications. They had yet to find out about preternaturals and the truly soulless. BUR was content to let daylight scientists blunder about without access to that particular knowledge. But Miss Tarabotti felt it was only a matter of time in this enlightened age before her kind were analyzed and dissected.

"You have been devising a way to measure the soul ever since?" She checked about casually for her supernatural shadow. Professor Lyall paced them several yards away, doffing his hat to ladies walking by: an everyday middle-class gentleman apparently unaware of their buggy nearby. But Alexia knew he was watching her the entire time. Professor Lyall knew his duty.

Mr. MacDougall nodded. "Wouldn't you like to know? Especially as a woman? I mean, ladies have a high risk of failing to survive metamorphosis."

Miss Tarabotti smiled. "I know exactly how much soul I have, thank you, sir. I need no scientist to tell me that."

Mr. MacDougall laughed, taking her confidence for jest.

A gaggle of dandified young men passed by. All were decked to the height of fashion: three-buttoned swallowtails instead of frock coats, knotted silk cravats, and high collars. Alexia was certain she knew several of them from somewhere, but she did not recognize them well enough to name. These tipped their hats to her. One tallish specimen in blueberry satin breeches slowed to look with inexplicable interest at Mr. MacDougall before being whisked onward by his cohorts. Off to one side, Professor Lyall took note of their antics with interest.

Alexia glanced at her companion. "If you are successful in the measuring of souls, Mr. MacDougall, shouldn't you be worried such knowledge might be misused?"

"By scientists?"

"By scientists, by hives, by packs, by governments. Right now, what keeps the power of the supernatural set in check is their small numbers. If they knew ahead of time who to recruit, they could turn more females and increase their population drastically, and the very fabric of our social world would be rearranged."

"Yet the fact that they need us to procreate gives us normal folk some small advantage," he demurred.

It occurred to Miss Tarabotti that hives and packs had probably been working to uncover a way to measure the human soul for hundreds of years. This young man stood little chance of success where generations of advanced supernatural researchers had failed. But she held her tongue. Who was she to destroy a man's dreams?

She pretended interest in a group of swans floating across a pond to one side of the track. In truth, it was Professor Lyall who had caught her attention. Had he stumbled? It looked as though he had, falling against another gentleman and causing that man to drop some sort of metal device.

"So what topic will you address at the Hypocras inauguration?" Miss Tarabotti asked.

Mr. MacDougall coughed. "Well"—he looked embarrassed—"primarily what I have found the soul *not* to be. My initial research would seem to indicate that it is not an aura of any kind nor a pigmentation of the skin. There are several working theories: some think it may reside in part of the brain; others believe it to be a fluid element in the eyes or perhaps electrical in nature."

"What do you think?" Alexia was still feigning interest in the swans. Professor Lyall seemed to recover himself. It was hard to tell at this distance, but, under his John Bull hat, his angular face seemed oddly pale.

"From what I know of metamorphosis—and I have never been privileged enough to observe it in action, mind you—I believe the conversion to be the result of a blood-borne pathogen. The same kind of pathogen Dr. Snow has suggested resulted in the recent cholera outbreaks."

"You oppose the miasmatic hypothesis of disease transfer?"

The scientist inclined his head, delighted to converse with a woman so well educated in modern medical theory.

Miss Tarabotti said, "Dr. Snow suggests cholera transmission occurred through the ingestion of contaminated water. How exactly would you suggest supernatural transmission occurs?"

"That remains a mystery. As does the reason why some respond positively and others do not."

"A condition that we currently refer to as the presence or absence of excess soul?" suggested Alexia.

"Exactly." The scientist's eyes brightened with enthusiasm. "Identifying a pathogen will only show us *what* occurs to drive metamorphosis. It will not tell us *why* or *how*. My research until now has focused on hematology, but I am beginning to think I have been pursuing the wrong hypothetical angle."

"You need to deduce what is different between those who die and those who survive?" Alexia tapped the brass handle of her parasol with her fingertips.

"And what the survivor is like before and after metamorphosis." Mr. MacDougall drew the horses up so he could turn fully to face Alexia, animated in his enthusiasm. "If the soul has substance, if it is an organ or part of an organ that some possess and others do not—the heart, perhaps, or the lungs—"

Miss Tarabotti was equally enthusiastic; she finished the hypothesis for him. "Then it should be quantifiable!" Her dark eyes sparkled with the very idea of such a thing. Brilliant in concept, but it would require much further study. She understood now why he had not thought his research appropriate dinner conversation the evening before. "You are undertaking a number of cadaverous dissections?" she asked.

Mr. MacDougall nodded, having forgotten her ladylike sensibilities in his excitement. "But I am finding it most difficult to acquire dead werewolves and vampires for comparison. Particularly in the United States."

Miss Tarabotti shuddered. No need to ask why. Everyone knew the Americans burned to death any accused of being supernatural, leaving little behind for any scientist to study. "You think to procure specimens here and transport them back?"

The scientist nodded. "I hope that it will be considered in the best interest of science to pursue this kind of inquiry."

"Well," Alexia said, "your speech at Hypocras should pave the way if it at all approaches the conversation we are having. You have some of the newest and best ideas I have yet heard on the subject. You would have my vote of confidence, were I allowed to be a member of the club."

The young man grinned at her praise and began to think ever more fondly of Miss Tarabotti, who possessed enough intelligence to not only follow his thoughts, but perceive their worth as well. He tsked his horses into motion once more, guiding them off to one side of the path. "Did I mention how lovely you are looking today, Miss Tarabotti?" He pulled the carriage to a full stop.

Of course, Alexia could hardly point out the many flaws in his theories after such a compliment. So instead she steered their conversation on to more general topics. Mr. MacDougall cranked up the mechanical water boiler and brewed a pot of tea. Alexia used the carriage's monocular distance viewing device while he did so. She tilted the lenses about, commenting on the pleasures of a sunny day and the statuesque grace of distant dirigibles floating above the park. She also trained them briefly on Professor Lyall, who was leaning in the shade of a tree a little way away, only to find he had donned his glassicals and was watching her through them. She hurriedly put the optical magnification device down and turned amiably back to her host and tea.

While she sipped cautiously at the tin mug, surprised to find the offering a delicious Assam, he lit up the small hydraulic engine she had noticed at the back of the carriage. With much creaking and groaning, a massive parasol pulled itself upright and then unfolded to shade the open carriage. Alexia snapped her own small parasol shut, glaring at it with an entirely unwarranted sense of inadequacy. It was a good little parasol and hardly deserving of such a jaundiced look.

They passed a distinctly pleasant additional hour in each other's company, sipping tea and nibbling a box of rosewater and lemon Turkish delight that Mr. MacDougall had invested in for this occasion especially. In no time, it seemed, Mr. MacDougall was lowering the gigantic parasol and driving Miss Tarabotti back home.

The young gentleman helped her down from his carriage at the Loontwills' front steps feeling justifiably pleased with the success of their outing, but Alexia forestalled him when he tried to see her all the way to the door.

"Please do not mistake my refusal for rudeness," she explained delicately. "But you do not wish to encounter my relations just now. They are not up to your caliber of intellect, I am ashamed to say." She suspected her mother and sisters were out shopping, but she needed some excuse. The way his eyes looked right now, he might make a declaration, and then where would she be?

The scientist nodded gravely. "I completely understand, my dear Miss Tarabotti. My own relatives are similarly afflicted. May I call again?"

Alexia did not smile. It would not do to be coy when she had no intention of returning his advances. "You may, but not tomorrow, Mr. MacDougall. You will be preparing for your speech."

"The next day?" He was persistent. "That way I can tell you how the opening celebrations went."

Very forward, American men. Alexia sighed inwardly but nodded her acquiescence.

Mr. MacDougall assumed the driver's seat, tipped his hat, and urged his chestnut beauties into a sedate withdrawal.

Miss Tarabotti pretended she was remaining on the stoop to wave him off. Once he was out of sight, however, she nipped furtively back down the front steps and round the side of the house.

"You certainly kept a close watch," she accused the man lurking there.

"Good afternoon, Miss Tarabotti," he said in a polite if mild voice—milder than usual, even for Professor Lyall, almost weak sounding.

Alexia frowned in concern. She tried to get a good look at his face under the ostentatious hat. "How came you to be on duty today, sir? I would have thought Lord Maccon required your expertise elsewhere."

The professor looked pale and drawn, normal in a vampire but not in a werewolf. The lines on his face had deepened with strain, and his eyes were bloodshot. "Miss Tarabotti, it is getting on to full moon; his lordship has to be careful who he puts out to guard you come daylight. The young ones are not very stable at this time of the month."

Alexia sniffed. "I appreciate his concern for my well-being. But I had thought there were others in BUR who might not be so taxed by daylight service. When is the moon?"

"Tomorrow night."

Miss Tarabotti frowned. "Same time as Mr. MacDougall's speech at the Hypocras Club," she said softly to herself.

"What?" The professor looked too tired to be interested.

Alexia waved a hand in the air. "Oh, nothing of import. You should go home, Professor, get some rest. You look absolutely awful. He should not work you so hard."

The Beta smiled. "It is part of my purpose."

"To exhaust yourself protecting me?"

"To safeguard his interests."

Miss Tarabotti gave him a horrified look. "I hardly think that an apt description."

Lyall, who'd seen the crested carriage parked just the other side of the Loontwill house, did not reply to that.

There was a pause.

"What did he do?" Alexia asked.

"Who?" replied Professor Lyall, although he knew perfectly well what she was asking about.

"The man you pretended to stumble into."

"Mmm." The werewolf was cagey. "It was more what he had."

Miss Tarabotti tilted her head and looked inquiring.

"I wish you a pleasant evening, Miss Tarabotti," said Professor Lyall.

Alexia gave him an exasperated look, then marched back up the front stairs and inside her house.

The family was clearly out, but Floote was waiting for her in the foyer with a most un-Floote-like expression of perturbation on his face. The door to the front parlor was open, a certain sign of visitors. Alexia was shocked. The Loontwills could not possibly have been expecting company, otherwise they would never have left the premises.

"Who is here, Floote?" she asked, fumbling with her hatpin.

The butler raised both eyebrows at her.

Alexia swallowed, suddenly nervous. She removed her hat and gloves and put them carefully on the hall table.

She took a moment to compose herself, checking her hair in the framed gilt hallway mirror. The dark mass was arranged a tad long for daytime, but she had a bite mark to cover up, and it was too hot for high necklines. She twitched several curls into place to better cover her bruise. Her own face looked back at her: firm chin, dark eyes, militant expression. Alexia touched her nose. *Mr. MacDougall thinks you are lovely,* she told her reflection.

Then she set her spine as straight as possible and marched into the front parlor.

Lord Conall Maccon whirled about from where he stood. He had been facing the closed velvet curtains of the front window, staring at them as though he might be able to see right through the heavy material. In the dim light of the room, his eyes looked accusatory.

Miss Tarabotti paused on the threshold. Without a word, she turned back around, reached out, and slammed the parlor door shut firmly behind her.

Floote gave the closed door a long, hard look.

Outside in the street, Professor Lyall set his bone-weary self toward the BUR offices—just a few more records to check before bed. With one free hand, he patted a new bulge in his many-pocketed waistcoat. Why, he wondered, was a man with a syringe wandering Hyde Park? He turned back once to look at the Loontwills' house. A sudden smile creased his angular face as he noted the Woolsey Castle carriage waiting nearby. Its crest shone in the late afternoon sun: a quartered shield, two parts a moon-backed castle, two parts a moonless starry night. He wondered if his lord and master would, in fact, grovel.

The Earl of Woolsey wore a suit of dark chocolate, a cravat of caramel silk, and an air of ill-disguised impatience. He had been holding his kid gloves in one hand and slapping them rhythmically into the other when Miss Tarabotti entered the front parlor. He stopped instantly, but she had noted the fidget.

"What bee has gotten into your britches?" Miss Tarabotti asked without any attempt at a formal greeting. Formality was wasted on Lord Maccon. She took up position, arms akimbo, standing on the round primrose rug before him.

The earl countered with a gruff "And where have you been all day?"

Miss Tarabotti was disposed to be elusive. "Out."

The earl would have none of it. "Out with whom?"

Alexia raised both eyebrows. He would find out from Professor Lyall eventually, so she said archly, "A nice young scientist."

"Not that butterball chap you were nattering away with at dinner last night?" Lord Maccon looked at her in horror.

Miss Tarabotti glared viciously down her nose at him. Inside she was secretly delighted. He had noticed! "It just so happens that Mr. MacDougall has some absolutely fascinating theories on a wide range of topics, and he is interested in *my* opinion. Which is more than I can say for certain other gentlemen of my acquaintance. It was a beautiful day and a lovely drive, *and* he makes for quite an enjoyable conversation partner. A position, I am certain, you are entirely unfamiliar with."

Lord Maccon looked suddenly very suspicious. His eyes narrowed, and their color lightened to the same caramel hue as his cravat. "What have you been telling him, Miss Tarabotti? Anything I should know?"

He was asking in his BUR tone of voice.

Miss Tarabotti looked around, expecting at any moment to see Professor Lyall emerge with a notepad or a metal plate and stylus. She sighed with resignation. Clearly, the earl had come to visit her only in his official capacity. Foolish of her to hope, she chided herself mentally. Then she wondered what exactly she was hoping for. An apology? From Lord Maccon! *Ha.* She sat down on a small wicker chair to one side of the sofa, careful to keep a proper distance between them. "What is interesting is more what *he* has been telling *me*," she said. "He thinks being supernatural is some kind of disease."

Lord Maccon, who was a werewolf and "cursed," had heard that description before. He crossed his arms and loomed at her.

"Oh, for goodness' sake," tsked Miss Tarabotti, "do sit down."

Lord Maccon sat.

Miss Tarabotti continued. "Mr. MacDougall . . . that *is* his name, you know? Mr. MacDougall. Anyhow, Mr. MacDougall believes that the supernatural state is brought about by a blood-borne pathogen that affects some humans but not others, because some possess a certain physical trait and others do not. Presumably under this theory, men are more likely to possess said trait, and that is why they survive metamorphoses more frequently than women."

Lord Maccon relaxed back, the tiny couch creaking under his weight. He snorted his contempt of the idea.

"There is, of course, one chief problem with his conjectures," Alexia went on, ignoring the snort.

"You."

"Mmmm." She nodded. There was no room in Mr. MacDougall's theory for those who had no soul at all and canceled out those who had too much. What *would* Mr. MacDougall make of a preternatural? Assume she was a kind of proximity antidote to the supernatural disease? "Still it is an elegant theory with what little knowledge he has to go on." She did not have to say that she respected the young man who had thought of it. Lord Maccon could see that in her face.

"So wish him joy of his delusions, and leave it be," the earl said grimly. His canines were beginning to show, and the color of his eyes had gone further toward the yellow end of brown.

Miss Tarabotti shrugged. "He shows interest. He is smart. He is wealthy and well connected, or so I understand." *He thinks I am lovely.* She did not say that out loud. "Who am I to complain at his attentions, or discourage them for that matter?"

Lord Maccon had cause to regret the words he had uttered to Professor Lyall the night Alexia killed the vampire. Apparently she *was* thinking of getting married. And she seemed to have found someone to marry her, despite being half Italian. "He will take you back to America, and you a preternatural. If he is as smart as you imply, he would figure that little fact out eventually."

Miss Tarabotti laughed. "Oh, I am not thinking of marrying him, my lord. Nothing so rash. But I enjoy his company; it relieves the monotony of the day, and it keeps the family off the offensive."

Lord Maccon felt a rush of palpable relief at this blithe assurance and was annoyed with himself for it. Why should he care so much? His canines retracted slightly. Then he realized she had specified *marry* and that in his experience, she was rather modern in her sensibilities for a spinster. "You are considering something else nonmarriage with him, perhaps?" His voice was practically a growl.

"Oh, for pity's sake. Would it bother you if I were?"

Lord Maccon actually sputtered slightly at that.

Alexia suddenly realized what she was doing. She was sitting, having a polite conversation with Lord Conall Maccon, Earl of Woolsey—whom she did not like and with whom she was supposed to be extremely annoyed—about her romantic involvement (or lack thereof). It was just that his presence caused her to become overall addlepated.

She closed her eyes and took a deep breath. "Wait a moment. Why am I speaking with you at all? My lord, your behavior last night!" She stood and began to swish about the cluttered little room, her eyes sparking fiercely. She pointed an accusatory finger at him. "You are not simply a werewolf; you, my lord, are a rake. That is what you are! You took advantage the other night, Lord Maccon. Admit it! I have no idea why you felt it necessary to do"—she paused, embarrassed—"what you did, the evening of my near abduction. But you have clearly since thought better

of it. Why, if you were not interested in me as anything more than a"—
she stumbled, trying to find the right terminology—"momentary plaything, you might at least have just told me outright afterward." She
crossed her arms and sneered at him. "Why didn't you? You think I was
not strong enough to take it without causing a scene? I assure you, no
one is better used to rejection than I, my lord. I think it very churlish of
you not to inform me to my face that your breach in manners was an
unfortunate impulse of the moment. I deserve *some* respect. We have
known each other long enough for that at the very least." At that, her
steam began to run out, and she felt a heat behind her eyes she refused to
believe might be tears.

Now Lord Maccon was getting angry but for different reasons.
"So you've figured it all out, have you? And why, pray tell, would I
suddenly be thinking better of my . . . what did you call it? Unfortunate impulse of the moment?" He sounded particularly Scottish. Alexia
would have been amused by the fact that the more angry the earl got,
the more burr crept into his speech. But she was too angry to notice.
All tears had retracted at that.

She stopped pacing and cast her hands heavenward. "I have no
earthly idea. You started it. You ended it. You treated me like a distant
and not-very-well-liked acquaintance all last evening. Then you turn
up in my front parlor today. You tell *me* what you were thinking yesterday at dinner. As sure as I am standing here, I have no clue as to
what you are about, Lord Maccon. That is the honest truth of it."

The earl opened his mouth and then closed it again. Truth be told,
he did not know what he was doing there either, so he could not very
well explain. Grovel, Lyall had said. He had no idea how to do such a
thing. Alphas simply did not grovel; arrogance was part of the job description. Lord Maccon might only recently have won leadership of the
Woolsey Castle pack, but he had always been an Alpha.

Miss Tarabotti could not help herself. It was rare that anyone left
the Earl of Woolsey at a loss for words. She felt both triumphant and
confused. She had tossed and turned most of the night over his disdain-
ful treatment. She had even thought to call on Ivy to ask her opinion of
his conduct. *Ivy* of all people! She must be desperate. Yet here before her
sat the object of her perturbation, apparently at her verbal mercy.

So, of course, being Alexia Tarabotti, she cut straight to the heart
of the matter. She looked down at the primrose rug, because, brave as
she was, she could not quite face his yellow eyes. "I am not very"—she
paused, thinking of the scandalous pictures in her father's books—
"experienced. If I did something wrong, you know"—she waggled a

hand in the air, even more embarrassed now but bound and determined to get it over with—"with the kissing, you must excuse my ignorance. I . . ."

Alexia trailed off, for Lord Maccon had stood up from the tiny couch, which creaked at the loss, and advanced purposefully toward her. He certainly was good at looming. Alexia was not used to feeling so small.

"That," the earl muttered gruffly, "was not the reason."

"Perhaps," Miss Tarabotti offered, hands up before her in a defensive position, "you thought better of it because you realized how ignoble it would be: the Earl of Woolsey and a twenty-six-year-old spinster?"

"Is *that* your real age?" he murmured, seemingly uninterested and still coming toward her. He moved in a hungry, stalking way, and under the brown of his expertly cut jacket, solid muscle shifted, all coiled energy directed at her.

Miss Tarabotti backed away and came up short against a large wingback armchair. "My father was an Italian; did you remember that all of a sudden?"

Lord Maccon moved closer, slowly, ready to pounce if she decided to bolt. His eyes were almost completely yellow now, with a ring of orange about the edge. Alexia had never noticed before how black and thick his eyelashes were.

He said, "And I hail from Scotland. Which origin is worse in the eyes of London society, do you think?"

Alexia touched her nose and considered the dark tenor of her skin. "I have . . . other . . . flaws. Perhaps time spent thinking over the matter made these more apparent?"

Lord Maccon reached forward and gently pulled her hand away from her face. Carefully he brought it down toward her other hand and then trapped both together in one big paw.

Miss Tarabotti blinked at him from a scarce few inches away. She hardly dared breathe, not quite certain if he was *actually* going to eat her or not. She tried to look away, but it was nigh impossible. His eyes had turned back to tawny brown as soon as he touched her—his human eyes. But instead of being a relief, this color was more frightening because no threat masked the hunger there.

"Uh, my lord, I am not actually food. You do realize this, yes?"

Lord Maccon bent forward.

Alexia watched him until she went almost cross-eyed. This close, she could smell open fields and dark cold nights all about him.

Oh no, she thought, *it is happening again.*

Lord Maccon kissed the very tip of her nose. Nothing more.

Startled, she shied back, then opened her generous mouth, a bit like a fish. "Wha?"

He drew her back in toward him.

His voice was low and warm against her cheek. "Your age is not an issue. What does it matter to me how old or how much a spinster you may be? Do you have any idea how old I am, and how long a bachelor?" He kissed her temple. "And I love Italy. Beautiful countryside, fabulous food." He kissed her other temple. "And I find perfect beauty excessively boring, don't you?" He kissed her nose again.

Alexia could not help herself; she drew back and gave him the once-over. "Clearly."

He winced. "Touché."

Alexia was not one to let the matter drop. "Then why?"

Lord Maccon groveled. "Because I am a foolish old wolf who has been too long in the company of the pack and too little in the company of the rest of the world."

It was not an explanation, but Alexia decided she would have to settle for it. "That was an apology, was it?" she asked, just to make perfectly certain.

It seemed to have taken almost everything out of him. Instead of answering her in the affirmative, he stroked her face with his free hand, as though she were an animal that needed soothing. Alexia wondered what he thought of her as—a cat perhaps? Cats were not, in her experience, an animal with much soul. Prosaic, practical little creatures as a general rule. It would suit her very well to be thought catlike.

"Full moon," said Lord Maccon, as though this were some kind of clarification, "is just round the corner." A pause. "You understand?"

Miss Tarabotti had no idea what he was on about. "Uh . . ."

His voice dropped, low, almost ashamed. "Not much control."

Miss Tarabotti widened her dark brown eyes and batted her eyelashes to try and hide her perplexed expression. It was an Ivy maneuver.

Then he did kiss her properly and fully. Which was not exactly what she had intended by applying eyelash flapping, but she was not about to complain at the consequences. Ivy might be onto something.

As before, he started slowly, lulling her with soft drugging kisses. His mouth was unexpectedly cool. He ran a path of little fluttering nibbles over her lower lip and then applied the same treatment to her upper one. It was delightful but maddening. The tongue phenomenon occurred once again. This time, Alexia did not find it quite so startling. In fact, she thought she might even like it. But, like caviar, she suspected she'd have to try it more than once to be confident in her enjoyment. Lord Maccon seemed willing to oblige. He also appeared to be staying quite maddeningly calm and cool. Alexia was beginning to find the cluttered front parlor overly oppressive. This polarity annoyed her.

Lord Maccon stopped nibbling and went back to long soft kisses. Alexia, never one for patience, was now finding them entirely unsatisfying. A whole new source of annoyance. Clearly, she would have to take matters into her own hands—or tongue, as the case may be. Experimentally, she darted her tongue against his lips. That got a whole new agreeable reaction out of the man. He deepened the kiss, almost roughly, angling his mouth over hers.

Lord Maccon shifted, drawing her closer. He let go of her hands and curved one of his up into her hair, tangling his fingers in the heavy curls. Alexia was certain, with a tiny modicum of offended sensibility, that he was probably mussing it up most dreadfully. He was using the maneuver to direct the angle of her head in harmony with his wishes. As his wishes appeared to prescribe further kissing, Alexia decided to let him have his way.

He began running his other hand up and down her back in long strokes. *Definitely a cat,* thought Alexia groggily. Her mind was becoming hazy. Those bizarre, sunshiny tingles that proximity to Lord Maccon seemed inevitably to produce were coursing through her body with alarming intensity.

The earl turned them both about where they stood. Alexia was not certain why, but she was inclined to cooperate so long as he did not stop kissing her. He did not. He arranged it so that he could sink slowly down onto the wingback armchair, taking her with him.

It was a most indelicate thing, but there Miss Alexia Tarabotti inexplicably found herself, bustle hiked up and all her layers of skirts askew, sitting in Lord Maccon's well-tailored lap.

He moved away from her lips, which was disappointing, but then began nibbling her neck, which was gratifying. He lifted one dark curl away from where the carefully arranged locks fell over one shoulder. He ran the strand between his fingertips and then pushed the silken mass aside.

Alexia tensed in anticipation, holding her breath.

Suddenly he stopped and jerked back. The wingback chair, already taxed by two occupants—neither of whom could be described as flimsy in physique—swayed alarmingly. "What the hell is that?" yelled Lord Maccon.

He had turned to anger so swiftly; Alexia could only stare at him, speechless.

She let out her pent-up breath in a *whoosh*. Her heart was beating a marathon somewhere in the region of her throat, her skin felt hot and stretched taut over her bones, and she was damp in places she was tolerably certain unmarried gentlewomen were not supposed to be damp in.

Lord Maccon was glaring at her coffee-colored skin, discolored between the neck and shoulder region by an ugly purple mark, the size and shape of a man's teeth.

Alexia blinked, and her brown eyes cleared of their dazed expression. A small crease of perturbation appeared between her brows.

"That is a bite mark, my lord," she said, pleased her voice was not shaking, though it was a little deeper than usual.

Lord Maccon was ever more enraged. "Who bit you?" he roared.

Alexia tilted her head to one side in utter amazement. "You did." She was then treated to the glorious spectacle of an Alpha werewolf looking downright hangdog.

"I did?"

She raised both eyebrows at him.

"I did."

She nodded, firmly, once.

Lord Maccon ran a distracted hand through his already messy hair. The dark brown strands stood up in small tufts. "Dog's bollocks," he said. "I am worse than a pup in his first season. I am sorry, Alexia. It is the moon and the lack of sleep."

Alexia nodded, wondering if she should point out that he had forgotten proper etiquette and used her first name. However, that seemed a little silly given their recent activities. "Yes, I see. Uh. What is?"

"This control."

She figured at some stage in the proceedings she might understand what was going on, but now did not seem to be that time. "What control?"

"Exactly!"

Miss Tarabotti narrowed her eyes and then said something very daring. "You could kiss the bruise and make it better." Well, perhaps not quite so daring for someone who was settled as intimately as she on Lord Maccon's lap. After all, she had read enough of her papa's books to know exactly what it was that pressed hard and flush against her nether regions.

Lord Maccon shook his head. "I do not think that is a very good idea."

"You do not?" Embarrassed by her own forwardness, Alexia squirmed against him, trying to extricate herself.

The earl swore and closed his eyes. There was a sheen of sweat on his brow.

Tentatively, Alexia squirmed again.

Lord Maccon groaned and leaned his head against her collarbone, clamping both hands about her hips to still the movement.

Alexia was scientifically intrigued. Had he gotten even larger down there? What was the maximum possible expansion ratio? she wondered. She grinned a tad maliciously. It had not occurred to her that she might have some sort of influence over the encounter. She decided then and there that, being a confirmed spinster and averse to allowing Mr. Mac-Dougall his druthers, this might be her only chance to test some long-held and rather interesting theories.

"Lord Maccon," she whispered, squirming again despite his firm grip.

He snorted and said in a strangled voice, "I suspect you could get away with calling me by my given name at this juncture."

"Um?" said Alexia.

"Um, Conall," prompted Lord Maccon.

"Conall," she said, relinquishing the last hold on her scruples—once the egg was broken, might as well make an omelet with it. Then she got distracted by the feel of his back muscles under her hands. Hands that had run afoul of his coat and unceremoniously managed to strip it off him without her knowledge.

"Aye, Alexia?" He looked up at her. Was that fear in his caramel eyes?

"I am going to take advantage of you," she said, and without giving him a chance to reply, she began untying his cravat.

CHAPTER SEVEN

Revelations Over Chopped Liver

U h, probably not a good idea." Lord Maccon was panting a little. "Hush, none of that, now," Miss Tarabotti admonished. "You started this."

"And it would be a devilish bad lot for all concerned were I to finish it," he said. "Or for you to finish it, for that matter." But he made no attempt to remove her from his lap. Instead, he seemed fascinated by the low neckline of her dress, which had sunk considerably during their exertions. One big hand was now tracing the lace frill tucked there, back and forth. Alexia wondered if he had a particular interest in ladies' fashions.

She dispensed with Lord Maccon's cravat, undid the buttons of his waistcoat and then those of his shirtwaist. "You are wearing entirely too much clothing," she complained.

Lord Maccon, who ordinarily could not agree more, was rather appreciative of it at the moment. Any additional time it took for her to undo buttons might give him back a modicum of restraint. He was sure his control was around somewhere, if he could simply find it. He tore his eyes away from the tops of those remarkable breasts of hers and tried to think unpleasant thoughts of particularly horrible things, like overcooked vegetables and cut-rate wine.

Alexia succeeded in her aim: peeling back Lord Maccon's clothing to expose his upper chest, shoulders, and neck. She had stopped kissing him for the moment. The earl considered that a godsend. He breathed a sigh of relief and looked up at her. Her expression seemed more one of avid curiosity than anything else.

Then Alexia bent forward and nibbled at his ear.

Lord Maccon writhed and let out an animal-in-pain sort of whimper. Alexia considered her experiment an unqualified success. Apparently what was good for the goose was, indeed, good for the gander.

She investigated further: moving along with little kisses down his throat and over his collarbone until she came to the same location on his neck that on hers was currently a decorative black and blue color. She bit him. Hard. Alexia never did anything by halves.

Lord Maccon almost reared right out of the armchair.

Alexia held on, teeth sinking into flesh. She did not want to draw blood, but she did intend to leave a mark and felt since he was a tough supernatural type, she had better do her worst. Any mark she left would not last long once they broke contact and he was out of her preternatural power. He tasted wonderful: of salt and meat—like gravy. She stopped biting and licked delicately at the red crescent-shaped brand she had left behind.

"Blast it all." Lord Maccon's breathing was very rapid. "We have got to stop."

Alexia nuzzled against him. "Why?"

"Because pretty bloody soon, I'm not going to be able to."

Alexia nodded. "I suppose that is sensible." She sighed. It felt like she had spent a lifetime being sensible.

The decision, it turned out, was taken away from them by some sort of commotion in the hallway.

"Well I never," said a lady's shocked voice.

Some quiet apologetic murmuring then ensued, the words of which were impossible to make out and probably emanated from Floote.

Then the woman issued forth once more, "In the front parlor? Oh, here on BUR business, is he? I understand. Surely not . . ." The voice trailed off.

Someone knocked loudly on the parlor door.

Miss Tarabotti slid hurriedly off Lord Maccon's lap. Much to her surprise, her legs seemed to be working properly. She yanked her bustle back into position and hopped up and down hurriedly to shake her skirts back into place.

Lord Maccon, in the interest of time, simply buttoned the top of his shirtwaist and bottom of his waistcoat and jacket. But he seemed defeated in any effort to rapidly tie his cravat.

"Here, let me do that." Miss Tarabotti gestured him autocratically over and tied it for him.

While she busied herself with an intricate knot, Lord Maccon tried, equally inexpertly, to fix her hair. His fingers brushed the bite mark on her lower neck.

"I am sorry about that," he said contritely.

"Do I detect an honest-to-goodness apology?" asked Alexia, but she smiled, still fiddling with his cravat. "I do not mind the bruise. What I mind is that I cannot produce the same." The bite mark she had given him only moments before had promptly vanished during the few seconds they separated while she straightened her dress. Then, she added, because Alexia never stayed silent when she ought, "These feelings you engender in me, my lord, are most indelicate. You should stop causing them immediately."

He gave her a quick look to assess the seriousness, and then, unable to determine if she was joking or not, remained silent.

Miss Tarabotti finished with the cravat. He had arranged her hair so that it at least covered all signs of his amorous attentions. She walked across the room to draw the curtains and look out the front window to see who might have arrived.

The knocking continued on the parlor door until finally it burst open.

Of all odd couples, Miss Ivy Hisselpenny and Professor Lyall entered the room.

Ivy was talking nonstop. She spotted Miss Tarabotti instantly and flitted over to her, looking like an excited hedgehog in a loud hat. "Alexia, my dear, did you know there was a BUR werewolf lurking in your hallway? When I came for tea, he was squaring off against your butler in a most threatening manner. I was terribly afraid there might be fisticuffs. Why would such a person be interested in visiting you? And why was Floote terribly set on keeping him away? And why . . . ?" She did not finish, having finally spotted Lord Maccon. Her large red and white striped shepherdess hat, with a curved yellow ostrich feather, quivered in agitation.

Lord Maccon was glaring at his second. "Randolph, you look awful. What are you doing here? I sent you home."

Professor Lyall took in his Alpha's disheveled appearance, wondering what atrocious thing had been done to his poor cravat. His eyes narrowed and shifted toward Miss Tarabotti's loose hair. However, Lyall had been Beta for three consecutive pack leaders, and he was nothing if not discreet. Instead of commenting or answering Lord Maccon's question, he simply walked over to the earl and whispered rapidly into his ear.

Miss Hisselpenny finally noticed her friend's tousled state. Solicitously, she urged Alexia to sit and took up residence next to her on the little settee. "Are you feeling quite well?" She removed her gloves and felt Alexia's forehead with the back of her hand. "You are very hot, my dear. Do you think you might be running a fever?"

Miss Tarabotti looked under her eyelashes at Lord Maccon. "That is one way of phrasing it."

Professor Lyall stopped whispering.

Lord Maccon's face flushed. He was newly upset about something. "They did *what*?" *Was he ever not upset?*

Whisper, whisper.

"Well, proud Mary's fat arse!" said the earl eloquently.

Miss Hisselpenny gasped.

Miss Tarabotti, who was getting very used to Lord Maccon's ribald mannerisms, snickered at her friend's shocked expression.

Issuing forth several additional creative statements of the gutter-born variety, the earl strode to the hat stand, shoved his brown topper unceremoniously on his head, and marched out of the room.

Professor Lyall shook his head and made a tut-tutting noise. "Fancy going out into public with a cravat like that."

The cravat in question, with head attached, reappeared in the doorway. "Watch her, Randolph. I will send Haverbink round to relieve you as soon as I get to the office. After he arrives, for all our sakes, go home and get some sleep. It is going to be a long night."

"Yes, sir," said Professor Lyall.

Lord Maccon disappeared once more, and they heard the Woolsey Castle carriage clattering off at a breakneck speed down the street.

Miss Tarabotti felt forsaken, bereft, and not entirely unworthy of the pitying glances Ivy was casting in her direction. What was it about kissing her that caused the Earl of Woolsey to feel it necessary to disappear with such rapidity?

Professor Lyall, looking uncomfortable, removed his hat and overcoat and hung them up on the stand just made vacant by vanished Lord Expletive. He then proceeded to check the room. What he was looking for, Alexia could not guess, but he did not seem to find it. The Loontwills kept to the height of what was required of a fashionable receiving parlor. It was greatly overfurnished, including an upright piano that none of the ladies of the house could play, and cluttered to capacity with small tables covered with embroidered drop cloths and crowded with assemblages of daguerreotypes, glass bottles with suspended model dirigibles, and other knickknacks. As he conducted his investigation, Professor Lyall avoided all contact with sunlight. In style since the supernatural set rose to prominence several centuries ago, the heavy velvet drapes over the front window nevertheless allowed some small amount of daylight to creep into the darkness. The Beta was fastidious in his avoidance of it.

Miss Tarabotti figured he must be very tired indeed to feel such ill effects. Older werewolves could go several days awake during the daytime. The professor must be pushing his time limit, or suffering some other ailment.

Miss Tarabotti and Miss Hisselpenny watched with polite curiosity as the urbane werewolf wandered about the room. He checked behind Felicity's insipid watercolors and underneath the infamous wingback armchair. Alexia blushed inwardly thinking about that chair and trying not to remember what had so recently occurred there. Had she really been so forward? Disgraceful.

When the silence became too unbearable, Miss Tarabotti said, "Do sit down, Professor. You look positively dead on your feet. You are making us dizzy wandering about the room like that."

Professor Lyall gave a humorless laugh but obeyed her order. He settled into a small Chippendale side chair, which he moved into the darkest recess of the room: a little nook near the piano.

"Should we order some tea?" Miss Hisselpenny asked, concern for both his peaked appearance and Alexia's obviously feverish condition outweighing all sense of propriety.

Miss Tarabotti was impressed by her friend's resource. "What an excellent notion."

Ivy went to the door to call for Floote, who magically appeared without needing to be summoned. "Miss Alexia is not feeling quite the thing and this gentleman here . . . ," she faltered.

Alexia was appalled at her own lack of manners. "Ivy! You don't mean to say you have not been introduced? And here I thought you knew each other. You came in together."

Miss Hisselpenny turned to her friend. "We encountered one another on the front stoop, but we never formally made each other's acquaintance." She turned back to the butler. "I am sorry, Floote. What was I saying?"

"Tea, miss?" suggested the ever-resourceful Floote. "Will there be anything else, miss?"

Alexia asked from the couch, "Do we have any liver?"

"Liver, miss? I shall inquire of the cook."

"If we do, simply have her chop it small and serve it raw." Miss Tarabotti double-checked with a glance at Professor Lyall, who nodded gratefully.

Both Ivy and Floote looked aghast, but there seemed to be nothing they could do to gainsay Alexia's request. After all, in the absence of the Loontwills proper, this was Miss Tarabotti's house to rule over.

"And some jam and bread sandwiches," said Miss Tarabotti firmly. She felt a bit more composed, now that Lord Maccon had vacated the premises. Miss Tarabotti, once composed, was generally of a peckish proclivity.

"Very good, miss," said Floote, and glided off.

Alexia performed introductions. "Professor Lyall, this is Miss Ivy Hisselpenny, my dearest friend. Ivy, this is Professor Randolph Lyall, Lord Maccon's second in command and protocol advisor, so far as I can tell."

Lyall stood and bowed. Ivy curtsied from the doorway. Formalities over with, both returned to their seats.

"Professor, can you tell me what has occurred? Why did Lord Maccon depart in such haste?" Miss Tarabotti leaned forward and peered into the shadows. It was hard to read the professor's expression in the dim light, which gave him a decided advantage.

"Afraid not, Miss Tarabotti. BUR business." He shut her down shamelessly. "Not to worry, the earl should get it all sorted through in short order."

Alexia leaned back in the settee. Idly she picked up one of the many pink ribbon-embroidered cushions and began plucking at one of the tassels. "Then I wonder, sir, if I might ask you somewhat about pack protocol?"

Miss Hisselpenny's eyes went very wide, and she reached for her fan. When Alexia got that look in her eye, it meant her friend was about to say something shocking. Had Alexia been reading her father's books again? Ivy shuddered to even think such a thing. She always knew no good would come of those reprehensible manuscripts.

Professor Lyall, startled by this sudden switch in topic, looked uncomfortably at Miss Tarabotti.

"Oh, is it secret?" asked Alexia. One was never quite certain with the supernatural set. She knew there existed such concepts as pack protocol and pack etiquette, but sometimes these things were learned via cultural acumen and never taught or talked of openly. It was true that werewolves were more integrated into everyday society than vampires, but, still, one never knew unless one was actually a werewolf. Their traditions were, after all, much older than those of daylight folk.

Professor Lyall shrugged elegantly. "Not necessarily. I should caution, however, that pack rules are often quite blunt and not necessarily intended for a lady of Miss Hisselpenny's delicacy."

Alexia grinned at him. "As opposed to mine?" she asked, putting him on the spot.

The professor was not to be trifled with. "My dear Miss Tarabotti, you are nothing if not resilient."

Ivy, blushing furiously, spread open her fan and began fluttering it to cool her hot face. The fan was bright red Chinese silk with yellow lace at its edge, clearly selected to match the reprehensible shepherdess hat. Alexia rolled her eyes. Was Ivy's dubious taste now extending to *all* her accessories?

The fan seemed to give Miss Hisselpenny some courage. "Please," she insisted, "do not forbear needlessly on my account."

Miss Tarabotti smiled approvingly and patted her friend on the upper arm before turning expectantly back to face Professor Lyall in his darkened corner. "Shall I come to the point, Professor? Lord Maccon's manners have been highly bewildering of late. He has made several"— she paused delicately—"interesting incursions in my direction. These began, as you no doubt observed, in the public street the other evening."

"Oh, dear Alexia!" breathed Miss Hisselpenny, truly shaken. "You do not mean to tell me you were *observed*!"

Miss Tarabotti dismissed her friend's concern. "Only by Professor Lyall here, so far as I am aware, and he is the soul of discretion."

Professor Lyall, though clearly pleased by her accolade, said, "Not to be rude, Miss Tarabotti, but your aspect of pack protocol is . . . ?"

Alexia sniffed. "I am getting there. You must understand, Professor Lyall, this is a smidgen embarrassing. You must permit me to broach the matter in a slightly roundabout manner."

"Far be it for me to require directness from *you*, Miss Tarabotti," replied the werewolf in a tone of voice Alexia felt might be bordering rudely on sarcasm.

"Yes, well, anyway," she continued huffily. "Only last night at a dinner event we both attended, Lord Maccon's behavior gave me to understand the previous evening's entanglement had been a . . . mistake."

Miss Hisselpenny gave a little gasp of astonishment. "Oh," she exclaimed, "how *could* he!"

"Ivy," said Miss Tarabotti a touch severely, "pray let me finish my story before you judge Lord Maccon too harshly. That is, after all, for me to do." Somehow Alexia could not endure the idea that her friend might be thinking ill of the earl.

Alexia continued. "This afternoon, I returned home to find him waiting for me in this very parlor. He seems to have changed his mind once again. I am becoming increasingly confused." Miss Tarabotti glared at the hapless Beta. "And I do not appreciate this kind of uncertainty!" She put down the ribbon pillow.

"Has he gone and botched things up again?" asked the professor.

Floote entered with the tea tray. At a loss for what proper etiquette required, the butler had placed the raw liver in a cut-glass ice-cream dish. Professor Lyall did not seem to care in what form it was presented. He ate it rapidly but delicately with a small copper ice-cream spoon.

Floote served the tea and then disappeared once more from the room.

Miss Tarabotti finally arrived at the point. "Why did he treat me with such hauteur last night and then with such solicitude today? Is there some obscure point of pack lore in play here?" She sipped her tea to hide her nervousness.

Lyall finished his chopped liver, set the empty ice-cream dish on the piano top, and looked at Miss Tarabotti. "Would you say that initially Lord Maccon made his interest clear?" he asked.

"Well," hedged Miss Tarabotti, "we have known each other for a few years now. Before the street incident, I would say his attitude has been one of apathy."

Professor Lyall chuckled. "*You* did not hear his comments after those encounters. However, I did mean more recently."

Alexia put down her teacup and started using her hands as she talked. It was one of the few Italian mannerisms that had somehow crept into her repertoire, despite the fact that she had barely known her father. "Well, yes," she said, spreading her fingers expansively, "but then again, not decisively. I realize I am a little old and plain for long-term romantic interest, especially from a gentleman of Lord Maccon's standing, but if he was offering claviger status, oughten I to be informed? And isn't it impossible for . . ." She glanced at Ivy, who did not know she was a preternatural. She did not even know that preternatural folk existed. "For someone as lacking in creativity as me to be a claviger? I do not know what to think. I cannot believe his overtures represent a courtship. So when he recently ignored me, I assumed the incident in the street had been a colossal mistake."

Professor Lyall sighed again. "Yes, that. How do I put this delicately? My estimable Alpha has been thinking of you instinctively, I am afraid, not logically. He has been perceiving you as he would an Alpha female werewolf."

Miss Hisselpenny frowned. "Is that complimentary?"

Seeing the empty ice-cream dish, Miss Tarabotti handed Professor Lyall a cup of tea.

Lyall sipped the beverage delicately, raising his eyebrows from behind the lip of the cup. "For an Alpha male? Yes. For the rest of us, I suspect, not quite so much. But there is a reason."

"Go on, please," urged Miss Tarabotti, intrigued.

Lyall continued. "When he would not admit his interest even to himself, his instincts took over."

Miss Tarabotti, who had a brief but scandalous vision of Lord Maccon's *instincts* urging him to do things such as throw her bodily over one shoulder and drag her off into the night, returned to reality with a start. "So?"

Miss Hisselpenny said to her friend, looking at Lyall for support, "It is an issue of *control*?"

"Very perceptive, Miss Hisselpenny." The professor looked with warm approval at Ivy, who blushed with pleasure.

Miss Tarabotti felt as though she was beginning to understand. "At the dinner party, he was waiting for *me* to make overtures?" She almost squeaked in shock. "But he was flirting! With a . . . a . . . Wibbley!"

Professor Lyall nodded. "Thereby trying to increase your interest—force you to stake a claim, indicate pursuit, or assert possession. Preferably all three."

Both Miss Tarabotti and Miss Hisselpenny were quite properly shocked into silence at the very idea. Though Alexia was less appalled than perturbed. After all, had she not *just* discovered, in this very room, the depth of her own interest in equalizing the male-female dynamic? She supposed if she could bite Lord Maccon on the neck and regret that she left no lasting mark, she might be able to claim him publicly.

"In pack protocol, we call it the Bitch's Dance," Professor Lyall explained. "You are, you will forgive my saying so, Miss Tarabotti, simply *too much* Alpha."

"I am not an Alpha," protested Miss Tarabotti, standing up and pacing about. Clearly, her father's library had failed her entirely on the niceties and mating habits of werewolves.

Lyall looked at her—hands on hips, full-figured, assertive. He smiled. "There are not many female werewolves, Miss Tarabotti. The Bitch's Dance refers to liaisons among the pack: *the female's* choice."

Miss Hisselpenny maintained an appalled silence. The very idea was utterly alien to her upbringing.

Miss Tarabotti mulled it over. She found she liked the idea. She had always secretly admired the vampire queens their superior position in hive structure. She did not know werewolves had something similar. *Did Alpha females,* she wondered, *trump males outside the romantic arena as well?* "Why?" she asked.

Lyall explained. "It *has* to be up to the female, with so few of them and so many of us. There is no battling over a female allowed. Werewolves rarely live more than a century or two because of all the infighting. The laws are strict and enforced by the dewan himself. It is entirely the bitch's choice every step of the dance."

"So, Lord Maccon was waiting for me to go to him." Miss Tarabo-

tti realized for the first time how strange it must be for the older supernatural folk to adjust to the changing social norms of Queen Victoria's
daylight world. Lord Maccon always seemed to have such things well
in hand. It had not even occurred to Alexia that he had made a mistake
in his behavior toward her. "Then what of his conduct today?"

Miss Hisselpenny sucked in a gasp. "What did he do?" She shivered in delighted horror.

Miss Tarabotti promised to tell her the particulars later. Although
this time, she suspected, she would not be able to reveal every detail.
Things had progressed a little too far for someone of Ivy's delicate sensibilities. If merely looking at that wingback chair could make Alexia
blush, it would certainly be too much for her dear friend.

Professor Lyall coughed. Miss Tarabotti believed he was doing so
to hide amusement. "That may have been my fault. I spoke to him most
severely, reminding him to treat you as a modern British lady, not a
werewolf."

"Mmm," said Miss Tarabotti, still contemplating the wingback
chair, "perhaps a little too modern?"

Professor Lyall's eyebrows went all the way up, and he leaned a
little out of the shadows toward her.

"Alexia," said Miss Hisselpenny most severely, "you must force
him to make his intentions clear. Persisting in this kind of behavior
could cause quite the scandal."

Miss Tarabotti thought of her preternatural state and her father,
who was reputed to have been quite the philanderer before his marriage. *You have no idea,* she almost said.

Miss Hisselpenny continued. "I mean to say, not that one could
bear to think such a thing, but it must be said, it really must . . ." She
looked most distressed. "What if he only intends to offer you *carte
blanche*?" Her eyes were big and sympathetic. Ivy was intelligent enough
to know, whether she liked to acknowledge it or not, what Alexia's prospects really were. Practically speaking, they could not include marriage
to someone of Lord Maccon's standing, no matter how romantic her
imagination.

Alexia knew Ivy did not intend to be cruel, but she was hurt none-
theless. She nodded glumly.

Professor Lyall, whose sensitivities were touched by Miss Tarabotti's suddenly sad eyes, said, "I cannot believe my lord's intentions are
anything less than honorable."

Miss Tarabotti smiled, wobbly. "That is kind of you to say, Professor. Still, it seems as though I am faced with a dilemma. Respond as your
pack protocol dictates"—she paused seeing Ivy's eyes widen—"risking

my reputation with ruination and ostracism. Or deny everything and maintain as I have always done."

Miss Hisselpenny took Miss Tarabotti's hand and squeezed it sympathetically. Alexia squeezed back and then spoke as though trying to convince herself. She was, after all, soulless and practical. "Mine is not precisely a bad life. I have material wealth and good health. Perhaps I am not useful nor beloved by my family, but I have never suffered unduly. And I have my books." She paused, finding herself perilously close to self-pity.

Professor Lyall and Miss Hisselpenny exchanged glances. Something passed between them. Some silent pact of purpose to do . . . Ivy knew not what. But, whatever the future, Miss Hisselpenny was certainly glad to have Professor Lyall on her side.

Floote appeared in the doorway. "A Mr. Haverbink to see you, Miss Tarabotti."

Mr. Haverbink entered the room, shutting the door behind him.

Professor Lyall said, "Forgive me not standing, Haverbink. Too many days running."

"Not a worry, sir, not a bit of it." Mr. Haverbink was an extraordinarily large and thuglike man of working-class extraction. What origins his cultivated speech left in doubt, his physical appearance demonstrated. He was the type of good farming stock that, when the oxen collapsed from exhaustion, picked up the plow, strapped himself to it, and finished tilling the fields by hand.

Miss Tarabotti and Miss Hisselpenny had never before seen so many muscles on one individual. His neck was the size of a tree. Both ladies were suitably impressed.

Professor Lyall made introductions. "Ladies, Mr. Haverbink. Mr. Haverbink, this is Miss Hisselpenny, and this is Miss Tarabotti, your charge."

"Oh!" said Ivy. "You are from BUR?"

Mr. Haverbink nodded affably. "Aye, miss."

"But you are not . . . ?" Miss Tarabotti could not tell how she knew. Perhaps it was because he seemed so relaxed in the bright sunlight or because how grounded and earthy he seemed. He showed none of the dramatic flair one expects with excess soul.

"A werewolf? No, miss. Not interested in being a claviger either, so I shan't ever become one. Gone up against a couple in the boxing ring once or twice, so do not worry yourself on that account. Besides, the boss does not seem to think we will have trouble from that quarter, leastways not during the daytime."

Professor Lyall stood slowly. He looked bent and old, his mercurial face thin and drawn.

Mr. Haverbink turned to him solicitously. "Begging your pardon, sir, but his lordship gave me strict instructions to see you into the carriage and off to the castle. He has got the situation well in hand back at the office."

Professor Lyall, nearly to the point of utter exhaustion, made his way haltingly to the door.

The hugely muscled young man looked like he would prefer to simply pick the Beta up and carry him out to the street, relieving the werewolf of his obvious distress. But, showing that he did indeed have experience working with the supernatural set, he respected his superior's pride and did not even try to assist him with an arm.

Polite to the last, Professor Lyall collected his hat and coat, donned both, and bowed his farewell from the parlor doorway. Alexia and Ivy were afraid he might topple right over, but he righted himself and made it out the front door and into the Woolsey Castle carriage with only a few stumbles here and there.

Mr. Haverbink saw him safely on his way and then came back into the parlor. "I'll be just out the front by yon lamppost if you need me, miss," he said to Miss Tarabotti. "I'm on duty until sundown, and then there'll be three vampires in rotation all night long. His lordship is not taking any chances. Not after what just happened."

Though dying of curiosity, Ivy and Alexia knew better than to hound the young man with questions. If Professor Lyall would not tell them anything about what had taken the earl away so suddenly, this man would be equally unforthcoming.

Mr. Haverbink bowed deeply, muscles rippling all up and down his back, and lumbered from the room.

Miss Hisselpenny sighed and fluttered her fan. "Ah, for the countryside, what scenery there abides . . . ," quoth she.

Miss Tarabotti giggled. "Ivy, what a positively wicked thing to say. Bravo."

CHAPTER EIGHT

Backyard Shenanigans

The Loontwills returned from their shopping expedition flushed with success. Except for Squire Loontwill, who was now less flush than he had been and wore an expression more often seen on men returning from battle—one that had been badly lost with many casualties. Floote appeared at his elbow with a large glass of cognac. The squire muttered something about Floote-liness being next to godliness and downed the liquor in one gulp.

No one was surprised to find Miss Tarabotti entertaining Miss Hisselpenny in the front parlor. The squire muttered a greeting only just long enough to satisfy politeness and then retreated to his office with a second glass of cognac and the mandate that he was not to be disturbed for any reason.

The ladies Loontwill greeted Miss Hisselpenny in a far more verbose manner and insisted on showing off all of their purchases.

Miss Tarabotti had the presence of mind to send Floote for more tea. It was clearly going to be a long afternoon.

Felicity pulled out a leather box and lifted the lid. "Look at these. Are they not utterly divine? Do you not wish you had some just like?" Lying in scrumptious grandeur on a bed of black velvet was a pair of lace elbow-length evening gloves in pale moss green with tiny mother-of-pearl buttons up the sides.

"Yes," agreed Alexia, because they were. "But you do not own an evening gown to match, do you?"

Felicity waggled her eyebrows excitedly. "Very perceptive, my dear sister, but I do now." She grinned in a most indecorous manner.

Miss Tarabotti thought she could understand her stepfather's deathly pallor. An evening gown to match such gloves would cost a small fortune, and whatever Felicity purchased, Evylin must have in equal value. Evylin proved this universal law by proudly displaying her own new evening gloves in silvery blue satin with rose-colored flowers embroidered about the edge.

Miss Hisselpenny was considerably impressed by such largesse. Her family's means did not extend into the realm of embroidered gloves and new evening gowns on a whim.

"The dresses are due next week," said Mrs. Loontwill proudly, as though her two daughters had accomplished something marvelous. "Just in time for Almack's, we hope." She looked down her nose at Ivy. "Will you be attending, Miss Hisselpenny?"

Alexia bridled at her mother, who was perfectly well aware that the Hisselpennys were not of a quality suitable to such an illustrious event. "And what new dress will you be wearing, Mama?" she asked sharply. "Something appropriate, or your customary style—a gown better suited to a lady half your age?"

"Alexia!" hissed Ivy, truly shocked.

Mrs. Loontwill turned flinty eyes on her eldest daughter. "Regardless of what I am wearing, it is clear *you* will not be there to see it." She stood. "Nor, I think, will you be permitted to attend the duchess's rout tomorrow evening." With that punishment, she swept from the room.

Felicity's eyes were dancing with merriment. "You are perfectly correct, of course. The gown she picked out is daringly low-cut, frilly, *and* pale pink."

"But really, Alexia, you should not say such things to your own mother," insisted Ivy.

"Who else should I say them to?" Alexia grumbled under her breath.

"Exactly, and why not?" Evylin wanted to know. "No one else will. Soon Mama's behavior will affect our chances." She gestured to Felicity and herself. "And *we* do not intend to end up old maids. No offense meant, my dear sister."

Alexia smiled. "None taken."

Floote appeared with fresh tea, and Miss Tarabotti gestured him over. "Floote, send my card round to Auntie Augustina, would you please? For tomorrow night."

Evylin and Felicity looked only mildly interested at this. They had no aunt named Augustina, but a meeting organized for a full-moon night with a personage of such a name must be a fortune-telling of some kind. Clearly, Alexia, unexpectedly and cruelly confined to the house by their mother's anger, must organize some kind of entertainment for herself.

Ivy was not so foolish as that. She gave Alexia a what-are-you-up-to? look.

Alexia only smiled enigmatically.

Floote nodded grimly and went off to do as he was bid.

Felicity changed the subject. "Have you heard? They are making jewelry out of this fantastic new lightweight metal—allum-ninny-um or something. It does not tarnish like silver. Of course, it is very dear at the moment, and Papa would not allow for the purchase of any." She pouted.

Miss Tarabotti perked up. Her scientific papers had been all agog over new ways of processing this metal, discovered twenty or so years ago. "Aluminum," she said. "I have read about it in several Royal Society publications. It has finally debuted in the London shops, has it? How splendid! You know, it is nonmagnetic, nonaetheric, and anticorrosive."

"It is what and what?" Felicity bit her bottom lip in confusion.

"Oh dear," said Evylin, "there she goes, no stopping her now. Oh, why did I have to have a bluestocking for a sister?"

Miss Hisselpenny stood. "Ladies," she said, "you really must excuse me. I should be getting on."

The Miss Loontwills nodded.

"Quite right. That is how we feel when she goes all scientificish as well," said Evylin with feeling.

"Only we have to live with her, so we cannot escape," added Felicity.

Ivy looked embarrassed. "No, really, it is simply that I must get home. My mother was expecting me a half hour ago."

Miss Tarabotti accompanied her friend to the door. Floote appeared with the offensive shepherdess hat, all white striped, red trim, and yellow ostrich glory. Alexia disgustedly tied it under Ivy's chin.

Looking out into the street, the two ladies observed Mr. Haverbink hovering across the way. Alexia gave him a tiny wave. He nodded to them politely.

Ivy flicked open her red parasol. "You never did intend to attend the duchess's rout tomorrow night at all, did you?"

Miss Tarabotti grinned. "You have caught me out."

"Alexia." Ivy's voice was deeply suspicious. "Who is Auntie Augustina?"

Miss Tarabotti laughed. "I believe you once referred to the individual in question as 'outrageous' and disapproved of our association."

Ivy closed her eyes in horror for a long moment. She had been thrown off by the gender switch, but that was simply the kind of code Alexia and her butler used around the Loontwills. "Twice in one week!"

she said, shocked. "People will begin to talk. They will think you are turning into a drone." She looked thoughtfully at her friend. A practical, statuesque, stylish woman, not the type vampires usually went in for. But then, everyone knew: Lord Akeldama was no ordinary vampire. "You are not actually taking up as a drone, are you? That is a very big decision."

Not for the first time, Alexia wished she could tell Ivy about her true nature. It was not that she did not trust Miss Hisselpenny; it was simply that she did not trust Miss Hisselpenny's tongue not to run away with her at an inopportune moment.

In answer, she said only, "You have no idea how impossible that is, my dear. Do not worry. I will be perfectly fine."

Miss Hisselpenny did not look reassured. She pressed her friend's hand briefly and then walked off down the street, shaking her head softly. The long curling yellow ostrich feather swished back and forth like the tail of an angry cat—the motion of her disapproval.

Only Ivy, thought Alexia, *could emit censure in such a sunny and fluffy manner.*

Miss Tarabotti returned to the tender mercies of her half sisters and prepared herself for an evening of familial bliss.

Miss Tarabotti was awakened in the small hours of the night by the most phenomenal ruckus. It seemed to be emanating from just below her bedroom window. She crept out of bed, throwing a white muslin pelisse over her nightgown, and went to see what was occurring.

Her window, as it belonged to one of the less prestigious rooms of the house, looked out over the servants' kitchen entrance and into a back alley where tradesmen made their deliveries.

The moon, only one night away from being full, illuminated the struggling forms of several men below her with a silvery sheen. They were apparently engaged in a bout of fisticuffs. Alexia was fascinated. They seemed evenly matched and fought mostly in silence, which lent a decided aura of menace to the proceedings. The noise that had awakened her was apparently caused by a dustbin overturning; otherwise, only the sound of flesh hitting flesh and a few muffled grunts rent the air.

Alexia saw one man strike out hard. His punch landed full in the face of one of the others. It was a palpable hit that ought to have set the second man flat. Instead, the opponent whipped around and hit back, using the momentum of his own spin. The sound of fist on skin echoed through the alleyway, an unpleasantly wet thudding.

Only a supernatural could take a hit like that and remain unfazed. Miss Tarabotti remembered Professor Lyall saying there would be vampires guarding her tonight. Was she witnessing a vampire-on-vampire battle? Despite the danger, she was excited by this idea. Rarely was such a thing to be seen, for while werewolves often brawled, vampires generally preferred subtler methods of confrontation.

She leaned out her window, trying to get a better look. One of the men broke free and headed toward her, looking up. His blank eyes met hers, and Alexia knew that he was no vampire.

She bit back a scream of horror, no longer fascinated by the battle below. It was a visage she had seen before: the wax-faced man from her botched abduction. In the light of the moon, his skin had a dull metallic sheen like pewter, so smooth and lifeless she shuddered in abject revulsion. The letters still marked his forehead, sootlike, VIXI. He saw her, pale nightgown against the darkened interior of the slumbering house, and grinned. As before, it was like no grin she had ever seen, a slashed unnatural opening full of perfect square white teeth, splitting across his head as a tomato will split when it is dropped into boiling water.

He ran toward her. A smooth three stories of brick lay between them, yet somehow Alexia knew there was no safety in that.

One of the other men broke away from the fighting group and sprinted after her attacker. Alexia doubted he would arrive in time. The wax-faced man moved with utter efficiency and economy of motion, less a man running than a water snake slithering.

But his pursuer clearly was a vampire, and as Miss Tarabotti watched, she realized she had never before seen a vampire run at full speed. He was all liquid grace, his fine Hessian boots making only a buzzlike whispering on the cobblestones.

The wax-faced man reached the Loontwills' house and began to climb up the brick side. Unhindered, spiderlike, he oozed up the wall. That utterly expressionless face of his remained tilted up at Alexia. It was as though he were hypnotized by her face, fixated on her and only her. VIXI. She read the letters over and over and over again. VIXI.

I do not want to die, thought Alexia. *I have not yet yelled at Lord Maccon for his most recent crass behavior!* Thrown into a panic, she was just reaching to slam her shutters closed, knowing they were but flimsy protection from such a creature, when the vampire struck.

Her supernatural protector leaped up and forward, landing on the wax-faced man's back. He grabbed the creature's head and yanked it around, hard. Either the added weight or the yank caused the wax-faced man to let go of the brick wall. They both fell, landing with a horrendous bone-crunching crash in the alley below. Neither screamed nor spoke, even after such a fall. Their companions continued their equally silent battle behind them, without pausing to observe the tumble.

Miss Tarabotti was certain the wax-faced man must be dead. He had fallen nearly an entire story, and only supernatural folk could survive such an experience unscathed. As no werewolf or vampire would ever look the way the wax-faced man looked, he must, perforce, be some kind of normal human.

Her supposition was in error, for the wax-faced man rolled about on top of the vampire's fallen form and then sprang once more to his feet, turned, and single-mindedly headed back toward the house. And Alexia.

The vampire, hurt but not incapacitated, anticipated this move and had an iron grip with both hands on one of the wax-faced man's legs. Instead of trying to fight off the vampire, the man behaved in an entirely illogical manner. He simply kept jerking in Alexia's direction, like a child denied a treat and incapable of being distracted by anything else. He dragged the vampire behind him by slow degrees. Every time he surged toward her, Alexia flinched, even though she was high above him in her third-story room.

Impasse reigned. The fight in the alley beyond seemed evenly matched, and the wax-faced man could not get to Alexia so long as the vampire held on to his leg.

The sound of heavy-booted footsteps and a sharp, high-pitched whistle rent the night air. Running around the corner of the back street came two constables. Rows of protective silver and wooden straight pins decorated the front of their uniforms, gleaming in the moonlight. One of them held an Adam's cross pistol, cocked and loaded with a deadly sharp wooden stake. The other held a Colt Lupis revolver, the silver-bullet-slinger out of America—only the best from that most superstitious of countries. Upon seeing the nature of the participants, he put the Colt away and pulled out a large wooden policeman's baton stake instead.

One of the men fighting in the alley yelled something sharp and commanding in Latin. Then he and his companion ran off, presumably leaving only BUR agents behind. The wax-faced man stopped jerking toward Alexia's window. Instead, he turned on the hapless fallen vampire and lashed out at the supernatural man's face. There was a scrunch of breaking bone. Still, the vampire would not let go. The wax-faced man stepped inward, put all his weight on his trapped leg, and then shifted downward with his free foot, slamming the vampire's wrists with all his might. Alexia heard another ghastly wet crunching sound. With both wrists shattered, the vampire was forced to relax his grip. With one final, emotionless grin up at Alexia, the wax-faced man turned and raced away, battering through the two policemen as though they were not even there. The one with the cross pistol got off an excellent shot, but the wooden bullet did not even cause the wax man to stumble.

Alexia's vampire protector stood, shaky. His nose was broken, and his wrists hung limply, but when he looked up at Miss Tarabotti, his face was full of satisfaction. Alexia winced in sympathy at the blood spattered over his cheeks and chin. She knew he would heal quickly enough, especially if they could get him to fresh blood soon, but she could not help feeling empathy for his current pain, which must be acute.

A stranger, Alexia realized, a vampire, had just saved her from she knew not what unpleasantness. Saved *her*, a preternatural. She put her hands together and raised her fingertips to her lips, bowing forward in a silent prayer of thanks. The vampire nodded acknowledgment and then motioned her to step back inside the bedroom.

Miss Tarabotti nodded and retreated into the shadows of her sleeping chamber.

"What's going on here, then, me lad?" she heard one constable ask as she closed the shutters firmly behind her.

"Attempted burglary, I believe, sir," the vampire replied.

A sigh came from the constable. "Well, let me see your registration papers, please." To the other vampires, "And yours as well, please, gentlemen."

Miss Tarabotti had an understandably difficult time getting back to sleep after that, and when she finally managed it, her dreams were full of vampires with lifeless faces and shattered wrists who kept turning multiple Lord Maccons into wax statues tattooed with the word VIXI over and over again.

Miss Tarabotti's family was unexpectedly en masse and entirely in an uproar when she arose for breakfast the next morning. Usually this was the calmest time of day, with Squire Loontwill up first, Alexia second, and the remainder of the household a distant third. But, due to the excitement of the night, Miss Tarabotti was the last to awaken. She deduced she must be uncommonly late indeed, for when she went down the stairs, it was to find that her nearest and dearest were crowded in the hallway rather than the breakfast room.

Her mother came toward her, wringing her hands and looking more than usually dippy. "Fix your hair, Alexia, do, dear, do. Hurry! He has been waiting for nearly an hour. He is in the front parlor. Of course the front; nowhere else would do at all. He would not let us wake you. Lord knows why he wants to see *you*, but no one else will do. I hope it is not official business. You have not been *up* to anything, have you,

Alexia?" Mrs. Loontwill left off wringing her hands to flutter them about her head like a herd of excited butterflies.

"He ate three cold roast chickens," said Felicity in a shocked voice. "Three, at breakfast time!" She spoke as though she was not certain which to be more offended by, the quantity or the hour.

"And he still does not look happy," added Evylin, big blue eyes even bigger and bluer than usual in awe.

"He arrived unfashionably early and did not even want to talk with Papa, and Papa was *willing* to visit with him." Felicity was impressed.

Alexia peeked in the hallway mirror and patted her hair into place. Today she had dealt with the bruises on her neck by donning a teal paisley shawl over her black and silver day dress. The shawl's pattern clashed with the geometric design trimming the fold of the dress, and it covered over the flattering square neckline of the bodice, but some things could not be helped.

Seeing nothing at all wrong with her hair, except that perhaps the simple knot was a bit old-fashioned, she turned to her mother. "Please calm yourself, Mama. *Who* exactly is waiting in the parlor?"

Mrs. Loontwill ignored the question, hustling her eldest daughter down the hall as though she were a blue frilly sheepdog and Alexia a reluctant black sheep.

Alexia opened the door to the parlor and, when her mother and sisters would have followed her inside, shut it firmly and unceremoniously in their faces.

The Earl of Woolsey was sitting in stony silence on the sofa farthest from the window, with the carcasses of three chickens on silver platters before him.

Before she could prevent herself, Miss Tarabotti grinned at him. He simply looked so bashful, with all those chickens, like poultry skeleton sentries, standing guard before him.

"Ah," said the earl, raising one hand as though to ward off her smile. "None of that, Miss Tarabotti. Business first."

Miss Tarabotti would have been crestfallen, except for the "first." She also remembered Professor Lyall's words. She was supposed to make the next move in this little dance of theirs. So, instead of taking offense, she lowered her eyelashes, filed her smile away for later, and took a seat near to him but not too near.

"Well, what brings you to call on me this morning, then, my lord? You certainly have thrown the Loontwill household into a tizzy." She tilted her head to one side and strove for cool politeness.

"Um, aye, apologies for that." He looked abashedly at the chicken carcasses. "Your family, they are a bit, well"—he paused, hunting for the right word and then appearing to have come up with a new one of his own—"fibberty-jibbitus, are they not?"

Alexia's dark eyes twinkled at him. "You noticed? Imagine having to live with them all the time."

"I'd as soon not, thank you. Though it certainly speaks highly of your strength of character," he said, smiling unexpectedly. The expression suffused his normally cross face.

Miss Tarabotti's breath caught. Until that moment, she had not actually thought of the earl as pretty. But when he smiled. Oh dear, it was most inconvenient to deal with. Particularly before breakfast. She wondered what exactly was entailed in her making a *first move*.

She removed her paisley shawl.

Lord Maccon, who had been about to speak, paused, arrested midthought by the low neckline of the dress. The stark silver and black coloration of the material brought out the creamy undertones of her Mediterranean skin. "That dress will make your complexion come over all tan," Mrs. Loontwill had criticized when she ordered it. But Lord Maccon liked that. It was delightfully exotic: the contrast of that stylish dress and the foreign tones of her complexion.

"It is unseasonably warm this morning, wouldn't you say?" said Miss Tarabotti, putting her wrap to one side in a way that caused her torso to dip forward slightly.

Lord Maccon cleared his throat and managed to track down what he had been about to say. "Yesterday afternoon, while you and I were . . . otherwise engaged, someone broke into BUR headquarters."

Miss Tarabotti's mouth fell open. "This cannot possibly be good. Was anyone grievously injured? Have you caught the culprits? Was anything of value stolen?"

Lord Maccon sighed. Trust Miss Tarabotti to get straight to the meat of the issue. He answered her questions in order. "Not seriously. No. And mostly rove vampire and loner wolf files. Some of the more detailed research documentation also vanished, and . . ." He looked upset, pursing his lips.

Miss Tarabotti was worried more by his expression than by his words. She had never seen the earl with a look of such worry on his face. "And?" she prompted, sitting forward anxiously.

"Your files."

"Ah." She leaned back.

"Lyall returned to the office to check on something or other, even though I had ordered him home to bed, only to find all those on duty insensate."

"Good gracious, how?"

"Well, there was not a mark on them, but they were quite solidly asleep. He checked the office and found it ransacked and those certain records stolen. That was when he came to alert me here. I verified his information, although, by the time I arrived, everyone was awake once more."

"Chloroform?" suggested Alexia.

The earl nodded. "That does seem to be the case. He said a lingering scent was on the air. It would have taken quite a considerable amount of it too. Few have access to such a quantity of the chemical. I have all available agents tracking major scientific and medical institutions for any recent orders for large shipments of chloroform, but my resources are always taxed at full moon."

Alexia looked thoughtful. "There are a number of such organizations around London these days, are there not?"

Lord Maccon shifted toward her, his eyes soft caramel and affectionate. "You can see that there is further concern for your safety? Before, we could assume that they did not know exactly *what* you were, they thought you just an interfering daylighter. Now they know you are a preternatural, and they know it means you can neutralize the supernatural. They will want to dissect you and understand this."

Lord Maccon hoped to impress upon Miss Tarabotti the full range of the danger. She could be very stubborn over these kinds of things. Tonight, being full moon, neither he nor his pack could keep watch over her. He trusted his other BUR agents, even the vampires, but they were not pack, and a werewolf could not help whom he trusted most. That would always be pack. But no werewolf could guard on full moon—all the human parts of them vanished in the space of one night. In fact, he himself should not even be outside right now. He should be home safe and asleep, with his claviger handlers keeping an eye on everything. Especially, he realized, he should not be around Alexia Tarabotti, whom, like it or not, his carnal urges had taken an overly proprietary interest in. There was a reason werewolf couples were locked in the same cell together on full moon. Everyone else had to take solitary vigil in bestial form, vicious and relentless, but passion was passion and could be channeled into more pleasurable and slightly less violent pursuits, so long as the female was equally cursed and so able to survive the experience. *How,* he wondered, *would it be to weather the moon in human form, held there by the touch of a preternatural lover?* What an experience that would be. His baser instincts urged such musings on, driven by the damnable neckline of Miss Tarabotti's dress.

Lord Maccon picked up the paisley shawl and shoved it at Alexia's chest area. "Put that back on," he ordered gruffly.

Miss Tarabotti, instead of taking offense, smiled serenely, lifted the garment from his grasp, and placed it carefully behind her and out of his reach.

She turned back and, greatly daring, took one of his large rough hands in both of hers.

"You are worried for my safety, which is sweet, but your guards were most efficacious last night. I have no doubt they will be equally competent this evening."

He nodded. He did not withdraw his hand from her tentative touch but turned it to curl about hers. "They reported the incident to me just before dawn."

Alexia shivered. "Do you know who he is?"

"He who?" asked the earl, sounding like a donkey. Absentmindedly, he ran his thumb over her wrist in a reassuring caress.

"The wax-faced man," said Miss Tarabotti, eyes glazed with memory and fear.

"No. Not human, not supernatural, not preternatural," he said. "A medical experiment gone astray, perhaps? He *is* filled with blood."

She was startled. "How would you know such a thing?"

He explained. "The fight, at the carriage? When they tried to abduct you. I bit him; do you not recall?"

She nodded, remembering the way the earl had only changed his head into wolf form and how he had wiped the blood from his face onto his sleeve.

One shapely male lip curled in disgust. "That meat was not fresh."

Alexia shuddered. *No, not fresh.* She did not like to think of the wax man and his compatriots having *her* personal information. She knew Lord Maccon would do his best to see her protected. And, of course, last night had proved that these mysterious enemies knew where to find her, so nothing had fundamentally changed with the theft of the BUR papers. But now that the wax-faced man and the shadowed man with his chloroform handkerchief knew she was soulless, Miss Tarabotti felt somehow terribly exposed.

"I know this will not please you," she said, "but I have decided to call on Lord Akeldama this evening while my family is out. Do not worry. I will make certain your guards can follow me. I am convinced Lord Akeldama's residence is extremely secure."

The Alpha grunted. "If you must."

"He knows things," she tried to reassure him.

Lord Maccon could not argue with that. "He generally knows too many things, if you ask me."

Miss Tarabotti tried to make her position clear. "He is not interested in me, as anything, well . . . *significant*."

"Why would he be?" wondered Lord Maccon. "You are a preternatural, soulless."

Alexia winced but strode doggedly onward. "However, you are?"

A pause.

Lord Maccon looked most put upon. His caressing thumb movement stopped, but he did not withdraw his hand from hers.

Alexia wondered if she should force the issue. He was acting as though he had not given the matter much thought. Perhaps he had not: Professor Lyall said the Alpha was acting entirely on instinct. And this *was* full moon, a notoriously bad time for werewolves and their instincts. *Was it appropriate to inquire as to his feelings on the matter of her good self at this particular time of the month?* Then again, wasn't this the time when she was most likely to get an honest answer?

"I am what?" The earl was not making this easy for her.

Alexia swallowed her pride, sat up very straight, and said, "Interested in me?"

Lord Maccon was quiet for a few long minutes. He examined his emotions. While admitting that at that moment—her small hands in his, the smell of vanilla and cinnamon in the air, the neckline of that damnable dress—his mind possessed all the clarity of pea soup full of hamhock–sized chunks of need, there was something else lurking in said soup. Whatever it was, it made him angry, for it would desperately complicate everything in his well-ordered life, and now was not the time to tackle it.

"I have spent a good deal of time and energy during the course of our association trying not to like you," he admitted finally. It was not an answer to her question.

"And yet *I* find not liking *you* comparatively easy, especially when you say things such as that!" Miss Tarabotti replied, trying desperately to extract her hand from his odious caress.

The action backfired. Lord Maccon tugged and lifted her forward as if she weighed no more than thistledown.

Miss Tarabotti found herself sitting flush against him on the small couch. The day was suddenly as warm as she had previously implied. She was scorched from shoulder to thigh by intimate contact with his lordship's prodigious muscles. *What is it,* she wondered, *about werewolves and muscles?*

"Oh my," said Alexia.

"I am finding," said the earl, turning toward her and caressing her face with one hand, "it very difficult to imagine not not disliking you on a regular and intimate basis for a very long time to come."

Miss Tarabotti smiled. The smell of open fields was all about her, that breezy scent only the earl produced.

He did not kiss her, simply touched her face, as though he were waiting for something.

"You have not apologized for your behavior," Miss Tarabotti said, leaning into his hand with her cheek. Best not to let him get the upper hand, so to speak, in this conversation by getting her all flustered. She wondered if she dared turn her face to kiss his fingertips.

"Mmm? Apologize? For which of my many transgressions?" Lord Maccon was fascinated by the smoothness of the skin of her neck, just below her ear. He liked the old-fashioned way she had put up her hair, all caught up at the back like a governess—better access.

"You ignored me at that dinner party," Alexia persisted. It still rankled, and Miss Tarabotti was not about to let him slide without some pretense at contrition.

Lord Maccon nodded, tracing her arched black brows with a fingertip. "Yet you spent the evening engaging in a far more interesting conversation than I and went driving the next morning with a young scientist."

He sounded so forlorn, Alexia almost laughed. Still no apology, but this was as close as an Alpha got, she supposed. She looked him dead-on. "*He* finds me interesting."

Lord Maccon looked livid at that revelation. "Of that I am perfectly well aware," he snarled.

Miss Tarabotti sighed. She had not meant to make him angry, fun as that could be. "What am I supposed to say at this juncture? What would you, or your pack protocol, like me to say?" she asked finally.

That you want me, his baser urges thought. *That there is a future, not too far away in space or time, involving you and me and a particularly large bed.* He tried to grapple with such salacious visions and extract himself from their influence. *Blasted full moon,* he thought, almost trembling with the effort.

He managed to control himself enough so that he did not actually attack her. But with the dampening down of his needs, he was forced to deal with his emotions. There it was, like a stone in the pit of his stomach. The one feeling he did not want to acknowledge. Further than just need, or want, or any of those less-civilized instincts he could so easily blame on his werewolf nature.

Lyall had known. Lyall had not mentioned it, but he had known. *How many Alphas,* Lord Maccon wondered, *had Professor Lyall watched fall in love?*

Lord Maccon turned a very wolflike gaze on the one woman who could keep him from ever becoming a wolf again. He wondered how much of his love was tied into that—the very uniqueness of it. Preternatural and supernatural—was such a pairing even possible?

Mine, said his look.

Alexia did not understand that glance. And she did not understand the silence that came with it.

She cleared her throat, suddenly nervous. "Bitch's Dance. Is it . . . my move?" she asked, naming pack protocol to give herself some credence. She did not know what was required, but she wanted him to know she had come to understand some part of his behavior.

Lord Maccon, still bowled over by the revelation he had just come to, looked at her as though he had never really seen her before. He stopped caressing her face and tiredly scrubbed at his own with both hands, like a little child. "My Beta has been talking, I see." He looked at her through his hands. "Well, Professor Lyall has assured me that I have committed a grave transgression in my handling of this situation. That Alpha you may be, but werewolf you are not. Though I will add that, appropriate or not, I have enjoyed our interactions immensely." He looked over at the wing chair.

"Even the hedgehog?" Miss Tarabotti was not certain what was happening. *Had he just admitted intentions? Were they purely physical? If so, should she pursue a liaison?* No word of marriage had yet crossed his lips. Werewolves, being supernatural and mostly dead, could not have children. Or so her father's books purported. They rarely married as a result, professional experts in bedsport or clavigers being the preferred approach. Alexia contemplated her own future. She was not likely to get another opportunity such as this, and there were ways to be discreet. Or so she had read. Although, no doubt, given the earl's possessive nature, all would be revealed eventually. *Reputation be damned,* she thought. *It is not as though I have any significant prospects to ruin. I would simply be following in my father's philandering footsteps. Perhaps Lord Maccon would stash me away in a little cottage in the countryside somewhere with my library and a nice big bed.* She would miss Ivy and Lord Akeldama and, yes, she must admit, her silly family and sillier London society. Alexia puzzled. *Would it be worth it?*

Lord Maccon chose that moment to tilt her head back and kiss her. No gentle approach this time, but straight to that long, hot branding of lips, and teeth, and tongue.

Plastering herself against him, annoyed, as always seemed to be the case when he accosted her, with the amount of clothing between her hands and his torso. *Only one possible answer to that: yes, it would be worth it.*

Miss Tarabotti smiled against his lordship's insistent mouth. *Bitch's Dance.* She drew back and looked up into his tawny eyes. She liked the predator hunger she saw there. It spiced the delicious salty taste of his skin, that sense of risk. "Very well, Lord Maccon. If we are going to play this particular hand, would you be interested in becoming my . . ." Miss Tarabotti scrabbled for the right word. *What does one properly call a male lover?* She shrugged and grinned. "Mistress?"

"*What* did you say?" roared Lord Maccon, outraged.

"Uh. The wrong thing?" suggested Alexia, mystified by this sudden switch in moods. She had no more time to correct her gaffe, for Lord Maccon's yell had reached out into the hallway, and Mrs. Loontwill, whose curiosity was chomping at the proverbial bit, burst into the room.

Only to find her eldest daughter entwined on the couch with Lord Maccon, Earl of Woolsey, behind a table decorated with the carcasses of three dead chickens.

CHAPTER NINE

A Problem of Werewolf Proportions

Mrs. Loontwill did what any well-prepared mother would do upon finding her unmarried daughter in the arms of a gentleman werewolf: she had very decorous, and extremely loud, hysterics.

As a result of this considerable noise, the entirety of the Loontwill household came rushing from whatever room they had formerly been occupying and into the front parlor. Naturally, they assumed someone had died or that Miss Hisselpenny had arrived in a bonnet of unmatched ugliness. Instead, they found something far less likely—Alexia and the Earl of Woolsey romantically enmeshed.

Miss Tarabotti would have moved off the couch and seated herself an appropriate distance from Lord Maccon, but he coiled one arm about her waist and would not let her shift.

She glared at him in extreme annoyance from under dark brows. "What are you doing, you horrible man? We are already in enough trouble. Mama will see us married; you see if she does not," she hissed under her breath.

Lord Maccon said only, "Hush up now. Let me handle this." Then he nuzzled her neck.

Which naturally made Miss Tarabotti even more put out and uncomfortable.

Felicity and Evylin paused in the doorway, eyes wide, and then commenced hysterical giggling. Floote appeared at their heels and hovered in a worried but mostly invisible manner next to the hat stand.

Mrs. Loontwill continued to scream, more in surprise than in outrage. The earl and *Alexia*? What would this do to their social standing?

Miss Tarabotti fidgeted under the warmth of Lord Maccon's arm. Surreptitiously, she tried to pry his fingers off where they gripped her waist, just above her hipbone. His arm rested across the top of her bustle—shocking. He merely winked at her subtle struggles in apparent amusement. Winked!

I mean, thought Alexia, *really!*

Squire Loontwill bumbled into the front parlor with a handful of household accounts he had been in the middle of reckoning. Upon observing Alexia and the earl, he dropped the accounts and sucked his teeth sharply. He then bent to retrieve the paperwork, taking his time so as to consider his options. He ought, of course, to call the earl out. But there were intricate layers to this situation, for the earl and he could not engage in a duel, being as one was supernatural and the other not. As the challenger, Squire Loontwill would have to find a werewolf to fight the earl as his champion. No werewolf of his limited acquaintance would take on the Woolsey Castle Alpha. As far as he knew, no werewolf in London would take on such a Herculean task, not even the dewan. On the other hand, he could always *ask* the gentleman to do the right thing by his stepdaughter. But who would willingly take on Alexia for life? That was more of a curse than even werewolf change. No, Lord Maccon would probably have to be forced. The real question was whether the earl could be persuaded in a nonviolent manner to marry Alexia or if the best the squire could hope for was for her to become simply one of Woolsey's clavigers.

Mrs. Loontwill, naturally, complicated the issue.

"Oh, Herbert," she said pleadingly to her silent husband, "you must *make* him marry her! Call for the parson immediately! Look at them . . . they are . . . ," she sputtered, "canoodling!"

"Now, now, Leticia, be reasonable. Being a claviger is not so bad in this day and age." Squire Loontwill was thinking of the expense of Alexia's continued upkeep. This situation might turn out to be profitable for all concerned, except Alexia's reputation.

Mrs. Loontwill did not agree. "My daughter is *not* claviger material."

Alexia muttered under her breath, "You have no idea how true a statement that is."

Lord Maccon rolled his eyes heavenward.

Her mother ignored her. "She is *wife* material!" Mrs. Loontwill clearly had visions of drastically improved social status.

Miss Tarabotti stood up from the couch to better confront her relations. This forced the earl to release her, which upset him far more than her mother's hysterics or her stepfather's cowardice.

"I will *not* marry under duress, Mama. Nor will I force the earl into such bondage. Lord Maccon has not tendered me an offer, and I will not have him commit unwillingly. Don't you dare press the issue!"

Mrs. Loontwill was no longer hysterical. There was instead a steel-edged gleam in her pale blue eyes. A gleam that made Lord Maccon wonder which side Alexia had gotten her flinty personality from. Until that moment, he had blamed the deceased Italian father. Now he was not so certain.

Mrs. Loontwill said, voice high-pitched and abrasive, "You brazen hussy! Such sentiments should have prevented you from allowing him such liberties in the *first* place."

Alexia was belligerent. "Nothing of significance has occurred. My honor is still intact."

Mrs. Loontwill stepped forward and slapped her eldest daughter smartly across the face. The cracking sound echoed like a pistol shot through the room. "You are in no position to argue this point, young lady!"

Felicity and Evylin gasped in unison and stopped giggling. Floote made an involuntary movement from his statuelike state near the door.

Lord Maccon, faster than anyone's eye could catch, suddenly appeared next to Mrs. Loontwill, a steel grip about her wrist. "I would not do that again, if I were you, madam," he said. His voice was soft and low and his expression bland. But there was a kind of anger in the air that was all predator: cold, impartial, and deadly. The anger that wanted to bite and had the teeth to back it up. This was a side of Lord Maccon that no one had seen before—not even Miss Tarabotti.

Squire Loontwill had the distinct impression that, regardless of his decision, Alexia was now no longer his responsibility. He also had the impression that his wife was actually in danger of her life. The earl looked both angry and hungry, and canines were inching down over his bottom lip.

Miss Tarabotti touched her hot cheek thoughtfully, wondering if she would have a handprint. She glared at the earl. "Let my mother go immediately, Lord Maccon."

The earl looked at her, not really seeing her. His eyes were entirely yellow, not simply the colored part either but the whites as well, just like a wolf. Miss Tarabotti thought werewolves could not change during daylight, but perhaps this close to full moon anything was possible. Or perhaps it was another one of those Alpha abilities.

She stepped forward and forcibly placed herself between Lord Maccon and her mother. He wanted an Alpha female, did he? Well, she would give him Alpha in spades.

"Mama, I will not marry the earl against his will. Should you or Squire Loontwill attempt to coerce me, I will simply not submit to the ceremony. You will be left looking like fools among family and friends, and me silent at the altar."

Lord Maccon looked down at her. "Why? What is wrong with me?"

This shocked Mrs. Loontwill into speaking again. "You mean you *are* willing to marry Alexia?"

Lord Maccon looked at her like she had gone insane. "Of course I am."

"Let us be perfectly clear here," said Squire Loontwill. "You are willing to marry our Alexia, even though she is . . . well . . . ," he floundered.

Felicity came to his rescue. "Old."

Evylin added, "And plain."

"And tan," said Felicity.

The squire continued. "And so extraordinarily assertive."

Miss Tarabotti was nodding agreement. "My point exactly! He cannot possibly *want* to marry me. I will not have him forced into such an arrangement merely because he is a gentleman and feels he ought. It is simply that it is near to full moon, and things have gotten out of hand. Or"— she frowned—"should I say too much *in* hand?"

Lord Maccon glanced about at Alexia's family. No wonder she devalued herself, growing up in this kind of environment.

He looked at Felicity. "What would I possibly want with a silly chit just out of the schoolroom?" At Evylin. "Perhaps our ideas on beauty do not ally with one another. I find your sister's appearance quite pleasing." He carefully did not mention her figure, or her smell, or the silkiness of her hair, or any of the other things he found so alluring. "After all, it is *I* who would have to live with her."

The more Lord Maccon considered it, the more he grew to like the idea. Certainly his imagination was full of pictures of what he and Alexia might do together once he got her home in a properly wedded state, but now those lusty images were mixing with others: waking up next to her, seeing her across the dining table, discussing science and politics, having her advice on points of pack controversy and BUR difficulties. No doubt she would be useful in verbal frays and social machinations, as long as she was on his side. But that, too, would be part of the pleasure of marrying such a woman. One never knew where one stood with Alexia. A union full of surprise and excitement was more than most could hope for. Lord Maccon had never been one to seek out the quiet life.

He said to the squire, "Miss Tarabotti's personality is a large measure of her appeal. Can you see me with some frippery young thing whom I could push around at any opportunity and cow into accepting all my decisions?"

Lord Maccon was not explaining himself for Alexia's family's benefit but for hers. Although, he certainly did not want the Loontwills to think they were forcing him into anything! He was Alpha enough for that. This whole marriage thing was *his* idea, curse it. No matter that it had only just occurred to him.

Squire Loontwill said nothing in response to that. Because he had, in fact, assumed the earl would want just such a wife. What man would not?

Lord Maccon and the squire were clearly birds of entirely different feathers. "Not with my work and position. I need someone strong, who will back me up, at least most of the time, and who possesses the necessary gumption to stand up to me when she thinks I am wrong."

"Which," interrupted Alexia, "she does at this very moment. You are not convincing anyone, Lord Maccon. Least of all me."

She held up her hand when he would have protested. "We have been caught in a compromising position, and you are trying to do the best by me." She stubbornly refused to believe his interest and intentions were genuine. Before her family had interrupted them, and during all previous encounters, no mention of marriage had ever passed his lips. Nor, she thought sadly, had the word *love.* "I *do* appreciate your integrity, but I will not have you coerced. Nor will I be manipulated into a loveless union based entirely on salacious urges." She looked into his yellow eyes. "Please understand my position."

As though her family were not watching, he touched the side of her face, stroking the cheek her mother had hit. "I understand that you have been taught for far too long that you are unworthy."

Miss Tarabotti felt inexplicably like crying. She turned her face away from his caress.

He let his arm drop. Clearly, the damage done could not be mended with a few words from him in the space of one disastrous morning.

"Mama," she said, gesturing expansively, "I will not have you manipulating this situation. No one need know what has occurred in this room. So long as you all hold your collective tongues for once." She glared at her sisters. "My reputation will remain intact, and Lord Maccon will remain a free man. And now I have a headache; please excuse me."

With that, she gathered what was left of her dignity and swept from the room. She retreated upstairs to the sanctity of her own boudoir to indulge in a most uncharacteristic but blessedly short-lived bout of tears. The only one who caught her at it was Floote, who placed a sympathetic tea tray on her bedside table, including some of Cook's extra-special apricot puffs, and issued orders with the household staff that she was not to be disturbed.

Lord Maccon was left in the bosom of her family.

"I believe, for the moment, we ought to do as she says," he said to them.

Mrs. Loontwill looked stubborn and militant.

Lord Maccon glared at her. "Do not interfere, Mrs. Loontwill. Knowing Alexia, your approbation is likely to turn her more surely against me than anything else possibly could."

Mrs. Loontwill looked like she would like to take offense, but given this was the Earl of Woolsey, she resisted the inclination.

Then Lord Maccon turned to Squire Loontwill. "Understand, my good sir, that my intentions are honorable. It is the lady who resists, but she must be allowed to make up her own mind. I, too, will not have her coerced. Both of you, stay out of this." He paused in the doorway, donning his hat and coat and baring his teeth at the Loontwill girls. "And, you two, keep quiet. Your sister's reputation is at stake, and never doubt that it drastically impacts your own. I am not one to be trifled with in this matter. I bid you good day." With that, he left the room.

"Well, I never," said Mrs. Loontwill, sitting down heavily on the couch. "I am not sure I want that man for a son-in-law."

"He is very powerful, my dear, no doubt, and a man of considerable means," said Squire Loontwill, attempting to establish a silver lining of some kind.

"But so rude!" persisted his wife. "And all that, after eating three of our best chickens!" She gestured limply at the carcasses in question, a blatant reminder that, whatever it was that had just occurred, she had clearly emerged the loser. The chickens were beginning to attract flies. She pulled the bell rope for Floote to come and clear them away, peeved with the butler for not disposing of them sooner.

"Well, I shall tell you one thing. Alexia is definitely not attending the duchess's rout tonight. Even if I had not already forbidden her, today's behavior would have sealed it. Full-moon celebration or not, she can stay at home and think long and hard on her many transgressions!"

Mr. Loontwill patted his wife's hand sympathetically. "Of course, my dear."

There was no "of course" about it. Miss Tarabotti, knowing her family's propensity for the dramatic, followed suit by keeping to her room most of the day and refusing to leave it even to see them depart that evening.

Appreciating the tragedy of it all, her two sisters made sympathetic cluck-clucking noises outside her closed door and promised to bring back all the latest gossip. She would have been more reassured if they had promised not to engage in any gossip of their own. Mrs. Loontwill refused to speak to her, an occurrence that did not tax Alexia in the slightest. Eventually the house fell silent. She breathed a prodigious sigh of relief. Sometimes her family could really be very trying.

She stuck her head out of her bedroom door and called, "Floote?"

The butler appeared on cue. "Miss?"

"Hail a cab, please, Floote. I am going out."

"Are you certain that is wise, miss?"

"To be wise, one might never leave one's room at all," quoted Miss Tarabotti.

Floote gave her a skeptical look but went downstairs as bidden to flag down a hackney.

Miss Tarabotti summoned her maid and went about changing into one of her more serviceable evening gowns. It was an ivory taffeta affair with small puffed sleeves, a modest scooped neckline, and trimmed out with raspberry pin-tucked ribbon and pale gold lace edging. True, it *was* two seasons old and probably should have been made over before now, but it was comfortable and wore well. Alexia thought of the dress as an old friend, and knowing she looked passably well in it, tended to don it in times of stress. Lord Akeldama expected grandeur, but Miss Tarabotti simply hadn't the emotional energy for her russet silk fancy, not tonight. She curled her hair over her still-marked shoulder, coiling part of it up with her two favorite hair pins, one of silver and one of wood. She braided the rest loosely with ivory ribbon. It contrasted becomingly with her dark tresses.

By the time she was ready, it was dark outside her window. All of London nested safely in those few hours after sunrise, before the moon climbed into the sky. It was a moment supernatural folk called twinight: just enough time to get werewolves under lock and key before the moon herself appeared and drove them to become mad unstoppable monsters.

Floote gave Miss Tarabotti one more long warning glance as he handed her up the steps of the cab. He did not approve of her going out on such a night. He was certain she would get into mischief. Of course, Floote tended to be under the impression that the young miss was up to no good *whenever* she was out of his sight. But on full moon in particular, no possible benefit could come of it.

Miss Tarabotti frowned, knowing exactly what the butler was thinking, despite his face remaining perfectly impassive. Then she smiled slightly. She must admit, he was probably correct in his opinion.

"Be careful, miss," Floote instructed severely but without much hope. He had, after all, been butler to her father before her, and just look what happened to Alessandro. Prone to willful and problematic lives, the Tarabottis.

"Oh, Floote, do stop mothering. It is most unbecoming in a man of your age and profession. I will only be gone a few hours, and I will be perfectly safe. Look." She pointed behind Floote to the side of the house, where two figures appeared out of the night shadows like bats. They moved with supernatural grace coming to stand several feet from Alexia's hackney, obviously prepared to follow it.

Floote did not look reassured. He snorted in a most unbutlerlike manner and shut the carriage door firmly.

Being vampires, Miss Tarabotti's BUR guards needed no cab of their own. Of course, they probably would have preferred one. It was not quite apropos to the supernatural mystique, jogging after a public transport. But they experienced no physical taxation of any kind from the exertion. So that is precisely what Miss Tarabotti forced them to do, instructing her driver to walk on, before they had a chance to find a conveyance of their own.

Miss Tarabotti's little cab wended its way slowly through the throngs of moon-party traffic, ending up in front of one of the most dashing abodes in London, the town residence of Lord Akeldama.

The foppish vampire was waiting for her at the door when she alighted from the cab. "Alexia, *sugarplumiest* of the plums, what a *lovely* way to spend the full moon, in your ambrosial company! Who could possibly wish for *anything* else in life?"

Miss Tarabotti smiled at the excessive gallantry, knowing full well Lord Akeldama would far rather be at the opera, or the theater, or the duchess's rout, or even down the West End in the blood-whores' den gorging himself until he could not see straight. Vampires liked to misbehave on full moon.

She paid the cab and made her way up the front steps. "Lord Akeldama, how lovely to see you again so soon. I am delighted you could accommodate my visit at such short notice. I have much to talk with you about."

Lord Akeldama looked pleased. Just about the only thing that could keep him home at full moon was information. In fact, he had been motivated to change his plans at Miss Tarabotti's request in light of the fact that she would only contact him if she needed to know something. And if she needed to know something, she must perforce know something else significant already. The vampire rubbed his elegant white hands together in delight. Information: reason for living. Well, that and fashion.

Lord Akeldama was dressed to the pink for the evening. His coat was of exquisite plum-colored velvet paired with a satin waistcoat of sea-foam green and mauve plaid. His britches were of a perfectly coordinated lavender, and his formal cravat a treble bow of white lawn secured with a massive amethyst and gold pin. His Hessian boots were polished to a mirror shine, and his top hat was plum velvet to match the coat. Miss Tarabotti was not certain if this elaborate outfit was because he intended to go out after their assignation, if he actually considered her that important, or if he just always dressed like a sideshow performer on full moon. Regardless, she felt shabby and severe by comparison in her outmoded gown and practical shoes. She was glad they were not going out on the town together. How the ton would laugh at such a mismatched pair!

Lord Akeldama guided her solicitously up the last few steps. He paused on the stoop and looked back over his plum-colored shoulder at the spot where her cab had been and now was not anymore. "Your shadows will have to stay outside my domain, little *creampuff*. You *know* vampire territory laws, don't you, my *dove*? Not even *your* safety, or *their* jobs at BUR, can countermand such regulations. They are more than law; they are instinct."

Miss Tarabotti looked at him, wide-eyed. "If you deem it necessary, my lord, of course they must stay off the premises."

"Well, my *ravishing* one, even if you do not comprehend to what I am referring, *they* certainly do." His eyes slitted as he glared out into the street.

Miss Tarabotti could not see what drew his attention, but she knew that did not mean they were not there: two vampire guards, standing supernaturally still in the night, watching them. She looked closely at her friend's face.

For a moment, Miss Tarabotti thought Lord Akeldama's eyes actually glowed, a sheen of warding, a spark of possession. She wondered if that look was the vampire equivalent of a dog peeing to mark his territory. *Stay out*, said Lord Akeldama's expression. *Mine*. What, then, did werewolves do? Lord Maccon had implied they were not as territorial as vampires, but still. The packs tended to stick to certain geographic regions; there was no doubt of that. Miss Tarabotti mentally shrugged. They actually were wolves, at least part of the time, and scent did seem to be particularly important to werewolves. They probably did pee. The thought of Lord Maccon cocking a leg to mark Woolsey Castle parklands was so absurd that Miss Tarabotti actually had to stop herself from chortling aloud. She filed the image away as an excellent and insulting question to ask the earl at an utterly inappropriate future moment.

A shadow across the street, empty darkness contrasting the light cast by flickering gas, materialized into the figure of two men. They doffed their hats at Lord Akeldama, who merely sniffed. Then they faded out of view once more.

Lord Akeldama grabbed Miss Tarabotti's hand, affectionately tucking it over his arm, and steered her into his fabulous house.

"Come along, my *dearest* girl." The sheen in his eyes vanished, as if it had never been, and he was back to his usual debonair self.

He shook his head as his butler closed the front door behind them. "Little better than drones, youngsters of the hive. They cannot even be bothered to think for themselves! First, obey the queen; second, obey BUR, spending their strongest years simply jumping from one set of orders to the next like trumped-up soldiers. Still, it is an uncomplicated life for the primitive of intellect." His tone was rancorous, but Miss Tarabotti thought she could detect an undercurrent of regret. He had a faraway look in his eyes, as if he were visiting some long-forgotten and far simpler time.

"Is that why you became a rove—too many orders?" Miss Tarabotti asked.

"What was that, my diminutive *gherkin*?" Lord Akeldama shook himself and blinked as though waking up from a long sleep. "Orders? No, the split was due to circumstances far *more* labyrinthine than that. It all started when gold buckles came back into vogue, progressed to heights of bitterness over spats versus gaiters, and wended down a slippery slope from there. I believe the defining moment was when certain persons, who shall remain nameless, objected to my fuchsia silk striped waistcoat. I loved that waistcoat. I put my foot down, right then and there; I do not mind telling you!" To punctuate his deeply offended feelings, he stamped one silver-and-pearl-decorated high heel firmly. "*No one* tells me what I can and cannot wear!" He snapped up a lace fan from where it lay on a hall table and fanned himself vigorously with it for emphasis.

It was clear he was skidding the conversation off track, but Miss Tarabotti did not mind. She responded to his distress with a noncommittal murmur of sympathy.

"Pardon me, my *fluffy cockatoo*," he said, pretending to rein in an excessively emotional state. "*Please* ignore my ramblings as those of a madman. It is just so uncomfortable to have two not of *my* bloodline in proximity to my home, you understand? It is a little like having those *disagreeable* shivers constantly running up and down one's spine. Something does not feel right with the *universe* when one's territory is invaded. I *can* bear it, but I do not *like* it. It makes me quite edgy and off kilter."

Lord Akeldama put the fan down. A personable young man appeared at his elbow with a solicitous cooling cloth draped artistically on a silver tray. Lord Akeldama dabbed at his brow delicately. "Oh, *thank* you, Biffy. *So* thoughtful." Biffy winked and skipped off again. He displayed impressive musculature for all his grace. Acrobat? wondered Alexia. Lord Akeldama watched the young man walk away appreciatively. "I should not have favorites, of course . . ." He sighed and turned to Miss Tarabotti. "But, now, on to more important topics! Such as your *scrumptious* self. To what do I owe the singular *pleasure* of your company this evening?"

Miss Tarabotti refrained from any direct answer. Instead, she looked about the interior of his house. She had never been inside before, and she was overwhelmed. Everything was to the height of style, if one were thinking in terms of style round about a hundred years ago. Lord Akeldama possessed real, substantial wealth and was not afraid to display it openly. Nothing in his home was substandard, or faux, or imitation, and all of it was well beyond the pale. The carpets were not Persian but were instead vibrant flower-ridden images of shepherds seducing shepherdesses under intense blue skies. Were those puffy white clouds? Yes, they were. The arched ceiling of the entrance hall was actually frescoed like the Sistine Chapel, only Lord Akeldama's ceiling depicted cheeky-looking cherubs up to nefarious activities. Alexia blushed. All kinds of nefarious activities. She turned her eyes hurriedly back down. Small Corinthian columns stood proudly all around, supporting marble statues of naked male gods that Miss Tarabotti had no doubt were authentically ancient Greek in origin.

The vampire led her through to his drawing room. It contained none of the style clutter but instead harkened back to a time before the French Revolution. The furniture was all white or gilded gold, upholstered in cream and gold striped brocade and riddled with fringe and tassels. Heavy layers of gold velvet curtains shielded the windows, and the plush rug on the floor sported yet another proximate shepherding event. Lord Akeldama's had only two nods to modern life. The first was evident in the room being well lit, with multiple gas lamps no less, elaborate candelabras appearing to be only for decorative purposes.

The second facet of modernity took the form of a gilded pipe with multiple joints, mounted on the mantel. Alexia figured it must be some modern artwork. *Such an expense!* thought Miss Tarabotti.

She took a seat in a thronelike armchair and removed her hat and gloves. Lord Akeldama sat across from her. He produced the strange crystal tuning fork device, flicking it into dissonant resonance and placing it on a side table.

Alexia wondered that he thought such caution necessary inside his own home. Then she figured no one would be more worried about eavesdropping than a lifelong eavesdropper.

"Well," he demanded, "what do you think of my humble abode?"

For all its gilt pomposity and grandeur, the room had a feeling of regular use. There were multiple hats and gloves strewn about, here-and-there notes on slips of paper, and the odd abandoned snuff-box. A fat calico cat lounged in possession of an overstuffed hassock and one or two dead tassels near the fire. A grand piano stood prominently in one corner, well dusted, with sheets of music lying atop it. It clearly underwent more regular use than the one in the Loontwills' front parlor.

"It is unexpectedly welcoming," Miss Tarabotti replied.

Lord Akeldama laughed. "So speaks one who has visited the Westminster hive."

"It is also very, uh, Rococo," she said, attempting not to intimate she found it at all old-fashioned.

Lord Akeldama clapped his hands delightedly. "Isn't it just? I am afraid I never quite left that particular era. It was *such* a glorious time to be alive, when men *finally* and *truly* got to wear sparkly things, and there was lace and velvet everywhere."

A gentle hubbub arose outside the drawing room door, then subsided, and then broke into raucous laughter.

Lord Akeldama smiled affectionately. His fangs showed clearly in the bright light. "There are my little drone-y-poos!" He shook his head. "Ah, to be young again."

They were left untroubled by whatever it was that was occurring in the hallway. Apparently a closed door meant a well-respected "stay out" in Lord Akeldama's household. However, Alexia soon discovered that her vampire friend's domicile seemed to exist in a constant state of tumult-in-the-hallway.

Miss Tarabotti imagined this must be what it was like inside a gentlemen's club. She knew that there were no women among Lord Akeldama's drones. Even if his taste had extended in that direction, Lord Akeldama could hardly hope to present a female to Countess Nadasdy for metamorphosis. No queen would willingly turn a woman of a rove household; the chance of making a renegade queen, however slim, would never be risked. The countess probably only bit Lord Akeldama's male drones under sufferance—for the good of increasing the population. Unless, of course, Lord Akeldama was allied to a different hive. Miss Tarabotti did not ask. She suspected such a question might be impertinent.

Lord Akeldama sat back and twiddled his amethyst cravat pin with thumb and forefinger, pinky raised high into the air. "Well, my *captivating* crumpet, *tell* me about your visit to the hive!"

Alexia told him, as briefly as possible, about the experience and her evaluation of the characters involved.

Lord Akeldama seemed to agree with her general assessments. "Lord Ambrose you can disregard; he is her pet favorite but hasn't the brains of a *peahen*, I am afraid, for all his pulchritude. *Such* a waste!" He tut-tutted and shook his blond head sadly. "Now, the Duke of Hematol, he is a tricky character and in an outright sense of a one-on-one match, the most perilous of the Westminster inner circle."

Alexia ruminated on that nondescript vampire who had reminded her so strongly of Professor Lyall. She nodded. "He certainly gave that impression."

Lord Akeldama laughed. "Poor old Bertie, he works so hard *not* to!"

Miss Tarabotti raised her eyebrows. "Which is exactly why he does."

"But you are, my *daffodil,* and I do not mean to cause offense, a tad *insignificant* for his attentions. The duke contents himself mainly with attempting to rule the world and other suchlike *nonsense.* When one is guiding the patterns of the social *universe,* a single spinster preternatural is unlikely to cause one undue distress."

Miss Tarabotti fully understood where he was coming from and was not in the least offended.

Lord Akeldama continued. "But, my *treasure,* under your *particular* circumstances, I suggest Dr. Caedes is the one to be most wary of. More mobile than the countess, and he is . . . How do I put this?" He stopped spinning his amethyst pin and began tapping it with one finger. "He is interested in *minutia.* You know he takes an interest in modern inventions?"

"That was his collection on display in the hallway of the hive house?"

Lord Akeldama nodded. "He dabbles himself, as well as investing and collecting like-minded drones. He is also not altogether *compos mentis* in the daylight sense of the term."

"As opposed to?" Alexia was confused. Sanity was sanity, was it not?

"Ah"—Lord Akeldama paused—"we vampires tend to have an unfettered approach to the concept of mental health." He twiddled his fingers in the air. "One's moral clarity goes a *little* fuzzy after the first two centuries or so."

Miss Tarabotti said, "I see," although she did not.

There came a timid knock on the drawing room door.

Lord Akeldama stilled the vibrating sound disrupter device. "Come!" he then sang out.

It opened to reveal a gaggle of grinning young men, captained by the one Lord Akeldama had referred to earlier as Biffy. All of them were handsome, charming, and in high spirits. They bustled into the room.

"My lord, we are going out to enjoy the full moon," said Biffy, top hat in hand.

Lord Akeldama nodded. "The usual instructions, my dear boys."

Biffy and the other young bloods nodded, their smiles slipping ever so slightly. They were all dressed to the nines—dandified gentry of the kind welcome at any gathering and noticed at none. Alexia reasoned no man of Lord Akeldama's household would ever be less than perfectly fashionable, entirely presentable, and patently invisible as a result. A few favored his more outrageous mode of costuming, but most were toned-down, less eccentric versions of their lord. A few looked faintly familiar, but Alexia could not, for the life of her, pinpoint where or when she had seen them before. They were simply so very *good* at being exactly what was expected.

Biffy looked hesitantly at Miss Tarabotti before asking Lord Akeldama, "Anything in particular desired for this evening, my lord?"

Lord Akeldama waggled a wrist limply in the air. "There is a *sizable* game in motion, my *darlings*. I depend upon you all to play it with your usual consummate skill."

The young men released a spontaneous cheer, sounding like they had already got into Lord Akeldama's champagne, and trundled out.

Biffy paused in the doorway, looking less jolly and more apprehensive. "You will be all right without us, my lord? I could stay if you wished." There was something in his eyes that suggested he would very much like to do just that, and not only out of concern for his master's welfare.

Lord Akeldama stood and minced over to the doorway. He pecked the young man on the cheek, which was for show, and then stroked it gently with the back of his hand, which was not. "I must know the players." He used no excessive emphasis when he spoke: no italic intonation, no endearments—just the flat sure voice of authority. He sounded old and tired.

Biffy looked down at the toe tips of his shiny boots. "Yes, my lord."

Alexia felt a little discomfited, as though she were witnessing an intimate moment in the bedchamber. Her face heated with embarrassment, and she looked away, feigning sudden interest in the piano.

Biffy placed his top hat on his head, nodded once, and left the room.

Lord Akeldama closed the door behind him softly and returned to sit next to Miss Tarabotti.

Greatly daring, she put a hand on his arm. His fangs retracted. The human in him, buried by time, surfaced at her touch. *Soul-sucker*, the vampires called her, yet Alexia always felt it was only in these moments that she actually got close to seeing the true nature of Lord Akeldama's soul.

"They will be fine," Miss Tarabotti said, trying to sound reassuring.

"I suspect that state would tend to depend on *what* my boys find out, and whether anyone *thinks* they have found out anything of import." He sounded very paternal.

"So far, no drones have gone missing," said Alexia, thinking about the French maid taking refuge at the Westminster hive, her rove master gone.

"Is that the *official* word? Or information from the source itself?" asked Lord Akeldama, patting the top of her hand with one of his appreciatively.

Alexia knew he was asking about BUR records. Since she did not know, she explained. "Lord Maccon and I are currently *not* on speaking terms."

"Good *gracious* me, why ever not? It is so much more fun when you are." Lord Akeldama had seen Miss Tarabotti and the earl through many an argument, but neither had ever resorted to silence before. That would defeat the purpose of their association.

"My mother wants him to marry me. And he agreed!" said Miss Tarabotti, as though that explained everything.

Lord Akeldama clapped a hand over his mouth in startlement, looking once more like his old frivolous self. He stared down into Alexia's upturned face to determine the veracity of her words. Upon realization that she was in earnest, he threw his head back and let out a quite unvampirelike bark of laughter.

"Showing his hand at last, is he?" He chuckled further, extracting a large perfumed mauve handkerchief from one waistcoat pocket to dab at his streaming eyes. "Lordy, what *will* the dewan have to say about such a union? Preternatural and supernatural! That has not happened in my lifetime. And Lord Maccon *already* so powerful. The hives will be outraged. And the potentate! Ha."

"Now, hold just a moment," insisted Alexia. "I refused him."

"You did *what*?" Now Lord Akeldama really was startled. "After leading him on for so many years! That is *just* plain cruel, my *rosebud*. How *could* you? He is only a werewolf, and they can be *terribly* emotional creatures, you understand? *Quite* sensitive about these things. You could do permanent damage!"

Miss Tarabotti frowned at this unexpected diatribe. Wasn't her friend supposed to be on her side? It did not occur to her how confoundingly odd it was for a vampire to be lauding a werewolf.

The vampire in question continued his admonition. "What is *wrong* with him? A little crude, I grant you, but a *robust* young beastie? *And*, rumor has it, he is endowed most generously with copious other . . . attributes."

Miss Tarabotti let go of his hand and crossed her arms. "I would not have him coerced into matrimony, simply because we were caught in flagrante delicto."

"You were caught . . . *what*? This simply gets better and better! I *demand* all the particulars!" Lord Akeldama looked like he anticipated a deliciously vicarious experience.

Outside in the hallway came another of those hubbubs that frequented the Akeldama household. For the moment, both were so involved in Alexia's gossip, neither remembered the house was supposed to be empty of such activity.

The door to the drawing room burst open.

"Here!" said the man at the entrance. A man who was not well dressed and clearly did not belong in Lord Akeldama's splendid house.

Lord Akeldama and Alexia both stood. Alexia grabbed her brass parasol, gripping it firmly in both hands. Lord Akeldama reached for the gold pipe art piece from the mantel. He pressed hard at a hidden button in the midpoint, and a curved, hooklike blade sprang out each end of the pipe and clicked into place. One was sharpened ironwood, the other solid silver. Not art, as it turned out.

"Where are my on-premises drones?" wondered Lord Akeldama.

"Never mind that," said Alexia. "Where are my vampire guards?"

The man in the doorway had no answer for either of them. He did not even appear to hear. He did not approach but merely stood, blocking their sole avenue of escape.

"He has got a female with him," he shouted back to someone in the hallway.

"Well, bring them both," came the sharp reply. Then some kind of complex Latin phrases were issued. The terms used were outside of

Miss Tarabotti's limited education and spoken in such a strange old-fashioned accent as to make them particularly difficult to decode.

Lord Akeldama tensed. He clearly understood what was said, or at least what it implied. "*No. That is impossible!*" he whispered.

Miss Tarabotti felt that if he had not been vampire-white already, he would have blanched. His supernatural reflexes seemed stalled by some horrific realization.

The stranger in the doorway vanished to be replaced by an all-too-familiar figure: a man with a stagnant, wax-like face.

CHAPTER TEN

For the Good of the Commonwealth

Miss Tarabotti's nemesis held a brown glass bottle up high in one hand.

She was momentarily hypnotized by the repulsive fact that he seemed to have no fingernails.

Closing the door firmly behind him, the wax-faced man advanced toward Miss Tarabotti and Lord Akeldama, unstopping the bottle and spilling its contents about the room as he went. He did so with infinite care, as a conscientious flower girl scatters petals before an advancing bride.

Invisible fumes rose up from the drops of liquid, and an odd smell permeated the air. Alexia knew that odor well by now: sugary turpentine.

Miss Tarabotti held her breath, plugging her nose with one hand and raising her parasol into guard position with the other. She heard a dull thud as Lord Akeldama collapsed to the floor, his golden pipe weapon rolled away, unused. Clearly, all his plethora of information did not include the latest medical pamphlets on the application, use, and smell of chloroform. Either that, or vampires were more quickly affected by the drug than preternaturals.

Alexia felt light-headed, not certain how long she could hold her breath. She fought the sensation as much as possible and then broke toward the drawing room door and fresh air.

The wax-faced man, apparently unaffected by the fumes, shifted to prevent her egress. Miss Tarabotti remembered from the night before how fast he could move. Supernatural? Perhaps not if the chloroform had no effect. But assuredly faster than she was. Miss Tarabotti cursed herself briefly for not bringing her conversation with Lord Akeldama more rapidly around to the topic of this man. She *had* meant to ask. It was just, now . . . too late.

She swung her deleterious parasol. Brass haft and silver tip made satisfying contact with the man's skull, yet neither seemed to have any effect.

She hit him again just below the shoulder. He brushed her weapon aside with the flick of one arm.

Alexia could not help but gasp in astonishment. She had hit him *very* hard. But no sound of breaking bone came when buckshot-filled ferrule met arm.

The wax-faced man grinned his horrible not-teeth grin.

Too late, Miss Tarabotti realized that she had breathed inward in her surprise. She cursed herself roundly for a fool. But self-recriminations were to no benefit. The sweet chemical smell of the chloroform invaded her mouth, permeated her nose and throat, and then her lungs. *Blast it,* thought Alexia, borrowing one of Lord Maccon's favorite curses.

She hit the wax-faced man one last time, mostly out of orneriness. She knew it would result in nothing. Her lips began to tingle and her head spun. She swayed dangerously and reached forward with her non-parasol hand, groping for the wax man, preternatural her last resort. Her hand came to rest against his horrible smooth temple, just below the *V* on VIXI. His skin felt cold and hard. Nothing at all happened to him at the contact. No change back to normal human, no return to life, no soul-sucking. Definitely not supernatural. *Here,* Miss Tarabotti realized, *was the real monster.*

"But," Alexia whispered, "I am the soulless one . . ." And with that, she dropped her parasol and pitched forward into darkness.

Lord Maccon arrived home in the nick of time. His carriage clattered up the long cobbled drive to Woolsey Castle just as the sun set behind the high trees planted along the western edge of its extensive grounds.

Woolsey Castle stood a respectable distance from town—far enough away for the pack to run and close enough for them to take advantage of all the amusements London afforded. Woolsey Castle was also not the impenetrable fortress its name implied but instead a sort of trumped-up family manor house with multiple stories and excessively excitable buttresses. Its most important feature, so far as the werewolves were concerned, was a very large and secure dungeon, designed to accommodate multiple guests. The original owner and designer was reputed to have had some rather indecent proclivities, outside of his fondness for flying buttresses. Whatever the cause, the dungeons were extensive. Also key, in the pack's opinion, was the large number of private bedchambers above dungeon level. Woolsey Castle had to house a goodly number of residents: werewolves, clavigers, and servants.

Lord Maccon jumped out of his carriage, already feeling those heady tingles and carnivorous urges only the full moon whipped into rampancy. He could smell the blood of prey on the evening air, and the urge to hunt, and maim, and kill, was approaching with the moon.

His clavigers were waiting for him in a large tense group at the door to the castle.

"You are cutting it a bit close for comfort, my lord," remonstrated Rumpet, head butler, taking the Alpha's cloak.

Lord Maccon grunted, shedding his hat and gloves onto a long hallway stand designed expressly for that purpose.

He squinted into the assembled masses, searching for Tunstell. Tunstell was his personal valet and default captain of the household clavigers. Spotting the gangly redhead, Lord Maccon barked, "Tunstell, you dreadful young blunt, report."

Tunstell bounced up and flourished a bow. His customary smile dimpled his freckled face. "All the pack's accounted for and locked down, sir. Your cell is clean and waiting. Best we get you down there right quick, I'm thinking."

"There you go with the thinking thing. What have I told you?"

Tunstell only grinned wider.

Lord Maccon held his wrists outward. "Precautionary measures, Tunstell."

Tunstell's chipper smile diminished. "Are you certain that is necessary, sir?"

The earl felt his bones beginning to self-fracture. "Drat it, Tunstell, are you questioning orders?" The small part of his logical brain still functioning was saddened by this lapse. He had great affection for the boy, but every time he thought Tunstell might be ready for the bite, he behaved like a fathead. He seemed to have plenty of soul, but did he have enough *sense* to become supernatural? Pack protocol was not to be taken lightly. If the redhead survived the change but continued with this cavalier attitude toward regulations, would *anyone* be secure?

Rumpet came to his rescue. Rumpet was no claviger. He had no intention of bidding for metamorphosis, but he did enjoy executing his job efficiently. He had been butler to the pack for a long time and was easily double the age of any of the clavigers present in that hallway. Usually he exhibited more aptitude than all of them combined.

Actors, thought Lord Maccon in exasperation. It was one of the downsides of fleecing that particular profession. Men of the stage were not always men of sagacity.

The butler proffered a copper tray with a set of iron manacles atop it. "Mr. Tunstell, if you would be so kind," he said.

The redheaded claviger already carried his own set of handcuffs, as all clavigers did. He sighed resignedly, plucking them off the tray and snapping them firmly around his master's wrists.

Lord Maccon sighed in relief. "Quickly," he insisted, already slurring his words as the change re-formed his jawbone away from any capacity for human speech. The pain was intensifying as well, the horrible bone-wrenching agony to which, in all his long life, Lord Maccon had never yet become accustomed.

The proto-pack of clavigers surrounded him and hustled him down the winding stone staircase and into the castle dungeon. Some, the earl noticed in relief, were sensibly armored and armed. All wore sharp silver cravat pins. A few carried silver knives sheathed at their waists. These stayed to the outskirts of the crowd, carefully distanced from him, until such a time when he might make it necessary for them to use those knives.

The Woolsey Castle dungeon was full of snarling, slathering occupants. The youngest pups of Lord Maccon's pack could not resist change for several nights leading up to the full moon, let alone the moon itself. These had been in residence for days. The rest went with the sun as soon as it set on the actual night. Only Lord Maccon was strong enough to still be outside of confinement so late in the evening.

Professor Lyall was sitting suavely on a small three-legged footstool in one corner of his cell, wearing only his ridiculous glassicals and reading the evening paper. He was struggling to slow the change. Most of the pack simply let themselves be taken, but Lyall always resisted as long as he could, testing his will against the inevitability of the moon. Through the heavy iron bars of his Beta's cell, Lord Maccon could see that Lyall's spine was curled forward inhumanly far, and he boasted considerably more hair than was acceptable for any more social occasion than reading the evening paper in the privacy of one's own . . . prison.

The professor gave his Alpha a long look from yellow eyes over the tops of his spectacles.

Lord Maccon, holding his manacled hands stiffly in front of him, ignored his Beta in a very pronounced manner. He suspected Lyall would have said something embarrassing about Alexia if his Beta's jaw were not already changed well beyond human speech.

The earl continued down the passageway. His pack settled down as he passed. As each wolf caught sight and scent of the Alpha, he instinctively quieted. Several flattened down their forelegs in a kind of bow, and one or two rolled over, presenting their stomachs. Even in the thrall of full moon, they acknowledged his dominance. None wished to even hint at a challenge. He would brook no disobedience, on this of all nights, and they knew it.

The earl stepped inside his own waiting cell. It was the largest but also the most secure, empty except for chains and bolts. Nothing was safe when he changed. No footstool or periodical was in residence, just stone and iron and emptiness. He sighed heavily.

His clavigers slammed and triple bolted the iron door behind him. They stationed themselves outside it but across the passageway, so as to be entirely out of reach. In this, at least, they followed his orders impeccably.

The moon rose above the horizon. Several youngsters of the pack began to howl.

Lord Maccon felt his bones completely breaking and reforming, his skin stretching and shrinking, his tendons realigning, his hair shifting downward and becoming fur. His sense of smell sharpened. He caught a faint whiff of some familiar scent riding an air current down from the castle above.

Those few older members of the pack still partly human completed their final changes with him. The air was rent with growls and whines as the dregs of daylight disappeared. Bodies always resisted the cursed change, making the pain ever more excruciating. With flesh held together only by the threads of what remained of their souls, all sensibility converted to frenzy. The noise they made was the rampaging death-lust cry of the damned.

Any who heard those particular howls felt nothing but fear: vampire, ghost, human, or animal, it mattered not. Nor would it, in the end, for any werewolf freed of his fetters would kill indiscriminately. On full-moon night, the blood moon, it was not a matter of choice or necessity. It simply was.

However, when Lord Maccon raised his muzzle up to howl, his was not a mindless cry of wrath. The low tones of the Alpha's voice were immeasurably mournful. For he had finally recognized the smell wafting down into the dungeon. Too late to say anything in human tongue. Too late to warn his clavigers.

Conall Maccon, Earl of Woolsey, crashed up against the bars of his cell, the last vestiges of his human side crying out: not to kill, not to be free, but to protect.

Too late.

For that little whiff bore the scent of sweet turpentine, and it was getting stronger.

*   *   *

The sign above the door to the Hypocras Club read PROTEGO RES PU-
BLICA, engraved into white Italian marble. Miss Alexia Tarabotti, gagged,
trussed, bound, and carried by two men—one holding her shoulders, the
other her feet—read the words upside down. She had a screaming headache, and it took her a moment to translate the phrase through the nauseating aftereffects of chloroform exposure.

Finally she deduced its meaning: *to protect the commonwealth.*

Huh, she thought. *I do not buy it. I definitely do not feel protected.*

There also appeared to be the emblem of some kind bracketing either side of the words. A symbol or some sort of excitable invertebrate?
Was it a brass octopus?

Miss Tarabotti was strangely unsurprised to be brought to the
Hypocras Club. She remembered Felicity reading out the *Post*'s proclamation detailing the "inception of an innovative social establishment
catering to gentlemen of a scientific inclination." Of course, she realized,
now that it made perfect sense. After all, it was at the duchess's ball, right
next door to the new club, that she had killed that first mysterious vampire who started it all. This made for a rather tidy full circle. And, with
all that chloroform, there would have to be scientists involved.

Had Lord Maccon discovered this as well? she wondered. *Did he
suspect just the club, or was the Royal Society itself implicated?* Alexia
doubted even the earl's suspicious nature would stretch as far as that.

Her captors carried her into a small boxlike room with a concertina-
style grating for a door. She could turn her head just enough to see the
violet-clad form of Lord Akeldama being treated with equal disrespect:
slung over someone's shoulder like a side of beef and crammed into the
tiny room with her.

Well, Miss Tarabotti reasoned, *at least we are still together.*

The wax-faced man, unfortunately still with them, was not engaged
directly in Tarabotti/Akeldama transport. He closed the grated door
and then cranked some sort of pulley device inset into one wall of the
chamber. The most peculiar thing resulted. The whole of the tiny room
began to move listlessly downward, carrying everyone inside with it. It
was like falling slowly, and Alexia's stomach, combining this with the
added bonus of chloroform exposure, was not particularly thrilled by
the experience.

She choked down a convulsive gag.

"This one does not like our ascension room," snickered the man
who held her feet, jiggling her rudely.

One of the other men grunted his agreement.

Through the grating, a flabbergasted Alexia watched as the first floor of the club vanished, and the ground itself appeared, then the foundations of the building, then a new ceiling, and, finally, the furniture and floor of underground chambers. It was really quite a remarkable experience.

The tiny room jolted to a stop. Miss Tarabotti's stomach joined up with them shortly thereafter. The human transport flunkies slid back the grating, carried her and Lord Akeldama out, and laid them side by side on a plush Oriental carpet in the middle of a respectably sized receiving room. One of them took the precautionary measure of sitting on Lord Akeldama's legs, although he was still asleep. They did not seem to feel Alexia warranted the same level of consideration.

A man, sitting in a comfortable brown leather armchair with silver studs and smoking a large ivory pipe, stood up at their arrival and walked over to look down at the two prisoners.

"Excellent work, gentlemen!" He bit down on his pipe and rubbed his hands together enthusiastically. "Akeldama, according to the BUR records, is one of the oldest vampires in London. Next to one of their queens, his blood should be the most potent we have yet analyzed. We are in the middle of a transverse-sanguinity procedure at the moment, so put him into storage for now. And what is this?" He turned to look down at Alexia.

There was something familiar about the set of his face, although at that particular angle it was almost completely in shadow. That shadow was also familiar. The man from the carriage! Miss Tarabotti had almost forgotten about him in the horror of her recent encounters with the wax-faced monster.

He clearly had not forgotten about her. "Well, what do you know? This one simply keeps turning up, does she not?" He puffed thoughtfully on his pipe. "First visiting the Westminster hive, now found in the august presence of specimen Akeldama. How does she fit into the picture?"

"We do not know yet, sir. We will have to consult the records. She is no vamp: has neither the teeth nor queen-level protection. Though she did have two vampire guards tailing her."

"Ah, so, and . . . ?"

"We eliminated them, of course. Could be BUR agents; difficult to tell these days. What do you want done in the meantime?"

Puff, puff, puff. "Put her into storage as well. If we cannot find anything out about how she fits into our investigations, we will have to force it out of her. Terribly gauche thing to do to a lady, of course, but she is clearly fraternizing with the enemy, and sometimes sacrifices must be made."

Miss Tarabotti was confused by the players in this little game. These men did not seem to know who or, more precisely, *what* she was. Yet, clearly they were the ones who wanted her. They had sent the wax-faced man to her house in the middle of the night only recently. Unless there existed two wax-faced men in London, both of them after her. Alexia shuddered at the very idea. They must have gotten her home address from her BUR records. Yet, now they did not seem to know who she was. It was as though they were thinking of her as two separate persons. The one who kept interfering with their plans, and the Miss Alexia Tarabotti, preternatural, of BUR's records.

Then Alexia recalled that BUR did not keep sketches on file, for safety reasons. Her record contained only words, notes, and brief descriptive details, and most of that in code. These men had not made the connection to the fact that she *was* Alexia Tarabotti, because they did not know what Alexia Tarabotti looked like. Excepting only the wax-faced man, who would have seen her face in her bedroom window. She wondered why he had not revealed her secret.

Her question remained unanswered. The thugs lifted her up, in response to the shadowed man's order, and carried her after Lord Akeldama out of the plush reception room.

"And, now, where is my precious baby?" she heard the shadowed man ask as they departed. "Ah, there he is! And how did he behave on this outing? Good? Of course he did, my darling." Then his words degenerated into Latin.

Miss Tarabotti was carried through a long narrow corridor, painted white and lined with institutional-looking doors. It was lit with white ceramic oil lamps atop short marble pedestals dispersed between the doors. It all looked very ritualistic, like some sort of ancient place of worship. Oddly, the door handles were made to look like octopuses and so, upon closer inspection, were the lamps.

Miss Tarabotti was maneuvered down a long flight of stairs and into another corridor with more doors and lamps, exactly the same as the first.

"Where shall we put them?" asked one of the men. "Space is scarce, since we have *vamped* up operations, so to speak."

The other three snickered at the terrible pun.

"Just put them in the cell at the end. It does not matter much if they are left together; the doctors will be taking Akeldama off soon enough for processing. The gray coats have been waiting to get their hands on him a good long while now."

One of the others licked his fatty lips. "We ought to be getting quite large bonuses for this little collection venture."

Murmurs of agreement met that statement.

They reached the last door in the corridor and slid aside the body section of its brass octopus handle, revealing a large keyhole. Opening the door, they unceremoniously deposited Miss Tarabotti and the supine form of Lord Akeldama inside the room. Alexia landed hard on her side and attempted not to cry out in pain. They slammed the door shut, and Alexia heard them chatting as they walked away.

"Bodes well for a success in the experiments, eh?"

"Hardly."

"What do we care so long as the pay is good?"

"Too true."

"You know what I think? I think . . ."

And then their voices became faint and faded to silence.

Miss Tarabotti lay wide-eyed, staring about at the chamber in which she now found herself. Her pupils took a while to adjust to the blackness, for there were no oil lamps here and no other source of illumination. The cell did not have bars, just a seamless door with no inside handle, and felt more like a closet than a prison. Nevertheless, she knew instinctively that it *was* a prison. It had no windows, no furniture, no rug, and no other decoration of any kind—just herself and Lord Akeldama.

Someone cleared his throat.

With difficulty, her limbs being tightly bound and her physical dexterity further impeded by her dratted corset and bustle, Miss Tarabotti wiggled from lying on her back to lying on her side, facing Lord Akeldama.

The vampire's eyes were open, and he was staring at her intently. It was as though he were trying to speak to her with simply the power of a glare.

Alexia did not speak glare-ish.

Lord Akeldama began undulating toward her. He managed to writhe his way across the floor, like some sort of purple snake, the velvet of his beautiful coat slippery enough to aid his progress. Eventually he reached her. Then he flipped about and twiddled his bound hands until Miss Tarabotti understood what he was after.

Alexia flipped back over, inched down, and pressed the back of her head to his hand. The vampire was able to undo the gag tied over her mouth with his fingertips. Her wrists and legs, unfortunately, were manacled with steel bonds, as were his. Such cuffs were beyond even a vampire's ability to break.

With great difficulty, they managed to reverse positions so that Miss Tarabotti could untie Lord Akeldama's gag. Then they were at least able to talk.

"Well," said Lord Akeldama, "this is a *pretty* kettle of fish. I think those miscreants have just *ruined* one of my best evening jackets. How *very* vexing. It is a *particular* favorite of mine. I am sorry to have dragged *you* into this, my dear, almost as much as having dragged the evening jacket into it."

"Oh, don't be so nonsensical. My head is still spinning from that blasted chloroform, and there is no need for you to be tiresome on top of it," remonstrated Miss Tarabotti. "This situation could not possibly be misconstrued as your fault."

"But they were after me." In the dark, Lord Akeldama actually looked guilty. But that could have been a trick of the shadows.

"They would have been after me as well, if they only knew my name," insisted Miss Tarabotti, "so let us hear nothing more about it."

The vampire nodded. "Well," he said, "my *buttercup,* I suggest we *keep* that name of yours quiet as long as possible."

Alexia grinned. "You should not find that a particularly difficult endeavor. You never do use my real name anyway."

Lord Akeldama chuckled. "Too true."

Miss Tarabotti frowned. "We may not need to bother with subterfuge. The wax-faced man knows. He saw me in the carriage outside the Westminster hive, *and* he saw me at my window one night when they came to abduct a known preternatural. He will put two and two together and realize I am the same person."

"Cannot be done, *dewdrop,*" said Lord Akeldama confidently.

Alexia shifted, trying to relieve the pain in her manacled wrists. "How could you possibly know that?" she asked, wondering at his confident tone.

"The wax-faced man, as you call it, cannot tell anyone *anything.* He has no voice, little tulip, *none* at all," replied Lord Akeldama.

Alexia narrowed her eyes at him. "You know what he is? Do tell! He is not supernatural; I can tell you that much."

"*It,* not *him,* my lightning bug. And, yes, I know what *it* is." Lord Akeldama wore a coy expression, one that usually accompanied his fiddling with his cravat pin. As his arms were cuffed behind his back, and his pin had been judiciously removed, he could do nothing to add to the expression but purse his lips.

"Well?" Miss Tarabotti was itching with curiosity.

"*Homunculus simulacrum,*" said Lord Akeldama.

Miss Tarabotti looked back at him blankly.

He sighed. "A *lusus naturae?*"

Alexia decided he was playing with her and gave him a nasty look.

He explained further. "A synthetic creature formed by science, an alchemical artificial man . . ."

Miss Tarabotti wracked her brain and finally came up with a word from some long-ago religious text in her father's library. "An automaton?"

"Exactly! They have existed before."

Miss Tarabotti's generous mouth fell open. She had thought them mere creatures of legend, like unicorns: freaks of a purely mythical nature. The scientific side of her intellect was intrigued. "But, what is it made of? How does it work? It seems so very much alive!"

Lord Akeldama took exception to her word choice once again. "It is moving, animated, and active, yes. But, my dear bluebell, *alive* it most certainly is *not*."

"Yes, but how?"

"Who knows what *dastardly* science went into its creation—a metal skeleton perhaps, a small aetheromagnetic or steam engine of some kind. Perhaps it has clockwork parts. I am no engineer to know the truth of it."

"But why should anyone wish to build such a creature?"

"*You* are asking *me* to explain the actions of a scientist? I hardly know how to put it, petunia petal. Your friend there would appear to be the perfect servant: unflagging and loyal to the last. Of course, one would suppose all orders must be *very* precise." He would have continued, but Miss Tarabotti interrupted him.

"Yes, yes, but what about killing them?" Alexia went straight for the heart of the matter. Really, she quite adored Lord Akeldama, but he did tend to blather on.

Lord Akeldama looked at her reprovingly. "Now, do not be *too* hasty, my darling. All in good time."

"That is easy for you to say," grumbled Miss Tarabotti. "You are a vampire; all you have is time."

"Apparently not. I need hardly remind you, sweetheart, that those men are coming back for *me*. Shortly. Or so they implied."

"You were awake the entire time." Miss Tarabotti was somehow unsurprised.

"I awoke in the carriage on the way here. I feigned sleep, as there seemed nothing advantageous in alerting them to my consciousness. Pretending afforded me an opportunity to overhear interesting information. Unfortunately, I heard *nothing* of any consequence. Those"—he paused as though searching for the right way to describe the men who had abducted them—"*degenerates* are mere minions. They know only what they have been told to do, not why they were told to do it. Just as bad as the automaton. They were not interested in discussing this business, *whatever* it is, among themselves. But, marigold—"

Miss Tarabotti interrupted him again. "Please, Lord Akeldama, I do not mean to be rude, but the *homunculus simulacrum?*"

"Quite right, my dear. If I am to be taken off presently, you should have as much information as I can relay. In my limited experience, automatons cannot be killed. Because how does one *kill* something that is not *alive?* The *homunculus simulacrum* can be disanimated, though."

Miss Tarabotti, who had developed rather unladylike homicidal tendencies toward the repulsive wax-faced thing, asked eagerly, "How?"

"Well," said Lord Akeldama, "activation and control is usually in the form of a word or phrase. If one can find a way to undo that phrase, one can, in effect, turn the *homunculus simulacrum* off, like a mechanical doll."

"A word like VIXI?" suggested Alexia.

"Very like. You have seen it?"

"Written across its forehead, in some kind of black powder," Miss Tarabotti confirmed.

"Magnetized iron dust, I would hazard a guess, aligned to the domain of the automaton's internal engine, possibly through an aetheric connection. You must find a way to undo it."

"Undo what?" she asked.

"The VIXI."

"Ah." Miss Tarabotti pretended to understand. "That simple, is it?"

In the darkness of their lonely cell, Lord Akeldama grinned at her. "Now you are playing *me* for a lark, my sweet. I am sorry I do not know any more. I have never had to deal with a *homunculus simulacrum* personally. Alchemic sciences have never been my forté."

Alexia wondered what *was* his forté but asked, "What else do you think they are doing at this club? Aside from building an automaton."

The vampire shrugged as much as his handcuffs would allow. "Whatever they do must, perforce, involve experimentation on vampires, possibly a *forcing* of metamorphosis. I am beginning to suspect that rove you killed—when was it, a week or so ago?—was not *actually* made supernatural at all but was manufactured as a counterfeit of some kind."

"They have been abducting loner werewolves too. Professor Lyall found out about it," Alexia told him.

"Really? *I* did not know that." Lord Akeldama sounded more disappointed in his own abilities than surprised at the news. "Stands to reason, I suppose; might as well work with both sides of the supernatural living. I assure you, even *these* scientists cannot figure out a way to cut open or replicate a ghost. The real question is, *what* are they doing with all of us in the end?"

Miss Tarabotti shuddered, remembering that Countess Nadasdy had said the new vampires rarely lived beyond a few days. "It cannot be pleasant, whatever it is."

"No," Lord Akeldama agreed quietly. "No, it cannot." He was silent for a long moment, and then he said soberly, "My dear child, may I ask you something, in all seriousness?"

Alexia raised her eyebrows. "I do not know. Can you? I did not think you actually possessed the capacity for seriousness, my lord."

"Ah, yes, it is an assumption I have taken great care to cultivate." The vampire cleared his throat. "But, let me give it my best attempt this once. It seems unlikely that I will survive this little misadventure of ours. But if I do, I should like to ask a favor of you."

Miss Tarabotti did not know what to say at that. She was struck by how bleak her life suddenly looked without Lord Akeldama to color it. She was also amazed by his calm acceptance of his impending demise. She supposed that after so many centuries, death was no longer a fearsome thing.

He continued. "It has been a very, very long time since I have experienced the sun. Do you think you might wake me early one evening, with contact, so that I could see it set?"

Miss Tarabotti was touched by such a request. It would be a very dangerous endeavor for him, for he would have to trust her implicitly not to let go. If they broke contact for even a moment, he would immolate instantly.

"Are you certain?"

He breathed out acknowledgment as though it were a benediction. "Absolutely positive."

Just then, the door to the cell banged open. One of the flunkies came in and unceremoniously lifted Lord Akeldama over one bulky shoulder.

"Promise?" said the vampire, hanging limply upside down.

Miss Tarabotti said, "I promise," hoping she would have the chance to live up to her vow.

With that, Lord Akeldama was carried from the room. The door was closed and bolted behind him. Miss Tarabotti, with nothing but her own thoughts for company, was left alone in the dark. She was particularly annoyed with herself; she had meant to ask about the brass octopuses appearing everywhere.

CHAPTER ELEVEN

Among the Machines

M iss Tarabotti could think of nothing to do but wiggle her hands and feet to keep up blood circulation within the tight confines of the manacles. She lay there for what seemed like an age, simply wiggling. She was beginning to infer she had been forgotten, for no one came to check up on her, nor, indeed, showed any interest at all in her physical condition. She was quite uncomfortable, for corsets, bustles, and all other accoutrements of a lady's appropriate dress were not conducive to lying, bound, on a hard floor. She shifted, sighed, and stared up at the ceiling, trying to think about anything but Lord Maccon, her current predicament, or Lord Akeldama's safety. Which meant she could do nothing but reflect on the complex plight of her mama's most recent embroidery project. This, in itself, was a worse torture than any her captors could devise.

Eventually, she was saved from her own masochistic meditations by the sound of two voices in the corridor outside her cell. Both seemed vaguely familiar. The conversation, when they were in close enough proximity for Alexia to overhear the particulars, bore a distinct semblance to a guided museum tour.

"Of course, you must acknowledge that in order to eliminate the supernatural threat, we must first understand it. Professor Sneezewort's most worthwhile research has shown . . . Ah, in *this* cell, we have another rove vampire: splendid example of *Homo sanguis,* although rather young for exsanguination. Unfortunately, his origin and original hive association are unknown. This is the sad result of having to rely so heavily on rove specimens. But, you understand, here in England, members of a hive tend to be too much in the public eye and too well guarded. We are having a very difficult time convincing this one to speak. He was transported over from France, you see, and has not been quite right in the head since. There appear to be some serious physical and mental repercussions when one removes a vampire from his immediate localized area: tremulations, disorientation, dementia, and the like. We have not determined the exact mathematical nature of the distance, whether bodies of water are key factors, and so forth, but it promises to be a fascinating branch of research. One of our younger, more enthusiastic, investigators is producing some interesting work utilizing this particular specimen as his main study source. He has been trying to convince us to mount a collecting trip across the Channel into the farther reaches of Eastern Europe. I believe he wants Russian specimens, but we are concerned with remaining inconspicuous at the moment. I am certain you understand. And, of course, there is the cost to consider."

A second male voice answered in a flattish accent, "This is quite fascinating. I had heard of the territorial aspect of vampire psychology. I did not know of the physiological repercussions. I would be quite interested to read the research once it is published. What little gem do you hold in the last cell?"

"Ah, well, it did house Akeldama, one of the oldest vampires in London. His capture this evening was quite the coup. But he is already on the exsanguination table, so we have our mystery guest in residence for the moment."

"A mystery?" The second voice sounded intrigued.

Miss Tarabotti was still unable to determine why this voice seemed so very familiar.

"Indeed," answered the first, "a spinsterly young lady of moderate breeding who has persisted in turning up during the course of our investigations. After one too many appearances, we brought her in."

The second voice said, shocked, "You have imprisoned a *lady*?"

"Unfortunately, she has made it increasingly necessary. It is the end result of her own meddling. Quite a puzzle she is too." The first man was sounding equal parts annoyed and enthralled. He continued. "Would you be interested in meeting her? You might be able to provide some insight. You are, after all, approaching the supernatural problem from an entirely unique perspective, and we would value your input."

The second man sounded genuinely pleased. "I would be delighted to offer my assistance. How kind of you to ask."

Miss Tarabotti frowned in ever increasing frustration at her terribly inconvenient inability to place the man's voice. There was something about his accent. What was it? Fortunately (or more accurately unfortunately), she did not have to live in confusion much longer.

The door to her closet of a prison swung open.

Miss Tarabotti blinked and inadvertently coiled away from the seemingly blinding light of the hallway.

Someone gasped.

"Why, Miss Tarabotti!"

Miss Tarabotti, eyes watering, squinted at the two backlit figures. Eventually, her eyes adjusted to the unsteady light of the oil lamps. She squirmed about, trying to assume a more elegant position on the floor. She was only mildly successful, remaining ungracefully prone and manacled. She did manage a better angle, which enabled her to see her visitors with greater clarity.

One proved to be the shadowed man, and for the first time in their unsavory acquaintance, his face was not actually in complete shadow. It was he who was playing the part of tour guide. Seeing his countenance at last was an unsatisfactory experience. Alexia had hoped for something particularly horrific and evil. But it was nothing singular, comprised of large graying muttonchops, excessive jowls, and watery blue eyes. She had expected at least some kind of dramatic scar. But there stood her great and sinister nemesis, and he was disappointingly ordinary.

The other man was plumpish, bespectacled, and in possession of a hairline midretreat. His was a countenance Alexia was quite familiar with.

"Good evening, Mr. MacDougall," she said. Even when one was horizontally prone, there was no call for rudeness. "How nice to see you again."

The young scientist, with a cry of profound surprise, came instantly over to kneel solicitously next to her. He helped her gently into a sitting position, apologizing profusely for having to manhandle her person.

Miss Tarabotti did not mind in the least; for, once upright, she felt considerably more dignified. She was also pleased to know Mr. MacDougall had no intentional hand in her abduction. That would have grieved her sorely, for she liked the young man and did not wish to think ill of him. She had no doubt his surprise and concern were genuine. She might, she thought, even be able to turn his presence to her advantage.

Miss Tarabotti then realized the state of her hair and was mortified. Her captors had, of course, removed her hair ribbon and her two deadly hair pins—the one of wood and the other of silver. Without them, heavy dark curls fell down her back in wild abandon. Pathetically, she raised a shoulder and bent to the side, trying to push it away from her face, not realizing, of course, how fetchingly exotic she looked with loose hair in combination with her strong features, wide mouth, and tan skin.

Very Italian, thought Mr. MacDougall when he could spare a moment in his concern for her well-being. He was genuinely worried. He also felt guilty, for if Miss Tarabotti was caught up in this mess, it must be of his doing. Had he not encouraged her interest in the supernatural during their drive together? And her, a lady of good breeding! What could he have been thinking to talk so unguardedly of scientific pursuits? A woman of Miss Tarabotti's caliber would not be content to let matters lie, if she was really intrigued. It *must* be his fault that she had been imprisoned.

"You know the young lady?" asked the shadowed man, pulling out his pipe and a small velvet tobacco pouch. There was an octopus embroidered on the outside of the pouch, golden thread on chocolate brown velvet.

Mr. MacDougall looked up from where he knelt. "I certainly do. This is Miss Alexia Tarabotti," he said angrily before Miss Tarabotti could stop him.

Oh dear, Alexia thought philosophically, *the cat is well and truly out of the bag now.*

Mr. MacDougall continued speaking, a flush staining his pasty, pudgy cheeks and a small sheen of sweat lining his brow. "To treat a young lady of such standing as shabbily as this!" he sputtered. "It is a grave blow, not only to the honor of the club, but also to that of the scientific profession as a whole. We should remove her restraints this moment! Shame on you."

How did that saying go? Alexia wondered. Ah, yes, "Brash as an American." Well, they had won their independence somehow, and it was not with politeness.

The man with the muttonchops filled his pipe bowl and nipped back into the hallway briefly to light it with one of the oil lamps. "Why does that name sound familiar?" He turned back and puffed for a moment, blowing fragrant vanilla-scented smoke into the cell. "Of course—the BUR records! Are you telling me this is *the* Alexia Tarabotti?" He took the pipe out of his mouth and pointed the long ivory stem at Alexia for emphasis.

"The only one I've met in your country so far," answered Mr. Mac-Dougall, sounding unbelievably rude—even for an American.

"Of course." The shadowed man finally put two and two together. "This explains everything: her involvement with BUR, her visiting the hive, and her association with Lord Akeldama!" He looked to Miss

Tarabotti severely. "You have led us a merry dance, young lady." Then he looked back at Mr. MacDougall. "Do you know *what* she is?"

"Aside from manacled? Which she should not be. Mr. Siemons, give me the keys this minute!"

Miss Tarabotti was suitably impressed by Mr. MacDougall's insistence. She had not thought he would be such a champion or possess such backbone.

"Ah, yes, of course," Mr. Siemons said. At last the shadow man had a name. He leaned backward out the doorway and yelled up the hallway. Then he came inside the cell and bent down toward Miss Tarabotti. He grabbed her face quite roughly and turned her toward the light in the hall. He continued to puff on his pipe, blowing smoke into her eyes.

Alexia coughed pointedly.

Mr. MacDougall was further shocked. "Really, Mr. Siemons, such crass treatment!"

"Amazing," said Siemons. "She seems perfectly normal. One would never be able to tell simply by looking, would one?"

Mr. MacDougall finally got over his gentlemanly instincts enough to allow the scientific part of his mental faculties to participate in the conversation. In a voice colored with both hesitation and dread, he asked, "Why shouldn't she be?"

Mr. Siemons stopped blowing smoke in Miss Tarabotti's face and blew it instead at the American scientist. "This young lady is a *preternatural:* a *Homo exanimus.* We have been looking for her since we first deduced her existence here in London. Which, I might add, was only shortly after finding out that preternaturals existed at all. Of course, if you follow the counterbalance theorem, her kind seems perfectly logical. I am surprised we never before thought to look. And, of course, we knew the supernatural set had ancient legends pertaining to certain dangerous creatures that were born to hunt *them.* The werewolves have their curse-breakers, the vampires their soul-suckers, and the ghosts their exorcists. But we did not know they were all the same organism and that that organism was a scientific fact, not a myth. They are startlingly uncommon, as it turns out. Miss Tarabotti here is a rare beast, indeed."

Mr. MacDougall looked shocked. "A *what?*"

Mr. Siemons did not share his shock; in fact, he looked particularly delighted all of a sudden—a lightning change of mood that did not strike Miss Tarabotti as entirely sane.

"A preternatural!" He grinned, waving his pipe about haphazardly. "Fantastic! There are so many things we need to know about her."

Alexia said, "*You* stole the paperwork from BUR."

Mr. Siemons shook his head. "No, my dear, we liberated and then secured important documents in order to prevent dangerous societal elements from fraudulently identifying themselves as normal. Our initiative in this matter will enhance our ability to assess threat and confirm identity of those enabling the supernatural conspiracy."

"She is one of them?" Mr. MacDougall said, still stuck on Miss Tarabotti's preternatural state. He jerked away from her and thus stopped supporting Alexia in her seated position. Luckily, she managed not to fall backward.

He seemed almost repelled by her. Alexia began to wonder about the story of his brother becoming a vampire. *How much of that had been truth?*

Mr. Siemons slapped Mr. MacDougall's back delightedly. "No, no, no, my good man. Quite the opposite! She is the antidote to the supernatural. If you can think of an entire living organism as an antidote. Now that we have her, the opportunities for study are endless! Simply think of what we could accomplish. Such possibilities." He was positively gregarious. His watery blue eyes shone with an excess of scientific enthusiasm.

Alexia shuddered at the idea of what such a study might entail.

Mr. MacDougall looked thoughtful and then stood and pulled his companion out into the hallway. They engaged in a whispered conversation.

During their brief absence, Miss Tarabotti tried frantically to slip free of her handcuffs. She had a sinking suspicion that she would not like anything they wanted to do to her in this ghastly place. But she could not even manage to stand upright.

She heard Mr. Siemons say, "It is an excellent suggestion and could not hurt. If she is as intelligent as you purport, she may yet perceive the merits of our work. It would certainly be novel to engage with a willing participant."

The most miraculous change in Miss Tarabotti's circumstances then proceeded to occur. She found herself gently lifted by a pair of subdued lackeys. She was carried upstairs into the lavish precincts of the foyer, with its plush Oriental carpets and luxuriant furnishings. Her restraints were unlocked and removed, and she was given a small private dressing room in which to wash and compose herself. Her ivory taffeta dress was a little worse for the experience; one of the puffed sleeves and some of the gold lace had ripped, and it was stained beyond redemption in several places. Alexia was annoyed. True, it was out of fashion, but she had liked the gown. She sighed and did her best to smooth out the wrinkles while looking with interest around the dressing room.

There was no means of escape, but there was a bit of ribbon for her to tie back her unruly hair and a looking glass in which she could check up on the generally disreputable state of her appearance. The mirror was ornate, framed but carved gilded wood, more suited to Lord Akeldama's house than a modern setting. The frame seemed to be made up of a long chain of octopuses, arms linked. Alexia was beginning to find the whole octopus prevalence slightly sinister.

She broke the looking glass as quietly as possible, tapping with the back of the ivory hairbrush she had been given. She wrapped a sharp shard of glass carefully in a handkerchief and tucked it down the front of her bodice, between dress and corset, for safekeeping.

Feeling slightly more the thing, she exited the changing room and was escorted downstairs back into the receiving area, with its brown leather armchair. There she found a hot cup of tea and an interesting proposition awaiting her.

Mr. MacDougall made introductions.

"Miss Tarabotti, this is Mr. Siemons. Mr. Siemons, Miss Alexia Tarabotti."

"Enchanted," said the pipe-smoking gentleman, bending over Alexia's hand as though he had not just abducted her, imprisoned her for several hours, and probably done unspeakable things to one of her dearest friends.

Miss Tarabotti decided to play whatever hand was dealt her, at least until she learned the rules of the game. It was typical of her character that she simply assumed she would, eventually, gain control over the situation. Only one man had ever consistently bested her in life's ongoing vocal scuffle, and Lord Maccon used underhanded nonverbal tactics. Thinking of Lord Maccon made Alexia cast a covert glance about the room, wondering if they had brought her parasol when they nabbed her.

"Let me come straight to the point, Alexia," said her jailer. Alexia had no doubt that, while her immediate bonds had been removed, she was still very far from free.

He sat in the leather chair and gestured for her to sit opposite him on a red chaise lounge.

She did so. "Please do, Mr. Siemons. Directness is a very admirable quality in kidnappers"—she paused in thought—"and scientists." She was nothing if not fair, and she had read her share of scientific articles that prevaricated and waffled most dreadfully. A strong thesis was very important.

Mr. Siemons proceeded on.

Miss Tarabotti sipped her tea and noted that the silver studs on the leather armchair were also very small octopuses. Really, why the obsession with invertebrates?

Mr. MacDougall hurried about worriedly while Mr. Siemons spoke, fetching this and that to make Alexia more comfortable. Would she like a cushion? Some sugar? Another spot of tea? Was she warm enough? Had the restraints harmed her wrists in any way?

Finally Mr. Siemons rounded on the young man and glared him into silent stillness.

"We should like very much to study you," he explained to Alexia. "And we should like to do so with your cooperation. It would be much easier and more civilized for all concerned if you were a willing participant in the proceedings." He sat back, a strange look of eagerness on his jowly face.

Alexia was confused. "You must understand," she said at length, "that I have several questions. Although, as you intend my participation whether willing or not, you can naturally refrain from answering them."

The man laughed. "I am a scientist, Miss Tarabotti. I appreciate a curious mind."

Miss Tarabotti raised her eyebrows. "Why do you wish to study me? What information do you hope to acquire? And what would these studies entail, exactly?"

He smiled. "Good questions, all of them, but none very enlightened in essence. Obviously, we wish to study you because you are a preternatural. And while both you and BUR might know much of what that means, we know very little and are quite eager to comprehend the whole. We hope, most importantly, to understand the sum components of your ability to cancel out the supernatural. To distill that ability and harness it, what a weapon you might make!" He rubbed his hands together gleefully. "Also, it would be a true joy simply to watch you in action."

"And the studies themselves?" Miss Tarabotti was beginning to feel most apprehensive, though she prided herself on the fact that it was not visible in her general demeanor.

"I understand you have heard some of Mr. MacDougall's theories?"

Miss Tarabotti thought back to that morning drive. It seemed to have occurred an age ago, to a different person, in a different time. However, she did remember much of the conversation, for it had been most diverting. "I recall some," she replied cautiously, "to the best of my recollection and limited feminine capacities, of course." Alexia hated to do it, but it was always advantageous to undermine one's enemy's confidence in one's intelligence.

Mr. MacDougall gave her a shocked glance.

As subtly as possible, Alexia winked at him.

He looked as though he might faint but sat back in his chair, clearly of a mind to let her deal with the situation in whatever way she saw fit.

Miss Tarabotti had the transitory idea that he might be suitable husband material after all. And then realized that a lifelong alliance with a man of such weak character would certainly turn her into a veritable tyrant.

She said, pretending timidity and lack of understanding, "He believes that the supernatural may either be blood-borne, a type of disease, or present as a special organ that those who can become supernatural possess and the rest of us do not."

Siemons smiled in a superior manner at this explanation. Alexia was seized with a quite unladylike desire to slap the smug expression right off his fat face. With those jowls, her hand would probably make a very satisfying smack. She took a hurried gulp of tea instead.

"That is near enough to the truth," he said. "We at the Hypocras Club find his theories intriguing but instead favor the idea that metamorphosis occurs as a result of energy transmission: a type of electricity. Although, a small minority holds out for aetheromagnetic fields. Have you heard of electricity, Miss Tarabotti?"

Of course I have, you nincompoop, was what Alexia wanted to say. Instead she said, "I believe I have read something on the subject. Why do you think this might be the answer?"

"Because supernatural beings react to light: werewolves to the moon and vampires to the sun. Light, we are beginning to theorize, is but another form of electricity; thus, we believe the two may be connected."

Mr. MacDougall leaned forward and joined in the conversation, as it had become one safely within his purview. "Some have suggested that the two theories are not mutually exclusive. After my lecture this evening, there was discussion of possible electricity within blood transfer, or organs whose purpose is to process this light-borne energy. In other words, that the two hypotheses could be combined." ·

Miss Tarabotti was interested despite herself. "And it is the capacity to process this electrical energy that you believe correlates to the soul?"

The two scientists nodded.

"How do I fit into this?"

The two men looked at each other.

Finally, Mr. Siemons said, "That is what we hope to find out. Do you somehow dampen this energy? We know that certain materials do not conduct electricity. Are preternaturals the living equivalent of a grounding agent?"

Great, Alexia thought, *I have gone from soul-sucker to electrical ground. The epithets just get sweeter and sweeter.* "And how, exactly, do you plan to figure this out?"

She did not expect them to say they wanted to cut her open. Though she had a pretty good idea that Mr. Siemons, at least, rather relished such an eventuality.

"Perhaps it would be best if we showed you some of our experimental equipment so you can get an idea of how we conduct research," suggested Mr. Siemons.

Mr. MacDougall blanched at that. "Are you certain that is such a good plan, sir? She is a lady of gentle breeding, after all. It might be a bit much."

Mr. Siemons gave Miss Tarabotti an assessing look. "Oh, I think she is of a strong enough constitution. Besides, it might . . . encourage . . . her willing participation."

Mr. MacDougall looked whiter at that. "Oh dear," he muttered under his breath, his forehead creased in a frown. He shoved his spectacles up his nose nervously.

"Come, come, my dear sir," said Mr. Siemons jovially. "Nothing is so bad as all that! We have a preternatural to study. Science will rejoice— our mission's conclusion is finally in sight."

Miss Tarabotti looked at him with narrowed eyes. "And what *exactly* is your mission, Mr. Siemons?"

"Why, to protect the commonwealth, of course," he replied.

Miss Tarabotti asked the obvious question. "From whom?"

"From the supernatural threat, what else? We Englishmen have allowed vampires and werewolves to roam openly among us since King Henry's mandate without a clear understanding of what they really *are.* They are predators. For thousands of years, they fed upon us and attacked us. What they have given us in military knowledge has allowed us to build an empire, true, but at what cost?" He became impassioned, his tone the high-voiced raving of a fanatic. "They permeate our government and our defenses, but they are not motivated to protect the best interest of the fully human species. They are only concerned with advancing their own agenda! We believe that agenda to be world domination at the very least. Our goal is mobilization of research in order to secure the homeland from supernatural attack and covert infiltration. This is an exceedingly complex and delicate mission, requiring the focused effort from our entire association. Our main scientific objective is to provide a framework of understanding that shall eventually lead to a unified national effort toward wide-scale extermination!"

Supernatural genocide, Alexia thought, feeling her face blanch. "Good Lord, you are not papal Templars, are you?" She looked about for religious paraphernalia. Was *that* the meaning of the octopuses?

Both men laughed.

"Those fanatics," said the pipe man. "Certainly not. Although some of their tactics have proved moderately useful in our collection expeditions. And, of course, we have recently realized that Templars have in the past employed preternaturals as covert agents. We had thought those rumors mere religious embellishment, the power of faith to cancel the devil's abilities. Now we see there were scientific underpinnings. Some of their information, should we manage to get possession of it, will pave the way toward better understanding of your physiology, if nothing else. But, to answer your question, no, we of the Hypocras Club are of a purely scientific bent."

"Though advocating a political agenda," accused Miss Tarabotti, forgetting her ploy to lull them into a false sense of her stupidity in her amazement at such flagrant disregard for the tenets of scientific objectivity.

"Say instead, Miss Tarabotti, that we have nobility of purpose," said Mr. Siemons. But his smile was not unlike that of a religious fanatic. "We are preserving the freedom of those who matter."

Alexia was confused. "Then why are you creating more of them? Why the experiments?"

Mr. Siemons said, "Know thy enemy, Miss Tarabotti. To eliminate the supernatural, we must first understand the supernatural. Of course, now that we have you, further supernatural vivisections may be unnecessary. We can turn all our attention to deducing the nature and reproducibility of the preternatural instead."

The two men escorted her proudly through the seemingly endless labyrinthine white laboratories of that nightmarish club. Each contained complex machinery of some kind. Most appeared to be steam-powered. There were great pumping bellows with enormous gears and coils to facilitate up-and-down motion. There were shiny engines, smaller than hatboxes, with overly organic curves that were, in their way, more terrifying than the larger contraptions. They all, regardless of size, boasted a brass octopus, riveted somewhere about their casings. The contrast of engine and invertebrate was oddly sinister.

The steam produced by the mechanicals discolored the walls and ceilings of the laboratories, causing the white wallpaper to buckle and pimple outward in yellowed boils. Oil from the gears leaked across the floors in dark viscous rivulets. There were other stains there, too, rust-colored ones that Alexia did not care to think about.

Mr. Siemons proudly detailed the function of each machine, as though relating the accomplishments of his favorite children.

Though Miss Tarabotti heard wheezing gasps and clunks in nearby rooms, she was never shown any machine in action.

She also heard the screams.

At first the keening was so high in pitch she thought it might be sourced in one of the machines. She was not certain *when* she realized it came from a human throat, but the absolute knowledge of its origin hit her so hard she stumbled under the weight of it. No machine could make such a noise as that high, agonized moaning squeal, like an animal being butchered. Alexia leaned heavily against one wall of the hallway, her skin clammy, swallowing down the sour bile her writhing stomach produced in sympathy. She thought she had never before heard so pure a sound of pain.

The machines she had been seeing took on new and horrific meanings as she realized what they might do to a physical body.

Mr. MacDougall was concerned by her sudden pallor. "Miss Tarabotti, you are unwell?"

Alexia looked at him with wide dark eyes. "This place is all madness. Do you realize that?"

Mr. Siemons's jowls swam into her field of view. "I take it you will not cooperate willingly with our research?"

Another high keening scream rent the air. Inside that cry, Alexia could hear Lord Akeldama's voice.

Mr. Siemons cocked his head at the sound and licked his lips, as though savoring a pleasant taste.

Miss Tarabotti shuddered. There was something almost lustful in his gaze. Only then did she finally come to a realization of the truth.

"What does it matter, if *that* is to be my fate either way?" Miss Tarabotti asked.

"Well, it would be easier all around if you were a willing participant."

And why, Alexia wondered, *should I make this easier for you?* She grimaced and said, "What do you want me to do?"

Mr. Siemons smiled like he had just won some competition. "We need to observe and verify the extent of your preternatural abilities.

There is no point in us undertaking extensive experimentation if we cannot determine if your purported soul-sucking curse-canceling powers are, in fact, genuine."

Miss Tarabotti shrugged. "So, bring me a vampire. All it takes is one touch."

"Really? Remarkable. Skin to skin, or does it work through clothing?"

"Through clothing most of the time. After all, I wear gloves like any respectable person. But I have not explored the particulars."

Mr. Siemons shook his head as though to clear it. "We will explore further, later. I was thinking of a little more definitive testing. After all, it is full moon night. As it happens, we have just received a substantial delivery of new werewolf specimens in full change. I should like to see if you can counteract such a substantial change."

Mr. MacDougall looked alarmed. "That could be dangerous, if her abilities are false or overexaggerated."

Mr. Siemons grinned wider. "That would be part of the test, would it not?" He turned to Miss Tarabotti. "How long does it usually take for you to neutralize the supernatural?"

Alexia lied instantly and without hesitation. "Oh, generally not much more than an hour."

The scientist, with no prior knowledge of the rapidity of her abilities, was forced to believe her. He looked at the goons, two of whom had been shadowing them throughout the tour. "Bring her."

Mr. MacDougall protested, but to no avail.

Once more prisoner instead of guest, Miss Tarabotti was dragged unceremoniously back toward the confinement area on the other side of the club grounds.

They took her to the other hallway, the one in which she and Lord Akeldama had not been ensconced. Previously silent, it now resounded with snarling cries and howls. Periodically, some door or another would vibrate violently as though a large body had hurled itself against it.

"Ah," said Mr. Siemons, "I see they have awoken."

"Chloroform works better initially on werewolves than on vampires but does not seem to last as long," reported a young man in a gray jacket who appeared seemingly out of thin air, clutching a leather notepad. He wore a pair of those monocular cross-whatsit lens things, the glassicals, which somehow looked less ridiculous on him than they had on Professor Lyall.

"And which room is *he* in?"

The man pointed with his notebook at one of the doors. One of the few that was not vibrating but stood ominously still and quiet. "Number five."

Mr. Siemons nodded. "He should be the strongest and thus the hardest to change back. Toss her in with him. I will check back in an hour." With that, he left them.

Mr. MacDougall protested vociferously. He even struggled against the two goons, attempting to stop the inevitable. Miss Tarabotti's valuation of his moral fiber rose substantially. But it was all to no avail. The two lackeys were of the overly muscled variety. They tossed the pudgy scientist aside with barely any effort whatsoever.

"But she'll never survive. Not with one in full change! Not if she takes so long to counteract them!" Mr. MacDougall continued to protest.

Even knowing the full extent and rapidity of her skills, Alexia, too, was worried. She had never changed an angry werewolf before, let alone one fully moon-mad. She was pretty certain he could manage to get in at least one bite before her abilities would take full effect. Even then, if she managed to survive that, what kind of man would she be trapped with? Werewolves tended to be physically strong even without their supernatural traits. Such a man could do her considerable harm, preternatural or no.

Miss Tarabotti had very little time to cogitate the possible shortness of her future before she was thrust into the portentously quiet chamber. So quiet, in fact, she could hear the door being locked and bolted behind her.

CHAPTER TWELVE

Nothing but Werewolf

The werewolf charged.

Miss Tarabotti, whose eyes were not yet accustomed to the darkness of the cell, perceived the monster as nothing more than a bulky blur of darkness heading at supernatural speed in her direction. She dove awkwardly to one side, only just fast enough. Her corset stays creaked in a most alarming manner as she tried desperately to twist out of the way. She stumbled upon landing, nearly falling to her knees.

The wolf hit the closed door hard, behind where she had just stood, and slid to the floor in an ungainly heap of long legs and sweeping tail.

Alexia backed away, hands up before her chest in an instinctive, and entirely useless, defensive position. She was not ashamed to admit she was deathly frightened. The werewolf was huge, and she was becoming convinced that what preternaturals *could* do would not be fast enough to cancel out what *he* might be able to do first.

The wolf resumed an upright position, shaking himself like a wet dog. He had a long glossy pelt, silky in texture and of some changeable color difficult to determine in the shadowy room. He crouched down to charge again, powerful muscles quivering, saliva leaking out one side of his mouth in silver rivulets.

He leaped forward in another burst of speed and then twisted before he struck, yanking himself back mid jump.

He could have killed her easily that time. There was no doubt in Alexia's head that his fangs were coming straight for her jugular. Her initial dodge had been pure luck. She was nowhere near fit enough to go up against a regular wolf, let alone a supernatural one. True, she was an inveterate walker and had a decent seat for the hunt, but no one would ever make the mistake of calling Miss Tarabotti a sportswoman.

In an apparent state of confusion, the great beast circled to one side of the cell, then the other, weaving about Alexia and sniffing the air. He gave an odd, frustrated little whine and backed slowly away from her, swaying his bushy head back and forth in profound mental distress. The yellow of his eyes glowed faintly in the dark room. Alexia thought that their expression was one of worry more than hunger.

Miss Tarabotti watched in amazement as for several minutes the werewolf continued his internal struggle, pacing back and forth. Her respite did not last long, however. It soon became clear that despite whatever held him back, the urge to attack was overpowering. The wolf's mouth opened in a snarl of bloodlust, and he coiled his muscles to spring at her once more.

This time, Alexia was pretty darn certain she would not escape unscathed. She had never before seen so many sharp teeth in one place.

The werewolf attacked.

Miss Tarabotti could make out his form more clearly now, her eyes having adjusted fully to the gloom. Yet all she could really process mentally was a great shaggy mass of killing frenzy plunging toward her throat. She wanted desperately to run, but there was nowhere for her to go.

Keeping her wits about her, Alexia stepped toward the charging monster and a little to one side. In the same movement, she tilted sideways as much as her corset would allow and crashed against the beast's ribs, knocking him out of his leap. He was a big wolf, but Alexia Tarabotti was no lightweight either, and she managed to broadside him just enough to throw him off kilter. They fell to the ground together in a coil of skirts and bustle wires and fur and fangs.

Alexia twined her arms, her legs—as much as her underpinnings would allow—and anything else she could manage about the wolf's huge furry body and held on as tightly as humanly possible.

With a profound sense of relief, she felt his fur disappear and his bones re-form under her fingers. The sound of muscle, sinew, and cartilage breaking was truly gruesome, like a cow being butchered, but the feel of it was even worse. The sensation of fur disappearing at her touch, crawling away from any point of contact with her body, and the bones, liquidlike, changing their very nature under his flesh, was one that would haunt her for months. But, eventually, she held only warm human skin and solid lean muscles.

Miss Tarabotti took a long, deep, shaky breath and from the smell alone had no doubt at all whom it was she held. For the scent was all open grassy fields and night air. Involuntarily, her hands moved against his skin in relief. Then, of course, she realized something else.

"Why, Lord Maccon, you are stark naked!" Alexia said. She was appalled beyond all reason by this last in the long string of indignities she had had to suffer in the space of one torturous evening.

The Earl of Woolsey was indeed completely nude. He did not seem particularly perturbed by this fact, but Miss Tarabotti felt the sudden need to close her eyes tight and think about asparagus or something equally mundane. Coiled about him as she was, her chin wedged over one of his massive shoulders, she was being forced to look down directly at a nicely round, but embarrassing bare, moon. And not the kind that caused werewolves to change either. Although it did seem to be changing aspects of her own anatomy that she would rather not think about. It was all a very heady—or bottomy?—experience.

But, Alexia reasoned, *at least he is no longer trying to kill me.*

"Well, Miss Tarabotti," admitted the earl, "nakedness happens, I am ashamed to say, particularly to us werewolves. To compound the offense, I must ask you most cordially *not* to let go." Lord Maccon was panting, and his voice sounded funny, all low and gruff and hesitant.

With her chest pressed hard against his, Alexia could feel the rapid beat of his overtaxed heart. A strange series of questions ran through her head. *Was his exertion the result of the attack or the change? What happened if he changed into wolf form in full evening dress? Would the clothes rip? That was sure to be inconveniently expensive! How come it was socially acceptable for werewolves in the wolf state to run around completely starkers, but not anyone else?*

Instead she asked, "Are you cold?"

Lord Maccon laughed. "Practical as always, Miss Tarabotti. It is a little chilly in here, but I am well enough for the moment."

Alexia looked at his long, powerful, but bare, legs dubiously. "I suppose I could loan you my underskirt."

The earl snorted. "I hardly think that would look very dignified."

Miss Tarabotti reared back so she could look him in the face for the first time. "I meant to drape over you like a blanket, not to wear, you ridiculous man!" She was blushing heatedly, but with her dark skin, she knew it was not noticeable. "Besides, remaining exposed is hardly a dignified condition either."

"Aye, I see. Thank you for the thought, but . . ." Lord Maccon trailed off, becoming distracted by something far more interesting. "Uh, where exactly are we?"

"We are guests of the Hypocras Club. That new scientific establishment that opened recently right next door to the Snodgroves' town residence." She did not even pause to let him interject but hurried agitatedly on. Partly because she wanted to relay everything she could

before she forgot something vital and partly because their intimate proximity was making her nervous. "It is the scientists here who are behind
the supernatural disappearances," she said, "as I am certain you are now
well aware. You yourself have become one of those very vanishing acts.
They have quite the arrangement here. We are currently in underground
facilities reached only by something called an ascension chamber. And
there are rooms upon rooms of exotic steam and electric current machinery on the other side of the foyer. They have got Lord Akeldama hooked
up to something called an exsanguination machine, and I heard the most
horrible screams. I think it was him. Conall"—this was said most earnestly—"I believe that they may be torturing him to death."

Miss Tarabotti's big dark eyes welled with tears.

Lord Maccon had never before seen her cry. It did the most remarkable thing to his own emotions. He became irrationally angry
that anything might make *his* stalwart Alexia sad. He wanted to kill
someone, and this time it was not at all tied into being a werewolf. It
couldn't be, as, held tightly in her arms, he was as human as possible.

Alexia paused to take a breath, and Lord Maccon said, in an attempt to distract her from her unhappiness and himself from homicidal
thoughts, "Aye, this is all very informative, but why are *you* here?"

"Oh, they put me in with you to check the authenticity of my
abilities as a preternatural," she answered, as though this fact were perfectly obvious. "They have your BUR files on me, the ones that were
stolen, and they wanted to see if the reports were true."

Lord Maccon looked ashamed. "Sorry about that. I still do not
know how they got through my security. But what I meant was, how
did you get here, to the club?"

She tried to find the least embarrassing place to rest her hands. Finally she decided the middle of his back was safest. She was seized with
a most irrational desire to rub her fingertips up and down the indenta-
tion of his spine. She resisted and said, "Technically, I believe they were
after Lord Akeldama, something about his being very old. Apparently
this is an important factor in their experimentation. I was having dinner with him. I told you I was going to, remember? They chloroformed
his entire residence and brought me along because I was with him.
They only realized who I was when Mr. MacDougall came into my cell
and saw me. He used my name, and the other man, he is called Siemons,
remembered it from your paperwork. Oh! And you should know, they
have an automaton." She tensed at the memory of that awful waxy
thing.

Lord Maccon rubbed his big hands over her back in an absent-
minded soothing motion. Miss Tarabotti took it as an excuse to loosen

her own grasp a mite. The temptation to begin her own rubbing was almost overwhelming.

He interpreted her relaxed hold the wrong way. "No, do not let go," he said, shifting his grip to pull her, if possible, even more intimately against his naked body. Then he answered her statement. "We had surmised that it was an automaton. Though I have never before encountered one filled with blood. It must be some newfangled construction. It may even be on a clockwork frame. I tell you, science can do amazing things these days." He shook his head. His hair brushed against Alexia's cheek. There was an edge of admiration mingled with the disgust in his voice.

"You knew it was an automaton, and you did not tell me?" Miss Tarabotti was most disgruntled, partly because she had not been informed and partly because Lord Maccon's hair was so very silky. So was his skin, for that matter. Alexia wished she had gloves on, for she had given up and was now running her fingers in circles against his back.

"I hardly see how your knowing might have improved matters. I am certain you would have continued to engage in your customary reckless behavior," said Lord Maccon rudely, not at all perturbed by her caress. In fact, though they were arguing, he had taken to nuzzling her neck between phrases.

"Ah-ha, I like that," replied Alexia. "I might remind you that *you,* too, have now been captured. Was that not a consequence of *your* reckless behavior?"

Lord Maccon looked worried. "Quite the opposite, actually. It was the consequence of too predictable nonreckless behavior patterns. They knew exactly where to find me and at what time I would return home on full-moon night. They used chloroform on the whole pack. Blast them! This Hypocras Club must hold a controlling interest in a chloroform company, given the sheer amount of the chemical that they seem to have access to." He cocked his head, listening. "From the number of howls, it sounds like they brought the entire pack in. I do hope the clavigers escaped."

"The scientists do not seem interested in drones or clavigers," said Miss Tarabotti reassuringly, "only fully supernatural and preternatural types. They seem to believe they must protect the commonwealth against some mysterious threat posed by yourself and others of your set. In order to do this, they are trying to *understand* the supernatural, to which end they have been conducting all sorts of horrendous experiments."

Lord Maccon stopped nuzzling, lifted his head, and growled, "They are *Templars?*"

"Nothing so church-bound as that," Miss Tarabotti said. "Purely scientific investigators, simply warped, so far as I can tell. And obsessed with octopuses." She looked sad, knowing the answer before she asked the next question. "Do you think the Royal Society is involved?"

Lord Maccon shrugged.

Alexia could feel the movement all up and down her body, even through her layers of clothing.

"I rather believe they must be," he said. "Though I suspect we would find that difficult to prove. There must have been others as well; the quality of the machinery and supplies alone would seem to indicate some considerable monetary investment on the part of several unknown benefactors. It is not entirely a surprise to us, you realize? After all, normal humans are right to suspect a supernatural agenda. We are basically immortal; our goals are likely to be a little different from those of ordinary people, sometimes even at odds. When all is said and done, daylight folk are still food."

Alexia stopped petting him and narrowed her eyes in mock suspicion. "Am I allied with the wrong side in this little war?"

In reality, she did not have much doubt. After all, she had never heard cries of pain and torture coming from the BUR offices. Even Countess Nadasdy and her hive seemed more civilized than Mr. Siemons and his machines.

"That depends." Lord Maccon lay passive in her arms. On full-moon night in human form, he was dependent upon her ability and her whim for his sanity. It did not sit well with an Alpha. All the choices were hers, including this one. "Have you decided which you prefer?"

"They did ask for my cooperation," she informed him coyly. Miss Tarabotti was enjoying having the upper hand over Lord Maccon.

The earl looked worried. "And?"

Alexia had never even contemplated Mr. Siemons's offer as a real possibility. Yet Lord Maccon was looking at her as though she had actually had a choice. How could she explain to the earl that, quite apart from anything else—including their constant arguments—*he* had her complete loyalty? She could not—not without having to admit, to herself or him, why that might be the case.

"Let us simply say," she said at last, "that I prefer your methods."

Lord Maccon went perfectly still. A gleam entered his beautiful tawny eyes. "Is that so? Which ones?"

Miss Tarabotti pinched him for such blatant innuendo. It did not matter where she pinched, as the earl was a bare canvas of pinchability.

"Ow!" said the Alpha, looking pained. "What was that for?"

"May I remind you we are in grave danger? I have managed to acquire for us, at most, an hour of grace time."

"How on earth did you finagle that?" he asked, rubbing the place she had just pinched.

Alexia smiled. "Luckily, your files on me did not report everything. I simply told Mr. Siemons my preternatural powers took an hour to activate."

"And they threw you into this cell with me anyway?" Lord Maccon was not pleased in the least by this bit of information.

"Did I not just say that I preferred your methods? Now you know why." Alexia twitched uncomfortably. She was getting a cramp in one of her shoulders. Lord Maccon's torso was rather too large to have one's arms wrapped around for an extended period of time, especially when one was lying on a hard wooden floor. Not that she was about to complain, mind you.

Her evident discomfort made the earl ask, in all seriousness, "I did not hurt you, did I?"

Miss Tarabotti cocked her head to one side and raised an eyebrow at him.

"I mean, when I attacked you just now, in wolf form? We werewolves do not remember much that happens during the full moon, you see. It is all embarrassingly instinctual," he admitted.

Miss Tarabotti patted him reassuringly. "I think you realized, almost despite yourself, that it was me you nearly killed."

"I smelled you," he admitted gruffly. "It sparked off a whole different set of instincts. I *do* remember being very confused, but not much else."

"What kind of different instincts?" Miss Tarabotti asked archly. She knew she was treading dangerous ground, but for some reason she could not resist encouraging him. She wanted to hear him say it. She wondered at what time she had become such a hardened flirt. *Well,* she reasoned, *one must get something from one's mother's side of the family.*

"Mmm. The reproductive variety." The earl began to nibble her neck with wholly concentrated interest.

Miss Tarabotti's innards turned toward a feel of mashed potatoes. Fighting her own urge to nibble back, she pinched him again, harder this time.

"Ow! Stop that!" He left off nibbling and glared at her. It was a funny thing to see such an expression of wounded dignity on the face of such an enormous and highly dangerous man—even if he was naked.

Alexia said practically, "We have no time for such monkeyshines. We must determine a way out of this predicament. We have to rescue Lord Akeldama, and we absolutely must close this wretched club down. Your amorous intentions are not currently part of the agenda."

"Is there a way they might become so, in the not-too-distant future?" Lord Maccon asked meekly, shifting against her in a manner that ensured she realized the nibbling had affected his outsides just as much as her insides. Alexia was partly shocked, partly intrigued by the idea that as he was naked, she might actually get to *see* what he looked like. She had seen sketches of the nude male, of course, for purely technical purposes. She was given to wonder if werewolves were anatomically bigger in certain areas. Of course, she was touching Lord Maccon, so such supernatural traits ought rightly to be canceled out, but in the interest of scientific curiosity, she shifted her lower body away from him a handbreadth and peeked downward. She was thwarted by the material of her own skirt wadded between them.

Taking her movement as withdrawal rather than curiosity, the earl pulled her back against him possessively. He slid one leg between her two, trying to shift multiple skirts and petticoats out of his way.

Miss Tarabotti sighed in long-suffering style.

He returned to nibbling and then nipping and kissing softly up and down the entire column of her throat. This was causing most distractingly invigorating frissons of sensation up and down her sides, over her ribs, and toward her nether regions. It was almost uncomfortable, as though her skin itched from underneath. Also, due to his unclothed state, Alexia was learning ever more about the veracity of some of those sketches. Still, her father's books had not entirely done the situation justice.

Lord Maccon slid one hand up into her hair.

So much for tying it back, thought Alexia as he loosed it from her hard-won ribbon.

The earl tugged at the black tresses, pulling her head back so as to more fully expose her neck to his lips and teeth.

Miss Tarabotti decided that there was something excruciatingly erotic about being fully dressed with a large naked man pressed against her from breast to foot.

Since she had not been able to see for herself exactly what the earl's frontal area looked like, Alexia decided to try the next best thing and began to work her hand around to touch. She was not entirely sure this was the kind of action a young lady undertook in such situations, but then again, most young ladies did not get themselves into them to start with. *In for a penny, in for a pound,* she decided. Miss Tarabotti always was one to seize the moment. So she seized.

Lord Maccon, and the certain portion of his anatomy now firmly in her grasp, jerked violently.

Miss Tarabotti let go. "Oops," she said. "Should I not have?" She trailed off, humiliated.

He hastened to reassure her. "Oh no, you most certainly should. It was simply unexpected." He pressed up against her receptively.

Embarrassed but more curious than anything else, purely scientifically, mind you, Alexia continued her explorations, a little more tenderly this time. His skin in that area was very soft, and there was hair nested at the base. He produced the most delicious noises under her tentative touch. She became increasingly intrigued but was also getting more and more concerned with the logistics of any further proceedings.

"Um, Lord Maccon?" she said finally in a cautious whisper.

The earl laughed. "No choice at this point, Alexia; you simply must call me Conall."

She swallowed. He could feel the movement under his lips.

"Conall, aren't we getting a tad carried away given the circumstances?"

The earl pulled her head back so he could look her directly in the eyes. "What are you blathering on about now, you impossible female?" His tawny eyes were glazed with passion, and he was breathing hard. Alexia was shocked to discover her own breathing was far from relaxed.

She scrunched up her forehead, trying to find the right words. "Well, should we not be abed for this kind of sport? Plus, they are scheduled to return at any moment."

"They? Who?" He was clearly falling behind the conversation.

"The scientists."

Lord Maccon gave a strangled laugh. "Aye, yes. And we wouldn't want them to learn too much about interspecies relations, now, would we?" He reached down with a free hand and pulled hers away from its questing.

Miss Tarabotti was faintly disappointed. Until he raised it to his lips and kissed it. "I do not mean to rush into these things, Alexia. You are inexplicably tempting."

She nodded, bumping his head slightly. "The feeling is mutual, my lord. Not to mention unexpected."

He seemed to take that as encouragement and rolled so that she was beneath him, and he loomed above her. He was now lying between her legs, component parts flush against hers.

Alexia squeaked at the sudden shift in positions. She was not certain whether she should be grateful or upset that women's fashion demanded so many copious layers of fabric, as this was now all that prevented more intimate contact and, she was pretty certain, sexual congress.

"Lord Maccon . . . ," she said in her best, most severe, spinster voice.

"Conall," he interrupted. He leaned back, and his hands began journeying over her chest.

"Conall! Now is *not* the time!"

He ignored her and asked, "How do I undo this blasted dress?"

Alexia's ivory taffeta gown was held together by a row of tiny mother-of-pearl buttons up the length of its back. Although she did not answer him, the earl eventually discovered this fact and began undoing them with a rapidity that bespoke consummate skill in the art of undoing ladies' clothing. Miss Tarabotti would have been disgruntled, except that she figured it was best if one of them knew what they were on about in the matter of fornication. And she could hardly expect a gentleman of over two hundred years or so to have remained celibate.

In no time at all, he had dexterously undone enough of the buttons to pull down the neckline of her dress and expose the tops of her breasts where they rose above her corset. He bent and began kissing them, only to stop, rear back very suddenly, and say in a voice harsh with suppressed need, "What in tarnation is that?"

Alexia lifted herself onto her elbows and looked down, trying to see what it was that had stopped the annoying but unfortunately delightful ravishment of her personage. However, given the nature of her copious endowments in the bosom department, she could not make out what it was about her corset that had so taken his attention.

Lord Maccon picked up the shard of mirror wrapped in a handkerchief and showed it to her.

"Oh, I forgot about that. I pinched it from the dressing room when the scientists left me alone for a moment. Thought it might come in handy."

Lord Maccon gave her a long, thoughtful, only mildly amorous look. "Very resourceful, my dear. It is at times like this when I really wish you could be on the BUR roster."

She looked up into his face, embarrassed more by the compliment and the endearment than she had been by their previous physical proceedings. "So, what is the plan?"

"*We* are not going to develop a plan," he growled, placing the mirror carefully down on the floor next to them, out of view of the doorway.

Alexia grinned at such foolish protectiveness. "Do not be ridiculous. You can hardly hope to accomplish anything more this night without my help. It is full moon, remember?"

Lord Maccon, who had, outrageously, forgotten the moon, had a momentary shock of terror that, in his absentmindedness, he might lose proximity with her. Alexia's preternatural abilities were the only thing currently keeping him sane. He quickly canvassed to make certain they were in firm physical contact. His body reminded him that, yes, *firm* was the operative word.

He tried to keep his head focused on their future nonamorous actions. "Well, in that case, you are to remain tangential as much as possible. None of those fire-eating antics you are so fond of. In order to get us out of here, I may have to use violence. In which case, you will need to hold on to me tightly and stay well out of the way. Do you ken?"

Alexia was going to get defensive and angry and explain quite severely that she was practical enough to avoid fisticuffs, especially when she had no brass parasol to protect herself with, but instead she said, "Did you just ask if I *kenned*?" She could not help grinning.

Lord Maccon looked ashamed of the verbal slip and muttered something about Scotland under his breath.

"You did! I was just kenned!" Miss Tarabotti's grin widened. She could not restrain herself; she did so like it when the earl's Highland lilt came out. It was currently her second favorite thing he did with his tongue. She leaned up on her elbows and kissed him softly on the cheek. Almost despite himself, Lord Maccon moved his own mouth toward her lips and turned it into a far deeper kiss.

When Alexia finally dropped back, they were both panting again.

"This has got to stop," she insisted. "We are in danger, remember? You know, ruination and tragedy? Calamity just beyond that door." She pointed behind him. "Any moment now, evil scientists may come charging in."

"All the more reason to grasp the opportunity," he insisted, leaning in and pressing his lower body against her.

Miss Tarabotti pressed against his torso defensively with both hands, trying to stop him from kissing her again. She cursed fate that had set life up so that when she finally did get to touch Lord Maccon's bare chest, there was no time to appreciate it.

He nibbled her earlobe. "Just think of this as a sort of wedding-night prelude."

Alexia was not certain which part of that particular statement gave the most offense—the fact that he assumed there would be a wedding night or the fact that he assumed it would take place on the hard floor of a barren room.

"Really, Lord Maccon!" she said, pushing harder.

"Oh dear, back to that, are we?"

"Where do you keep getting this idea that we should marry?"

Lord Maccon rolled his tawny eyes and gestured expressively to his naked flesh. "I assure you, Miss Tarabotti, I do not do these kinds of things with a woman of your caliber without contemplating marriage in the very near future. I may be a werewolf and Scottish, but despite what you may have read about both, we are not cads!"

"I do not want to force you into anything," Alexia insisted.

Keeping hold of her with one hand, the Alpha rolled off her prone body and sat back. Although he kept in contact to keep himself from changing, most of him was now separated from Alexia.

Miss Tarabotti's eyes, having entirely adjusted to the dim interior of the room, received a full-frontal view. Those sketches in her papa's books had been far more restrained than she realized.

"Really, we must discuss this silly notion of yours," he said with a sigh.

"What?" she croaked, goggling at him.

"That you will not marry me."

"Must we discuss it here and now?" she said, not realizing what she was saying. "And why is it silly?"

"Well, at least we have some privacy." He shrugged. The movement shifted all the muscles of his chest and stomach.

"Uh . . . uh . . . ," stuttered Miss Tarabotti, "couldn't it wait until I am home and you are, uh, clothed?"

Lord Maccon realized he had the advantage over Alexia; he was not about to sacrifice it. "Why, you think your family will allow us some privacy? My pack certainly will not. They have been eager to meet you ever since I came home covered in your scent. Not to mention Lyall and his gossiping."

"Professor Lyall gossips?" Alexia tore her eyes away from his body to look up into his face.

"Like an old churchyard biddy."

"And what exactly has he told them?"

"That the pack is getting an Alpha female. I am not giving up, you realize?" He said it with deadly calm.

"But I thought it was my move? Isn't that the way this works?" Miss Tarabotti was confused.

Lord Maccon's grin was all wolf. "Up to a certain point. Let us simply say you have made your preferences known."

"I thought you found me utterly impossible."

He grinned cheerfully. "Most assuredly."

Alexia's stomach flipped over, and she was seized with the sudden impulse to tackle him and rub up against him. Lord Maccon naked was one thing; naked and smiling that gently crooked smile of his— devastating.

"I thought I was too bossy," she said.

"And I shall provide you with an entire pack to boss around. They could use the discipline. I have been getting lax in my old age."

Miss Tarabotti highly doubted that. "I thought you found my family impossible."

"I shall not be marrying them," he began, inching back in toward her, sensing a weakness in her resolve.

Miss Tarabotti was not certain his return was a good thing. True, that most disturbing view was blurring as he moved toward her, but he had that look on his face that said the kissing would start up again presently. She wondered exactly how she had managed to get herself into such an untenable position.

"But I am tall, and brown, and have a large nose, and large everything else." She gestured ineffectually at her hips and chest.

"Mmm," said the earl, agreeing with her entirely, "you most certainly do." He found it interesting she did not mention those things that had worried him from the start: his age (advanced) and her state (preternatural). But he was not about to assist in her protestations by giving her more ammunition in objecting to his suit. They could talk about his own concerns later—preferably after they were married; that is, he grimaced mentally, if they managed to survive their current predicament and make it to the altar.

Finally, Alexia came round and about to the thing that really troubled her. She looked down at her free hand as though finding its palm fascinating. "You do not love me."

"Ah," said the Alpha, looking pleased at this, "says who? You never asked me. Should it not be *my* opinion you take into account?"

"Well," sputtered Miss Tarabotti, at a loss for words. "Well, I never."

"So?" He raised an eyebrow.

Alexia bit her lip, white teeth gnawing at the full swollen flesh. Finally, she lifted trembling lashes and cast a very worried glance up at him, now too close to her once more.

Naturally, because fortune is a fickle beast, it was precisely at that moment that the door to their cell opened.

Standing in the doorway was a backlit figure, clapping slowly but with evident approval.

CHAPTER THIRTEEN

The Last Room

In a lightning-fast movement, which bespoke his dexterity as a human before he had become a werewolf, Lord Maccon shifted around Miss Tarabotti so that his back was to the intruder and he was shielding her with his body. In the same motion, Alexia saw he had managed to grab the shard of mirror off the floor next to them. He held it between them, protected from Mr. Siemons's view.

"Well, Miss Tarabotti," said the scientist, "you certainly do excellent work. I never thought to see a werewolf Alpha in human form on full-moon night."

Alexia moved to sit, lifting the bodice of her dress over her shoulders as subtly as possible. The back had entirely come undone. She glared at Lord Maccon, who looked back at her in an utterly unapologetic way.

"Mr. Siemons," she said flatly.

As the scientist moved into the room, she saw that behind him stood at least six other men of varying sizes, mostly on the larger end of the spectrum. He was clearly taking no chances should her preternatural abilities be simply a superstitious hoax. But, having found no werewolf in residence, he stared at Lord Maccon's back with a decidedly clinical expression.

"Does his brain return to human reason as well as his body to human form, or is he still essentially a wolf inside?" the scientist asked.

Alexia saw the earl's intent in the narrowing of his eyes and the way he shifted his grip on the shard. With his back to the door, Lord Maccon had not seen Mr. Siemons's large retinue. Miss Tarabotti shook her head almost imperceptibly at him. Taking the hint, he subsided slightly.

Mr. Siemons came closer. Bending over their prone forms, he

made to grab the earl's head so he could tilt it up and look into his face. With a spark of malicious humor, Lord Maccon growled loudly and snapped at him as though he were still a wolf. Mr. Siemons hurriedly backed away.

He looked at Alexia. "Really," he said, "quite remarkable. We are going to have to study your abilities extensively, and there are several tests . . ." He trailed off. "Are you certain I cannot persuade you to our cause—that of justice and security? Now that you have experienced the true terror of a werewolf attack, you must admit to how incontrovertibly hazardous these creatures are! They are nothing more than a plague on the human race. Our research will lead to empire-wide prevention and protection against this threat. With your capabilities, we could determine new neutralization tactics. Don't you see how valuable you could be to us? We would simply want to do a few physical assessments now and again."

Alexia was not quite sure what to say. She was both repulsed and frightened by the eminently reasonable way in which the man spoke. For there she sat, flush against a werewolf, a man whom this kidnapper, this torturer, thought of as an abomination. Yet a man whom, she realized with no surprise whatsoever, she loved.

"Thank you for the kind offer—" she began.

The scientist interrupted her. "Your cooperation would be invaluable, but it is not necessary, Miss Tarabotti. Understand, we will do what we must."

"Then I would act in accordance with my conscience, not yours," she said firmly. "Your perception of me must logically be as warped as your perception of him." She dipped her chin at Lord Maccon. He was glaring at her intently, as though trying to get her to stay silent. But Miss Tarabotti's tongue had always gotten the better of her—hinged in the middle as it undoubtedly was. "I would as soon not be a willing participant in your fiendish experiments."

Mr. Siemons smiled a tight little psychopathic smile. Then he turned away and yelled something in Latin.

A brief silence descended.

There was a rustle among the scientists and thugs gathered in the doorway, and the automaton pushed them aside to enter the cell.

Lord Maccon could see the revulsion on Miss Tarabotti's face, but he still did not turn around to find out what had caused it. He remained resolutely facing away from the scientist and those who stood behind him, keeping his naked back to the events. He had grown tenser and tenser as Alexia and Mr. Siemons exchanged barbs.

Miss Tarabotti could feel his vibrating aggravation at every point of contact between their bodies. She could see it in the hard muscles under his bare skin. He practically quivered, like a dog straining at its lead.

Alexia knew he was going to break a moment before he did.

In one smooth movement, Lord Maccon turned and lashed out with the mirror shard. Mr. Siemons, seeing a certain apprehension enter Alexia's face, stepped out of range.

At the same time, the automaton came forward and to one side, lunging for Miss Tarabotti.

Caught midswing and hampered by having to stay in physical contact with her, Lord Maccon could not switch to strike against the automaton quickly enough.

Alexia was not so restricted. As soon as the evil thing closed in on her, she screamed and lashed out, certain she would die if that repulsive imitation of a man touched her.

Notwithstanding her aversion, the automaton grabbed Miss Tarabotti under the armpits with its cold fingernailless hands and picked her up bodily. The monster was amazingly strong. Alexia kicked out, and though she made definitive contact with the heel of her boot, it did not seem to affect the creature. It threw her, still kicking and screeching like a banshee, over one waxy shoulder.

Lord Maccon whirled back toward her, but the combination of his lunge and the automaton's attack had broken contact between them. Alexia, draped facedown, caught his panicked expression through the tangle of her hair and then the flash of something sharp. With his last conscious thought, Lord Maccon had thrown the shard of mirror into the automaton's lower back, just under where she hung suspended.

"He is changing back!" yelled Mr. Siemons, retreating rapidly from the room. The automaton, carrying the squirming Miss Tarabotti, followed.

"Neutralize him! Quickly!" Mr. Siemons ordered the men waiting in the doorway. They rushed into the chamber.

Miss Tarabotti felt a little sorry, realizing they had no idea how fast the change would occur. She had claimed it would take her an hour to change a werewolf back into human form. They must have thought it took equally long to change back. She hoped this gave Lord Maccon some kind of advantage. It would be a mixed blessing in any event, his animal instincts now taking over completely, placing everyone, even her, at risk.

As they moved rapidly down the corridor, Miss Tarabotti heard a portentous snarl, a sad wet crunching sound, and then terrified screams. Those cries being so much more impressively bloodcurdling than her own, she stopped her bansheelike screeching and turned her attention to trying to get the automaton to drop her. She kicked and writhed with animalistic vigor. Unfortunately, the construct's grip was like iron about her waist. Since she had no idea exactly what the monstrosity was made of, she figured its grip could actually *be* iron.

Whatever the skeletal superstructure of the *homunculus simulacrum,* it was coated in a layer of fleshy substance. Miss Tarabotti eventually stopped struggling, a waste of energy, and stared morosely down at the shard of mirror sticking out of its back. A small amount of dark viscous liquid was leaking from where it stuck. In fascinated horror, she realized Lord Maccon was right. The being was filled with blood—old, black, dirty blood. *Was everything,* she wondered, *about blood with these scientists?* And then: *Why had Lord Maccon been so intent on wounding the automaton?* It came to her. *He needs a trail to follow. This will never do,* she thought. *It's not bleeding enough to leave drops behind.*

Trying not to think about it too closely, she reached for the piece of mirror embedded in the automaton's oozing flesh. She slashed the soft underside of her arm against an exposed corner of the sharp shard. Her own blood, a healthy bright red, welled fast and clean and dripped in perfect droplets onto the carpeted floor. She wondered if even her blood smelled of cinnamon and vanilla to Lord Maccon.

No one noticed. The automaton, following its master, carried her back through the receiving room of the club and toward the machinery chambers. They passed by those rooms Miss Tarabotti had visited on her tour of the Hypocras facilities and on toward parts she had not been allowed to see. This was the area from which she had heard those terrible screams.

They reached the last room at the very end of the corridor. Alexia managed to twist about enough to read a small slip of paper tacked to the side of the door. It said, in neat black calligraphy, framed on either side by an etched octopus, EXSANGUINATION CHAMBER.

Miss Tarabotti could see nothing of the interior from where she hung, until Mr. Siemons issued instructions in that undecipherable Latin of his, and the automaton put her down. Alexia bounced away from the creature like a not-very-agile gazelle. Undeterred, the automaton grabbed both her arms and wrenched her back to itself, holding her immobilized.

She stiffened in revulsion. No matter that it had just carried her the length of the club, her skin still shivered away in horror whenever the monster touched her.

Swallowing down bile, she took a deep breath and tried to calm herself. Reaching some kind of equilibrium, she shook her hair out of her face and looked about.

The room contained six iron platforms of equal size and shape, bolted to the floor and paired off into three groups of two. Each platform, the size of a large man, was equipped with a plethora of restraints made of various materials. Two young scientists in gray frock coats and glassicals bustled about. They clutched leather-bound notepads and were jotting observations in them using sticks of graphite wrapped in sheepskin. An older man, about Mr. Siemons's age, was also in attendance. He wore a tweed suit, of all horrible things, and a cravat tied with such carelessness it was almost as much a sin as his actions. He also wore glassicals, but of a larger, more elaborate kind than Alexia had seen before. All three gentlemen paused to look at them when they entered the room, their eyes distorted to hugeness by the optical glass. Then they were back to moving between the lifeless figures of two men lying on one pair of platforms. One figure was tied down with sisal rope, and the other . . .

Alexia cried out in horror and distress. The other wore an extravagant plum-colored velvet evening coat stained with blood and a satin waistcoat of sea-foam green and mauve plaid torn in several places. He, too, was tied down with rope, but he had also been crucified through both hands and feet with wooden stakes. The stakes were bolted into the platform on which he lay, and Alexia could not tell if he lay still because of the pain they caused him or because he could no longer move at all.

Miss Tarabotti wrenched toward her friend convulsively, but the automaton held her fast. Finding reason only at the very last, Alexia figured this was probably a good thing. If she touched Lord Akeldama when he was in such a weakened state, her preternatural abilities might bring about his immediate demise. Only his supernatural strength was keeping him alive—that is, if he *was* still alive.

"You," she sputtered at Mr. Siemons, searching for a word horrible enough to describe these so-called scientists, "you *philistines*! What have you done to him?"

Not only had Lord Akeldama been strapped and nailed down, but they had hooked him into one of their infernal machines. One sleeve of his beautiful coat had been cut away, as had the silk shirt underneath, and a long metal tube emerged from under the skin of his upper arm. The tube ran into a mechanical steam-driven contraption of some kind, from which came another tube, which hooked into the other man. This second man was clearly not supernatural; his skin was tan and his cheeks rosy. But he, too, lay as still as death.

"How far along are we, Cecil?" Mr. Siemons asked one of the gray-clad scientists, completely ignoring Miss Tarabotti.

"Nearly done, sir. We think you may be correct about the age. This seems to be going much more smoothly than our previous procedures."

"And the application of the electrical current?" Mr. Siemons scratched his sideburns.

The man looked down at his notations, twiddling the side of his glassicals for focus. "Within the hour, sir, within the hour."

Mr. Siemons rubbed his hands together delightedly. "Excellent, quite excellent. I shall not disturb Dr. Neebs; he looks to be concentrating deeply. I know how involved he gets in his work."

"We are trying to moderate the intensity of the shock, sir. Dr. Neebs thinks this might extend survival time in the recipient," explained the second young scientist, looking up from some large levers he was fiddling with on the side of the machine.

"Fascinating thought. Very interesting approach. Proceed, please, proceed. Do not mind me. Just bringing in a new specimen." He turned and gestured at Miss Tarabotti.

"Very good, sir. I'll just get on, then," said the first scientist, who went back to what he had been doing before they entered the room with barely a glance in Miss Tarabotti's direction.

Alexia looked Mr. Siemons full in the face. "I am beginning to understand," she said in a quiet, deadly voice, "who is the monster. What you are doing is farther from natural than vampires or werewolves could ever get. You are profaning creation, not only with this"—she gestured rudely with her thumb at the automaton holding her tightly—"but with that." She pointed to the machine with its suckerlike metal tubes reaching hungrily inside the body of her dear friend. The horrible contraption seemed to be drinking him dry, more hungry for blood than any vampire she had ever seen. "It is you, Mr. Siemons, who is the abomination."

Mr. Siemons stepped forward and slapped her hard across the face. The sound, a sharp crack, caused Dr. Neebs to look up from his work. No one said anything, though, and all three scientists immediately returned to their activities.

Alexia recoiled back against the cold stillness of the automaton. Instantly, she jerked forward away from it once more, blinking away tears of frustration. When her vision had cleared, she could see that Mr. Siemons was once more smiling his tight little psychopathic smile.

"Protocol, Miss Tarabotti," he said. Then he said something in Latin.

The automaton hauled Alexia over to one of the other sets of platforms. One of the young scientists stopped what he was doing and came to strap her down while the creature held her immobile. Mr. Siemons helped to secure her ankles and wrists with rope tied so tight Miss Tarabotti was certain she would lose all circulation to her extremities. The platform was decked out with massive manacles made of solid metal that looked to be iron coated in silver, and there were more of those awful wooden stakes, but the scientists clearly did not think she needed such extreme measures.

"Bring in a new test recipient," Mr. Siemons ordered once she was secure. The gray-coated young man nodded, put his leather notebook on a small shelf, took off the glassicals, and left the room.

The automaton took up residence in front of the closed door, a silent wax-faced sentry.

Alexia twisted her head to one side. She could see Lord Akeldama to her left, still lying silent and unmoving on his platform. The older scientist, Dr. Neebs, seemed to have completed his task. He was now hooking another machine into the one with all the tubes. This new apparatus was a small engine of some kind, all gears and cogs. At its heart was a glass jar with metal plates at each end.

The remaining gray-clad young scientist came around and began to rigorously turn a crank attached to this device.

Eventually there issued a sharp crackling sound, and a vibrating beam of extraordinarily white light ran up the tube attached to Lord Akeldama's arm and penetrated his body. The vampire jerked and writhed, pulling involuntarily on the wooden stakes impaling his hands and feet. His eyes shot open, and he let out a keening scream of pain.

The young scientist, still cranking with one hand, pulled a small lever down with his other, and the beam of light shifted through the exsanguination machine to run up the tube attached to the seemingly comatose human subject on the platform next to Lord Akeldama.

This man's eyes also opened. He, too, jerked and screamed. The scientist stopped cranking, and the electrical current, for Alexia surmised that must be what it was, dissipated. Ignoring Lord Akeldama, who slumped with eyes closed, looking small and sunken and very old, Mr. Siemons, Dr. Neebs, and the young scientist rushed over to the other man. Dr. Neebs checked his pulse and then lifted his now-closed eyelids to check his pupils, staring hard through the glassicals. The man lay perfectly still.

Then, suddenly, he began to whimper, like a child at the end of a tantrum—out of tears, with only small dry heaving sobs left. All the muscles in his body seemed to lock up, his bones stiffened, and his eyes practically bulged right out of his head. The three scientists backed away but continued to watch him intently.

"Ah, there he goes," said Mr. Siemons with satisfaction.

"Yes, yes." Dr. Neebs nodded, slapping his hands together and rubbing. "Perfect!"

The gray-clad youngster busily scratched notes into his leather pad.

"A much more rapid and efficient result, Dr. Neebs. This is commendable progress. I shall write a most favorable report," said Mr. Siemons, smiling widely and licking his lips.

Dr. Neebs beamed with pride. "Much obliged, Mr. Siemons. However, I am still concerned by the charge current intensity. I should like to be able to direct soul transfer with even greater accuracy."

Mr. Siemons looked over at Lord Akeldama. "Do you think you left any behind?"

"Difficult to tell with such an ancient subject," Dr. Neebs prevaricated, "but perhaps—"

He was cut off by a loud knock on the door.

"Me, sir!" said a voice.

"*Expositus*," said Mr. Siemons.

The automaton turned stiffly and opened the door.

In came the other young scientist accompanied by Mr. MacDougall. They carried between them the body of a man, wrapped tightly in a long length of linen, looking like nothing so much as an ancient Egyptian mummy.

Upon seeing Miss Tarabotti, strapped to her own platform, Mr. MacDougall dropped his end of the body and rushed over to her.

"Good evening, Mr. MacDougall," said Alexia politely. "I must say, I do not think very highly of your friends here. Their behavior is"—she paused delicately—"immodest."

"Miss Tarabotti, I am so very sorry." The American worried his hands together in a little ball and fluttered about her anxiously. "If I had only known *what* you were at the commencement of our acquaintance, I might have prevented this. I would have taken proper precautions. I would have . . ." He covered his mouth with both pudgy hands, shaking his head in an excess of troubled emotion.

Alexia attempted a little smile. *Poor thing*, she thought. *It must be hard to be so weak all the time.*

"Now, Mr. MacDougall," Mr. Siemons interrupted their little tête-à-tête. "You know what is at stake here. The young lady refuses to cooperate willingly. So this is how it must be. You may stay to observe, but you must behave yourself and not interfere with the procedure."

"But, sir," the American protested, "shouldn't you test the extent of her abilities first? Make some notations, formulate a hypothesis, take a more scientific approach? We know so little about this so-called preternatural state. Shouldn't you utilize caution? If she is as unique as you say, you can hardly afford to take unnecessary risks with her well-being."

Mr. Siemons raised an autocratic hand. "We are only performing a preliminary transfer procedure. The vampires call her kind 'soulless.' If our predictions are correct, she will not require any kind of electro-shock treatment for revival. No soul, you see?"

"But what if it is *my* theory that is correct and not yours?" Mr. MacDougall looked worried beyond all endurance. His hands were shaking, and a sheen of sweat had appeared across his brow.

Mr. Siemons smiled maliciously. "We had better hope, for her sake, that it is not." He turned away and issued instructions to his compatriots. "Prepare her for exsanguination. Let us analyze the true extent of this woman's capabilities. Dr. Neebs, if you are finished with that subject?"

Dr. Neebs nodded. "For the time being. Cecil, please continue to monitor his progress. I want immediate notification of dental protuberance." He began rummaging about, unhooking the two machines from each other and then from Lord Akeldama and his companion sufferer. He pulled the tubes out of their respective arms roughly. Alexia was disturbed to see that the gaping hole in Lord Akeldama's flesh did not immediately begin to close and heal itself.

Then there was no more time for her to worry about Lord Akeldama, for they were moving the machine in her direction. Dr. Neebs approached her arm with a very sharp-looking knife. He ripped away the sleeve of her gown and poked about with his fingers at the underside of her elbow, looking for a vein. Mr. MacDougall made nonsensical murmurs of distress the entire time but did nothing to help her. In fact, he backed timidly away and turned his head as though afraid to watch. Alexia struggled futilely against her restraints.

Dr. Neebs focused his glassicals and placed the knife into position.

A great crash reverberated through the room.

Something large, heavy, and very angry hit the outside of the door hard enough to jar the automaton that stood in front of it.

"What the hell's that?" Dr. Neebs asked, pausing with the knife resting against her skin.

The door reverberated again.

"It will hold," said Mr. Siemons confidently.

But with the third great crash, the door began to split.

Dr. Neebs lifted the knife he had been about to use on Alexia and took up a defensive position with it instead. One of the younger scientists began to scream. The other ran about looking for a weapon of some kind among the scientific paraphernalia littering the room.

"Cecil, calm yourself!" yelled Mr. Siemons. "It will hold!" Clearly, he was trying to convince himself as much as anyone else.

"Mr. MacDougall," Alexia hissed under the hubbub, "could you, perhaps, see yourself toward untying me?"

Mr. MacDougall, trembling, looked at her as though he could not understand what she was saying.

The door cracked and caved inward, and through the splintered mess charged a massive wolf. The fur about his face was matted and clotted with blood. Pink-tinged saliva dribbled from around long sharp white teeth. The rest of his pelt was brindled black and gold and brown. His eyes, when they turned toward Miss Tarabotti, were hot yellow, with no humanity in them at all.

Lord Maccon probably weighed a good fourteen stone. Alexia now possessed intimate knowledge supporting the fact that a good deal of that weight of his was muscle. This made for a very large, very strong wolf. And all of it was angry, hungry, and driven by full-moon madness.

The werewolf hit the exsanguination chamber in a vicious storm of fang and claw and began unceremoniously tearing everything apart. Including the scientists. Suddenly, there was noise and blood and panic everywhere.

Miss Tarabotti turned her head away as much as possible, flinching from the horror of it. She tried Mr. MacDougall again. "Mr. MacDougall, please untie me. I can stop him." But the American had pressed himself back into a far corner of the room, trembling with fear, eyes riveted on the rampaging wolf.

"Oh!" said Miss Tarabotti in frustration. "Untie me this instant, you ridiculous man!"

Where requests had failed, orders seemed to work well enough. Her sharp words broke through his terror. Trancelike, the American began fumbling at her bonds, eventually freeing her hands enough for her to bend down and untie her ankles herself. She swung to the edge of the platform.

A stream of Latin sang out above the sounds of carnage, and the automaton slid into action.

By the time Alexia could stand—it took a few moments for the blood to return to her feet—the automaton and the werewolf were grappling in the doorway. What was left of Dr. Neebs and the two young scientists lay crumpled on the floor, swimming in small pools of blood, glassical parts, and entrails.

Miss Tarabotti tried very hard not to be sick or faint. The smell of carnage was truly appalling—fresh meat and molten copper.

Mr. Siemons remained unscathed, and while his construct fought the supernatural creature, he turned to seek out Alexia.

He picked up Dr. Neebs's long sharp surgical knife and moved at her unexpectedly fast for such a well-fed man. Before Alexia had time to react, he was upon her, knife pressed to her throat.

"Do not move, Miss Tarabotti. You neither, Mr. MacDougall. Stay where you are."

The werewolf had its massive jaw about the throat of the automaton and appeared to be putting concerted effort into decapitating it. It was to no avail, however, because the construct's bones were made of a substance too strong even for a werewolf's jaw. The head remained attached. Wobbly, but attached. The automaton's sluggish blackened blood spilled out of massive neck gashes over the wolf's muzzle. The supernatural creature sneezed and let go.

Mr. Siemons began inching toward the door, which was mostly blocked by the battling monsters. He pushed Miss Tarabotti in front of him, knife to her throat, trying for a side approach behind the wolf.

The werewolf's massive head swung toward them, and his lips pulled back in a snarl of warning.

Mr. Siemons jerked back, slicing through the first few layers of skin on Alexia's neck. She squeaked in alarm.

The wolf sniffed at the air, and its bright yellow eyes narrowed. It turned its attention completely onto Alexia and Mr. Siemons.

The automaton charged from behind and grabbed for the wolf's throat, trying to choke it to death.

"Godth's truth, I am hungry!" someone lisped. All forgotten, the human half of the Lord Akeldama experiment stood up from his platform. He had long, well-developed fangs and was looking around the room with single-minded interest. His eyes flitted about, dismissing Lord Akeldama, the werewolf, and the automaton but lingering with interest on Miss Tarabotti and Mr. Siemons before zeroing in on the most accessible meal in the chamber: Mr. MacDougall.

The American, huddled in his corner, shrieked as the newly created vampire vaulted over Lord Akeldama and across the intervening space with supernatural agility and speed.

Miss Tarabotti did not have time to watch further, as her attention was drawn back to the entranceway. She heard Mr. MacDougall scream again and then the thumping sounds of fighting.

The werewolf was trying to shake the automaton off his back. But the construct had established a death grip around his furry neck and would not budge. With the wolf momentarily distracted, the broken door was partly freed up, and Mr. Siemons began forcing Alexia once more toward it.

Miss Tarabotti wished, for about the hundredth time that evening, for her trusty parasol. Not having it, she did the next best thing. She elbowed Mr. Siemons hard in the gut while stomping down onto his insole with the heel of her boot.

Mr. Siemons cried out in pain and surprise and let her go.

Miss Tarabotti twisted away with a yell of triumph, and the werewolf's attention switched back toward them at the sound.

Choosing his own safety above all else, Mr. Siemons gave Miss Tarabotti up for a bad risk and fled the chamber, calling for his fellow scientists at the top of his lungs as he ran pell-mell down the hallway outside.

The automaton continued to fight, its hands tightening ever more surely around the wolf's brindled throat.

Alexia did not know what to do. Lord Maccon undoubtedly stood a better chance against the automaton in werewolf form. But, wheezing from restricted air flow, he was coming toward *her* and ignoring the automaton attempting to strangle him. She could not allow him to touch her if she wanted him to survive.

A hoarse voice said, "Rub out the word, my darling *tulip*."

Alexia glanced over. Lord Akeldama, still pale and clearly in unmitigated pain, had tilted his head up from where he lay. He was watching the brutal proceedings with glazed eyes.

Miss Tarabotti gave a cry of relief. He was alive! But she did not understand what he wanted her to do.

"The word," he said again, his voice wrecked by his suffering, "on the *homunculus simulacrum's* forehead. Rub it out." He collapsed back, exhausted.

Miss Tarabotti dodged sideways, positioning herself. Then, shuddering in revulsion, she reached forward and brushed her hand over the automaton's waxy face. She missed all but the very end of the word so that VIXI became VIX.

It seemed sufficient to do some good. The automaton stiffened and let go enough for the werewolf to shake him off. The creature was still moving but now did so with apparent difficulty.

The werewolf turned all his concentrated yellow attention on Miss Tarabotti.

Before he could even begin to spring at her, Alexia moved forward, unafraid, and wrapped both arms about his furry neck.

The change was a little less horrible the second time around. Or, perhaps, she was simply getting used to the feel of it. Fur retreated from where she touched him, bone and skin and flesh re-formed, and she held, once again, the naked body of Lord Maccon in her arms.

He was coughing and spitting.

"That automaton thing tastes awful," he announced, wiping his face with the back of one hand. It did nothing more effective than smudge the red over his chin and cheek.

Miss Tarabotti refrained from pointing out he had also been snacking on scientists and wiped his face with the skirt of her dress. It was already beyond salvation anyway.

Tawny brown eyes turned to her face. Alexia noted with relief that they were full of intelligence and entirely lacking in ferocity or hunger.

"You are unharmed?" he asked. One big hand came up, stroking over her face and down. He paused upon reaching the cut on her neck.

His eyes, even though he was touching her, went slightly back to feral yellow. "I'll butcher the bastard," he said softly, all the more anger in his voice for its quiet tone. "I'll pull his bones out through his nostrils one by one."

Alexia shushed him impatiently. "It is not that deep." But she did lean into his touch and let out a shaky breath she had not even known she was holding.

His hand, now trembling in fury, kept up its gentle assessment of her injuries. It smoothed softly over the bruises appearing on her exposed upper torso and down her shoulder to the slice on her arm.

"The Norse had it right—flay a man open from the back and eat out his heart," he said.

"Do not be disgusting," admonished the object of his interest. "Besides, I did that one to myself."

"What?!"

She shrugged dismissively, "You needed a trail to follow."

"You little fool," he said affectionately.

"It worked, didn't it?"

His touch became insistent for just a moment. Pulling her in against his large naked form, he kissed her roughly, a deeply erotic and oddly desperate melding of tongue and teeth. He kissed as though he needed her to subsist. It was unbearably intimate. Worse than allowing one's ankles to be seen. Alexia leaned into him, opening her mouth eagerly.

"I do so *hate* to intrude, my little lovebirds, but if you could see your way clear to maybe releasing me?" came a soft voice, interrupting their embrace. "And your business here, it is not quite finished."

Lord Maccon surfaced and looked about, blinking as though he had just woken from sleep: half nightmare, half erotic fantasy.

Miss Tarabotti shifted so that their only point of contact was her hand nested inside his big one. It was still enough contact to be comforting, not to mention preternaturally effective.

Lord Akeldama still lay on his platform. In the space between him and where Alexia had been strapped down, Mr. MacDougall still fought with the newly created vampire.

"Goodness me," said Miss Tarabotti in surprise, "he is still alive!" No one was sure, even her, whether she meant Mr. MacDougall or the manufactured vampire. They seemed equally matched, the vampire unused to his new strength and abilities, and Mr. MacDougall stronger than expected in his desperation and panic.

"Well, my love," said Alexia with prodigious daring to Lord Maccon, "shall we?"

The earl started to move forward and then stopped abruptly and looked down at her, not moving at all. "Am I?"

"Are you what?" She peeked up at him through her tangled hair, pretending confusion. There was no possible way she was going to make this easy for him.

"Your love?"

"Well, you are a werewolf, Scottish, naked, and covered in blood, and I am *still* holding your hand."

He sighed in evident relief. "Good. That is settled, then."

They moved over to where Mr. MacDougall and the vampire fought. Alexia was not certain she could effectively change two supernatural persons at once, but she was willing to try.

"Pardon me," she said, and grabbed the vampire by one shoulder. Surprised, the man turned toward this new threat. But his fangs were already retracting.

Miss Tarabotti smiled at him, and Lord Maccon had him by the ear like a naughty schoolboy before he could even make an aggressive move in her direction.

"Now, now," said Lord Maccon, "even new vampires may choose only willing victims." Releasing the ear, he punched the man extremely hard up under the chin. It was an expert boxer's move that laid the poor man out flat.

"Will it last?" Alexia asked of the fallen vampire. She was no longer touching him, so he should recuperate quickly.

"For a few minutes," said Lord Maccon in his BUR voice.

Mr. MacDougall, bleeding only slightly from a row of punctures in one side of his neck, blinked at his saviors.

"Tie him up, would you? There is a good lad. I have only one working hand, you see?" said Lord Maccon to the American, handing him rope from one of the platforms.

"Who, sir, are you?" Mr. MacDougall asked, looking the earl up and down and then focusing in on his and Alexia's linked hands. Or Alexia assumed that is what he was focusing in on.

Miss Tarabotti said, "Mr. MacDougall, your questions will have to wait."

Mr. MacDougall nodded submissively and began to tie the vampire.

"My love." Alexia looked at Lord Maccon. It was much easier to say the words the second time around, but she still felt very daring. "Perhaps you might see to Lord Akeldama? I dare not touch him in such a weakened state."

Lord Maccon refrained from commenting that when she called him "my love," he was pretty much willing to do whatever she asked.

They walked together over to Lord Akeldama's platform.

"Hello, princess," said Lord Maccon to the vampire. "Got yourself into quite a pickle this time, didn't you?"

Lord Akeldama looked him up and down. "My *sweet* young naked boy, you are *hardly* one to talk. Not that *I* mind, of course."

Lord Maccon blushed so profoundly it extended all the way down his neck to his upper torso. Alexia thought it entirely adorable.

Without another word, the earl untied Lord Akeldama and, as gently as possible, slid his hands and feet off the wooden stakes. The vampire lay still and silent for a long time after he had finished.

Miss Tarabotti worried. His wounds should be healing themselves. But, instead, they remained large, gaping holes. There wasn't even any blood dripping from them.

"My *dearest* girl," said the vampire finally, examining Lord Maccon with an exhausted but appreciative eye, "such a banquet. Never been one to favor werewolves myself, but he is *very* well equipped, now, is he not?"

Miss Tarabotti gave him an arch look. "My goodies," she warned.

"Humans," chuckled the vampire, "so possessive." He shifted weakly.

"You are not well," commented Lord Maccon.

"Quite right, Lord Obvious."

Miss Tarabotti looked at the vampire's wounds more closely, still careful not to touch him. She wanted desperately to hug her friend and offer some consolation, but any contact with her and he was certain to die. He was near enough to it already, and returning to human form would end him undoubtedly.

"You are dry," she remarked.

"Yes," agreed the vampire. "It all went into him." He gestured with his chin toward where the new vampire lay under Mr. MacDougall's ministrations.

"I suppose you might take a donation from me?" suggested Lord Maccon dubiously. "Would that work? I mean to say, how fully human does preternatural touch make me?"

Lord Akeldama shook his head weakly. "Not enough for me to feed from you, I suspect. It might work, but it also might kill you."

Lord Maccon unexpectedly jerked backward, pulling Alexia with him. Two hands were wrapped around his throat, squeezing tightly. The fingers on those hands had no fingernails.

The automaton had crawled all the way across the floor, slowly but surely, and was trying to fulfill the last order given to it: to kill Lord Maccon. This time, with the earl in human form, it stood a fairly good chance of succeeding.

CHAPTER FOURTEEN

Royal Interference

Lord Maccon sputtered and gasped for breath, trying to fight off the repulsive creature with only one hand. Miss Tarabotti beat at the automaton with her free arm. But nothing they did seemed capable of wresting the construct from around the earl's neck. Alexia was about to let go of Lord Maccon's hand and back away, knowing he could free himself in werewolf form, when Lord Akeldama stood shakily up from the platform on which he rested.

The vampire produced a still miraculously immaculate white lace handkerchief from a waistcoat pocket, stumbled over, and wiped the rest of the smudged word off the automaton's forehead.

The monstrosity let go of Lord Maccon and collapsed onto the floor.

The most remarkable thing then occurred. Its skin began melting away in slow rivulets, like warm honey. Slow black blood, mixed with some black particulate matter, leaked out and intermingled with the skin substance. Both slid off a mechanical skeletal structure. Soon, all that was left of the automaton was a metal frame wearing shabby clothing and lying in a gooey puddle of old blood, wax, and small black particles. Its internal organs appeared to be all gears and clockwork mechanisms.

Miss Tarabotti's attention was drawn away from the fascinating mess by Lord Maccon saying, "Oops, whoa there," and reaching for Lord Akeldama with his free arm.

The vampire was toppling over as well, having utterly exhausted what few resources of energy he had left in administering the deadly handkerchief. Lord Maccon, attached to Alexia with one hand, managed only to slow his fall with the other but not catch him completely.

The vampire crumpled to the floor in a sad little heap of plum-colored velvet.

Miss Tarabotti bent over him, still desperately careful not to touch him in any way. He was still, miraculously, alive.

"Why?" she stuttered, glancing over at the automaton, or what *had* been the automaton. "Why did that work?"

"You only wiped off the *I*?" asked Lord Maccon, looking thoughtfully at the puddle of *homunculus simulacrum* residue.

Alexia nodded.

"So you turned VIXI—*to be alive*—into VIX, *with difficulty.* Thus, the automaton could still move, but only barely. In order to destroy it entirely, you needed to remove the word and the activation particulate completely, breaking the aetheromagnetic connection."

"Well," huffed Miss Tarabotti, "how was I supposed to know that? That was my first automaton."

"And a *very* good job you made of it, too, *my pearl,* on such short acquaintance," complimented Lord Akeldama tenderly from his prone position without opening his eyes. He had yet to succumb to the Grand Collapse, but he looked in imminent danger of doing so.

They heard a great clattering and a quantity of yelling from the hallway behind them.

"Arse over apex, what now?" wondered Lord Maccon, standing up and dragging Miss Tarabotti with him.

A conglomeration of impeccably well-dressed young men bustled into the room, carrying with them the trussed and bound form of Mr. Siemons. They let out a collective shriek upon seeing Lord Akeldama crumpled on the floor. Several rushed over and began billing and cooing about him in an excess of emotional concern.

"Lord Akeldama's drones," Alexia explained to Lord Maccon.

"I would never have known," he replied sarcastically.

"Where did they all come from?" wondered Miss Tarabotti.

One of the young men whom Alexia remembered from before—had it only been a few hours ago?—deduced the cure to his master's ailments quickly enough. He pushed the other dandies aside, pulled off his blue silk evening jacket, rolled up his shirtsleeve, and offered his arm to the destabilized vampire. Lord Akeldama's eyes blinked slowly open.

"Ah, my capable Biffy. Do not let me drink too long from you alone."

Biffy leaned forward and kissed Lord Akeldama on the forehead, as though he were a small child. "Of course not, my lord." Gently he put his wrist to the vampire's pale lips.

Lord Akeldama bit down with a sigh of relief.

Biffy was both smart enough and strong enough to pull away half-way through the feeding. He summoned one of the other drones to take his place. Lord Akeldama, as thirsty as he was from his recent abuse, could easily damage a solo donor beyond repair. Luckily, none of his drones was foolish enough to try and stay the course. The second young man gave way to a third and then a fourth. At this point, Lord Akel-dama's wounds began to close, and his skin went from frighteningly gray to its normal porcelain white.

"Explain yourselves, my darlings," ordered Lord Akeldama as soon as he was able.

"Our little information-gathering excursion into high society's fes-tivities yielded up far more fruit than we had hoped, and more quickly, my lord," said Biffy. "When we returned home early to find you gone, we proceeded immediately to act upon the information most recently acquired—namely, that which bespoke suspicious activity and bright white lights late at night emanating from the recently opened scientific club, near the Duke of Snodgrove's town residence."

"And a good thing we did too," continued Biffy, wrapping a salmon-pink embroidered handkerchief about his own wrist and tying a knot with his teeth. "Not that I doubt your ability to handle the situation, sir," he said respectfully to Lord Maccon, without the sarcasm the state-ment ought to have elicited considering the Alpha was still entirely na-ked. "I will say that the moving room contraption transport device gave us some stick. Figured it out in the end, though. We ought to get one of those installed at the town house, my lord."

"I will think about it," said Lord Akeldama.

"You did very well," complimented Miss Tarabotti to the dandies. She believed in giving praise where it was due.

Biffy rolled down his sleeve and pulled his evening jacket back on over broad muscular shoulders. A lady was present, after all—even if her hair was most scandalously loose.

Lord Maccon said, "Someone must go to BUR and get a couple of agents over here to handle the formalities." He looked about, taking stock: three dead scientists, one new vampire, a trussed-up Mr. Siemons, a blathering Mr. MacDougall, the other mummylike body intended for Alexia's blood, and the remains of an automaton. The chamber was a veritable battlefield. He winced at the mounds of paperwork ahead of him. His own three kills alone would not be too much of a bother. He *was* chief sundowner, sanctioned killer for queen and country. But ex-plaining the automaton would require eight forms that he could think of, and probably a few more that he could not.

He sighed. "Whoever we send will also need to tell BUR we need sweeps here posthaste to clean up the mess. Have them check to see if there is a local ghost tethered nearby. See if it can be recruited to check for hidden chambers. This is a logistical nightmare."

Miss Tarabotti stroked his knuckles with her thumb sympathetically. Absentmindedly, Lord Maccon raised her hand to his lips and kissed the inside of her wrist.

Biffy signaled to one of the other drones. With a grin of eagerness, the man clapped his topper to his head and minced out of the room. Alexia wished she had that kind of energy. She was starting to feel the strain of the evening. Her muscles were sore, and all the little points of abuse—the rope burns about her ankles, the cut on her throat, the slice on her arm—had started to ache.

Lord Maccon said to Biffy, "We will need the potentate if we are to shut this operation down completely. Does your master have any drones with high enough rank to get into the Shadow Council without question? Or will I need to do that myself?"

Biffy gave the Alpha an appreciative but courteous once-over. "Looking like that, sir? Well, I am certain many a door might be opened to you, but not the potentate's."

Lord Maccon, who seemed to be periodically forgetting he was naked, sighed at this. Alexia figured, delightedly, that this meant he did, in fact, tend to traipse around his private apartments in the altogether. Marriage was becoming more and more of an attractive prospect. Though, she suspected, such a practice might get distracting in the long term.

Biffy continued, unabashed, to rib the Alpha's appearance. "To the best of our knowledge, the potentate's inclinations lie elsewhere. Unless he is with the queen, of course, in which case you might get right inside." He paused significantly. "We all know the queen likes a bit of Scottish now and again." He waggled his eyebrows in a highly suggestive manner.

"You do not say?" gasped Miss Tarabotti, genuinely shocked for the first time that evening. "Those rumors about Mr. Brown, they were true?"

Biffy settled in. "Every word, my dear. You know what I heard just the other day? I heard—"

"Well?" interrupted Lord Maccon.

Biffy shook himself and pointed to one of the young men fussing solicitously over Lord Akeldama: a slight, effete blond, with an aristocratic nose, wearing top-to-toe butter-yellow brocade. "See the canary over there? That is Viscount Trizdale, believe it or not. Heya Tizzy, come over here. Got a bit of sport for you."

The yellow-clad dandy pranced over.

"Our lord does not look well, Biffy. I am telling you. Quite ill, in fact," he said.

Biffy patted a yellow shoulder reassuringly. "Not to worry your pretty head. He will be just fine. Now, Lord Maccon here has a bit of a task for you. Should only take a jiffy. Wants you to nip round to old Bucky and rustle up the potentate. Needs some political clout, if you know what I mean, and it is not like the dewan's going to be much use this night. Full moon and all, haw haw. Go on now, shove off."

With one more worried look in Lord Akeldama's direction, the young viscount wandered out.

Alexia stared at Biffy. "Does the Duke of Trizdale know his only son is a drone?"

Biffy pursed his lips in a cagey manner. "Not as such."

"Huh," said Miss Tarabotti thoughtfully—so much gossip in one night!

A different dandy appeared, proffering one of the long gray frock coats sported by the younger scientists around the club.

Lord Maccon took it with a grumbled "thank you" and pulled it on. He was such a large man that it was quite scandalously short on him without trousers, but it covered the most important bits.

Alexia was a little disappointed.

So, apparently, was Biffy. "Now, Eustace, what did you go and do a thing like that for?" he said to his fellow drone.

"It was getting incommodious," said the unapologetic Eustace.

Lord Maccon interrupted them all by issuing forth a series of orders, which, with only minor dissembling, the assembled gentlemen took in hand. They did, collectively, keep trying to arrange matters so that Lord Maccon had to bend over. There was a twinkle in the earl's eye suggesting the Alpha knew what they were about and was humoring their attempts.

One small gaggle left to canvas the premises for other scientists, upon whom they pounced and locked away in the very cells formerly dedicated to vampires. Lord Akeldama's boys might *look* like fruits of the first water, but they all boxed at Whites, and at least a half dozen wore clothing specially cut to *disguise* musculature. As per Lord Maccon's instructions, they left his imprisoned pack alone. No need to test Miss Tarabotti's abilities any further than was necessary. The trapped vampires they released, asking them to please stay behind and help with the BUR reports. A few did, but most needed desperately to get home to their respective territories or down to the blood alley for a feeding. A few took off about the club tracking down and exterminating, in a most horrific manner, those last remaining scientists who had until then believed themselves lucky in evading Lord Akeldama's dandies.

"Bah," said Lord Maccon upon hearing this, "more paperwork, and on a night without Lyall too. How aggravating."

"I will help," said Miss Tarabotti brightly.

"Oh, you will, will you? I knew you were going to take every opportunity to interfere with my work, insufferable woman."

Miss Tarabotti knew how to handle his grumbling well enough now. She glanced about: everyone seemed to be suitably busy, so she slid in close to him and nibbled delicately at one side of his neck.

Lord Maccon jumped a little and clapped his hand to the front of the gray frock coat. The hemline rose slightly.

"Stop that!"

"I am very effective," Alexia insisted, breathing into his ear. "You should put me to good use. Otherwise, I will have to come up with other ways to entertain myself."

He groaned. "Fine, right. You can help with the paperwork."

She sat back. "Was that so hard?"

He raised both eyebrows and shifted his protective hand so she could partly see the result of her teasing.

Miss Tarabotti cleared her throat. "Was that so difficult?" She rephrased her question.

"I suspect you are much better at paperwork than I am anyway," he admitted grudgingly.

Miss Tarabotti had a brief horrific flashback to the state of his office last she had visited. "I am certainly more organized."

"You and Lyall are going to run me ragged, aren't you?" grumbled the earl, sounding most put-upon.

After that, cleanup proceeded with remarkable rapidity. Miss Tarabotti was beginning to understand how Lord Akeldama always seemed to know so much. His young men were amazingly efficacious. They managed to be everywhere at once. She wondered how many occasions in her past had contained some young fop, apparently too silly or too drunk, watching everything.

By the time the five BUR agents—two vampires, two humans, and a ghost—arrived, everything was basically in order. The premises had been searched thoroughly, vampire statements taken, prisoners and werewolves secured, and someone had even managed to find Lord Maccon a pair of ill-fitting knickerbockers. Above and beyond the call of duty, Biffy, utilizing a few stray metal coils from one of Dr. Neebs's machines, had twisted Miss Tarabotti's hair into a beautiful rendition of the latest updo out of Paris.

Lord Akeldama, now sitting on one of the platforms, watching, with the eyes of a proud parent, his boys work, said approvingly to Biffy, "Lovely job, my *dear.*" Then to Alexia, "Do you see, my little marshmallow, you simply *must* get yourself a nice French maid."

Mr. Siemons was carted off to prison by two of the BUR agents. Miss Tarabotti had to speak most severely to Lord Maccon about not paying him a call when she was no longer around.

"Justice must take its course," she insisted. "If you are going to work for BUR and support the system, you must do so all the time, not simply when you find it convenient."

Eyes riveted on the line of congealed blood across the lower part of her neck, he wheedled, "Just a short visit, enough for a mild dismemberment?"

She gave him a dour look. "No."

The rest of the BUR agents and a competent-looking sweeps crew bustled about, scribbling notations and passing things to the earl to sign. At first they had been entirely shocked to find him in human form, but the sheer mountain of cleanup to be done at the Hypocras Club made them quickly more grateful than surprised to have him available and competent.

Miss Tarabotti tried to be helpful, but her eyes were becoming scratchy, and she was leaning more and more heavily against Lord Maccon's broad side. Eventually, the earl shifted his operation to the entry room of the club and sat them both down on the red couch there. Someone made tea. Lord Akeldama enthroned himself in the brown leather studded armchair. Despite the indignity, Miss Tarabotti soon found herself curled up on the couch, head pillowed on Lord Maccon's hard thigh, snoring softly.

The earl, issuing orders and signing forms, stroked her hair with one hand, in defiance of Biffy's protestations that this would mess up her new hairdo.

Miss Tarabotti, dreaming of brass octopuses, slept through the remains of the night. She did not awaken upon the arrival or the departure of the potentate and his argument with Lord Maccon, whose growls of annoyance at the politician's obtuseness only seemed to lull her further into dreamland. Nor was she awake to see Lord Maccon square off against Dr. Caedes over the disposition of the Hypocras Club's gadgetry and research notes. She slept through Lord Akeldama and his young men leaving, the sunrise, the release of the werewolves—now back in human form—and Lord Maccon's explanation of events to his pack.

She even slept through the earl gently transferring her into Professor Lyall's arms and the Beta carrying her rapidly past the arriving press, her head, and thus identity, covered by one of Lord Akeldama's ever-present lace handkerchiefs.

She did not, however, sleep through her mother's shrieks upon her arrival back at the Loontwill town house. Mrs. Loontwill was waiting up for them in the front parlor. And she was *not* pleased.

"Where have you been all night, young lady?" said her mother in the sepulchral tones of the deeply put-upon.

Felicity and Evylin appeared in the doorway of the parlor, wearing nightdresses and draped in heavy pelisses and shocked expressions. Upon noticing Professor Lyall, they squeaked in alarm and dashed back up to their rooms to dress as quickly as possible, horrified that decorum dictate they miss any part of the undoubted drama occurring downstairs.

Miss Tarabotti blinked at her mother sleepily. "Uh . . ." She could not think. *I was off meeting with a vampire, got abducted by scientists, attacked by a werewolf, and then spent the remainder of the night holding hands with a naked peer of the realm.* She said, "Uh . . ." again.

"She was with the Earl of Woolsey," said Professor Lyall firmly, in a tone of voice that brooked no objection, as though that settled the matter.

Mrs. Loontwill ignored his tone entirely and made a move as if to strike her daughter. "Alexia! You wanton hussy!"

Professor Lyall twisted fast so that his charge, still held in his arms, was well out of the woman's reach and glared furiously.

Mrs. Loontwill turned her wrath on him, like a rabid poodle. "I will have you know, young man, no daughter of mine spends an entire night away from home with a gentleman without being securely married to that gentleman first! I do not care if he *is* an earl. You werewolf types may have different rules for this kind of affair, but this *is* the nineteenth century, and we do not hold with such shenanigans. Why, I ought to have my husband call your Alpha out right now!"

Professor Lyall raised one refined brow. "He is welcome to the attempt. I would not recommend that particular course of action. To the best of my recollection, Lord Maccon has never actually lost a fight." He looked down at Alexia. "Except to Miss Tarabotti, of course."

Alexia grinned up at him. "You can put me down now, Professor. I am quite awake and able to stand. Mama will do that to a person. She is like a glass of cold water."

Professor Lyall did as she requested.

Miss Tarabotti found that she had not actually spoken the truth. Her whole body ached most awfully, and her feet did not seem to wish to work as instructed. She stumbled heavily to one side.

Professor Lyall made to grab her and missed.

With the majestic efficiency of all good butlers, Floote appeared at her side and took her arm, preventing her from falling.

"Thank you, Floote," said Alexia, leaning gratefully against him.

Felicity and Evylin, both properly attired in cotton day dresses, reappeared and went immediately to sit on the chesterfield before they could be told to leave.

Alexia looked about and noticed one family member still absent. "Where *is* the squire?"

"Never you mind that, missy. What is going on? I demand an immediate explanation," insisted her mother, waggling a finger.

Just then, there came the most imperious knocking on the front door. Floote transferred Alexia back to Professor Lyall and went to answer it. Lyall ushered Miss Tarabotti over to the wingback chair. With a nostalgic smile, Alexia sat down in it.

"We are *not* at home!" yelled Mrs. Loontwill after Floote. "To anyone!"

"You are at home to me, madam," said a very autocratic voice.

The Queen of England swept into the room: a petite woman, in late middle life but wearing it very well.

Floote trailed in after and said, in tones of shock Alexia had never thought to hear from her unflappable butler, "Her Most Royal Highness, Queen Victoria, to see Miss Tarabotti."

Mrs. Loontwill fainted.

Alexia thought it the best, most sensible thing her mama had done in a very long while. Floote uncorked a bottle of smelling salts and went to revive her, but Alexia shook her head firmly. Then she made to rise and curtsy, but the queen raised her hand.

"No formality, Miss Tarabotti. I understand you have had an interesting night," she said.

Miss Tarabotti nodded mutely and made a polite gesture for the queen to sit. She was mortified by what now seemed the shabby clutter of her family's front parlor. Her Most Royal Highness did not seem to notice, sitting down on a mahogany side chair next to Alexia, moving it so her back was to the collapsed form of Mrs. Loontwill.

Miss Tarabotti turned to her sisters. Both had their mouths open and were flapping about like ineffectual fish.

"Felicity, Evylin, out, now," she ordered quite curtly.

Professor Lyall helped hustle the two girls from the room and would have followed, but the queen said curtly, "Stay, Professor. We may need your expertise."

Floote glided out with an expression that said he would keep all prying ears at bay, although probably not his own.

The queen looked at Alexia a long moment. "You are not at all what I expected," she said at last.

Miss Tarabotti refrained from saying, "Neither are you." Instead she said, "You knew to expect something?"

"Dear girl, you are one of the only preternaturals on British soil. We approved your father's immigration papers all those many years ago. We were informed the moment of your birth. We have watched your progress since then with interest. We even considered interfering when all this folderol with Lord Maccon began to complicate matters. It has gone on quite long enough. You will be marrying him, I understand?"

Alexia nodded mutely.

"Good, we approve." She nodded as though she had somehow had a hand in this outcome.

Professor Lyall said, "Not everyone does."

The queen actually snorted at that. "*We* are the one whose opinion counts, are we not? The potentate and the dewan are trusted advisors, but they are only that: advisors. No legal records for our empire or any previous one forbid marriage between supernatural and preternatural outright. Yes, the potentate informs us hive tradition bans such a union, and werewolf legend warns against fraternization, but we require this business settled. We will not have our best BUR agent distracted, and we need this young lady married."

"Why?" Alexia asked, confused that her single state should concern the Queen of England.

"Ah, that. You are aware of the Shadow Council?" The queen settled herself in the hard chair, as much as queens do, which is to say her shoulders relaxed slightly.

Alexia nodded. "The potentate acts as your official vampire consultant and the dewan in the werewolf capacity. Rumors are that most of your political acumen comes from the potentate's advice and your military skill from the dewan's."

"Alexia," Professor Lyall growled a warning.

The queen looked more amused than insulted at this. She even dropped the royal "we" for the space of a few moments. "Well, I suppose my enemies must blame somebody. I will say that those two are invaluable, when they are not bickering with each other. But there is a third post that has been vacant since before my time. An advisor meant to break the stalemate between the other two."

Miss Tarabotti frowned. "A ghost?"

"No, no. We have plenty of those flitting around Buckingham Palace; cannot keep them quiet half the time. We certainly do not need one in any official capacity. Not when they cannot maintain solidity that long. No, what we require is a muhjah."

Alexia looked confused.

The queen explained. "Traditionally the third member of the Shadow Council is a preternatural, the muhjah. Your father declined the post." She sniffed. "Italians. Now, there simply is not enough of your set left to vote on your nomination, so it will have to be an appointed position. But voting is mostly a formality, even for the positions of dewan and potentate. At least it has been during my reign."

"No one else wants the job," said Professor Lyall with feeling.

The queen gave him a reproving look.

He leaned forward and explained further. "It is a political post," he said. "Lots of arguing and paperwork and books being consulted all the time. It is not at all like BUR, you understand?"

Miss Tarabotti's eyes positively sparkled. "Sounds delightful." Yet she remained suspicious. "Why me? What could I possibly offer against two such experienced voices?"

The queen was not used to being questioned. She looked at Professor Lyall.

He said, "I told you she was difficult."

"Aside from breaking a stalemate, our muhjah is the only truly mobile unit of the three councilors. Our potentate is confined to a narrow territory, like most vampires, and cannot function during the day. Our dewan is more mobile, but he cannot travel by dirigible and is incapacitated every full moon. We have relied upon BUR to make up for the Shadow Council's weakness in this regard, but we would prefer a muhjah whose attention is solely on the Crown's concerns and who can come to us directly."

"So there *will* be some active duty?" Miss Tarabotti was even more intrigued.

"Uh-oh," muttered Professor Lyall, "I do not think Lord Maccon fully comprehended this aspect of the position."

"The muhjah is the voice of the modern age. We have faith in our potentate and our dewan, but they are old and set in their ways. They require balance from someone who keeps up with current lines of scientific inquiry, not to mention the interests and suspicions of the daylight world. We are concerned that this Hypocras Club is a symptom of greater unrest. We are worried that our BUR agents did not uncover it sooner. You have proven yourself an able investigator and a well-read young woman. As Lady Maccon, you would also possess the standing needed to infiltrate the highest levels of society."

Alexia looked between Professor Lyall and the queen. Lyall looked worried. That decided her. "Very well, I accept."

The queen nodded happily. "Your future husband indicated you would not be averse to the position. Most excellent! We convene twice a week, Thursday and Sunday nights, unless there is a crisis of some kind, in which case you are expected to be readily available. You will be answerable to the Crown alone. We will expect you to start the week after your wedding. So do hurry it up."

Alexia smiled foolishly and looked at Professor Lyall from under her lashes. "Conall approves?"

The werewolf grinned. "He recommended you to the job months ago. The first time you interfered in one of his operations and he knew BUR would not be allowed to hire you. Of course, he did not know the muhjah engaged in active investigations on the queen's behalf."

The queen said, "Of course, initially we objected to the recommendation. We cannot have a single young lady in such a powerful position. It simply is *not* done." She looked almost mischievous and lowered her voice. "In all confidentiality, my dear, we do believe the Woolsey Alpha thinks being muhjah will keep you out of his way."

Alexia slapped a hand to her mouth in an excess of embarrassment. To have the Queen of England thinking of her as an interfering busybody!

Professor Lyall crossed his arms and said, "Begging your pardon, Your Majesty, but I think he wants to set Miss Tarabotti at the dewan and watch the fur fly."

Queen Victoria smiled. "They never have gotten along, those two."

Professor Lyall nodded. "Both are too much alpha."

Miss Tarabotti looked suddenly worried. "That is not why he is marrying me, is it? So I can be muhjah?" A little bit of her old insecurity came back to haunt her.

"Do not be ridiculous," admonished the queen curtly. "He has been mad for you these many months, ever since you prodded him in the nether regions with a hedgehog. It has been driving everyone balmy, all this dancing about. Glad it is finally getting settled. This wedding of yours is going to be *the* social event of the season. Half the guests in attendance will be there simply to make certain you both go through with it. Outside of enough, that is our opinion."

Miss Tarabotti, for one of the first and last times in her life, was entirely at a loss for words.

The queen stood up. "Well, that is settled, then. We are most pleased.

And now we suggest you go to bed, young lady. You look exhausted." With that, she swept from the house.

"She is so short," said Miss Tarabotti to Professor Lyall once the queen had gone.

"Alexia," said a tremulous voice from the other side of the room. "what *is* going on?"

Alexia sighed and struggled to her feet, wobbling over to her confused mama. All of Mrs. Loontwill's anger had evaporated upon waking to find her daughter in conversation with the Queen of England.

"Why was the queen here? Why were you discussing the Shadow Council? What is a muhjah?" Mrs. Loontwill was very confused. She seemed to have utterly lost control of the situation.

Me, thought Alexia with pleasure. *I will be muhjah. This is going to be such fun.* Aloud she said the only thing calculated to shut her mother up. "Do not worry about a thing, Mama. I am going to marry Lord Maccon."

It worked. Mrs. Loontwill's mouth snapped closed. Her expression evolved rapidly from perturbation to uncontrollable elation. "You caught him!" she breathed in delight.

Felicity and Evylin reentered the room, both wide-eyed. For the first time in their entire lives, they regarded their older sister with something other than mild contempt.

Noticing her other two daughters had arrived, Mrs. Loontwill added hastily, "Not that I approve your methods of catching him, of course. Out all night, indeed. But thank heavens you did!" Then in an aside, "Girls, your sister is going to *marry* Lord Maccon."

Felicity and Evylin looked even more shocked, but they recovered quickly enough.

"But, Mama, why was the queen here?" Evylin wanted to know.

"Never mind that now, Evy," said Felicity impatiently. "The important question is, what will you wear for a wedding dress, Alexia? You look horrible in white."

The afternoon papers reported the bulk of the news accurately enough. Miss Tarabotti and Lord Akeldama's names were left out, and the exact makeup of the experiments was omitted in favor of emphasizing their sensational grisliness and illegal nature.

The reports threw all of London into a fervor of speculation. The Royal Society scrambled to deny any association with the Hypocras Club, but BUR commenced a whirlwind of undercover operations. A good many other scientists, some with well-known names indeed, suddenly found themselves without funding, on the run, or in prison. No one ever explained the octopuses.

The Hypocras Club was shut down permanently and its premises impounded and placed on the market. It was bought by a nice young couple from East Duddage whose success in the chamber-pot business had brought them up in the world. The Duchess of Snodgrove regarded the entire affair as a travesty designed solely to impinge on her social standing. The fact that her new neighbors, nice young couple or no, hailed from Duddage and were involved in *trade* sent her into a fit of hysteria so pervasive her husband removed her instantly to the country ducal estates in Berkshire for the sake of everyone's health. He sold their town house.

As far as Miss Tarabotti was concerned, the worst thing to result from the whole sordid affair was that, although both club premises and Lord Akeldama's house had been searched top to bottom, BUR never did recover her brass parasol.

"Bah," she complained to her intended as they strolled through Hyde Park late one evening, "I did so love that parasol."

A carriage of dowagers swept past. One or two nodded in their direction. Lord Maccon tipped his hat to them.

Society had come, albeit reluctantly, to accept the fact that one of the most eligible bachelors was going off the market by marrying a spinster nobody. One or two, witness the nods, had even come around to extending cautious overtures of friendship to Miss Tarabotti. Miss Tarabotti further improved her standing among the aristocracy as a force to be reckoned with by turning her large nose up at such sycophancy. Lady Maccon-to-be was clearly as formidable as her intended.

Lord Maccon took Miss Tarabotti's arm soothingly. "I shall have them make you a hundred such parasols, one for every dress."

Miss Tarabotti raised her eyebrows at him. "Silver tipped, you realize?"

"Well, you will be facing down the dewan several times a week; you might need some silver. Though I do not anticipate he will give you too much trouble."

Alexia, who had not yet had an opportunity to meet the other members of the Shadow Council and would not until after her wedding, looked at Lord Maccon curiously. "Is he really that fainthearted?"

"Nope. Simply ill-prepared."

"For what?"

"You, my love," the earl said, tempering the insult with an endearment.

Alexia sputtered in such a charming way that Lord Maccon simply had to kiss her, right there, in the middle of Hyde Park. Which made her sputter even more. Which made him kiss her more. It was a vicious cycle.

Of course, it was Mr. MacDougall who had taken possession of the brass parasol. The poor young man had slipped everyone's mind, including Alexia's, as soon as the Hypocras investigation was put to rest. He took the parasol back to America with him—as a sort of memento. He had been genuinely heartbroken to read the announcement of Miss Tarabotti's engagement in the *Gazette*. He returned to his mansion in Massachusetts and threw himself with renewed scientific vigor and a more cautious attitude into measuring the human soul. Several years later, he married a veritable battle-ax of a woman and happily allowed himself to be bossed around for the remainder of his days.

EPILOGUE

MISS Alexia Tarabotti did not wear white to her wedding. Apart from the fact that Felicity was perfectly correct in stating that it clashed something terrible with her skin tone, she figured that when one has seen one's affianced naked and covered in blood, one is no longer quite pure enough for white.

Instead, she wore ivory: a sumptuous French-made dress selected and designed with Lord Akeldama's consummate assistance. It took into account the new trend in cleaner lines and long sleeves, hugging her upper torso and showing her curves to perfection. The square neckline of the bodice was cut quite low, much to Lord Maccon's approval, but it came up high in the back and around her neck in a demi-collar, reminiscent of some exotic robe from the Rococo era. It was held closed by an exquisite opal brooch at her throat and started a fashion trend in necklines that persisted for nearly three whole weeks.

Miss Tarabotti told no one the dress's design was a last-minute alteration due entirely to the fact that, two days before the wedding, the earl got her alone in the dining room for almost an hour. As always, the bite marks *she* had left on *him* faded the moment they separated. She sighed, not unhappily. *Really, the amount of attention he paid to her neck, one would think he was a vampire.*

Biffy did her hair for the prestigious event. He had been loaned to Miss Tarabotti for the duration of the wedding planning. He knew a phenomenal amount about who *must* be invited, who *should* be invited, what the invitations ought to look like, which flowers to order, and so forth. As bridesmaid, Ivy Hisselpenny did her best, but the poor thing was a tad overwhelmed by the particulars. Biffy developed a dab hand at keeping Ivy well out of tasks that involved style of any kind, so that, in the end, everything looked lovely and managed not to clash. Even Ivy.

The ceremony was to take place just after sunset on a quarter-moon night so that everyone could attend. Just about *everyone* did: including the queen, Lord Akeldama and *all* his drones, and the cream of London society. Most notably absent were the vampires, who had not even bothered to politely refuse invitations but instead snubbed the couple outright.

"They have good reason to object," said Lord Akeldama.

"But not you?"

"Oh, I have good reason, too, but I trust you, little innovator. And I like change." He left it at that, despite Alexia's pointed further inquiries.

The Westminster hive proved the exception of the mass vampire cut direct. Countess Nadasdy sent Lord Ambrose to observe the ceremony, but clearly under duress. She also sent Alexia an unexpected gift, which arrived while she was dressing the afternoon of the wedding.

"Did I not say she would get rid of me?" said Angelique with a self-deprecating smile.

Miss Tarabotti was a little overwhelmed. "You are in favor of a new position? With me?"

The violet-eyed girl shrugged in a blasé French kind of way. "My master, he iz dead because of ze scientists. Lady's maid, it iz better than housemaid."

"But what about your drone status?"

Angelique looked coy. "Zer iz always claviger, yez?"

"Very well, then, welcome," said Miss Tarabotti. Of course, the French girl must, perforce, be a spy, but Alexia reasoned it was better to know and keep her close than force the hive into more desperate maneuvering. It did cause a twinge of worry. Why were the vampires fussing so?

Angelique began immediately to assist Biffy in finishing the last of Alexia's coiled updo, arguing mildly on the subject of a flower above the right ear.

They both protested when Alexia stood, not yet fully dressed, and waved them off.

"I must pay someone a visit," she said imperiously. It was late afternoon: the sun had not yet set, and there was still much to do before the big event that night.

"But right now?" sputtered Biffy. "It is your wedding evening!"

"And we have only just finished ze hair!"

Miss Tarabotti could tell that these two were going to be a force to be reckoned with. But so was she. Alexia instructed them to get her dress ready and that she would be back within the hour, so not to fret. "It is not like anything can actually occur without me, is it? I have to see a friend about the sun."

She took the Loontwills' carriage without asking and went round to Lord Akeldama's gilt-edged town house. She sailed in the front door past various drones and woke Lord Akeldama from his deadlike daytime sleep with a touch.

Human, he blinked at her groggily.

"It is almost sunset," said Miss Tarabotti with a tiny smile, her hand on his shoulder. "Come with me."

Clad only in his sleeping robe, she took the vampire firmly by the hand and led him up through the splendor of his gilt house and out onto the rooftop into the waning light.

Alexia rested her cheek on his shoulder, and they stood silently together and watched the sun set over the city.

Lord Akeldama refrained from pointing out she would be late for her own wedding.

Miss Tarabotti refrained from pointing out that he was crying.

She figured it was a good way to end her career as a spinster.

Lord Akeldama also cried during the ceremony, which took place at Westminster Abby. Well, he was a bit of a weeper. So did Mrs. Loontwill. Miss Tarabotti, rather callously, figured her mama's tears were more for the loss of her butler than for the loss of her daughter. Floote had given notice and moved, along with Alexia's father's entire library, into Woolsey Castle that very morning. Both were settling in nicely.

The wedding was hailed as a masterpiece of social engineering and physical beauty. Best of all, as Alexia's bridesmaid, Miss Hisselpenny was not permitted to choose her own hat. The ceremony went unexpectedly smoothly, and in no time at all, Miss Tarabotti found herself Lady Maccon.

Afterward, everyone assembled in Hyde Park, which was admittedly unusual, but exceptions had to be made when werewolves were involved. And there certainly were a goodly number of werewolves. Not simply Lord Maccon's pack but all the loners, other packs, and clavigers within traveling distance had attended the celebration.

Luckily, there was enough meat for them all. The only aspect of wedding procedure Alexia had invested genuine involvement and time into was the food. As a result, the tables set about their corner of the park fairly groaned under their burdens. There were galantines of guinea fowl stuffed with minced tongue quivering in aspic jelly and decorated with feathers made of lemon-soaked apple peel. No fewer than eight pigeons in truffle gravy nesting in coils of pastry made their appearance and disappearance. There were stewed oysters, fried haddock fillets in anchovy sauce, and grilled sole with peach compote. Having noted Lord Maccon's fondness for poultry, the Loontwill cook provided woodcock pie, roast pheasant in butter sauce with peas and celery, and a brace of grouse. There was a baron of beef, a forequarter of mutton glazed with red wine, and lamb cutlets with fresh mint and broad beans—all offered on the rarer side. Corner dishes included lobster salad, spinach and eggs, vegetable fritters, and baked potatoes. In addition to the massive bride's cake and the piles of nutty groom's cakes for the guests to take home, there were rhubarb tarts, stewed cherries, fresh strawberries and purple grapes, gravy boats of clotted cream, and plum pudding. The food was declared an unqualified success, and many a plan was made to visit Woolsey Castle for luncheon once Alexia took over supervision of its kitchens.

Miss Hisselpenny took the entire event as an excuse to flirt with anything male and on two legs, and a few on four. This seemed perfectly acceptable, until Alexia spotted her going goggle-eyed over the repulsive Lord Ambrose. The new Lady Maccon crooked an imperious finger at Professor Lyall and sent him to salvage the situation.

Professor Lyall, muttering something about "new brides having more to concern themselves with than meddling," did as ordered. He insinuated himself seamlessly into the conversation between Lord Ambrose and Miss Hisselpenny, and hustled Ivy away for a waltz without anyone the wiser to his militarylike intervention tactics. He then carried Ivy off to the other side of the lawn, which was serving as the dance floor, and introduced her to Lord Maccon's redheaded claviger, Tunstell.

Tunstell looked at Ivy.

Ivy looked at Tunstell.

Professor Lyall noted with satisfaction that they wore identical expressions of the stunned-donkey variety.

"Tunstell," instructed the Beta, "ask Miss Hisselpenny if she would like to dance."

"Would you, um, like to, um, dance, Miss Hisselpenny?" stuttered the normally loquacious young man.

"Oh," said Ivy. "Oh yes, please."

Professor Lyall, all forgotten, nodded to himself. Then he dashed off to deal with Lord Akeldama and Lord Ambrose who seemed to be getting into some sort of heated argument on the subject of waistcoats.

"Well, wife?" asked Alexia's new husband, whisking her about the lawn.

"Yes, husband?"

"Think we can officially escape yet?"

Alexia looked about nervously. Everyone seemed to be suddenly fleeing the dance floor, and the music was changing. "Um, I think, perhaps, not just yet."

They both stopped and looked about.

"This was not part of the wedding plan," she said in annoyance. "Biffy, what is happening here?" she yelled.

From the sidelines, Biffy shrugged and shook his head.

The clavigers were causing the disturbance. They had arranged themselves in a large circle about Lord Maccon and Alexia and were slowly pushing everyone else away. Alexia noticed that Ivy, little traitor, was helping them.

Lord Maccon slapped his forehead with his hand. "God's truth, they aren't really? That old tradition?" He trailed off as the howling began. "Aye, they are. Well, my dear, best get used to this kind of thing."

The wolves burst into the open circle like a river of fur. Under the quarter moon, there was no anger or bloodlust in their movements. Instead it was like a dance, liquid and beautiful. The fuzzy throng was comprised of not just the Woolsey Pack but also all the visiting werewolves. Almost thirty of them jumped and pranced and yipped as they coiled around the newly married couple.

Alexia held very still and relaxed into the dizzying movement. The wolves circled closer and closer until they pressed against her skirts, all hot predator breath and soft fur. Then one wolf stopped directly next to Lord Maccon—a thin, sandy, vulpinelike creature—Professor Lyall.

With a wink at Alexia, the Beta threw his head back and barked, once, sharply.

The wolves stopped stock-still and then did the most organized, politely amusing thing. They lined up in a neat circle all about and one by one came forward. As each wolf stood before the newly married pair, he lowered his head between his forelegs, showing the back of his neck in a funny little bow.

"Are they paying homage to you?" Alexia asked her husband.

He laughed. "Lord, no. Why would they bother with me?"

"Oh," replied Alexia, realizing it was meant to honor her. "Should I *do* something?"

Conall kissed her cheek. "You are wonderful as you are."

The last to come forward was Lyall. His bow was somehow more elegant and more restrained than anyone else's.

Once completed, he barked again, and they all leaped into action: running three times around the couple and dashing off into the night.

After that, everything else was anticlimactic, and as soon as civility allowed, Alexia's new husband hustled her into the waiting carriage and on the road out of London toward Woolsey Castle.

A few of the werewolves returned then, still in wolf form, to run alongside the carriage.

Just outside of town, Lord Maccon stuck his head out the coach window and told them unceremoniously to "shove off."

"I gave the pack the evening out," he informed Alexia, retracting his head and closing the window.

His wife issued him an arch look.

"Oh, very well. I told them if they showed their furry faces round Woolsey Castle for the next three days, I would personally eviscerate them."

Alexia smiled. "Good gracious, where will they all stay?"

"Lyall muttered something about invading Lord Akeldama's town house." Conall looked smugly amused.

Alexia laughed. "Would I were a fly on that wall!"

Her husband turned about and without further ado began unclasping the brooch that held the neck of her beautiful gown together.

"Intriguing design, this dress," he commented without real interest.

"Rather say, necessary design," replied his lady as the neck fell away to show a neat pattern of tiny love bites all about her throat. Lord Maccon traced them with proprietary pride.

"What are you up to?" Alexia asked as he gently kissed the tiny bruises. She was distracted by the delicious tingly sensation this caused, but not enough to forgo noticing his hands were round the back of the bodice of her dress, sliding open the row of buttons there.

"I should think that would be obvious by now," he replied with a grin. He pushed back the top of her dress and became intent on undoing her corset. His lips moved down from her neck to delve into the region of her décolletage.

"Conall," Alexia murmured hazily, almost losing her objections as new and delicious sensation extended from nipples turned strangely tight and hard. "We are in a moving *carriage*! Why this constant preference for inappropriate locations for amorous activities?"

"Mmm, not to worry," he purposefully misconstrued her protestations. "I gave the coachman instructions to take the long way round." He helped her to stand and shucked her out of her dress, skirts, and corset with consummate rapidity.

Alexia, in only a shift, stockings, and shoes, crossed her arms over her breasts self-consciously.

Her new husband ran large calloused hands around the hem of her chemise, stroking at the soft skin of her upper thighs. Then he lifted the material up to cup her buttocks before raising that last bastion of her admittedly deteriorated dignity over her head and discarding it.

Until that moment, Alexia realized she had never before seen real hunger in his eyes. They were in physical contact, supernatural and preternatural, but nevertheless, his eyes had turned to pure wolf yellow. He looked at her, clad in nothing but stockings and ivory button boots, as though he wanted to eat her alive.

"You are trying to get back at me, are you?" she said accusingly, trying to calm him a little. The intensity was scaring her. She was, after all, relatively new to this kind of activity.

He paused and looked at her, yellow fading in genuine surprise. "For what?"

"Back at the Hypocras Club, when you were naked and I was not."

He pulled her toward him. She had no idea how he managed to attend to himself as well as her, but somehow he had opened the flap at the front of his breeches. Everything else remained covered. "I'll admit the thought had crossed my mind. Now sit."

"What, there?"

"Aye, there."

Alexia looked dubious. However, there were destined to be some arguments in their relationship she could not hope to win. This was one of them. The carriage, rather too conveniently, pitched slightly to one side, and she stumbled forward. Conall caught her and guided her into his lap in one smooth movement.

He did not do anything else with that particular proximity for a moment; instead he turned his attention to her generous breasts, first kissing, then nibbling, then biting, a progression that had Alexia squirming in such a way as to force the very tip of him inside her whether she willed it or no.

"Really," she insisted, panting, "this is a most unseemly location for such activities."

Just then, the carriage lurched over a rut in the road and silenced all further objections. The movement brought her flush on top of him, naked thighs pressed against the material of his breeches. Lord Maccon groaned, a rapt expression on his face.

Alexia gasped and winced. "Ouch!" She leaned forward against her husband and bit his shoulder hard in revenge. Hard enough to draw blood. "That hurt."

He took the bite without complaint and looked worried. "Does it still?"

The carriage bumped again. This time Alexia sighed. Something extremely odd and tingly was beginning to occur in her nether regions.

"I shall take that as a no," said her husband, and began to move, rocking with the motion of the carriage.

What happened after that was all sweat, and moans, and pulsing sensation to which Alexia decided, after about one second of deep deliberation, she was not averse. It culminated in the most intriguing second heartbeat emerging right around the area where he had impaled himself. Shortly thereafter, her husband gave a long low groan and collapsed back on the carriage cushions, cradling her against him.

"Ooo," said Alexia, fascinated, "it shrinks back down again. The books didn't detail that occurrence."

The earl laughed. "You must show me these books of yours."

She folded forward on top of him and nuzzled down into his cravat, pleased to be with a man who was strong enough to be untroubled at having her draped atop him. "Books of my father's," she corrected.

"I hear he had an interesting reputation."

"Mmmm, so his library would suggest." She closed her eyes, relaxing against her husband. Then she thought of something, reared back, and whacked him on the waistcoat with one balled-up fist.

"Ouch," said her long-suffering husband. "Now what are you upset about?"

"Isn't that just *like* you!" she said.

"What?"

"You took it as a challenge, didn't you? My stopping you from seducing me back at the Hypocras Club."

Lord Maccon grinned wolfishly, though his eyes had gone back to their human tawny brown color. "Naturally."

She frowned, considering how best to handle this situation. Then she shifted back toward him and began busily untying his cravat and divesting him of coat, waistcoat, and shirt.

"Well, then," she said.

"Aye?"

"I am still holding that the carriage is an entirely inappropriate place for conjugal activities. Would you like to prove me wrong a second time?"

"Are you challenging me, Lady Maccon?" asked Lord Maccon in mock annoyance. But he was already lifting himself up to facilitate her removal of his clothing.

Alexia smiled down at his bare chest and then looked once more into his eyes. The yellow was back. "All the time."

CHANGELESS

The Parasol Protectorate:
Book the Second

Acknowledgments

With grateful thanks to the three least-appreciated and hardest-working proselytizers of the written word: independent bookstores, librarians, and teachers.

CHAPTER ONE

Wherein Things Disappear,
Alexia Gets Testy Over Tents,
and Ivy Has an Announcement

They are what?"

Lord Conall Maccon, Earl of Woolsey, was yelling. Loudly. This was to be expected from Lord Maccon, who was generally a loud sort of gentleman—the earbleeding combination of lung capacity and a large barrel chest.

Alexia Maccon, Lady Woolsey, muhjah to the queen, Britain's secret preternatural weapon extraordinaire, blinked awake from a deep and delicious sleep.

"Wasn't me," she immediately said, without having the barest hint of an idea as to what her husband was carrying on about. Of course, it usually *was* her, but it would not do to fess up right away, regardless of whatever it was that had his britches in a bunch this time. Alexia screwed her eyes shut and squirmed farther into the warmth of down-stuffed blankets. Couldn't they argue about it later?

"What do you mean *gone*?" The bed shook slightly with the sheer volume behind Lord Maccon's yell. The amazing thing was that he wasn't nearly as loud as he could be when he really put his lungs into it.

"Well, I certainly did not tell them to go," denied Alexia into her pillow. She wondered who "they" were. Then she came about to the realization, taking a fluffy-cottony sort of pathway to get there, that he wasn't yelling at her but at someone else. In their bedroom.

Oh dear.

Unless he was yelling at himself.

Oh *dear*.

"What, *all* of them?"

Alexia's scientific side wondered idly at the power of sound waves—hadn't she heard of a recent Royal Society pamphlet on the subject?

"All at once?"

Lady Maccon sighed, rolled toward the hollering, and cracked one eyelid. Her husband's large naked back filled her field of vision. To see any more, she'd have to lever herself upright. Since that would probably expose her to more cold air, she declined to lever. She did, however, observe that the sun was barely down. What was Conall doing awake and aloud so freakishly early? For, while her husband roaring was not uncommon, its occurrence in the wee hours of late afternoon was. Inhuman decency dictated that even Woolsey Castle's Alpha werewolf remain quiet at this time of day.

"How wide of a radius, exactly? It canna have extended this far."

Oh dear, his Scottish accent had put in an appearance. That never bode well for anyone.

"All over London? No? *Just* the entire Thames embankment and city center. That is simply not possible."

This time Lady Maccon managed to discern a mild murmuring response to her husband's latest holler. Well, she consoled herself, at least he hadn't gone entirely potty. But who would dare attempt to rustle up Lord Maccon in his private quarters at such an abysmal hour? She tried once more to see over his back. *Why* did he have to be so substantial?

She levered.

Alexia Maccon was known as a lady of regal bearing and not much more. Society generally considered her looks too swarthy to give much credence despite her rank. Alexia, herself, had always believed good posture was her last best hope and was proud to have acquired the "regal bearing" epithet. This morning, however, blankets and pillows thwarted her; she could only flounder gracelessly up to her elbows, her backbone as limp as a noodle.

All that her Herculean effort revealed was a hint of wispy silver and a vaguely human form: Formerly Merriway.

"Mummer murmur," said Formerly Merriway, straining for full apparition in the not-quite darkness. She was a polite ghost, relatively young and well preserved, and still entirely sane.

"Oh, for goodness' sake." Lord Maccon seemed to be getting only more irritated. Lady Maccon knew that particular tone of voice well—it was usually directed at her. "But there is nothing on this Earth that can *do* that."

Formerly Merriway said something else.

"Well, have they consulted all the daylight agents?"

Alexia strained to hear. Already gifted with a low, sweet voice, the ghost was difficult to understand when she intentionally dampened her tone. Formerly Merriway might have said, "Yes, and they have no idea either."

The ghost seemed frightened, which caused Alexia more concern than Lord Maccon's irritation (which was sadly frequent). Little could frighten the already dead, with the possible exception of a preternatural. And even Alexia, soulless, was only dangerous under very specific circumstances.

"What, no idea at all? Right." The earl tossed his blankets aside and climbed out of bed.

Formerly Merriway gasped and shimmered about, presenting her transparent back to the completely naked man.

Alexia appreciated the courtesy, even if Lord Maccon did not. Polite to the core was poor little Merriway. Or what was left of her core. Lady Maccon, on the other hand, was not so reticent. Her husband had a decidedly fine backside, if she did say so herself. And she had said so, to her scandalized friend Miss Ivy Hisselpenny, on more than one occasion. It may be far too early to be awake, but it was never too early to admire something of that caliber. The artistically pleasing body part drifted out of view as her husband strode toward his dressing chamber.

"Where is Lyall?" he barked.

Lady Maccon tried to go back to sleep.

"What! Lyall's gone too? Is *everyone* going to disappear on me? No, I did not send him. . . ." A pause. "Oh yes, you are perfectly correct, I did. The pack was"—*blub blub blub*—"coming in at"—*blub, blub*—"station." *Splash.* "Shouldn't he have returned by now?"

Her husband was obviously washing, as periodically his bellowing was interrupted by soggy noises. Alexia strained to hear Tunstell's voice. Without his valet, her louder half was bound to look quite disastrously disheveled. It was never a good idea to let the earl dress unsupervised.

"Right, well, send a claviger for him posthaste."

At which point, Formerly Merriway's spectral form vanished from view.

Conall reappeared in Alexia's line of sight and gathered up his gold pocket watch from the bedside table. "Of course, they will take it as an insult, but nothing to be done about it."

Ha, she had been right. He was, in fact, not dressed at all but was wearing only a cloak. *No Tunstell then.*

The earl seemed to remember his wife for the first time.

Alexia counterfeited sleep.

Conall shook Alexia gently, admiring both the tousled mound of inky hair and the artfully feigned disinterest. When his shaking became insistent, she blinked long lashes at him.

"Ah, good evening, my dear."

Alexia glared at her husband out of slightly red-rimmed brown eyes. This early evening tomfoolery wouldn't be so horrible if he had not kept her up half the day. Not that those particular exertions had been unpleasant, simply exuberant and lengthy.

"What are you about, husband?" she inquired, her voice laced buttery-smooth with suspicion.

"All apologies, my dear."

Lady Maccon absolutely hated it when her husband called her his "dear." It meant he was up to something but was not going to tell her about it.

"I must run off to the office early tonight. Some important BUR business has cropped up." From the cloak and the fact that his canines were showing, Alexia surmised that he literally meant run, in wolf form. Whatever was going on must need urgent attention, indeed. Lord Maccon usually preferred to arrive at BUR in carriage, comfort, and style, not fur.

"Has it?" muttered Alexia.

The earl began to tuck the blankets about his wife. His large hands were unexpectedly gentle. Touching his preternatural spouse, his canines disappeared. In that brief moment, he was mortal.

"Are you meeting with the Shadow Council tonight?" he asked.

Alexia considered. Was it Thursday? "Yes."

"You are in for an interesting conference," advised the earl, goading her.

Alexia sat up, undoing all of his nice tucking. "What? Why?" The blankets fell, revealing that Lady Maccon's endowments were considerable and not fabricated through fashionable artifice such as stuffed corset or too-tight stays. Despite nightly familiarity with this fact, Lord Maccon was prone to dragging her onto secluded balconies at balls in order to check and "make certain" this remained the case.

"I *am* sorry for waking you so early, my dear." There was that dreaded phrase again. "I promise I shall make it up to you in the morning." He waggled his eyebrows at her lasciviously and leaned down for a long and thorough kiss.

Lady Maccon sputtered and pushed at his large chest ineffectually. "Conall, *what* is going on?"

But her irritating werewolf of a husband was already away and out of the room.

"Pack!" His holler resounded through the hallway. At least this time he had made a pretense of seeing to her comfort by shutting the door first.

Alexia and Conall Maccon's bedroom took up the whole of one of the highest towers Woolsey had to offer, which, admittedly, was more of a dignified pimple off the top of one wall. Despite this comparative isolation, the earl's bellow could be heard throughout most of the massive building, even down to the back parlor, where his clavigers were taking their tea.

The Woolsey clavigers worked hard about their various duties during the day, looking after slumbering werewolf charges and taking care of daylight pack business. For most, tea was a brief and necessary respite before they were called to their other nonpack work. As packs tended to favor boldly creative companions, and Woolsey was close to London, more than a few of its clavigers were actively engaged in West End theatricals. Despite the lure of Aldershot pudding, Madeira cake, and gunpowder black tea, their lord's yodel had them up and moving as fast as could be desired.

The entire house suddenly became a hubbub of activity: carriages and men on horseback came and went, clattering on the stone cobbles of the forecourt; doors slammed; voices called back and forth. It sounded like the dirigible disembarkation green in Hyde Park.

Emitting that heaviest of sighs that denotes the gravely put-upon, Alexia Maccon rolled herself out of bed and picked up her nightgown from where it lay, a puddle of frills and lace, on the stone floor. It was one of her husband's wedding gifts to her. Or more probably gifts to *him,* as it was made of a soft French silk and had scandalously few pleats. It was quite fashion-forward and daringly French, and Alexia rather liked it. Conall rather liked taking it off her. Which was how it had ended up on the floor. They had negotiated a temporal relationship with the nightgown; most of the time, she was able to wear it only out of the bed. He could be very persuasive when he put his mind, and other parts of his anatomy, to it. Lady Maccon figured she would have to get used to sleeping in the altogether. Although there was that niggling worry that the house might catch fire and cause her to dash about starkers in full view of all. The worry was receding slowly, for she lived with a pack of werewolves and was acclimatizing to their constant nudity—by necessity if not preference. There was, currently, far more hairy masculinity in her life than any Englishwoman should really have to put up with on a monthly basis. That said, half the pack was away fighting in northern India; someday there would be even more full-moon maleness. She thought of her husband; him she had to deal with on a *daily* basis.

A timid knock sounded, followed by a long pause. Then the door to the bedchamber was pushed slowly open, and a heart-shaped face paired with dark blond hair and enormous violet eyes peered in. The eyes were apprehensive. The maid to whom they belonged had learned, to her abject mortification, to give her master and mistress extra time before disturbing them in the bedchamber. One could never predict Lord Maccon's amorous moods, but one could certainly predict his temper if they were interrupted.

Noting his absence with obvious relief, the maid entered carrying a basin of hot water and a warm white towel over one arm. She curtsied gracefully to Alexia. She wore a modish, if somber, gray dress with a crisp white apron pinned over it. Alexia knew, though others did not, that the high white collar about her slender neck disguised multiple bite marks. As if being a former vampire drone in a werewolf household were not shocking enough, the maid then opened her mouth and proved that she was also, quite reprehensibly, French.

"Good evening, madame."

Alexia smiled. "Good evening, Angelique."

The new Lady Maccon, barely three months in, had already established her taste as quite daring, her table as incomparable, and her style as trendsetting. And while it was not generally known among the ton that she sat on the Shadow Council, she was observed to be on friendly terms with Queen Victoria. Couple that with a temperamental werewolf husband of considerable property and social standing, and her eccentricities—such as carrying a parasol at night and retaining an overly pretty French maid—were overlooked by high society.

Angelique placed the basin and a towel on Alexia's dressing table and disappeared once more. She reappeared a polite ten minutes later with a cup of tea, whisked away the used towel and dirty water, and returned with a determined look and an air of quiet authority. Usually, there was a minor contest of wills when dressing Lady Maccon, but recent praise in the society column of the *Lady's Pictorial* had bolstered Alexia's faith in Angelique's decisions à la toilette.

"Very well, you harridan," said Lady Maccon to the silent girl. "What am I wearing tonight?"

Angelique made her selection from the wardrobe: a military-inspired tea-colored affair trimmed in chocolate brown velvet and large brass buttons. It was very smart and appropriate to a business meeting of the Shadow Council.

"You will have to leave off the silk scarf," said Alexia, her token protest. "I shall need to show neck tonight." She did not explain that bite marks were monitored by the palace guards. Angelique was not one of those who knew Alexia Maccon sat as muhjah. She may be Alexia's personal maid, but she was still French, and despite Floote's feeling on the matter, the domestic staff didn't have to know *everything*.

Angelique acquiesced without protest and put Lady Maccon's hair up simply, complementing the severity of the dress. Only a few loops and tendrils peeked out from under a small lace cap. Then Alexia made good her escape, aflutter with curiosity over her husband's early departure.

There was no one to ask. No one waited at the dinner table; clavigers and pack alike had vanished along with the earl. The house was empty but for the servants. Alexia turned her concentrated interest on them, but they scattered about their various tasks with the ease of three months' practice.

The Woolsey butler, Rumpet, refused, with an air of affronted dignity, to answer her questions. Even Floote claimed to have been in the library all afternoon and overheard nothing.

"Floote, truly, you simply *must* be acquainted with what has transpired. I depend upon you to know what is going on! You always do."

Floote gave her a look that made her feel about seven years of age. Despite graduating from butler to personal secretary, Floote had never quite lost his severe aura of butlerness.

He handed Alexia her leather dispatch case. "I reviewed the documents from last Sunday's meeting."

"Well, what is your opinion?" Floote had been with Alexia's father before her, and, despite Alessandro Tarabotti's rather outrageous reputation (or perhaps because of it), Floote had learned *things.* Alexia was finding herself, as muhjah, more and more reliant upon his opinion, if only to confirm her own.

Floote considered. "My concern is with the deregulation clause, madam. I suspect that it is too soon to release the scientists on their own recognizance."

"Mmm, that was my assessment as well. I shall recommend against that particular clause. Thank you, Floote."

The elderly man turned to go.

"Oh, and, Floote."

He turned back, resigned.

"Something substantial has happened to overset my husband. I suspect research in the library may be called for when I return tonight. Best to clear your schedule."

"Very good, madam," said Floote with a little bow. He glided off to summon her a carriage.

Alexia finished her repast, gathered up her dispatch case, her latest parasol, and her long woolen coat, and wandered out the front door.

Only to discover exactly where everyone had gone—outside onto the sweeping front lawn that led up to the cobbled courtyard of the castle. They had managed to multiply themselves, don attire of a military persuasion, and, for some reason known only to their tiny little werewolf brains, proceed to engage in setting up a considerable number of large canvas tents. This involved the latest in government-issue self-expanding steam poles, boiled in large copper pots like so much metal pasta. Each one started out the size of a spyglass before the heat caused it to suddenly expand with a popping noise. As was the general military protocol, it took far more soldiers than it ought to stand around watching the poles boil, and when one expanded, a cheer erupted forth. The pole was grasped between a set of leather potholders and taken off to a tent.

Lady Maccon lost her temper. "What *are* you all doing out here?"

No one looked at her or acknowledged her presence.

Alexia threw her head back and yelled, "*Tunstell!*" She had not quite the lung capacity to match that of her massive husband, but neither was she built on the delicate-flower end of the feminine spectrum. Alexia's father's ancestors had once conquered an empire, and it was when Lady Maccon yelled that people realized how that was accomplished.

Tunstell came bouncing over, a handsome, if gangly, ginger fellow with a perpetual grin and a certain carelessness of manner that most found endearing and everybody else found exasperating.

"Tunstell," Alexia said calmly and reasonably, she thought, "*why* are there tents on my front lawn?"

Tunstell, Lord Maccon's valet and chief among the clavigers, looked about in his chipper way, as if to say that he had not noticed anything amiss and was now delighted to find that they had company. Tunstell was always chirpy. It was his greatest character flaw. He was also one of the few residents of Woolsey Castle who managed to remain entirely unfazed by, or possibly unaware of, either Lord or Lady Maccon's wrath. This was his second-greatest character flaw.

"He didn't warn you?" The claviger's freckled face was flushed with exertion from helping to raise one of the tents.

"No, *he* most certainly did not." Alexia tapped the silver tip of her parasol on the front stoop.

Tunstell grinned. "Well, my lady, the rest of the pack has returned." He flipped both hands at the canvas-ridden chaos before her, waggling his fingers dramatically. Tunstell was an actor of some note—everything he did was dramatic.

"Tunstell," said Alexia carefully, as though to a dim child, "this would indicate that my husband possessed a very, very big pack. There are no werewolf Alphas in England who can boast a pack of such proportions."

"Oh, well, the rest of the pack brought the rest of the regiment with them," explained Tunstell in a conspiratorial way, as though he and Alexia were partners engaged in the most delightful lark.

"I believe it is customary for the pack and fellow officers of a given regiment to separate upon returning home. So that, well, one doesn't wake up to find hundreds of soldiers camping on one's lawn."

"Well, Woolsey has always done things a little differently. Having the biggest pack in England, we're the only ones who split the pack for military service, so we keep the Coldsteam Guards together for a few weeks when we get home. Builds solidarity." Tunstell gestured expansively once more, his fine white hands weaving about in the air, and nodded enthusiastically.

"And does this solidarity have to occur on Woolsey's front lawn?" *Tap tap tap* went the parasol. The Bureau of Unnatural Registry (BUR) was experimenting with new weaponry of late. At the disbanding of the Hypocras Club several months previous, a small compressed steam unit had been discovered. It apparently heated continually until it burst. Lord Maccon had shown it to his wife. It made a ticking noise just prior to explosion, rather like that of Alexia's parasol at this precise moment. Tunstell was unaware of this correlation or he might have proceeded with greater caution. On the other hand, being Tunstell, he might not.

"Yes, isn't it jolly?" crowed Tunstell.

"But why?" *Tap tap tap.*

"It is where we have always camped," said a new voice, apparently belonging to someone equally unfamiliar with the ticking, exploding steam device.

Lady Maccon whirled to glare at the man who dared to interrupt her midrant. The gentleman in question was both tall and broad, although not quite to her husband's scale. Lord Maccon was Scottish-big; this gentleman was only English-big—there was a distinct difference. Also, unlike the earl, who periodically bumped into things as though his form were larger than his perception of it, this man seemed entirely comfortable with his size. He wore full officer formals and knew he looked good in them. His boots were spit-shined, his blond hair coiffed high, and he boasted an accent that very carefully was no accent at all. Alexia knew the type: education, money, and blue blood.

She gritted her teeth. "Oh, it is, is it? Well, not anymore." She turned back to Tunstell. "We are hosting a dinner party the evening after next. Have them remove those tents immediately."

"Unacceptable," said the large blond gentleman, moving closer.

Alexia began to believe that he was no gentleman, despite his accent and immaculate appearance. She also noticed that he had the most cutting blue eyes, icy and intense.

Tunstell, a look of worry behind his cheery grin, seemed unable to decide whom to obey.

Alexia ignored the newcomer. "If they must camp here, move them around to the back."

Tunstell turned to do her bidding but was stopped by the stranger, who put a large white-gloved hand on his shoulder.

"But this is preposterous." The man's perfect teeth snapped at Lady Maccon. "The regiment has always taken up residence in the forecourt. It is far more convenient than the grounds."

"Now," said Alexia to Tunstell, still ignoring the intruder. Imagine talking to her in such a tone of voice, and they hadn't yet been introduced.

Tunstell, less cheerful than she had ever seen him, was looking back and forth between her and the stranger. Any moment now, he might place his hand upon his head and enact a swoon of confusion.

"Stay precisely where you are, Tunstell," instructed the stranger.

"Who the devil are you?" Alexia asked, the man's cavalier interference irritating her into using actual profanity.

"Major Channing Channing of the Chesterfield Channings."

Alexia gawked. No wonder he was so very full of himself. One would have to be, laboring all one's life under a name like that.

"Well, Major Channing, I shall ask you not to interfere with the running of the household. It is *my* domain."

"Ah, you are the new housekeeper? I was not informed that Lady Maccon had made any such drastic changes."

Alexia was not surprised by this assumption. She was very well aware of the fact that she was not of the appearance others patently expected of a Lady Maccon, being too Italian, too old, and too, frankly, ample. She was going to correct his error before further embarrassment ensued, but he did not provide her with the opportunity. Clearly Channing Channing of the Chesterfield Channings enjoyed the cadence of his own voice.

"Don't you worry your pretty little head about our camping arrangements. I assure you, neither his lordship nor her ladyship will take you to task." The ladyship in question flushed at his presumption. "You simply let us get on with our business and return to your duties."

"I can assure you," said Alexia, "everything that occurs in or around Woolsey Castle concerns me."

Channing Channing of the Chesterfield Channings smiled his

perfect smile and twinkled his blue eyes in a way Alexia was certain he believed to be alluring. "Now, really, neither of us has time for this, do we? Just you scamper off and get about your daily chores, and we shall see about a bit of a reward later for your obedience."

Was that a leer? Alexia actually thought it might be. "Are you philandering with me, sir?" She was imprudently startled into asking.

"Would you like me to be?" he replied, grin widening.

Well, that certainly settled that. *This* was no gentleman.

"Uh-oh," said Tunstell very softly, backing away slightly.

"What a nauseating thought," said Lady Maccon.

"Oh, I don't know," said Major Channing, moving in closer, "a fiery Italian thing like you, with a nice figure and not too old, might have a few lively nights left. I always did fancy a bit of the foreign."

Alexia, who was only half Italian, and that only by birth, having been raised English to the bone, could not decide which part of that sentence offended her most. She sputtered.

The repulsive Channing person looked like he might actually try to touch her.

Alexia hauled off and hit him, hard, with her parasol, right on the top of his head.

Everyone in the courtyard stopped what they were about and turned to look at the statuesque lady currently engaged in whacking their third in command, Woolsey Pack Gamma, commander of the Coldsteam Guards abroad, with a parasol.

The major's eyes shifted to an even icier blue and black about the rim of each iris, and two of his perfect white teeth turned pointed.

Werewolf, was he? Well, Alexia Maccon's parasol was tipped with silver for a reason. She walloped him again, this time making certain the tip touched his skin. At the same time, she rediscovered her powers of speech.

"How dare you! You impudent"—*whack*—"arrogant"—*whack*—"overbearing"—*whack*—"unobservant dog!" *Whack, whack*. Normally Alexia wasn't given to such language or unadulterated violence, but circumstances seemed to warrant it. He was a werewolf and, without her touching him and canceling out his supernatural abilities, practically impossible to damage. Thus, she felt justified in clobbering him a couple of times for discipline's sake.

Major Channing, shocked by a physical attack from an apparently defenseless housekeeper, shielded his head and then grabbed the parasol, using it to yank her toward him. Alexia lost her grip, and Major Channing stumbled back in possession of the accessory. He looked like he wanted to hit her back with it, which could have done Alexia some real damage, as she had no supernatural healing abilities at all. But instead, he tossed the parasol aside and made as if to slap her.

Which was when Tunstell leaped onto his back. The redhead wrapped long arms and legs about the major, trapping Channing's limbs at his sides.

The assembled newcomers gasped in horror. For a claviger to attack a member of the pack was unheard of and was grounds for instant expulsion. However, those of the pack and their companion clavigers who knew who Alexia was all dropped whatever they were doing and rushed forward to assist.

Major Channing shook Tunstell off and backhanded him hard across the face. The strike sent Tunstell to the ground easily. The claviger gave a loud groan and collapsed.

Alexia gave the blond blackguard a glare of wrath and bent to check on the fallen redhead. His eyes were closed, but he appeared to be breathing. She stood and said calmly, "I would stop this now, if I were you, Mr. Channing." She dropped the "major" out of contempt.

"I should say not," said the man, unbuttoning his uniform and stripping off his white gloves. "Now you both need discipline."

In the next second, he began to change. In polite company, this would have been shocking, but most everyone there had witnessed the event before. Over the decades since pack integration, the military had become as comfortable with werewolf change as they were with profanity. But to change in front of a lady, even if one did think she was a housekeeper? Murmurs of alarm rippled through the crowd.

Alexia was also surprised. It was only just nightfall, and it was nowhere near full moon. Which meant this man was older and more experienced than his brash behavior indicated. He was also darn good at the change, polished in its execution despite what her husband had once described as the worst pain a man could stand and still live. Alexia had seen youngsters of the pack writhe and whimper, but Major Channing shifted smoothly from human to wolf. Skin, bone, and fur rearranged itself, resulting in one of the most beautiful wolves Alexia had ever seen: large and almost pure white, with icy blue eyes. He shook off the remains of his clothing and circled slowly about her.

Alexia braced herself. One touch from her and he would be human again, but that was no guarantee of safety. Even mortal, he would still be bigger and stronger than she, and Alexia was without her parasol.

Just as the huge white wolf charged forward, a new wolf leaped in front of Alexia and Tunstell, teeth bared. The newcomer was considerably smaller than Major Channing, with sandy fur frosted black about the head and neck, pale yellow eyes, and an almost foxlike face.

There was an awful thud of fur-covered flesh, and the two scrabbled against one another, claws and teeth ripping. The white wolf was bigger, but it presently became clear that the smaller wolf possessed greater speed and cunning. He used the other's size against him. In a matter of moments, the smaller wolf had twisted about and taken a clean firm death grip on Major Channing's throat.

Quick as it had started, the fight ended. The white wolf flopped instantly down, rolling to present his belly in submission to his diminutive opponent.

Alexia heard a groan and dragged her eyes away from the fight to see that Tunstell was now sitting upright and blinking blearily. He was bleeding copiously from the nose but otherwise appeared merely dazed. Alexia passed him a handkerchief and bent to look for her parasol. She used it as an excuse not to watch as the two werewolves changed back into human form.

She did peek. What hot-blooded woman wouldn't? Major Channing was all muscle, longer and leaner than her husband but, honesty compelled her to admit, not at all unsightly. What surprised her was the small sandy-haired man of indeterminate age standing calmly next to him. She would never have accused *Professor Lyall* of gratuitous musculature. But there he was, assuredly fit. What profession had Lyall had before he became a werewolf? Alexia wondered, not for the first time. A couple of claviger appeared with long cloaks and covered over the object of Lady Maccon's speculation.

"What the hell is going on?" Major Channing spat as soon as his jaw had sufficiently returned to human form. He turned to glare at the urbane man standing quietly next to him.

"I did not challenge *you*. You know I would never challenge you. We settled that years ago. This was a perfectly acceptable matter of pack discipline. Misbehaving claviger must be tamed."

"Unless, of course, one of them is no claviger," said Professor Randolph Lyall, long-suffering Beta of the Woolsey Pack.

The blond man looked nervous. His face lost most of its arrogance. Alexia thought he was considerably more attractive that way.

Professor Lyall sighed. "Major Channing, Woolsey Pack Gamma, allow me to introduce you to Lady Alexia Maccon, curse-breaker, and your new Alpha female."

Alexia disliked the term *curse-breaker;* it sounded terribly sportsmanlike, as though she were about to engage in a protracted bout of unremitting cricket. Since some werewolves still considered their immortality a curse, she supposed it was an odd kind of accolade, praise that she could stave off the bestiality of full moon. To be called curse-breaker was certainly more complimentary than *soul-sucker.* Trust the vampires to come up with a term that implied an even more crass kind of sport than cricket—if such a thing could be conceived.

Alexia found her parasol and stood. "I could say it was a pleasure to meet you, Major Channing, but I would not wish to perjure myself so early in the evening."

"Well, confound it," said Major Channing, glaring first at Lyall and then at everyone else around him, "why didn't any of you *tell* me?"

Alexia did feel a little guilty at that. She had let her temper get the better of her. But really, he hadn't given her time to introduce herself.

"I take it you were not informed of my appearance, then?" Alexia asked, prepared to chalk another thing up onto the board of her husband's mistakes for the night. He was going to get a ruddy earful when he got home.

Major Channing said, "Well, no, not precisely. I mean, yes, we had a short missive a couple months back, but the description was not . . . you understand . . . and I thought you would be . . ."

Alexia hefted her parasol thoughtfully.

Channing backpedaled rapidly. ". . . less Italian," he said finally.

"And my dear husband did not warn you of the truth of it when you arrived?" Alexia was looking more thoughtful than angry. Perhaps Major Channing was not so bad. After all, she, too, had been surprised at Lord Maccon's choosing *her* to wed.

Major Channing looked irritated at that. "We have not yet seen him, my lady. Or this faux pas might have been avoided."

"I do not know about that." Lady Maccon shrugged. "He is prone to exaggerating my virtues. His descriptions of me are generally a tad unrealistic."

Major Channing dialed his charm back up to the highest setting— Lady Maccon could practically see the gears crunching and the steam spiraling off his body. "Oh, I doubt that, my lady." Unfortunately for the Gamma, who did genuinely recognize Alexia's appeal, Alexia chose to take offense.

She went cold, her brown eyes hard and her generous mouth compressed into a straight line.

He hurriedly switched the subject, turning to Professor Lyall. "Why was our venerated leader not at the station to meet us? I had some fairly urgent business to discuss with him."

Lyall shrugged. There was an air about him that suggested the major not push this particular subject. It was the nature of a Gamma to criticize, but equally common was a Beta's support, no matter how rude the Alpha's actions. "Urgent BUR matters," was all he answered.

"Yes, well, my business might also be urgent," snapped Major Channing. "Hard to know, especially when he is unavailable to see to the needs of the pack."

"What exactly happened?" Professor Lyall's tone implied that whatever this urgent business, it was probably Major Channing's fault.

"The pack and I experienced something unusual on board ship." Major Channing clearly felt that if the Beta could be cagey, so could he. He turned pointedly to Alexia. "A pleasure to make your acquaintance, Lady Maccon. I apologize for the dust-up. Ignorance is no excuse; I assure you I am well aware of that. Nevertheless, I shall endeavor to make it up to you to the best of my poor abilities."

"Apologize to Tunstell," replied Lady Maccon.

That was a blow: the pack Gamma, third in command, apologizing to a lowly claviger. Major Channing sucked in his breath but did exactly as he was told. He made a pretty speech to the redhead, who looked progressively more and more embarrassed as it rattled on, terribly conscious of his Gamma's humiliation. By the end, Tunstell was so flushed his freckles had disappeared entirely behind the red. After which Major Channing disappeared in a huff.

"Where is he going?" wondered Lady Maccon.

"Most likely to move the regiment's camping arrangements to the back of the house. It will have to wait a short while, my lady, for the tent poles to cool."

"Ah." Alexia grinned. "I win."

Professor Lyall sighed, looked briefly up toward the moon, and said as though appealing to a higher deity, "Alphas."

"So"—Alexia gave him an inquiring look—"would you mind explaining Channing Channing of the Chesterfield Channings to me? He does not seem like a man my husband would choose to run with his pack."

Professor Lyall tilted his head to one side. "I am not privy to his lordship's feelings on the gentleman, but regardless of Lord Maccon's preferences, Channing was inherited along with Woolsey. As was I. Conall had no choice. And, quite frankly, the major is not so bad. A good soldier to have guarding one's back in a battle, and that is the honest truth. Try not to be too put off by his manner. He has always behaved himself in the capacity of Gamma, a decent third in command, despite disliking both Lord Maccon and myself."

"Why? I mean, why you? I can perfectly comprehend not liking my husband. *I* dislike him intensely most of the time."

Professor Lyall stifled a chuckle. "I am given to understand that he does not approve of spelling one's name with two *ll*'s. He finds it inexcusably Welsh. I suspect he may be quite taken with you, however."

Alexia twirled her parasol, embarrassed. "Pity's sake, was he being honest under all that syrupy charm?" She wondered what it was about her physique or personality that only large werewolves seemed to find her alluring. And would it be possible to change that quality?

Professor Lyall shrugged. "I should steer well clear of him in that arena, if I were you."

"Why?"

Lyall struggled for the polite way of putting it and then finally settled on the indelicate truth. "Major Channing likes his woman feisty, to be sure, but that is because he likes"—a delicate pause—"refining them."

Alexia wrinkled her nose. She sensed the indelicate underpinning to Professor Lyall's comment. She would have to research it later, confident that her father's library would provide. Alessandro Tarabotti, preternatural, had lived a racy life and passed on to his daughter a collection of books, some of them with terribly wicked sketches, which attested to his raciness. Alexia had those books to thank for the fact that some of her husband's more innovative desires did not provoke her into fainting fits on a regular basis.

Professor Lyall merely shrugged. "Some women like that kind of thing."

"And some women like needlepoint," replied Alexia, resolving to think no more on her husband's problematic Gamma. "And some women like extraordinarily ugly hats." This comment was sparked by the fact that she had just caught sight of her dear friend, Miss Ivy Hisselpenny, disembarking from a hackney at the end of Woolsey's long entranceway.

Miss Hisselpenny was a long way away, but there was no doubt it was her—no one else would dare sport such a hat. It was a mind-numbing purple, trimmed in bright green, with three high feathers emerging from what looked to be an entire fruit basket arranged about the crown. Fake grapes spilled down and over one side, dangling almost to Ivy's pert little chin.

"Fiddlesticks," said Lady Maccon to Professor Lyall. "Am I ever going to make it to my meeting?"

Lyall took that as a hint and turned to go. Unless, of course, he was fleeing from the hat. His mistress stopped him.

"I truly do appreciate your unexpected intervention just now. I did not think he would actually attack."

Professor Lyall looked at his Alpha's mate thoughtfully. It was a rare unguarded look, his face free of its customary glassicals, his mild hazel eyes puzzled. "Why unexpected? Didn't you think I was capable of defending you in Conall's place?"

Lady Maccon shook her head. It was true she had never had much confidence in the physical abilities of her husband's Beta, with his slight frame and professorial ways. Lord Maccon was massive and treelike; Professor Lyall was built more on the shrub scale. But that wasn't what she had meant. "Oh no, unexpected because I had assumed you would be with my husband tonight, if this BUR problem is so very bad."

Professor Lyall nodded.

Lady Maccon tried one last time. "I don't suppose it was the arrival of the regiment that had my husband in a dither?"

"No. He knew the regiment was due in; he sent me to meet them at the station."

"Oh, he did, did he? And he did not see fit to inform me?"

Lyall, realizing he might have just gotten his Alpha into some very hot water indeed, dissembled. "I believe he was under the impression you knew. It was the dewan who ordered the military recall. Withdrawal papers came through the Shadow Council several months ago."

Alexia frowned. She remembered vaguely the potentate arguing vociferously with the dewan on this subject at the beginning of her stint as muhjah. The dewan had won, since the strength of Queen Victoria's regiments and the building of her empire was dependent upon her alliance with the packs. The vampires held controlling interest in the East India Company and its mercenary troops, of course, but this had been a matter for the regulars and so the werewolves. Still, Lady Maccon had not realized the results of that decision would end up encamping on her doorstep.

"Don't they have a proper barracks somewhere they should be shambling off to?"

"Yes, but it is tradition for them all to stay here for several weeks while the pack re-forms—before the daylight soldiers head homeward."

Lady Maccon watched Ivy wend her way through the chaos of military tents and baggage. She moved with such purpose it was as though she walked with exclamation marks. Hydrodine engines emitted small puffs of yellow smoke at her as she passed and compressed expansion tent stakes hissed as they were pulled prematurely from the ground. All were now being taken back down and moved around the side of the house and into Woolsey's extensive grounds.

"Have I mentioned recently how much I dislike tradition?" Alexia said, and then panicked. "Are we expected to feed them all?"

The grape bunches bobbed in time with Ivy's rapidly mincing footsteps. She did not even pause to investigate the disarray. She was clearly *in a hurry*, which meant Ivy had *news of note*.

"Rumpet knows what to do. Don't concern yourself," advised Professor Lyall.

"You really cannot tell me what is going on? He was up so very early, and Formerly Merriway was definitely involved."

"Who, Rumpet?"

That earned the Beta a look of profound disgust.

"Lord Maccon did not inform me of the particulars," Professor Lyall admitted.

Lady Maccon frowned. "And Formerly Merriway won't. You know how she gets, all-over nervous and floaty."

Ivy attained the steps to the front door.

As she neared, Professor Lyall said hastily, "If you will excuse me, my lady, I should be getting on."

He bowed to Miss Hisselpenny and vanished around the corner of the house after Major Channing.

Ivy curtsied to the departing werewolf, a strawberry on a long silk stem wiggling about in front of her left ear. She didn't take offense at Lyall leaving so precipitously. Instead, she trotted up to the stoop, blithely ignoring Alexia's dispatch case and waiting carriage, certain in the knowledge that her news was far more important than whatever affair was causing her friend to depart forthwith.

"Alexia, did you know there is an entire regiment decamping on your front lawn?"

Lady Maccon sighed. "Really, Ivy, I would never have noticed."

Miss Hisselpenny ignored the sarcasm. "I have the most splendid *news*. Should we go in for tea?"

"Ivy, I have business in town, and I am already late." Lady Maccon refrained from mentioning that business was with Queen Victoria. Ivy knew nothing of her preternatural state, nor her political position, and Alexia thought it best to keep her friend ignorant. Ivy was particularly adept at being ignorant but could cause extensive havoc with the smallest scrap of information.

"But, *Alexia,* this is very important gossip!" The grapes vibrated in agitation.

"Oh, have the winter shawls from Paris come into the shops?"

Ivy tossed her head in frustration. "Alexia, must you be so tiresome?"

Lady Maccon could barely tear her eyes off of the hat. "Then, please, do not keep it to yourself one moment longer. Pray tell me at once." Anything to get her dearest friend gone posthaste. Really, Ivy could be too inconvenient.

"Why is there a regiment on your lawn?" Miss Hisselpenny persisted.

"Werewolf business." Lady Maccon dismissed it in the manner cal-culated to most efficiently throw Ivy off the scent. Miss Hisselpenny had never quite accustomed herself to werewolves, even after her best friend had the temerity to marry one. They were not exactly common-place, and she had never had to cope with their brand of gruffness and sudden nudity. She simply couldn't seem to acclimatize to it the way Alexia had. So she preferred, in typical Ivy fashion, to forget they ex-isted.

"Ivy," said Lady Maccon, "what exactly *are* you doing here?"

"Oh, Alexia, I am terribly sorry for descending upon you so unex-pectedly! I hadn't the time to send round a card, but I simply had to come and tell you as soon as it was decided." She opened her eyes wide and flipped both hands toward her head. "*I* am engaged."

CHAPTER TWO

A Plague of Humanization

L ord Conall Maccon was a very large man who made for an exceedingly large wolf. He was bigger than any natural wolf could ever hope to be and less rangy, with too much muscle and not enough lank. No passerby would be in any doubt, had they seen him, that he was a supernatural creature. That said, those few people traveling the cold winter road on this particular early evening could not see him. Lord Maccon was moving fast, and he boasted a dark brindled pelt so that, but for his yellow eyes, he faded almost completely into the shadows. On more than one occasion, his wife had called him handsome in his wolf form, yet she had never called him so as a human. He would have to ask her about that. Conall ruminated a moment; then again, perhaps he would not.

Such were the mundane thoughts that passed through a werewolf's head as he ran the country lanes toward London. Woolsey Castle was some distance away from the metropolis, just north of Barking, a good two hours by carriage or dirigible and a little less on four legs. Time passed and eventually wet grass, neat hedgerows, and startled bunnies gave way to muddy streets, stone walls, and disinterested alley cats.

The earl found himself enjoying the run a good deal less when, just after entering the city proper, right around Fairfoot Road, he abruptly and completely lost his wolf form. It was the most astonishing thing—one moment he was dashing along on four paws, and the next his bones were crunching, his fur retreating, and his knees crashing down upon the cobbles. It left him, shivering and panting, naked in the road.

"Great ghosts!" exclaimed the aggrieved nobleman.

Never had he experienced the like. Even when his gloriously frustrating wife used her preternatural touch to force him back into humanity, it was not so sudden. She generally gave him some warning. Well, a little warning. Well, a yell or two.

He looked about, worried. But Alexia was nowhere near, and he was pretty darn certain he had managed to leave her safe, if fuming, back at the castle. There were no other preternaturals registered for the greater London area. What, then, had just happened?

He looked to his knees, which were bleeding slightly and quite definitely not healing. Werewolves were supernatural: such minor scrapes ought to be closing up right before his eyes. Instead they leaked his slow old blood onto the muddy stones.

Lord Maccon tried to change back, reaching for that place from which he drove his body to split its biological nature. Nothing. He tried for his Anubis Form, the Alpha's ace, with the head of the wolf and the body of a man. Still nothing. Which left him sitting on Fairfoot Road, completely unclothed, and deeply confused.

Struck with the spirit of investigation, he backtracked a short way. He tried for Anubis Form, changing just his head into that of a wolf, an Alpha trick that was faster than full shift. It worked but left him in a conundrum: dally about as a wolf, or press on to the office naked? He changed his head back.

Normally, when there was a chance he might have to change publicly, the earl carried a cloak in his mouth. But he had thought to make it safely to the BUR offices and into the cloakroom there before decency became necessary. Now he regretted such careless confidence. Formerly Merriway had been right—something was terribly wrong in London, and that apart from the fact that he was currently lollygagging about starkers inside it. It would appear that it was not only the ghosts who were being affected. Werewolves, too, were undergoing alteration. He gave a tight smile and retreated hurriedly behind a pile of crates. He would lay good money that the vampires weren't growing any feeding fangs tonight either—at least not the ones living near the Thames. Countess Nadasdy, queen of the Westminster hive, must be positively frantic. Which, he realized with a grimace, meant he was likely to get the unparalleled pleasure of a visit from Lord Ambrose later that evening. It was going to be a long night.

The Bureau of Unnatural Registry was not situated, as many a confused tourist expected, in the vicinity of Whitehall. It was in a small, unassuming Georgian building just off Fleet Street, near the *Times* offices. Lord Maccon had made the switch ten years ago, when he discovered that it was the press, not the government, that generally had a handle on what was truly transpiring around the city—political or otherwise. This particular evening, he had cause to regret his decision, as he now had to make his way through the commercial district as well as several crowded thoroughfares in order to get to his office.

He almost managed the trek without being seen, skulking through the grubby streets and around the mudspattered corners—London's finest back alleys. It was quite the feat, as the streets were crawling with soldiers. Fortunately, they were intent on celebrating their recent return to London and not his large white form. But he was spotted by the most unexpected individual, near St. Bride, the unfragrant scent of Fleet Street in the air.

A toff of the highest water, dressed to the nines in a lovely cut-front jacket and stunning lemon-yellow cravat tied in the Osbaldeston style, materialized out of the darkness behind a brewing pub, where no toff had a right to be. The man doffed his top hat amiably at the naked werewolf.

"Why, I do declare, if it isn't Lord Maccon. How *do* you do? Fancy, aren't we a tad underdressed for an evening's stroll?" The voice was mildly familiar and laced with amusement.

"Biffy," said the earl on a growl.

"And how is your lovely wife?" Biffy was a drone of reputation, and his vampire master, Lord Akeldama, was a dear friend of Alexia's. Much to Lord Maccon's annoyance. So, come to think of it, was Biffy. Last time the drone had visited Woolsey Castle with a message from his master, he and Alexia had spent hours discussing the latest hairstyles out of Paris. His wife had a penchant for gentlemen of the frivolous persuasion. Conall paused to deduce what that said about his own character.

"Hang my lovely wife," he answered. "Get into that tavern there and wrestle me up a coat of some kind, would you?"

Biffy arched an eyebrow at him. "You know, I would offer you my coat, but it's a swallowtail, hardly useful, and would never fit that colossal frame of yours anyway." He gave the earl a long, appraising look. "Well, well, isn't my master going to be all of a crumble for not having seen this?"

"Your impossible patron has seen me naked already."

Biffy tapped his bottom lip with a fingertip and looked intrigued.

"Oh for goodness' sake, you were there," said Lord Maccon, annoyed.

Biffy only smiled.

"A cloak." A pause, then the added grumble of, "Please!"

Biffy vanished and returned with alacrity, bearing an oilskin greatcoat of ill design and briny smell but that was at least large enough to cover the earl's indignities.

The Alpha shrugged it on and then glared at the still-smiling drone. "I smell like parboiled seaweed."

"Navy's in town."

"So, what do you know of this madness?" Biffy might be a pink, and his vampire master even more so, but Lord Akeldama was also London's main busybody, and he ran his ring of impeccably clad informants so efficiently it put anything the government could muster to shame.

"Eight regiments came into port yesterday: the Black Scotts, Northumberland, the Coldsteam Guards—" Biffy was pointedly obtuse.

Lord Maccon interrupted him. "Not that—the mass exorcism."

"Mmm, *that*. That is why I was waiting for you."

"Of course you were," sighed Lord Maccon.

Biffy stopped smiling. "Shall we walk, my lord?" He took up position next to the werewolf, who was no werewolf at all anymore, and they strode together toward Fleet Street. The earl's bare feet made no noise on the cobbles.

"What!" The amazed exclamation emanated from not one, but two sources: Alexia *and* the heretofore forgotten Tunstell. The claviger had sat down behind the corner of the stoop to nurse the results of Major Channing's discipline.

Upon hearing Miss Hisselpenny's news, however, the gangly actor reappeared. He was sporting a large red mark about the right eye, which was destined to darken in a most colorful manner, and was pinching his nose to stanch the flow of blood. Both Alexia's handkerchief and his own cravat appeared much the worse for the experience.

"Engaged, Miss Hisselpenny?" In addition to his disheveled aspect, Tunstell was looking quite tragic, in a Shakespearean comedy kind of way. From behind the handkerchief, his eyes were wide in distress. Tunstell had been mighty taken with Miss Hisselpenny ever since they danced together at Lord and Lady Maccon's wedding, but they had not been allowed to mingle socially since. Miss Hisselpenny was a lady of consequence, and Tunstell was but a lowly claviger and an actor to boot. Alexia had not comprehended the extent of his attachment. Or perhaps the attachment meant more now that it was no longer possible.

"To whom?" Lady Maccon asked the obvious question.

Ivy ignored her and dashed to Tunstell's side.

"You are injured!" she gasped, bunches of grapes and silk strawberries bobbing about. She pulled out her own minuscule handkerchief, embroidered with small clusters of cherries, and dabbed at his face unhelpfully.

"A mere scratch, Miss Hisselpenny, I assure you," said Tunstell, looking pleased by her ministrations, as ineffectual as they may be.

"But you are bleeding, simply gouts and gouts of it," insisted Ivy.

"Not to worry, not to worry, the business end of a fist will do that to a person, you know."

Ivy gasped. "Fisticuffs! Oh, how *perfectly* horrid! Poor Mr. Tunstell." Ivy petted an unbloodied corner of the man's cheek with her white-gloved hand.

Poor Mr. Tunstell did not seem to mind, if this was the result. "Oh, please, do not trouble yourself so," he said, leaning into her caress. "My, what an enchanting hat, Miss Hisselpenny, so"—he hesitated, searching for the right word—"fruity."

Ivy blushed beet red at that. "Oh, do you like it? I bought it specially."

That did it. "Ivy," said Alexia sharply, bringing her friend back around to the important business at hand. "To whom have you gotten yourself engaged, exactly?"

Miss Hisselpenny snapped back to the present, drifting away from the alluring Mr. Tunstell. "His name is Captain Featherstonehaugh, and he has just returned with the Northumberling Fusilli, all the way from Inja."

"You mean the Northumberland Fusiliers."

"Is that not what I just said?" Ivy was all big-eyed innocence and excitement.

The dewan's army reshuffling clearly involved far more regiments than Alexia had thought. She would have to find out what the queen and her commanders were about at the Shadow Council meeting.

The meeting she was now inexcusably late for.

Miss Hisselpenny continued. "It is not a bad match, although Mama would have preferred a major at the very least. But you know"—she lowered her voice to almost a whisper—"I haven't really the luxury of choice at my age."

Tunstell looked quite put out upon hearing that. He thought Miss Hisselpenny a grand catch, older than he to be sure, but imagine her having to settle on a mere captain. He opened his mouth to say so but showed unexpected restraint upon receipt of a high-stakes glare from his mistress.

"Tunstell," instructed Lady Maccon, "go away and be useful. Ivy, felicitations on your impending nuptials, but I really must be off. I have an important meeting, for which I am now late."

Ivy was watching Tunstell's retreating back. "Of course, Captain Featherstonehaugh was not exactly what I had hoped for. He is quite the military man, you understand, very stoic. That kind of thing would seem to suit you, Alexia, but *I* had hoped for a man with the soul of a bard."

Alexia threw her hands up into the air. "*He* is a claviger. You know what that means? Someday, relatively soon, he will petition for metamorphosis and then probably die in the attempt. Even if he came through intact, he would then be a werewolf. You don't even *like* werewolves."

Ivy gave her an even-wider-eyed look as if butter wouldn't melt in her mouth. The grapes bobbed. "He could always leave before that."

"To be what? A professional actor? Living on a penny a day and the approbation of a fickle public?"

Ivy sniffed. "Who says we are discussing Mr. Tunstell?"

Alexia was driven to distraction. "Get into the carriage, Ivy. I shall take you back to town."

Miss Hisselpenny nattered on about her impending marriage and its companion apparel, invitation list, and comestibles for the entirety of the two-hour ride into London. Not much was said, however, about the prospective groom. Alexia was made to realize, during the course of that drive, that he apparently was of little consequence to the proceedings. She watched her friend climb down and trot inside the Hisselpenny's modest town house with a slight pang of concern. What was Ivy doing? But with no time at the moment to worry over Miss Hisselpenny's *situation*, Lady Maccon directed the driver on to Buckingham.

The guards were expecting her. Lady Maccon was always at the palace two hours after dark on Sundays and Thursdays without fail. And she was one of the most unproblematic of the queen's regular visitors, being the least high-and-mighty, for all her forthright tone and pointed opinions. After the first two weeks, she had even gone to the trouble of learning all of their names. It was the little things that made someone grand. The ton were suspicious of Lord Maccon's choice, but the military was rather pleased with it. They welcomed straightforward talk, even from a female.

"You are late, Lady Maccon," said one, checking her neck for bite marks and her dispatch case for illegal steam devices.

"Don't I know it, Lieutenant Funtington, don't I know it," replied the lady.

"Well, we shan't keep you. Go on in, my lady."

Lady Maccon gave him a tight smile and went.

The dewan and the potentate were already waiting for her. Queen Victoria was not. The queen usually arrived nearer to midnight, after presiding over her family and supper, and stayed only to hear the results of their debate and formulate any final decisions.

"I cannot apologize enough for having kept you both," said Alexia. "I had unexpected squatters on my front lawn and an equally unexpected engagement to handle this evening. No excuses, I know, but those are my reasons."

"Well, there you have it," snarled the dewan, "The affairs of the British Empire must wait on squatters and your good graces." Landed as the Earl of Upper Slaughter but without any real country seat, the dewan was one of the few werewolves in England who could give the Earl of Woolsey a fight for his fur and had had occasion to prove it. He was almost as big as Conall Maccon but slightly older-looking, with dark hair, a wide face, and deep-set eyes. He ought to have been handsome, except that his mouth was a little too full, the cleft in his chin a little too pronounced, and his mustache and muttonchops astonishingly assertive.

Alexia had spent long hours wondering over that mustache. Werewolves did not grow hair, as they did not age. Where had it come from? Had he always had it? For how many centuries had his poor abused upper lip labored under the burden of such vegetation?

Tonight, however, she ignored both him and his facial protuberances. "So," she said, sitting down and placing the dispatch case on the table next to her, "shall we on to business?"

"By all means," replied the potentate, his voice honeyed and cool. "Are you feeling well this evening, muhjah?"

Alexia was surprised by the question. "Quite."

The vampire member of the Shadow Council was the more dangerous of the two. He had age on his side and much less to prove than the dewan. Also, while the dewan made a show of disliking Lady Maccon for form's sake, Alexia knew for a fact that the potentate actually loathed her. He had registered an official complaint in writing on the occasion of her marriage to the Woolsey Pack Alpha and the same again when Queen Victoria brought her in to sit on the Shadow Council. Alexia had never discerned exactly why. But he had the support of the hives in this as in most things, which made him far more powerful than the dewan, for whom pack loyalty seemed wobbly.

"No stomach ailments?"

Alexia gave the vampire a suspicious look. "No, none. Could we get on?"

Generally, the Shadow Council administered supernatural interaction with the Crown. While BUR handled enforcement, the Shadow Council dealt with legislative issues, political and military guidance, and the occasional sticky-residue snafu. During Alexia's few months on board, discussions had ranged from hive authorization in the African provinces, to military code covering the death of an Alpha overseas, to neck-exposure mandates in public museums. They had not yet had a genuine crisis to deal with. This, Alexia felt, was going to be interesting.

She snapped open the lid of her dispatch case and extracted her harmonic auditory resonance disruptor, a spiky little apparatus that looked exactly like two tuning forks sticking out of a crystal. She tapped one fork with her finger, waited a moment, and then tapped the other. The two produced a discordant, low-pitched humming noise, amplified by the crystal that would prevent their conversation from being overheard. She placed the device carefully in the middle of the massive meeting table. The sound was annoying, but they had all learned to deal with it. Even inside the security of Buckingham Palace, one could never be too careful.

"What, exactly, has happened in London this evening? Whatever it was had my husband up scandalously early, just after sunset, and my local ghost informant in a positive fluster." Lady Maccon removed her favorite little notebook and a stylographic pen imported from the Americas.

"You do not know, muhjah?" sneered the dewan.

"Of course I know. I am simply wasting everyone's time by inquiring, for my own amusement." Alexia was sarcastic to the last.

"Neither of us look any different to you this evening?" The potentate steepled his long fingers together on the tabletop, pure white and snakelike against the dark mahogany, and looked at her out of beautiful, deep-set green eyes.

"Why are you humoring her? Obviously she *must* have something to do with it." The dewan stood and began to pace about the room—his customary restless state during most of their meetings.

Alexia pulled her favorite glassicals out of her dispatch case and put them on. They were properly called *monocular cross-magnification lenses with spectral modifier attachment,* but everyone was calling them *glassicals* these days, even Professor Lyall. Alexia's were made of gold, inset with decorative onyx around the side that did not boast multiple lenses and a liquid suspension. The many small knobs and dials were also made of onyx, but the expensive touches did not stop them from looking ridiculous. All glassicals looked ridiculous: the unfortunate progeny of an illicit union between a pair of binoculars and opera glasses.

Her right eye became hideously magnified out of all proportion as she twiddled one dial, homing in on the potentate's face. Fine even features, dark eyebrows, and green eyes—the face seemed totally normal, natural even. The skin looked healthy, not so pale. The potentate gave a little smile, all his teeth in perfect boxlike order. Remarkable.

There would be the problem. No fangs.

Lady Maccon stood and went to stand in front of the dewan, stopping him in his impatient movements. She trained the glassicals upon his face, focusing on the eyes: plain old brown. No yellow about the iris, no hidden quality of open-field or hunter instincts.

In silence, thinking hard, she sat back down. Carefully, she removed the glassicals and put them away.

"Well?"

"Am I to understand you are both laboring under a state, that is, afflicted with, um"—she groped for the correct way of putting it—"that is, infected by . . . normality?"

The dewan gave her a disgusted look. Lady Maccon made a note in her little journal.

"Astonishing. And how many of the supernatural set are also contaminated into being mortal?" she asked, stylographic pen poised.

"Every vampire and werewolf in London central." The potentate was incurably calm.

Alexia was truly stunned. If all of them were no longer supernatural, that meant that any or all of them could be killed. She wondered, as a preternatural, if she was being affected. She went introspective for a moment. She felt like herself—difficult to tell, though.

"What's the geographical extent of those disabled?" she asked.

"It seems to be concentrated around the Thames embankment area, extending in from the docklands."

"And if you leave the affected zone, do you return to your supernatural state?" the scientific side of Alexia instantly wanted to know.

"Excellent inquiry." The dewan disappeared out the door, presumably to send a runner to find out the answer to that question. Normally they would have had a ghost agent handle such a job. Where was she?

"And the ghosts?" Lady Maccon asked, frowning.

"That is how we know the extent of the afflicted area. Not a single ghost tethered in that zone has appeared since sundown. Every one has vanished. Exorcised." The potentate was watching her closely. He, of course, would assume Alexia had something to do with this. Only one creature had the inherent power to exorcise ghosts, as unpleasant a job as it was, and that creature was a preternatural. Alexia was the only preternatural in the London locale.

"Gods," breathed Lady Maccon. "How many ghosts lost were in the Crown's employ?"

"Six worked for us; four worked for BUR. Of the remaining spec-
ters, eight were in the poltergeist stage, so no one misses them, and
eighteen were at the end stages of disanimus." The potentate tossed a
pile of paperwork in Alexia's direction. She flipped through the stack,
looking at the details.

The dewan came back into the room. "We will know your answer
within the hour." He resumed his pacing.

"In case you are curious, gentlemen, I spent the entire day asleep at
Woolsey Castle. My husband can attest to that fact, as we do not maintain
separate bedrooms." Alexia blushed slightly but felt her honor demanded
she stand up for herself.

"Of course he can," said the vampire who currently was no vampire
at all but a natural human. For the first time in hundreds of years. He
must be absolutely shaking in those hugely expensive Hessian boots of
his. To face mortality after so very long. Not to mention the fact that
one of the hives was in the afflicted zone—which meant a queen was in
danger. Vampires, even roves like the potentate, would do almost anything to protect a queen.

"You mean, your werewolf husband who sleeps daylight solid. And
whom I highly doubt you touch while you sleep?"

"Of course I do not." Alexia was taken aback that he need ask.
Staying in contact with Conall all night, every night, would cause him
to age, and while she abhorred the idea of growing old without him,
she wasn't about to inflict mortality on him. He would also grow facial
hair and come over more than usually scruffy of a morning.

"So you admit you could have snuck out of the house?" The dewan
stopped pacing and glared at her.

Lady Maccon made a clucking noise of denial. "Have you met my
staff? If Rumpet didn't stop me, Floote would, not to mention Angelique running about fussing over my hair. Sneaking out, I am sorry
to say, is a thing of my past. But you are welcome to blame me if you
are too lazy to try and figure out what is really going on here."

The potentate, of all people, seemed a little more convinced. Perhaps it was simply that he did not want to believe she had access to such
an ability.

Alexia continued. "I mean, really, how could one preternatural,
however powerful, affect an entire area of the city? I have to touch you
in order to force your humanity. I have to touch a dead body in order to
exorcise its ghost. I could not possibly manage to be in all those places at
once. Besides which, I am not touching you right now, am I? And you
are both mortal."

"So what are we dealing with? A whole pack of preternaturals?" That was the dewan. He was prone to thinking in numbers, the consequence of an overabundance of military training.

The potentate shook his head. "I have seen BUR's records. There are not enough preternaturals in all of England to exorcise so many ghosts at once. There are probably not enough in the civilized world."

Alexia wondered *how* he had seen such records. She would have to tell her husband about that. Then she returned her attention to the business at hand. "Is there anything more powerful than a preternatural?"

The not-vampire shook his head again. "Not in this particular way. Vampire edict tells us that soul-suckers are the second most deadly creatures on the planet. But it also says that the most deadly of all is no leech, but a different kind of parasite. This cannot be the work of one of them."

Lady Maccon scribbled this down in her book. She was intrigued and a little put out. "Worse than us soul-suckers? Is that possible? And here I was thinking myself a member of the most hated set. And what do you call *them*?"

The potentate ignored this question. "That will teach you to get full of yourself."

Alexia would have pressed the issue but suspected that line of questioning would be ignored. "So this must be the result of a weapon, a scientific apparatus. That is the only possible explanation."

"Or we could take that ridiculous man Darwin's theories to heart and postulate a newly evolved species of preternatural."

Alexia nodded. She had her reservations about Darwin and his prattle on origins, but there might be some little merit to his ideas.

The dewan, however, pooh-poohed the idea. Werewolves were, largely, of a much less scientific bent than vampires, except where advances in weaponry were concerned. "I am more sympathetic to the muhjah on this point if nothing else. If she isn't doing it herself, then it must be some newfangled contrivance of technical origin."

"We *are* living in the Age of Invention," agreed the potentate.

The dewan looked thoughtful. "The Templars have finally managed to unify Italy and declare themselves Infallible; perhaps they are turning their attention outward once more?"

"You think this may herald a second Inquisition?" The potentate blanched. He could do that now.

The dewan shrugged.

"There is no point in wild speculation," said the ever-practical Lady Maccon. "Nothing suggests that the Templars are involved."

"You are Italian," grumbled the dewan.

"Oh, fiddlesticks, is everything in this meeting going to come back around to my being my father's daughter? My hair is curly too—could that somehow be involved? I am the product of my birth, and there is nothing I can change about that, or believe you me, I might have opted for a smaller nose. Let us simply agree that the most likely explanation for this kind of wide-scale preternatural effect is a weapon of some kind." She turned to the potentate. "You are *positive* you have never heard of this kind of thing happening before?"

He frowned and rubbed at the crease between his green eyes with the tip of one white finger. It was an oddly human gesture. "I will consult the edict keepers on the subject, but, no, I do not think so."

Alexia looked to the dewan. He shook his head.

"So the question is, what could someone hope to gain by this?"

Her supernatural colleagues looked at her blankly.

A tap came on the closed door. The dewan went to answer it. He spoke softly for a moment through the crack and then returned with an expression transformed from scared to bemused.

"The effects would appear to be negated just outside the afflicted zone we discussed earlier. Werewolves, at least, revert back to fully supernatural. The ghosts, of course, cannot relocate to take advantage of this fact. And I cannot speak for the vampires."

What he did not say was that what changed werewolves was also likely to change vampires—they were more alike than either race preferred to admit.

"I shall look into this myself, personally, as soon as our meeting is concluded," said the potentate, but he was clearly relieved. It had to be a product of his human condition; normally his emotions were not so obvious.

The dewan sneered at him. "You will be able to move that endangered queen of yours, should you deem it necessary."

"Do we have any further business to address?" asked the potentate, ignoring the comment.

Alexia reached forward to tap at the harmonic auditory resonance disruptor with the butt end of her stylographic pen, getting it vibrating once more. Then she looked to the dewan. "Why have so many regiments returned home recently?"

"Indeed, I had noticed something of an overabundance of the military roaming the streets as I left my house this evening." The potentate looked curious.

The dewan shrugged, trying for casualness and failing. "Blame Cardwell and his blasted reforms."

Alexia sniffed pointedly. She approved of the reforms, far more humane to cut out flogging and change enlistment tactics. But the dewan was an old-timer; he liked his soldiers disciplined, poor, and mildly bloody.

He continued as though she hadn't sniffed. "We had that steamer in from West Africa several months ago crying that the Ashantis were giving us hell. The Secretary of War pulled everyone we could spare out of the east and back here for rotation."

"Do we still have that many troops in India? I thought the region was pacified."

"Not hardly. But we have the numbers to pull several regiments out and leave the East India Company and its mercenaries to take the brunt of it. The empire should stay sound. The duke wants proper regiments with werewolf attachments down in West Africa, and I can't say I blame him. It's a nasty business down there. These incoming regiments you see around London are to reconfigure as two separate battalions and ship back out within a month. It's causing a moon's worth of mess. Most had to be routed through Egypt in order to get back here fast enough, and I still don't know how we are going to stretch to fill the orders. Still, they're here now, clogging up the London taverns. Best get them fighting again right quick."

He rounded on Lady Maccon. "Which reminds me. Get your husband to keep his ruddy packs under control, would you?"

"Packs? There was only the one last time I checked, and let me inform you, it is not my husband who has to discipline them. Constantly."

The dewan grinned, causing his massive mustache to wiggle. "I am guessing you met Major Channing?" There were just few enough werewolves in England that, as Alexia had come to learn, they all seemed to know one another. And gracious did they enjoy a good gossip.

"You would be guessing correctly." Lady Maccon made a sour face.

"Well, I was referring to the earl's other pack, the Highland one, Kingair," said the dewan. "They were running with the Black Watch regiment, and there's been a bit of a dust-up. I thought your husband might stick a paw in."

Lady Maccon frowned. "I doubt it."

"Lost their Alpha out there, the Kingair Pack, you do realize? Niall something-or-other, a full colonel, nasty business. The pack was ambushed during high noon, when they were at their weakest and couldn't change shape. Threw the whole regiment over for a while there. Losing a ranking officer like that, werewolf Alpha or not, caused quite a fuss."

Alexia's frown deepened. "No, I was not aware." She wondered if her husband knew of this. She tapped her lip with the back of her pen. It was highly unusual for a former Alpha to survive the loss of his pack, and she had never managed to extract from Conall the whys and where-fores of his abandonment of the Highlands. But Alexia was pretty darn certain that a leadership void placed him under some sort of obligation to his former pack, even if it had been decades.

The discussion moved on to speculation as to who might be re-sponsible for the weapon: various not-as-secret-as-they-wanted societ-ies, foreign nations, or factions within the government. Lady Maccon was convinced it was Hypocras Club style scientists and held firm on her stance over deregulation. This frustrated the potentate, who wanted the surviving Hypocras Club members released to his tender mercies. The dewan sided with the muhjah. He wasn't particularly interested in scientific research of this kind, but he wasn't about to see it fall wholly into vampire hands. This derailed the conversation onto distribution of Hypocras goods. Alexia suggested they go to BUR, and despite her husband's charge of the institution, the potentate agreed so long as a vampire agent was attached.

By the time Queen Victoria arrived to confer with her council, they had come to several decisions. They informed her of the plague of humanization and their theory that it was some kind of secret weapon. The queen was appropriately worried. She knew perfectly well that the strength of her empire rested on the backs of her vampire advisors and her werewolf fighters. If they were at risk, so was Britain. She was par-ticularly insistent that Alexia look into the mystery. After all, exorcism was supposed to be under the muhjah's jurisdiction.

Since she would have gone out of her way to investigate regardless, Lady Maccon was happy to have official sanction. She left the Shadow Council meeting with a feeling of unexpected accomplishment. She desperately wanted to pigeonhole her husband in his BUR den, but, knowing that would only end in a row, she headed home to Floote and the library instead.

Lady Alexia Maccon's father's collection of books, normally an excel-lent, or at least distracting, source of information, proved a disappoint-ment on the matter of large-scale negation of the supernatural. Nor did it have anything to say on the potentate's tantalizing comment con-cerning a threat to vampires worse than soul-suckers. After hours of flipping through the worn leather-covered books, ancient scrolls, and personal journals, Lady Maccon and Floote had uncovered absolutely nothing. There were no further notes in her little leather book and no further insight into the mystery.

Floote's silence was eloquent.

Alexia nibbled a light breakfast of toast with potted ham and kippered salmon and went to bed just before dawn, defeated and frustrated.

She was awakened in the early morning by her husband, in an entirely dissimilar state of frustration. His big rough hands were insistent, and she was not unwilling to awaken thus, especially as she had some very pressing questions that needed answers. Still, it was daylight, and most respectable supernatural folk ought to be asleep. Fortunately, Conall Maccon was a strong enough Alpha to be awake several days running without the ill effects younger members of a pack would sustain from such solar contamination.

His approach was unique this time. He was squirming his way up under the covers from the foot of the bed toward where she lay. Alexia's newly opened eyes met the ludicrous sight of an enormous lump of bedclothes, swaying back and forth like some sort of encumbered jellyfish, laboring toward her. She was lying on her side, and his chest hair tickled the backs of her legs. He was lifting up her nightgown as he went. A little kiss whiskered just behind one knee, and Alexia jerked her leg in reaction. It tickled something dreadful.

She flipped the blankets and glared down at him. "What are you doing, you ridiculous man? You are acting like some sort of deranged mole."

"Being stealthy, my little terror. Do I not *seem* stealthy?" He spoke with mock affront.

"Why?"

He looked a little bashful, which was a categorically absurd expression for an enormous Scotsman to wear. "I was after the romanticism of an undercover approach, wife. The BUR agent mystique. Even if this BUR agent is disgracefully late home."

His wife propped herself up on one elbow and raised both eyebrows, clearly trying to suppress laughter but still look intimidating.

"No?"

The eyebrows went, if possible, higher.

"Humor me."

Alexia swallowed down a bubble of mirth and pretended a gravity suitable to a Lady Maccon. "If you insist, husband." She placed a hand to her heart and sank back into the pillows with a sigh of the type she imagined emitted by the heroine of a Rosa Carey novel.

Lord Maccon's eyes were halfway between caramel and yellow, and he smelled of open fields. Alexia wondered if he had traveled home in wolf form.

"Husband, we must talk."

"Aye, but later," he muttered. He began hiking her nightgown up farther, turning his attention to less ticklish but no-less-sensitive areas of her body.

"I loathe this article of clothing." He pulled the offending garment off and tossed it to its customary repose on the floor.

Lady Maccon went almost cross-eyed in her attempt to watch him as he moved predatorily the rest of the way up her body.

"You purchased it." She squirmed down to bring herself in greater contact with his body, her excuse being that it was cold and he had yet to replace the covers.

"So I did. Remind me to stick to parasols from now on."

His tawny eyes turned almost completely yellow; they tended to do that at this stage in the proceedings. Alexia loved it. Before she could protest, had she thought to, he swooped in for a full, all-absorbing kiss of the kind that, when they were standing, tended to make her knees go wobbly.

But they were not standing, and Alexia was now fully awake and unwilling to give in to the persuasions of her knees, her husband's mouth, or any other area of the body for that matter.

"Husband, I am very angry with you." She panted slightly as she made the accusation and tried to remember why.

He bit down softly at the meaty place between her shoulder and neck. Alexia let out a small moan.

"What have I done this time?" he paused to ask before continuing with his oral expedition about her body: her husband, the intrepid explorer.

Alexia writhed, attempting to get away.

But her movements only caused him to groan and become more insistent.

"You left me with an entire regiment encamping on my front lawn," she finally remembered to accuse.

"Mmm." Warm kisses littered her torso.

"And there was a certain Major Channing Channing of the Chesterfield Channings to boot."

He husband left off his nibbling to say, "You make him sound like some sort of disease."

"You *have* met him, I assume?"

The earl snorted softly and then began kissing her again, moving down toward her stomach.

"You knew they were coming, and you did not see fit to inform me."

He sighed, a puff of breath across her bare belly. "Lyall."

Alexia pinched his shoulder. He returned his amorous attentions to her lower body. "Yes! Lyall had to introduce me to my own pack. I've never met the soldier element before. Remember?"

"I am given to understand, from my Beta, that you handled a particularly hard situation perfectly adequately," he said between kisses and little licks. "Care to handle something else hard?"

Alexia thought maybe she might care to. After all, why should she be the only one panting? She pulled him up for a proper kiss and reached downward.

"And what about this mass exorcism in London? You did not see fit to tell me about that either?" she grumbled, squeezing softly.

"Um, well, that . . ." He huffed against her hair. Persuasive mouth. Mutter mutter. ". . . ended." He nibbled her neck, his attentions becoming even more insistent.

"Wait," Alexia squeaked. "Were we not having a conversation?"

"I believe *you* were having a conversation," replied Conall before remembering there was only one surefire way to shut his wife up. He bent forward and sealed her mouth with his.

CHAPTER THREE

Hat Shopping and Other Difficulties

Alexia lay staring thoughtfully up at the ceiling, feeling about as wet and as limp as a half-cooked omelet. Suddenly she stiffened. "*What* did you say had ended?"

A soft snore greeted her question. Unlike vampires, werewolves did not appear dead during the day. They simply slept very, very heavily.

Well, not *this* werewolf. Not if Lady Maccon had anything to say about it. She poked her husband hard in the ribs with a thumb.

It might have been the poke or it might have been the preternatural contact, but he awoke with a soft snuffle.

"What ended?"

With his wife's imperious face peering down at him, Lord Maccon took a moment to wonder why he had thought to crave such a woman in his life. Alexia bent over and nibbled at his chest. Ah, yes, initiative and ingenuity.

The nibbles stopped. "Well?"

And manipulation.

His bleary tawny eyes narrowed. "Does that brain of yours never stop?"

Alexia gave him an arch, "Well, yes." She looked at the angle of the sunlight creeping in around the edge of one heavy velvet drape. "You do seem to be able to give it pause for a good two hours or so."

"Was that all? What do you say, Lady Maccon—shall we try for three?"

Alexia batted at him without any real annoyance. "Aren't you supposed to be too old for this kind of continuous exercise?"

"What a thing to say, my love," snorted the earl, offended. "I am only just over two hundred, a veritable cub in the woods."

But Lady Maccon was not to be so easily distracted a second time. "So, what ended?"

He sighed. "That strange mass preternatural effect ceased at about three a.m. this morning. Everyone who should have returned to supernatural normal did, except for the ghosts. Any ghost tethered in the Thames embankment area seems to have been permanently exorcised. We brought in a volunteer ghost with a body about an hour after normality returned. He remained perfectly fine and tethered, so any new ghosts should establish in the area without difficulty, but all the old ones are gone for good."

"So that is it? Crisis averted?" Lady Maccon was disappointed. She must remember to jot this all down in her little investigation notebook.

"Oh, I think not. This isn't something that can be swept under the proverbial carpet. We must determine what exactly occurred. Everyone knows of the incident, even the daylight folk. Although they are, admittedly, much less upset about it than the supernatural set. Everybody wants to know what happened."

"Including Queen Victoria," interjected Alexia.

"I lost several excellent ghost agents in that mass exorcism. So did the Crown. I also had office visits from the *Times,* the *Nightly Aethograph,* and the *Evening Leader,* not to mention a very angry Lord Ambrose."

"My poor darling." Lady Maccon petted his head sympathetically. The earl hated dealing with the press, and he could barely tolerate being in the same room as Lord Ambrose. "I take it Countess Nadasdy was in a tizzy over the matter."

"To say nothing of the rest of her hive. After all, it has been thousands of years since a queen was in such danger."

Alexia sniffed. "It probably did them all some good." It was no secret she bore little love for and had absolutely no trust in the Westminster Hive queen. Lady Maccon and Countess Nadasdy were carefully polite to each other. The countess *always* invited Lord and Lady Maccon to her rare and coveted soirees, and Lord and Lady Maccon pointedly *always* attended.

"You know, Lord Ambrose had the audacity to threaten me? Me!" The earl was practically growling. "As though it were my fault!"

"I would have suspected he thought it was mine," suggested his wife.

Lord Maccon became even more angry. "Aye, well, he and his whole hive are deuced ignorant arses, and their opinion is of little consequence."

"Husband, language please. Besides, the potentate and the dewan felt the same."

"Did they threaten you?" The earl reared upright and grumbled several dockside phrases.

His wife interrupted his tirade by saying, "I completely see their point."

"What?"

"Be reasonable, Conall. I am the only soulless in this area, and so far as anyone knows, only preternaturals have this kind of effect on supernaturals. It is a logical causal leap to take."

"Except that we both know it was not you."

"Exactly! So who was it? Or what was it? What really did happen? I am certain you have some theory or other."

At that her husband chuckled. He had, after all, attached himself to a woman without a soul. He should not be surprised by her consistent pragmatism. Amazed by how quickly his wife could improve his mood by simply being herself, he said, "You first, woman."

Alexia tugged him down to lie next to her and pillowed her head in the crook between his chest and shoulder. "The Shadow Council has informed the queen that we believe it to be a newly developed scientific weapon of some kind."

"Do you agree?" His voice was a rumble under her ear.

"It is a possibility in this modern age, but it is only, at best, a working hypothesis. It might be that Darwin is right, and we have attained a new age of preternatural evolution. It might be that the Templars are somehow involved. It might be that we are missing something vital." She directed a sharp glare at her silent spouse. "Well, what has BUR uncovered?"

Alexia had a private theory that this was part of her role as muhjah. Queen Victoria had taken an unexpectedly favorable interest in seeing Alexia Tarabotti married to Conall Maccon, prior to Alexia's assumption of the post. Lady Maccon often wondered if that wasn't a wish to see greater lines of communication open between BUR and the Shadow Council. Although, Queen Victoria probably did not think such communication would take place quite so carnally.

"How much do you know about Ancient Egypt, wife?" Conall dislodged her and leaned up on one arm, idly rubbing the curve of her side with his free hand.

Alexia tucked a pillow under her head and shrugged. Her father's library included a large collection of papyrus scrolls. He had had some fondness for Egypt, but Alexia had always been more interested in the classical world. There was something unfortunately fierce and passionate about the Nile and its environs. She was much too practical for Arabic with its flowery scrawl when Latin, with all its mathematic precision, made for such an attractive alternative.

Lord Maccon pursed his lips. "It was ours, you know? The werewolves'. Way back, four thousand years or more, lunar calendar and everything. Long before the daylight folk built up Greece and before the vampires extruded Rome, we werewolves had Egypt. You have seen how I can keep my body and turn only my head into wolf shape?"

"The thing that only true Alphas can do?" Alexia remembered it well from the one time she had seen him do it. It was unsettling and mildly revolting.

He nodded. "To the present day, we still call it the Anubis Form. Howlers say that, for a time, we were worshipped as gods in Ancient Egypt. And that was our downfall. For there are legends of a disease, a massive epidemic that struck only the supernatural: the God-Breaker Plague, a pestilence of unmaking. They say it swept the Nile clean of blood and bite, of werewolves and vampires alike, all of them dying as mortals within the space of a generation, and no metamorphosis came again to the Nile for a thousand years."

"And now?"

"Now in all of Egypt, there exists just one hive, near Alexandria, as north as it can get and still be delta. They represent what remains of the Ptolemy Hive. Just that one, and it came in with the Greeks, and is only six vampires strong. A few mangy packs roam the desert far up the Nile, way to the south. But they say the plague still dwells in the Valley of the Kings, and no supernatural has ever practiced any form of archaeology. It is our one forbidden science, even now."

Alexia processed this information. "So you believe we may be facing down an epidemic? A disease like this God-Breaker Plague?"

"It is possible."

"Then why would it simply disappear?"

Conall rubbed his face with his large callused hand. "I do not know. Werewolf legends are kept in the oral tradition, from howler to howler. We have no written edicts. Thus, they shift through time. It is possible the plague of the past was not so bad as we remember or that they simply did not know to leave the area. Or it is possible that what we have now is some completely new form of the disease."

Alexia shrugged. "It is at least as good a theory as our weapon hypothesis. I suppose there is only one way to find out."

"The queen has placed you on the case, then?" The earl never liked the idea of Alexia undertaking field operations. When he first recommended her for the job of muhjah, he thought it a nice, safe political position, full of paperwork and tabletop debate. It had been so long since England had a muhjah, few remembered what the preternatural advisor to the queen actually did. She was indeed meant to legislatively balance out the potentate's vampire agenda and the dewan's military obsession. But she was also meant to take on the role of mobile information gatherer, since preternaturals were confined by neither place nor pack. Lord Maccon had been spitting angry when he found out the truth of it. Werewolves, by and large, loathed espionage as dishonorable—the vampire's game. He'd even accused Alexia of being a kind of drone to Queen Victoria. Alexia had retaliated by wearing her most voluminous nightgown for a whole week.

"Can you think of someone better suited?"

"But, wife, this could become quite dangerous, if it is a weapon. If there is malice behind the action."

Lady Maccon let out a huff of disgust. "For everyone but *me.* I am the only one who would not be adversely affected, and, so far as I can tell, I seem to be essentially unchanged. Well, me and one other type of person. Which reminds me—the potentate said something interesting this evening."

"Really. What an astonishingly unusual occurrence."

"He said that according to the edicts, there exists a creature worse than a soul-sucker. Or perhaps it *used* to exist. You would not know anything about this, would you, husband?" She watched Conall's face quite closely.

There was a flicker of genuine surprise in his tawny eyes. In this, at least, he appeared to have no ready answer carefully prepared.

"I have never heard talk of such a thing. But then again, we are different in our perceptions, the vampires and the werewolves. We see you as a curse-breaker, not a soul-sucker and, as such, not so bad. So for werewolves, there are many things worse than you. For the vampires? There are ancient myths from the dawn of time that tell of a horror native to both day and night. The werewolves call this the *skin-stealer.* But it is only a myth."

Alexia nodded.

A hand began gently stroking the curve of her side.

"Are we done talking now?" the earl asked plaintively.

Alexia gave in to his demanding touch, but only, of course, because he sounded so pathetic. It had nothing, whatsoever, to do with her own quickening heartbeat.

She entirely failed to remember to tell Conall about his former pack's now-dead Alpha.

Alexia awakened slightly later than usual to find her husband already gone. She expected to encounter him at the supper table so was not overly troubled. Her mind already plotting investigations, she did not bother to protest the outfit her maid chose, replying only with, "That should do well enough, dear," to Angelique's suggestion of the pale blue silk walking dress trimmed in white lace.

The maid was astonished by her acquiescence, but her surprise was not sufficient to affect her efficiency. She had her mistress smartly dressed, if a tad too de mode for Alexia's normal preferences, and down at the dining table in a scant half hour—a noteworthy accomplishment by anyone's standards.

Everyone else was already seated at the supper table. In this particular case, "everyone else" included the pack, both residents and returnees, half the clavigers, and the insufferable Major Channing—about thirty or so. "Everyone else" did not, however, appear to include the master of the house. Lord Maccon made for a tangibly large absence, even in such a crowd.

Sans husband, Lady Maccon plonked herself down next to Professor Lyall. She gave him a little half-smile as a partial greeting. The Beta had not yet commenced his meal, preferring to begin with a hot cup of tea and the evening paper.

Startled by her sudden appearance, the rest of the table scrambled to stand politely as she joined them. Alexia waved them back to their seats, and they returned with much clattering. Only Professor Lyall managed a smooth stand, slight bow, and reseat with the consummate grace of a dancer. And all that without losing his place in his newspaper.

Lady Maccon quickly served herself some haricot of veal and several apple fritters and began eating so the others about the table could stop fussing and continue with their own meals. Really, sometimes it was simply too vexatious to be a lady living with two dozen gentlemen. Not to mention the hundreds now encamped on the Woolsey grounds.

After only a moment to allow her husband's Beta to acclimatize to her presence, Lady Maccon struck. "Very well, Professor Lyall, I shall bite: where has he gone now?"

The urbane werewolf said only, "Brussels sprouts?"

Lady Maccon declined in horror. She enjoyed most foods, but brussels sprouts were nothing more than underdeveloped cabbages.

Professor Lyall said, crinkling his paper, "*Shersky and Droop* are offering the most interesting new gadget for sale, just here. It is a particularly advanced form of teakettle, designed for air travel, to be mounted on the sides of dirigibles. It harnesses the wind via this small whirligig contraption that generates enough energy to boil water." He pointed out the advertisement to Alexia, who was distracted despite herself.

"Really? How fascinating. And so very useful for those more frequent dirigible travelers. I wonder if . . ." She trailed off and gave him a suspicious look. "Professor Lyall, you are trying to persuade me away from the point. Where has my husband gone?"

The Beta put down the now-useless newspaper and dished himself a fine piece of fried sole from a silver platter. "Lord Maccon left at the crack of dusk."

"That was not what I asked."

On the far side of Lyall, Major Channing chuckled softly into his soup.

Alexia glared at him and then turned a sharp look onto the defenseless Tunstell, seated at the other side of the table among the clavigers. If Lyall would not talk, perhaps Tunstell would. The redhead met her glare with wide eyes and quickly stuffed his face with a large mouthful of veal, trying to look as if he knew absolutely nothing.

"At least tell me if he was dressed properly?"

Tunstell chewed slowly. Very slowly.

Lady Maccon turned back to Professor Lyall, who was calmly slicing into his sole. Lyall was one of the few werewolves she had met who actively preferred fish to meat.

"Did he head off to Claret's?" she asked, thinking the earl might have business at his club before work.

Professor Lyall shook his head.

"I see. Are we to play at guessing games, then?"

The Beta sighed softly through his nose and finished his bite of sole. He put down his knife and fork with great precision on the side of his plate and then dabbed, unnecessarily, at his mouth with the corner of his serviette.

Lady Maccon waited patiently, nibbling at her own dinner. After Professor Lyall had put the damask serviette back into his lap and shoved his spectacles up his nose, she said, "Well?"

"He had a message this morning. I'm not privy to the particulars. He then swore a blue streak and set off northward."

"Northward to where, exactly?"

Professor Lyall sighed. "I believe he has gone to Scotland."

"He did *what*?"

"And he did not take Tunstell with him." Professor Lyall stated the obvious in clear annoyance, pointing to the redhead who was looking ever more guilty and ever more eager to continue chewing rather than participate in the conversation.

Lady Maccon worried at that information. Why should Conall take Tunstell? "Is he in danger? Shouldn't you have gone with him, then?"

Lyall snorted. "Yes. Picture the state of his cravat without a valet to tie him in." The Beta, always the height of understated elegance, winced in imagined horror.

Alexia privately agreed with this.

"Could not take me," muttered the Tunstell in question. "Had to go in wolf form. Trains are down, what with the engineer's strike. Not that I should mind going; my play's finished its run, and I've never seen Scotland." There was a note of petulance in his tone.

Hemming, one of the resident pack members, slapped Tunstell hard on the shoulder. "Respect," he growled without looking up from his meal.

"Where, precisely, has my husband taken himself off to in Scotland?" Lady Maccon pressed for details.

"The southern part of the Highlands, as I understand it," replied the Beta.

Alexia recovered her poise. What little she had. Which admittedly wasn't generally considered much. The southern Highland area was the vicinity of Conall's previous abode. She thought she understood at last. "I take it he found out about his former pack's Alpha being killed?"

Now it was Major Channing's turn to be surprised. The blond man practically spat out his mouthful of fritter. "How did *you* know that?"

Alexia looked up from her cup of tea. "I know many things."

Major Channing's pretty mouth twisted at that.

Professor Lyall said, "His lordship did say something about dealing with an embarrassing family emergency."

"Am I not family?" wondered Lady Maccon.

To which Lyall muttered under his breath, "And often embarrassing."

"Careful there, Professor. Only one person is allowed to say insulting things about me to my face, and you are certainly not large enough to be he."

Lyall actually blushed. "All apologies, *mistress*. I forgot my tongue." He emphasized her title and pulled his cravat down to show his neck ever so slightly.

"*We* are all his family! And he simply left us." Major Channing seemed to be even more annoyed by Alexia's husband's departure than she was. "Pity he didn't talk to me beforehand. I might have given him reason to stay."

Alexia turned hard brown eyes on Woolsey's Gamma. "Oh yes?"

But Major Channing was busy puzzling over something else. "Of course, he might have known, or at least guessed. What *did* they get up to those months without an Alpha to guide them?"

"I don't know," pressed Alexia, although his talk was clearly not directed at her. "Why don't *you* tell *me* what you were going to tell him?"

Major Channing started and managed to look both guilty and angry at the same time. Everyone's attention was on him.

"Yes," came Lyall's soft voice, "why don't you?" There was steel there, behind the studied indifference.

"Oh, it is nothing much. Only that, while we were on the boat and for the entirety of the journey over the Mediterranean and through the straits, none of us could change into wolf form. Six regiments with four packs, and we all grew beards. Basically, we were mortal the whole time. Once we left the ship and traveled some ways toward Woolsey, we suddenly became our old supernatural selves once more."

"That is very interesting given recent occurrences, and you didn't manage to tell my husband?"

"He never had time for me." Channing seemed angrier than she was.

"You took that as a slight and did not make him listen? That is not only stupid but could prove dangerous." Now Alexia was getting angry. "Is someone a little jealous?"

Major Channing slammed his palm down on the table, rattling the dishes. "We have only *just* arrived back after six years abroad, and *our* illustrious Alpha takes off, leaving his pack to go and see to the business of another!" The major practically spat the words out in his self-righteousness.

"Yup," said Hemming from nearby, "definitely jealous."

Major Channing pointed a threatening finger at him. He had wide, elegant hands, but they were callused and rough, making Alexia wonder what backcountry he had fought to tame in the years before he became a werewolf. "Take greater caution with your words, runt. I outrank you."

Hemming tilted his head, exposing his throat in acknowledgment of the threat's validity, and then proceeded to finish his supper and keep his opinions to himself.

Tunstell and the rest of the clavigers watched the conversation with wide-eyed interest. Having the entire pack home was a novel experience for them. The Coldsteam Guards had been stationed in India long enough for most of the Woolsey clavigers to have never met the full pack.

Lady Maccon decided she had had enough of Major Channing for one evening. With this new information, it was even more urgent she head into town, and so she rose from her chair and called for the carriage.

"Back into London again this evening, my lady?" wondered Floote, appearing in the hallway with her mantle and hat.

"Unfortunately, yes." His lady was looking perturbed.

"Will you be needing the dispatch case?"

"Not tonight, Floote. I am not going as muhjah. Best to remain as innocuous-looking as possible."

Floote's silence was eloquent, as so many of Floote's silences were. What his beloved mistress made up for in brains she lacked in subtlety; she was about as innocuous as one of Ivy Hisselpenny's hats.

Alexia rolled her eyes at him. "Yes, well, I take your point, but there is something I am missing about last night's incident. And now we know that whatever it was came into town with the regiments. I simply must see if I can catch Lord Akeldama. What BUR did not uncover, his boys will have."

Floote looked slightly perturbed by this. One eyelid fluttered almost imperceptibly. Alexia would never have noticed had she not labored under twenty-six years of acquaintance with the man. What it meant was that he did not entirely approve of her fraternization with the most outlandish of London's vampire roves.

"Do not alarm yourself, Floote. I shall take prodigious care. Pity I do not have a legitimate excuse for going into town tonight, though. People will remark upon my break from the normal schedule."

A timid feminine voice said, "My lady, I may be able to assist with that."

Alexia looked up with a smile. Female voices were rare about Woolsey Castle, but this was one of the few commonly heard ones. As ghosts went, Formerly Merriway was an amenable one, and Alexia had grown fond of her over the last few months. Even if she was timid.

"Good evening, Formerly Merriway. How are you tonight?"

"Still holding myself together, mistress," replied the ghost, appearing as nothing more than a shimmery grayish mist in the brightness of the gas-lit hallway. The front hall was at the farthest end of her tether, so it was difficult for her to solidify. It also meant her body must be located somewhere in the upper portion of Woolsey Castle, probably walled in somewhere, a fact Alexia preferred not to think about and hoped fervently never to smell.

"I have a personal message to deliver to you, my lady."

"From my impossible husband?" It was a safe guess, as Lord Maccon was the only one who would employ a ghost rather than some sensible means of communication, like perhaps waking up his own wife and talking to her before he left for once.

The ghostly form swayed a bit up and down, Formerly Merriway's version of a nod. "From his lordship, yes."

"Well?" barked Alexia.

Formerly Merriway skittered back slightly. Despite copious promises from Alexia that she was not going to wander about the castle looking to lay hands on Merriway's corpse, the ghost could not get over her fear of the preternatural. She persisted in seeing imminent exorcism behind every threatening attitude Alexia took, which, given Alexia's character, made for a constant state of nervousness.

Alexia sighed and modified her tone. "What was his message to me, Formerly Merriway, please?" She used the hall mirror to pin on her hat, careful not to upset Angelique's hairdo. It perched far to the back of the head in an entirely useless manner, but as the sun was not out, Alexia supposed she did not have to mind the lack of shade.

"You are to go hat shopping," said Formerly Merriway, quite unexpectedly.

Alexia wrinkled her forehead and pulled on her gloves. "I am, am I?"

Formerly Merriway gave her bobbing nod once again. "He recommends a newly opened establishment on Regent Street called Chapeau de Poupe. He emphasized that you should visit it without delay."

Lord Maccon rarely took an interest in his own attire. Lady Maccon could hardly believe he would suddenly take an interest in hers.

She said only, "Ah, well, I was just thinking how I did not like this hat. Not that I really require a new one."

"Well, I certainly know someone who does," said Floote with unexpected feeling from just behind her shoulder.

"Yes, Floote, I *am* sorry you had to see those grapes yesterday," Alexia apologized. Poor Floote had very delicate sensibilities.

"Suffering comes unto us all," quoth Floote sagely. Then he handed over a blue and white lace parasol and saw her down the steps and into the waiting carriage.

"To the Hisselpenny town residence," he instructed the driver, "posthaste."

"Oh, Floote." Lady Maccon stuck her head out the window as the carriage wheeled off down the drive. "Cancel tomorrow's dinner party, would you? Since my husband has chosen to absent himself, there is simply no point."

Floote tipped his head at the retreating carriage in acknowledgment and went to see to the details.

Alexia felt justified in turning up on Ivy's doorstep without announcement, as Ivy had done that very thing to her the evening before.

Miss Ivy Hisselpenny was sitting listlessly in the front parlor of the Hisselpennys' modest town address, receiving visitors. She was delighted to see Alexia, however unexpected. The whole Hisselpenny household was generally elated to receive Lady Maccon; never had they thought Ivy's odd little relationship with bluestocking spinster Alexia Tarabotti would flower into such a social coup de grace.

Lady Maccon swept in to find Mrs. Hisslepenny and her clacking knitting needles, keeping wordless vigil to her daughter's endless chatter.

"Oh, Alexia! Tremendous."

"And a good evening to you too, Ivy. How are you tonight?"

This was rather an imprudent question to ask Miss Hisselpenny, as Miss Hisselpenny was prone to telling one the answer—in excruciating detail.

"Would you believe? The announcement of my engagement to Captain Featherstonehaugh was in the *Times* this morning, and practically *no one* has called all day! I have received only twenty-four visitors, and when Bernice got engaged last month, she had twenty-seven! Shabby, I call it, perfectly shabby. Although, I suppose you would make it twenty-five, dearest Alexia."

"Ivy," said Alexia without further shilly-shallying, "why bother to lay about here awaiting insult? You clearly require some diversion. And I am in just the humor to provide it. For I do believe you are in dire need of a new hat. You and I should go shopping for one."

"Right this very instant?"

"Yes, immediately. I hear there is a divine new shop just opened on Regent Street. Shall we give it our patronage?"

"Oh." Ivy's cheeks pinkened in delight. "The Chapeau de Poupe? It is supposed to be very daring, indeed. Some ladies of my acquaintance have even referred to it as *fast*." A little gasp at that word emitted from Ivy's perennially quiet mama, but that good lady did not offer any comment to companion her inhalation, so Ivy continued. "You know, only the most forward ladies frequent that establishment. The actress Mabel Dair is supposed to stop in regularly. And the proprietress is said to be quite the scandal herself."

Everything about her friend's outraged tone told Alexia that Ivy was dying to visit Chapeau de Poupe.

"Well, it sounds like just the place to find something a little more unusual for the winter season, and as a newly engaged lady, you do realize you simply must have a new hat."

"Must I?"

"Trust me, my dearest Ivy, you most definitely must."

"Well, Ivy dear," said Mrs. Hisselpenny in a soft voice, setting down her knitting and looking up. "You should go and change. It would not do to keep Lady Maccon waiting on such a generous offer."

Ivy, pressed most firmly into doing something she wished to do more than anything else in the world, trotted upstairs with only a few more token protests.

"You will try to help her, won't you, Lady Maccon?" Mrs. Hisselpenny's eyes were quite desperate over her once-again clicking needles.

Alexia thought she understood the question. "You are also worried about this sudden engagement?"

"Oh no, Captain Featherstonehaugh is quite a suitable match. No, I was referring to Ivy's headwear preferences."

Alexia swallowed down a smile, keeping her face perfectly serious. "Of course. I shall do my very best, for queen and country."

The Hisselpennys' manservant appeared with a welcome tea tray. Lady Maccon sipped a freshly brewed cup in profound relief. All in all, it had been quite the trying evening thus far. With Ivy and hats in her future, it was only likely to get worse. Tea was a medicinal necessity at this juncture. Thank goodness Mrs. Hisselpenny had thought to provide.

Lady Maccon resorted to painfully pleasant discussion of the weather for a quarter of an hour. None too soon, Ivy reappeared in a walking dress of orange taffeta ruffled to within an inch of its life, and a champagne brocade overjacket, paired with a particularly noteworthy flowerpot hat. The hat was, not unexpectedly, decorated with a herd of silk mums and here and there a tiny feather bee on the end of a piece of wire.

Alexia forbore to look at the hat, thanked Mrs. Hisselpenny for the tea, and hustled Ivy into the Woolsey carriage. Around them, London's night society was coming to life, gas lights being lit, elegantly dressed couples hailing cabs, here and there a reeling group of rowdy young blunts. Alexia directed her driver to proceed on to Regent Street, and they arrived in short order at Chapeau de Poupe.

At first Alexia was at a loss as to why her husband wanted her to visit Chapeau de Poupe. So she did what any young lady of good breeding would do. She shopped.

"Are you certain you wish to go hat shopping with me, Alexia?" asked Ivy as they pushed in through the wrought-iron door. "Your taste in hats is not mine."

"I should most profoundly hope not," replied Lady Maccon with real feeling, looking at the flower-covered monstrosity atop her friend's sweet round little face and glossy black curls.

The shop proved to be as reported. It was exceptionally modern in appearance, all light airy muslin drapes, with soft peach and sage striped walls and bronze furniture with clean lines and matched cushions.

"Ahooo," said Ivy, looking about with wide eyes. "Isn't this simply too French?"

There were a few hats on tables and on wall hooks, but most were hanging from little gold chains suspended from the ceiling. They fell to different heights so that one had to brush through the hats to get around the shop, and they swayed slightly, like some alien vegetation. And such hats—caps of embroidered batiste with Mechlin lace, Italian straw shepherdesses, faille capotes, velvet toques that put Ivy's flowerpot to shame, and outrageous pifferaro bonnets—dangled everywhere.

Ivy was immediately entranced by the ugliest of the bunch: a canary-yellow felt toque trimmed with black currants, black velvet ribbon, and a pair of green feathers that looked like antennae off to one side.

"Oh, not that one!" said both Alexia and another voice at the same time when Ivy reached to pull it off the wall.

Ivy's hand dropped to her side, and both she and Lady Maccon turned to see the most remarkable-looking woman emerging from a curtained back room.

Alexia thought, without envy, that this was quite probably the most beautiful female she had ever seen. She had a lovely small mouth, large green eyes, prominent cheekbones, and dimples when she smiled, which she was doing now. Normally Alexia objected to dimples, but they seemed to suit this woman. Perhaps because they were offset by her thin angular frame and the fact that she had her brown hair cut unfashionably short, like a man's.

Ivy gasped upon seeing her.

This was not because of the hair. Or, not entirely because of it. This was because the woman was also dressed head to shiny boots in perfect and impeccable style—for a man. Jacket, pants, and waistcoat were all to the height of fashion. A top hat perched upon that scandalously short hair, and her burgundy cravat was tied into a silken waterfall. Still, there was no pretense at hiding her femininity. Her voice, when she spoke, was low and melodic, but definitely that of a woman.

Alexia picked up a pair of burnt umber kid gloves from a display basket. They were as soft as butter to the touch, and she looked at them to stop herself from staring at the woman.

"I am Madame Lefoux. Welcome to Chapeau de Poupe. How may I serve you fine ladies?" She had the hint of a French accent, but only the barest hint, utterly unlike Angelique, who could never seem to handle the "th" sound.

Ivy and Alexia curtsied with a little tilt to their heads, the latest fashion in curtsies, designed to show that the neck was unbitten. One wouldn't want to be thought a drone without the benefit of vampiric protection. Madame Lefoux did the same, although it was impossible to tell if her neck was bitten under that skillfully tied cravat. Alexia noted with interest that she wore two cravat pins: one of silver and one of wood. Madame Lefoux might keep night hours, but she was cautious about it.

Lady Maccon said, "My friend Miss Hisselpenny has recently become engaged and is in dire need of a new hat." She did not introduce herself, not yet. Lady Maccon was a name best kept in reserve.

Madame Lefoux took in Ivy's copious flowers and feather bees. "Yes, this is quite evident. Do walk this way, Miss Hisselpenny. I believe I have something over here that would perfectly suit that dress."

Ivy dutifully trotted after the strangely clad woman. She gave Alexia a look over her shoulder that said, as clearly as if she had the gumption to say it aloud, *what the deuce is she wearing?*

Alexia wandered over to the offensive yellow toque she and Madame Lefoux had so hastily warned Ivy off of. It completely contrasted with the general sophisticated tenor set by the other hats. Almost as though it wasn't meant to be purchased.

As the extraordinary patroness seemed to be thoroughly distracted by Ivy (well, who wouldn't be?), Alexia used the handle of her parasol to gently lift the toque and peek underneath. It was at that precise moment she deduced why it was her husband had sent her to Chapeau de Poupe.

There was a hidden knob, disguised as a hook, secreted under the hideous hat. Alexia quickly replaced the hat and turned away to begin innocently wandering about the shop, pretending interest in various accessories. She began to notice that there were other little hints as to a second nature for Chapeau de Poupe: scrape marks on the floor near a wall that *seemed* to have no door and several gas lights that were not lit. Alexia would wager good money that they were not lights at all.

Lady Maccon would not have thought to be curious, of course, had her husband not been so insistent she visit the establishment. The rest of the shop was quite unsuspicious, being the height of la mode, with hats appealing enough to hold even *her* unstylish awareness. But with the scrapes and the hidden knob, Alexia became curious, both about the shop and its owner. Lady Maccon might be soulless, but the liveliness of her mind was never in question.

She wandered over to where Madame Lefoux had actually persuaded Miss Hisselpenny to don a becoming little straw bonnet with upturned front, decorated about the crown with a few classy cream flowers and one graceful blue feather.

"Ivy, that looks remarkably well on you," she praised.

"Thank you, Alexia, but don't you find it a tad reserved? I'm not convinced it quite suits."

Lady Maccon and Madame Lefoux exchanged a *look*.

"No, I do not. It is nothing like that horrible yellow thing at the back you insisted on at first. I went to take a closer look, you know, and it really is quite ghastly."

Madame Lefoux glanced at Alexia, her beautiful face suddenly sharp and her dimples gone.

Alexia smiled, all teeth and not nicely. One couldn't live around werewolves and not pick up a few of their mannerisms. "It cannot possibly be your design?" she said mildly to the proprietress.

"The work of an apprentice, I do assure you," replied Madame Lefoux with a tiny French shrug. She put a new hat onto Ivy's head, one with a few more flowers.

Miss Hisselpenny preened.

"Are there any more . . . like it?" wondered Alexia, still talking about the ugly yellow hat.

"Well, there is that riding hat." The proprietress's voice was wary.

Lady Maccon nodded. Madame Lefoux was naming the hat nearest to the scrape marks Alexia had observed on the floor. They understood one another.

There came a pause in conversation while Ivy expressed interest in a frosted pink confection with feather toggles. Alexia spun her closed parasol between two gloved hands.

"You seem to be having problems with some of your gas lighting as well," said Alexia, all mildness and sugar.

"Indeed." A flicker of firm acknowledgment crossed Madame Lefoux's face at that. "And, of course, there is the door handle. But you know how it goes—there are always kinks to work out after opening a new establishment."

Lady Maccon cursed herself. The door handle—how had she missed that? She wandered over casually, leaning on her parasol to look down at it.

Ivy, all insensible of the underpinnings to their conversation, went on to try the next hat.

The handle on the inside of the front door was far larger than it ought to be and seemed to be comprised of a complicated series of cogs and bolts, far more security than any ordinary hat shop required.

Alexia wondered if Madame Lefoux was a French spy.

"Well," Ivy was telling Madame Lefoux in a chatty manner when Alexia rejoined them, "Alexia always says my taste is abysmal, but I can hardly see how she has much ground. Her choices are so often banal."

"I lack imagination," admitted Alexia. "Which is why I keep a highly creative French maid."

Madame Lefoux looked mildly interested at that. Her dimples showed in a little half-smile.

"And the eccentricity of carrying a parasol even at night? I take it I am being honored by a visit from Lady Maccon?"

"Alexia," Miss Hisselpenny asked, scandalized, "you never introduced yourself?"

"Well I—" Alexia was grappling for an excuse, when . . .

Boom!

And the world about them exploded into darkness.

CHAPTER FOUR

___

The Proper Use of Parasols

An enormous noise shook the structure around them. All of the hats on the ends of their long chains swung about violently. Ivy let out the most milk-curdling scream. Someone else yelled, rather soberly by comparison. The gas lighting went out, and the shop descended into darkness.

It took a moment for Lady Maccon to realize that the explosion had not, in fact, been intended to kill *her*. Given her experiences over the past year, this was a novel change of pace. But it also made her wonder if the explosion had been intended to kill someone else.

"Ivy?" Alexia asked the darkness.

Silence.

"Madame Lefoux?"

Further silence.

Alexia crouched down, as much as her corset would allow, and felt about, willing her eyes to acclimatize to the black. She felt taffeta: the ruffles attached to Ivy's prone form.

Alexia's heart sank.

She patted Ivy all about for injury, but Miss Hisselpenny seemed unscathed. Light puffs of breath hit the back of Lady Maccon's hand when she passed it under Ivy's nose, and there was a pulse—shallow but solid. Apparently, Miss Hisselpenny had simply fainted.

"Ivy!" she hissed.

Nothing.

"Ivy, please!"

Miss Hisselpenny shifted slightly and murmured, "Yes, Mr. Tunstell?" under her breath.

Oh dear, thought Alexia. What a terribly unsuitable match, and Ivy already engaged to someone else. Lady Maccon had no idea that things had progressed so far as to involve *murmurings* in times of distress. Then she felt a stab of pity. Better to let Ivy have her dreams while she could.

So Lady Maccon left her friend as she lay and did not reach for the smelling salts.

Madame Lefoux, on the other hand, was nowhere to be found. She had apparently vanished into the blackness. Perhaps seeking the source of the explosion. Or perhaps being the source of the explosion.

Alexia could guess as to where the Frenchwoman had disappeared. Her eyes now partly adjusted to the gloom, she made her way along the wall toward the back of the shop, where the scrape marks were located.

She felt all about the wallpaper for a switch or a knob of some kind, finally finding a lever hidden under a glove display box. She pressed it sharply down, and a door swung open before her, nearly cracking her on the nose.

Lady Maccon managed to determine that it was no room or passageway but a large shaft with several cables down the middle and two guide rails on the side. She craned her head inside and looked up, hanging on to the doorjamb. What appeared to be a steam-powered windlass occupied the whole of the top of the shaft. She found a cord to one side of the doorway that, when pulled upon, engaged the windlass. With many puffs of steam and some creaking and groaning, a boxy cage appeared from out of the shaft depths. Alexia was familiar with the concept—an ascension room. She'd had previous dealings with a less sophisticated version at the Hypocras Club. She had found that they did not suit her stomach, but she stepped into the cage regardless, closing the grate behind her, and turned a crank on one side to lower the contraption.

The cage bumped when it hit the ground, causing Alexia to stumble violently up against the side. Parasol held defensively before her as though it were a cricket bat, she opened the grate and stepped out into an illuminated underground passageway.

The lighting mechanism was like nothing Lady Maccon had ever seen. It must be some kind of gas, but it appeared as an orange tinted mist inside glass tubing set along the ceiling. The mist swirled about within its confines, causing the illumination to be patchy and faint in odd, shifting patterns. *Light cast as clouds,* thought Alexia fancifully.

At the end of the passage was an open doorway, out of which spilled a mass of brighter orange light and three voices raised in anger. As she neared, Alexia realized the passage must traverse directly underneath Regent Street. She also realized the voices were arguing in French.

Alexia had a good grasp of the modern languages, so she followed the gist of the conversation without difficulty.

"What could possibly have possessed you?" Madame Lefoux was asking, her voice still smooth despite her annoyance.

The entranceway appeared to service a laboratory of some kind, although it was nothing like those Alexia had seen at the Hypocras Club or the Royal Society. It had more the look of an apparatus factory, with massive machine components and other gadgetry.

"Well, you see, I could not for the life of me get the boiler running."

Alexia peeked into the room. It was huge and in a complete and utter muddle. Containers had been knocked off tables, glass had shattered, and thousands of tiny gears were scattered across the dirt floor. A jumble of cords and wire coils lay on the ground along with the hat stand they had once been hanging on. There was black soot everywhere, coating both those tubes, gears, and springs that had not fallen and the larger pieces of machinery. Outside the blast zone, things were also in disarray. A pair of glassicals lay atop a pile of research books. Large diagrams drawn in black pencil on stiff yellow paper were pinned haphazardly to the walls. It was clear that some accident had disrupted matters, but it was equally clear the place had been untidy well before the unfortunate event.

It was noisy, as many of those mechanisms and gadgets not affected by the blast were running. Steam puffed out in little gasps and whistles, gears clanked, metal chain links clicked, and valves squealed. Such a cacophony of noises as only the great factories of the north might make. But it wasn't an invasive noise, more a symphony in engineering.

Partly hidden behind the piles, Madame Lefoux stood, hands on angular trouser-clad hips, legs wide like a man, glaring down at some species of grubby child. The urchin came complete with grease-smeared face, filthy hands, and jaunty tilt to his newsboy cap. He was clearly in a hot spot of bother but seemed less apologetic than excited about his inadvertent pyrotechnics.

"So, what did you do, Quesnel?"

"I just soaked a bit of rag in ether and tossed it into the flame. Ether catches fire, no?"

"Oh, for goodness sake, Quesnel. Don't you ever listen?" This came from a new voice, a ghost, who was making a show of sitting side-saddle on an overturned barrel. She was a very solid-looking specter, which meant her dead body must be relatively close and well preserved.

Regent Street was well north of the exorcised zone, so she would have escaped last night's incident undead. If the ghost's speech was anything to go by, her body must have traveled over from France, or she had died in London an immigrant. Her face was sharply defined, her visage that of a handsome older woman who resembled Madame Lefoux. Her arms were crossed over her chest in annoyance.

"Ether!" shrieked Madame Lefoux.

"Well, yes," said the ragamuffin.

"Ether is explosive, you little . . ." After which followed a stream of unpleasant words, which still managed to sound pleasant in Madame Lefoux's mellow voice.

"Ah," replied the boy with a shameless grin. "But it did make a fantastic bang."

Alexia could not help herself; she let out a little giggle.

All three gasped and looked over at her.

Lady Maccon straightened up, brushed her blue silk walking dress smooth, and entered the cavernous room, swinging her parasol back and forth.

"Ah," said Madame Lefoux, switching back to her impeccable English. "Welcome to my contrivance chamber, Lady Maccon."

"You are a woman of many talents, Madame Lefoux, an inventor as well as a milliner?"

Madame Lefoux inclined her head. "As you see, the two more often cross paths than one would think. I should have realized you would deduce the function of the windlass engine and the location of my laboratory, Lady Maccon."

"Oh," replied Alexia. "Why should you have?"

The Frenchwoman dimpled at her and bent to retrieve a fallen vial of some silvery liquid, which had managed to escape Quesnel's explosion unbroken. "Your husband informed me that you were clever. And prone to interfering overmuch."

"That sounds like something he would say." Alexia made her way through the shambles, lifting her skirts delicately to keep them from getting caught on fragments of glass. Now that she could see them closer up, the gadgets lying about Madame Lefoux's contrivance chamber were amazing. There seemed to be an entire assembly line of glassicals in midconstruction and a massive apparatus that looked to be composed of the innards of several steam engines welded to a galvanometer, a carriage wheel, and a wicker chicken.

Alexia, tripping only once over a large valve, completed her trek across the room and nodded politely to the child and the ghost.

"How do you do? Lady Maccon, at your service."

The scrap of a boy grinned at her, made an elaborate bow, and said, "Quesnel Lefoux."

Alexia gave him an expressionless look. "So, *did* you get the boiler started?"

Quesnel blushed. "Not exactly. But I did get a fire started. That should count for something, don't you feel?" His English was superb.

Madame Lefoux cast her hands heavenward.

"Indubitably," agreed Lady Maccon, endearing herself to the child for all time.

The ghost introduced herself as Formerly Beatrice Lefoux.

Alexia nodded to her politely, which surprised the ghost. The undead were often subjected to rudeness from the fully alive. But Lady Maccon always stood on formality.

"My impossible son and my noncorporeal aunt," explained Madame Lefoux, looking at Alexia as though she expected something.

Lady Maccon filed away the fact that they all had the same last name. Had Madame Lefoux not married the child's father? How very salacious. But Quesnel did not look at all like his mother. She need not have claimed him. He was a towheaded, pointy-chinned little creature with the most enormous violet eyes and not a dimple in sight.

The lady inventor said to her family, "This is Alexia Maccon, Lady Woolsey. She is also muhjah to the queen."

"Ah, my husband saw fit to tell you that little fact, did he?" Alexia was surprised. Not many knew about her political position, and, as with her preternatural state, both she and her husband preferred to keep it that way: Conall, because it kept his wife out of danger; Alexia, because it caused most individuals, supernatural or otherwise, to come over all funny about soullessness.

The ghost of Beatrice Lefoux interrupted them. "You are ze muhjah? Niece, you allow an exorcist into ze vicinity of my body? Uncaring, thoughtless child! You are ze worse than your son." Her accent was far more pronounced than her niece's. She moved violently away from Alexia, floating back and upward off the barrel upon which she had pretended to sit. As though Alexia could *do* anything damaging to her spirit. Silly creature.

Lady Maccon frowned, realizing that the aunt's presence eliminated Madame Lefoux as a suspect in the case of the mass exorcism. She could not have invented a weapon that acted like a preternatural, not here, not if her aunt's spirit resided in the contrivance chamber.

"Aunt, do not get so emotional. Lady Maccon can only kill you if she touches your body, and only I know where that is kept."

Alexia wrinkled her nose. "Please do not agitate yourself so. Formerly Lefoux. I prefer not to perform exorcisms in any event: decomposing flesh is very squishy." She shuddered delicately.

"Oh, well, thank you for that," sneered the ghost.

"Ew!" said Quesnel, fascinated. "Have you conducted simply masses of them?"

Alexia narrowed her eyes at him in a way she hoped was mysterious and cunning, and then turned back to his mother. "So, in what capacity did my husband see fit to inform you of my nature and my position?"

Madame Lefoux was leaning back slightly, a faint look of amusement on her lovely face. "What could your ladyship possibly mean?"

"Was he in attendance upon you as Alpha, as earl, or as the head of BUR investigations?"

Madame Lefoux dimpled once more at that. "Ah, yes, the many faces of Conall Maccon."

Alexia bridled at the Frenchwoman's use of Conall's first name. "And how long, exactly, have you known my husband?" Abnormal dress was one thing, but loose morals were an entirely different matter.

"Calm yourself, my lady. My interest in your husband is purely professional. He and I know each other through BUR transactions, but he visited me here a month ago as the earl and your husband. He wished me to make you a special gift."

"A gift?"

"Indeed."

"Well, where is it?"

Madame Lefoux looked to her son. "Scat, you. Go find the cleaning mechanicals, hot water, and soap. Listen to your former great-aunt; she will tell you what can take water immersion and what will need to be cleaned and repaired by some other means. You have a very long night ahead of you."

"But, *Maman*, I simply wanted to see what would happen!"

"So, now you see. What happens is it makes your *maman* angry and gets you nights and nights of cleaning as punishment."

"Aw, *Maman*!"

"Right this very minute, Quesnel."

Quesnel sighed loudly and scampered off with a "nice to meet you" directed over his shoulder at Lady Maccon.

"That will teach him to run experiments without some valid hypothesis. Go after him, please, Beatrice, and keep him away for at least a quarter of an hour while I finish my business with Lady Maccon."

"Fraternizing with a preternatural! You run a far more dangerous game than I did in my day, niece," grumbled the ghost, but she dispersed easily enough, presumably after the boy.

"Pleasure to make your acquaintance, Formerly Lefoux," said Alexia defiantly to the now-empty air.

"Please do not concern yourself with her attitude. Even when alive, my aunt was difficult. Brilliant, but difficult. An inventor like me, you see, but less socially indoctrinated, I am afraid."

Lady Maccon smiled. "I have met many such scientists, and most of them could not claim brilliance as an excuse. That is not to say they didn't claim it, of course, just that . . ." She trailed off. She was babbling. She wasn't certain why, but something about the beautiful, strangely dressed Frenchwoman made Alexia nervous.

"So." The inventor moved closer to her. Madame Lefoux smelled of vanilla and mechanical oil. "We find ourselves alone. It is a genuine pleasure to meet you, Lady Maccon. The last time I was in the company of a preternatural, I was but a small child. And, of course, he was nowhere near as striking as you."

"Well, uh, thank you." Alexia was a little taken aback by the compliment.

The inventor took her hand gently. "Not at all."

The skin of the inventor's palm was callused. Lady Maccon could feel the roughness even through her gloves. At the contact, Alexia experienced certain slight palpitations that had, heretofore, been associated only with the opposite sex and, more specifically, her husband. Not much truly shocked Alexia. This did.

As soon as was seemly, she withdrew her hand, blushing furiously under her tan. Considering it a rude betrayal by her own body, Alexia ignored the phenomenon and grappled ineffectually for a moment, trying to remember the direction of her inquiry and the reason they were now alone together. Which was? Ah, yes, at her *husband's* insistence.

"I believe you may have something for me," she said at long last.

Madame Lefoux doffed her top hat in acknowledgment. "Indeed I do. One moment, please." With a sly smile, she moved off to one side of the lab and rummaged about for a moment in a large steamer trunk. Eventually, she emerged with a long skinny wooden box.

Lady Maccon held her breath in anticipation.

Madame Lefoux carried it over and flipped open the lid.

Inside was a not-very-prepossessing parasol of outlandish shape and indifferent style. Its shade was slate gray in color, edged in embroidered lace, with a thick cream ruffle trim. It had a peculiarly long spike at its tip, decorated with two egg-sized metal globules, like seedpods, one near the fabric and another closer to the tip. Its ribs were oversized, making it bulky and umbrella-like, and its shaft was extremely long, ending in a chubby, knobby, richly decorated handle. The handle looked like something that might top an ancient Egyptian column, carved with lotus flowers—or a very enthusiastic pineapple. The parasol's parts were entirely of brass, in what looked to be variable alloys, giving it a wide-ranging coloration.

"Well, Conall's taste strikes again," commented Alexia, whose own taste, while not particularly imaginative or sophisticated, at least did not tend toward the bizarre.

Madame Lefoux dimpled. "I did my best, given the carrying capacity."

Alexia was intrigued. "May I?"

The inventor offered her the box.

Lady Maccon lifted out the monstrosity. "It's heavier than it looks."

"That is one of the reasons I made it so very long. I thought it might serve double as a walking stick. Then you would not have to carry it everywhere."

Alexia tested it. The height was ideal for just that. "Is it likely to be something I must carry everywhere?"

"I believe your esteemed husband would prefer it so."

Alexia demurred. It leaned heavily toward the ugly end of the parasol spectrum. Many of her favorite day dresses would clash most horribly with all that brass and gray, not to mention the decorative elements.

"Also, of course, it had to be tough enough to serve as a defensive weapon."

"A sensible precaution, given my proclivities." Lady Maccon had destroyed more than one parasol through the application of it against someone else's skull.

"Would you like to learn its anthroscopy?" Madame Lefoux became gleeful as she made the offer.

"It has anthroscopy? Is that healthy?"

"Why, certainly. Do you believe I would design an object so ugly without sufficient cause?"

Alexia passed her the heavy accessory. "By all means."

Madame Lefoux took hold of the handle, allowing Alexia to maintain a grip on the top spire. Upon closer examination, Alexia realized the tip had a tiny hydraulic hinge affixed to one side.

"When you press here"—Madame Lefoux indicated one of the lotus petals on the shaft just below the large handle—"that tip opens and emits a poisoned dart equipped with a numbing agent. And if you twist the handle so . . ."

Alexia gasped as, just above where she gripped the end, two wickedly sharp spikes flipped out, one of silver and one of wood.

"I did notice your cravat pins," Lady Maccon said.

Madame Lefoux chuckled, touching them delicately with her free hand. "Oh, they are more than simply cravat pins."

"Of that I have no doubt. Does the parasol do anything else?"

Madame Lefoux winked at her. "Ah, that is just the beginning. In this, you understand, Lady Maccon, I am an artist."

Alexia licked her bottom lip. "I am certainly beginning to comprehend that fact. And here I thought only your hats were exceptional."

The Frenchwoman blushed slightly, the color visible even in the orange light. "Pull this lotus petal here, and so."

Every noise in the lab fell silent. All the whirring, clanking, and puffs of steam that had faded into the background as ambient sound became suddenly noticeable by way of their absence.

"What?" Alexia looked about. All was still.

And then, moments later, the mechanisms started up once more.

"What happened?" she asked, looking in awe down at the parasol.

"The nodule here"—the inventor pointed to the egg attachment near the shade section of the parasol—"emitted a magnetic disruption field. It will affect any metal of the iron, nickel, or cobalt family, including steel. If you need to seize up a steam engine for any reason, this will probably do the trick, but only for a brief amount of time."

"Remarkable!"

Again the Frenchwoman blushed. "The disruption field is not of my own invention, but I did make it substantially smaller than Babbage's original design." She continued on. "The ruffles contain various hidden pockets and are fluffy enough to disguise small objects." She reached inside the wide ruffle and pulled out a little vial.

"Poison?" asked Lady Maccon, tilting her head to one side.

"Certainly not. Something far more important: perfume. We cannot very well have you fighting crime unscented, now, can we?"

"Oh." Alexia nodded gravely. After all, Madame Lefoux *was* French. "Certainly not."

Madame Lefoux pushed the shade up, revealing that the parasol was of an old-fashioned pagoda shape. "You can also turn it thus"—she flipped the parasol around so that the shade was pointing the wrong direction—"and twist and press here." She pointed to a small nodule just above the magnetic disruption emitter, in which a tiny dial was set. "I have designed it to be quite difficult to operate, to prevent any unfortunate accidents. The rib caps of the parasol will open and emit a fine mist. At one click, these three will emit a mixture of *lapis lunearis* and water. At two clicks, the other three ribs will emit *lapis solaris* diluted in sulfuric acid. Make certain that you, and anyone you care about, stay well out of the blast area and upwind. Although the *lunearis* will cause only mild skin irritation, the *solaris* is toxic and will kill humans as well as disabling vampires." With a sudden grin, the scientist added, "Only werewolves are resistant. The *lunearis* is, of course, for them. A direct spray should render the species in question helpless and gravely ill for several days. Three clicks and both will emit at once."

"Quite outstanding, madame." Alexia was suitably impressed. "I did not know there were any poisons capable of disabling either species."

Madame Lefoux said mildly, "I once had access to a partial copy of the Templar's Amended Rule."

Lady Maccon's mouth dropped. "You what?"

The Frenchwoman elucidated no further.

Alexia took the parasol, turning it about in her hands reverently. "I shall have to change over half my wardrobe to match it, of course. But I suspect it will be worth it."

Madame Lefoux dimpled in pleasure. "It *will* also keep the sun at bay."

Lady Maccon snorted in amusement. "As to the cost, has my husband dealt with the necessities?"

The Frenchwoman held up a small hand. "Oh, I am well aware that Woolsey can see to the expense. And I have had dealings with your pack before."

Alexia smiled. "Professor Lyall?"

"Mainly. He is a curious man. One wonders, sometimes, as to his motivations."

"He is not a man."

"Just so."

"And you?"

"I, too, am not a man. I simply enjoy dressing like one," replied Madame Lefoux, purposefully choosing to misinterpret Alexia's question.

"So you say," replied Lady Maccon. Then she frowned, remembering something Ivy had said about the new hat shop: that actresses like Mabel Dair were known to frequent it. "You are dealing with the hives as well as the packs."

"And why would you say that?"

"Miss Hisselpenny mentioned that Miss Dair visited your establishment. She is drone to the Westminster Hive."

The Frenchwoman turned away, busying herself with tidying the laboratory. "I provide to those who can afford my services."

"Does that include loners and roves? Have you catered to, for example, Lord Akeldama's taste?"

"I have not yet had the pleasure," replied the inventor.

Alexia noted that the Frenchwoman did not say that she had not *heard* of him.

Lady Maccon decided to meddle. "Ah, this is a grave lapse! It ought to be rectified immediately. Would you be free for tea later this evening, say around midnight? I shall consult with the gentleman in question and see if he is available."

Madame Lefoux looked curious but wary. "I believe I could arrange to get away. How very kind of you, Lady Maccon."

Alexia inclined her head in grand-dame fashion, feeling silly. "I shall send around a card with the address, if he is amenable." She wanted to meet with Lord Akeldama alone first.

Just then, a new noise made itself heard through the hubbub of machinery, a querulous, high-pitched, "Alexia?"

Lady Maccon whirled about. "Oh dear, Ivy! She has not made her way down here, has she? I believe I closed the door to the ascension chamber behind me."

Madame Lefoux looked unperturbed. "Oh, do not concern yourself. It is only her voice. I have an auditory capture and dispersal amplifier funneling sounds in from the shop." She pointed to where a trumpet-shaped object was cabled to the ceiling. Lady Maccon had thought it some kind of gramophone. But Ivy's voice emanated from it, as clearly as if she were in the laboratory with them. Astonishing.

"Perhaps we should return to the shop and attend her," suggested the inventor.

Alexia, clutching her new parasol to her ample bosom like a newborn child, nodded.

They did so, to find that the gas lighting was up and running once more. And that, under the bright lights of the empty shop, Miss Hisselpenny was still reposing on the floor, but now seated upright and looking pale and confused.

"What happened?" she demanded as Lady Maccon and Madame Lefoux approached.

"There was a loud bang, and you fainted," replied Alexia. "Really, Ivy, if you did not lace your corset so tight, you would not be so prone to the vapors. It is reputed to be terribly bad for your health."

Miss Hisselpenny gasped at the mention of *underclothing* in a public hat shop. "Please, Alexia, do not spout such radical folderol. Next thing, you will want me to engage in dress reform!"

Lady Maccon rolled her eyes. The very idea: *Ivy* in bloomers!

"What have you got there?" Miss Hisselpenny asked, focusing on the parasol Lady Maccon clasped to her chest.

Alexia crouched down to show the parasol to her friend.

"Why, Alexia, that is quite beautiful. It does not reflect your customary taste at all," approved Miss Hisselpenny with glee.

Trust Ivy to like the hideous thing for its looks.

Miss Hisselpenny glanced eagerly up at the Frenchwoman. "I should like one just like it, in perhaps a nice lemon yellow with black and white stripes. Would you have such an item to hand?"

Alexia giggled at Madame Lefoux's shocked expression.

"I should think not," the inventor croaked out finally, having cleared her throat twice. "Should I"—she winced slightly—"order you one?"

"Please do."

Alexia stood and said softly in French, "Perhaps without the additional garnishing."

"Mmm," replied Madame Lefoux.

A little bell chimed cheerfully as someone new wandered into the shop. Miss Hisselpenny struggled to rise from her undignified lounge upon the floor.

The newcomer approached them, parting the forest of dangling hats and, upon seeing Ivy's plight, leaped to her aid.

"Why, Miss Hisselpenny, are you unwell? Let me offer my most humble services."

"Tunstell," interjected Alexia, glaring at the young man. "What are *you* doing *here*?"

The redheaded claviger ignored her, cooing over Miss Hisselpenny solicitously.

Ivy attained her feet and clutched at his arm, leaning against his side weakly and looking up at him out of big dark eyes.

Tunstell seemed to be taking a long, leisurely swim in those eyes, like some sort of gormless guppy.

Actors, the lot of them. Alexia poked at his bottom, nicely packaged in some excessively tight britches, with the tip of her new parasol. "Tunstell, explain your presence at once."

Tunstell jumped slightly and looked at her in a maltreated manner.

"I have a message from Professor Lyall," he said, as though she were somehow to blame for this.

Lady Maccon did not ask how Lyall had known she would be at Chapeau de Poupe. The ways of her husband's Beta were often mysterious and better left unquestioned.

"Well?"

Tunstell was staring once more into Miss Hisselpenny's eyes.

Alexia tapped the parasol on the wooden floor, enjoying the metallic clicking noise it made. "The message."

He requests for you to visit with him at BUR as a matter of some urgency," said Tunstell without looking at her.

A matter of urgency was pack code for activation of Lady Maccon as muhjah. Lyall had some information for the Crown. Alexia nodded. "In that case, Ivy, you would not mind if I left you under Tunstell's care while you complete your shopping? He will see you safely off. Won't you, Tunstell?"

"It would be my very great pleasure." Tunstell beamed.

"Oh, I believe that would suit adequately," breathed Ivy, smiling back.

Lady Maccon wondered if she had ever been so foolish over Lord Maccon. Then she recalled that her affection generally took the form of threats and verbal barbs. She gave herself a pat on the back for avoiding sentimentality.

The inventor-cum-milliner walked her to the front door.

"I shall send a card around presently when I determine Lord Akeldama's availability. He should be at home, but you never can tell with roves. This summons from Professor Lyall cannot possibly take long." Alexia looked back at Tunstell and Ivy, engaged in an overly familiar tête-à-tête. "Please, do try to prevent Miss Hisselpenny from purchasing anything too hideous, and see that Tunstell puts her into a hackney but does not get into it himself."

"I shall do my level best, Lady Maccon," replied Madame Lefoux with an abbreviated bow—so short as to be almost rude. Then, in a quick-fire movement, she caught one of Alexia's hands with her own. "It was a great pleasure to meet you at last, my lady." Her grip was firm and sure. Of course, lifting and building all that machinery below street level would give anyone a certain degree of musculature, even the rail-thin woman before her. The inventor's fingers caressed Alexia's wrist just above the perfect fit of her gloves, so quickly that Alexia was not certain the action had occurred. There was that faint scent of vanilla mixed with gear oil once more. Then Madame Lefoux smiled, dropped Alexia's hand, and turned back into the shop, disappearing among the swinging jungle of fashionable headgear.

Professor Lyall and Lord Maccon shared an office at BUR headquarters, on Fleet Street, but it was always considerably cleaner whenever the earl was not in residence. Lady Alexia Maccon breezed in, swinging her new parasol proudly and hoping Lyall would ask about it. But Professor Lyall was mightily distracted behind a pile of paperwork and a stack of metal scrolls with acid-etched notes upon them. He stood, bowed, and sat back down again as a matter of course rather than courtesy. Whatever had occurred was clearly occupying all of his considerable attention. His glassicals were perched upon his head, mussing his coiffure. Was it possible that his cravat could be minutely askew?

"Are you well, Professor Lyall?" Alexia asked, quite worried by the cravat.

"I am in perfect health, thank you for asking, Lady Maccon. It is your husband who concerns me, and I have no way to get through to him at present."

"Yes," said the earl's wife, deadpan, "I daily face a similar dilemma, frequently when he and I are in conversation. What has he gone and done now?"

Professor Lyall smiled slightly. "Oh no, nothing like that. It is simply that the plague of humanization has struck again, moving northward as far as Farthinghoe."

Alexia frowned at this new information. "Curious. It is on the move, is it?"

"And heading in the same direction as Lord Maccon. Though slightly ahead of him."

"And he doesn't know that, does he?"

Lyall shook his head.

"That family matter, it's the dead Alpha, isn't it?"

Lyall ignored this and said, "Don't know quite how it's moving so fast. The trains have been down since yesterday—strike. Trust the daylight folk to become inefficient at a time like this."

"By coach, perhaps?"

"Could be. It seems to be moving quickly. I should like to make the earl aware of this information, but there is no way to contact him until he arrives at the Glasgow offices. Not to mention Channing's blather about the boat ride over. This thing is mobile and Conall doesn't know that."

"You think he might overtake it?"

The Beta shook his head again. "Not at the rate it is moving. Lord Maccon is fast, but he said he was not going to push this run. If it keeps traveling north at the rate I predict, it will hit Scotland several days before he does. I have sent a note to our agents in the north, but I thought you should know as well, as muhjah."

Alexia nodded.

"Will you inform the other members of the Shadow Council?"

Lady Maccon frowned at that. "I do not think that is entirely wise just yet. I think it might wait until our next meeting. You should file a report, of course, but I shall not go out of my way to tell the potentate and the dewan."

The Beta nodded and did not inquire as to her reasons.

"Very well, Professor Lyall. If there is nothing else, I should be off. I have need of Lord Akeldama's council."

Professor Lyall gave her an unreadable look. "Well, I suppose someone must. Good evening, Lady Maccon."

Alexia left without ever having shown Professor Lyall her new parasol.

CHAPTER FIVE

Lord Akeldama's Latest

Lord Akeldama was indeed in residence and willing to receive Alexia. Despite the rudeness of her unannounced visit, he seemed genuinely pleased to see her. It was difficult to tell through the vampire's self-consciously frivolous mannerisms, but Alexia thought she detected real warmth beneath the flatterings and flutterings.

The ancient vampire sashayed forward to greet her, both arms extended, dressed in his version of the "casual gentleman at home." For most men of means and taste, this meant a smoking jacket, opera scarf, long trousers, and soft-soled derbies. For Lord Akeldama, this meant that the jacket was of pristine white silk with black embroidered birds of some lean oriental persuasion splashed about, the scarf a bright peacock-patterned teal, the trousers the latest in tight-fitting black jacquard, and the shoes cut in a flashy wingtip style with a black and white spectator coloration that was held by many to be rather vulgar.

"My *darling* Alexia. How fortuitous. I have just received delivery of the most divine new *plaything*. You *must* take a gander and give me your expert opinion!" Lord Akeldama addressed Lady Maccon by her given name and had done so since the night they met. And yet, Alexia realized for the first time as she took his hands in a firm grip, she had no idea what his was.

At the preternatural contact, Lord Akeldama turned from supernaturally beautiful, his skin ice white and his blond hair shining gold, to the merely pretty young man he had once been before his metamorphosis.

Lady Maccon kissed him softly on both cheeks, as though he were a child. "And how are you this evening, my lord?"

He leaned against her, momentarily calm in his fully human state, before resuming his animated chatter. "Perfectly *splendid*, my little tea biscuit, perfectly *splendid*. There is a mystery waffling about London town, and I am immersed in the thick of it. You know how I do so dearly *love* a mystery." He kissed her back, a loud smack to the forehead, and then released her hands to curl his arm affectionately with hers.

"And it has certainly been all abuzz around my humble little abode since the excitement of yesterday." He led her into said abode, which was anything but humble. It had an extravagant arched and frescoed hallway with marble busts of pagan gods. "I suppose, *you* know *all* about it, you high-powered political *daffodil*, you."

Alexia loved Lord Akeldama's drawing room, not that she could tolerate it in her own house, but it was a nice place to visit. It was quite old-fashioned in appearance, white and gilded gold like something from a French painting of pre-Napoleonic times.

The vampire unceremoniously ejected a fat calico from her slumbering possession of a gold brocade love seat with tasseled trim and settled gracefully into her place. Lady Maccon seated herself in an armchair nearby, one that felt deliciously thronelike.

"Well, my creamy *pudding* cup, Biffy told me *the* most attractive little story last night." Lord Akeldama's ethereal face was intent under its unnecessary coating of white powder and pink blush. "Quite the bedtime romance."

Lady Maccon was not certain she wanted to hear this story. "Oh, uh, did he? Where is Biffy, by the way? Is he about?"

Lord Akeldama fiddled with his gold monocle. The glass was, of course, plain. Like all vampires, he had perfect vision. "La, the troublesome boy is causing mischief somewhere not too far away, I am certain. He is in a bit of a kerfuffle over a necktie, but never mind that; you must permit me to tell you what he saw yester eve."

Lady Maccon forestalled him. "Before you do, my lord, might we send round an invitation to a new acquaintance I have made? I should very much like the two of you to know one another."

That stalled Lord Akeldama. "*Really*, my darling little kumquat, how thoughtful. Who is he?"

"*She* is one Madame Lefoux."

Lord Akeldama smiled slightly at that. "I did hear you had been hat shopping recently."

Alexia gasped. "How did you know that? Oh, how vexatious! Do you mean to say that you are already acquainted with the lady? Madame Lefoux indicated nothing to that effect."

"You can hardly expect *me* to reveal *my* sources, snow drop. As to the rest, I do not know her; I merely know *of* her, and I should enjoy meeting her socially very much indeed. I hear she affects masculine garb! I shall send a card directly." He reached to pull a small bell rope. "So, do tell: *what* did you purchase from the *scandalous* Frenchwoman, my little clementine?"

Alexia showed him the parasol.

Lord Akeldama was alarmed by its appearance. "Oh dear, it is rather"—he cleared his throat—"*loud,* is it not?"

Alexia thought that rich coming from a man wearing black and white wingtip shoes and a teal scarf. She said only, "Yes, but it does the most delicious things." She was about to explain further when a polite knock interrupted them, and Biffy trotted into the room.

"You rang?" Biffy was an agreeable young blunt with stylish proclivities and prodigious physical charms who always seemed to turn up when least expected and most wanted. Had he not been born into wealth and status, he might have made for an excellent butler. He was Lord Akeldama's favorite drone, although the vampire would never confess openly to having favorites any more than he would wear the same waistcoat two days running. Alexia had to admit there was something special about Biffy. He was certainly a dab hand with the curling iron, better at hair arrangements than even the otherwise unparalleled Angelique.

"Biffy, my *dove,* dash round to that scrumptious new hat shop on Regent Street and collect the proprietress for a bit of a hobnob, would you, darling? There's a good fellow. She should be expecting something of the kind."

Biffy smiled. "Certainly, my lord. Good evening, Lady Maccon. Is this arrangement of your making? You know the master here has been dying to meet Madame Lefoux ever since she opened that shop, with no excuse to do so for an age."

"Biffy!" hissed Lord Akeldama.

"Well, you have," replied Biffy truculently.

"Off with you, you impossible infant, and keep that *lovely* mouth shut."

Biffy bowed shortly and tripped lightly out, lifting his hat and gloves from a nearby side table as he went.

"That young whippersnapper will be the death of me. However, he has an *admirable* knack for being in the right place at the right time. Yesterday evening, for example, he was outside the Pickled Crumpet, that *horrible* little pub near St. Bride, known for a preponderance of military and blood whores. Not his normal watering hole by *any* means. And you will *never* guess whom he encountered skulking about the back alleyway, just behind the pub."

Lady Maccon sighed. "My husband?"

Lord Akeldama was crestfallen. "He told you."

"No, it simply seems like the exact kind of place where my husband would be skulking."

"Well, let *me* tell *you*, my petunia blossom! Biffy says that he was in a perfectly indelicate condition, trying to make his way toward Fleet Street."

"Inebriated?" Lady Maccon was doubtful. Generally speaking, werewolves were not prone to intoxication. Their constitutions did not allow for it. Besides which, that simply was not *like* her husband.

"Oh no. The poor dear had encountered that *disastrous* malady ravaging the downtown area and found himself entirely human and unclothed quite suddenly in the heart of London."

Lord Akeldama's eyes were twinkling.

Lady Maccon could not help herself; she began to laugh. "No wonder he did not tell me about the incident. Poor thing."

"Not that Biffy complained about the spectacle."

"Well, who would?" Alexia had to give credit where it was due, and her husband did have quite the splendid physique. "That is interesting, though. It means that one does not have to be present when this antisupernatural blight attacks. One can wander into the infected area and be struck down."

"You think it is a *disease* of some kind, do you, my little pumpernickel?"

Lady Maccon cocked her head to one side. "I do not know with any certainty what it may be. What do you think it is?"

Lord Akeldama rang a different bell rope for tea. "I believe it to be a weapon of some kind," he said, unusually blunt.

"You have heard of something like it before?" Lady Maccon sat up straight, intent on her friend. Lord Akeldama was a very old vampire. There were rumors he was older even than Countess Nadasdy, and everyone knew she was five hundred or more.

The vampire tossed his queue of long blond hair back off his shoulder. "No, I have not. But it does not have the *feel* of a sickness about it, and my experience with the Hypocras Club has taught me not to underestimate modern scientists and their vulgar technological *dabblings*."

Lady Maccon nodded. "I agree, and so does the rest of the Shadow Council. BUR is holding out that it is a disease, but I am leaning in favor of a newly fashioned weapon. Have your boys found out anything of significance?"

Lord Akeldama puffed out his cheeks. He did not like open acknowledgment that his collection of apparently decorative and inconsequential drones, possessed of high family connection and little evident sense, were in fact consummate spies. He resigned himself to Alexia, and, via Alexia, to Lord Maccon and BUR, knowing of his activities, but he did not like them mentioned openly.

"Not as much as I had hoped. Although one of the ships, the *Spanker*, transporting multiple regiments and associated packs, was said to be afflicted by a *human condition* the *entire* passage home."

"Yes, Major Channing mentioned something of the kind. Although the Woolsey Pack had returned to supernatural normalcy by the time they reached the castle."

"And what do *we* think of Major Channing?"

"*We* try *not* to think on that repulsive individual at all."

Lord Akeldama laughed, and a handsome young butler entered with the tea tray. "You know, I once tried to recruit him, decades ago."

"Did you really?" Lady Maccon could not countenance the idea; for one thing, she did not believe Major Channing leaned in Lord Akeldama's direction, although there were rumors about military men.

"He was a *splendid* sculptor before he turned. Did you know? We all knew he had a good chance of having excess soul; vampires and werewolves were vying to be his patron. Such a sweet young talented thing."

"We *are* discussing the same Major Channing, are we not?"

"He rebuffed *me* and went into soldiering, thought it more *romantic*. Eventually, he was converted to the fuzzy side of the supernatural during the Napoleonic war."

Alexia was not clear on what to make of this information. So she returned to the original topic. "If it is a weapon, I must find where it has gone. Lyall said it was headed north, and we believe it to be going by coach. The question is, where, and who is carrying it?"

"And *what* exactly is it?" added the vampire, pouring the tea. Lady Maccon took hers with milk and a little sugar. He took his with a dash of blood and a squeeze of lemon.

"Well, if Professor Lyall claims it is heading northward, then northward it is. Your husband's Beta is *never* wrong." There was an odd tone in Lord Akeldama's voice. Alexia looked at him sharply. He added only, "When?"

"Just before I came here."

"No, no, primrose. I mean, when did *it* begin to move northward?" He passed a small plate of some excellent biscuits, declining the comestibles himself.

Lady Maccon did some quick calculations. "Seems like it would have had to depart London late yesterday evening or early this morning."

"Just as the humanization in London stopped?"

"Precisely."

"So what we need to know is what regiments, or packs, or individuals came in on the *Spanker,* then proceeded north yesterday morning."

Lady Maccon had a sinking feeling all fingers were about to point in one particular direction. "I place great confidence in the fact that Professor Lyall is already hunting down just that information."

"But you already have a good idea of who the perpetrators might be, don't you, my little *periwinkle*?" Lord Akeldama stopped relaxing back into the love seat and tilted forward to peer at her through his monocle.

Lady Maccon sighed. "Call it instinct."

The vampire smiled, showing his two long fangs, pointed and strikingly lethal. "Ah, yes, your preternatural ancestors were hunters for generations, *sugardrop.*" Delicacy did not permit him to remind her that they hunted vampires.

"Oh no, not that kind of instinct."

"Oh?"

"Perhaps instead I should say 'wifely intuition.'"

"Ah." Lord Akeldama's smile widened. "You believe your oversized husband to be connected to the weapon?"

Lady Maccon frowned and nibbled a biscuit. "No, not exactly, but where my dear spouse goes . . ." She trailed off.

"You think this whole thing may be connected to his visiting Scotland?"

Alexia sipped her tea and remained silent.

"You think this has something to do with the Kingair Pack losing their Alpha?"

Alexia started. She did not realize that little fact was common knowledge. How *did* Lord Akeldama come by his information so quickly? It was really remarkable. If only the Crown could be so efficient. Or BUR for that matter.

"A pack without an Alpha can behave badly, but on this kind of scale? You think—"

Lady Maccon interrupted her friend. "*I think* Lady Maccon may suddenly feel quite oppressed by the dirty London air. I think Lady Maccon may have need of a vacation. Perhaps to the north? I hear Scotland is lovely this time of year."

"Are you barmy? Scotland is wholly *abysmal* this time of year."

"Indeed, why would one wish to travel there, especially with the trains down?" This was a new voice, tinged with a very faint French accent.

Madame Lefoux had not forgone her men's garb, although she had formalized it for visiting, changing her colorful cravat for one of white lawn and her brown top hat for a black one.

"Lady Maccon fancies herself in need of air," replied Lord Akeldama, rising and going forward to greet his new guest. "Madame Lefoux, I presume?"

Alexia blushed at not having jumped in to make proper introductions, but the other two seemed to have matters well in hand.

"How do you do? Lord Akeldama? A pleasure to make your acquaintance at last. I have heard much of your charms." The inventor gave the vampire's startling black and white shoes and smoking jacket an intent look.

"And I yours," replied the vampire, casting an equally critical eye to the inventor's stylish masculine garb.

Alexia noted a certain undercurrent of wariness, as though they were two vultures circling the same carcass.

"Well, there is no accounting for taste," said the Frenchwoman softly. Lord Akeldama appeared about to take offense, but the lady added, turning slightly to the side, "Scotland, Lady Maccon, are you certain?"

A flash of wary approval crossed the vampire's face at that. "Do sit," he offered. "You smell divine by the way. Vanilla? A lovely scent. And so very *feminine.*"

Was that a return jibe? wondered Alexia.

Madame Lefoux accepted a cup of tea and sat on another little settee, next to the relocated calico cat. The cat clearly believed Madame Lefoux was there to provide chin scratches. Madame Lefoux provided.

"Scotland," replied Lady Maccon firmly. "By dirigible, I think. I shall make the arrangements directly and depart tomorrow."

"You shall find that difficult. Giffard's is not open to nighttime clientele."

Lady Maccon nodded her understanding. Dirigibles catered to daylight folk, *not* the supernatural set. Vampires could not ride them, as they flew too high out of territory range. Ghosts were usually inconveniently tethered. And werewolves did not like to float—prone to terrible airsickness, her husband had explained the first and only time she intimated interest in such a mode of transport.

"Tomorrow afternoon," she amended, "but let us talk of more pleasant things. Lord Akeldama, are you interested in hearing about some of Madame Lefoux's inventions?"

"Indeed."

Madame Lefoux described several of her more recent devices. Despite his old-fashioned house, Lord Akeldama was fascinated with modern technological developments.

"Alexia has shown me her new parasol. You do *impressive* work. You are not seeking a patron?" he asked after some quarter of an hour's talk, clearly impressed with the Frenchwoman's intelligence, if nothing else.

Understanding fully the unspoken code, the inventor shook her head. Given Madame Lefoux's appearance and skills, Alexia was in no doubt she had received offers of a similar nature in the past. "Thank you kindly, my lord. You do me particular favor, as I know you prefer male drones. But I am happily situated and of independent means, with no wish to bid for immortality."

Lady Maccon followed this interchange with interest. So Lord Akeldama thought Madame Lefoux had excess soul, did he? Well, if her aunt had turned into a ghost, excess soul might run in the family. She was about to ask an impolitic question when Lord Akeldama rose, rubbing his long white hands together.

"Well, my little *buttercups.*"

Uh-oh, Alexia winced in sympathy. Madame Lefoux had achieved Akeldama-appellative status. They would now have to suffer together.

"Would you *charming* blossoms like to see my newest acquisition? Quite the beauty!"

Alexia and Madame Lefoux exchanged a look, put down their teacups, and rose to follow him with no argument.

Lord Akeldama led them out into the arched and gilded hallway and up several sets of increasingly elaborate staircases. Eventually they attained the top of the town house, entering what should have been the attic. It proved, instead, to have been made over into an elaborate room hung with medieval tapestries and filled with an enormous box, large enough to house two horses. It was raised up off the floor via a complex system of springs and was quilted in a thick fabric to prevent ambient noise from reaching its interior. The box, itself, comprised two small rooms filled with machinery. The first, Lord Akeldama described as the transmitting room, and the second the receiving room.

Alexia had never seen such a thing before.

Madame Lefoux had. "Why, Lord Akeldama, such an expense! You have purchased an aethographic transmitter!" She looked about the crowded interior of the first room with enthusiastic appreciation. Her dimples were in danger of reappearing. "She's beautiful." The inventor ran reverent hands over the many dials and switches that controlled the transmitting room's tangled gadgetry.

Lady Maccon frowned. "The queen is reputed to own one. I understand she was urged to acquire it as a replacement for the telegraph, shortly after the telegraph proved itself an entirely unviable method of communication."

Lord Akeldama shook his blond head sadly. "I was *vastly* disappointed to read of the report of that failure. I had such hopes for the telegraph." There'd been a noted gap in long-distance communication ever since, with the scientific community scrabbling to invent something that was more compatible with highly magnetic aetheromagnetic gasses.

"The aethographor is a wireless communication apparatus, so it does not suffer from such severe disruption to the electromagnetic currents as the telegraph," Lord Akeldama explained.

Lady Maccon narrowed her eyes at him. "I *have* read of the new technology. I simply had not thought to *see* it so soon." As a matter of course, Alexia had been angling for an invitation to see the queen's aethographor for over a fortnight, with little success. There was some delicacy to its function that would not allow it to be interrupted during operation. She had also tried, unsuccessfully, to visit BUR's aethographor. She knew that they had one at the London offices, because she saw rolls of etched metal lying about. Her husband had been utterly impossible about it. "Wife," he had finally stated in abject frustration, "I canna interrupt business simply to satisfy your curiosity." Unfortunately for Alexia, since they had come into government possession, both aethographors had been in constant operation.

Lord Akeldama picked up an etched metal roll, flattened it out, and slotted it into a special frame. "You put the message for transfer, so, and activate the aetheric convector."

Madame Lefoux, looking about with avid interest, interrupted him mid-explanation. "You would, of course, first have to input an outgoing crystalline valve frequensor, just here." She pointed to the control board, then started. "Where is the resonator cradle?"

"Aha!" crowed the vampire, apparently thrilled she had noticed this flaw. "This is the latest and greatest design, *squash blossom*. It does not operate via *crystalline* compatibility protocol!"

Madame Lefoux looked to Lady Maccon. "Squash blossom," she mouthed silently, her expression half offended, half amused.

Alexia shrugged.

"Usually," explained Lord Akeldama to Alexia, misinterpreting the shrug, "the transmitting component of the aethographor requires the installation of a specific valve, depending on the message's intended destination. You see, a companion valve must also be installed in the other party's receiving room. Only with both in place can a message transfer from point A to point B. The problem is, of course, that exact times must be agreed upon beforehand by both parties, and each must possess the appropriate valve. The queen has an entire library of valves linked to different aethographors dotted all about the empire."

Madame Lefoux was frowning. "And yet your device has none? It is not very useful, Lord Akeldama, to transmit a message into the aether with no one at the other end to receive it."

"Aha!" The vampire pranced about the tiny room in his ridiculous shoes, looking far too pleased with himself. "*My* aetheric transponder does not need one! I have had it installed with the latest in frequency transmitters so that I can tune to whatever aetheromagnetic setting is desired. All I need is to know the crystalline valve's orientation on the receiving end. And to receive all I need is the right time, a good scan, and someone who has my codes. Sometimes I can even pick up messages intended for *other* aethographors." He frowned a moment. "Story of my life, if you think about it."

"Good Lord." Madame Lefoux was obviously impressed. "I had no idea such technology even existed. I knew they were working on it, of course, but not that it had finally been built. Impressive. May we witness it in action?"

The vampire shook his head. "I have no messages to go out at the present time and am not expecting any incoming."

Madame Lefoux looked crestfallen.

"So what happens, exactly?" asked Lady Maccon, who was still looking closely at the equipment.

Lord Akeldama was all too delighted to explain. "Ever notice that the metal paper has a faint grid on it?"

Alexia switched her attention to a scroll of metal Lord Akeldama handed her. The surface was, indeed, divided into a standardized grid. "One letter per square?" she hypothesized.

Lord Akeldama nodded and explained further. "The metal is exposed to a chemical wash that causes the etched letters to burn through. Then two needles pass over each grid square, one on top and the other on the bottom. They spark whenever they are exposed to one another through the letters. *This* causes an aether wave that is bounced off the upper aethersphere and, in the absence of solar interference, *transmits globally.*" His gesturing throughout became wilder and wilder, and on the last phrase, he did a little pirouette.

"Astounding." Lady Maccon was impressed, both with the technology and Lord Akeldama's ebullience.

He paused, recovering his equanimity, then continued with the explanation. "Only a receiving room tuned to the appropriate frequency will be able to pick up the message. Come with me."

He led them into the receiving room section of the aethographor.

"Receivers, mounted on the roof *directly* above us, pick up the signals. A skilled operator is required to tune out ambient noise and amplify the signal. The message then displays there"—he gestured, hands waving about like flippers, at two pieces of glass with black particulate sandwiched between and a magnet mounted to a small hydraulic arm hovering above—"one letter at a time."

"So someone must be in residence to read and record each letter?"

"And they must do so utterly silently," added Madame Lefoux, examining the delicacy of the mounts.

"And they must be ready in an instant, for the message destroys itself as it goes," Lord Akeldama added.

"Now I comprehend the reason for the noise-proof room and the attic location. This is clearly a most delicate device." Lady Maccon wondered if *she* could operate such an apparatus. "You have, indeed, made an impressive acquisition."

Lord Akeldama grinned.

Alexia gave him a sly look. "So what precisely *is* your compatibility protocol, Lord Akeldama?"

The vampire pretended offense, looking coquettishly up at the ceiling of the box. "Really, Alexia, what a thing to ask on your *very* first showing."

Lady Maccon only smiled.

Lord Akeldama sidled over and slotted her a little slip of paper upon which was written a series of numbers. "I have reserved the eleven o'clock time slot especially for you, my dear, and will begin monitoring all frequencies at that time starting a week from today." He bustled off and reappeared with a faceted crystalline valve. "And here is this, tuned to my frequency, just in case the apparatus you employ is less progressive than my own."

Alexia tucked the little slip of paper and the crystalline valve into one of the hidden pockets of her new parasol. "Does any other private residence own one?" she wondered.

"Difficult to know," replied Lord Akeldama. "The receiver *must* be mounted upon the roof, so one could conceivably hire a dirigible for air reconnaissance and float about looking for them, but I hardly think that an efficient approach. They are very dear, and there are few private individuals who could see to the expense. The Crown, of course, has two, but others? I only have the list of official compatibility protocols: that is a little under one hundred aethographors dotted about the empire."

Reluctantly, Alexia realized that time was getting on, and if she intended to leave for Scotland, she had much to do in the space of one night. For one thing, she would have to send round to the queen to alert her to the fact that her muhjah would be missing meetings of the Shadow Council for the next few weeks.

She made her excuses to Lord Akeldama. Madame Lefoux did the same, so that the two ladies found themselves exiting his residence at the same time. They paused to take leave of one another on the stoop.

"Do you really propose to float to Scotland tomorrow?" inquired the Frenchwoman, buttoning her fine gray kid gloves.

"I think it best I go after my husband."

"Should you travel alone?"

"Oh, I shall take Angelique."

Madame Lefoux started slightly at the name. "A Frenchwoman? Who is that?"

"My maid, inherited from the Westminster Hive. She is a dab hand with the curling iron."

"I am certain she is, if she was once under Countess Nadasdy," replied the inventor with a kind of studied casualness.

Alexia felt there was some kind of double meaning to the comment.

Madame Lefoux did not give her the chance for further inquiry, as she nodded her good-bye, climbed into a waiting hackney, and was gone before Lady Maccon had time to say more than a polite good night.

Professor Randolph Lyall was impatient, but no one would ever guess it to look at him. Partly, of course, because currently he looked like a slightly seedy and very hairy dog, skulking about the bins in the alley next to Lord Akeldama's town house.

How much time, he was wondering, *could possibly be required to take tea with a vampire?* A good deal, apparently, if Lord Akeldama and Lady Maccon were involved. Between the two of them, they could talk all four legs off a donkey. He had encountered them in full steam on only one memorable occasion and ever since had avoided the experience assiduously. Madame Lefoux had been a surprise addition to the party, although she probably was not adding much to the conversation. It was odd to see her out of her shop and paying a social call. He made a mental note: this was something his Alpha should know about. Not that he had orders to watch the inventor. But Madame Lefoux *was* a dangerous person to know.

He shifted about, nose to the wind. Some strange new scent on the air.

Then he noticed the vampires. Two of them, lurking in the shadows well away from Lord Akeldama's house. Any closer and the effete vampire would sense their alien presence, larvae not of his line in his territory. So, what were they there for? What were they about?

Lyall lowered his tail between his legs and slunk a quick circle behind them, coming at them from downwind. Of course, vampires had nowhere near as fine a sense of smell as werewolves but they had better hearing.

He crept in close, trying to be as silent as possible.

Neither of the vampires were BUR agents, that was for certain. Unless Lyall missed his guess, these were Westminster's get.

They did not appear to be doing anything but simply watching.

"Fangs!" said one of them finally. "How bloody long can it take to have tea? Especially if one of them ain't drinking it?"

Professor Lyall wished he had brought his gun. Difficult to carry, though, in one's mouth.

"Remember, he wants it done stealthy; we are simply checking. Don't want to go at it with the werewolves over nothing. You know . . ."

Lyall, who did *not* know, wanted to very badly, but the vampire, most unhelpfully, did not continue.

"I think he's paranoid."

"Ours is not to question, but I believe the mistress agrees with you. Doesn't stop her from humoring—"

The other vampire suddenly held up a hand, cutting his companion off.

Lady Maccon and Madame Lefoux emerged from Lord Akeldama's town house and made their good-byes on the stoop. Madame Lefoux swung herself up into a cab, and Lady Maccon was left alone, looking thoughtful on the front steps.

The two vampires moved forward toward her. Lyall did not know what they intended, but he guessed it was probably not good. It certainly was not worth risking his Alpha's wrath to find out. Quick as a flash, he slithered underneath one of the vampires, tripping him up, in the next movement lunging for the other, teeth snapping hard around anklebone. The first vampire, reacting rapidly, jumped so fast to one side as to be almost impossible to follow, at least for normal sight. Lyall, of course, was not normal.

He leaped, meeting the vampire halfway, lupine body slamming into the man's side, throwing him off. The second vampire lunged toward him, grabbing for his tail.

The entire scuffle took place in almost complete silence, only the sound of snapping jaws marking the activity.

It gave Lady Maccon just enough time, although she did not know she needed it, to climb into the Woolsey carriage and set off down the street.

The two vampires both stilled as soon as the vehicle was out of sight.

"Well, that's a sticky wicket," said one.

"Werewolves," said the other in disgust. He spat at Lyall, who paced, hackles raised, between them, forestalling any idea of pursuit. Lyall paused to sniff delicately at the wad of spit—eau de Westminster Hive.

"Really," said the first to Lyall, "we weren't going to harm one hair of that swarthy Italian head. We simply had a little test in mind. No one would have even known."

The other elbowed him, hard. "Hush you, that's Professor Lyall, that is. Lord Maccon's Beta. The less he knows about anything, the better."

With that, the two doffed their hats at the still growling, still bristling wolf in front of them and, turning, took off at a leisurely pace toward Bond Street.

Professor Lyall would have followed, but he decided on more precautionary measures and set a brisk trot to follow Alexia and ensure she arrived home safely.

Lady Maccon caught Professor Lyall when he came in, just before dawn. He looked exhausted, his already lean face pinched and drawn.

"Ah, Lady Maccon, you have waited up for me? How kind."

She searched for the sarcasm in his words, but if it was there, it was cleverly disguised. He was good. Alexia often wondered if Professor Lyall had been an actor before metamorphosis and somehow managed to hold on to his creativity despite sacrificing most of his soul for immortality. He was so very skilled at doing, and being, what was expected.

He confirmed her suspicions. Whatever it was that had caused the wide-scale lack of supernatural was definitely heading north. BUR had determined that the hour of London's return to supernatural normal correlated with the departure of the Kingair Pack toward Scotland. He was not surprised that Lady Maccon had arrived at the same conclusion.

He was, however, decidedly against the idea that she should go trailing after.

"Well, who else should go? I, at least, will remain entirely unaffected by the affliction."

Professor Lyall glared at her. "*No one* should go after it. The earl is perfectly capable of handling the situation, even if he doesn't yet know he has two problems to deal with. You seem to have failed to realize we all wandered around undamaged for centuries before you appeared in our lives."

"Yes, but look what a mess you have made of things prior to my arrival." Lady Maccon was not to be dissuaded from her chosen course of action. "Someone has to tell Conall that Kingair is to blame."

"If none of them are changing, he'll find out as soon as he arrives. His lordship would not like you following him."

"His lordship can eat my fat—" Lady Maccon paused, thought the better of her crass words, and said, "—does not have to like it. Nor do you. The fact remains that this morning Floote will secure for me passage on the afternoon's dirigible to Glasgow. His lordship can take it up with me when I arrive."

Professor Lyall had no doubt that his poor Alpha would do just that and be similarly humbled. Still, he would not give in so easily. "You shall have to take Tunstell with you, at the very least. The lad has been pining to visit the north ever since his lordship left, and he will be able to keep an eye on you."

Lady Maccon was truculent. "I do not need him. Have you seen my new parasol?"

Lyall had seen the purchase order and been suitably impressed, but he was no fool. "A woman, even a married woman, cannot float without proper escort. It is simply not done. You and I are both well aware of that fact."

Lady Maccon frowned. He was right, bother it. She sighed and figured that at least Tunstell was a pushover.

"Oh, very well, if you insist," she conceded with ill grace.

The intrepid Beta, older than most werewolves still living in the greater London environs—Lord Maccon and the dewan included—did the only thing he could under the circumstances. Pulled his cravat aside to expose his neck, gave a little bow, and took himself off to bed without another word, leaving Lady Maccon in possession of the field.

Her ladyship sent the hovering Floote to rouse poor Tunstell from his bed and give him the unexpected news that he would be departing for Scotland. The claviger, who had only just climbed into bed, having spent the better part of the night looking at ladies' hats, wondered a tad about the sanity of his mistress.

Just after sunrise, having gotten very little sleep, Lady Maccon commenced packing. Or, it should be said more precisely that Lady Maccon commenced arguing with Angelique over what should be packed. She was interrupted by a visit from the only person on the planet capable of consistently routing her in verbal skirmishes.

Floote brought up the message.

"Good gracious, what on earth is *she* doing here? And at such an early hour!" Alexia put the calling card back down on the little silver tray; checked her appearance, which was only just passable for receiving; and wondered if she should take the time to change. Should one risk keeping a caller waiting or face criticism for being dressed in attire unbecoming to a lady of rank? She chose the latter, deciding to get the encounter over and done with as quickly as possible.

The woman waiting for her in the front parlor was a diminutive blond with a rosy complexion that owed more to artifice than nature, wearing a visiting dress of pink and white stripes that would better suit a lady half her age.

"Mama," said Lady Maccon, presenting her cheek for the half-hearted kiss her mother wafted in her direction.

"Oh, Alexia," cried Mrs. Loontwill, as though she had not seen her eldest in years. "I am quite overset with the most nervous misery; such a to-do is afoot. I require your immediate assistance."

Lady Maccon was dumbfounded—a state that did not afflict her often. Firstly, her mother had not insulted her appearance. Secondly, her mother actually seemed to be seeking her help in some matter. *Her* help.

"Mama, do sit. You are quite discombobulated. I shall order tea." She gestured to a chair, and Mrs. Loontwill sank into it gratefully. "Rumpet," Alexia addressed the hovering butler, "tea, please. Or would you prefer sherry, Mama?"

"Oh, I am not *that* overset."

"Tea, Rumpet."

"However, the situation *is* very dire. Such poopitations of the heart as you would not *believe.*"

"Palpitations," corrected her daughter softly.

Mrs. Loontwill relaxed slightly, and then all of a sudden sat up straight as a poker, looking wildly about. "Alexia, none of your husband's *associates* are in residence, are they?"

This was her mother's delicate way of referring to the pack.

"Mama, it is full daylight. They are all in residence, but they are also all abed. I, myself, have been up most of the night." She said this last as a subtle hint, but her mother existed well beyond subtlety.

"Well, you *would* marry into the supernatural set. Not that I am complaining about your catch, my dear, far from it." Mrs. Loontwill puffed up her chest like a pink-striped quail. "My daughter, Lady Maccon."

It was a constant source of amazement to Alexia that the only thing she had ever done in her entire life that pleased her mama was marry a werewolf.

"Mama, I really have a great deal to accomplish this morning. And you indicated you were visiting regarding a matter of some considerable urgency. What has happened?"

"Well, you see, it is your sisters."

"You finally comprehend what intolerable little ninnies they both are?"

"Alexia!"

"What about them, Mama?" Lady Maccon was wary. It wasn't that she did not love her sisters; it was simply that she did not *like* them very much. They were half sisters to be precise: Misses Loontwills the pair of them, while Alexia had been a Miss Tarabotti before her marriage. They were as blond, as silly, and as nonpreternatural as their pink-striped mama.

"They are in the most terrible argument at the moment."

"Evylin and Felicity are fighting? How surprising." The sarcasm was entirely lost on Mrs. Loontwill.

"I know! But I speak nothing but truth. You must comprehend perfectly my distress at this. You see, Evylin has become engaged. Not a catch quite up to your standards, of course—we cannot expect lightning to strike twice—but a tolerable match. The gentleman is not supernatural, thank heavens; one irregular in-law is more than enough. Regardless, Felicity cannot countenance the fact that her younger sister will marry before her. She is being perfectly beastly over the whole thing. So Evylin suggested, and I agree, that perhaps she needs to get out of London for a spell. So I suggested, and Mr. Loontwill agreed, that a trip to the countryside would be just the thing to brighten up her spirits. So I have brought her here, to you."

Lady Maccon did not quite follow. "You have brought Evylin?"

"No, dear, no. Do pay attention! I have brought Felicity." Mrs. Loontwill produced a ruffled fan and began waggling it about violently.

"What, here?"

"Now you are being purposefully dull-witted," accused her mother, prodding her with the fan.

"I am?" Where *was* Rumpet with the tea? Lady Maccon was in desperate need. Her mother often caused that kind of reaction.

"I have brought her here to stay with you, of course."

"What! For how long?"

"As long as is required."

"But, what?"

"I am certain you could use the company of family," insisted her mother. She took a moment to glance about the parlor, a cluttered but friendly room, full of books and large pieces of leather furnishing. "And this place could certainly benefit from additional feminine influence. There is not a single doily in sight."

"Wait . . ."

"She has packed for a two-week stay, but, you understand, as I have a wedding to arrange, she may need to remain at Woolsey longer. In which case, you will have to go shopping."

"Now wait just a moment—" Alexia's voice rose in aggravation.

"Good, that is settled, then."

Alexia was left gaping like a fish.

Mrs. Loontwill stood, apparently recovered from her palpitations. "I shall go fetch her from the carriage, shall I?"

Lady Maccon trailed her mother out of the parlor and down the front steps to find Felicity, surrounded by a prodigious amount of baggage, on her front lawn.

Without further ado, Mrs. Loontwill kissed both of her daughters on the cheek, climbed back into the carriage, and departed in a whirl of lavender perfume and pink stripes.

Lady Maccon looked her sister over, still in shock. Felicity was dressed in the latest of velvet long coats, white with a red front, hundreds of tiny black buttons running up it, and a long white skirt with red and black bows. Her blond hair was up, and her hat was perched back on her head in just the kind of precarious manner Angelique would approve of most.

"Well," Lady Maccon said brusquely, "I guess you had best come in."

Felicity looked about at her bags and then maneuvered delicately around them and swept up the front steps and into the house.

"Rumpet, would you please?" Lady Maccon, left behind with the luggage, indicated the massive pile with her chin.

Rumpet nodded.

Lady Maccon stopped him as he passed. "Do not bother to see them unpacked, Rumpet. Not just yet. We shall see if we can arrange this differently."

The butler nodded. "Very good, my lady."

Lady Maccon followed her sister into the house.

Felicity had found her way into the front parlor and was pouring herself some of the tea. Without asking. She glanced up when Lady Maccon entered. "I do declare, you are looking rather puffy about the face, sister. Have you gained weight since I saw you last? You know, I do so worry about your health."

Alexia refrained from commenting that the only worry Felicity felt was over next season's gloves. She sat down across from her sister, folded her arms ostentatiously over her ample chest, and glared. "Out with it. Why would you possibly allow yourself to be foisted off on me?"

Felicity cocked her head to one side, sipped her tea, and demurred. "Well, your complexion seems to have improved. One might even mistake you for an Englishwoman. That is nice. I should never have believed it had I not seen it for myself."

Pale skin had been popular in England since vampires officially emerged into, and took over, much of the higher ranks. But Alexia had her father's Italian skin and no interest in fighting its inclinations merely to look like one of the undead. "Felicity," she said sharply.

Felicity looked to one side and tutted in annoyance. "Well, if I must. Let me simply say it has become desirable for me to absent myself from London for a short while. Evylin is being overly smug. You know how she gets if she has something and she knows you want it."

"The truth, Felicity."

Felicity glanced about as though looking for some clue or hint, and then said finally, "I was under the impression that the regiment was in residence here at Woolsey."

Ah, thought Alexia, so that was what was going on. "Oh, you were, were you?"

"Well, yes, I was. Are they?"

Lady Maccon narrowed her eyes. "They are encamped around the back."

Felicity immediately stood, brushing down her skirts and plumping her curls.

"Oh no, you don't. Sit right back down there, young lady." Alexia took great satisfaction in treating her sister as though she were an infant. "There is no point; you simply cannot stay with me."

"Why ever not?"

"Because I am not stopping here. I have business in Scotland, and I depart this afternoon. I cannot very well leave you at Woolsey alone and without a chaperone, especially as the regiment *is* in residence. Simply think how that would look."

"But why Scotland? I should hate to have to go to Scotland. It is such a barbaric place. It is *practically Ireland!*" Felicity was clearly perturbed at this disruption in her carefully wrought plans.

Alexia came up with the most Felicity-safe reason for traveling that she could think of, off of the top of her head. "My husband is in Scotland on pack business. I am to join him there."

"Well, piffle!" exclaimed Felicity, sitting back down with a *whump.* "What a frightful bother. Why do you always have to be so inconvenient, Alexia? Can you not think of *me* and my needs for a change?"

Lady Maccon interrupted what looked to be a long diatribe. "I am confident your suffering is quite beyond all description. Shall I call for the Woolsey carriage so you can at least travel back to town in style?"

Felicity looked glum. "It cannot be countenanced, Alexia. Mama will have your head if you send me back now. You know how impossible she can be about these things."

Lady Maccon did know. But what was to be done?

Felicity sucked on her teeth. "I suppose I shall simply have to accompany you to Scotland. It will be a terrible bore, of course, and you know how I hate traveling, but I shall bear it with grace." Felicity looked oddly cheered by this idea.

Lady Maccon blanched. "Oh no, absolutely not." A week or more in her sister's company and she would go categorically bonkers.

"I think the idea has merit." Felicity grinned. "I could instruct you on the subject of appearance." She gave Alexia a sweeping up-and-down look. "It is clear you are in need of expert guidance. Now, if I were Lady Maccon, I should not choose such somber attire."

Lady Maccon rubbed at her face. It would make for a good cover story, removing her deranged sister from London for a desperately needed airing. Felicity was just self-involved enough not to notice or remark upon any of Alexia's muhjah activities. Plus, it would give Angelique someone else to fuss over for a change.

That decided matters.

"Very well. I hope you are prepared to travel by air. We are catching a dirigible this afternoon."

Felicity looked uncharacteristically unsure of herself. "Well, if I must, I must. But I am certain I did not pack the correct bonnet for air travel."

"Cooee!" A voice reverberated down the hallway outside the open parlor door. "Anyone home?" it rang forth, singsong.

"Now what?" wondered Lady Maccon, fervently hoping she would not miss float-off. She did not want to delay her travel, particularly now that she must keep the regiment and Felicity separated.

A head appeared around the edge of the doorjamb. The head was wearing a hat comprised almost entirely of red feathers, all standing straight upright, and a few tiny puffy white ones, looking like nothing so much as an overly excited duster with a case of the pox.

"Ivy," stated Alexia, wondering if her dear friend was perhaps secretly the leader of a Silly Hat Liberation Society.

"Oh, Alexia! I let myself in. I do not know where Rumpet has taken himself off to, but I saw the parlor door open, so I deduced you must be awake, and I thought I ought to tell you . . ." She trailed off upon realizing Alexia was not alone.

"Why, Miss Hisselpenny," purred Felicity, "what are *you* doing *here*?"

"Miss Loontwill! How do you do?" Ivy blinked at Alexia's sister in utter surprise. "I might ask you the same question."

"Alexia and I are taking a trip to Scotland this afternoon."

The feather duster trembled in confusion. "You are?" Ivy looked rather hurt that Alexia would not see fit to inform her of such a trip. And that Alexia would choose Felicity as a companion, when Ivy knew how much Alexia loathed her sister.

"By dirigible."

Miss Hisselpenny nodded sagely. "So much more sensible. Rail is such an undignified way to travel. All that rapid racing about. Floating has so much more gravitas."

"It was decided at the last minute," said Lady Maccon, "both the trip and Felicity joining me. There has been some domestic difficulty at the Loontwills'. Frankly, Felicity is jealous that Evy is getting married." There was no way Lady Maccon would allow her sister to seize control of a conversation at the expense of her dear friend's feelings. It was one thing to put up with Felicity's jibes herself and another to witness them turned upon defenseless Miss Hisselpenny.

"What a lovely hat," Felicity said to Ivy snidely.

Lady Maccon ignored her sister. "I am sorry, Ivy. I would have invited you. You know I would, but my mother insisted, and you know how utterly impossible *she* can be."

Miss Hisselpenny nodded, looking gloomy. She came fully into the room and sat down. Her dress was subdued for Ivy: a simple walking gown of white with red polka dots, boasting only one row of red ruffles and fewer than six bows—although the ruffles were very puffy, and the bows were very large.

"I am assured floating is terribly unsafe, even so," added Felicity, "Us two women traveling alone. Don't you think you should ask several members of the regiment to accompany—?"

"No, I most certainly should not!" replied Lady Maccon sharply. "But I do believe Professor Lyall will insist upon Tunstell joining us as escort."

Felicity pouted. "Not that horrible redheaded thespian chap? He is so fearfully jolly. Must he come? Could we not get some nice soldier instead?"

Miss Hisselpenny quite bristled upon hearing Tunstell disparaged. "Why, Miss Loontwill, how bold you are with your opinions of young men you should know nothing of. I'll thank you not to cast windles and dispersions about like that."

"At least I am smart enough to have an opinion," snapped Felicity back.

Oh dear, thought Alexia, *here we go.* She wondered what a "windle" was.

"Oh," Miss Hisselpenny gasped. "I certainly do have an opinion about Mr. Tunstell. He is a brave and kindly gentleman in every way."

Felicity gave Ivy an assessing look. "And now here I sit, Miss Hisselpenny, thinking it is *you* who is probably overly familiar with the gentleman in question."

Ivy blushed as red as her hat.

Alexia cleared her throat. Ivy should not have been so bold as to reveal her feelings openly to one such as Felicity, but Felicity was behaving like a veritable harpy. If this was a window into her behavior of late, no wonder Mrs. Loontwill wanted her out of the house.

"Stop it, both of you."

Miss Hisselpenny turned big, beseeching eyes upon her friend. "Alexia, are you certain you cannot see your way to allowing me to accompany you as well? I have never been in a dirigible, and I should so very much like to see Scotland."

In truth, Ivy was vastly afraid of floating and had never before showed any interest in geography outside of London. Even inside London, her geographic concerns centered heavily on Bond Street and Oxford Circus, for obvious pecuniary reasons. Alexia Maccon would have to be a fool not to realize that Ivy's interest lay in Tunstell's presence.

"Only if you believe your mother and your *fiancé* can spare you," said Lady Maccon, emphasizing that last in the hopes that it might remind Ivy of her prior commitment and force her to see reason.

Miss Hisselpenny's eyes shone. "Oh, thank you, Alexia!"

And there went the reason. Felicity looked as though she had just been forced to swallow a live eel.

Lady Maccon sighed. Well, if she must have Felicity as companion, she could do worse than to have Miss Hisselpenny along as well. "Oh dear," she said. "Am I suddenly organizing the Lady's Dirigible Invitational?"

Felicity gave her an inscrutable look and Ivy beamed.

"I shall just head back to town to obtain Mama's permission and to pack. What time do we float?"

Lady Maccon told her. And Ivy was off and out the front door, never having told Alexia why she had jaunted all the way out to Woolsey Castle in the first place.

"I shudder to think what that woman will choose as headgear for floating," said Felicity.

CHAPTER SIX

The Lady's Dirigible Invitational

Alexia could see it all in the society papers:

Lady Maccon boarded the Giffard Long-Distance Airship, Standard Passenger Class Transport Model, accompanied by an unusually large entourage. She was followed up the gangplank by her sister, Felicity Loontwill, dressed in a pink traveling dress with white ruffled sleeves, and Miss Ivy Hisselpenny, in a yellow carriage dress with matching hat. The hat had an excessive veil, such as those sported by adventurers entering bug-infested jungles, but otherwise the two young ladies made for perfectly appropriate companions. The party was outfitted with the latest in air-travel goggles, earmuffs, and several other fashionable mechanical accessories designed to facilitate the most pleasant of dirigible experiences.

Lady Maccon was also accompanied by her French maid and a gentleman escort. There was some question as to the appropriateness of the gentleman, a ginger fellow who might have trod the boards on more than one occasion. It was thought odd that Lady Maccon was seen off by her personal secretary, a former butler, but the presence of her mother more than made up for this gaffe. Lady Maccon is one of London's premiere eccentrics; these things must be taken in stride.

The lady herself wore a floating dress of the latest design, with tape-down skirt straps, weighted hem, a bustle of alternating ruffles of teal and black designed to flutter becomingly in the aether breezes, and a tightly fitted bodice. There were teal-velvet-trimmed goggles about her neck and a matching top hat with an appropriately modest veil and drop-down teal velvet earmuffs tied securely to her head. More than a few of the ladies walking through Hyde Park that afternoon stopped to wonder as to the maker of her dress, and a certain matron of low scru-

ples plotted openly to hire away Lady Maccon's excellent maid. True,
Lady Maccon carried a garish foreign-looking parasol in one hand and
a red leather dispatch case in the other, neither of which matched her
outfit, but one must be excused one's luggage when traveling. All in all,
Hyde Park's afternoon perambulators reported favorably on the elegant
departure of one of the season's most talked-about brides.

Lady Maccon thought they must look like a parade of stuffed pigeons and found it typical of London society that what pleased them
annoyed her. Ivy and Felicity would not leave off bickering, Tunstell
was revoltingly bouncy, and Floote had refused to accompany them to
Scotland on the grounds that he might be suffocated by an overabundance of bustle. Alexia was just thinking it was going to be a long and
tedious journey when an impeccably dressed young gentleman hove
into view. The leader of their procession, a frazzled ship's steward trying to steer them to their respective rooms, paused in the narrow passageway to allow the gentleman to pass.

Instead, the gentleman stopped and doffed his hat at the parade of
newcomers. The smell of vanilla and mechanical oil tickled Lady Maccon's nose.

"Why," said Alexia in startlement, "Madame Lefoux! What on
Earth are *you* doing *here*?"

Just then, the dirigible jerked against its tethers as the massive
steam engine that drove it through the aether rumbled into life. Madame Lefoux stumbled forward against Lady Maccon and then righted
herself. Alexia felt that the Frenchwoman had taken a good deal longer
to do so than was necessary.

"Clearly we are not 'on Earth' for much longer, Lady Maccon," said
the inventor, dimpling. "I thought, after our conversation, that I, too,
would enjoy visiting Scotland."

Alexia frowned. To travel so soon after opening a brand-new shop,
not to mention leaving both her son and her ghostly aunt behind, seemed
unwarranted. Clearly the inventor must be a spy of some kind. She
would have to keep her guard up around the Frenchwoman, which was
sad, as Alexia rather enjoyed the inventor's company. It was a rare
thing for Lady Maccon to encounter a woman more independent and
eccentric than herself.

Alexia introduced Madame Lefoux to the rest of her party, and the
Frenchwoman was unflaggingly polite to all, although there might
have been a slight wince upon seeing Ivy's eyeball-searing ensemble.

The same could not be said of Alexia's entourage. Tunstell and Ivy
bowed and curtsied, but Felicity openly snubbed the woman, clearly taken
aback by her abnormal attire.

Angelique, too, seemed uncomfortable, although the maid did curtsy as required by someone in her position. Well, Angelique had very decided opinions on proper attire. She probably did not approve of a woman dressing as a man.

Madame Lefoux gave Angelique a long and hard look, almost predatory. Lady Maccon assumed it had something to do with both of them being French, and her suspicions were confirmed when Madame Lefoux hissed something at Angelique in a rapid-fire undertone in her native tongue, too fast for Alexia to follow.

Angelique did not respond, turning her lovely little nose up slightly and pretending to be busy fluffing the ruffles on Lady Maccon's dress.

Madame Lefoux bade them all farewell.

"Angelique," Lady Maccon addressed her servant thoughtfully, "what was that?"

"It waz nothing of import, my lady."

Lady Maccon decided the matter might wait for a later time and followed the steward into her cabin.

She did not remain inside for long, as she wished to explore the ship and be on deck to witness float-off. She had waited years to float the skies, having followed the development of airship technology detailed in the Royal Society papers from a very young age. To be on board a dirigible at last was a joy not to be dampened by French mannerisms.

Once the last of the passengers had boarded and been shown to their respective cabins, the crew cast off the rope tethers, and the great balloon hoisted them slowly into the sky.

Lady Maccon gasped to see the world retreating below them, people disappearing into the landscape, landscape disappearing into a patchwork quilt, and final, irrevocable proof that the world was, indeed, round.

Once they floated through normal air and were high up into the aether, a young man, dangerously perched at the very back of the engines, spun up the propeller, and, with steam emitting in great puffs of white out the back and sides of the tank, the dirigible floated forward in a northerly direction. There came a slight jolt as it caught the aetheromagnetic current and picked up speed, going faster than it looked like it ought to be able to go, with its portly boatlike passenger decks dangling below the massive almond-shaped canvas balloon.

Miss Hisselpenny, who had joined Lady Maccon on deck, recovered from her own awe and began singing. Ivy had a good little voice, untrained but sweet. "Ye'll take the high road," she sang, "and I'll take the low road, and I'll be in Scotland afore ye."

Lady Maccon grinned at her friend but did not join her. She knew the song. Who didn't? It had been a forerunner in Giffard's dirigible travel marketing campaign. But Alexia's was a voice meant for commanding battles, not singing, as anyone who ever heard her sing took great pains to remind her.

Lady Maccon found the whole experience invigorating. The air up high was colder and somehow fresher than that of London or the countryside. She felt strangely comforted by it, as though this were her element. It must be the aether, she supposed, replete with its gaseous mix of aetheromagnetic particles.

However, she liked it far less the next morning when she awoke with a queasy stomach and a feeling of floating inside as well as out.

"Air travel takes some over like that, my lady," said the steward, adding by way of explanation, "derangement of the digestive components." He sent round one of the ship's hostesses with a tincture of mint and ginger. Very little put Alexia off her food, and with the help of the tincture, she recovered a measure of her appetite by midday. Part of the queasiness, she supposed, was the fact that she was readjusting her routine to that of daylight folk, after spending months conducting her business mainly at night.

Felicity only noticed that Alexia was getting new color in her cheeks.

"Of course, not just anyone looks good in a sun hat. But I do believe, Alexia, that you ought to make that sacrifice. If you are wise, you will take my advice in this matter. I know sun hats are not often worn these days, but I think someone of your unfortunate propensities might be excused the old-fashioned nature of the accessory. And why do you go gadding about with that parasol at all times of day and yet never use it?"

"You are sounding more and more like our mama," replied Lady Maccon.

Ivy, who was flitting from one railing to the other, cooing over the view, gasped at the cutting nature of such a statement.

Felicity was about to respond in kind when Tunstell appeared, entirely distracting her. She'd deduced Ivy and Tunstell's regard for one another and thus was now committed to securing Tunstell's affection for herself, for no other reason than to show Ivy that she could.

"Oh, Mr. Tunstell, how lovely of you to join us." Felicity batted her eyelashes.

Tunstell reddened slightly and bobbed his head at the ladies. "Miss Loontwill. Lady Maccon." A pause. "And how do you feel today, Lady Maccon?"

"The airsickness fades by luncheon."

"How terribly convenient of it," remarked Felicity. "You might hope it would hold on a trifle longer given your inclination toward robustness and obvious affection for food."

Lady Maccon did not rise to the bait. "It would be better if the luncheons were not so consistently subpar." All food on board the dirigible appeared to favor the bland and steamed approach. Even the much-lauded high tea had been disappointing.

Felicity carefully knocked her gloves off the little table next to the deck chair in which she lounged.

"Oh, how careless of me. Mr. Tunstell, would you mind?"

The claviger stepped forward and bent to retrieve them for her.

Felicity shifted quickly and angled herself in such a way that Tunstell was now bending over her legs, practically facedown in the skirts of her green dress. It was a rather intimate arrangement, and, of course, Ivy came bouncing around the corner of the deck right at that very moment.

"Oh!" said Ivy, somewhat deflated in her bounciness.

Tunstell straightened, handing Felicity her gloves. Felicity took them from him slowly, allowing her fingers to trail over his hand.

Ivy's countenance looked remarkably similar to that of a bilious poodle.

Lady Maccon wondered that her sister had not gotten herself into trouble before now, with such behavior. When had Felicity turned into such a hardened little flirt?

Tunstell bowed to Ivy. "Miss Hisselpenny. How do you do?"

"Mr. Tunstell, please do not let my presence disturb you."

Lady Maccon stood up, ostentatiously fixing the ear flaps of her flying hat. Really, it was too vexing: Felicity overly bold, Ivy engaged to another, and poor Tunstell stuck making puppy eyes at the both of them in his confusion.

Tunstell went to bow over Miss Hisselpenny's hand. The dirigible encountered turbulence in the aether and lurched, causing Ivy and Tunstell to blunder into one another. Tunstell caught at her arm, helping her to stay upright while Ivy blushed like an overripe strawberry, her eyes downcast.

Alexia decided she needed a brisk walk on the forward deck.

Usually uninhabited, the forward deck was the windiest the dirigible had to offer. Both ladies and gentlemen tended to give it a miss, as it upset the hair something dreadful, but Alexia had no such qualms, even knowing she would earn a heavily accented chiding from Angelique upon her return. She turned the muffs down about her ears, donned her goggles, grabbed her parasol, and sallied forth.

The forward deck was, however, already occupied.

Madame Lefoux, dressed as impeccably and as inappropriately as always, stood next to that very same Angelique at the rails to one side,

looking down over the patchwork of the British landscape spread below them like some sort of ill-designed and asymmetrical quilt. The
two were whispering to each other heatedly.

Lady Maccon cursed the wind of air travel, for it carried their
words away before reaching her, and she would have dearly loved to
know what was being said. She thought of her dispatch case. Had Floote
packed any listening mechanicals?

Deciding there was nothing else for it but a direct frontal attack,
Alexia moved as quietly as possible across the deck, hoping to catch
some part of the conversation before they noticed her presence. She was
in luck.

". . . assume proper responsibility," Madame Lefoux was saying in
French.

"Cannot happen, not yet." Angelique moved closer to the other
woman, placing small, pleading hands on the inventor's arm. "Please
do not ask it of me."

"Better happen soon or I'll tell. You know I will." Madame Lefoux
tossed her head, top hat tilting dangerously but staying in place, as it
was tied on for travel. She shrugged off the blond woman's grip.

"Soon, I promise." Angelique pressed herself against the inventor's
side and nested her head on the other woman's shoulder.

Again Madame Lefoux shrugged her off. "Games, Angelique.
Games and fancying up a lady's hair. That is all you have now, isn't it?"

"It is better than selling hats."

Madame Lefoux rounded on the maid at that, gripping the woman's
chin in her hand, one set of goggle-covered eyes meeting another. "Did
she really kick you out?" Her tone was both vicious and disbelieving.

Lady Maccon was close enough by then to meet her maid's big violet eyes behind the plain brass goggles when the girl looked away. Angelique started at the appearance of her mistress, and her eyes filled
with tears. With a little sob, she cast herself at Lady Maccon so that
Alexia had no choice but to catch her.

Alexia was disturbed. Even though she was French, Angelique was
rarely given to displays of emotion. Angelique composed herself, hurriedly withdrew from her mistress's arms, bobbed a curtsy, and rushed
away.

Alexia had liked Madame Lefoux, but she could hardly condone
her distressing the domestic staff. "The vampires rejected her, you
know. It is a sensitive subject. She does not like to talk about the hive
giving her up to me."

"I wager she doesn't."

Lady Maccon bristled. "Any more than you would tell me the real reason you are on board this dirigible." The Frenchwoman would have to learn: a pack protected its own. Alexia might only be pack by proxy, but Angelique was still in its service.

Green eyes met her brown ones for a long moment. Two sets of goggles were no impediment, but Lady Maccon could not interpret that expression. Then the inventor reached up and stroked the back of her hand down the side of Alexia's face. Alexia wondered why the French were so much more physically affectionate than the English.

"Did you and my maid have some kind of *association* in the past, Madame Lefoux?" Alexia asked, not responding to the touch, although it made her face feel hot even in the cold aether wind.

The inventor dimpled. "We did once, but I assure you I am currently free of all such entanglements." Was she being purposefully obtuse? She moved closer.

Alexia, always blunt, cocked her head to one side and asked, "Who are you working for, Madame Lefoux? The French government? The Templars?"

The inventor backed away slightly, strangely upset by the question. "You misconstrue my presence here, Lady Maccon. I assure you, I work only for myself."

"I would not trust her if I were you, my lady," said Angelique, fixing Alexia's hair before supper that evening. The maid was ironing it straight with a specially provided steam iron, much to both their disgust. Straight and loose was Ivy's idea. Miss Hisselpenny had insisted Alexia be the one to try the fancy iron invention out, because Alexia was married and could suffer the burden of risky hair.

"Is there something I should know, Angelique?" Lady Maccon asked gently. The maid so rarely offered up an opinion that was not fashion related.

Angelique paused in her ministrations, her hand fluttering a moment about her face as only the French could flutter. "Only zat I knew her before I became drone, in Paris."

"And?"

"And we did not part with ze friendly terms. A matter, how do you say, personal."

"Then I would not dream of prying further," replied Alexia, dearly wishing to pry.

"She did not say anything about me to you, my lady?" the maid asked. Her hand went up to stroke the high collar about her neck.

"Nothing of consequence," replied Lady Maccon.

Angelique did not look convinced. "You do not trust me, do you, my lady?"

Alexia looked up in surprise, meeting Angelique's eyes in the looking glass. "You were drone to a rove, but you also served the Westminster Hive. *Trust* is a strong word, Angelique. I trust that you will do my hair to the height of fashion and that your taste should govern my own disinterest in the matter. But you cannot ask me for more than that."

Angelique nodded. "I see. So it iz not something Genevieve said?"

"Genevieve?"

"Madame Lefoux."

"No. Should it be?"

Angelique lowered her eyes and shook her head.

"You will tell me nothing more about your previous relationship?"

Angelique remained silent but her face seemed to indicate that she thought this inquiry excessively personal.

Lady Maccon excused her maid and went to find her little leather journal, the better to collect her thoughts and make a few notations. If she suspected Madame Lefoux of being a spy, she ought to jot this down, along with her reasoning. Part of the purpose of the notebook was to leave adequate record should anything untoward happen to her. She had commenced the practice upon assuming her position as muhjah, though she used the journal for personal notes, not state secrets. Her father's journals had proved helpful on more than one occasion. She would like to think her own might be of equal assistance to future generations. Although probably not in quite the same way as Alessandro Tarabotti's. She didn't go in for recording *that* type of information.

The stylographic pen was where she had left it, on the nightstand, but her notebook had vanished. She checked all about—under the bed, behind the furniture—but could find it nowhere. With a sinking feeling, she went looking for her dispatch case.

A knock came at her door, and before she could come up with some excuse to keep the visitor at bay, Ivy trotted into the room. She looked flushed and nervous, her hat of the day a floof of black lace draped over masses of dark side curls, the earmuffs underneath only visible because Ivy was tugging at them.

Alexia paused in her hunt. "Ivy, what is wrong? You look like a perturbed terrier with an ear mite problem."

Miss Hisselpenny cast herself dramatically facedown on Alexia's small bed, clearly in some emotional distress. She mumbled into the pillow. Her voice was suspiciously high.

"Ivy, what is wrong with your voice? Have you been up in engineering, on the Squeak Deck?" Since the dirigible maintained buoyancy through the application of helium, it was a legitimate assumption for any vocal abnormalities.

"No," squeaked Ivy. "Well, maybe for a short while."

Lady Maccon stifled a laugh. Really, it was too absurd-sounding. "Who were you up there with?" she inquired archly, although she could very well hazard a guess.

"No one," squeak, squeak. "Well, in actuality, I mean to say, I might have been with . . . uh . . . Mr. Tunstell."

Lady Maccon snickered. "I wager he sounded pretty funny too."

"A slight leak occurred while we were up there. But there was grave need for a small moment of privacy."

"How romantic."

"Really, Alexia, this is no time for levity! I am all aquiver, facing a ghastly emotional crisis, and you issue forth nothing more than scads of unwanted jocularity."

Lady Maccon composed her features and tried to look like she was not amused at her friend's expense, annoyed at her friend's appearance, nor still glancing about her room in search of the missing dispatch case. "Let me hazard a guess. Tunstell has professed his undying love?"

"Yes," Ivy wailed, "and I am engaged to another!" On the word *engaged*, she finally stopped squeaking.

"Ah, yes, the mysterious Captain Featherstonehaugh. And let us not forget that, even if you were not affianced, Tunstell is an entirely unsuitable match. Ivy, he makes his living as a *thespian*."

Ivy groaned. "I know! In addition, he is your husband's *valet!* Oh, it is all so messily plebeian." Ivy rolled over on the bed, the back of her wrist pressed to her forehead. She kept her eyes tightly shut. Lady Maccon wondered if Miss Hisselpenny did not have a possible future career on the stage herself.

"Which also makes him a claviger. Well, well, well, you have got yourself into a pretty pickle." Lady Maccon tried to sound sympathetic.

"Oh, but, Alexia, I am quite fearfully afraid that I might just possibly, maybe a little itty-bitty bit, love him back."

"Shouldn't you be certain of a thing like that?"

"I do not know. Should I be? How does one determine one's own state of enamorment?"

Lady Maccon snickered. "I am hardly one to elucidate. It took me ages to realize I had feelings for Conall beyond abhorrence, and quite frankly, I am still not certain that feeling does not persist unto this very moment."

Ivy was taken aback. "Surely you jest?"

Alexia cast her mind back to the last time she had engaged in a protracted encounter with her husband. There had been a good deal of moaning at the time, if memory served. "Well, he has his uses."

"But, Alexia, what do *I* do?"

At that moment, Lady Maccon spotted her missing dispatch case. Someone had shoved it in the corner between the wardrobe and the door to the washroom. Alexia was quite certain that was not where she had left it.

"Aha, how did you get there?" she said to the missing accoutrement, and went to retrieve it.

Ivy, eyes still shut, pondered this question. "I have no idea how I allowed myself into such an untenable position. You must help me, Alexia. This is a *cataplasm* of epic proportions!"

"Too true," agreed Lady Maccon, considering the state of her beloved dispatch case. Someone had tried to break open the catch. Whomever it was must have been disturbed in the act, or they would have stolen the case as well as her notebook. Her little leather journal would fit inside a vest or under a skirt, but the dispatch case would not. The villain must have left it behind as a result. Lady Maccon considered possible suspects. The ship's domestic staff had access to her rooms, of course, and Angelique. But, really, given the state of the locks on board, it could have been anyone.

"He kissed me," Miss Hisselpenny keened.

"Ah, well, that *is* something like." Alexia decided nothing more could be determined from the dispatch case, at least not with Ivy still in the room. She went to sit next to her friend's prostrate form. "Did you enjoy kissing him?"

Ivy said nothing.

"Did you enjoy kissing Captain Featherstonehaugh?"

"Alexia, the very idea. We are only engaged, not married!"

"So you have not kissed the good captain?"

Ivy shook her head in an excess of embarrassment.

"Well, then, what about Tunstell?"

Miss Hisselpenny flushed even redder. Now she looked like a spaniel with a sunburn. "Well, maybe, just a little."

"And?"

Miss Hisselpenny opened her eyes, still blushing furiously, and looked at her married friend. "Is one supposed to enjoy kissing?" she practically whispered.

"I believe it is generally thought to be a pleasant pastime. You read novels, do you not?" replied Lady Maccon, trying desperately to keep a straight face.

"Do you enjoy doing . . . *that* with Lord Maccon?"

Lady Maccon did not hesitate, credit where it was due and all. "Unreservedly."

"Oh, well, I thought it was a little"—Ivy paused—"damp."

Lady Maccon cocked her head to one side. "Well, you must understand, my husband has considerable experience in these matters. He is hundreds of years older than I."

"And that does not trouble you?"

"My dear, he will live hundreds of years longer than I as well. One must come to terms with these things if one fraternizes with the supernatural set. I admit it is hard, knowing we will not grow old together. But if you choose Tunstell, you may eventually have to face the same concerns. Then again, your time together could be cut short, as he may not survive metamorphosis."

"Is that likely to occur soon?"

Lady Maccon knew very little about this aspect of pack dynamics. So she only shrugged.

Ivy sighed, a long, drawn-out exhalation that seemed to encompass all the problems of the empire. "It is all too much to think about. My head is positively awhirl. I simply do not know what to do. Don't you see? Don't you comprehend my cacophony?"

"You mean catastrophe?"

Ivy ignored her. "Do I throw over Captain Featherstonehaugh, and his five hundred a year, for Mr. Tunstell and his unstable"—she shuddered—"working-class station? Or do I continue with my engagement?"

"You could always marry your captain and pursue a dalliance with Tunstell on the side."

Miss Hisselpenny gasped, sitting fully upright in her outrage at such a proposal. "Alexia, how could you even *think* such a thing, let alone suggest it aloud!"

"Well, yes, of course, those damp kisses *would* have to improve."

Ivy threw a pillow at her friend. "Really!"

Lady Maccon, it must be admitted, gave little further thought to her dear friend's dilemma. She transferred all the most delicate documents and important smaller instruments and devices out of her dispatch case and into the pockets of her parasol. Since she was already known as an eccentric parasol-carrier, no one remarked upon its continued presence at her side, even well after dark.

Dinner was a strained affair, stiff with tension and suspicion. Worse, the food was horrible. True, Alexia had very high standards, but the fare continued to be ghastly. Everything—meat, vegetables, even pudding—

appeared to have been steamed into flaccid colorless submission, with no sauce, or even salt, to bolster the flavor. It was like eating a wet handkerchief.

Felicity, who had the palate of a country goat and tucked in without pause to anything laid before her, noticed that Alexia was only picking at her food. "Nice to see you are finally taking measures, sister."

Lady Maccon, lost in thought, replied with an unguarded, "Measures?"

"Well, I am terribly concerned for your health. One simply should not weigh so much at your age."

Lady Maccon poked at a sagging carrot and wondered if anyone would miss her dear sister were she to be oh-so-gently tipped over the rail of the upper deck.

Madame Lefoux glanced up. She gave Alexia an appraising look. "I think Lady Maccon appears in fine health."

"I think you are being fooled by her unfashionable robustness," said Felicity.

Madame Lefoux continued as though Felicity hadn't spoken. "You, on the other hand, Miss Loontwill, are looking a touch insipid."

Felicity gasped.

Alexia wished, yet again, that Madame Lefoux were not so clearly a spy. She would be a good egg otherwise. Was it she who had tried to get into the dispatch case?

Tunstell came wandering in, full of excuses for his tardiness, and took his seat between Felicity and Ivy.

"How nice of you to join us," commented Felicity.

Tunstell looked embarrassed. "Have I missed the first course?"

Alexia examined the steamed offering before her. "You can have mine if you like. I find my appetite sorely taxed these days."

She passed the graying mass over to Tunstell, who looked at it doubtfully but began eating.

Madame Lefoux continued talking to Felicity. "I have an interesting little invention in my rooms, Miss Loontwill, excellent for enlivening the facial muscles and imparting a rosy hue to the cheeks. You are welcome to try it sometime." There was a slight dimpling at that, suggesting this invention was either sticky or painful.

"I would not think, with your propensities, that you would be concerned with feminine appearances," shot back Felicity, glaring at the woman's vest and dinner jacket.

"Oh, I assure you, they concern me greatly." The Frenchwoman looked at Alexia.

Lady Maccon decided Madame Lefoux reminded her a little bit of

Professor Lyall, only prettier and less vulpine. She looked to her sister. "Felicity, I seem to have misplaced my leather travel journal. You have not seen it anywhere, have you?"

The second course was presented. It looked only slightly more appetizing than the first: some unidentifiable grayish meat in a white sauce, boiled potatoes, and soggy dinner rolls. Alexia waved it all away in disgust.

"Oh dear, sister, you have not taken up writing, have you?" Felicity pretended shock. "Quite frankly, all of that reading is outside of enough. I had thought that being married would cure you of such an unwise inclination. I never read if I can help it. It is terribly bad for the eyes. And it causes one's forehead to wrinkle most horribly, just there." She pointed between her eyebrows and then said pityingly to Lady Maccon, "Oh, I see you do not have to worry about *that* anymore, Alexia."

Lady Maccon sighed. "Oh, pack it in, Felicity, do."

Madame Lefoux hid a smile.

Miss Hisselpenny said suddenly in a loud and highly distressed voice, "Mr. Tunstell? Oh! Mr. Tunstell, are you quite all right?"

Tunstell was leaning forward over his plate, his face gone pale and drawn.

"Is it the food?" wondered Lady Maccon. "Because if it is, I entirely understand your feelings on the subject. I shall have a conversation with the cook."

Tunstell looked up at her. His freckles were standing out and his eyes watering. "I feel most unwell," he said distinctly before lurching to his feet and stumbling out the door.

Alexia looked after him for a moment with her mouth agape, then glared suspiciously down at the food set before them. She stood. "If you will excuse me, I think I had best check on Tunstell. No, Ivy, you stay here." She grabbed her parasol and followed the claviger.

She found him on the nearest observation deck, collapsed on his side against a far rail, clutching at his stomach.

Alexia marched up to him. "Did this come over you quite suddenly?"

Tunstell nodded, clearly unable to speak.

There came a faint smell of vanilla, and Madame Lefoux's voice behind them said, "Poison."

CHAPTER SEVEN

Problematic Octopuses
and Airship Mountaineering

Randolph Lyall was old, for a werewolf. Something on the order of three hundred or so. He had long since stopped counting. And through all that time, he had played this little game of chess with local vampires: they moved their pawns and he moved his. He'd been changed shortly before King Henry absorbed supernaturals legally into the British government, so he'd never known the Dark Ages, not personally. But he, like every other supernatural on the British Isles, worked hard to keep them from returning. Funny how such a simple objective could so easily become adulterated by politics and new technology. Of course, he could simply march up to the Westminster Hive and *ask* them what they were about. But they would no more tell him than he would tell them Lord Maccon had BUR agents watching the hive twenty-four hours a day.

Lyall reached his destination in far less time than it would have taken by carriage. He changed into human form in a dark alley, throwing the cloak he'd carried in his mouth about his naked body. Not precisely dress appropriate for paying a social visit, but he was confident his host would understand. This *was* business. Then again, one never could tell with vampires. They had, after all, dominated the fashion world for decades as a kind of indirect campaign against werewolves and the uncivilized state shifting shape required.

He reached forward and pulled the bell rope on the door in front of him.

A handsome young footman opened it.

"Professor Lyall," said Professor Lyall, "to see Lord Akeldama."

The young man gave the werewolf a very long look. "Well, well.

You will not mind, sir, if I ask you to wait on the stoop while I inform the master of your presence?"

Vampires were odd about invitations. Professor Lyall shook his head.

The footman disappeared, and a moment later, Lord Akeldama opened the door in his stead.

They had met before, of course, but Lyall had never yet had occasion to visit the vampire at home. The decoration was—he discerned as he peered into the glittering interior—very loud.

"Professor Lyall." Lord Akeldama gave him an appraising look through a beautiful gold monocle. He was dressed for the theater, and one pinky pointed out as he lowered the viewing device. "And *alone*. To what do I owe this honor?"

"I have a proposition for you."

Lord Akeldama looked the werewolf up and down once more; his blond eyebrows, darkened by artificial means, rose in surprise. "Why, Professor Lyall, how *charming*. I think you had best come inside."

Without looking up at Madame Lefoux, Alexia asked, "Is there anything built into my parasol to counteract poison?"

The inventor shook her head. "The parasol was designed as an offensive device. Had I known we would need an apothecary's kit, I would have added that feature."

Lady Maccon crouched down over Tunstell's supine form. "Run to the steward and see if he has an emetic on board, syrup of ipecac or white vitriol."

"At once," said the inventor, and dashed off.

Lady Maccon envied Madame Lefoux the masculine attire. Her own skirts were getting caught about her legs as she tried to tend to the afflicted claviger. His face was paper white, freckles stark against it, and there was a sheen of sweat on his forehead dampening his red hair.

"Oh no, he is suffering so. Will he recover soon?" Miss Hisselpenny had defied Alexia's order and tracked them down to the observation deck. She, too, crouched over Tunstell, her skirts spilling about her like a great over-iced meringue. She patted uselessly at one of Tunstell's hands, which were clenched over his stomach.

Alexia ignored her. "Tunstell, you must try to purge yourself." She made her voice as authoritative as possible, disguising her worry and fear with gruffness.

"Alexia!" Miss Hisselpenny was appalled. "Imagine suggesting such a thing. How undignified! Poor Mr. Tunstell."

"He must eject the contents of his stomach before the toxin enters his system any further."

"Do not be a ninnyhammer, Alexia," replied Ivy with a forced laugh. "It is just a bit of food poisoning."

Tunstell groaned but did not move.

"Ivy, and I mean this with the kindest and best of intentions, bugger off."

Miss Hisselpenny gasped and stood up, scandalized. But at least she was out of the way.

Alexia helped Tunstell to turn over so he was on his knees. She pointed a finger over the side of the dirigible autocratically. She made her voice as low and as tough as possible. "Tunstell, this is your Alpha speaking. Do as I tell you. You must regurgitate now." Never in all her time had Alexia supposed she would someday be ordering someone to throw up their supper.

But the command in her voice seemed to get through to the claviger. Tunstell stuck his head under the rail and over the side of the dirigible and tried to retch.

"I can't," he said finally.

"You must try harder."

"Regurgitation is an involuntary action. You cannot simply order me to do it," replied Tunstell in a small voice.

"I most certainly can. Besides which, you are an actor."

Tunstell grimaced. "I've never had cause to vomit onstage."

"Well, if you do this, you shall know how if you need to in the future."

Tunstell tried again. Nothing.

Madame Lefoux returned clutching a bottle of ipecac.

Alexia made Tunstell take a large gulp.

"Ivy, run and fetch a glass of water," she ordered her friend, mostly to get her out of the way.

In moments, the emetic took effect. As unsavory as the supper had been to eat, it was even less pleasant going the other direction. Lady Maccon tried not to look or listen.

By the time Ivy returned with a goblet of water, the worst was over.

Alexia made Tunstell drink the entirety of the glass. They waited a full quarter of an hour more while his color returned, and he was finally able to attain an upright position.

Ivy was in a flutter over the whole incident, agitating about the recovering man with such vigor that Madame Lefoux was driven to desperate measures. She extracted a small flask from her waistcoat pocket.

"Have a little nip of this, my dear. Calm your nerves." She handed it to Ivy.

Ivy nipped, blinked a couple times, nipped again, and then graduated from frantic to loopy. "Why, that *burns* all the way down!"

"Let's get Tunstell to his room." Alexia hoisted the redhead to his feet.

With Ivy walking backward before them and weaving side to side like an iced tea cake with delusions of shepherding, Lady Maccon and Madame Lefoux managed to get Tunstell to his rooms and onto bed.

By the time all the excitement had ended, Lady Maccon found she had lost her appetite entirely. Nevertheless, appearances must be kept up, so she returned to the dining cabin with Ivy and Madame Lefoux. She was in a mental quandary: why on earth, or in aether for that matter, would someone try to kill Tunstell?

Ivy walked into one or two walls on their way back.

"What did you give her?" Alexia hissed to the inventor.

"Just a bit of cognac." Madame Lefoux's dimples flashed. "Very effective stuff."

The rest of the meal passed without incident, if one ignored Ivy's evident inebriation, which occasioned two spills and one bout of hysterical giggling. Alexia was about to rise and excuse herself when Madame Lefoux, who had been silent throughout most of the postpurge meal, spoke to her.

"Do you think you might take a little turn with me about the ship before bed, Lady Maccon? I should like a private word," she asked politely, dimples safely stored away.

Not entirely surprised, Alexia acquiesced, and the two left Felicity to sort out after-dinner activities on her own.

As soon as they were alone, the inventor got straight to the point. "I do not think the poison was meant for Tunstell."

"No?"

"No. I believe it was meant for you, secreted in the first dish that you turned away and Tunstell consumed in your stead."

"Ah, yes, I recall. You may be right."

"What a strange temperament you have, Lady Maccon, to accept near-death so easily as that." Madame Lefoux tilted her head to one side.

"Well, the whole episode does make far more sense that way."

"It does?"

"Why, yes. I cannot imagine Tunstell has many enemies, but people are always trying to exterminate me." Lady Maccon was relieved and strangely comfortable with this revelation, as though things were not right with the universe unless someone was actively trying to kill her.

"Do you have a suspect?" the inventor wanted to know.

"Aside from you?" Lady Maccon shot back.

"Ah."

The Frenchwoman turned away, but not before Alexia spotted a little tinge of hurt in her eyes. Either she was a good actress or she was not guilty.

"I am sorry to offend," said Lady Maccon, not sorry in the least. She followed the inventor over to the rail, leaning on it next to her. The two women stared out into the evening aether.

"I am not upset that you think me capable of poison, Lady Maccon. I am offended you should think I would be so ham-handed with it. Had I wished you dead, I have had ample opportunity and access to numerous techniques far less clumsy than the one employed this evening." She pulled a gold watch out of the pocket of her vest and pressed a little catch on the back. A small injection needle sprang out of the bottom.

Alexia did not ask what was in the needle.

Madame Lefoux folded it back in and tucked the watch away once more.

Alexia took a long assessing look at the amount and type of jewelry the Frenchwoman wore. Her two cravat pins were in place, one wood, one silver. And there was another chain leading to her other vest pocket. A different kind of watch, or some other gadget, perhaps? The buttoner pin seemed suddenly suspicious, as did the metal cigar case tucked into the band of her top hat. Come to think on it, Alexia had never seen the woman smoke a cigar.

"True," said Alexia, "but the primitive nature of the attempt could be to throw me off the scent."

"You are of a suspicious inclination, are you not, Lady Maccon?" The Frenchwoman still did not look at her but seemed to find the cold night sky infinitely fascinating.

Lady Maccon came over philosophical. "Possibly that has something to do with having no soul. I prefer to think of it as pragmatism rather than paranoia."

Madame Lefoux laughed. She turned toward Alexia, dimples back.

And just like that, something solid hit Alexia hard across the back at exactly the correct angle to tilt her forward and over the railing. She tumbled, ass over teakettle, right over the edge of the deck. She felt herself falling, and screaming, scrabbling with both hands for purchase on the side of the dirigible. Why was the darn thing so smooth? The carrier body of the dirigible was shaped like a huge duck, and the observation deck was at its fattest point. In falling down, she was also falling away.

There was a horrible long moment when Alexia *knew* all was lost.

She knew that all her future held in store was the long cold rush of aether and then air followed by a sad, wet thud. And then she was stopped with an abrupt jerk and flipped upside down, her head crashing hard into the side of the ship. The reinforced metal hem of her dress, designed to keep her copious skirts from floating about in the aether breezes, had wrapped fast around a spur that stuck out of the side of the ship two decks down, part of the docking mechanism.

She hung, suspended, her back against the ship's side. Carefully, cautiously, she twisted, climbing her own body with her hands, seeking out the spur of metal, until she could wrap her arms around it. She reflected that this was probably the first and last time in her life she would have cause to value the ridiculous fashions society foisted upon her sex. She realized she was still screaming and stopped, slightly embarrassed with herself. Her mind became a blur of worries. Could she trust in the security of the little metal spur to which she now clung? Was Madame Lefoux safe? Had her parasol fallen over the edge with her?

She took several calming breaths and assessed the situation: *not dead yet, but not precisely safe either.* "Ha-looo," she called out. "Anyone? A little assistance if you would be so kind."

The cold aether rushed past her, wrapping a loving chill about her legs, which were protected now only by her underdrawers and were unused to such exposure. No one answered her call.

Only then did she realize that, despite the fact that she had stopped screaming, the screaming had not stopped. Above her, she could see the figure of Madame Lefoux struggling against a cloaked opponent against the white backdrop of the blimp. Whoever had pushed Alexia over the edge obviously intended Madame Lefoux to follow. But the inventor was putting up a good deal of fight. She was struggling valiantly, arms pinwheeling, top hat tilting frantically from side to side.

"Help!" Alexia cried, hoping someone might hear her above the racket.

The struggling continued. First Madame Lefoux, then the covert enemy, leaned back over the railing, only to twist aside at the last moment and fight on. Then Madame Lefoux jerked away, fumbling with something. There came the sound of a loud burst of compressed air. The whole dirigible jerked suddenly to one side.

Alexia's grip loosened. She was distracted from the battle above by her own, more pressing, danger as she tried to reestablish her purchase on the helpful little spur.

The sound of forced air rang forth again, and the cloaked villain vanished from sight, leaving Madame Lefoux slumped back against the railing above. The dirigible lurched again, and Alexia let out a little *eep* of distress.

"Halloo! Madame Lefoux, a little assistance if you please!" she yelled up at the top of her voice. She had cause to appreciate her lung capacity and the vocal practice that living with a confrontational husband and a pack of unruly werewolves had given her.

Madame Lefoux turned and looked down. "Why, Lady Maccon! I was convinced you had fallen to your death! How wonderful that you are still alive."

Alexia could barely make out what the Frenchwoman was saying. The inventor's normally melodic voice was high and tinny, a helium-afflicted squeak. The inflation apparatus for the blimp must have developed a severe leak to be affecting voices all the way down to the observation deck.

"Well, I am not going to be here much longer," yelled back Alexia.

The top hat nodded agreement. "Hold on, Lady Maccon, I shall fetch crewmen to collect you directly."

"What?" yelled Alexia. "I cannot make you out at all. You have come over all squeaky."

Madame Lefoux's top hat and associated head disappeared from view.

Alexia entertained herself by concentrating on holding on as hard as she could and yelling a bit more for form's sake. She was indebted to those few puffy clouds floating below her, for they obscured the distant ground. She did not want to know exactly how far she had to fall.

Eventually, a small porthole window popped open near one of her booted feet. A familiar ugly hat stuck out the tiny hole. The face wearing the hat tilted up and back and witnessed Alexia's indecorous position.

"Why, Alexia Maccon, what *are* you doing? You appear to be dangling." The voice was a little slurred. Ivy was clearly still laboring under the effects of Madame Lefoux's cognac. "How undignified of you. Stop it at once!"

"Ivy. Assist me, would you?"

"I hardly see what I can do," replied Miss Hisselpenny. "Really, Alexia, what could have possessed you to attach yourself to the side of the ship in such a juvenile fashion? It is positively barnacle-like."

"Oh, for goodness' sake, Ivy, it is not like I intended to end up this way." Ivy tended toward dense, it was true, but alcohol evidently caused her to attain new heights of fatheadedness.

"Oh? Well, then. But honestly, Alexia, I do not mean to be boorish, but do you realize that your underdrawers are exposed to the night air, not to mention the public view?"

"Ivy, I am hanging on for dear life to the side of a floating dirigible, leagues up in the aether. Even you must admit there are some instances wherein protocol should be relaxed."

"But why?"

"Ivy, I fell, obviously."

Miss Hisselpenny blinked bleary dark eyes at her friend. "Oh, deary me, Alexia. Are you actually in real danger? Oh no!" Her head retreated.

Alexia wondered what it said about her character that Ivy had genuinely believed she would intentionally go climbing about the side of a floating dirigible.

Some sort of silky material was shoved out the window and up at her.

"What is that?"

"Why, my second-best cloak."

Lady Maccon gritted her teeth.

"Ivy, did you miss the part where I am hanging, an inch from death? Do get help."

The cloak vanished, and Miss Hisselpenny's head reappeared. "As bad as that, is it?"

The dirigible lurched, and Alexia swayed to one side with a squeal of alarm.

Ivy fainted, or possibly passed out from the alcohol.

As was to be expected, it was Madame Lefoux who provided the rescue in the end. Mere moments after Ivy vanished from view, a long rope ladder flopped down next to Alexia. She was able, with some difficulty, to transfer her grip from the metal spur to the ladder and climb up. The steward, several worried crewmembers, and Madame Lefoux stood anxiously awaiting her ascent.

Strangely, once Lady Maccon had attained the deck, her legs no longer seemed to function as nature intended. She slid gracelessly onto the wooden deck.

"I think I might reside here for a moment," she said after her third attempt to rise resulted only in wobbly knees and bones akin to jellyfish tentacles.

The steward, an immaculate if portly man dressed in a uniform of yellow canvas and fur, hovered about her in great concern, wringing his hands. He was clearly most upset that such a thing as a Lady of Quality falling off his craft had occurred. What would the company say if word got out? "Is there anything I can get you, Lady Maccon? Some tea perhaps, or something a little stronger?"

"Tea, I think, would be quite the restorative," replied Alexia, mostly to get him to stop hovering about like a worried canary.

Madame Lefoux crouched down next to her. Yet another reason to envy the Frenchwoman her mode of dress. "Are you certain you are in good health, my lady?" Her squeaky voice had gone, the helium leak having apparently been fixed while Lady Maccon was rescued.

"I am finding myself less delighted by the height and notion of floating than I was at the onset of our journey," replied Alexia. "But never mind that. Quickly now, before the steward returns, what happened after I fell? Did you see the attacker's face, ascertain his purpose or intention?" She left off the "Were you in cahoots?" part of that question.

Madame Lefoux shook her head, looking serious. "The miscreant wore a mask and a long cloak; I could not even say with certainty if it was a male or a female. I do apologize. We struggled for a time, and eventually I managed to disentangle myself and get off a shot with the dart emitter. The first one missed and cut a hole through one of the dirigible helium ports, but the second caught our enemy a glancing blow to the side. Apparently that was sufficient to instill fear, for the attacker took flight and managed to escape mostly unharmed."

"Bollix," swore Lady Maccon succinctly. It was one of her husband's favorite words, and she would normally never deign to use it, but current circumstances seemed to warrant its application. "And there are far too many crew and passengers on board to stage an inquest, even if I did not want to keep my preternatural state and role as muhjah a comparative secret."

The Frenchwoman nodded.

"Well, I think I may be able to stand now."

Madame Lefoux bent to help her up.

"Did I lose my parasol in the fall?"

The inventor dimpled. "No, it tumbled to the floor of the observation deck. I believe it is still there. Shall I have one of the hands bring it to your room?"

"Please."

Madame Lefoux signaled to a nearby deckhand and sent him off to find the missing accessory.

Lady Maccon was feeling a little dizzy and was annoyed with herself for it. She had been through worse during the preceding summer and saw no reason to come over weak and floppy due to a mere dabbling with gravity. She allowed the inventor to assist her to her room but refused to call Angelique.

She sat gratefully down on her bed. "A little sleep and I shall be right as rain tomorrow."

The Frenchwoman nodded and bent over her solicitously. "You are certain you do not need assistance to disrobe? I would be happy to help in your maid's stead."

Alexia blushed at the offer. Had she been wrong to doubt the inventor? Madame Lefoux did seem to be quite the best sort of ally to have. And, despite her masculine attire, she smelled amazing, like vanilla custard. Would it be so awful if this woman were to become a friend?

Then she noticed that the cravat around Madame Lefoux's neck was stained on one side with a small amount of blood.

"You were injured while fighting off the attacker and said nothing!" she accused, worried. "Here, let me see." Before the inventor could stop her, Lady Maccon pulled her down to sit on the bed and began untying the long length of Egyptian cotton wound about Madame Lefoux's elegant neck.

"It is of little consequence," the Frenchwoman asserted, blushing.

Lady Maccon ignored all protestations and tossed the cravat to the floor—it was ruined anyway. Then, with gentle fingers, she leaned in close to check the woman's neck. The wound appeared to be nothing more than a scratch, already clotted.

"It looks quite shallow," she said in relief.

"There, you see?" Self-consciously, Madame Lefoux shifted away from her.

Alexia caught a glimpse of something else upon the woman's neck. Something that the cravat had kept hidden: near the nape, partly covered by a few short curls of hair. Lady Maccon craned her head about to see what it might be.

A mark of some kind, dark against the woman's fine white skin, was inked in careful black lines. Alexia brushed the hair aside in a soft caress, startling the Frenchwoman, and leaned in, overcome with curiosity.

It was a tattoo of an octopus.

Lady Maccon frowned, oblivious to the fact that her hand still lay softly against the other woman's skin. Where had she seen that image before? Abruptly, she remembered. Her hand twitched, and only through sheer strength of character did she stop herself from jerking away in horror. She had seen that octopus depicted in brass over and over again, all about the Hypocras Club just after Dr. Siemons kidnapped her.

An awkward silence ensued. "Are you certain you are quite well, Madame Lefoux?" she inquired finally, for lack of anything better to say.

Misinterpreting her continued physical contact, the lady inventor twisted to face her, their noses practically touching. Madame Lefoux slid her hand up Alexia's arm.

Lady Maccon had read that Frenchwomen were much more physically affectionate than British women in their friendship, but there was something unbearably personal in the touch. And no matter how good she smelled and how helpful she had been, there was that octopus mark to consider. Madame Lefoux could not be trusted. The fight could have been staged. She could have an associate on board. She could still be a spy, intent on procuring the muhjah's dispatch case through any possible means. Alexia pulled away from the caressing hand.

At the withdrawal, the inventor stood. "I shall excuse myself. We could probably both use some rest."

Breakfast the next morning saw everyone back about their regular routine, bruises, bonnets, and all. Miss Hisselpenny forbore to mention Alexia's clumsy attempt at scaling Mt. Dirigible out of mortification over her dear friend's exposed underpinnings. Madame Lefoux was impeccably, if incorrectly, dressed and unflaggingly polite, with no comment on the previous evening's aerial escapade. She inquired kindly after Tunstell's health, to which Alexia responded favorably. Felicity was horrible and snide, but then Felicity had been a repulsive earwig ever since she first grew a vocabulary. It was as though nothing untoward had occurred at all.

Lady Maccon only nibbled at her food, not from any concern that there would be another attempted poisoning, but because she was still feeling slightly airsick. She was looking forward to having solid, unpretentious ground under her feet once more.

"What are your plans for the day, Lady Maccon?" inquired Madame Lefoux when all other pleasantries were exhausted.

"I envision an exhausting day of lying about in a deck chair, broken up with small but thrilling strolls about the ship."

"Capital plan," replied Felicity.

"Yes, sister, but I was going to sit in that deck chair with a book, not a supercilious expression and a hand mirror," shot back Alexia.

Felicity only smiled. "At least I possess a face worth looking at for extended periods of time."

Madame Lefoux turned to Ivy. "Are they always like this?"

Miss Hisselpenny had been staring dreamily off into space. "What? Oh, them, yes, as long as I've know them. Which is a dog's age now. I mean to say, Alexia and I have been friends for quite these four years. Imagine that."

The inventor took a bite of steamed egg and did not respond.

Lady Maccon realized she was exposing herself to ridicule by bickering with her sibling.

"Madame Lefoux, what did you do before you came to London? You resided in Paris, I understand? Did you have a *hat shop* there too?"

"No, but my aunt did. I worked with her. She taught me everything I know."

"Everything?"

"Oh yes, *everything.*"

"A remarkable woman, your aunt."

"You have no idea."

"Must be the excess soul."

"Oh." Ivy was intrigued. "Did your aunt come over all phantomy after death?"

Madame Lefoux nodded.

"How nice for you." Ivy smiled her congratulations.

"I suspect *I* will be a ghost in the end," said Felicity, preening. "I am the type to have extra soul. Don't you all agree? Mama says I am remarkably creative for someone who does not play or sing or draw."

Alexia bit her tongue. Felicity was about as likely to have excess soul as a hassock. She turned the conversation forcibly back to the inventor. "What made you leave your home country?"

"My aunt died, and I came over here looking for something precious that had been stolen from me."

"Oh, really? Did you find it?"

"Yes, but only to come to the understanding that it was never mine to begin with."

"How tragic for you," sympathized Ivy. "I had just such a thing happen with a hat once."

"It matters little. It had changed beyond all recognition by the time I located it."

"How mysterious and cryptic you are." Lady Maccon was intrigued.

"It is not entirely my story to tell and others may be injured in the telling if I am not careful."

Felicity yawned ostentatiously. She was little interested in anything not directly connected to herself. "Well, this is all very fascinating, but I am off to change for the day."

Miss Hisselpenny rose as well. "I believe I shall go check on Mr. Tunstell, to ascertain if he has been provided with an adequate breakfast."

"Highly unlikely—none of us were," said Alexia, whose delight in the imminent end to their voyage was encouraged by the idea of eating food that was not bland and steamed into submission.

They parted ways, and Alexia was about to pursue her highly strenuous plans for the day when she realized that if Ivy had gone to check on Tunstell, the two would be isolated together, and that was *not a good idea*. So she hightailed it after her friend toward the claviger's cabin.

She found Miss Hisselpenny and Tunstell engaged in what both probably thought was an impassioned embrace. Their lips were, in fact, touching, but nothing else was, and Ivy's greatest concern throughout the kiss seemed to be keeping her hat in place. The hat was of a masculine shape but decorated with the most enormous bow of purple and green plaid.

"Well," said Lady Maccon loudly, interrupting the couple, "I see you have recovered with startling alacrity from your illness, Tunstell."

Miss Hisselpenny and the claviger jumped apart. Both turned red with mortification, though it must be admitted that Tunstell, being a redhead, was far more efficient at this.

"Oh dear, Alexia," exclaimed Ivy, leaping back. She made for the door as rapidly as the strapped-down floating skirts of her travel dress would allow.

"Oh no, Miss Hisselpenny, please, come back!" Tunstell cried, and then, shockingly, "Ivy!"

But the lady in question was gone.

Alexia gave the ginger-haired young man a hard look. "What are you up to, Tunstell?"

"Oh, Lady Maccon, I am unreservedly in love with her. That black hair, that sweet disposition, those capital hats."

Well goodness, thought Alexia, *he really must be in love if he likes the hats.* She sighed and said, "But, really, Tunstell, be serious. Miss Hisselpenny cannot possibly have a future with you. Even if you were not up for metamorphosis presently, you are an *actor,* with no substantial prospects of any kind."

Tunstell donned a tragic-hero expression, one she had seen more than once in his portrayal of Porccigliano in the West End production of *Death in a Bathtub*. "True love will overcome all obstacles."

"Oh bosh. Be reasonable, Tunstell. This is no Shakespearian melodrama; this is the 1870s. Marriage is a practical matter. It must be treated as such."

"But you and Lord Maccon married for love."

Lady Maccon sighed. "And how do you figure that?"

"No one else would put up with him."

Alexia grinned. "By which you mean that no one else would put up with me."

Tunstell judiciously ignored that statement.

Lady Maccon explained. "Conall is the Earl of Woolsey and as such is permitted the eccentricity of a highly inappropriate wife. You are not. And *that* is a situation unlikely to alter in the future."

Tunstell still looked starry-eyed and unrelenting.

Lady Maccon sighed. "Very well, I see you are unmoved. I shall go determine how Ivy is coping."

Miss Hisselpenny was coping by engaging in a protracted bout of hysteria in one corner of the observation deck.

"Oh, Alexia, what am I to do? I am overcome with the injustice of it all."

Lady Maccon replied with a suggestion. "Seek the assistance of an ugly-hat-addiction specialist this very instant?"

"You are horrible. Be serious, Alexia. You must recognize that this is a travesty of unfairness!"

"How is that?" Lady Maccon did not follow.

"I love him so very much. As Romeo did Jugurtha, as Pyramid did Thirsty, as—"

"Oh, please, no need to elaborate further," interjected Alexia, wincing.

"But what would my family *say* to such a union?"

"They would say that your hats had leaked into you head," muttered Alexia, unheard under her breath.

Ivy continued wailing. "What would they *do*? I should have to break off my engagement with Captain Featherstonehaugh. He would be so *very* upset." She paused, and then gasped in horror. "There would have to be a *printed* retraction!"

"Ivy, I do not think that is the best course of action, throwing Captain Featherstonehaugh over. Not that I have met the man, mind you. But to go from a sensible, income-earning military man to *an actor*? I am very much afraid, Ivy, that it would be generally regarded as reprehensible and even indicative of"—she paused for dramatic effect—"*loose morals.*"

Miss Hisselpenny let out an audible gasp and stopped crying. "You truly believe so?"

Lady Maccon went in for the kill. "Even, dare I say it, *fastness*?"

Ivy gasped again. "Oh no, Alexia, say not so. Truly? To be thought such a thing. How absolutely grisly. Oh what a pickle I am in. I suppose I shall have to throw over Mr. Tunstell."

"To be fair," admitted Lady Maccon, "Tunstell has confessed openly to appreciating your choice of headgear. You may very well be giving up on true love."

"I know. Is that not simply the worst thing you have *ever* heard, *ever*?"

Lady Maccon nodded, all seriousness. "Yes."

Ivy sighed, looking forlorn. To distract her, Alexia asked casually, "You did not perchance *hear* anything unusual last night after supper, did you?"

"No, I did not."

Alexia was relieved. She did not want to explain to Ivy the fight on the observation deck.

"Wait, come to think on it, yes," Ivy corrected herself, twisting a coil of black hair about one finger.

Uh-oh. "What was that?"

"You know, it was a most peculiar thing—just before I drifted off to sleep, I heard someone yelling in French."

Now that *was* interesting, "What did they say?"

"Do not be absurd, Alexia. You know perfectly well I do not speak French. Such a nasty slippery sort of language."

Lady Maccon considered.

"It could have been Madame Lefoux talking in her sleep," Ivy suggested. "You know she has the cabin next to mine?"

"I suppose that is possible." Alexia was not convinced.

Ivy took a deep breath. "Well, I should get on with it, then."

"On with what?"

"Throwing over poor Mr. Tunstell, possibly the love of my life." Ivy was looking nearly as tragic as the young man had moments earlier.

Alexia nodded. "Yes, I think you better had."

Tunstell, in grand thespian fashion, did not take Miss Hisselpenny's rejection well. He staged a spectacular bout of depression and then sank into a deep sulk for the rest of the day. Overwrought, Ivy came pleading to Alexia. "But he has been so very dour. And for a whole three hours. Could I not relent, just a little? He may never recover from this kind of heartache."

To which Alexia replied, "Give it more time, my dear Ivy. I think you will find he may recuperate eventually."

Madame Lefoux came up at that moment. Seeing Miss Hisselpenny's crestfallen face, she inquired, "Has something untoward occurred?"

Ivy let out a pathetic little sob and buried her face in a rose-silk handkerchief.

Alexia said in a hushed voice, "Miss Hisselpenny has had to reject Mr. Tunstell. She is most overwrought."

Madame Lefoux's face took on an appropriately somber cast. "Oh, Miss Hisselpenny, I am sorry. How ghastly for you."

Ivy waved the wet handkerchief, as much as to say, *words cannot possibly articulate my profound distress.* Then, because Ivy never settled for meaningful gestures when verbal embellishments could compound the effect, she said, "Words cannot possibly articulate my profound distress."

Alexia patted her friend's shoulder. Then she turned to the Frenchwoman. "Madame Lefoux, might I beg a small word in private?"

"I am always at your disposal, Lady Maccon. For *anything.*" Alexia failed to examine the possible meaning of that "anything."

The two women moved out of Miss Hisselpenny's earshot over to a secluded corner of the relaxation deck, out of the ever-present aether breezes. To Alexia, these felt faintly tingly, almost like charged particles, but friendlier. She imagined the aether gasses as a cloud of fireflies swarming close to her skin and then flitting off as the dirigible rode one strong current and passed through others. It was not unpleasant but could be distracting.

"I understand you got into an argument late last night, after our little escapade." Lady Maccon did not sugarcoat her words.

Madame Lefoux puffed out her lips. "I might have yelled at the steward for his negligence. He did take an inexcusably long time to get that rope ladder."

"The argument was in French."

Madame Lefoux made no response to that.

Lady Maccon switched tactics. "Why are you following me to Scotland?"

"Are you convinced it is you, my dear Lady Maccon, that I am following?"

"I hardly think you have also developed a sudden passion for my husband's valet."

"No, you would be correct in that."

"So?"

"So, I am no danger to you or yours, Lady Maccon. I wish you could believe that. But I cannot tell you more."

"Not good enough. You are asking me to trust you without reason."

The Frenchwoman sighed. "You soulless are so very logical and practical, it can be maddening."

"So my husband is prone to complaining. You have met a preternatural before, I take it?" If she could not convince the inventor to explain her presence, perhaps she could learn more about the mysterious woman's past.

"Once, a very long time ago. I suppose I could tell you about it."

"Well?"

"I met him with my aunt. I was perhaps eight years old. He was a friend of my father's—a very good friend, I was given to believe. Formerly Beatrice is the ghost of my father's sister. My father himself was a bit of a bounder. I am not exactly legitimate. When I was dumped on his doorstep, he gave me to Aunt Beatrice and died shortly thereafter. I remember a man coming to see him after that, only to find that I was all that was left. The man gave me a present of honey candy and was sad to learn of my father's death."

"He was the preternatural?" Despite herself, Lady Maccon was intrigued.

"Yes, and I believe they were once very close."

"And?"

"You understand my meaning: very close?"

Lady Maccon nodded. "I fully comprehend. I am, after all, a friend of Lord Akeldama's."

Madame Lefoux nodded. "The man who visited was your father."

Alexia's mouth fell open. Not because of this insight into her father's preferences. She knew his taste to run to both the exotic and the eclectic. From reading his journals, she guessed him to be, at best, an opportunist in matters of the flesh. No, she gasped because it was such an odd coincidence, to find out that this woman, not so much older than herself, had once met her father. Had known what he was like—alive.

"I never knew him. He left before I was born," Lady Maccon said before she could stop herself.

"He was handsome but stiff. I remember believing that all Italian men would be like him: cold. I could not have been more wrong, of course, but he made an impression."

Lady Maccon nodded. "So I have been given to understand by others. Thank you for telling me."

Madame Lefoux switched topics abruptly. "We should continue to keep the full details of the incident last night a secret from your companions."

"No point in worrying the others, but I shall have to tell my husband after we land."

"Of course."

The two women parted at that; Lady Maccon was left wondering. She knew why *she* wanted to keep the scuffle a secret, but why did Madame Lefoux?

CHAPTER EIGHT

Castle Kingair

They landed just before sunset on a patch of green near the Glasgow train station. The dirigible came to rest as lightly as a butterfly on an egg, if the butterfly were to stumble a bit and list heavily to one side and the egg to take on the peculiar characteristics of Scotland in winter: more soggy and more gray than one would think possible.

Alexia disembarked with pomp and circumstance similar to her embarkation. She spearheaded a parade of bustle-swaying ladies, like so many fabric snails, onto firm (well, truthfully, rather squishy) land. The bustles were particularly prevalent due to the general relief at being able to wear a proper one once more and to pack the floating skirts away. The snails were followed by Tunstell, laden with a quantity of hatboxes and other package; four stewards with various trunks; and Lady Maccon's French maid.

No one, thought Alexia smugly, could accuse her of traveling without the dignity due to the Earl of Woolsey's wife. She might gad about town alone or in the care of only one unwed young lady, but clearly she *traveled* in company. Unfortunately, the effect of her arrival was undermined by the fact that the ground persisted in reeling about under her, causing Lady Maccon to tilt to one side and take an abrupt seat atop one of her trunks.

She dismissed Tunstell's concern by sending him away to hire an appropriate conveyance to take them into the countryside.

Ivy wandered about the green to stretch her legs and look for wildflowers. Felicity came to stand next to Alexia and began immediately to carry on about the horrible weather.

"Why must it be so gray? Such a greeny sort of gray goes so badly

with the complexion. And it is so awful to travel by coach anywhere in
such weather. Must we go by coach?"

"Well," said Lady Maccon, driven to annoyance, "this *is* the north.
Do stop being silly about it."

Her sister continued to complain, and Alexia watched out of the
corner of her eye as Tunstell veered near to Ivy on his way across the
landing green and hissed something in her ear. Ivy said something back,
an excess of emotion coloring the sharp movements of her head. Tunstell's back straightened and he turned away to walk on.

Ivy came to sit next to Alexia, trembling lightly.

"I do not know what I *ever* saw in that man." Miss Hisselpenny
was clearly overwrought.

"Oh dear, has something come between the lovebirds? Is there
trouble afoot?" said Felicity.

When no one answered her, she trotted after the rapidly departing
claviger. "Oh, Mr. Tunstell? Would you like some company?"

Lady Maccon looked to Ivy. "Am I to understand that Tunstell did
not take your rejection well?" she inquired, trying not to sound as
weak as she felt. She was still dizzy, and the ground seemed quite taken
with shifting about like a nervous squid.

"Well, no, not as such. When I . . ." Ivy started and then broke off,
her attention diverted by an exceedingly large dog charging in their
direction. "Mercy me, what is that?"

The immense dog resolved into being, in actuality, a very large wolf,
with a wad of fabric wrapped about its neck. Its fur was a dark brown
color brindled gold and cream, and its eyes were pale yellow.

Upon reaching them, the wolf gave Miss Hisselpenny a polite little
nod and then put its head in Lady Maccon's lap.

"Ah, husband," said Alexia, scratching him behind the ears, "I figured you would find me, but not so quickly as this."

The Earl of Woolsey lolled his long pink tongue at his wife good-
naturedly and tilted his head in Miss Hisselpenny's direction.

"Yes, of course," replied Alexia to the unspoken suggestion. She
turned to her friend. "Ivy, my dear, I suggest you look away at this juncture."

"Why?" wondered Miss Hisselpenny.

"Many find a werewolf's shape change rather unsettling and—"

"Oh, I am certain I should not be at all disconcerted," interrupted
Miss Hisselpenny.

Lady Maccon was not convinced. Ivy was, circumstances had
shown, prone to fainting. She continued her explanation. "*And* Conall
will not be clothed when the transformative event has completed."

"Oh!" Miss Hisselpenny put a hand to her mouth in alarm. "Of course." She turned quickly away.

Still, one could not help but hear, even if one did not look: that slushy crunchy noise of bones breaking and reforming. It was similar to the echoing sound that dismembering a dead chicken for the stew pot makes in a large kitchen. Alexia saw Ivy shudder.

Werewolf change was never pleasant. That was one of the reasons pack members still referred to it as a curse, despite the fact that, in the modern age of enlightenment and free will, clavigers *chose* metamorphosis. The change comprised a good deal of biological rearranging. This, like rearranging one's parlor furniture for a party, involved a transition from tidy to very messy to tidy once more. And, as with any redecoration, there was a moment in the middle where it seemed impossible that everything could possibly go back together harmoniously. In the case of werewolves, this moment involved fur retreating to become hair, bones fracturing and mending into new configurations, and flesh and muscle sliding about on top of or underneath the two. Alexia had seen her husband change many times, and every time she found it both vulgar and scientifically fascinating.

Conall Maccon, Earl of Woolsey, was considered proficient at the change. No one could beat out Professor Lyall for sheer elegance, of course, but at least the earl was fast, efficient, and made none of those horribly pugilistic grunting noises the younger cubs were prone to emitting.

In mere moments, he stood before his wife: a big man, without being fat. Alexia had commented once that, given his love of food, he probably would have become portly had he aged as normal humans did. Luckily, he had elected for metamorphosis sometime in his midthirties and so had never gone to seed. Instead he remained forever a well-muscled mountain of a man who needed the shoulders of his coats tailored, his boots specially ordered, and near constant reminding that he must duck through doorways.

He turned eyes, only a few shades darker than they had been in wolf form, to his wife.

Lady Maccon stood to help him pull on his cloak but sat back down before she could do so. She was still not steady on her feet.

Lord Maccon immediately stopped shaking out the garment in question and knelt, naked, before her.

"What's wrong?" he practically yelled.

"What?" Ivy turned to see what was going on, caught a glimpse of the earl's naked backside, squeaked, and turned back away, fanning herself with one gloved hand.

"Do not fuss, Conall. You are upsetting Ivy," grumbled Lady Maccon.

"Miss Hisselpenny is always upset over something. *You* are a different matter. You don't *do* these kinds of things, wife. You are not that feminine."

"Well, I like that!" Lady Maccon took offense.

"You understand my meaning perfectly. Stop trying to distract me. What's wrong?" He drew entirely the wrong conclusion. "You're sickening! Is that why you've come, to tell me you're ill?" He looked like he wanted to shake her but did not dare.

Alexia looked straight into his worried eyes and said slowly and carefully, "I am perfectly fine. It is simply taking a little time for me to get my land legs back. You know how it can be after a long air or sea journey."

The earl looked vastly relieved. "Not a very good floater, my love, as it turned out?"

Lady Maccon gave her husband a reproachful look and replied petulantly, "No, not so very good at the floating. No." Then she changed the subject. "But, really, Conall, you know I welcome the spectacle, but poor Ivy! Put your cloak on, do."

The earl grinned, straightened under her appreciative eye, and wrapped his long cloak about his body.

"How did you know I was here?" Alexia asked as soon as he was decent.

"The lewd display has ended, Miss Hisselpenny. You are safe," Lord Maccon informed Ivy, settling his massive frame next to his wife. The trunk creaked at the added weight.

Lady Maccon snuggled against her husband's side happily.

"Simply knew," he grumbled, wrapping one long, fabric-shrouded arm about her and hauling her closer against him. "This landing patch is just off my route to Kingair. I caught your scent about an hour ago and saw the dirigible coming in for a landing. Figured I had better come see what was going on. Now you, wife. What are you doing in Scotland? With Miss Hisselpenny no less."

"Well, I had to bring some kind of companion. Society would not very well condone my floating across the length of England by myself."

"Mmm." Lord Maccon glanced over, eyes heavy-lidded, at the still-nervous Ivy. She had not yet reconciled herself to talking with an earl dressed only in a cloak so was standing a little distance off with her back to them.

"Give her a bit more recuperation time," advised Alexia. "Ivy's sensitive, and you are such a shock to the system, even fully dressed."

The earl grinned. "Praise, wife? How unusual from you. Nice to know I still have the capacity to unsettle others, even at my age. But stop trying to avoid the subject. Why *are* you here?"

"Why, darling"—Lady Maccon batted her eyelashes at him—"I was coming to Scotland to see *you* of course. I missed you so."

"Ah, wife, how romantic of you," he replied, not believing a word of it. He looked down at her fondly. Not as far down as he would have had to on most women, mind you. His Alexia was rather strapping. He preferred her that way. Undersized women reminded him of yippy dogs.

He rumbled softly, "Lying minx."

She leaned in. "It will have to wait until later, when others cannot overhear," she whispered against his ear.

"Mmm." He turned in toward her and kissed her lips, warm and adamant.

"Ahem." Ivy cleared her throat.

Lord Maccon took his time breaking off the kiss.

"Husband," said Lady Maccon, her eyes dancing. "You remember Miss Hisselpenny?"

Conall gave his wife *a look,* and then stood and bowed. As though he and the nonsensical Miss Hisselpenny had not formed a lasting acquaintance these three months since his marriage.

"Good evening, Miss Hisselpenny. How do you do?"

Ivy curtsied. "Lord Maccon, how unexpected. You were notified of our arrival time?"

"No."

"Then how?"

"It is a werewolf machination, Ivy," explained Alexia. "Do not trouble yourself."

Ivy did not.

Lady Maccon said to her husband carefully, "I also have my sister and Tunstell accompanying me. And Angelique, of course."

"I see, an unexpected wife and reinforcements. Are we anticipating a battle of some kind, my dear?"

"If I were, I should only have to set the enemy against the sharp barbs of Felicity's tongue to rout them thoroughly. The size of my traveling party is, however, entirely unintentional."

Miss Hisselpenny acted a bit guilty at that statement.

Lord Maccon gave his wife a look of profound disbelief.

Alexia went on. "Felicity and Tunstell are procuring transportation as we speak."

"How thoughtful of you, to bring me my valet."

"Your valet has been a resounding nuisance."

Miss Hisselpenny gasped.

Lord Maccon shrugged. "He usually is. There is an art to irritation that only few of us can achieve."

Lady Maccon said, "That must be how werewolves select personalities for metamorphosis. Regardless, Tunstell was required. Professor Lyall insisted upon a male escort, and as we were traveling by dirigible, we could not bring a member of the pack."

"Better not to anyway, seeing as this is someone else's territory."

A polite clearing of the throat occurred at that juncture, and the Maccons turned about to find Madame Lefoux hovering nearby.

"Ah, yes," said Lady Maccon. "Madame Lefoux was also on board the dirigible with us. Quite *unexpectedly.*" She emphasized the last word for her husband's benefit so that he might understand her concern over the inventor's presence. "I believe you and my husband are already acquainted, Madame Lefoux?"

Madame Lefoux nodded. "How do you do, Lord Maccon?"

The earl bowed slightly and then shook Madame Lefoux's hand, as he would a man. Lord Maccon's opinion appeared to be that if Madame Lefoux dressed as a male, she should be treated as such. Interesting approach. Or perhaps he knew something Alexia did not.

Lady Maccon said to her husband, "Thank you for the lovely parasol, by the way. I shall put it to good use."

"I never doubted that. I am a little surprised you have not already."

"Who says I have not?"

"That's my sweet, biddable little wife."

Ivy said, surprised, "Oh, but Alexia is not sweet."

Lady Maccon only grinned.

The earl seemed genuinely pleased to see the Frenchwoman. "Delighted, Madame Lefoux. You have business in Glasgow?"

The inventor inclined her head.

"I don't suppose I could persuade you to visit Kingair? I just heard in town that the pack is experiencing some technical difficulties with its aethographic transmitter, newly purchased, secondhand."

"Good Lord, husband. Does everyone have one but us?" his wife wanted to know.

The earl turned sharp eyes on her. "Why? Who else acquired one recently?"

"Lord Akeldama, of all people, and he has the latest model. Would you be very cross if I said I rather covet one myself?"

Lord Maccon reflected upon the state of his life wherein he had somehow gained a spouse who could not give a pig's foot for the latest dresses out of Paris but who whined about not owning an aethographic transmitter. Well, at least the two were comparable obsessions so far as expense was concerned.

"Well, my little bluestocking bride, someone has a birthday coming up."

Alexia's eyes shone. "Oh, splendid!"

Lord Maccon kissed her softly on the forehead and then turned back to Madame Lefoux. "Well, can I persuade you to stop over at Kingair for a few days and ascertain if there is anything you can do to help?"

Alexia pinched her husband in annoyance. When would he learn to ask her about these things first?

Lord Maccon captured his wife's hand in one big paw and shook his head ever so slightly at her.

The inventor frowned, a little crease in her creamy forehead. Then, as though the crease had never been, the dimples appeared, and she accepted the invitation.

Alexia managed only a brief, private word with her husband as they piled their luggage into two hired carriages.

"Channing says the werewolves couldn't change all the boat ride over."

Her husband blinked at her, startled. "Really?"

"Oh, and Lyall says the plague is moving northward. He thinks it beat us to Scotland."

Lord Maccon frowned. "He thinks it's something to do with the Kingair Pack, doesn't he?"

Alexia nodded.

Strangely, her husband grinned. "Good, that gives me an excuse."

"Excuse for what?"

"Showing up on their doorstep; they'd never let me in otherwise."

"What?" Alexia hissed at him. "Why?" But they were interrupted by Tunstell's return and unparalleled excitement at seeing Lord Maccon.

The rented carriages rattled down the track to Kingair in ever-growing darkness. Alexia was bound to either silence or inanities by the presence of Ivy and Madame Lefoux in their carriage. It was too dark and rainy to see much outside the window, a fact that upset Ivy.

"I did so want to *see* the Highlands," said Miss Hisselpenny. As though there would be some sort of line, drawn on the ground, that indicated transition from one part of Scotland to the next. Miss Hisselpenny had already commented that Scotland looked a lot like England, in a tone of voice that suggested this a grave error on the landscape's part.

Inexplicably tired, Alexia dozed, her cheek resting on her husband's large shoulder.

Felicity, Tunstell, and Angelique rode in the other carriage, emerging with an air of chummy gaiety that confused Alexia and tormented Ivy. Felicity was flirting shamelessly, and Tunstell was doing nothing to dissuade her. But the sight of Castle Kingair dampened everyone's spirits. As if to compound matters, as soon as they and all their luggage had alighted and the carriages trundled off, the rain began to descend in earnest.

Castle Kingair was like something out of a Gothic novel. Its foundation was a huge rock that jutted out over a dark lake. It put Woolsey Castle to shame. There was the feel of real age about the place, and Alexia would bet good money that it was a drafty, miserably old-fashioned creature on the inside.

First, however, it appeared that they would have to get past a drafty, miserably old-fashioned creature on the outside.

"Ah," said Lord Maccon upon seeing the reception committee of one, standing, arms crossed, outside the castle front gates. "Gird your loins, my dear."

His wife looked up at him, her wet hair falling from its fancy arrangement. "I do not think you should be discussing my loins just now, husband," she said in a sprightly manner.

Miss Hisselpenny, Felicity, and Madame Lefoux came to stand next to them, shivering in the rain, while Tunstell and Angelique began organizing the baggage.

"Who is that?" Ivy wanted to know.

The personage stood shrouded in a long, shapeless plaid cloak, face shadowed under a beaten coachman's hat of oiled leather that had seen better days and barely survived them.

"One might well ask instead, *what* is that?" corrected Felicity, her nose wrinkled in disgust, her parasol raised ineffectually against the deluge.

The woman—for upon closer inspection, the personage did appear to be, to some slight degree, of the female persuasion—did not move forward to greet them. Nor did she offer them shelter. She simply stood and glared. And her glaring was most definitely centered on Lord Maccon.

They approached cautiously.

"You're nae welcome here, Conall Maccon, you ken!" she yelled, long before they were within any reasonable conversational distance. "Hie yourself back away now afore you be fighting all what's left of this here pack."

Under the shade of the hat, she appeared to be of middling years, handsome but not pretty, with strong features and coarse thick hair, tending toward gray. She boasted the general battle-ax demeanor of an especially strict governess. This was the kind of woman who took her tea black, smoked cigars after midnight, played a mean game of cribbage, and kept a bevy of repulsive little dogs.

Alexia liked her immediately.

The woman shouldered a rifle with consummate skill and pointed it at Lord Maccon.

Alexia liked her less.

"And dinna be thinking you can change on me. Pack's been free of yon werewolf's curse for months, since we started out across the sea."

"Which would be why I'm here, Sidheag." Lord Maccon continued to advance. He was a good liar, her husband, thought Lady Maccon proudly.

"You be doubting these bullets be silver?"

"What matters that, if I'm as mortal as you?"

"Och, you always were a sharp one with the tongue."

"We have come to help, Sidheag."

"Who's been saying we need help? You're na wanted here. Hie yourself off Kingair territory, the lot of ye."

Lord Maccon sighed heavily. "This is BUR business, and your pack's behavior has called me down on you, willing or nae. I'm not here as Woolsey Alpha. I am not even here as mediator for your Alpha gap. I am here as sundowner. What did you expect?"

The woman flinched away, but she also put down the gun. "Aye. I see it now to rights. 'Tis na that you care what happens to the pack— *your* old pack. You're simply here touting queen's will. Turn-tail coward, that's what you are, Conall Maccon, and naught more."

Lord Maccon had almost reached her by now. Only Lady Maccon still trailed behind him. The rest had stopped at the sight of the woman's gun. Alexia glanced back over her shoulder to see Ivy and Felicity huddled near Tunstell, who had a small pistol pointed steadily at the woman. Madame Lefoux stood next to him, her wrist held at just such an angle to suggest some more exotic form of firearm was concealed but enabled just inside the sleeve of her greatcoat.

Lady Maccon, parasol at the ready, moved toward her husband and the strange woman. He was speaking in a low voice so that the party behind them could not hear through the rain. "What did they get up to overseas, Sidheag? What mess did you get into over there after Niall died?"

"What do you care? You up and abandoned us."

"I had no choice." Conall's voice was weary with remembered arguments.

"Bollix to that, Conall Maccon. 'Tis a cop-out, well and truly, and we both be knowing it. You fixing the mess you left behind these twenty years gone, now that you're back?"

Alexia looked at her husband, curious. Perhaps she would get the answer to something she'd always wondered about. Why would an Alpha abdicate one pack, only to seek out and fight to rule another?

The earl remained silent.

The woman pushed the worn old hat back off her head to look up at Lord Maccon. She was tall, almost as tall as he, so she did not have to look up far. She was no slight thing either. There was muscle rolling about noticeably under that massive cloak. Alexia was suitably impressed.

The woman's eyes were a terribly familiar tawny brown color.

Lord Maccon said, "Let us inside out of this muck and I will think about it."

"Pah!" spat the woman. Then she marched up the beaten stone path toward the keep.

Lady Maccon looked to her husband. "Interesting lady."

"Dinna you start," he growled at her. He turned back to the rest of their party. "That is about as much of an invitation as we're likely to receive around these parts. Come on inside. Leave the luggage. Sidheag will send a man out to get it."

"And you are convinced she will not simply toss it all into the lake, Lord Maccon?" wondered Felicity, clutching her reticule protectively.

Lord Maccon snorted. "No guarantees."

Lady Maccon immediately left his side and retrieved her dispatch case from the mound of luggage.

"Does this thing work as an umbrella?" she asked Madame Lefoux on her way back, waving the parasol.

The inventor looked sheepish. "I forgot that part."

Alexia sighed and squinted up into the rain. "Capital. Here I stand, about to meet the dreaded in-laws looking like nothing so much as a drowned rat."

"Be fair, sister," contradicted Felicity. "You look like a drowned toucan."

And with that, the little band entered Castle Kingair.

It was just as drafty and old-fashioned on the inside as its appearance would suggest from the outside. *Neglected* was too fine a term for it. The carpets were gray-green, threadbare relics from the time of King

George; the chandelier in the entranceway supported *candles,* of all ridiculous forms of lighting; and there were actual medieval tapestries hanging against the walls. Alexia, who was fastidious, ran one gloved finger along the banister railing and tutted at the dust.

The Sidheag woman caught her at it.

"Na up to yon high-falutin' London standards, young miss?"

"Uh-oh," said Ivy.

"Not up to standards of common household decency," shot back Alexia. "I heard the Scots were barbarians, but this"—she brushed her fingers together, releasing a small cloud of gray powder—"is ridiculous."

"I'm na stopping you from heading back out into the rain."

Lady Maccon cocked her head to one side. "Yes, but would you stop me from dusting? Or do you have a particular attachment to grime?"

The woman chuckled at that.

Lord Maccon said, "Sidheag, this is my wife, Alexia Maccon. Wife, this is Sidheag Maccon, Lady Kingair. My great-great-great-granddaughter."

Alexia was surprised. Her guess would have been a grand-niece of some kind, not a direct descendent. Her husband had been married before he changed? Now *why* hadn't he told her that?

"But," objected Miss Hisselpenny, "she looks older than Alexia." A pause. "She looks older than you, Lord Maccon."

"I would not try to understand, if I were you, dear," consoled Madame Lefoux with a slight dimpling at Ivy's distress.

"I am just about forty," replied Lady Kingair, unabashed at stating her age before strangers and in polite company. Really, this part of the country was just as primitive as Floote had said. Lady Maccon shuddered delicately and adjusted her grip on her parasol, prepared for anything.

Sidheag Maccon looked pointedly at the earl. "Nigh on too old."

Felicity wrinkled her nose. "Ew, this is simply too revoltingly peculiar. Why did you *have* to involve yourself in the supernatural set, Alexia?"

Lady Maccon merely gave her sister an arch look.

Felicity answered her own question. "Oh yes, I remember now—no one else would have you."

Alexia ignored that and looked with interest at her husband. "You never told me you had a family *before* you became a werewolf."

Lord Maccon shrugged. "You never asked." He turned to introduce the rest of the party. "Miss Hisselpenny, my wife's companion. Miss Loontwill, my wife's sister. Tunstell, my primary claviger. And Madame Lefoux, who would be happy to examine your broken aethographor."

Lady Kingair started. "How did you ken that we . . . ? Never mind. You always were uncanny with the knowing. You being BUR has na improved that to anyone else's comfort. Weel, that's one welcome guest. Delighted to meet ye, Madame Lefoux. I have, of course, heard of your work. We've a claviger who's familiar with your theories, a bit o' an amateur inventor himself."

Then the Scotswoman looked at her great-great-great-grandfather. "I'm supposing you'd as lief see the rest o' the pack?"

Lord Maccon inclined his head.

The Lady of Kingair reached off to the side of the darkened stairwell and clanged a bell hidden there. It made a noise halfway between a moo and a steam engine coming to an abrupt halt, and suddenly the hallway was filled with large men, most of them in skirts.

"Good heavens," exclaimed Felicity, "what *are* they wearing?"

"Kilts," explained Alexia, amused at her sister's discomfort.

"Skirts," replied Felicity, deeply offended, "and short ones at that, as though they were opera dancers."

Alexia swallowed a giggle. Now there was a funny image.

Miss Hisselpenny did not seem to know where to look. Finally she settled on staring up at the candelabra in abject terror. "Alexia," she hissed to her friend, "there are knees positively everywhere. What do I do?"

Alexia's attention was on the faces of the men around her, not their unmentionable leg areas. There seemed to be an equal mix of disgust and delight at seeing Lord Maccon.

The earl introduced her to those he knew. The Kingair Pack Beta, nominally in charge, was one of the unhappy ones, while the Gamma was one of those pleased to see Conall. The remaining four members fell two for and two against and ranged themselves to stand accordingly, as though at any moment fisticuffs might spontaneously break out. Kingair was smaller than the Woolsey Pack, and less unified. Alexia wondered what kind of man the post-Conall Alpha had been, to lead this contentious lot.

Then, with unseemly haste, Lord Maccon grabbed the surly Beta, who responded in a halfhearted manner to the name of Dubh, and dragged him off into a private parlor, leaving Alexia to mitigate the tense social atmosphere he left behind.

Lady Maccon was equal to the task. No one of her stalwart character, required since birth to supervise first Mrs. Loontwill and later two equally improbable sisters, was unprepared for even such trying circumstances as large, kilted werewolves en masse.

"We heard about you," said the Gamma, whose name sounded like something slippery to do with bogs. "Knew the old laird had suckered himself to a curse-breaker." He paced about Alexia slowly in a circle as though examining her for flaws. It felt very doglike to Alexia. She was prepared to jump back if he cocked a leg.

Luckily, his statement was misconstrued by both Ivy and Felicity. Alexia was not *known* as a preternatural to either of them and she preferred to keep it that way. Both young ladies seemed to assume that the phrase *curse-breaker* was some queer Scottish term for wife.

Felicity said, sneering at the enormous man in front of her, "Really, can you not speak English?"

Lady Maccon said quickly, ignoring her sister, "You have the upper hand on me. I know nothing of you." They were all so very large. She was not used to feeling diminutive.

The Gamma's broad face went pinched at that. "Over a century he was master o' this pack and he na mentioned us to ye?"

"Could be *me* he does not want to know you, rather than you he does not want to talk about," offered Alexia.

The werewolf gave her a long, assessing look. "I'm thinking 'tis that he never brought us up, did he?"

Sidheag interrupted them. "Enough gossip. We'll show you to your rooms. Lads, go grab in the extras—blasted English canna travel light."

The upstairs bedrooms and guest accommodations seemed no better off than the rest of the castle, muted in color and dank in smell. The room given to Lord and Lady Maccon was tidy enough but musty, with decorations of brownish red some hundred years or so outdated. There was a large bed, two small wardrobes, a dressing table for Alexia, and a dressing chamber for her husband. The color scheme and general appearance reminded Lady Maccon of nothing so much as a damp, malcontented squirrel.

She checked about the chamber for a safe place to secrete her dispatch case, with little success. There seemed nowhere acceptably discreet, so she trundled three doors down to where Miss Hisselpenny was billeted.

As she passed one of the other chambers, she heard Felicity say, in a breathy voice, "Oh, Mr. Tunstell, shall I be safe in the room right next to yours, do you think?"

Seconds later, she witnessed Tunstell, panic in every freckle, emerge from Felicity's room and dive into the refuge of his small valet accommodations just off of Conall's dressing chamber.

Ivy was busy unpacking her trunk when Alexia tapped politely on her door and wandered in.

"Oh, thank heavens, Alexia. I was just pondering, do you think there might be ghosts in this place? Or worse, poltergeists? Please do not think I am at all bigoted against the supernatural set, but I simply cannot withstand an overabundance of ghosts, especially not those at the final stage of disanimus. I heard they get all over funny in the head and go wafting about losing bits of their noncorporeal selves. One rounds a corner of some perfectly respectable passageway only to find a disembodied eyebrow floating halfway between ceiling and potted palm." Miss Hisselpenny shuddered as she carefully stacked her twelve hatboxes next to the wardrobe.

Alexia thought back to what her husband had said. If the werewolves here could not change, then the plague of humanization must be infecting Castle Kingair. The castle would have been completely exorcised.

"I have a funny feeling, Ivy," she said with confidence, "that ghosts will definitely not be frequenting this locale."

Ivy looked unconvinced. "But, Alexia, really you must admit to the fact that this building seems like the kind of place that *ought* to have ghosts."

Lady Maccon clicked her tongue in exasperation. "Oh, Ivy, do not be ridiculous. Appearances have nothing to do with it; you know that. Only in Gothic novels are ghosts linked so, and we both know how utterly fanciful fiction has become recently. Authors never *do* get the supernatural correct. I mean to say, the last one I read essentially claimed metamorphosis had to do with *magic*, when everyone knows there are perfectly valid scientific and medical explanations for excess soul. Why, just the other day, I read that—"

Miss Hisselpenny interrupted her hastily before she could go on. "Yes, well, no need to overset me with bluestocking explanations and Royal Society papers. I shall take your word for it. What time did Lady Kingair say supper was to commence?"

"Nine, I believe."

Another look of panic suffused her friend's face. "Will they be serving"—she gulped—"haggis, do you think?"

Lady Maccon made a face. "Surely not for our first meal. But best prepare yourself; one never knows." Conall had described the disastrous foodstuff, with unwarranted delight, during their carriage ride in. The ladies were living in mortal terror as a result.

Ivy sighed. "Very well. We had better get dressed, then. Would my periwinkle taffeta be appropriate for the occasion?"

"For the haggis?"

"No, silly, for dinner."

"Does it have a matched hat?"

Miss Hisselpenny looked up from tidying her stack of hatboxes with a disgusted expression. "Alexia, do not talk such folderol. It is a *dinner* gown."

"Then I think it will serve very well. May I ask you a favor? I have a gift for my husband in this case. Do you think I might conceal it in your room for the time being so he does not accidentally uncover it? I wish it to be a surprise."

Miss Hisselpenny's eyes shone. "Oh, really! How lovely and wifely of you. I should never have pegged you for a romantic."

Lady Maccon winced.

"What is it?"

Alexia grappled with her brain for an appropriate answer. What would one possibly buy for a man and then hide in a dispatch case? "Uh. Socks."

Miss Hisselpenny was crushed. "Only socks? I hardly think socks cry out for secrecy."

"They are lucky, special socks."

Miss Hisselpenny saw no apparent illogicality in that and carefully tucked Lady Maccon's dispatch case behind her stack of hatboxes.

"I may need to access it from time to time," said Alexia.

Miss Hisselpenny was bemused. "Why?"

"To, uh, check on the condition of the, uh, socks."

"Alexia, are you feeling quite the thing?"

Lady Maccon instantly spoke, in order to throw Miss Hisselpenny off the scent. "Did you know, I just passed Tunstell leaving Felicity's rooms."

Ivy gasped. "No!" She immediately began furiously arranging her accessories for dinner, tossing gloves, jewelry, and lacy hair cap on top of the dress already laid out upon the bed.

"Alexia, I do not mean to be at all rude. But I really do believe your sister may be an actual nincompoop."

"Oh, that is perfectly all right, Ivy dear. I cannot stomach her myself," replied Lady Maccon. And then, because she felt guilty for having told her about Tunstell, "Would you like to borrow Angelique this evening to do up your hair? The rain's ruined mine beyond all repair I'm afraid, so it would be a wasted effort."

"Oh, really? Thank you, that would be lovely." Ivy perked up immediately.

With that, Lady Maccon retreated to her own room to dress.

"Angelique?" The maid was busy unpacking when Lady Maccon reentered her bedroom.

"I have told Ivy she may have you for her hair this evening. Not a thing could possibly be done to help mine at this point." Alexia's dark locks were a mass of frizzy curls in reaction to the unpleasant Scottish climate. "I shall simply pop on one of those horrible lace matron's caps you are always trying to get me to wear."

"Yez, my lady." The maid bobbed a curtsy and went to do as she was bid. She paused in the doorway, looking back at her mistress. "Please, my lady, why is Madame Lefoux still with us?"

"You really do not like her, do you, Angelique?"

A quintessentially French shrug met that statement.

"It was my husband's idea, I am afraid to say. I do not trust her either, mind you. But you know how Conall gets. Apparently, Kingair has a malfunctioning aethographic transmitter. I know, you might well look surprised. Who would have thought a backwater place like this could possess anything so modern? Apparently they do, and it has been having difficulties. Secondhand goods, I understand. Well, what do you expect? Anyhow, Conall brought Madame Lefoux along to give it the old once-over. Nothing I could do to stop him."

Angelique looked blank at that and bobbed a quick curtsy, and went off to see to Ivy.

Alexia ruminated over the outfit the maid had selected for her to wear. And then, because she really could not count on her own sense of style to do any better, put it on.

Her husband came in just as she was struggling to fasten the buttons up the back of the bodice.

"Oh, good, there you are. Do this up for me, would you, please?"

Entirely ignoring her command, Lord Maccon strode over to her in three quick steps and buried his face in the side of her neck.

Lady Maccon emitted an exasperated sigh but at the same time swiveled around to wrap her arms about his neck.

"Well, that is very helpful, darling. You do realize we are due for—" He kissed her.

When breathing eventually became a necessity, he said, "Well, wife, been wanting to do that the entire carriage ride here." He moved his large hands down to her posterior and hoisted her against his big, firm body.

"And here I thought you were thinking about politics most of the ride; you sported such a terrible frown," replied his wife with a grin.

"Well, that too. I *can* do two things at once. For example, right now I am talking to you and also devising a means by which to extract you from this gown."

"Husband, you cannot take it off of me. I just put it on."

He seemed disinclined to agree with that statement, instead putting a concerted effort into undoing all her careful work and shoving the dress aside.

"Did you really like the parasol I gave you?" he asked, sweetly hesitant, drifting his fingertips up over her now-bare shoulders and upper back.

"Oh, Conall, such a lovely gift, with magnetic disruption field generator, poison darts, and everything. So very thoughtful. I was delighted to find I had not lost it during the fall."

The fingers stopped drifting abruptly. "Fall? What fall?"

Lady Maccon knew that burgeoning roar well. She squirmed against him in an effort to distract him. "Uh," she hedged.

Lord Maccon pushed her slightly away, holding her by the shoulders.

She patted him as best she could on the chest. "Oh, it was nothing, dear—simply a little tumble."

"Little tumble! Little tumble off of what, wife?"

Alexia looked down and away and tried to mumble. Since she had a naturally assertive voice, this did not work at all well. "A dirigible."

"A dirigible." Lord Maccon's tone was hard and flat. "And did that dirigible happen to be floating in the air at the time?"

"Umm, well, possibly, not quite air . . . more in the region of, well, aether . . ."

A hard glare.

Alexia hung her head and peeked at him through her eyelashes.

Lord Maccon steered his wife, as though she were an unwieldy rowboat, backward toward the bed and forced her to sit down upon it. Then he flopped down next to her.

"Start at the beginning."

"You mean the evening I woke up to find you had taken yourself off to Scotland without even speaking to me about it?"

Lord Maccon sighed. "It was a serious family matter."

"And what am I, a nodding acquaintance?"

Conall actually had the grace to look slightly shamefaced at that. "You must allow me some little time to get used to having a wife."

"You mean you did not acclimatize to it the last time you were wed?"

He frowned at her. "*That* was a long time ago."

"I certainly hope so."

"Before I changed. And it was a matter of duty. In those days, one simply didna turn werewolf without leaving an heir behind. I was to be laird; I could not possibly become supernatural without first ensuring the prosperity of the clan."

Alexia was not inclined to let him off lightly for keeping her in the dark on this matter, even if she perfectly understood his reasons. "I gathered as much by the fact that you seem to have produced a child. What I question is the fact that, for some reason, you elected not to tell me you still had living descendants."

Lord Maccon snorted, grabbing his wife's hand and caressing her wrist with his callused thumbs. "You met Sidheag. Would you want to claim her as a relation?"

Alexia sighed and leaned against his broad shoulder. "She seems like a fine, upstanding woman."

"What she is is an impossible grouch."

Lady Maccon smiled into her husband's shoulder. "Well, there can be no doubt as to which side of the family she gets that from." She switched tactics. "Are you going to tell me anything substantial about this previous family of yours? Who was your wife? How many children did you have? Am I likely to encounter any other Maccons of import scattered about?" She stood, continuing about her preparations for dinner, trying not to show how much she cared about his answers. This was one aspect of being married to an immortal she had not figured into her equation. Of course, she knew he had taken previous lovers; at two centuries, she would be concerned if he had not, and she had almost nightly reason to be grateful for his experience. But previous wives? This she had not considered.

He lay back on the bed, folding his arms behind his head, looking at her out of predatory eyes. There was no denying it—impossible man her husband, but also a terribly sexy beast.

"Are *you* going to tell me about falling off the dirigible?" he countered.

Alexia fastened earrings to her ears. "Are *you* going to tell *me* why you hightailed it off to Scotland without your valet, leaving me to deal with Major Channing at the supper table, Ivy hat shopping, and half of London still recovering from a severe bout of humanization? Not to mention the fact that I had to travel the length of England *all by myself.*"

They heard Miss Hisselpenny squealing in the hallway and then a chatter of other voices, Felicity perhaps, and Tunstell.

Lord Maccon, still lounging poetically upon the bed, sniffed.

"Very well, travel the length of England accompanied by Ivy and my sister, which is very possibly worse—and still your fault."

The earl rose, came over, and buttoned up the back of her dress. Alexia was only mildly disappointed. They were running late for dinner, and she was starving.

"Why are you here, wife?" he asked bluntly.

Lady Maccon leaned back, exasperated. They were getting nowhere with this conversation. "Conall, answer me this: have you been able to change since we arrived at Kingair?"

Lord Maccon frowned. "I had not thought to try."

She gave him an aggrieved look via the mirror, and he let go of her and stepped back. She watched him, his busy hands stilled. Nothing happened.

He shook his head and came back. "Not possible. It feels a little as though I am in contact with you and trying for my wolf form. Not difficult, or even elusive, simply unavailable. That part of me, the werewolf part, has vanished."

She turned to him. "I came because I am muhjah, and this changelessness is connected to the Kingair Pack. I saw you sneak away and talk to the Beta. None of this pack has been able to shift in months, have they? For how long exactly has this been going on? Since boarding the *Spanker* and traveling home? Or before? Where did they find the weapon? India? Egypt? Or is it a plague they have brought back? What happened to them overseas?"

Lord Maccon looked at his wife in the looking glass, his big hands on her shoulders. "They willna tell me. I am no longer Alpha here. They owe me no explanation."

"But you are BUR's chief sundowner."

"This is Scotland; BUR's authority is weak here. Besides, these people were my pack for generations. I may have no wish to lead them anymore, but I do not want to kill any of them either. They know that. I simply want to know what is happening here."

"You and I both, my love," replied his wife. "You don't mind if I wish to question your brethren on the matter?"

"I dinna see how you will make over any better than I." Conall was doubtful. "They do not know you are muhjah, and you'd be wise to keep it that way. Queen Victoria isna so loved in this part of the world."

"I'll be discreet." Her husband's eyebrows reached for the sky at that. "Very well, as discreet as possible for me."

"It canna hurt," he said, and then thought better of it. This was Alexia, after all. "So long as you refrain from using that parasol."

His lady wife grinned maliciously. "I shall be direct, but not that direct."

"Why do I doubt you? Well, watch out for Dubh; he can be difficult."

"Not up to Professor Lyall's caliber as a Beta, shall we say?"

"Um, that's not for me to say. Dubh was never my Beta, not even my Gamma."

That *was* interesting news. "But this Niall, the one who was killed in battle over seas, he wasn't your Beta either?"

"Na. Mine died," he replied shortly, in a tone of voice that said he did not want to discuss the matter further. "Your turn. This dirigible fall, wife?"

Alexia stood, finished with her ablutions. "Someone else is on the scent: a spy of some kind or some other agent, a member of the Hypocras Club, perhaps. While Madame Lefoux and I were strolling the observation deck, someone tried to push us over the side. I fell and Madame Lefoux fought off whomever it was. I managed to stay my fall and climbed to safety. It was nothing, really, except that I nearly lost the parasol. And I am no longer partial to dirigible travel."

"I should think not. Well, wife, try not to get yourself killed for at least a few days?"

"Are you going to tell me the real reason you came back to Scotland? Do not think you have thrown me off the scent so easily."

"I never doubted you, my sweet demure little Alexia."

Lady Maccon gave him her best, most fierce, battle-ax expression, and they went down to dinner.

CHAPTER NINE

In Which Meringues Are Annihilated

Lady Maccon wore a dinner gown of black with white pleated trim and white satin ribbon about the neck and sleeves. It would have cast her in a suitably subdued and dignified tone except that, due to the protracted argument with her husband, she had entirely forgotten to stuff her hair under a cap. Her dark tresses rioted about her head, only partially confined by the morning's updo, a heaven of frizz and feathering. Lord Maccon adored it. He thought she looked like some exotic gypsy and wondered if she might be amenable to donning gold earrings and dancing topless about their room in a loose red skirt. Everyone else was outraged—imagine the wife of an earl appearing at dinner with frizzy hair. Even in Scotland such things were simply not done.

The rest of the company was already at dinner when they arrived. Ivy had rejected the blue gown for a more excitable puce monstrosity, with multiple poufs of ruffles like so many taffeta puffballs, and a wide belt of bright crimson tied in an enormous bow above the bustle. Felicity had chosen an uncharacteristic white and pale green lace affair, which made her look deceptively demure.

Conversation was already in flow. Madame Lefoux was in deep consult with one of the Kingair clavigers, a bespectacled young man with high-arched eyebrows that gave him a perpetual expression of equal parts panic and curiosity. They appeared to be ruminating on the malfunction of the aethographor and formulating plans to investigate it after the meal.

Kingair's Beta, Gamma, and four other pack members all looked glum and uninterested in the world about them, but spoke comfortably enough to Ivy and Felicity on the inanities of life, such as the appalling Scottish weather and the appalling Scottish food. Both of which the ladies made a show of liking more than was the case and the gentlemen a show of liking less.

Lady Kingair was in a fine fettle, waxing sharp and grumpy at the head of the table. She paused in the act of waving austere hands at the footmen to glower at her distant grandfather and his new wife for their unpardonable tardiness.

Lord Maccon hesitated upon entering the room, as though unsure of where to sit. The last time he'd been in residence he would have sat at the foot of the table, a spot now ostentatiously vacant. As a guest in his old home, his precedence was unknown. An earl would sit in one chair, a family member in another, and a BUR representative in still another. There was a cast to his expression that said eating with his former pack at all was burden enough. What had they done, Alexia wondered, to earn his disgust and his neglect? Or was it something he had done?

Lady Kingair noticed the hesitation. "Canna choose? Is that not just like you? May as well take Alpha position, Gramps, naught else for it."

The Kingair Beta paused in his discussion with Felicity (aye, Scotland was terribly green) and looked up at this.

"He's na Alpha here! Have you run mad?"

The woman stood. "Shut your meat trap, Dubh. Someone's gotta fight challengers, and you'd go belly-up to the first man capable of Anubis Form."

"I'm not a coward!"

"Tell that to Niall."

"I had his back. He missed the signs and the scent. Shoulda known they'd ambush."

Conversation deteriorated at that point. Even Madame Lefoux and Mr. Querulous Brows paused in their pursuit of scientific superiority as tension spread about the supper table. Miss Loontwill stopped flirting with Mr. Tunstell. Mr. Tunstell stopped glancing hopefully in Miss Hisselpenny's direction.

In a desperate bid to reestablish civilized talk and decorum, Miss Hisselpenny said, quite loudly, "I see they are bringing in the fish course. What a pleasant surprise. I do so love fish. Don't you Mr., uh, Dubh. It is so very, um, salty."

The Beta sat back down at that, bemused. Alexia sympathized. What could one say to such a statement? The gentleman, for he still was such despite a hot temper and lupine inclinations, replied to Ivy, as required by the standards of common decency, with a, "I, too, am mighty fond of fish, Miss Hisselpenny."

Some more daring scientific philosophers claimed that the manners of the modern age had partly developed in order to keep werewolves calm and well behaved in public. Essentially, the theory was that etiquette somehow turned high society into a kind of pack. Alexia had never given it much credence, but seeing Ivy, through the mere application of fish-riddled inanities, tame a man like that was quite remarkable. Perhaps there was something to the hypothesis after all.

"What is your very favorite kind?" persisted Miss Hisselpenny breathily. "The pink, the white, or the bigger sort of grayish fishes?"

Lady Maccon exchanged a look with her husband and tried not to laugh. She took her own seat on his left-hand side, and with that, the fish in question was served and dinner continued.

"I like fish," chirruped Tunstell.

Felicity drew his attention immediately back to herself. "Really, Mr. Tunstell? What is your preferred breed?"

"Well"—Tunstell hesitated—"you know, the um, ones that"—he made a swooping motion with both hands—"uh, swim."

"Wife," murmured the earl, "what is your sister up to?"

"She only wants Tunstell because Ivy does."

"Why should Miss Hisselpenny have any interest whatsoever in my actor-cum-valet?"

"Exactly!" replied his lady wife enthusiastically. "I am glad we are in agreement on this matter: a most unsuitable match."

"Women," said her still-perplexed husband, reaching over and serving himself a portion of fish—the white kind.

The conversation never did improve much after that. Alexia was too far away from Madame Lefoux and her scientifically inclined dinner companion to engage in any intellectual conversation, much to her regret. Not that she could have contributed: they had moved on to magnetic aether transmogrification, which was far beyond her own cursory knowledge. Nevertheless, it verbally surpassed her end of the table. Her husband concentrated on eating as though he had not fed in several days, which he probably hadn't. Lady Kingair seemed incapable of multisyllabic sentences that were not crass or dictatorial in tone, and Ivy kept up a constant flow of fish-related commentary to a degree Alexia would never have countenanced had she been the intended target. The problem being, of course, that Miss Hisselpenny knew nothing on the subject of fish—a vital fact that seemed to have escaped her notice.

Finally, in desperation, Alexia grasped the conversational reins and inquired rather casually as to how the pack was enjoying its vacation from the werewolf curse.

Lord Maccon rolled his eyes heavenward. Hardly had he supposed even his indomitable wife would confront the pack so directly, en masse, and over dinner. He thought she would at least approach members individually. But then, subtlety never had been her style.

Lady Maccon's comment interrupted even Miss Hisselpenny's talk of fish. "Oh dear, have you become afflicted too?" said the young lady, glancing sympathetically around the table at the six werewolves present. "I had heard members of the supernatural set were, well, indisposed, last week. My aunt said that all the vampires took to their hives, and most of the drones were called in. She was supposed to see a concert, but it was canceled due to the absence of a pianist belonging to the Westminster Hive. All of London was on its ear. Really, there are not all that many of"—she paused, having talked herself into a corner—"well, you know, the *supernatural persuasion* in London, but there certainly is a *fuss* when they cannot leave their homes. Of course, we knew werewolves must be affected, too, but Alexia never said anything to me about it, did you, Alexia? Why, I even saw you, just the next day, and you said not a word on the subject. Was Woolsey unaffected?"

Lady Maccon did not bother to respond. Instead, she turned sharp brown eyes upon the Kingair Pack sitting about the table. Six large, guilty-looking Scotsman who apparently had nothing to say for themselves.

The pack exchanged glances. Of course, they assumed Lord Maccon would have told his wife they were unable to change, but they did think it a tad injudicious of her, not to say overly direct, to bring the subject up publicly at supper.

Finally, the Gamma said awkwardly, "It has been an interesting few months. Of course, Dubh and myself have been supernatural long enough to safely experience daylight with few of the, uh, associated difficulties, at least during new moon. But the others have rather enjoyed their vacation."

"I've only been a werewolf for a few decades, but I hadna realized how much I missed the sun," commented one of the younger pack members, speaking for the first time.

"Lachlan's been singing again—hard to be mad about that."

"But now it's beginning to annoy," added a third. "The humanity, not the singing," he added hastily.

The first grinned. "Yeah, imagine, at first we missed the light; now we miss the curse. Once one is accustomed to being a wolf part of the time, it is hard to be denied it."

The Beta gave them all a warning look.

"Being mortal is so inconvenient," complained a third, ignoring the Beta.

"These days, even the tiniest of cuts take forever to heal. And one is so verra weak without that supernatural strength. I used to be able to lift the back end of a carriage; now, carrying in Miss Hisselpenny's hatboxes gave me heart palpitations."

Alexia snorted. "You should see the hats inside."

"I'd forgotten how to shave," continued the first with a little laugh.

Felicity gasped and Ivy blushed. Bringing up a gentleman's toilette at the table—imagine being so indiscreet!

"Cubs," barked Lady Kingair, "that is by far enough of that."

"Aye, my lady," bobbed the three gentlemen, who were all two or three times her age. They had probably seen her grow up.

The table fell silent.

"So, are you all *aging*?" Lady Maccon wanted to know. She was blunt, but then, that was part of her charm. The earl looked to his great-great-great-granddaughter. It must drive Sidheag batty that she could not order Alexia, a guest, to be silent.

No one answered Lady Maccon. But the pack's collective worried expression spoke volumes. They were back to being entirely human, or as human as creatures who had once partially died could get. *Mortal* was perhaps a better word for it. It meant they could finish dying now, just like any other daylight mundane. Of course, Lord Maccon was in the same situation.

Lady Maccon chewed a small bite of hare. "I commend you for not panicking. But I am curious—why not ask for medical assistance while in London? Or perhaps seek out BUR to make inquiries? You did come through London with the rest of the regiments."

The pack looked to Lord Maccon to rescue them from his wife. Lord Maccon's expression said it all: they were at her mercy, and he was enjoying witnessing the carnage. Still, she needn't have asked. She was perfectly well aware of the fact that most supernatural creatures mistrusted modern doctors, and this pack would hardly seek out the London BUR offices with Lord Maccon in charge. Of course, they would want to get out of London as quickly as possible, retreat to the safety of their home den, hiding their shame with tails between their legs—proverbially, of course, as this was no longer literally possible. No tails to be seen.

Much to the pack's relief, the next course arrived, veal and ham pie with a side of beet and cauliflower mash. Lady Maccon waved her fork about expressively and asked, "So, how did it happen? Did you eat some polluted curry or something while you were over in India?"

"You must excuse my wife," said Lord Maccon with a grin. "She is a bit of a gesticulator, all that Italian blood."

Awkward silence persisted.

"Are you all ill? My husband thinks you have a plague. Will you be infecting him in addition to yourselves?" Lady Maccon turned to look pointedly at the earl sitting next to her. "I am not entirely sure how I would feel about that."

"Thank you for your concern, wife."

The Gamma (what had her husband called him? Oh yes, Lachlan) said jokingly, "Come off it, Conall. You canna expect sympathy from a curse-breaker, even if you did wed her."

"I heard of this phenomenon," piped up Madame Lefoux, turning her attention to their conversation. "It did not extend to my neighborhood, so I did not experience it firsthand; nevertheless, I am convinced there must be a logical scientific explanation."

"Scientists!" muttered Dubh. Two of his fellow pack members nodded in agreement.

"Why do you people keep calling Alexia a curse-breaker?" wondered Ivy.

"Precisely. Isn't she simply a curse?" said Felicity unhelpfully.

"Sister, you say the sweetest things," replied Lady Maccon.

Felicity gave her a dour look.

The pack Gamma seized this as an opportunity to change the subject. "Speaking of which, I was under the impression that Lady Maccon's former name was Tarabotti. But you are a Miss Loontwill."

"Oh"—Felicity smiled charmingly—"we have different fathers."

"Ah, I see." The Gamma frowned. "Oh, I *see. That* Tarabotti."

He looked at Alexia with newfound interest. "I should never have thought *he* would marry."

The Beta also looked at Lady Maccon curiously. "Indeed, and to produce offspring. Civic duty, I suppose."

"You knew my father?" Lady Maccon was suddenly intrigued, and, it must be admitted, distracted from her course of inquiry.

The two werewolves exchanged a look. "Not personally. We knew *of* him, of course. Quite the traveler."

Felicity said with a sniff, "Mama always said she could never remember why she leg-shackled herself to an Italian. She claimed it was a marriage of convenience, although I understand he was very good-looking. It did not last, of course. He died, just after Alexia was born. Such a terribly embarrassing thing to do, simply to up and die like that. Goes to show, Italians cannot be trusted. Mama was well rid of him. She married Papa shortly thereafter."

Lady Maccon turned to look hard at her husband. "Did *you* know my father too?" she asked him in a low voice to keep things private.

"Not as such."

"At some point, husband of mine, we must have a discussion, you and I, about the proper methods of fully transferring information. I am tired of feeling consistently behind the times."

"Except that, wife, I have two centuries on you. I can hardly tell you everything I have learned and about everyone I have met during all those years."

"Do not trouble me with such weak excuses," she hissed.

While they were arguing, the suppertime conversation moved on without them. Madame Lefoux began explaining that she felt the aethographic transmitter's crystalline valve resonator's magnetic conduction might be out of alignment. Compounded, of course, by the implausibility ratio of transference during inclement weather.

No one, except the bespectacled claviger, was able to follow a word of her explanation, but everyone was nodding sagely as though they did. Even Ivy, who had the look of a slightly panicked dormouse on her round face, pretended interest.

Tunstell solicitously passed Miss Hisselpenny the plate of potato fritters, but Ivy ignored him.

"Oh, thank you, Mr. Tunstell," said Felicity, reaching across to take one as though he had offered them to her.

Ivy huffed.

Tunstell, apparently frustrated by Miss Hisselpenny's continued rejection, turned in Miss Loontwill's direction, and began chatting with her about the recent influx of automated eyelash-curling implements imported from Portugal.

Ivy was more annoyed by this and turned away from the redhead to join in the werewolves' discussion on a possible hunting outing the next morning. Not that Miss Hisselpenny knew a whit about guns or hunting, but dearth of knowledge on a subject had never yet kept Ivy from waxing poetical upon it.

"I believe there is considerable range in the bang of most guns," she said sagely.

"Uh . . ." The gentlemen about her drifted in confusion.

Ah, Ivy, thought Alexia happily, *spreading a verbal fog wherever she goes.*

"Since we can go out during the day, we might as well take advantage and get a little dawn shooting in for old times' sake," said Dubh finally, ignoring Miss Hisselpenny's comment.

"Is Dubh his given name or surname?" Alexia asked her husband.

"Good question," he replied. "Hundred and fifty years I have had to put up with that blighter and he never told me the which way of it. I dinna know much about his past before Kingair. Came in as a loner, back in the early seventeen hundreds. Bit of a troublemaker."

"Ah, and you wouldn't know anything about secrecy or trouble-making, would you, husband?"

"Touché, wife."

The dinner drew to a close, and eventually the ladies left the gentlemen to their drinks.

Lady Maccon had never much supported the vampire-derived tradition of after-dinner gender segregation. After all, what had begun as an honor to the hive queen's superiority and need for privacy now felt like a belittling of the feminine ability to imbibe quality alcohol. Still, Alexia recognized the opportunity for what it was and made an effort to fraternize with Lady Kingair.

"You are fully human, yet you seem to act as female Alpha. How is that?" she asked, settling herself on the dusty settee and sipping a small sherry.

"They lack leadership, and I'm the only one left." The Scotswoman was blunt to the point of rudeness.

"Do you enjoy leading?" Alexia was genuinely curious.

"It'd work a mite better if I were a werewolf proper."

Lady Maccon was surprised. "Would you really be willing to try? It's such a grave risk for the gentler sex."

"Aye. But yon husband of yers didna care for my wishes." Left unsaid was the fact that Conall's was the only opinion that mattered. Only an Alpha capable of Anubis Form could breed more werewolves. Alexia had never witnessed a metamorphosis, but she had read the scientific papers on the subject. Something about soul reclamation needing both forms at once.

"He thinks you would die in the attempt. And it would be at his hand. Well, at his teeth."

The woman sipped her own sherry and nodded. Suddenly she looked every bit of her forty years and then some.

"And I the last of his mortal line," said Sidheag Maccon.

"Oh." Alexia nodded. "I see. And he would have to give you the full bite. It is a heavy burden you ask of him, to end his last mortal holding. Is that why he left the pack?"

"You think I drove him out with my asking? You dinna ken the truth of it?"

"Obviously not."

"Then it isna my place to be telling you. You married the blighter; you should be asking him."

"You think I have not tried?"

"Cagey old cuss, my gramps, that's for pure certain. Tell me something, Lady Maccon, why *did* you cleave to him? 'Cause he's seated right proper in an earldom? 'Cause he heads up BUR and they watchdog your kind? What could one such as you gain from such a union?"

It was clear what the Lady of Kingair thought. She saw Alexia as nothing more than some kind of pariah who had married Lord Maccon out of either social or pecuniary avarice.

"You know," replied Lady Maccon, not playing into her trap, "I ask myself that question daily."

"It ain't natural, a blending like that."

Alexia looked over to ensure that the other ladies were out of earshot. Madame Lefoux and Ivy were engaged in complaining about long-distance travel in the mild manner of those who had thoroughly enjoyed the experience. Felicity stood on the far side of the room, looking out into the rainy night.

"Of course it is not natural. How could it be natural when neither of us are?" Lady Maccon sniffed.

"I canna make you out, curse-breaker," replied Sidheag.

"It is really very simple. I am just like you, only without a soul."

Lady Kingair leaned forward. Those familiar tawny eyes of hers were set in an equally familiar frown. "I was raised by the *pack*, child. 'Twas always intended I become Alpha female and lead them, whether he changed me or not. You merely married into the role."

"And in that you have the advantage over me. But then again, instead of adapting, I am simply retraining *my* pack to accept my ways."

A half-smile appeared on Sidheag's dour face. "I wager Major Channing is cracked over your presence."

Alexia laughed.

Just when Lady Maccon felt like she might be gaining ground with Lady Kingair, an enormous crash reverberated against the wall nearest the dining chamber.

The ladies all exchanged startled looks. Madame Lefoux and Lady Maccon immediately leaped to their feet and went swiftly back toward the supper room. Lady Kingair was but a few steps behind, and all three burst through to find Lord Maccon and the Kingair Beta, Dubh, grappling fiercely on top of the massive table, rolling about among the remnants of what once had been a most excellent brandy and plate of sticky meringues. The other members of the pack, the Kingair claviers in residence, and Tunstell had arranged themselves well out of the way and seemed to be viewing the fisticuffs in the manner of sportsmen at the races.

Tunstell was running a commentary. "Oh, nice uppercut from Lord Maccon there, and, oh, did Dubh *kick*? Bad form, terribly bad form."

Alexia paused, regarding the two large Scotsman rolling about among the sticky powder of crushed meringue.

"Lachlan, report!" barked Lady Kingair over the racket. "What's going on?"

The Gamma, who Alexia had thought of as rather sympathetic up until that point, shrugged. "It needs getting out right to the open, mistress. You know how we like to settle things."

The woman shook her head, gray-streaked plait flying back and forth. "We settle things by teeth and claw, na fist and flesh. This isna our way. This isna pack protocol!"

Lachlan shrugged again. "Having na teeth possible, this be the next best option. You canna stop it, mistress, challenge was issued. We all witnessed the wording of it."

The other pack members nodded gravely.

Dubh landed a good right punch to Lord Maccon's chin, sending him flying backward.

Lady Kingair stepped hastily to one side to avoid a silver platter as it skidded off the table toward her.

"Oh my goodness!" came Ivy's voice from the doorway. "I do believe they are actually skirmishing!"

Tunstell immediately sprang into action. "This is not a thing a lady should witness, Miss Hisselpenny," he exclaimed, rushing over and shepherding her out of the room.

"But . . ." came Ivy's voice.

Lady Maccon smiled proudly at the fact that the redhead hadn't considered her sensibilities. Madame Lefoux, noting that Felicity still stood watching with wide, interested eyes, gave Alexia a look and left the room, shutting the door behind her and sweeping Felicity in her wake.

Lord Maccon slammed into Dubh's stomach with his head, propelling the werewolf backward into the wall. The whole room shook at the impact.

Now, thought Alexia maliciously, *Kingair will have to remodel.*

"At least take the disagreement outside!" yelled Lady Kingair.

There was blood everywhere, as well as spilled brandy, broken glass, and crushed meringues.

"For goodness' sake," said Lady Maccon, exasperated, "don't they realize that as humans, they could seriously injure one another if they carry on like this? They do not have the supernatural strength to take those kinds of blows, nor the supernatural healing to recover from them."

Both men rolled to the side and fell off the tabletop with a loud thud.

Good Lord, thought Lady Maccon, noting that a good deal of the blood seemed to be emerging from her husband's nose, *I do hope Conall has brought a spare cravat.*

She was not particularly worried, for she had little doubt in her husband's pugilistic skills. He boxed regularly at Whites, and he was *her* chosen mate. Of course, he would win the fight, but still, the disarray being generated was unacceptable. Things could not be allowed to continue much longer. Imagine, the poor Kingair staff, having to clean up such a mess.

With that thought, Lady Maccon whirled about and went purposefully to fetch her parasol.

She need not have bothered. By the time she returned, numbing darts loaded and parasol ready to fire, both men were slumped in opposite corners of the room. Dubh was clutching his head and coughing in sharp painful little gasps, and Lord Maccon was listing to one side, blood dribbling out of his nose and one eye nearly swollen shut.

"Well don't you two look a picture," Alexia said, resting her parasol against the wall and crouching down to examine Conall's face with gentle fingers. "Nothing a spot of vinegar won't put to rights." She turned to one of the clavigers. "Run and get me some cider vinegar, my good man." Lord Maccon looked at her over the top of his cravat, which he was now holding to his nose. Ah well, the cravat was ruined already.

"Didna ken you cared, wife," he grumbled, but leaned in against her gentle ministrations nevertheless.

So as not to seem too sympathetic, Alexia began vigorously brushing off the meringue crumbs covering his jacket.

At the same time, she looked over at the Kingair Beta and said, "Settle the issue to your mutual satisfaction, did you, gentlemen?"

Dubh gave her a deadpan expression that still managed to indicate a certain profound level of deep disgust in her very existence, let alone her question. Alexia only shook her head at such petulance.

The Kingair claviger returned bearing a flask of cider vinegar. Lady Maccon immediately began to copiously douse her husband about the face and neck with it.

"Ouch! Steady on, that stings!"

Dubh made to rise.

Lord Maccon instantly struggled to his feet. He would have to, Alexia surmised, to maintain dominance. Or it could be that he was trying to get away from her vinegar-riddled attentions.

"I know it stings," she said. "Not nice to have to heal the old-fashioned way, now, is it, my brave table warrior? Perhaps you will pause to consider next time before you commence fighting in a confined space. I mean really, look at this room." She tutted. "You both should be thoroughly ashamed of yourselves."

"Nothing has been settled," Dubh said, returning hastily to his slumped position on the carpeted floor. He appeared to have gotten the worse end of things. One of his arms looked broken, and there was a nasty gash in his left cheek.

However, Lady Maccon's brisk application of vinegar seemed to have shattered everyone else's collective inertia, for they began bustling around the fallen Beta, splinting up his arm and tending to his wounds.

"You still abandoned us." Dubh sounded like a petulant child.

"You all know *exactly* why I left," Lord Maccon growled.

"Uh," said Alexia timidly, raising a questioning hand, "I do not." Everyone ignored her.

"You couldna control the pack," Dubh accused.

Everyone present in the room gasped. Except Alexia, who did not comprehend the gravity of the insult and was occupied trying to pick the last of the meringue off her husband's dinner jacket.

"That isna fair," said Lachlan, not moving from his stance. Unsure of his allegiance, the Gamma simply stayed away from both Conall and Dubh.

"*You* betrayed *me*." Lord Maccon did not yell, but the words carried and, even though he could not change to wolf form, there was wolf anger in them.

"And you pay us back in kind? The emptiness you left, was that fair?"

"There is naught fair about pack protocol. You and I both know that; there is simply protocol. And there was none to cover what you did. It was entirely unprecedented. So I was cursed with the dubious pleasure of having to make it up myself. Abandonment seemed to be the best solution, since I didna want to spend another night in your presence."

Alexia looked over at Lachlan. The Gamma had tears in his eyes.

"Besides"—Lord Maccon's voice softened—"Niall was a perfectly good Alpha alternative. He led you well, I hear. He married my progeny. You were tame enough for decades under his dominance."

Lady Kingair finally spoke. Her voice was oddly soft. "Niall was my mate, and I pure loved him. He was a brilliant tactician and a good soldier, but he wasna a true Alpha."

"Are you saying he wasna dominant enough? I heard naught of lack of discipline. Whenever I ran a recognizance on Kingair, you all seemed to be perfectly content." Conall's voice was soft.

"So you did check up on us, did you, old wolf?" Lady Kingair looked hurt at that rather than relieved.

"Of course I did. You *were* once my pack."

The Beta looked up from where he still lay on the floor. "You left us weak, Conall, and you knew it. Niall had na Anubis Form, and the pack couldna procreate. Clavigers abandoned us as a result, the local loners rebelled, and we didn't have an Alpha fighting for the integrity of the pack."

Lady Maccon glanced at her husband. His face was carved in stone, relentless. Or what little she could see behind the puffy eye and blood-stained cravat seemed that way.

"You betrayed me," he repeated, as though that settled the matter. Which, in Conall's world, it probably did. He valued few things more than loyalty.

Alexia decided to make her presence known. "What is the point of recriminations? Nothing can be done about it now, since none of you can change into any form at all, Anubis or otherwise. No new wolves can be made, no new Alpha found, no challenge battles fought. Why argue over what was when we are immersed in what isn't?"

Lord Maccon looked down at her. "So speaks my practical Alexia. Now do you understand why I married her?"

Lady Kingair said snidely, "A desperate, if ineffectual, attempt at control?"

"Oooh, she has claws. Are you positive you never bit her to change, husband? She has the temper of a werewolf." Alexia could be just as snide as the next person.

The Gamma stepped forward, looking at Lady Maccon. "Our apologies, my lady, and you a newly arrived guest among us. We must truly seem the barbarians you English take us for. 'Tis only that na Alpha these many moons is making us nervous."

"Oh, and here I thought your behavior sprang from the whole not-being-able-to-change-shape quandary," she quipped back sharply.

He grinned. "Well, that too."

"Werewolves without pack leaders tend to get into trouble?" Lady Maccon wondered.

No one said anything.

"I don't suppose you are going to tell us what trouble you got into overseas?" Alexia tried to look as though she wasn't avidly interested, taking her husband's arm casually.

Silence.

"Well, I think we have all had enough excitement for one evening.

Since you have been human these many months, I assume you are keeping daylight hours?"

A nod from Lady Kingair.

"In that case"—Lady Maccon straightened her dress—"Conall and I shall bid you good night."

"We shall?" Lord Maccon looked dubious.

"Good night," said his wife firmly to the pack and clavigers. Grabbing her parasol in one hand and her husband's arm in the other, she practically dragged the earl from the room.

Lord Maccon lumbered obediently after her.

The room they left behind was filled with half-thoughtful, half-amused faces.

"What are you about, wife?" Conall asked as soon as they were upstairs and out of everyone's earshot.

His wife plastered herself up against him and kissed him fiercely.

"Ouch," he said when they pulled apart, although he had participated with gusto. "Busted lip."

"Oh, look what you did to my dress!" Lady Maccon glared down at the blood now decorating the white satin trim.

Lord Maccon refrained from pointing out that she had initiated the kiss.

"You are an impossible man," continued his ladylove, swatting him on one of the few undamaged portions of his body. "You could have been killed in such a fight, do you realize?"

"Oh, phooey." Lord Maccon waved a dismissive hand in the air. "For a Beta, Dubh is not a verra good fighter even in wolf form. He is hardly likely to be any more capable as a human."

"He is *still* a trained soldier." She was not going to let this rest.

"Have you forgotten, wife, that so am I?"

"*You* are out of practice. Woolsey Pack Alpha has not been on campaign in years."

"Are you saying I'm getting old? I'll show you old." He swept her up like some exaggerated Latin lover and carried her into their bedchamber.

Angelique, who was engaged in some sort of tidying of the wardrobe, quickly made herself scarce.

"Stop trying to distract me," said Alexia several moments later. During which time her husband had managed to divest her of a good percentage of her clothing.

"Me, distract you? You are the one who dragged me off and up here right when things were getting interesting."

"They are not going to tell us what is going on no matter how hard we push," said Alexia, unbuttoning his shirt and hissing in concern at the array of harsh red marks destined to become rather spectacular bruises by the morning. "We are simply going to have to figure this out for ourselves."

He paused in kissing a little path along her collarbone and looked at her suspiciously. "You have a plan."

"Yes, I do, and the first part of it involves you telling me exactly what happened twenty years ago to make you leave. No." She stopped his wandering hand. "Stop that. And the second part involves you going to sleep. You are going to hurt in places your little supernatural soul forgot it could hurt in."

He flopped back on the pillows. There was no reasoning with his wife when she got like this. "And the third part of the plan?"

"That is for me to know and you not to know."

He let out a lusty sigh. "I hate it when you do that."

She waggled a finger at him as though he were a schoolboy. "Uh-uh, you just miscalculated, husband. I hold all the high cards right now."

He grinned. "Is that how this works?"

"You have been married before, remember? You should know."

He turned on his side toward her, wincing at the pain this caused. She lay back against the pillows, and he ran one large hand over her stomach and chest. "You are perfectly correct, of course; that is exactly how this works." Then he made his tawny eyes wide and batted his eyelashes at her, pleading. Alexia had learned that expression from Ivy and had employed it effectively on her husband during their, for lack of a better word, courtship. Little did she know how persuasively it could be applied in the opposite direction.

"Are you going to at least see me settled?" he murmured, nibbling her neck, his voice gravelly.

"I might be persuaded. You would, of course, have to be very very nice to me."

Conall agreed to be nice, in the best nonverbal way possible.

Afterward, he lay staring fixedly up at the ceiling and told her why he had left the Kingair Pack. He told her all of it, from what it was like for them, as both werewolves and Scotsmen, at the beginning of Queen Victoria's rule, to the assassination attempt on the queen planned by the then Kingair Beta, his old and trusted friend, without his knowledge.

He did not once look at her while he talked. Instead his eyes remained fixed on the stained and smudged molding of the ceiling above them.

"They were all in on it. Every last one of them—pack and clavigers.

And not a one told me. Oh, not because I was all that loyal to the queen; surely you know packs and hives better than that by now. Our loyalty to a daylight ruler is never unreserved. No, they lied to me because I was loyal to the cause, always have been."

"What cause?" wondered his wife. She held his big hand in both of hers as she lay curled toward him, but otherwise she did not touch him.

"Acceptance. Can you imagine what would have happened if they had succeeded? A Scottish pack, attached to one of the best Highland regiments, multiple campaigns served in the British Army, killing Queen Victoria. It would have thrown over the whole government, but not only that, it would have taken us back to the Dark Ages. Those daylight conservatives who have always been against integration would call it a nationally supported supernatural plot, the church would regain its foothold on British soil, and we would be back to the Inquisition quicker than you could shake a tail."

"Husband"—Alexia was mildly startled, but only because she'd never given Conall's political views much consideration—"you are a progressive!"

"Damn straight! I couldna believe *my pack* would put all werewolves into such a position. And for what? Old resentments and Scottish pride? A weak alliance with Irish dissidents? And the worst of it was, not a one had told me of the plot. Not even Lachlan."

"Then how did you find out about it in the end?"

He huffed in disgust. "I caught them mixing the poison. Poison, mind you! Poison has no place on pack grounds or in pack business. It isna an honest way to kill anyone, let alone a monarch."

Alexia suppressed a smile. This would appear to be the aspect of the conspiracy that upset him the most.

"We werewolves are not known for our subtlety. I had realized they were plotting something for weeks. When I found the poison, I forced a confession out of Lachlan."

"And you ended up having to fight and kill your own Beta over it. Then what, you simply took off for London, leaving them without leadership?"

He finally turned and looked at her, propping himself on his elbow. Seeing no judgment or accusation in her eyes, he relaxed slightly. "There is no pack protocol to cover this kind of situation. A large-scale betrayal of an Alpha with no qualified reason or ready replacement. Led by my own Beta." His eyes were agonized. "My *Beta*! They deserved to be without metamorphosis. I could have killed them all, and not a one would have objected, least of all the dewan, save that they were not plotting against me; they were plotting against a daylight queen."

He looked to her and his eyes were sad.

She tried to distill the story down into one manageable chunk. "So your leaving was a point of pride, honor, and politics?"

"Essentially."

"I suppose it could have been worse." She smoothed away the frown creasing his forehead.

"They could have succeeded."

"You realize, as muhjah, I am forced to ask: will they try again, do you think? After two decades? Could that explain the mysterious weapon?"

"Werewolves have long memories."

"In the interest of Queen Victoria's safety, is there a way for us to provide a surety against this?"

He sighed softly. "I dinna know."

"And that's why you came back? If it's true, you'll have to kill them all, won't you, sundowner?"

He turned away from her words, his broad back stiff, but he did not deny them.

CHAPTER TEN

Aether Transmissions

Using the information Lord Akeldama had provided, and with the assistance of a personable young man the vampire referred to only as Biffy, Professor Lyall set up an operation. "Ambrose has been meeting with various members of the incoming regiments," Lord Akeldama had informed him over an aged scotch—a warm fire in the grate and a plump calico cat on his knee. "At first I thought it was *simply* opiates or some other form of illegal trade, but now I believe it to be something more sinister. The hive is not only employing its vampire contacts—it's approaching any common soldier. Even the ill-dressed. It's *horrible*." The vampire gave a delicate little shudder. "I cannot discern what it is they are buying up so greedily. You want to find out what Westminster is up to? Tap into those werewolf military connections of yours, *darling*, and set up an offer. Biffy can take you to the preferred venue."

And so it was, on the information provided by a rove vampire, that Professor Lyall now sat in a very seedy pub, the Pickled Crumpet, accompanied by a spectacularly well-dressed drone and Major Channing. A few wobbly tables away sat one of Major Channing's most trusted soldiers, clutching several suspicious packages and looking nervous.

Professor Lyall slouched down and nursed his beer. He hated beer, a vile common beverage.

Major Channing was twitchy. He shifted long legs, jostling the table and sloshing their drinks.

"Stop that," his Beta instructed. "No one's come yet. Be patient."

Major Channing only glared at him.

Biffy offered them a pinch of snuff. Both werewolves declined in thinly veiled horror. Imagine mucking about with one's sense of smell! Such a vampiric kind of affectation.

Some while later, with Professor Lyall's beer barely touched but Major Channing on his third pint, the vampire entered the pub.

He was a tall, exceedingly comely individual, who looked exactly as a novelist might describe a vampire—sinister and pensive with an aquiline nose and unfathomable eyes. Professor Lyall sipped his beer in salute. He had to give Lord Ambrose tribute—the man put on an excellent show. Top marks for dramatic flair.

Lord Ambrose made his way straight to the soldier's table and sat down without introduction. The tavern was loud enough to make an auditory disruptor unnecessary, and even Lyall and Channing with their supernatural hearing caught only about one word in ten.

The exchange moved quite rapidly and culminated in the soldier showing Lord Ambrose his collection of goods. The vampire looked each one over, then shook his head violently and stood to leave.

The soldier stood as well, leaning forward to ask a question.

Lord Ambrose clearly took offense, for he lashed out with supernatural speed, striking the man across the face so fast even a soldier's reflexes stood him in poor stead.

Major Channing immediately jumped to his feet, his chair crashing back as he surged forward. Professor Lyall grabbed his wrist, halting his protective instinct. Channing all too often thought of his soldiers as pack.

The vampire's head swiveled around, focusing in on their little band. He hissed through his teeth, the tips of both fangs visible over thin lips. Then with a swirl of long burgundy greatcoat, he swept majestically from the inn.

Professor Lyall, who had never done anything majestically in all his life, faintly envied the man.

The young soldier came over to them, a harsh red welt about the side of his mouth.

"I'll murder the liverless bastard," swore Major Channing, making as if to follow Lord Ambrose out into the street.

"Stop." Professor Lyall's hand tightened on the Gamma's arm. "Burt here is perfectly fine. Aren't you, Burt?"

Burt spat out a bit of blood but nodded. "Dealt with worse at sea."

Biffy picked his snuffbox off the table and tucked it into a coat pocket. "So"—the young man gestured for the soldier to pull up a chair and join them—"what did he say? What are they looking for?"

"It's the weirdest thing. Artifacts."

"What?"

The soldier bit his bottom lip. "Yeah, *Egyptian* artifacts. But not objects as we might have thought. Not a weapon as such. That's why he was so angry with my offerings. Thems is looking for scrolls. Scrolls with a certain image on 'em."

"Hieroglyphic?"

Burt nodded.

"What image, did he say?"

"Seems they're quite desperate, 'cause it was pretty indiscreet of him to tell me, but, yeah, he said. Something called an ankh, only they want it broken. You know, in the picture, like the symbol was cut in half."

Professor Lyall and Biffy looked at one another. "Interesting," they both said at the same time.

"I wager the edict keepers have some kind of record of the symbol." Biffy, of course, had some knowledge of vampire information sources.

"Which means," Lyall said thoughtfully, "this has happened before."

Alexia left her husband soundly asleep. After centuries as an immortal, he had forgotten how a mortal body seeks succor in slumber when it has injuries to deal with. Despite the excitement, the night was young and most of the rest of the castle was still awake.

She nearly ran full tilt into a rapidly scuttling Ivy in the hallway. Miss Hisselpenny had a fierce frown decorating her normally amiable face.

"Good Lord, Ivy, what an expression." Lady Maccon leaned casually on her parasol. The way things were progressing this evening, she was unwilling to part with the accessory.

"Oh, Alexia. I do not mean to be forward, but I really must venture: I simply loathe Mr. Tunstell."

"Ivy!"

"Well, I mean to say, well, really! He is so very impossible. I was given to understand that his affection for me was secure. And one little objection and he switches allegiance quite flippantly. One might even call him flighty! To bill and coo around another female so soon after I went to such prodigious lengths to break his heart. It gives him the countenance of a, well, a vacillating butterfly!"

Lady Maccon was arrested trying to imagine a cooing butterfly. "Really, I thought you were still quite enamored of him, despite rejecting his suit."

"How *could* you think such a thing? I positively detest him. I am in full agreement with myself on this. He is nothing more than a billing-cooing *vacillator*! And I shall have nothing more to do with a person of such weakened character."

Lady Maccon was not quite certain how to converse with Miss Hisselpenny when she was in such a mood. She was accustomed to

Ivy-overset and Ivy-chatterbox, but Ivy-full-of-wrath was a new creature altogether. She opted for the fallback position. "You are clearly in need of a fortifying cup of tea, my dear. Shall we go and see if we can hunt one down? Even the Scots must stock some form of libation."

Miss Hisselpenny took a deep breath. "Yes, I think you may be right. Excellent notion."

Lady Maccon solicitously shepherded her friend down the stairs and into one of the smaller drawing rooms, where they ran into two clavigers. The young gentlemen were more than eager to hunt down the requisite tea, see to Miss Hisselpenny's every whim, and generally prove to the ladies that all good manners had not fled the Highlands along with its complement of trousers. As a result, Ivy forgave them their kilts. Lady Maccon left her friend to their stimulating accents and tender care and went in search of Madame Lefoux and the broken aethographor, hoping for a peek at its functional component parts.

It took her some time to track the massive machine down. Castle Kingair was a real castle, with none of Woolsey's practical notions on conservation of space and gridlike layout. It was very large, with a propensity for confusing itself with additional rooms, towers, and gratuitous staircases. Lady Maccon was logical in her approach (which may have been her mistake). She surmised that the aethographor must be located in one of the many castle turrets, but *which one* proved to be the difficulty. There was a decided overabundance of towers. Very concerned with defensibility, the Scots. It took a good deal of time to climb the winding steps to each turret. She knew she was in the right area, however, when she heard the cursing. In French, of course, and not words that she was familiar with, naturally, but she was in no doubt as to their profane nature. Madame Lefoux appeared to be experiencing some form of inconvenience.

When she finally attained the room, Alexia came face-to-face, or as is were, face-to-bottom, with yet another good reason for the lady inventor to don trousers. Madame Lefoux was on her back, half underneath the apparatus, only her legs and backside visible. Had she been in skirts, it would have been a most indelicate position.

Kingair's aethographic transmitter was raised up on little legs above the stone floor of the castle. It looked somewhat like two attached privy houses with footstool feet. Everything was brightly lit with gas lamps, as the pack had clearly spared no expense on this room. It was also clean.

Lady Maccon craned her neck to see into the darkened interior of the chamber that Madame Lefoux worked under. It appeared that the transmitting mechanicals were the ones being problematical. The

Frenchwoman had with her a hatbox that appeared to be no hatbox at all but a cleverly disguised toolkit. Lady Maccon instantly coveted one herself—so much less *obvious* than a dispatch case.

The bespectacled claviger, with the ever-present expression of panic, crouched nearby, passing the inventor, one after another, a string of exciting-looking tools.

"The magnetomotor modulating adjustor, if you please," Madame Lefoux would say, and a long, sticklike object with a corkscrew of copper at one end and a glass tube full of an illuminated liquid at the other was passed over. Shortly after, there would emit another curse, the tool would be passed back to the claviger, and a new one called for.

"Goodness gracious," exclaimed Alexia. "What *are* you doing?"

There came the sound of a thump, Madame Lefoux's legs jerked, and further cursing ensued. Moments later, the Frenchwoman wormed her way out and stood up, rubbing her head. The action only added to a vast collection of grease smudges covering her pretty face.

"Ah, Lady Maccon, how lovely. I did wonder when you would track us down."

"I was unavoidably delayed by husbands and Ivys," explained Alexia.

"These things, regrettably, are bound to occur when one is married and befriended." Madame Lefoux was sympathetic.

Lady Maccon leaned forward and, using her parasol as a prop, tried to see underneath the contraption. Her corset made this action mostly impossible, so she turned back to the Frenchwoman. "Have you determined the nature of the problem?"

"Well, it is definitely the transmitting chamber that is malfunctioning. The receiving room seems fully operational. It is hard to tell without an actual transmission of some kind."

Alexia looked to the claviger for confirmation, and the young man nodded. He did not appear to have much to say for himself, but he was eager to help. The best kind of person, felt Alexia.

"Well," said Lady Maccon, "what time is it?"

The young gentleman took out a small pocket watch and flipped it open. "Half past ten."

Lady Maccon turned to Madame Lefoux. "If you can get it ready by eleven, we can try to raise Lord Akeldama on his aethographor. Remember, he gave me the codes, a valve frequensor, *and* an eleven o'clock time slot for open-scan transmission."

"But if he doesna have our resonance, what good is that? He willna be able to receive." The claviger snapped his watch closed and stashed it once more in his waistcoat pocket.

"Ah," Madame Lefoux jumped in, "he has a multi-adaptive model that does not operate using crystalline compatibility protocol. All he need do is scan for a transmission to his frequency during the allotted time. We can receive back because Lady Maccon *does* have the appropriate valve component."

The claviger looked even more surprised than usual.

"I understand they are dear friends." Madame Lefoux appeared to feel this would explain everything.

Alexia smiled. "On the evening of my wedding, I held his hand so he could watch the sunset."

The claviger looked confused. Again, more confused than usual (his was a difficult face for expressing the full range of human emotion).

Madame Lefoux explained, "Lord Akeldama is a vampire."

The young man gasped. "He trusted you with his life?"

Lady Maccon nodded. "So trusting me with a crystalline valve, however technologically vital, is no very great thing by comparison."

Madame Lefoux shrugged. "I do not know about that, my lady. I mean to say, one's life is one thing; one's technology is an entirely different matter."

"Nevertheless, I can provide you the means to test this aethographor's effectiveness, once it has been repaired."

The claviger gave her a look of burgeoning respect. "Efficient female, aren't you, Lady Maccon?"

Alexia was not certain whether she should be pleased or offended by the statement, so she chose to ignore it.

"So, I had better get to it, hadn't I?" Madame Lefoux turned and crawled back under the transmitter, returning to her tinkering.

Muffled words emanated a few moments later.

"What was that?"

Madame Lefoux's head reappeared. "I said, would you like to inscribe a message to Lord Akeldama while you are waiting?"

"Superb idea." Lady Maccon turned to the claviger. "Would you mind finding me a blank scroll, a stylus, and some acid?"

The young man jumped to oblige. While she waited for the supplies, Alexia poked about looking for the pack's valve frequensor library. Who did Kingair communicate with? Why had they bothered to invest in the aethographor at all? She found the crystalline valves in a small set of unlocked drawers off to one side. There were only three, but they were all entirely unlabeled and without any other identification.

"What are you doing, Lady Maccon?" The claviger came up behind her, looking suspicious (an expression entirely unsuited to his face).

"Just pondering why a Scottish pack would need an aethographor," replied Alexia. She was never one to dissemble when forthrightness could keep others off guard.

"Mmm," the young man replied, noncommittal. He handed her a metal scroll, a small vial of acid, and a stylus.

Lady Maccon set herself up in one corner of the room, tongue sticking out slightly as she attempted to be as neat as possible inscribing one letter into each grid square on the scroll. Her penmanship had never won her any school awards, and she wanted to make it as clear as possible.

The message read, "Testing Scots. Please reply."

She removed Lord Akeldama's crystalline valve from the secret pocket of her parasol, carefully using her copious skirts to shroud her movements so the claviger could not see where it was hidden.

Madame Lefoux was still puttering, so Lady Maccon entertained herself by exploring the receiving room, the part of the aethographor on which Madame Lefoux was not working. She tested her own memory on the parts. They were, in general, larger and less streamlined than on Lord Akeldama's transmitter, but they were in the same place: filter to eliminate ambient noise, dial for amplifying incoming signals, and two pieces of glass with black particulate between.

Madame Lefoux surprised Alexia with a gentle touch on her arm.

"We are almost ready. It is five minutes until eleven. Shall we set the machine to transmit?"

"Will I be allowed to watch?"

"Of course."

The three of them crammed into the tiny transmitting room, which, like the receiving room, was packed with machinery that looked like Lord Akeldama's—except that the gadgetry was more tangled, something Alexia had not thought possible, and the dials and switches were more numerous.

Madame Lefoux smoothed out and slotted Alexia's metal scroll into the special frame. Alexia placed Lord Akeldama's valve into the resonator cradle. After confirming the time, Madame Lefoux pulled down on a large knob-ended switch and engaged the aetheric convector, activating the chemical wash. The etched letters began to phosphoresce. The two small hydrodine engines spun to life, generating opposing aethero-electric impulses, and the two needles raced across the slate. Sparking brightly whenever they were exposed to one another through the letters, transmission commenced. Alexia worried about the rain causing delay, but she had faith that Lord Akeldama's improved technology was capable of greater sensitivity and could cut though climatic interference.

"Testing . . . Scots . . . please . . . reply" sped invisibly outward.

And leagues to the south, at the top of a posh town house, a well-trained vampire drone, dressed like a candied orange peel, who looked as though his gravest concern was whether winter cravats permitted paisley or not, sat up straight and began recording an incoming transmission. The source was unknown, but he had been told to sweep on broad receiving at eleven o'clock for several nights straight. He took down the message and then noted the transmission coordination frequency and the time before dashing off to find his master.

"It is hard to know for certain, but I believe everything went smoothly." Madame Lefoux switched off the transmitter, the little hydrodine engines spinning quietly down. "Of course, we will not know if communication has been established until we receive an answering transmission."

The claviger said, "Your contact will have to determine the correct frequency from the incoming message so that he can dial it in from his end, without a companion valve frequensor. How long will such an endeavor take?"

"No way to know," replied the Frenchwoman. "Could be quite rapid. We had best go turn the receiving room on."

So they let themselves into the other chamber and lit the silent little steam engine located under the instrument board. Then came a long quarter of an hour simply sitting, as quietly as possible, waiting.

"I think we will give it just a few more minutes," Madame Lefoux whispered. Even her whisper caused the magnetic resonator coils to shake slightly.

The claviger frowned at her and went to retune the ambient noise filtration component.

Then, with no warning at all, Lord Akeldama's message slowly began to appear between the two pieces of glass on the receiver. The small hydraulic arm with its mounted magnet began painstakingly moving back and forth, shifting the magnetic particulate one letter at a time.

The claviger, whose name Alexia still did not know, began carefully and quietly copying down the incoming letters on a soft piece of washed canvas using a stylographic pen. Lady Maccon and Madame Lefoux held their collective breaths and tried not to move. Silence was vital. After each letter was complete, the arm reset itself and the glass shook softly, erasing the previous letter and preparing for the next.

Eventually, the arm stopped moving. They waited a few more minutes, and when Alexia went to speak, the claviger held up his hand autocratically. Only when he had switched everything off did he nod, allowing them to talk. Lady Maccon realized why he had charge of the aethographor. The Scots were a silent, dour lot, but he seemed to have the least to say of any of them.

"Well? Read out the message," she demanded.

He cleared his throat and, blushing slightly, read out, " 'Got you. Scots taste good?' "

Lady Maccon laughed. Lord Akeldama must have misread her message. Instead of "testing Scots," he had read "tasting Scots." "Regardless of the reply, we know that this transmitter is working. And I can gossip with Lord Akeldama."

The claviger looked offended. "An aethographor isna intended for *gossip,* Lady Maccon!"

"Tell that to Lord Akeldama."

Madame Lefoux's dimples appeared.

"Could we send him one more message to be certain as to the efficaciousness of the transmitting room?" Lady Maccon asked hopefully.

The claviger sighed. He was reluctant to agree but was apparently also unwilling to resist the request of a guest. He wandered off and returned with another metal scroll.

Alexia inscribed, "Spy here?"

From what she could recall, Lord Akeldama's newer model had the ability to overhear other transmissions, if it knew where to look.

Minutes later in the other room, the reply came. "Not mine. Probably chatty bats."

While the other two looked confused, Alexia only nodded. Lord Akeldama thought that any spy would belong to the vampires. Knowing her friend, he would now take it upon himself to start monitoring the Westminster Hive and nearby roves. She could just imagine him rubbing pink-gloved hands together, thrilled with the challenge. With a smile, she removed Lord Akeldama's valve and, when the claviger was not looking, stashed it back in her trusty parasol.

Lady Maccon was exhausted by the time she sought her bed. It was not a small bed by any means, yet her husband seemed to be occupying the entirety of it. He was sprawled, snoring softly, wrapped every which way in a ragged and much-abused (clearly throughout its long and not very successful life) coverlet.

Alexia climbed in and applied a tried-and-true technique she had developed over the last few months. She braced herself against the headboard and used her legs to push him as much to one side as possible, clearing sufficient space for her to worm her way down before he took to sprawling once more. She supposed he had spent decades, even centuries, sleeping alone; it would take some time to retrain him. In the meantime, she was developing some decent thigh muscles from her nightly ritual. The earl was no lightweight.

Conall growled at her slightly but seemed pleased enough to find her next to him once she snuggled against his side. He rolled toward her, nuzzled the back of her neck, and wrapped a heavy arm about her waist.

She tugged hard at the coverlet, which would not budge, and settled for arranging the earl's arm about her instead of the blanket. As a supernatural creature, Conall was supposed to be cold most of the time, but Alexia never felt it. Whenever she touched him, he was mortal, and his mortal body seemed to run at temperatures something akin to a high-end steam boiler. It was nice to be able to sleep touching him for once, with no worries she might cause him to age.

And on that note, Lady Maccon drifted off.

She awoke still warm. But her husband's affection, or possibly his hidden murderous tendencies, had shoved her so far toward the edge of the bed that she was partly suspended in midair. Without his arm about her waist, she would most certainly have tumbled off the side. Her nightgown was, of course, gone. How did he always manage to do that? The nuzzling at the back of her neck had turned into nibbles.

She cracked an eyelid: it was just about dawn, or the gray and depressing Highland winter version of dawn. Kingair heralded the day with a sad, reluctant spit of light, which in no way encouraged one to spring swiftly from the bed and trip lightly the morning dew. Not that Alexia was any kind of springer or tripper first thing on normal occasions.

Conall's nibbles turned into slightly more insistent bites. He was fond of a bite here or there. Sometimes Alexia was given to wonder if, had she not been a preternatural, he would not have actually eaten a chunk of her once in a while. There was something in the way his eyes came over yellow and hungry when he was in an amorous mood. She had ceased fighting the fact that she loved Conall, but that did not stop her from being practical about his requirements. Baser instincts were baser instincts, after all, and, her touch aside, he was still a werewolf. On occasions like this, she had reason to be glad her own powers kept his teeth nice and square. Although, of course, the way things stood in Kingair, had she been in full possession of a soul, she still would not have had to worry.

He turned his attention to her ear.

"Stop that. Angelique will be in presently to see me dressed."

"Bother her."

"For goodness' sake, Conall. Think of her delicate sensibilities."

"Your maid is a prude," was her husband's grumbled reply. He did not leave off his romantic attentions. Instead he moved his arm to better facilitate his notion of acceptable morning activities. Unfortunately, he neglected to realize his arm was all that was holding his wife in the bed.

With an undignified squawk, Alexia tumbled to the floor.

"Good Lord, woman, what'd you do *that* for?" her husband asked in profound confusion.

Lady Maccon checked to see that everything was unbroken and then stood, angrier than a hornet. She was just about to sting her husband into oblivion with the sharper side of her already-sharp tongue when she remembered that she was naked. At that same moment, she came to the sudden realization of exactly how cold a stone castle could get during a Highland winter. Cursing her husband a blue streak, she jerked the covers off of him and launched herself at him, burrowing into his warmth.

Seeing how this put her naked body plastered on top of him, Lord Maccon had no objection. Except that his wife was still annoyed and was now wide awake and twitchy, and he was aching something awful from his fight the night before.

"I am going to find out what is going on with this pack of yours today if it is the last thing I do," she said, swatting at his hands when they attempted to make interesting forays. "The longer I spend lazing about in bed, the less time I have to investigate."

"I wasna planning on being lazy," came the growl.

Lady Maccon decided that, in the interest of economy, she would have to face the cold, or her husband would carry on about this for hours. When he took it into his head to do a thing, he liked to see it done properly.

"It will have to wait until this evening," she said, extracting herself from his embrace. In a swift movement, she rolled off of him to one side, spinning the coverlet around herself. She part rolled, part hopped off the edge of the bed to her feet and shuffled across the floor toward her pelisse. This left her poor husband naked on the bed behind her. He was less disturbed by the cold, for he simply propped himself up on a pillow, folded his hands behind his head, and watched her out of heavy-lidded eyes.

Which was the scene poor Angelique came in upon—her mistress wrapped in a blanket like a large upended sausage roll, and her master sprawled naked for all the world to see. The maid had been living among werewolves, and in the presence of Lord and Lady Maccon, long enough not to have this bother her overmuch. She squeaked, winced, averted her eyes, and carried the basin of washing water over to the little stand provided.

Lady Maccon hid a smile. Poor Angelique. To come from the world of hives into the chaos that was pack life must be disconcerting. After all, no one was more civilized than the vampires, and no one less civilized than werewolves. Alexia wondered if vampires ever even made it to bed sport; they were so busy being polite to one another. At least the werewolves lived large: loud and messy, but also large.

She thanked the maid and took pity on her, sending her off to find tea. Then she quickly dropped the blanket to wash.

Conall lumbered off the bed and came over to see if he could "help" with her ablutions. His assistance caused some giggling, and a lot of splashing, and a certain degree of wetness that was not necessarily water related. But she did manage to be safely enshrouded in her pelisse and to see him shoved off into his dressing chamber and under the tender ministrations of Tunstell's waistcoat choices before Angelique reappeared.

She sipped tea while the maid picked out a perfectly serviceable tweed day dress and underthings. She pulled these on in an apologetic silence, with not even a token complaint, figuring they had already put the poor woman's finer feelings through the wringer that morning.

She huffed a little as the corset went on. Angelique was merciless. Soon enough Alexia was seated, docile and dressed, while the Frenchwoman did her hair.

Angelique asked, "So, ze machine, iz it fixed?"

Alexia gave her a suspicious look through the mirror. "Yes, we believe so. But I wouldn't be too excited; Madame Lefoux shows no inclination to depart anytime soon."

Angelique made no reply.

Alexia was positively aquiver with the need to know the history between the two women but resigned herself to the fact that French caginess beat out British stubbornness, in this at least. So she sat in silence while the maid finished her work.

"Tell him this is good enough," came her husband's roar.

Lady Maccon stood and turned around.

Conall came striding in, trailed by the long-suffering Tunstell.

Lady Maccon looked at her husband with a critical eye.

"Your shirt is untucked, your cravat has no finish, and your collar is bent at one side." She stood and began fussing with his rumpled clothing.

"I dinna ken why I bother; you always side with him." Conall submitted to her ministrations with ill grace.

"Did you know your accent has gotten stronger since we arrived in Scotland?"

That got her a dour look. Lady Maccon rolled her eyes at Tunstell over Conall's shoulder and gestured with her head that he could leave.

"*We* didna arrive in Scotland. *I* arrived; *you* followed." He ran a finger under his high collar.

"Stop that—you'll dirty the white."

"Have I mentioned recently how loathsome I find the current fashions?"

"Take it up with the vampires; they set the trends."

"Hence the high collars," he grumbled. "I and mine, however, have no need to hide our necks."

"No," quipped his wife, "simply your personalities." She stepped back, brushing down the shawl collar of his waistcoat. "There. Very handsome."

Her large supernatural husband looked shy at that. "You think so?"

"Stop fishing for compliments and go get your jacket. I am positively starving."

He pulled her against him and administered a long, deep, and distracting kiss. "You are always hungry, wife."

"Mmm." She could not take umbrage with a true statement. "So are you. Simply for different things."

They were only slightly late for breakfast.

Most of the rest of the house was not yet up. Lady Kingair was there—Alexia wondered if the woman slept—and two claviers, but none of the Kingair Pack. Of course, Ivy and Felicity were still abed. They kept London hours, even in the country, and could not be expected to appear until midmorning. Tunstell, Lady Maccon suspected, would find things to occupy himself until the ladies came down.

The castle put on a decent breakfast, for the middle of nowhere. There were cold cuts of pork, venison, and woodcock; potted shrimp; fried wild mushrooms; sliced pears; boiled eggs and toast; as well as a nice collection of fruit preserves. Lady Maccon helped herself, then settled down to tuck in.

Lady Kingair, who was eating a bowl of unseasoned porridge and a piece of plain toast, gave Alexia's loaded plate a telling look. Alexia, who had never let the opinions of others sway her overmuch, especially where food was concerned, merely chewed loudly and with appreciative gusto.

Her husband shook his head at her antics, but as he himself sported a plate piled nearly twice as high as his wife's, he could not cast aspersions.

"If you are back to being human," Lady Maccon said after a pause, "you will get rotund eating like that."

"I shall have to take up some sort of abrasively atrocious athletic sport."

"You could go in for the hunt," suggested Alexia. "Tallyho and view halloo."

Werewolves, as a general rule, were not big on riding. Precious few horses were willing to carry a wolf on their back, even if he did look temporarily human. Driving a team was about as close as most werewolves could get. Since they could run faster in wolf form than a horse anyway, this fact did not tend to trouble the packs much. Except, of course, those men who had enjoyed riding before their metamorphosis.

Lord Maccon was not one of those men. "Foxhunting? I should think not," he said, gnawing on a bit of pork. "Foxes are practically cousins; wouldna sit well with the family, if you take my meaning."

"Oh, but how dashing you would look in shiny boots and one of those flashy red jackets."

"I was contemplating boxing or possibly lawn tennis."

Lady Maccon stifled a giggle by stuffing her face with a forkful of mushroom. The very idea of *her* husband prancing around all in white with a little netted baton in his hand. She swallowed. "Those sound like lovely ideas, dear," she said, deadpan, eyes bright and dancing. "Have you considered golf? Highly suited to your heritage and sense of style."

Conall glared at her, but there was a bit of a smile playing about his lips. "Now, now, wife, there's no cause for blatant insult."

Alexia was not certain whether she was insulting him by suggesting golf or insulting golf by suggesting he was its ideal participant.

Lady Kingair watched this byplay with both fascination and repugnance. "Goodness, I had heard it said that yours was a love match, but I couldna countenance it."

Lady Maccon huffed. "Why else would any woman marry him?"

"Or her," agreed Lord Maccon.

Something caught Alexia's attention out of the corner of one eye. Something small and moving near the door to the room. Taken with curiosity, she stood, arresting the table conversation, and went to investigate.

Upon closer examination, she squealed in a most un-Alexia-like manner and jumped away in horror. Lord Maccon leaped to her rescue.

Lady Maccon looked at her great-great-whatever-daughter-in-law. "Cockroaches!" she accused, horrified out of any politeness that dictated she not mention the filthiness of the abode. "Why does your castle have *cockroaches*?"

Lord Maccon, with great presence of mind, removed his shoe and went to crush the offending insect. He paused, examined it for a split second, and then squished it flat.

Lady Kingair turned to one of the clavigers. "How did that get in here?"

"Canna keep them confined, my lady. They seem to be breeding, they do."

"Then summon an exterminator."

The young man glanced furtively in Lord and Lady Maccon's direction. "Would he ken how to deal with"—a pause—"this particular type?"

"Only one way to find out. Hie yourself into town immediately."

"Very good, madam."

Alexia returned to the dining table, but her appetite had deserted her. She made to rise shortly thereafter.

Lord Maccon inhaled a few last bites and then took off after his wife, catching up to her in the hallway.

"That was not a cockroach, was it?" she asked.

"Aye. It wasna."

"Well?"

He shrugged, his big hands spread wide in confusion. "Strangely colored, all shiny."

"Oh, thank you for that."

"Why bother? 'Tis dead now."

"Point taken, husband. So, what are we planning for today?"

He nibbled a fingertip thoughtfully. "You know, I thought we might discern exactly why the supernatural isna working properly here."

"Oh, darling, what a unique and original idea."

He paused. The subject of Kingair's little affliction of humanity seemed not to actually be foremost in his mind. "Red jacket and shiny boots, you say?"

Lady Maccon looked at her husband, confused for a moment. Where was he going with this line of reasoning? "Boots are causing the illness?"

"No," he grumbled, shamefaced, "on me."

"Ah!" She grinned hugely. "I believe I might have mentioned something to that effect."

"Anything else?"

The grin widened. "Actually, I was envisioning boots, jacket, and nothing else at all. Mmm, perhaps just boots."

He swallowed, nervous.

She turned to him, upping the odds. "If you were to make this fashion event happen, I might be open to a little negotiating about which of us will be doing the riding."

Lord Maccon, werewolf of some two hundred years, blushed beet red at that. "I am eternally grateful you have not taken up gambling, my dear."

She wormed herself into his arms and raised her lips to be kissed. "Give me time."

CHAPTER ELEVEN

Chief Sundowner

That afternoon, Lord and Lady Maccon decided to take a walk. The rain had let up slightly, and it looked to be turning into a passable day, if not precisely pleasant. Lady Maccon decided she was in the country and could relax her standards slightly, so did not change into a walking dress, instead simply slipping on practical shoes.

Unfortunately for Lord and Lady Maccon, Miss Loontwill and Miss Hisselpenny decided to join them. This occasioned a wait while both ladies changed, but since Tunstell had made himself scarce, there was less competition than there might otherwise have been in this endeavor. Alexia was beginning to think they wouldn't get out of the house before teatime when both girls appeared sporting parasols and bonnets. This reminded Alexia to get her own parasol, causing yet another delay. Really, mobilizing an entire fleet for a great naval battle would probably have been easier.

Finally they set forth, but no sooner had they attained the small copse on the southern end of the grounds than they came across the Kingair Gamma, Lachlan, and Beta, Dubh, having some sort of heated argument in low, angry voices.

"Destroy it all," the Gamma was saying. "We canna continue ta live like this."

"Not until we ken to which and why."

The two men spotted the approaching party and fell silent.

Politeness dictated they join the larger group, and, with Felicity and Ivy's assistance, Alexia actually managed to get some semblance of polite conversation going. Both men were reluctant to say much at the best of times, and, clearly, the pack was under a gag order. However, such orders did not take into account the success with which sharp determination and frivolity could loosen the tongue.

"I know you gentlemen were on the front lines in India. How brave you must be, to fight primitives like that." Miss Hisselpenny widened her eyes and looked at the two men, hoping for tales of heroic bravery.

"Not much fighting left to do out there anymore. Simply some minor pacification of the locals," objected Lord Maccon.

Dubh gave him a dirty look. "And how would you know?"

"Oh, but what's it really like?" asked Ivy. "We get the stories in the papers now and again, but no real feel for the place."

"Hotter than hell's—"

Miss Hisselpenny gasped in anticipation of lewd talk.

Dubh civilized himself. "Well, hot."

"And the food doesna taste verra good," added Lachlan.

"Really?" That interested Alexia. Food always interested Alexia. "How perfectly ghastly."

"Even Egypt was better."

"Oh." Miss Hisselpenny's eyes went wide. "You were in Egypt too?"

"Of course they were in Egypt," Felicity said snidely. "Everyone knows it is one of the main ports for the empire these days. I have a passionate interest in the military, you know? I heard that most regiments have to stop over there."

"Oh, do they?" Ivy blinked, trying to comprehend the geographic reason behind this.

"And how did you find Egypt?" asked Alexia politely.

"Also hot," snapped Dubh.

"Seems to me most places would be, compared to Scotland," Lady Maccon snapped back.

"*You* chose to visit *us*," he reminded her.

"And you chose to go to Egypt." Alexia was not one to back down from a verbal battle.

"Not entirely. Pack service to Queen Victoria is mandatory." The conversation was getting tense.

"But it does not have to take the form of military service."

"We are not loners to slink about the homeland with tails twixt our legs." Dubh actually looked to Lord Maccon for assistance in dealing with his irascible wife. The earl merely winked at him.

Help came from an unlooked-for source. "I hear Egypt has some very nice, old"—Ivy was trying to keep matters civil—"stuff."

"Antiquities," added Felicity, proud of herself for knowing the word.

In a desperate attempt to keep Lady Maccon and the Beta from killing one another, Lachlan said, "We picked up quite a collection while we were there."

Dubh growled at his pack mate.

"Isn't that illegal?" Lord Maccon wondered softly in his BUR voice. No one paid him any attention, except for his wife, who pinched him.

She said, "Oh, really? What kind of artifacts?"

"A few bits of jewelry and some statuary to add to the pack vault and, of course, a couple of mummies."

Ivy gasped. "Real live mummies?"

Felicity snorted. "I should hope they are not alive." But even she seemed excited by the idea of mummies in residence. Alexia supposed that, in her sister's world, such things were considered glamorous.

Lady Maccon said, pressing her advantage, "We should have a mummy-unwrapping party. They are all the rage in London."

"Well, we shouldna want to be thought backward," said Lady Kingair's abrasive voice. She had come upon them all unnoticed, looking gray and severe. Lord Maccon, Lachlan, and Dubh all started upon hearing her speak. They were accustomed to having their supernatural sense of smell tell them when anyone approached, no matter how stealthily.

Sidheag turned to the Gamma. "Lachlan, get the clavigers to arrange it."

"Are you certain, my lady?" he questioned.

"We could do with a bit of fun. We wouldna want to disappoint the visiting ladies, now, would we? We are in possession of the mummies. Might as well unwrap them. We were after the amulets anyway."

"Oh, how thrilling," said Miss Hisselpenny, practically bouncing in her excitement.

"Which mummy, my lady?" asked Lachlan.

"The smaller one, with the more nondescript coverings."

"As you say." The Gamma hurried off to arrange for the event.

"Oh, I shall find this so very diverting," crowed Felicity. "You know Elsie Flinders-Pooke was lording it over me just last week that she had been to an unwrapping. Imagine what she will say when I tell her I experienced one in a haunted castle in the Scottish Highlands."

"How do you know Kingair is haunted?"

"I know because, obviously, it *must* be haunted. You could not possibly convince me otherwise. No ghosts have appeared since we arrived, but that is no proof to the contrary," Felicity defended her future tall tale.

"Delighted we could provide you with some significant social coup," sneered Lady Kingair.

"Your pleasure, I'm sure," replied Felicity.

"My sister is a woman of mean understanding," explained Lady Maccon apologetically.

"And what are you?" asked Sidheag.

"Oh, I am simply mean."

"And here I was, thinking you were the sister with the understanding."

"Not just yet. Give me time."

They turned around and headed back toward the castle. Lord Maccon moved to draw his wife back slightly so they could converse privately.

"You believe one of the artifacts to be a humanization weapon?"

She nodded.

"But how would we know which one?"

"You may have to come allover BUR on the Kingair Pack and simply confiscate all their collected antiquities as illegal imports."

"And then what? See them all incinerated?"

Lady Maccon frowned. She fancied herself a bit of a scholar and was not generally in favor of wanton destruction. "I had not thought to take things quite so far."

"It would be a terrible destruction, and I should be opposed, save that we canna simply have these things wandering around the empire. Imagine if they fell into the wrong hands?"

"Such as the Hypocras Club?" Lady Maccon shuddered to even think it.

"Or the vampires." No matter how integrated the two became into civilized society, werewolves and vampires would never really trust one another.

Lady Maccon stopped suddenly. Her husband got four long strides ahead before he realized she had paused. She was staring thoughtfully up into the aether, twirling the deadly parasol about her head.

"I have just remembered something," Alexia said when he returned to her side.

"Oh, that explains everything. How foolish of me to think you could walk and remember at the same time."

She stuck her tongue out at him but began drifting toward the house once more. He slowed to match her pace. "That bug, the one that scared me at breakfast. It was not a cockroach at all. It was a scarab beetle. From Egypt. It must have something to do with the artifacts they brought back."

Lord Maccon's lip curled. "Yuck."

They had fallen some distance behind the rest of the party. The others were busy entering the castle just as someone else emerged. There was a pause while they all politely greeted one another, and then the new figure headed purposefully in the direction of Lord and Lady Maccon.

The figure rapidly resolved itself into the personage of Madame Lefoux.

Alexia waved a "how do you do" at the Frenchwoman. She was wearing her beautiful morning coat of dove-gray, striped trousers, a black satin waistcoat, and a royal-blue cravat. It made for a pretty picture, the Kingair castle—mist-shrouded and gray in the background— and the attractive woman, as improperly dressed as she may be, hurrying toward them. Until Madame Lefoux neared enough for them to realize she was also wearing something else: a concerned expression.

"I am glad I 'ave found you two." Her accent was unusually strong. She sounded almost as bad as Angelique. "Ze most extraordinary thing, Lady Maccon. I waz looking for you just now to let you know, we went to check on the aethographor; then I saw—"

The most tremendous clap resounded through the Scottish air. Alexia felt certain she could see the mist shake with the noise. Madame Lefoux, her face changing from worry to surprise, stopped midsentence and mid-step and tumbled forward, as limp as overcooked pasta. A bloom of red appeared on one immaculate gray lapel.

Lord Maccon caught the inventor before she could fall completely to the ground and carefully lowered her there instead. He held his hand briefly before her mouth to see if she was breathing. "She is still alive." Alexia quickly pulled her shawl from about her shoulders and handed it to him to use as a bandage. No sense in his spoiling the last of his good cravats.

Alexia looked up at the castle, scoping the battlements for a glint of sun on a rifle barrel, but there were too many battlements and there was too little sun. The sharpshooter, whoever he might be, was not visible.

"Get down this instant, woman," ordered her husband, grabbing her by one skirt ruffle and yanking her down next to the fallen Frenchwoman. The ruffle ripped. "We dinna know if the shooter was aiming at her or at us," he growled.

"Where's your precious pack? Shouldn't they be hightailing it to our rescue?"

"How do you ken it isna them shooting?" her husband wondered.

"Good point." Lady Maccon shifted her open parasol defensively so that it shielded them as much as possible from sight of the castle.

Another shot rang out. It hit the ground next to them, splattering turf and small pebbles.

"Next time," grumbled the earl, "I shall pay extra and have that thing made with metal shielding."

"Oh, that will be tremendously practical for hot summer afternoons. Come on, we need to find cover," hissed his wife. "I shall leave the parasol propped here as a diversion."

"Break for that hedge?" suggested Conall, looking over to their right, where a little berm covered in wild roses seemed to be the Kingair formal garden hedge substitute.

Alexia nodded.

Lord Maccon hoisted the Frenchwoman over one shoulder easily. He might no longer have superhuman strength, but he was still strong.

They dashed toward the berm.

Another shot rang forth.

Only then did they hear yelling. Alexia peeked around the rosebush. Members of the pack poured out of the castle, looking about for the source of the shooting. Several yelled and pointed up. Clavigers and pack reentered the castle at a run.

Lord and Lady Maccon stayed hidden until they were convinced that no one would be taking any more shots at them. Then they emerged from behind the bushes. Lord Maccon carried Madame Lefoux, and Lady Maccon retrieved her parasol.

Upon attaining the house, it was found that Madame Lefoux was in no serious medical danger but had simply fainted from the wound, her shoulder badly gouged by the bullet.

Ivy appeared. "Oh dear, has something untoward ensued? Everyone is gesticulating." Upon catching sight of the comatose form of Madame Lefoux, she added, "Has she come over nonsensical?" At the sight of the blood, Ivy became rather breathless and looked near to fainting herself. Nevertheless, she trailed them into the back parlor, unhelpfully offering to help and interrupting, as they lowered Madame Lefoux to the small settee, with, "She hasn't caught a slight fatality, has she?"

"What happened?" demanded Lady Kingair, ignoring Ivy and Felicity, who had also entered the room.

"Someone seems to have decided to dispose of Madame Lefoux," Lady Maccon said, bustling about ordering bandages and vinegar. Alexia believed that a generous application of cider vinegar could cure most ills, except, of course, for those bacterial disorders that required bicarbonate of soda.

Felicity decided to immediately absent herself from any possible associated danger via proximity to Madame Lefoux. Which, as it absented everyone else from her, was no bad thing.

Only Lady Kingair had the wherewithal to respond. "Good Lord, why? She's naught more than a two-bit French inventor."

Alexia thought she saw the Frenchwoman twitch at that. Was Madame Lefoux shamming? Alexia leaned in on the pretext of checking bandages. She caught a whiff of vanilla, mixed with the coppery smell of blood this time instead of mechanical oil. The inventor remained absolutely still under Alexia's gentle ministrations. Not even her eyelids moved. If she was shamming, she was very, very good at it.

Lady Maccon glanced toward the door and thought she caught a flicker of servant black. Angelique's white, horrified face peeked around the corner. Before Alexia could summon her in, the maid disappeared.

"An excellent question. Perhaps she will be so kind as to tell us once she has awakened," Lady Maccon said, once more watching Madame Lefoux's face. No reaction to that statement.

Unfortunately for everyone's curiosity, Madame Lefoux did not awaken, or did not allow herself to be awakened, for the entirety of the rest of the afternoon. Despite the assiduous attentions of Lord and Lady Maccon, half the Kingair Pack, and several clavigers, her eyes remained stubbornly shut.

Lady Maccon took her tea in the sickroom, hoping the smell of baked goods would awaken Madame Lefoux. All that resulted was that Lady Kingair came to join her. Alexia had settled into not liking this relation of her husband's, but she had not the constitution that would allow for anything to interfere with her consumption of tea.

"Has our patient awakened yet?" inquired Lady Kingair.

"She remains dramatically abed." Alexia frowned into her cup. "I do hope nothing is seriously wrong with her. Should we call a doctor, do you think?"

"I've seen and tended to much worse on the battlefield."

"You go with the regiment?"

"I may not be a werewolf, but I'm Alpha female for this pack. My place is with them, even if I dinna fight alongside."

Alexia selected a scone from the tea tray and plopped a dollop of cream and marmalade on top of it. "Did you side with the pack when they betrayed my husband?" she asked in forced casualness.

"He told you about it."

Lady Maccon nodded and ate a bite of scone.

"I was just sixteen when he left, away at finishing school. I didna have a say in the pack's choices."

"And now?"

"Now? Now I ken they all behaved like fools. You dinna piss up-wind."

Alexia winced at the vulgarity of the statement.

Sidheag sipped her tea, relishing the effect of her barracks language on her guest. "Queen Victoria might not chase the tails of a werewolf agenda, but she isna bleeding to the vampire fang either. She's no Henry or Elizabeth to be throwing her support full tilt behind the supernatural cause, but she hasna been as bad as we'd feared either. Perhaps she doesna watch the scientists as careful as she might, and she sure plays us close and fast, but I dinna think she is the worst monarch we could be having."

Lady Maccon wondered if Sidheag was attempting to guarantee the pack's safety or if the woman was talking truth. "Do you consider yourself a progressive, then, like my husband?"

"I'm saying, everyone handled the incident poorly. An Alpha abandoning his pack is extreme. Conall ought to have killed all the ringleaders, not just the Beta, and restructured. I love this pack, and to leave it leaderless and turn to a *London* pack instead is worse than death. It was a national embarrassment, what your husband did." Lady Kingair leaned forward, eyes fierce. She was close enough for Alexia to see that her graying hair, pulled tightly back into a braid, was frizzing slightly in the humid air.

"I thought he left them Niall?"

"Na. I brought Niall back with me. He was naught more than a loner I met abroad. Handsome and dashing, just what all schoolroom misses want in a husband. I thought I'd be bringing him home to meet the pack and gramps, get permission, and post the bans. Only to find the old wolf gone and the pack in shambles."

"You took on the responsibility of leadership?"

Sidheag sipped her tea. "Niall was an excellent soldier and a good husband, but he'd have made a better Beta. He took on Alpha for my sake." She rubbed at her eyes with two fingers. "He was a good man, and a good wolf, and he did his best. I willna speak against him."

Alexia knew enough about herself to realize she couldn't have taken on leadership like that so young, and she considered herself a capable person. No wonder Sidheag was bitter.

"And now?"

"Now we're even worse off. Niall killed in battle and no one able enough to take Alpha role, let alone be Alpha in truth. And I'm knowing full well Gramps willna come back to us. Marrying you cemented that. We've lost him for good."

Lady Maccon sighed. "Regardless, you need to trust him. You should take your concerns to him and talk this out. He will see reason. I know he will. And he will help you find a solution."

Lady Kingair put her cup down with a sharp clatter. "There is only one solution. And he willna take it. I have written and asked every year for the last decade, and time is running out."

"What is that?"

"He needs to see me changed."

Lady Maccon sat back, puffing out her cheeks. "But that is so very perilous. I do not have the statistics on hand, but aren't the odds completely against a woman surviving the metamorphosis bite?"

Lady Kingair shrugged. "No one has tried in hundreds of years. 'Tis one of the ways packs beat out hives. At least we dinna need females to sustain ourselves."

"Yes, but vampires still manage to survive longer—less fighting. Even if you do survive the bite, you're setting yourself up to Alpha for the rest of your life."

"Hang the danger!" Sidheag Maccon practically yelled. Alexia thought the woman had never looked more like Conall. Her eyes also turned toward yellow when she was overset with extreme emotion.

"And you want Conall to do this for you? Risk killing off the last of his living relatives?"

"For me, for the pack. I'm na having any bairns at my age. He willna be able to continue the Maccon line through me. He's needing to move on from that. He owes Kingair some kind of salvation."

"You'll likely die." Lady Maccon poured herself another spot of tea. "You have held this pack together as a human."

"And what happens after I die of old age? Better to take the risk now."

Alexia was silent. Finally she said, "Oddly enough, I agree with your assessment."

Lady Kingair stopped drinking her tea and simply clutched the saucer for a long moment, fingertips white with tension. "Would *you* talk to him for me?"

"You want me to involve myself in Kingair's problems? Is that wise? Couldn't you simply go to another pack's Alpha for the bite?"

"Never!" There went that stiff werewolf pride, or was it Scottish pride? Difficult to tell the difference sometimes.

Alexia sighed. "I will discuss it with him, but it is a moot point: Conall cannot bite you or anyone else to change, as he cannot take Anubis Form. Until we find out why this pack is changeless, nothing else can happen. No Alpha challenge, no metamorphosis."

Lady Kingair nodded, relaxing her grip enough to sip at her tea once more.

Alexia noted that the woman did not crook her finger properly.

What kind of finishing school had she been sent to, where they did not teach the basics of teacup holding? She cocked her head. "Is this humanization plague some kind of foolish self-flagellation? Do you want to take the rest of the pack with you into mortality because my husband will not bite you to metamorphosis?"

Lady Kingair's tawny eyes, so much like Conall's, narrowed at that. "It isna my fault," she practically yelled. "Dinna you understand? *We* canna tell you because we *dinna ken* why this has happened to us. I dinna know. None of us know. We dinna ken what's doing it!"

"So can I count on your support to figure it out?" Alexia asked.

"What's it to you, Lady Maccon?"

Alexia backpedaled hurriedly. "I encourage my husband's BUR concerns. It keeps him out of household affairs. And I am interested in these things, as a new Alpha of my own pack. If you have some kind of dangerous disease, I should very much like to understand it fully and prevent it from spreading."

"If he agrees to try for my metamorphosis, I'll agree to help."

Knowing she couldn't make any such promise on her husband's behalf, Lady Maccon nevertheless said, "Done! Now, shall we finish our tea?"

They finished drinking in companionable discussion of the Women's Social and Political Union, whose stance both ladies supported but whose tactics and working-class routes neither was inclined to ally with publicly. Lady Maccon refrained from commenting that, from her more intimate knowledge of Queen Victoria's character, she could practically guarantee that lady's continued low opinion of the movement. She could not make such a statement, however, without revealing her own political position. Even an earl's wife would not be on such intimate terms with the queen, and she did not wish Lady Kingair to know that she was muhjah. Not yet.

Their pleasant conversation was interrupted by a knock at the parlor door.

At Lady Kingair's call, Tunstell's copious freckles came wandering in, attached to a somber-looking Tunstell.

"Lord Maccon sent me to sit with the patient, Lady Maccon."

Alexia nodded her understanding. Worried and unsure of whom to trust, Lord Maccon was placing Tunstell as a surety against further attacks on Madame Lefoux's person. Essentially, her husband was utilizing Tunstell's claviger training. Tunstell may look like a git of the first water, but he could handle werewolves in full-moon thrall. Of course, that meant both Ivy and Felicity were soon likely to take up residence in the sickroom as well. Poor Tunstell. Miss Hisselpenny was still convinced she did not want him, but she was equally convinced she must protect him from Felicity's wickedness. Lady Maccon felt that the presence of both women would provide a better defense than anything else. It was hard to get up to serious shenanigans under the enthusiastic interest of two perennially bored, unmarried ladies.

Eventually, however, it became necessary for everyone but Tunstell to leave the still-unconscious Frenchwoman and dress for dinner.

Upon attaining her chamber, Lady Maccon received her second major shock of the day. It was a good thing she was a woman of stalwart character. Someone had upended her room. Again. Probably looking for the dispatch case. Shoes and slippers were everywhere, and the bed had been torn apart; even the mattress was slashed open. Feathers coated flat surfaces like so much snow. Hatboxes lay broken, hats disemboweled, and the contents of Alexia's wardrobe lay strewn across the floor (a condition familiar to only the nightgowns).

Alexia propped her parasol safely to one side and took stock of the situation. The chaos was greater than it had been on board the dirigible, and the crisis was compounded shortly thereafter when Lord Maccon discovered the carnage.

"This is a gross outrage! First we are shot at, and now our rooms are ransacked," he roared.

"Does this kind of thing always happen around a pack without an Alpha?" wondered his wife, nosing about, trying to determine if anything significant was missing.

The earl grunted at her. "A terrible bother, leaderless packs."

"And messy." Lady Maccon picked her way delicately about the room. "I wonder if this was the information Madame Lefoux had to impart before she was shot. She said something about trying to find me regarding the aethographor. Perhaps she disturbed the culprits in action when she came looking for me here." Alexia began to form three piles: things beyond salvation, items for Angelique to repair, and the undamaged.

"But why would someone shoot at her?"

"Perhaps she saw their faces?"

The earl pursed his well-formed lips. "It is possible. Come here, woman; stop your fussing. The dinner bell is about to go, and I'm hungry. We shall tidy later."

"Bossy britches," said his wife, but she did as she was bid. It wouldn't do to get into an argument with him on an empty stomach.

He helped her unbutton her dress, so well distracted by the day's proceedings that he only fluttered kisses down her spine and did not even nibble. "What do you believe they were looking for? Your dispatch case again?"

"Difficult to know. Could be someone else, I suppose. I mean, not the same miscreant as when I was floating." Alexia was confused. Initially, on board the dirigible, she had suspected Madame Lefoux, but that lady had been asleep and in company all day long. Unless the inventor managed it before she was shot at, this chaos must be attributed to someone else. A different spy with a different motive? Things certainly were getting complicated.

"What else might they be looking for? Did you bring something I should know about, husband?"

Lord Maccon said nothing, but when Alexia turned about and gave him the wifely eye of suspicion, he looked like a guilty sheepdog. He left off unbuttoning and went to the window. Throwing aside the shutters, he stuck his head far out, reached around, retrieved something, and returned to her side with a look of relief, carrying a small package wrapped in oiled leather.

"Conall," said his wife, "*what* is that?"

He unwrapped and showed her: a strange chubby little revolver with a square grip. He clicked open the chamber to display its armament: hardwood bullets inlaid with silver in a cagelike pattern and capped to take the powder explosion. Alexia wasn't big on guns, but she knew enough about the mechanics to realize this little creature was expensive to make, used only the most modern technology, and was capable of taking down either a vampire or a werewolf.

"A Galand Tue Tue. This is the Sundowner model," he explained.

Lady Maccon took her husband's face in her hands. His skin was rough with a day's growth of beard; she would have to remind him to shave, now that he was human all the time. "Husband, you are not here to kill someone, are you? I should hate to find out that you and I were working at cross purposes."

"Simply a precautionary measure, my love, I assure you."

She was not convinced. Her fingers tightened about his jaw. "When did you start carrying the deadliest supernatural weapon known to the British Empire as a *precaution*?"

"Professor Lyall had Tunstell bring it for me. He guessed I'd be mortal while I was here and thought I might want the added security."

Alexia let go of his face and watched as he wrapped the deadly little device back up and returned it to its hidey-hole just outside the window.

"How easy is that to use?" she asked, all innocence.

"Dinna even consider it, wife. You've got that parasol of yours."

She pouted. "You are no fun as a mortal."

"So," he said, deliberately changing the subject, "where did you hide your dispatch case, then?"

She grinned, pleased that he would not think her so feeble as to have kept it where it could be stolen. "In the least likely place, of course."

"Of course. And are you going to tell me where?"

She widened her large brown eyes at him, batting her eyelashes and attempting to look innocent.

"What is in it that someone might want?"

"That's the odd thing. I really have no idea. I took the smallest things out and stashed them in my parasol. So far as I can tell, there is nothing too valuable left: the royal seal; my notes and paperwork on this latest issue with the humanization plague, minus my personal journal, which got pinched; the codes to various aethographors; a stash of emergency tea; and a small bag of gingersnaps."

Her husband gave her his version of the *look*.

Lady Maccon defended herself. "You would not believe how long those Shadow Council meetings are prone to running, and being as the dewan and the potentate are supernatural, they don't seem to notice when it's teatime."

"Well I hardly think anyone is ransacking our rooms in a desperate bid to acquire gingersnaps."

"They are very *good* gingersnaps."

"I suppose it could be something other than the dispatch case?"

Lady Maccon shrugged. "This is useless speculation for the time being. Here, help me on with this. Where is Angelique?"

In the absence of the maid, Lord Maccon buttoned his wife up into her dinner dress. It was a gray and cream affair with a multitude of pleated gathers all up the front and a long, rather demure ruffle at the hem. Alexia liked the gown, except that it had a cravatlike bow at the neck, and she wasn't entirely behind this latest fashion for incorporating masculine elements into women's garb. Then again, there was Madame Lefoux.

Which reminded her that, since Tunstell was on French-inventor guard detail, she would have to help her husband dress. It was a mild disaster: his cravat came out lopsided and his collar limp. Alexia was resigned. She had, after all, been a spinster most of her life, and cravat-tying was not a proficiency generally acquired by spinsters.

"Husband," she said as they finished their preparations and headed downstairs for dinner, "have you considered biting your many-times great-granddaughter to change?"

Lord Maccon stopped abruptly at the head of the staircase and growled, "How on God's green earth did that bloody woman persuade *you* to *her* cause?"

Alexia sighed. "It makes sense, and it is an elegant solution to

Kingair's current problems. She is already acting like an Alpha; why not make it official?"

"It isna as simple as that, wife, and you verra well know it. And her chances of survival—"

"Are very slim. Yes, I am well aware of that."

"Not simply slim—they are beyond salvation. You are essentially suggesting that I kill the last living Maccon."

"But if she survived . . ."

"If."

Lady Maccon tilted her head. "Isn't it her risk to take?"

He remained silent and continued on down the massive staircase.

"You should think about it, Conall, as BUR, if nothing else. It is the most logical course of action."

He kept on walking. There was something about the set of his shoulders.

"Wait a moment." She was suddenly suspicious. "That was the reason you came back here all along, wasn't it? The family problem. You intend to fix the Kingair Pack? Despite the betrayal."

He shrugged.

"You wanted to see how Sidheag was handling things. Well?"

"There's this changeless issue," he prevaricated.

Alexia grinned. "Yes, well, apart from that. You must agree I have a point."

He turned to frown up at her. "I hate it when you come over all correct."

Alexia trotted down the staircase until they were nose to nose. She had to stand one step up from him for it to be so. She kissed him softly. "I know. But I am so very good at it."

CHAPTER TWELVE

The Great Unwrapping

They decided the mummy would be unwrapped, for the titillation of the ladies, just after dinner. Alexia was not convinced as to the cleverness of this plan. Knowing Miss Hisselpenny's constitution, if the mummy were gruesome enough, dinner might just be revisited. But it was believed that darkness and candlelight best suited such an illustrious event.

None of the ladies present had ever before been to a mummy-unwrapping party. Lady Maccon expressed some distress that Madame Lefoux and Tunstell would be missing the fun. Lord Maccon suggested that as he had little interest and he would go relieve Tunstell, thus allowing the claviger at least to participate. Tunstell, everyone knew, enjoyed drama.

Alexia looked sharply at Miss Hisselpenny, but Ivy held herself composed and untroubled by the possibility of a redheaded thespian and naked mummy in the same room. Felicity licked her lips in anticipation, and Lady Maccon prepared herself for inevitable histrionics. But it was she, not Felicity or Ivy, who felt most uncomfortable in the presence of the ancient creature.

Truth be told, it was a rather sad-looking mummy. It resided in a not-very-big boxlike coffin that had only minimal hieroglyphic decorations upon it. Once removed from the coffin, the wrappings on the mummy were revealed to be minimally painted with one repeated motif: what looked to be an ankh, broken. The dead thing did not disgust or frighten Alexia in any way, and she had seen mummies before in museums without desultory effects. But there was something about this particular mummy that, simply put, repulsed her.

Lady Maccon was not given to bouts of sentimentality, so she did not think her reaction an emotional one. No, she was being literally repulsed, in the scientific definition of the word. It was as though she and the mummy both had some kind of magnetic field, and they were the same charge, with forces violently repelling one another.

The actual unwrapping seemed to take an exceptionally long time. Who knew there would be so dreadfully many bandages? They also kept breaking. Every time an amulet was uncovered, the whole operation stopped and people gasped in delight. As more and more of the mummy was revealed, Alexia found herself instinctively backing toward the door of the room, until she was at the fringe of the crowd, standing on tiptoe to witness the proceedings.

Being soulless, Alexia had never given death much consideration. After all, for preternaturals like her, death was the end—she had nothing whatsoever to look forward to. In BUR's special documentation vaults, an inquisition pamphlet lamented the fact that preternaturals, the church's last best weapon against the supernatural threat, were also the only human beings who could never be saved. What Alexia felt, most of the time, was indifference to her own mortality. This was the result of an ingrained practicality that was also due to her soullessness. But there was something about this mummy that troubled her even as it repulsed: the poor, sad, wrinkled thing.

Finally they worked their way up to his head, exposing a perfectly preserved skull with dark brown skin and some small portion of hair still adhered to it. Amulets were removed from ears, nose, throat, and eyes, revealing the empty eye sockets and slightly gaping mouth. Several scarab beetles crawled out of the exposed orifices, plopped to the floor, and skittered about. At which both Felicity and Ivy, who had until that moment remained only mildly hysterical, fainted.

Tunstell caught Miss Hisselpenny, clutching her close to his breast and murmuring her given name in tones of marked distress. Lachlan caught Miss Loontwill and was nowhere near as affectionate about it. Two sets of expensive skirts draped themselves artistically in ruffled disarray. Two sets of bosoms heaved in heart-palpitating distress.

The evening's entertainment was pronounced a definitive success.

The gentlemen, marshaled into action by Lady Kingair's barked commands, carried the two young ladies into a sitting room down the hall. There the ladies were duly revived with smelling salts, and rosewater was patted across the brow.

Alexia was left alone with the unfortunate mummy, unwitting cause of all the excitement. Even the scarab beetles had scuttled off. She cocked her head to one side, resisting the insistent push, which seemed even worse now that there was only the two of them. It was as though the very air were trying to drive her from the room. Alexia narrowed her eyes at the mummy, something niggling the back of her brain. Whatever it was, she could not recall it. Turning away, still thinking hard, she made her way into the other room.

Only to find Tunstell kissing Miss Hisselpenny, who was apparently wide awake and participating with gusto. Right there in front of everyone.

"Well, I say!" said Alexia. She had not thought Ivy possessed that degree of gumption. Apparently, she was finding Tunstell's kisses less damp than she had previously.

Felicity blinked awake, probably desirous to see what had pulled everyone's attention so thoroughly away from her own prostrate form. She caught sight of the embrace and gasped, joining Alexia in amazement. "Why, Mr. Tunstell, what *are* you doing?"

"That should be perfectly clear, even to you, Miss Loontwill," Lady Kingair snapped, not nearly so scandalized as she ought.

"Well," said Alexia, "I take it you are feeling more the thing?"

No one answered her. Ivy was still occupied with kissing Tunstell. It appeared there might even be tongue involved at this juncture. And Felicity was still occupied watching them with all the good-humored interest of an irritated chicken.

The touching scene was broken by Lord Maccon's fantastically loud yell, which welled suddenly forth from the downstairs front parlor. It was not one of his angry yells either. Lady Maccon would hardly have bestirred herself for one of those. No, this yell sounded like pain.

Alexia was out the door and galloping pell-mell down the staircase, heedless of the very real danger to her delicate apparel, waving her parasol about madly.

She crashed into the parlor door, which refused to budge. Something heavy was blocking it. She heaved against it desperately, finally shoving it open far enough to find that it was her husband's fallen body that blocked her entrance.

She bent over him, checking for injuries. She could find none on his back, so with prodigious effort, she rolled him over, checking his front. He was breathing slowly and laboriously, as though drugged.

Alexia paused, frowning suspiciously at her parasol, lying near her at the ready. *The tip opens and emits a poisoned dart equipped with a numbing agent,* she heard Madame Lefoux's voice say in her head. How easy, then, would it be to create a sleeping agent? A quick glance about the room showed Madame Lefoux was still unconscious but otherwise undamaged.

Lady Kingair, Dubh, and Lachlan appeared at the door. Lady Maccon held up a hand indicating she was not to be disturbed and stripped her husband bare to the waist, examining him more closely, not for injuries but for . . . aha!

"There it is." A small puncture wound just below his left shoulder.

She pushed her way through the crowd at the door and yelled up the stairs, "Tunstell, you revolting blighter!" In Woolsey Castle, such affectionate terminology for the claviger meant for him to come quickly, and come armed. Lord Maccon's idea.

She turned back into the room and marched over to the prone form of Madame Lefoux. "If this is your fault," she hissed to the still-apparently-comatose woman, "I shall see you hanged as a spy; you see if I don't." Heedless of the others listening and watching in avid interest, she added, "And you know very well I have the power to do so."

Madame Lefoux lay as still as death.

Tunstell muscled his way into the room and immediately bent over his fallen master, reaching to check his breath.

"He is alive."

"Barely," replied Alexia. "Where did you—"

"What has happened?" interrupted Lady Kingair impatiently.

"He has been put to sleep, some kind of poisoned dart. Tincture of valerian perhaps," explained Lady Maccon without looking up.

"Goodness, how remarkable."

"Woman's weapon, poison." Dubh sniffed.

"I beg your pardon!" replied Lady Maccon. "None of that, or you shall meet the blunt end of *my* preferred weapon, and let me assure you, it isn't poison."

Dubh wisely beat a retreat to avoid offending the lady further.

"You will have to leave off your tender ministrations of Miss Hisselpenny's delicate constitution for the moment, Tunstell." Lady Maccon stood and strode purposefully to the door. "If you will excuse us," she said to the assembled Kingair Pack. Then she shut them firmly out of their own front parlor. Terribly rude, of course, but sometimes circumstances required rudeness, and there was simply nothing else for it. Luckily, under such circumstances, Alexia Maccon was always equal to the task.

She proceeded on to another unpardonably rude offense. Leaving Tunstell to see her husband comfortable—which he did by dragging the earl's massive frame over to another small couch, then folding him onto it before covering him with a large plaid blanket—Lady Maccon marched over and began stripping Madame Lefoux of her garments.

Tunstell did not ask, only turned his head away and tried not to look. Alexia did this carefully, feeling about and checking every layer and fold for hidden gadgets and possible weapons. The Frenchwoman did not stir, although Alexia could have sworn the woman's breath quickened. By the end, Alexia had a fine pile of objects, some of them familiar: a pair of glassicals, an aether transponder cable, an encephalic valve, but most of them unknown to her. She knew Madame Lefoux normally boasted a dart emitter, because she'd said she used it during the fight on board the dirigible. But none of the objects in the pile looked to be such a device, even disguised as something else. Had it been stolen? Or had Madame Lefoux used it on Conall and then contrived to hide it somewhere else?

Lady Maccon slid her hands under the sleeping woman. Nothing there. Then she tucked them down Madame Lefoux's side where it rested against the back of the settee. Still nothing. Then she looked under and behind the couch. If the inventor had hidden it, she had done so quite thoroughly.

With a sigh, Lady Maccon set about putting the Frenchwoman's clothing back together again. It was odd to think, but she had never before seen another woman's naked body until now. She must admit Madame Lefoux did have a rather nice one. Not so well endowed as Alexia's own, of course, but trim and tidy with neat small breasts. It was a good thing the inventor opted for masculine garb, she reflected, as it was much easier to manage. Once the task was completed, Lady Maccon's hands were trembling slightly—from embarrassment, of course.

"Keep a close eye on her, Tunstell. I shall return directly." With that, Lady Maccon stood and marched out of the room, shutting the door behind her and ignoring the Kingair Pack, still milling about confusedly in the vestibule. She went immediately upstairs and inside her bedchamber. Angelique was already there, rummaging about.

"Out," she said to the maid.

Angelique bobbed a curtsy and scurried away.

Lady Maccon went directly to the window and, standing on tiptoe, reached around for Conall's precious little oiled leather package. It was well beyond her reach, stashed behind a jutting brick. Impatient, she balanced on the sill precariously, bemoaning her overly skirted state, bustle squeezing up tight against the side of the window. Despite the hazardous position, she managed to grab hold of the package without mishap.

Unwrapping the little weapon, she stashed it under her ridiculous lace cap, nested among her copious dark curls, and marched on to Ivy's room to retrieve her dispatch case.

Ivy was lying in half-faint, half-flutter on her bed.

"Oh, Alexia, thank goodness. What am I to do? This is such a terrible crisis of apex proportions. Such palpitations of the heart. Did you see? Oh, of course you saw. He kissed me, right there in public. I am *ruined!*" She sat up. "Yet I love him." She flopped back. "Yet I am ruined. Oh, woe is me."

"Did you actually just utter the phrase 'woe is me'? I'm just going to, uh, check on those socks."

Miss Hisselpenny was not to be distracted from her majestic problems. The removal of the dispatch case, not to mention her friend's militant expression, went unnoticed.

"He told me he would love me forever."

Lady Maccon flipped through the various stacks of papers and rolls of parchments inside her case, looking for her muhjah letter of marque. Where had she put the bedamned thing?

"He said that this was the true, the one, the only."

Lady Maccon gave a noncommittal murmur at that. What else could one say to such folderol?

Miss Hisselpenny, unconcerned by a lack of response, continued to bemoan her fate. "And I love him. I really and truly do. You could never understand this type of love, Alexia. Not such true love as ours. Marrying for practical gain is all very well and good, but this . . . this is the real thing."

Lacy Maccon tilted her head in sham surprise. "Is that what I did?"

Ivy continued without acknowledgment. "But we cannot possibly marry."

Alexia continued to rummage. "Mmm, no, I see that."

That made Miss Hisselpenny sit up and look daggers down at her friend. "Really, Alexia, you are not being even remotely helpful."

Lady Maccon remembered she had transferred her most important papers to her parasol after the first break-in and quickly snapped the dispatch case shut, locked it, and tucked it back behind Ivy's stack of hatboxes.

"Ivy, my dear, I am terribly sympathetic to your plight. Honestly, I am, most sincerely. But you must excuse me. Necessity demands I handle a situation downstairs rather hurriedly."

Miss Hisselpenny flopped back onto the bed, hand to her head. "Oh, what kind of friend are you, Alexia Maccon? Here I lie, in crisis and abject suffering. This is the worst evening of my whole life, you realize? And *you* care only for your husband's lucky socks!" She flipped over and buried her head in the pillow.

Alexia departed the room before Ivy could come up with further histrionics.

Most of the pack still stood outside the parlor door, looking confused. Alexia glared at them with her best Lady Maccon glare, opened the door, and shut it once more in their faces.

She handed the gun to Tunstell, who took it but swallowed nervously.

"You know what this is?"

He nodded. "Tue Tue Sundowner. But why would I need it? There are no vampires here, or werewolves for that matter. Not with the way things currently stand."

"They are not going to stand like this for much longer, not if I have anything to say about it. Poison does not work on a werewolf, and I intend to see my husband wide awake sooner than it would take for that stuff, whatever it may be, to run its course through a human system. Besides, that deadly little gun will work just as well on daylight folk. Are you authorized to use it?"

Tunstell shook his head slowly. His freckles stood out starkly on his white face.

"Well, you are now."

Tunstell looked like he would like to argue the point. Sundowner was a BUR position. Technically the muhjah had no real say in the matter. But his mistress was looking dreadfully belligerent, and he had no wish to try her patience.

She pointed an autocratic finger at him. "No one is to come in or out of this room. *No one*, Tunstell. No staff, no pack, no claviger, not even Miss Hisselpenny. Speaking of which, I really must insist you refrain from embracing her in public. It is most discomforting to watch." Her nose wrinkled slightly.

Tunstell flushed at that, his freckles fading under the red, but he kept to the main point. "What are you going to do now, my lady?"

Lady Maccon glanced up at the grandfather clock ticking sonorously in the corner of the room. "Send an aetherogram, and soon. This is all getting terribly out of hand."

"To whom?"

She shook her head, hair falling down now that she wore no cap. "Just you do your job, Tunstell, and let me do mine. I will want to know immediately if either of them awaken or worsen. Understood?"

The redhead nodded.

She scooped up the large pile of Madame Lefoux's gadgets, stuffing them into her lace cap as a kind of bag. Her hair was loose about her face, but sometimes one must sacrifice appearance to cope with trying circumstances. Grasping the cap of booty in one hand and her parasol in the other, she exited the parlor, pulling the door firmly closed with her foot.

"I am afraid I must inform you, Lady Kingair, that no one is to go in or out of that room, including yourself, for the foreseeable future. I have left Tunstell exceedingly well armed and with strict instructions to fire on any who attempt to enter. You would not want to test his obedience to me, now, would you?"

"Under whose authority have you done this? The earl's?" Lady Kingair was shocked.

"My husband has become"—Alexia paused—"indisposed at the moment. So, no, this is no longer a BUR matter. I have taken it under my own jurisdiction. I have tolerated this shilly-shallying and hedging of yours long enough. I have pandered to your pack problems and your pack ways, but *this* is outside of enough. I want this plague of humanization lifted, and I want it lifted now. I will not have anyone else shot at, or attacked, or spied upon, or any further rooms ransacked. Things are getting far too messy, and I cannot abide a mess."

"Temper, Lady Maccon, temper," remonstrated Lady Kingair.

Alexia narrowed her eyes.

"Why should we do what you say?" Dubh was militant.

Alexia shoved the letter of marque under the Beta's nose. He left off his grumbling, and the oddest expression suffused his wide, angry face.

Lady Kingair grabbed the paperwork and held it up to the indifferent light of a nearby oil lamp. Satisfied, she passed it on to Lachlan, who appeared the least surprised by its contents.

"I take it you were not informed of my appointment?"

Sidheag gave her a hard look. "I take it you didna marry Lord Maccon purely for love?"

"Oh, the political position was a surprise advantage, I assure you."

"And one that wouldna have been given to a spinster."

"So you know the queen's disposition sufficiently to predict that at least?" Alexia took her marque back and tucked it carefully down the front of her bodice. It would not do for the pack to be made aware of her parasol's hidden pockets.

"Muhjah has been vacant for generations. Why you? Why now?" Dubh was looking less angry and more thoughtful than Alexia had yet seen him. Perhaps there was brain behind all that brawn and bluster.

"*She* did offer it to your father," Lachlan pointed out.

"I had heard something to that effect. I understand he turned it down."

"Oh no, no." Lachlan gave a little half-smile. "We filibustered."

"The werewolves?"

"The werewolves and the vampires and one or two ghosts as well."

"What *is* it with you people and my father?"

At that Dubh snorted. "How much time do you have?"

The grandfather clock, locked in the room with Tunstell and his two comatose charges, tolled a quarter 'til.

"Apparently, not enough. I take it you accept the letter as authentic?"

Lady Kingair was looking at Alexia as though a good number of her previous questions about one Lady Maccon had now all been answered. "We will accept it, and we will defer to your authority in this." She gestured to the closed parlor door. "For the time being," she added, so as not to lose face in front of the pack.

Lady Maccon knew this was as good as she was going to get, so, in characteristic fashion, she took it and asked for more. "Very good. Next I will need to compose and send a message on your aethographor. While I am doing that, if you would please collect all the artifacts you brought back from Egypt into one room. I should very much like to peruse them as soon as my message has been sent. If I cannot determine which artifact is most likely causing the humanity problem, I shall have my husband removed to Glasgow, where he should return to supernatural and recover with no ill effects." With that, she headed up to the top of the castle and the aethographor.

She was in for a prodigious surprise. For what should she find on the floor of the aethographor room but the comatose form of the bemused claviger who was caretaker of the machine and every single valve frequensor in Kingair's library broken to smithereens. The place was littered with glittering crystalline shards.

"Oh dear, I knew they ought to have been locked away." Lady Maccon checked the claviger, who was still breathing and as fast asleep as her husband, and then picked her way through the wreckage.

The apparatus itself was undamaged. Which made Alexia wonder; if the objective in destroying the valve frequensors was to prevent outside communication, why not take down the aethographor itself? It was, after all, an awfully delicate gadget easily and quickly disabled. Why smash all the valves instead? Unless, of course, the culprit wanted continued access to the aethographor.

Alexia rushed into the transmitting chamber, hoping that the fallen claviger had disturbed the vandal in the act. It looked like he had, for there, still sitting in the emitter cradle, was a unrolled scroll of metal with a burned-through message clearly visible upon it. And it was *not* the message she had sent to Lord Akeldama the evening before. Oh no, this message was in French!

Lady Maccon was not quite as good at reading French as she should have been, so it took her long precious moments to translate the burned-through metal.

"Weapon here but unknown," it said.

Lady Maccon was disgruntled that the bloody thing did not read like an old-fashioned ink-and-paper letter, with a "dear so-and-so" and a "sincerely, so-and-so," thus revealing all to her without fuss. Who had Madame Lefoux sent the message to? When had the message been sent—just before she was shot, or earlier? Was it really the inventor who had also destroyed the valve frequensors? Lady Maccon could not believe that wanton destruction of technology was Madame Lefoux's style. The woman adored all gadgetry; it would be against her nature to destroy it with such abandon. And, regardless of all else, what *had* she been trying to tell them right before she was shot?

With a start, Alexia realized it was getting on toward eleven o'clock, and she had best etch her message and prepare it to send right away. Currently, the only concrete action she could think to take was consultation with Lord Akeldama. She did not have the valves to contact the Crown or BUR, so the outrageous vampire would have to do.

Her message read simply, "Floote check library: Egypt, humanization weapon? BUR send agents to Kingair."

It was a long message for the aethographor to handle, but it was the shortest she could formulate. Lady Maccon hoped she could remember the pattern of movements the young claviger had used the evening before. She was generally good about such things, but she might have missed a button or two. Still, there was nothing for it but to try.

The tiny transmitting room was much less crowded with only one person. She extracted Lord Akeldama's valve from her parasol and placed it carefully into the resonator cradle. She slotted the inscribed metal into the frame and pulled down the switch that activated the aetheric convector and chemical wash. The etched letters burned away, and the hydrodine engines spun to life. It was easier than she had thought. The director of the Crown's aethographic transmitter said one needed special schooling and certification to run the complicated apparatus— little liar.

The two needles raced across the slate, sparking as they met. Alexia sat in perfect silence throughout the transmission, and when it was finished, she removed the slate from the cradle. She wouldn't want to be so careless as the spy had been.

Lady Maccon bustled into the other chamber, which proved far more difficult to operate. No matter how many knobs she twiddled or cogs she turned, she could not get the ambient noise down far enough to receive. Luckily, Lord Akeldama took his sweet time replying. She had nearly half an hour to get the receiving chamber quiet. She did not manage to get it down nearly so low as the claviger had, but it was eventually quiet enough.

Lord Akeldama's response began to appear inside the black magnetic particulates between the two pieces of glass, one letter at a time. Trying to breathe quietly, Alexia copied down the message. It was short, cryptic, and totally unhelpful.

"Preternaturals always cremated," was all it said. Then there was some kind of image, a circle on top of a cross. Some kind of code? That was rich! Blast Lord Akeldama for being coy at a time like this!

Alexia waited another half an hour, past midnight, for any additional communication, and when nothing further materialized, she turned the aethographor off and left in a huff.

The house was abuzz. In the main drawing room across from the front parlor, in which remained Tunstell and his charges, a cheery fire burned in the fireplace and maids and footmen bustled about setting out artifacts.

"Good gracious, you did do a little shopping in Alexandria, now, didn't you?"

Lady Kingair looked up from the small mummy she was arranging carefully on a side table. It appeared to have started life as some kind of animal, perhaps of the feline persuasion? "We do what we must. The regimental pay isna adequate to cover Kingair's upkeep. Why should we not collect?"

Lady Maccon began looking through all the artifacts, not quite certain what she was looking for. There were little wooden statues of people, necklaces of turquoise and lapis, strange stone jars with animal-head lids, and amulets. All of them were relatively small except for two mummies, both still properly clothed. These were more impressive than the one they had unwrapped. They resided inside curvy, beautifully painted coffins, the surfaces of which were covered in colorful images and hieroglyphics. Cautiously, Alexia moved toward them but felt no overwhelming repulsion. None of the artifacts, mummies included, seemed any different from those she had seen on display in the halls of the Royal Society or, indeed, in the Museum of Antiquities.

She looked suspiciously at Lady Kingair. "Are there no others?"

"Only the entertainment mummy we unwrapped, still upstairs."

Lady Maccon frowned. "Did they all come from the same seller? Were they all looted from the same tomb? Did he say?"

Lady Kingair took offense. "They are *all* legal. I have the paperwork."

Alexia sucked her teeth. "I am certain you do. But I understand very well how the antiquities system works in Egypt these days."

Sidheag looked like she would like to take umbrage at that, but Alexia continued. "Regardless, their origins?"

Frowning, Lady Kingair said, "All different places."

Lady Maccon sighed. "I will want to see the other mummy again in just a moment, but first . . ." Her stomach went queasy at the very idea. It was so uncomfortable, to be in the same room with that thing. She turned to look at the rest of the Kingair Pack, who were milling about looking unsure of themselves, large men in skirts with scruffy faces and lost expressions. For a moment Alexia softened. Then she remembered her husband, comatose in another room. "None of you purchased anything privately that you are not telling me about? Things will go dreadfully ill for you if you did"—she looked directly at Dubh—"and I find out later."

No one stepped forward.

Lady Maccon turned back to Sidheag. "Very well, then, I shall take one more look at that mummy. Now, if you would be so kind."

Lady Kingair led the way up the stairs, but once there, Alexia did not follow her into the room. Instead she stood at the door, looking intently at the thing. It pushed against her, so that she had to fight a strange urge to turn and run. But she resisted, staring at the withered dark brown skin, almost black, shrunken down to hug those old bones. Its mouth was slightly open, bottom teeth visible, gray and worn. She could even see its eyelids, half-lidded, over the empty eye sockets. Its arms were crossed over its chest as though it were trying to hold itself together against death, clutching its soul inward.

Its soul.

"Of course," Alexia gasped. "How could I have been so blind?"

Lady Kingair looked to her sharply.

"I have been thinking all along that it was an ancient weapon, and Conall that it was some plague your pack caught and brought back with you from Egypt. But, no, it is simply *this* mummy."

"What? How could a mummy do such a thing?"

Resisting the terrible pushing sensation, Lady Maccon strode into the room and picked up a piece of the mummy's discarded bandage, pointing to the image depicted on it. An ankh, broken in half. Like the circle on top of a cross in Lord Akeldama's aethographic message, only fractured.

"This is not a symbol of death, nor of the afterlife. That is the name"—she paused—"or perhaps the title, of the person the mummy was in life. Do you not see? The ankh is the symbol for eternal life, and here it is shown broken. Only one creature can end eternal life."

Sidheag gasped, one hand to her lips, and then she slowly lowered it and pointed to Lady Maccon. "A curse-breaker. You."

Alexia smiled a tight little smile. She looked to the dead thing sadly. "Some long-ago ancestor, perhaps?" Despite herself she began to back away from it once more, the very air about the creature driving her away.

She looked to Lady Kingair, already knowing her answer. "Do you feel that?"

"Do I feel what, Lady Maccon?"

"I thought as much. Only I *would* notice." She frowned again, mind racing. "Lady Kingair, do you know anything about preternaturals?"

"Only the basics. I should know more, were I a werewolf, for the howlers would have told me the stories that, as a human, I am not allowed to hear."

Alexia ignored the bitterness in the older woman's voice. "Who, then, is the oldest of the Kingair Pack?" She had never missed Professor Lyall more. He would have known. Of course he would. He was probably the one who told Lord Akeldama.

"Lachlan," Lady Kingair answered promptly.

"I must speak with him directly." Alexia whirled away, almost bumping into her maid, who stood behind her in the hallway.

"Madame." Angelique's eyes were wide and her cheeks pink. "Your room, what haz 'appened?"

"Not again!"

Lady Maccon dashed to her bedchamber, but it looked the same as when she had last left it. "Oh, this is nothing, Angelique. I simply forgot to tell you about it. Please see it is tidied."

Angelique stood forlornly among the carnage and watched her mistress rush back downstairs. Lady Kingair followed sedately after.

"Mr. Lachlan," Alexia called, and that earnest gentleman appeared in the vestibule, a look of concern on his pleasant face. "A private word if you would be so kind."

She led the Gamma and Lady Kingair across the hall into a tight huddle away from the other pack members.

"This may come as a strange question, but please answer to the best of your knowledge."

"Of course, Lady Maccon. Your wish is my command."

"I am muhjah." She grinned. "My command is your command."

"Just so." He inclined his head.

"What happens to us when we die?"

"A philosophical conversation, Lady Maccon? Is now the time?"

She shook her head, impatient. "No, not us here. I mean to say we as in preternaturals. What happens to preternaturals when we die?"

Lachlan frowned. "I have not known very many of your kind, rare as they fortunately are."

Alexia bit her lip. Lord Akeldama's message said preternaturals were cremated. What would happen if one was not? What would happen if the body was never allowed to decompose? Ghosts displayed, in their very nature, the fact that excess soul was tethered to the body. As long as the body could be preserved, the ghost would stick around— undead and progressively more insane, but around. Surely the ancient Egyptians would have discovered this for themselves through the process of mummification? It might even be the reason they mummified. Was there something about *not* having a soul that was also connected to the body? Perhaps soul-sucking abilities were coupled to a preternatural's skin. After all, it was through her touch that Alexia managed to negate supernatural power.

She gasped and, for the first time in her stalwart life, actually felt near to fainting. The implications were endless and terrifying. The dead bodies of preternaturals could be turned into weapons against the supernatural. Preternatural mummies, like the one below, could be divided up and transported about the empire, or even turned into a powder and made into a poison! A *humanity* poison. She frowned. Such a drug might pass through the body after digestive processing, but still, for a time, a werewolf or vampire would be mortal.

Lachlan and Lady Kingair remained silent, staring at Alexia. It was almost as though they could see the gears and cogs in her head moving. Only one question remained to be answered: why was she repelled by the mummy? She asked Lachlan, "What happens when two preternaturals meet?"

"Oh, they dinna. Not even their own bairns. You never met your father?" Lachlan paused. "Course, he wouldna been the type. But, regardless, they simply dinna. Preternaturals canna stand to share the same air as one another. 'Tis naught personal, simply unbearable, so they tend to avoid the same social circles." He paused. "Are you saying somehow yon dead mummy is doing all this?"

"Maybe death expands our soulless abilities so they no longer require touch. Just as a ghost's excess soul can move outward from its body to the limits of its tether." Alexia looked at them both. "It would explain the mass exorcism within a specific radius."

"And the fact that this pack cannot change." Lady Kingair was nodding.

"Mass curse-breaking." Lachlan frowned.

Just then they heard the murmur of voices from behind the locked door near them. The parlor door clicked open, and Tunstell stuck his red head out. He started back upon seeing the three of them standing so close.

"Mistress," he said, "Madame Lefoux has awakened."

Alexia followed him inside, turning to Lady Kingair and Lachlan before shutting the door. "I need hardly tell you how dangerous the information we just discussed."

Both looked appropriately grave. Behind them, the rest of the pack emerged from the artifact room, curious at Tunstell's appearance.

"Please do not tell the rest of your pack," Alexia asked, but it sounded like a command.

They nodded and she shut the door.

CHAPTER THIRTEEN

The Latest Fashion from France

Tunstell was bent over the inventor, helping her to sit upright on the small settee, when Alexia entered. Madame Lefoux was looking groggy, but her eyes were open. They focused on Alexia as she walked into the room, and the Frenchwoman gave a slow smile—there were the dimples.

"My husband," asked Lady Maccon, issuing forth her own brief upturn of the lips, "has his condition changed also?" She went to Conall's side, a mountain of a man on the tiny little couch. Its bowed, claw-foot legs looked like they were buckling under his weight. She reached down to touch his face: slightly scruffy. She had *told* him he needed a shave. But his eyelids remained closed, ridiculously long eyelashes flat against his cheek. Such a waste of good eyelashes. She'd said only last month how much she resented him for them. He'd laughed and tickled her neck with them.

Her reminiscences were interrupted, not by Tunstell's voice answering her question, but by Madame Lefoux's slightly accented musical one. It was a little dry and croaky from lack of water.

"He will not regain his senses for some time, I am afraid. Not if he was disabled by one of the new sleeping darts."

Lady Maccon went over to her. "What was it, Madame Lefoux? What happened? What were you trying to tell us this morning? Who shot at you?" Her voice became very cold. "Who shot my husband?" She was confident she knew the answer, but she wanted Madame Lefoux to be the one to tell her. It was time the inventor chose a side.

The inventor swallowed. "Please do not be angry with her, Lady Maccon. She does not do it intentionally, you understand? I am convinced she doesn't. She is simply a little thoughtless—that is all. She has a good heart, under it all. I know she has.

"I found the aethographor, all those beautiful valves smashed to bits. How could she do such a thing? How could anyone?" There were tears now leaking out of those green eyes. "She went too far with that, and then when I came to tell you, instead I found her searching your room. That was when I knew it had gotten out of hand. She must have been looking for your crystalline valve, the one she knew you had, the one for Lord Akeldama's transmitter. To destroy it as well. Such destruction. I never knew she was capable. To push someone off a ship is one thing, but to destroy such perfectly functional beauty as a crystalline valve frequensor—what kind of monster does that?"

Well, that certainly told Alexia where Madame Lefoux's priorities lay.

"Who is Angelique working for? The vampires?"

Madame Lefoux, having talked herself out, nodded.

Lady Maccon swore, using words her husband would have been proud of.

Tunstell was shocked. He blushed.

"I suspected she was a spy, of course, but I did not think she would become an active agent. She did such lovely things with my hair."

Madame Lefoux tilted her head as though she could understand perfectly.

"What is she after? Why has she been doing this?"

The Frenchwoman shook her head. With her top hat off and her cravat untied, she looked almost feminine, most unlike herself. Softer. Alexia was not certain she liked it. "I can only suggest—the same thing you are after, muhjah. The humanization weapon."

Lady Maccon swore again. "And, of course, Angelique was standing just there. Right behind me in the hallway when I figured out what it was."

Madame Lefoux's eyes widened.

But it was Tunstell who said, voice full of awe, "You figured it out?"

"Of course I did. Where have you been?" Lady Maccon immediately headed toward the door. "Tunstell, my orders stand."

"But, mistress, you need—"

"They stand!"

"I do not think she wants to kill anyone but me," Madame Lefoux called after her. "I really do not. Please, my lady, do not do anything . . . terminal."

Lady Maccon whirled back at the door and bared her teeth, looking for all the world like a bit of a werewolf herself.

"She shot my husband, madame," she said.

Outside, where the Kingair Pack should have still stood, was only silence. Silence and a whole mess of plaid-skirted, large, sleeping bodies—quite the grand collapse.

Lady Maccon closed her eyes and took a long, annoyed breath. Really, must she do everything herself?

Gripping her parasol firmly, she armed the numbing spike, her finger hovering over the dart-ejection button, and charged up the stairs toward the mummy room. Unless she missed her guess, Angelique would try to get the creature out and on the road, probably by carriage, and back to her masters.

She missed her guess. The moment she opened the door to the room, it became patently clear the mummy was still in residence and Angelique was not.

Lady Maccon frowned. "What?"

She tapped the tip of her parasol on the floor in annoyance. Of course! A vampire spy's priority would be the transfer of information. It was the thing vampires valued most. Alexia changed her grip on the parasol and hurtled up too many staircases for her corset-clad self, arriving, panting, at the aethographic transmitter room.

Without even bothering to see if it was in use, she aimed her parasol and pulled down on the appropriate lotus leaf in the handle, activating the magnetic disruptor emitter. For just one moment everything stopped.

Then Alexia rushed forward and into the transmitting room of the apparatus.

Angelique was already standing up from the station. The little arms of the spark emitters were stopped midmessage. The French maid looked directly at Lady Maccon and, without pause, dashed toward her.

Alexia deflected the charge, but the girl's intention obviously had not been to attack, for she simply shoved Alexia to one side and leaped from the room. Lady Maccon fell back against a tangle of gadgetry on one wall of the chamber, lost her balance, and hit the floor hard, landing on her side.

She floundered among skirts, bustle, and petticoats, trying to regain her footing. As soon as she had, she raced to the transmitter cradle and grabbed out the metal scroll. Only three-quarters had burned through. Was it enough? Had her blast stopped the transmission, or did the vampires now have access to possibly the most dangerous information both about and to preternaturals?

With no time to check, Lady Maccon thrust the slate to one side, whirled about, and dashed after Angelique, convinced that now the young woman would be after the mummy.

This time she was correct.

"Angelique, stop!"

Alexia saw her from the landing above, struggling with the corpse of the long-dead preternatural, half carrying, half dragging the gruesome thing down the first set of stairs toward the front door of the castle.

"Alexia? What is going on?" Ivy Hisselpenny emerged from her room, cheeks blotchy and tearstained.

Lady Maccon took aim with her parasol, through the mahogany railing of the banister, and fired a numbing dart at her maid.

The French girl twisted, holding the mummy up as a shield. The dart hit and hung half inside of wrinkled brown skin thousands of years old. Alexia pounded down the next set of stairs.

Angelique pulled the mummy across her back so that it could protect her as she ran, but her progress was hampered by the awkwardness of having to carry the creature.

Lady Maccon paused on the staircase and took aim once more.

Miss Hisselpenny appeared in Alexia's line of view, standing on the landing above the first staircase, looking down at Angelique, entirely blocking Alexia's chance at a second shot.

"Ivy, move!"

"Goodness, Alexia, what is your maid up to? Is she *wearing* a mummy?"

"Yes, it is the latest Paris fashion, didn't you know?" replied Lady Maccon before, quite rudely, shoving her friend out of the way.

Miss Hisselpenny squeaked in outrage.

Alexia took aim and shot again. This time the dart missed entirely. She swore. She would have to get in some target practice if she were to continue this line of work. The parasol carried only a two-dart armament, so she increased her speed and went for the old-fashioned option.

"Really, Alexia, language. You sound like a fishmonger's wife!" said Miss Hisselpenny. "What is going on? Did your parasol just *emit* something? How untoward of it. I must be seeing things. It must be my deep love for Mr. Tunstell clouding my vision."

Lady Maccon entirely ignored her dear friend. The power of the mummy to repel her notwithstanding, she charged down the staircase, parasol at the ready. "Stay out of the way, Ivy," she ordered.

Angelique stumbled over the fallen form of one of the pack members.

"Just you stop right there," yelled Lady Maccon in her best muhjah voice.

French maid and mummy were almost at the door when Lady Maccon pounced, prodding Angelique viciously with the tip of the parasol.

Angelique froze, turning her head toward her former mistress. Her big violet eyes were wide.

Lady Maccon gave her a tight little smile. "Now, then, my dear, one lump or two?" Before the girl could answer her, she hauled her arm back and bashed Angelique as hard as she could over the head.

The maid and the mummy both fell.

"Apparently, just one is sufficient."

At the top of the stairs, Miss Hisselpenny gave a little cry of alarm and then clapped her hand to her mouth. "Alexia," she hissed, "how could you possibly behave so forcefully? With a parasol! To your own maid. It simply is not the thing to discipline one's staff so barbarically! I mean to say, your hair always looked perfectly well done to me."

Lady Maccon ignored her and kicked the mummy out of the way.

Ivy gasped again. "What are you doing? That is an ancient artifact. You love those old things!"

Lady Maccon could have done without the commentary. She had no time for historical scruples. The blasted mummy was causing too many problems and, if left intact, would become a logistical nightmare. There was no way it could be allowed to exist. Hang the scientific consequences.

She checked Angelique's breathing. The spy was still alive.

The best thing to do, Lady Maccon decided, was eliminate the mummy. Everything else could be dealt with subsequently.

Resisting the intense pushing sensation that urged her to get as far away from the awful thing as possible, Alexia dragged the mummy out onto the massive stone blocks that formed the front stoop of the castle. No sense in putting anyone else in danger.

Madame Lefoux had not designed the parasol to emit anything particularly toxic to preternaturals, if there existed such a substance, but Alexia was confident sufficient application of acid could destroy most anything.

She opened the parasol and flipped it so she was holding the spike. Just to be on the safe side, she turned the tiny dial above the magnetic disruption emitter all the way to the third click. The parasol's six ribs opened, and a fine mist clouded over the mummy, drenching dehydrated skin and old bone. She swayed the parasol back and forth, to be sure the liquid covered the entire body, and then propped it over the mummy's torso and backed away, leaving mummy and parasol alone together. The pungent aroma of burning acid permeated the air, and Alexia moved even farther away. Then came an odor like nothing she had ever smelled before: the final death of ancient bones, a mix of musty attic, and coppery blood.

The repelling sensation emitted by the mummy began to decrease. The creature itself was gradually disintegrating, turning into a lumpy puddle of brown mush, irregular bits of bone and skin sticking out. It was no longer recognizable as human.

The parasol kept spraying, the stone steps becoming pitted.

Behind Alexia, inside Kingair Castle, at the top of the grand staircase, Ivy Hisselpenny screamed.

On the other side of the British isle, in a hired, unmarked cab outside what looked to be a quite innocent, if expensive, town house in a discreetly fashionable neighborhood near Regent's Park, Professor Randolph Lyall and Major Channing Channing of the Chesterfield Channings sat and waited. It was a dangerous place for two werewolves to be, just outside the Westminster Hive. Doubly dangerous in that they were not there in any official capacity. If this got back to BUR, Lyall was tolerably certain he would be out of a job and the major cashiered.

They both practically jumped out of their skins, a true skill for a werewolf, when the cab door crashed open and a body tumbled inside.

"Drive!"

Major Channing banged on the roof of the cab with his pistol and the hack jumped forward. The horse's hooves emitted a shockingly loud clatter in the London night air.

"Well?" questioned Channing, impatient.

Lyall reached down to help the young man regain his feet and his dignity.

Biffy tossed back the black velvet cape that had fallen askew during his mad dash to safety. Lyall was at a loss to know how a cape could be of assistance when breaking and entering, but Biffy had insisted. "Dressing the part," he had said, "is *never* optional."

Professor Lyall grinned at the youngster. He really was a rather good-looking gentleman. Whatever else one might say about Lord Akeldama, and one might say a lot, he had excellent taste in drones. "So, how did it go?"

"Oh, they have one, all right. Right up near the roof. A slightly older model than my master's, but it looked to be in good working order."

A good-looking and *effective* gentleman.

"And?" Professor Lyall quirked an eyebrow.

"Let us simply say, for the time being, that it is most likely not as useful as it was a little while ago."

Major Channing looked at Biffy suspiciously. "What did you do?"

"Well, you see, there was this pot of tea, simply sitting there . . ." He trailed off.

"Useful thing, tea," commented Lyall thoughtfully.

Biffy grinned at him.

It was not one of Ivy's normal breathy, about-to-faint sort of screams. It was a scream of real terror, and it caused Lady Maccon to abandon her parasol to its acidic work and rush back inside, alone.

The scream's assertiveness had attracted the attention of others as well. Tunstell and a wobbly-looking Madame Lefoux both emerged from the downstairs parlor, despite Alexia's orders to the contrary.

"What are you doing?" she yelled at them. "Get back in there this instant!"

But their collective attention was entirely held elsewhere. It was fixed on the landing above, where Angelique stood close behind Miss Hisselpenny, a deadly looking knife held to that young lady's throat.

"Miss Hisselpenny!" yelled Tunstell, his face suffused with horror. And then, abandoning all decency and decorum, "Ivy!"

At the same time Madame Lefoux yelled, "Angelique, no!"

Everyone charged toward the stairs. Angelique dragged Ivy back with her toward the room that had once housed the mummy.

"Stay back or she will die," said the maid in her native tongue, hand steady and eyes hard.

Tunstell, not understanding, drew the Tue Tue and pointed it at the maid. Madame Lefoux pulled down on his arm. She proved surprisingly strong for one so recently injured. "You'll hit the hostage."

"Angelique, this is madness," said Lady Maccon, trying to be reasonable. "I have destroyed the evidence. Soon the pack will be awake and recovered. Whatever drug you gave them will not last once they reclaim their supernatural state. It cannot possibly be long now. You simply will not be able to escape."

Angelique continued to move backward, dragging the hapless Miss Hisselpenny with her. "Zen I have nothing to lose, non?" She continued into the room.

As soon as she was out of sight, Lady Maccon and Tunstell both dashed up the stairs after her. Madame Lefoux tried to follow, but her progress was much slower. She was clutching at her wounded shoulder and breathing with difficulty.

"I need her alive," Alexia panted at Tunstell. "I have questions."

Tunstell tucked the Tue Tue into his breeches and nodded.

They attained the room at about the same time. They found Angelique, still armed, directing Ivy to open the shutters to the far window. Alexia bitterly regretted her lack of parasol. Really, she would have to chain the bloody thing to her side. Every time she did not have it, she found herself in grave need of its services. Before Angelique caught sight of them, Tunstell ducked down and to one side, using the various furnishings about the room to shield himself from the maid's view.

While he approached in secret, making his way cautiously about the room, Lady Maccon took it upon herself to distract the spy. It was not easy; Tunstell was not what one could describe as subtle. His flaming red hair bobbed up with each pointed and articulated footstep, as though he were some cloaked Gothic villain creeping across a stage. Melodramatic fat-head. It was a good thing the room was darkened, lit by only one gas lamp in the far corner.

"Angelique," Lady Maccon called.

Angelique turned, jerking roughly at Miss Hisselpenny with her free hand, the other still clutching the wicked-looking knife at Ivy's neck. "Hurry up," she growled at Miss Hisselpenny. "You"—she jerked her chin at Alexia—"stay back and let me see your hands."

Lady Maccon waved her empty hands about, and Angelique nodded, clearly pleased by the lack of weaponry. Alexia privately urged Ivy to faint. It would make matters much easier. Ivy remained stubbornly conscious and distraught. She never did faint when it was actually warranted.

"Why, Angelique?" Lady Maccon asked, genuinely curious, not to mention eager to keep the maid's attention off of the blatantly skulking Tunstell.

The French girl smiled, her face even more beautiful. Her large eyes shone in the light of the gas lamp. "Because she asked me to. Because she promised she would try."

"She. *She* who?"

"Who do you think?" Angelique practically snapped back.

Lady Maccon caught a whiff of vanilla scent, and then a soft voice spoke from her side. Madame Lefoux leaned weakly against the doorjamb next to her. "Countess Nadasdy."

Lady Maccon frowned and bit at her lip, confused. She continued to speak to Angelique, only half acknowledging the inventor's presence. "But I thought your former master was a rove. I thought you were at the Westminster Hive under sufferance."

Angelique prodded at Ivy again, this time using the tip of the knife. Ivy squeaked and fumbled with the latch of the shutters, finally managing to throw them back. The castle was old, with no glass in its windows. Cool, wet night air rushed into the room.

"You think too much, my lady," sneered the spy.

Tunstell, having finally made his way about the room, sprang forward at that moment, launching himself at the Frenchwoman. For the first time in their acquaintance, Alexia felt he was finally showing some of the grace and dexterity one would expect in a soon-to-be werewolf. Of course, it could all be showmanship, but it was impressive nevertheless.

Miss Hisselpenny, seeing who it was who had come to her rescue, screamed and fainted, collapsing to one side of the open window.

Finally, thought Alexia.

Angelique reeled around, brandishing the knife.

Tunstell and the maid grappled. Angelique struck out at the claviger with a wicked slash, training and practice behind the movement. He ducked, deflecting the blade with his shoulder. A bloody gash appeared on the meat of his upper arm.

Lady Maccon jerked forward to go to Tunstell's aid, but Madame Lefoux held her back. Her foot came down with a sad little crunch noise, and Alexia tore her gaze away from the grappling forms to see what had caused it. *Ugh!* The floor was littered with dead scarab beetles.

The claviger was unsurprisingly stronger than Angelique. She was a delicate little thing, and he was built on the larger end of the scale, as both werewolves and stage directors preferred. What he lacked in technique, he more than made up for in brawn. He came up out of the crouch, twisting to push his uninjured shoulder to the maid's gut. With a scream of anger, the woman fell backward out the window. This was probably not quite what she had originally intended upon opening it, if the rope ladder was any indication. She let forth a long, high scream that ended in a crunchy kind of thud.

Madame Lefoux screamed herself and left off holding back Lady Maccon. The two dashed over to look out the window.

Below, Angelique lay in a crumpled heap. Probably not the landing she had intended either.

"Did you miss the part where I said I needed her alive?"

Tunstell's face was white. "Then she isn't? I killed her."

"No, she flew off into the aether. Of course you killed her, you—"

Tunstell forestalled his mistress's wrath by fainting into a freckled heap.

Alexia turned her ire on Madame Lefoux. The inventor was staring, white-faced, down at the fallen maid.

"Why did you hold me back?"

Madame Lefoux opened her mouth, and a sound like stampeding elephants halted whatever she had been about to say.

The members of the Kingair Pack appeared around the open doorway. They were minus their human companions, as the clavigers and Lady Kingair still labored under the effects of Angelique's sleep drug. The fact that they were up and about indicated that the mummy must have finally and completely dissolved.

"Move, you mongrels," growled a vehement voice behind them. Just as quickly as they had appeared, the pack disappeared, and Lord Conall Maccon strode into the room.

"Oh, good," said his wife, "you are awake. What took you so long?"

"Hello, my dear. What have you done now?"

"Be so kind as to leave off insulting me, and see to Ivy and Tunstell, would you, please? They may both require vinegar. Oh, and keep an eye on Madame Lefoux. I have a body to check on."

Noting his wife's general demeanor and expression, the earl did not question her dictates.

"I take it the body is that of your maid?"

"How did you know?" Lady Maccon was understandably peeved. After all, she had only just figured this all out. How dare her own husband be a step ahead of her?

"She shot me, remember?" he replied with a sniff.

"Yes, well, I had better check."

"Are we hoping for dead or alive?"

Lady Maccon sucked her teeth. "Mmm, dead would make for less paperwork. But alive would make for fewer questions."

He waved a hand flippantly. "Carry on, my dear."

"Oh, really, Conall. As if it were your idea," said his wife, annoyed but already trotting out the door.

"And I chose to marry that one," commented her husband to the assembled werewolves in resigned affection.

"I heard that," Lady Maccon said without pausing.

She made her way quickly back down the stairs. She was certainly getting her exercise today. She picked her way through the still-slumbering clavigers and out the front door. She took the opportunity to check the mummy, which was no more than a pile of brown slush. The parasol was no longer emitting its deadly mist, obviously having used up its supply. She would have to see about a tune-up, as she had already used much of its complement of weaponry. She closed it with a snap and took it with her around the side of the castle to where the crumpled form of Angelique lay, unmoving on the damp castle green.

Lady Maccon poked at her with the tip of the parasol from some distance. When that elicited no reaction, she bent to examine the fallen woman closer. Without a doubt, Angelique's was not a condition that could be cured through the application of vinegar. The French girl's head listed far to one side, her neck broken by the fall.

Lady Maccon sighed, stood, and was just about to poodle off, when the air all about the body shivered, as heat will ripple the air about a fire.

Alexia had never before witnessed an unbirth. As with normal births, they were generally considered a little crass and unmentionable in polite society, but there was no doubt about what was happening to Angelique. For there before Lady Maccon appeared the faint shimmering form of her dead maid.

"So, you might have survived Countess Nadasdy's bite in the end."

The ghost looked at her. For a long moment, as though adjusting to her new state of existence—or nonexistence as it were. She simply floated there, the leftover part of Angelique's soul.

"I always knew I could have been something more," replied Formerly Angelique. "But you had to stop me. Zey told me you were dangerous. I thought it was because zey feared you, feared what you were and what you could produce. But now I realized zey feared *who* you are az well. Your lack of soul, it haz affected your character. You are not only preternatural, you also think differently az a result."

"I suppose I might," replied Alexia. "But it is hard for me to know with any certainty, having only ever experienced my own thoughts."

The ghost floated, hovering just over her body. For some time she would be tethered close, unable to stretch her limits until her flesh began to erode away. Only then, doomed to deterioration as the connection to the body became weaker and weaker, would she be able to venture farther away, at the same time dissolving into poltergeis and madness. It was not a nice way to enter the afterlife.

The Frenchwoman looked at her former mistress. "Will you be preserving my body, or letting me go mad, or will you exorcise me now?"

"Choices, choices," said Lady Maccon rather harshly. "Which would *you* prefer?"

The ghost did not hesitate. "I should like to go now. BUR will persuade me to spy, and I should not wish to work against either my hive or my country. And I could not stand to run mad."

"So, you do have some scruples."

It was hard to tell, but it seemed as though the specter smiled at that. Ghosts were never more than passing solid; one scientific hypothesis was that they were the physical representation of the mind's memory of itself. "More zan you will ever know," said Formerly Angelique.

"And if I exorcise you, what will you give me in return?" Alexia, preternatural, wanted to know.

Formerly Angelique sighed, although she no longer had lungs with which to sigh or air with which to emit sound. Lady Maccon spared a thought to wonder how ghosts managed to talk.

"You are curious, I suppose. A bargain. I will answer you ten questions az honest az I am able. Zen, you will set me to die."

"Why did you do all of this?" Lady Maccon asked immediately, and without hesitation: the easiest and most important question first.

Formerly Angelique held up ten ghostly fingers and ticked one down. "Because ze comtesse offered me ze bite. Who does not want eternal life?" A pause. "Aside from Genevieve."

"Why were you trying to kill me?"

"I waz never trying to kill you. I waz always after Genevieve. I waz not very good at it. Ze fall, in ze air, and ze shootings, zat was for her. You were an inconvenience; she iz ze danger."

"And the poison?"

Formerly Angelique now had three fingers bent. "Zat was not me. I am thinking, my lady, zat someone else wants you dead. And your fourth question?"

"Do you believe it is Madame Lefoux trying to kill me?"

"I think not, but it iz hard to tell with Genevieve. She iz, how do you say? Ze smart one. But should she want you dead, it would be your body lying there, not mine."

"So why do *you* wish our little inventor dead?"

"Your fifth question, my lady, and you waste it on Genevieve? She 'az something of mine. She insisted on giving it back or telling the world."

"What could be so horrible?"

"It would have ruined my life. Ze comtesse, she insists, no family. She will not bite to change if there iz children—part of vampire edict. A lesser regulation but the comtesse 'az always played hive politics close. And seeing how Lady Kingair complicates your husband's life, I begin to understand why the rule waz in place."

Lady Maccon put all things together. She knew those violet eyes had been familiar. "Madame Lefoux's son, Quesnel. He is not her child, is he? He is yours."

"A mistake that no longer matters." Another finger went down. Three questions left.

"Madame Lefoux was on board the dirigible tracking you, not me! Was she blackmailing you?"

"Yez, either I take up my maternal duty or she'd tell the countess.

I could not have that, you understand? When I had worked so hard for immortality."

Alexia blushed, grateful for the cool night air. "You two were . . ."

The ghost gave a kind of shrug, the gesture, still so casual, even in specter form. "Of course, for many years."

Lady Maccon felt her face go even hotter, erotic images flashing through her brain: Madame Lefoux's dark head next to Angelique's blond one. A pretty picture the two of them would have made, like something out of a naughty postcard. "Well, I say, how extraordinarily French."

The ghost laughed. "Hardly that. How do you think I caught Comtesse Nadasdy's interest? Not with ze hairdressing skills, let me assure you, my lady."

Alexia had seen something of the kind in her father's collection, but she had never imagined it might be based on anything more than masculine wistfulness or performances put on to titillate a john's palate. That two women might do such things voluntarily with one another and do so with some degree of romantic love. Was this possible?

She did not realize she had voiced this last question aloud.

The ghost snorted. "All I can say iz, I am certain she loved me, at one time."

Lady Maccon began to see much more in the inventor's actions and comments over the past week than she had originally. "You are a hard little thing, aren't you, Angelique?"

"What a waste of your last question, my lady. We all become what we are taught to be. You are not so hard as you would like. What will that husband of yours say, when he finds out?"

"Finds out what?"

"Oh, you really do not know? I thought you were playacting." The ghost laughed, a genuine laugh, harsh and directed at the confusion and future misery of another.

"What? What do I not know?"

"Oh no, I have fulfilled my half of the bargain. Ten questions, fairly answered."

Alexia sighed. It was true. She reached forward, albeit reluctantly, to perform her very first exorcism. Odd that the government had known of her preternatural state for her whole life, had recorded her in the BUR Files of Secrecy and Import as the only preternatural in all of London, yet never used her in her kind's most common capacity—that of exorcist. Odd, too, that her first use of this ability should be at a ghost's request, in the Highlands of Scotland. And odd, last of all, that it should be so dreadfully easy.

She simply laid her hand upon Angelique's broken body, performing the literal application of the term *laying the body to rest*. As quick as that, the ghostly form disappeared, tethers broken, and all excess soul was terminated. With no living body to call it back when Alexia raised her hands, it was gone forever: complete and total disanimus. The soul could never return, as it did with werewolves and vampires. With the body dead, such a return was fatal. Poor Angelique, she might have been immortal, had she made different choices.

Lady Maccon found a very strange scene when she made her way back inside the castle and up the stairs into the mummy room. Tunstell was awake, his shoulder and upper arm bandaged with a red-checked handkerchief of Ivy's origination, and he was busy applying a good deal of excellent brandy to his mouth as a curative addendum. Miss Hisselpenny was kneeling next to him, cooing unhelpfully, having recovered her senses, at least enough to attain wakefulness, if not actual sense.

"Oh, Mr. Tunstell, how exceedingly brave you were, coming to my rescue like that. So heroic," she was saying. "Imagine if it got known that I had been knifed by a maid, a *French* maid, no less? Had I died, I should *never* have lived it down! How can I possibly thank you enough?"

Madame Lefoux stood next to Lord Maccon, looking composed, if a little drawn about the eyes and mouth, her dimples secured away for the time being. Alexia could not interpret this expression. She was not yet confident in the inventor's trustworthiness. Madame Lefoux had entertained some considerable vested interest in the proceedings from the start. Not to mention that suspicious octopus tattoo. If nothing else, Alexia's experience with the bedeviled scientists of the Hypocras Club had taught her not to trust octopuses.

She strode up to the Frenchwoman and said, "Angelique has had her say. It is time, Madame Lefoux, for you to do the same. What did you really want—simply Angelique or something more? Who was trying to poison me on board the dirigible?" Without pause, she turned her attention onto Tunstell, eyeing his wound critically. "Did he get vinegar put on that?"

"Had?" Madame Lefoux asked, apparently grappling with only one of the many words Lady Maccon had uttered. "Did you say *had*? Is she dead, then?"

"Angelique?"

Teeth nibbling fretfully at her bottom lip, the Frenchwoman nodded. "Quite."

Madame Lefoux did the most curious thing. She opened her green eyes wide, as though in surprise. And then, when that did not seem to help, turned her dark head aside and began to cry.

Lady Maccon envied her the skill of crying with aplomb. She herself went allover splotchy, but Madame Lefoux seemed to be able to execute the emotional state with minimal fuss: no gulps, no sniffles, just silent fat tears falling down her cheeks and dripping off her chin. It seemed all the more painfully sad, immersed in unnatural silence.

Lady Maccon, never one to be moved by sentiment, cast her hands up to heaven. "Oh, by glory, what now?"

"I ken, wife, now is the time for us all to be a tad more forthcoming with one another," said Conall. He was a softer touch. He steered both Alexia and Madame Lefoux away from the scene of battle (and Ivy and Tunstell, who were now making horrible kissy noises at one another) to a different part of the room.

"Oh dear." Lady Maccon glared at Lord Maccon. "You said 'us all.' Were you involved as well, my darling husband? Have you, perhaps, been less forthcoming than you should with your loving wife?"

Lord Maccon sighed. "Why must you always be so difficult, woman?"

Lady Maccon said nothing, simply crossed her arms over her ample bosom and stared pointedly at him.

"Madame Lefoux was working for me," he admitted, his voice so low it was almost a growl. "I asked her to keep an eye on you while I was away."

"And you did not tell me?"

"Well, you know how you get."

"I most certainly do. Really, Conall, imagine assigning a BUR agent to track me, as though I were a fox in the hunt. That is simply the living end! How could you?"

"Oh, she isn't BUR. We've known each other a long time. I asked her as a friend, not an employee."

Alexia frowned. She wasn't sure how she felt about *that*. "How long a time and how good a friend?"

Madame Lefoux gave a watery little smile.

Lord Maccon looked genuinely surprised. "Really, wife, you are not usually given to such denseness. I dinna fit Madame Lefoux's preferences."

"Ah, any more than I fit Lord Akeldama's?"

Lord Maccon, who was prone to getting a mite jealous of the effete vampire and resented the man's close relationship with Alexia, nodded his understanding. "Verra well, I take your point, wife."

"Admittedly," interjected Madame Lefoux, her voice soft and tear-strained, "I was also interested in contacting Angelique, and she *is* Lady Maccon's maid."

"You had your own agenda," accused Lord Maccon, looking with suspicion at the Frenchwoman.

"Who doesn't?" wondered Lady Maccon. "Angelique told me you used to be intimate and that Quesnel is hers, not yours."

"When did she tell you this, before she died?" wondered Lord Maccon.

Alexia patted his arm. "No, dear, after."

Madame Lefoux brightened considerably. "She is a ghost?"

Lady Maccon waggled her fingertips about. "Not anymore."

The inventor gasped, what appeared to have been a strange kind of hope quickly followed by a return to sadness. "You exorcised her? How cruel."

"She asked, and we struck a bargain. I am sorry. I did not think to take your feelings into account."

"These days, no one seems to." The inventor sounded bitter.

"There is no need to wallow," replied Lady Maccon, who did not approve of maudlin humors.

"Really, Alexia, why such sharpness with the woman? She is over-set."

Lady Maccon looked more closely into Madame Lefoux's face. "I believe there may be cause. You are not so sad over lost love as you are over a lost past. Is that not so, madame?"

Madame Lefoux's face lost a modicum of its grief, and her eyes narrowed, sharpening on Alexia. "We were together for a long time, but you are right. I did want her back—not for me but for Quesnel. I thought perhaps a son would ground her in the daylight world. She changed so very much after she became a drone. They tapped into the hardness Quesnel and I had once managed to temper."

Alexia nodded. "I deduced as much."

Lord Maccon looked at his wife appreciatively. "Good Lord, woman, how could you have possibly known that?"

"Well"—Lady Maccon grinned—"Madame Lefoux here did play a bit of the coquette with me while we were traveling. I do not think she was entirely shamming."

Madame Lefoux flashed a sudden smile. "I did not know you were even aware."

Alexia arched both eyebrows. "I was not until recently; hindsight can be most illuminating."

Lord Maccon glowered at the Frenchwoman. "You were flirting with *my wife!*" he roared.

Madame Lefoux straightened her spine and looked up at him. "No need to raise your hackles and get territorial, old wolf. You find her attractive—why shouldn't I?"

Lord Maccon actually sputtered.

"Nothing happened," corroborated Alexia, smiling broadly.

Madame Lefoux added, "Not that I wouldn't like—".

Lord Maccon growled and loomed even more menacingly in Madame Lefoux's direction. The inventor rolled her eyes at his posturing.

Alexia's grin widened. It was rare to have someone else around brave enough to tease the earl. She shot a quick glance in the Frenchwoman's direction. At least, she thought they were teasing. Just to be on the safe side, she hastily switched topics. "This is all very flattering, but could we return to the subject at hand? If Madame Lefoux was on board the dirigible to keep an eye on me and to blackmail Angelique with parental duties, then it was not she who tried to poison me and got Tunstell instead. And I now know it was not Angelique either."

"Poison! You didna tell me about a poisoning, wife! You only mentioned the fall." Lord Maccon began to vibrate with suppressed anger. His eyes had turned feral, solid yellow now instead of tawny brown. Wolf eyes.

"Yes, well, the fall *was* Angelique."

"Dinna change the subject, you impossible woman!"

Lady Maccon switched to defending herself. "Well, I did suppose Tunstell would have told you. He took the brunt of the incident, after all. And he is your claviger. Normally he tells you everything. Regardless"— she turned back to Madame Lefoux—"*you* are after the humanization weapon as well, aren't you?"

Madame Lefoux smiled again. "How did you guess?"

"Someone keeps trying to break into or steal my dispatch case. Since you knew about the parasol and all its secret pockets, I figured it had to be you, not Angelique. And what could you possibly want with it except my records as muhjah on the London humanization and the dewan and potentate's findings?" She paused, her head cocked to one side. "Would you mind stopping now? It is most aggravating. There is nothing of import in the case, you do realize?"

"But I am still eager to know where you hid it."

"Mmm, ask Ivy about lucky special socks."

Lord Maccon gave his wife a funny look.

Madame Lefoux ignored that bizarre statement and moved on. "You did figure it out in the end, didn't you? The source of the humanization? You must have, because"—she gestured to Lord Maccon's wolf eyes—"it seems to have been reversed."

Lady Maccon nodded. "Of course I did."

"Yes, I thought you might. That was the real reason I followed you."

Lord Maccon sighed. "Really, Madame Lefoux, why not wait until BUR had it cleared and simply ask what had happened?"

The inventor gave him a hard look. "When has BUR, or the Crown for that matter, ever shared such information openly with anyone? Let alone a French scientist? Even as a friend, you would never tell me the truth of it."

Lord Maccon looked like he would rather not comment on that statement. "Were you, like Angelique, being paid by the Westminster vampires to find this information out?" he asked, looking resigned.

Madame Lefoux said nothing.

Alexia felt rather smug at this point. It was rare for her to be able to put one over on her husband. "Conall, you mean to say you did not know? Madame Lefoux is not really working for you. She is not working for the hives either. She is working for the Hypocras Club."

"What! That canna be possible."

"Oh yes, it can. I saw the tattoo."

"No, really it is not," Lord Maccon and Madame Lefoux said at the same time.

"Trust me, my dear, we saw to it that the entire operation was disbanded," added the earl.

"That explains why you turned so cold toward me all of a sudden," said Madame Lefoux. "You saw my tattoo and jumped to conclusions."

Lady Maccon nodded.

"Tattoo, what tattoo?" Lord Maccon growled. He was looking ever more annoyed.

Madame Lefoux yanked down her collar, which was easy without her cravat, exposing the telltale mark upon her neck.

"Ah, my dear, I see the source of the confusion." The earl seemed suddenly much calmer, rather than launching into violence over the octopus as Alexia had expected.

He took his wife's hand softly in his large paw. "The Hypocras was a militant branch of the OBO. Madame Lefoux is a member in good standing. Are you not?"

The inventor gave a little half-smile and nodded.

"And what, pray tell, is the OBO?" Lady Maccon yanked her hand out of her husband's patronizing grip.

"The Order of the Brass Octopus, a secret society of scientists and inventors."

Lady Maccon glared at the earl. "And you did not think to tell me about this?"

He shrugged. "It is meant to be *secret*."

"We really must work on our communication. Perhaps if you were not so constantly interested in other forms of intimacy, I might actually have access to the information I need to survive with my temper intact!" Alexia poked at him with a sharp finger. "More talk, less bed sport."

Lord Maccon looked alarmed. "Fine, I shall make time to discuss these things with you."

She narrowed her eyes.

"I promise."

She whirled about to look at Madame Lefoux, who was unsuccessfully trying to hide her amusement at Lord Maccon's discomfort.

"And this Order of the Brass Octopus, what are its policies?"

"Secret."

A hard look met that remark.

"In all honesty, we do agree with the Hypocras Club to a certain degree: that the supernatural must be monitored, that there should be checks in place. I am sorry, my lord, but it is true. Supernaturals continue to tamper with the world, particularly the vampires. You get greedy. Look at the Roman Empire."

The earl snorted but was not particularly offended. "As though the daylight folk have done so well: never forget, your lot boasts the Inquisition."

Madame Lefoux turned to Alexia, trying to explain. Her green eyes were oddly desperate, as though this, of all things, was terribly important. "You, as a preternatural, must understand. You are the living representation of the counterbalance theorem in action. You are supposed to be on *our* side."

Alexia did understand. Having worked alongside the dewan and the potentate for several months, she could comprehend this desperate need the scientists felt to constantly monitor the supernatural set. She wasn't yet quite certain which side she came down on, but she said firmly, "You understand Conall has my loyalty? Well, him and the queen."

The Frenchwoman nodded. "And now that you know my allegiances, will you tell me what caused the mass negation of the supernatural?"

"You want to harness it into an invention of some kind, don't you?"

Madame Lefoux looked arch. "I am convinced there is a market. How about it, Lord Maccon? Imagine what I could do for a sundowner, with the ability to turn vampires and werewolves mortal. Or, Lady Maccon, what new gadget I might install in your parasol? Think of the control we could have over supernaturals."

Lord Maccon gave the inventor a long, hard look. "I didna realize you were a radical, Madame Lefoux. When did that happen?"

Lady Maccon decided then and there not to tell the inventor about the mummy. "I am sorry, madame, but it would be best if I kept this to myself. I have removed the cause, obviously"—she gestured to the pack, still hovering hopefully in the doorway—"with the help of your excellent parasol, but I am thinking this is knowledge best kept out of the public domain."

"You are a hard woman, Lady Maccon," replied the inventor, frowning. "But you do realize, we *will* figure it out eventually."

"Not if I have anything to do with it. Although it may be too late. I believe our little spy may have managed to get the word out to the Westminster Hive despite my precautions," said Lady Maccon, suddenly remembering the aethographic transmitter and Angelique's message.

She turned and strode toward the door. Madame Lefoux and Lord Maccon followed.

"No." She looked at the inventor. "I am sorry, Madame Lefoux. It is not that I do not like you. It is simply that I do not trust you. Please remain here. Oh, and give me back my journal."

The inventor looked confused. "I did not take it."

"But I thought you said . . ."

"I looked for the dispatch case, but it was not me who broke into your room on board the dirigible."

"Then who did?"

"The same person who tried to poison you, I suppose."

Alexia threw her hands up. "I don't have time for this." And with that, she led her husband from the room at a brisk trot.

CHAPTER FOURTEEN

Changes

Lord Maccon checked the hall. It was empty, the pack having filed into the mummy room or gone to collect Angelique's body. Seeing no one around to forestall his action, the earl slammed his wife up against the wall, pressing the full length of his body against hers.

"Ooomph," said his wife. "Not now."

He nuzzled in at her neck, kissing and licking her softly just below her ear. "Just a moment," he said. "I need a small reminder that you are here, you are whole, and you are mine."

"Well, the first two should be patently obvious, and the last one is always in question," replied his lady unhelpfully. But she wrapped her arms about his neck and pressed against him despite all protestations to the contrary.

He resorted, as always, to action over words and sealed his lips atop hers, stopping that wicked tongue.

Alexia, who had, until that moment, managed to remain rather pulled together and tidy, despite all of her dashing about the castle, cast herself into a willing state of hopeless disarray. There was really nothing else to do when Conall was in one of these moods but enjoy it. Her husband drove his hands into her hair, tilting her head to the correct angle for ravishment. Ah well, at least he was good at it.

Alexia sacrificed herself on the altar of wifely duty, enjoying every minute of it, of course, but still determined to pull him back and get on to the aethographor.

Her determination notwithstanding, it was several long moments before he finally raised his head.

"Right," he said, as though he had just finished a refreshing beverage. "Shall we continue on, then?"

"What?" Alexia asked, dazed, trying to recall what they had been about before he started kissing her.

"The transmitter, remember?"

"Oh yes, right." She swatted him out of habit. "Why did you want to go and distract me like that? I was quite in my element and everything."

Conall laughed. "Someone has to keep you off balance; otherwise you'll end up ruling the empire. Or at least ordering it into wretched submission."

"Ha-ha, very funny." She started down the hallway at a brisk trot, bustle waggling suggestively back and forth. Halfway down, she paused and looked back at him over one shoulder coquettishly. "Oh, Conall, *do* get a move on."

Lord Maccon growled but lumbered after her.

She stopped again, cocking her head. "What is that preposterous noise?"

"Opera."

"Really? I should never have guessed."

"I believe Tunstell is serenading Miss Hisselpenny."

"Good heavens! Poor Ivy. Ah well." She started onward again.

As they wound their way up through the castle toward the top turret where the aethographor resided, Alexia explained her theory that the now-destroyed mummy had once been a preternatural, that, after death, it had turned into some strange sort of soul-sucking weapon of mass disintegration. And that Angelique, believing the same, had tried to steal the mummy. Probably to get it into the hands of the Westminster Hive and Countess Nadasdy's pet scientists.

"If Angelique did manage to reveal all to the hive, no possible good can come of it. We might as well tell Madame Lefoux; at least she will use the knowledge to make weapons for our side."

Lord Maccon looked at his wife oddly. "Are there sides?"

"It would appear to be that way."

Lord Maccon sighed, his face worn with care, if not the passage of time. Alexia realized she was gripping his hand tightly and had thus brought him back into mortal state. She let go. He probably needed to be a werewolf right now, tapping into his reserves of supernatural strength.

He grumbled. "The last thing we need is a competition over weaponry based on dead preternaturals. I shall issue standing orders that all soulless are to be cremated after death. Covertly, of course." He looked to his wife, for once not angry, simply concerned. "They would all be after you and those of your kind dotted about the empire. Not only that, but you would also be more valuable dead if they knew that mummification worked as a preservation technique for your power."

"Luckily," Alexia said, "no one knows how the ancients conducted mummification. It gives us some time. And perhaps the transmission did not go through. I did manage to blast the aethographor with my magnetic disruption emitter."

She retrieved Angelique's metal scroll from where she had stashed it. It was not reassuring. The spy's message was burned completely through, and the track marks from the spark readers were evident across most of it.

Lady Maccon swore an impressive blue streak. The earl gave her a look that was half disapproval, half respect.

"I take it the message was sent on successfully?"

She passed the slate over to him. It read simply, "Dead mummy is soul-sucker." Not so many words in the end, but enough to complicate her life considerably in the future.

"Well, that has gone and torn it," was Lady Maccon's first cogent sentence.

"How can we be certain it went through to the other side?"

Alexia picked up a faceted crystalline valve, completely intact, from where it rested in the resonator cradle. "This must belong to the Westminster Hive." She tucked it into her parasol, in the pocket next to the one for Lord Akeldama's valve.

Then, with a thoughtful frown, she pulled that one out and examined it, twisting it this way and that in her gloved hand. What had Lord Akeldama's message said when they were testing Madame Lefoux's repairs? Something about rats? Oh no, no, it had been bats. Old-fashioned slang for the vampire community. If Lord Akeldama was monitoring the Westminster Hive, as she'd thought at the time, would he, too, have received the transmission about the mummy? Would him knowing be any worse or better?

Only one way to find out. Try sending him a message and see if he responded.

It was well past her arranged transmission time, of course, but Lord Akeldama's was the kind of apparatus that, if it was on and directed toward the appropriate frequency, would receive whatever was sent. If he *had* intercepted something significant, he would be expecting Alexia to contact him.

Instructing her husband to please stay as silent as possible, with a glare that indicated real consequences should he misbehave, Alexia went to work. She was getting quite adept at running the aethographor.

She etched in her message as quickly as possible. Fitting Lord Akeldama's valve into the cradle and the slate into its holder and activating the machine to transmit was much less difficult this time. Her message consisted of two things: "?" and "Alexia."

As soon as the transmission was complete, she went into the receiving chamber. Her husband merely continued to stand outside the aethographor, arms crossed, watching his wife's frilly form. She scuttled about, twiddling various dials and flipping large, important-looking switches. He might approve of her bluestocking tendencies, but he would never understand them. Back at BUR, he had people to run his aethographor for him.

Lady Maccon appeared to have things well in hand, however, as a message began to appear, letter by letter, in the magnetic particulate. As quietly as possible, she copied it down. It was rather longer than any transmission she had received before. It took a good deal of time to come in and even longer for her to determine where the breaks were between words and how it should read. When she finally managed it, Lady Maccon began to laugh. "My *petal*." The italics were visible even across the length of England. "Westminster's toy had tea issues. Thank Biffy and Lyall. Toodle pip. A."

"Fantastic!" said Lady Maccon, grinning.

"What?" Her husband's head looked in at the door to the receiving chamber.

"My favorite vampire, with the help of your illustrious Beta, managed to get his fangs into the Westminster Hive's transmitter. Angelique's last message never made it through."

Lord Maccon frowned darkly. "Randolph was working *with* Lord Akeldama?"

Lady Maccon patted his arm. "Well, he is far more accepting than you about these things."

The frown increased. "Clearly." A pause. "Well, then, let me just . . ." Her husband, still holding the slate with Angelique's message on it, twisted the dangerous thing around itself, his muscles expanding impressively, and then crushed the scroll together until all that remained was a crumpled metal ball. "We had better melt it down as well," he said, "just to be on the safe side." He looked to his wife. "Does anyone else know?"

"About the mummy?" She bit her lip in thought. "Lachlan and Sidheag. Possibly Lord Akeldama and Professor Lyall. And Ivy, but only in that way Ivy knows things."

"Which is to say, not with any real cogency?"

"Exactly."

They smiled at each other and, after Alexia shut down the machine, made their way leisurely back downstairs.

"Miss Hisselpenny has eloped."

After the general chaos of the night before, everyone had retired to their respective beds. Those still affected by Angelique's sleep drug were carried up by the pack. Then most of them, werewolves driven once more by antisun instincts and everyone else through pure exhaustion, slept the day away.

When Alexia came down for her first meal of the day, right about teatime, the sun had just set. It was as though her old pattern of nighttime living had miraculously transplanted itself to the Scottish Highlands.

The Kingair Pack sat about munching down fried kippers at the rate of knots, all looking brighter and bushier of tail, seeing as they now could go back to having tails. Even Lady Kingair seemed in slightly better spirits. She certainly relished delivering the news that Tunstell and Ivy had set out for Gretna Green sometime that morning, while everyone was still abed.

"What?" barked Lady Maccon, genuinely surprised. Ivy was silly, but was she really *that* silly?

Felicity, whom Alexia had, it must be admitted, entirely forgotten about in the chaos of the night before, looked up from her meal. "Why, yes, sister. She left you a note, with me of course."

"Did she, by George?" Alexia snatched the scribbled missive from her sister's pink-gloved hand.

Felicity grinned, enjoying Alexia's discomfort. "Miss Hisselpenny was awfully distraught when she composed it. I noticed no less than ten exclamation marks."

"And why, pray tell, would she leave it with you?" Alexia sat down and served herself a small portion of haggis.

Felicity shrugged, biting into a pickled onion. "I was the only one keeping respectable hours?"

Alexia was instantly suspicious. "Felicity, did you encourage them in any way into this rash course of action?"

"Who, me?" Her sister blinked wide eyes at her. "I never."

Lady Maccon was confident that if Felicity had helped, she had done so out of malice. She rubbed at her face with one hand. "Miss Hisselpenny will be ruined."

Felicity grinned. "Yes, yes, she will. I knew no good could possibly come of their association. I never liked Mr. Tunstell. I never even thought to look in his direction."

Lady Maccon gritted her teeth and opened Ivy's message.

All about the dining table, fascinated eyes watched her and less fascinated jaws masticated even more kipper.

Dearest Alexia, the message read. *Oh, please absolve me of this guilt I already feel squishing on my very soul!* Lady Maccon huffed, trying not to laugh. *My troubled heart weeps!* Oh dear, Ivy was getting flowery. *My bones ache with the sin that I am about to commit. Oh, why must I have bones? I have lost myself to this transplanting love. You could not possibly understand how this feels! Yet try to comprehend, dearest Alexia, I am like a delicate bloom. Marriage without love is all very well for people like you, but I should wilt and wither. I need a man possessed of a poet's soul! I am simply not so stoic as you. I cannot stand to be apart from him one moment longer! The caboose of my love has derailed, and I must sacrifice all for the man I adore! Please do not judge me harshly! It was all for love! ~ Ivy.*

Lady Maccon passed the missive to her husband. Several lines in, he began to guffaw.

His wife, eyes twinkling, said unhelpfully, "Husband, this is a serious matter. There are derailed cabooses to consider. You have lost your valet, for one, not to mention a promising claviger for the Woolsey Pack."

Lord Maccon wiped his eyes with the back of his hand. "Ah Tunstell, the nitwit, he was never a very good claviger. I was having doubts about him anyhow."

Lady Maccon took Ivy's note back from him. "But we must feel sorry for poor Captain Featherstonehaugh."

Lord Maccon shrugged. "Must we? He has had a lucky escape, if you ask me. Imagine having to look at those hats for the rest of one's life."

"Conall." His wife slapped his arm in reprimand.

"Well," Lord Maccon said truculently.

"You realize, husband, this puts us in an exceptionally embarrassing position? Ivy was in my charge. We shall have to inform her parents of this sad affair."

Lord Maccon shrugged. "The newlyweds will probably make it back to London before we do."

"You believe they are headed there after Gretna Green?"

"Well, Tunstell is hardly likely to give up the stage. Besides, all of his possessions are at Woolsey."

Lady Maccon sighed. "Poor Ivy."

"Why poor Ivy?"

"Well, my dear, you must admit, she has come rather down in the world."

Lord Maccon waggled his eyebrows. "I always thought your friend had a flair for the dramatic, *my dear.*"

Alexia winced. "You suppose she will join him in treading the boards?"

Lord Maccon shrugged.

Felicity, who had been avidly listening in to their conversation, slapped her fork down on her empty plate with a clank. "Well, I *say!* You mean she will not be completely ruined?"

Lord Maccon only smiled.

"You know, husband"—Lady Maccon glanced at her sister—"I think you may be right. She might make for a passing good actress. She certainly has the looks for it."

Felicity stood up from the table and marched out of the room.

Lord and Lady Maccon exchanged grins.

Alexia figured this was as good a time as any. "Husband," she said, casually helping herself to another small portion of haggis and assiduously avoiding the kippers. Her stomach was still feeling a little queasy, having never really recovered from the dratted dirigible experience, but a body had to eat.

"Aye?" Conall loaded his plate down with mounds of various dead critters.

"We will be departing presently, will we not?"

"Aye."

"I *ken* it is time you bit Lady Kingair, then," she stated baldly into the quiet munching of the dinner table.

The pack was immediately in an uproar, everyone talking at once.

"You canna change a woman," objected Dubh.

"She's the only Alpha we got left," added Lachlan, as though Alpha were a cut of meat to be acquired at the butcher.

Lady Kingair did not say anything, looking pale but resolute.

Alexia, rather boldly, took her husband's chin in one gloved hand, turning him mortal and turning him toward her.

"You need to do this, regardless of your pack laws and your werewolf pride. Take my counsel in this matter; remember, you married me for my good sense."

He grumbled but did not jerk his head away. "I married you for your body and to stop that mouth of yours. Look where that's got me."

"Aw, Conall, what a sweet thing to say." Lady Maccon rolled her eyes and then kissed him swiftly, on the lips, right there in front of the whole dinner table.

It was the surest way to silence a pack—scandalize them all. Even Conall was left speechless, with his mouth hanging slightly open.

"Good news, Lady Kingair," said Alexia. "My husband has agreed to change you."

The Kingair Beta laughed, breaking the dumbfounded hush. "I'm guessing she *is* a proper Alpha for all she was born a curse-breaker. Never thought I'd see you line up short to the petticoats, old wolf."

Lord Maccon stood up slowly and leaned forward, staring across at Dubh. "Want to try me again, pup? I can beat you down just as soundly in wolf form as I could in human."

Dubh quickly turned to one side, baring his neck. Apparently he agreed with the earl in this matter.

Lord Maccon made his way over to where Lady Kingair sat, still and straight in her chair at the head of the table. "You certain about this, lass? You ken 'tis probably death that's facing you?"

"We need an Alpha, Gramps." She looked to him. "Kingair canna survive much longer without one. I be the only option we've got left, and at least I'm Maccon. You owe the pack."

Lord Maccon's voice was a low rumble. "I dinna owe this pack anything. But you, lass, you're the last of my line. And it's time I took your wishes into consideration."

Lady Kingair sighed softly. "Finally."

Conall nodded once more. Then he changed. Not entirely. There was no full breaking of bone, no complete melting from one form to the next, and no shifting of hair into fur—except about his head. Only there did Lord Maccon transform: his nose elongating, his ears expanding upward, and his eyes shifting from brown to full yellow and lupine. The rest of him remained fully human-looking.

"Goodness me!" exclaimed Lady Maccon. "Are you going to do it right here, right now?" She swallowed. "At the dinner table?"

No one responded. They all stopped eating—a serious business, indeed, to put a Scotsman off his food. Pack and claviger alike became still and focused, staring hard at Lord Maccon. It was as though, by sheer strength of will, they could all see this metamorphosis through to a successful conclusion. Either that, or they were about to regurgitate their meals.

Then Lord Conall Maccon proceeded to eat his great-great-great-granddaughter.

There was really no other way of putting it.

Alexia watched in wide-eyed horror as her husband, wearing the head of a wolf, began to bite down on Lady Kingair's neck and then kept on chomping. Never before had she thought to behold such a thing.

And he was doing it right there, supper dishes not yet cleared away.

The blood leaking down from Lady Kingair's throat seeped into the lace collar and silk bodice of her dress, a dark spreading stain.

The Earl of Woolsey savaged Sidheag Maccon. Not one of the pack stepped in to save her. Sidheag flailed against the full bite. Instinct would not deny such a reaction. She clawed and hit at Conall, but he remained unmoved and unhurt, his werewolf strength easily outmatching her pathetic human struggles. He simply clamped those big hands about her shoulders—and they were still simply hands, without claws—and kept on biting. His long white teeth ripped through skin and muscle right down to the bone. Blood covered his muzzle, clotting the fur there.

Lady Maccon could not pull her eyes away from the gruesome sight. There seemed to be blood everywhere, and the copper smell of it battled against the scent of haggis and fried kipper. She was beginning to discern the inner workings of the woman's neck, as though this were some kind of horrific tableside anatomy lesson. Sidheag stopped struggling, her eyes rolling far back, showing almost all the whites. Her head, barely still attached to the rest of her body, lolled dangerously far to one side.

Then, in some farcical mockery of death, out came Conall's big pink tongue, and like an excessively friendly dog, he began licking over all the flesh he had just butchered. And he kept on licking, covering Sidheag's face and her partly open mouth, spreading lupine saliva about Lady Kingair's gaping wounds.

I am never going to be able to perform my wifely duty with that man ever again, thought Alexia, her eyes wide and fixed on the repulsive sight. Then, entirely unexpectedly and without even knowing it was about to happen, she actually fainted. A real honest-to-goodness faint, right there, face forward into her half-eaten haggis.

Lady Maccon blinked awake to her husband's worried, looming face. "Conall," she said, "please do not take this the wrong way. But that may have been the most disgusting thing I have ever seen in my life."

"Have you ever attended the birthing of a human child?"

"No, of course not. Don't be vulgar."

"Well, perhaps you had best wait to pass judgment, then."

"Well?" Alexia levered herself up slightly and glanced about. She appeared to have been carried into one of the drawing rooms and put to rest upon a brocade settee of considerable age.

"Well what?"

"Did it work? Did the metamorphosis work? Is she going to survive?"

Lord Maccon sat back slightly on his haunches. "A remarkable thing, a full Alpha female. Rare even in our oral histories. Boudica was an Alpha, did you know?"

"Conall!"

The head of a wolf came into Alexia's line of vision. It was not one she was personally familiar with: a craggy, rangy creature, graying about the muzzle but muscled and fit despite evident signs of age. Lady Maccon struggled to prop herself farther up onto the pillows.

The wolf's neck was covered in blood, the fur matted with a dark red crust, but otherwise it showed no injury. As though the blood were not her own. Which, technically, as she had now become supernatural, it might not be anymore.

Sidheag Maccon lolled a tongue out at Alexia. Alexia wondered how the wolf would respond to a scratch about the ears and decided, given the dignity of the woman when mortal, not to risk such an approach.

She looked at her husband. At least he seemed to have changed his shirt and washed his face during her mental absence. "I take it it worked?"

He grinned hugely. "My first successful change in years, and a female Alpha at that. The howlers will cry it to the winds."

"Somebody's proud of himself."

"Except that I should have remembered how distressing metamorphosis is to outsiders. I am sorry, my dear. I didna mean to upset you."

"Oh pish tosh, it wasn't that! I'm hardly one to be overcome by a bit of blood. It was simply a little dizzy spell."

Lord Maccon shifted forward against her and ran a large hand down the side of her face. "Alexia, you have been entirely comatose for well over an hour. I had to send for smelling salts."

Madame Lefoux came around the side of the couch and crouched down next to Alexia as well. "You had us very worried, my lady."

"So what happened?"

"You fainted," accused Lord Maccon, as though she had committed some egregious crime against him personally.

"No, with the metamorphosis. What did I miss?"

"Well," said Madame Lefoux, "it was all very exciting. There was this crash of thunder and a bright blue light and then—"

"Don't be ridiculous," snapped Lord Maccon. "You sound like a novel."

Madame Lefoux sighed. "Very well, Sidheag started to convulse and then collapsed to the floor, dead. Everyone stood around staring at her body, until all of a sudden, she began spontaneously changing into a wolf. She screamed a lot—I understand the first change is the worst. Then we realized you had collapsed. Lord Maccon threw a conniption fit, and we ended up here."

Lady Maccon turned accusing eyes to her husband. "You didn't, and on your granddaughter's metamorphosis day!"

"You fainted!" he said again, disgruntled.

"Stuff and nonsense," replied his wife sharply. "I never faint." A bit of her old color was returning. Really, who would have suspected she could turn quite that ashen?

"There was that one incident, in the library, when you killed the vampire."

"I was shamming and you knew it."

"How about that time we visited the museum after hours and I trapped you in a corner behind the Elgin Marbles?"

Lady Maccon rolled her eyes. "That was an entirely different kind of passing out."

Conall crowed. "My point exactly! Just now, you actually, positively, did faint. You never do that kind of thing; you're not that kind of female. What's wrong with you? Are you ill? I *forbid* you to be ill, wife."

"Oh, really. Stop fussing. There is absolutely nothing wrong with me. I'm just a tad off-kilter, have been since the dirigible ride." Alexia pushed herself more upright, trying to smooth her skirts and ignore her husband's still-stroking hand.

"Someone could have poisoned you again."

Alexia shook her head decisively. "As it wasn't Angelique who tried before, and it wasn't Madame Lefoux who stole my journal, and both occurred on board the dirigible, I believe the perpetrator never followed us to Kingair. Call it a preternatural hunch. No, I'm not being poisoned, husband. I'm just a little bit weak, that's all."

Madame Lefoux snorted, looking back and forth between the two of them as though they were both batty. She said, "She is just a little bit pregnant is what she is."

"What!" Lord Maccon's exclamation was echoed by Alexia. Lady Maccon stopped smoothing out her skirts, and Lord Maccon stopped smoothing out his wife's face.

The French inventor looked at them, genuinely amazed. "You did not know? Neither of you knew?"

Lord Maccon recoiled away from his wife, violently, jerking to stand upright, arms stiff by his sides.

Alexia glared at Madame Lefoux. "Don't talk piffle, madame. I cannot possibly be pregnant. That is not scientifically feasible."

Madame Lefoux dimpled. "I was with Angelique during her confinement. You show every possible sign of a delicate condition—nausea, weakness, increased girth."

"What!" Lady Maccon was genuinely shocked. True, she had been slightly sick to her stomach and unreasonably off some foods, but was it really possible? She supposed she might be in an indelicate condition. The scientists could be wrong, after all; there didn't exist very many soulless females, and none of them were married to werewolves.

She turned a suddenly grinning face to her husband. "You know what this means? I am not a bad dirigible floater! It was being pregnant that made me ill on board. Fantastic."

But her husband was not reacting in quite the manner anticipated. He was clearly angry, and not the sort of angry that made him bluster about, or shout, or change form, or any of those normal Lord Maccon-ish kinds of things. He was quietly, white-faced, shivering angry. And it was terribly, terribly frightening.

"*How?*" he barked at his wife, backing away from her as though she were infected with some terrible disease.

"What do you mean, how? The *how* should be perfectly obvious, even to you, you impossible man!" Alexia shot back, becoming angry herself. Shouldn't he be delighted? This was evidently a scientific miracle. Wasn't it?

"We only *call* it 'being human' when I touch you, for lack of a better term. I'm still dead, or mostly dead. Have been for hundreds of years. No supernatural creature has ever produced an offspring. *Ever.* It simply isna possible."

"You believe this can't be your child?"

"Now, hold on there, my lord, don't be hasty." Madame Lefoux tried to intervene, placing one small hand on Lord Maccon's arm.

He shook her off with a snarl.

"Of course it's your child, you pollock!" Now Alexia was livid. If she hadn't still been feeling weak, she would have stood and marched about the room. As it was, she groped for her parasol. Maybe whacking her husband atop his thick skull would drive some sense into him.

"Thousands of years of history and experience would seem to suggest you are lying, wife."

Lady Maccon sputtered in offense at that. She was so overset she couldn't even find the words, a remarkably novel experience for her.

"Who was he?" Conall wanted to know. "What daylight-dependent dishtowel did you fornicate with? One of my clavigers? One of Akeldama's poodle-faking drones? Is that why you're always visiting him? Or just some milk-curling mortal blowhard?"

Then he began calling her things, names and words, dirtier and harsher than she had ever heard before—let alone been called—and Alexia had encountered more than her fair share of profanity over the past year. They were horrible, cruel things, and she could comprehend the meanings of most, despite her lack of familiarity with the terminology.

Conall had committed many a violent act around Alexia during their association, not the least of which was savage a woman into metamorphosis at the supper table, but Alexia had never been actually afraid of him before.

She was afraid of him now. He did not move toward her—in fact, he'd backed farther away toward the door—but his hands were fisted white at his thighs, his eyes had changed to wolf yellow, and his canines were long and extended. She was immeasurably grateful when Madame Lefoux physically interposed herself between Alexia and the earl's verbal tirade. As though, somehow, the inventor could provide a barrier to his horrible words.

He stayed there, on the other side of the room, yelling at Alexia. It was as though he'd placed the distance between them, not because he didn't want to come at her and tear her apart, but because he really thought he might. His eyes were such a pale yellow they were almost white. Alexia had never seen them that color before. And, despite the filthy words coming out of his mouth, those eyes were agonized and bereft.

"But I didn't," Alexia tried to say. "I wouldn't. I'd never do those things. I am no adulteress. How could you even think? I would never." But her protestations of innocence only seemed to injure him. Eventually, his big, good-natured face crumpled slightly about the mouth and nose, drawing down into lines of pain, as though he might actually cry. He strode from the room, slamming the door behind him.

The silence he left behind was palpable.

Lady Kingair had, during the chaos, managed to change back into human form. She came around the front of the couch and stood a moment before Alexia, entirely naked, shielded only by her long gray-brown hair, loose over her shoulders and chest.

"You will understand, *Lady* Maccon," she said, eyes cold, "if I ask you to leave Kingair territory at once. Lord Maccon may have abandoned us once, but he is still pack. And pack protects its own."

"But," Alexia whispered, "it is his child. I swear it. I was never with anyone else."

Sidheag only stared at her, hard. "Come now, Lady Maccon. Shouldna you come up with a better story than that? 'Tis na possible. Werewolves canna breed children. Never have done, never will do." Then she turned and left the room.

Alexia turned to Madame Lefoux, shock written all over her face.

"He really believes I was unfaithful." She herself had reflected recently how much Conall valued loyalty.

Madame Lefoux nodded. "I'm afraid it is a belief most will share." Her expression sympathetic, she placed a small hand on Alexia's shoulder and squeezed.

"I wasn't, I swear I wasn't."

The Frenchwoman winced. "I believe that, Lady Maccon. But I will be in the minority."

"Why would you trust me when even my husband does not?" Alexia looked down at her own stomach and then rested shaking hands upon it.

"Because I know how very little we understand about preternaturals."

"You are interested in studying me, aren't you, Madame Lefoux?"

"You are a remarkable creature, Alexia."

Alexia widened her eyes, trying not to cry, her mind still vibrating with Conall's words. "Then how is this possible?" She pressed hard against her stomach with both hands, as though asking the tiny creature inside to explain itself to her.

"I imagine that is something we had best figure out. Come on, let's get you out of this place."

The Frenchwoman helped Alexia to stand and supported her weight out into the hallway. She was surprisingly strong for such a delicate-looking creature, probably all that lifting of heavy machinery.

They ran into Felicity, looking remarkably somber.

"Sister, there was the most awful to-do," she said as soon as she saw them. "I believe your husband just smashed one of the hall tables into a thousand pieces with his fist." She cocked her head. "It *was* an astonishingly ugly table, but still, one could always give it to the deserving poor, couldn't one?"

"We must pack and leave immediately," said Madame Lefoux, keeping one arm supportively about Alexia's waist.

"Good Lord, why?"

"Your sister is pregnant, and Lord Maccon has cast her out."

Felicity frowned. "Well, *that* does not follow."

Madame Lefoux had clearly had enough. "Quickly, girl, run off and gather your things together. We must quit Kingair directly."

Three-quarters of an hour later, a borrowed Kingair carriage sped away toward the nearest train station. The horses were fresh and made good time, even in the slush and mud.

Alexia, still overcome with the most profound shock, opened the small window above the carriage door and poked her head out into the rushing wind.

"Sister, come away from the window. That will wreak havoc with your hair. And, really, your hair doesn't need the excuse," Felicity jawed on. Alexia ignored her, so Felicity looked to the Frenchwoman. "What *is* she doing?"

Madame Lefoux gave a sad little grimace of a smile—no dimples. "Listening." She put a gentle hand on Alexia's back, rubbing it softly. Alexia did not appear to notice.

"For what?"

"Howling, running wolves."

And Alexia was listening, but there was only the damp quiet of a Scottish night.

BLAMELESS

The Parasol Protectorate: Book the Third

Acknowledgments

This book really wouldn't have happened without Kristin, Devi, and Francesca. No, really, you'd be reading a big fat collection of blank pages right now. Thanks, ladies, I owe you all wine and cheese! Lots of cheese. And a million hugs to J. Daniel Sawyer, who was more helpful, more often, than he realized.

CHAPTER ONE

Wherein the Misses Loontwill Cope with Scandal in Their Midst

How much longer, Mama, must we tolerate this gross humiliation?" Lady Alexia Maccon paused before entering the breakfast room. Cutting through the comfortable sounds of chinking teacups and scrunching toast shrilled her sister's less-than-dulcet tones. In an unsurprising morning duet of well-practiced whining, Felicity's voice was soon followed by Evylin's.

"Yes, Mumsy darling, such a scandal under our roof. We really shouldn't be expected to put up with it any longer."

Felicity championed the cause once more. "This is ruining our chances"—*crunch, crunch*—"beyond all recuperation. It isn't to be borne. It really isn't."

Alexia made a show of checking her appearance in the hall mirror, hoping to overhear more. Much to her consternation, the Loontwill's new butler, Swilkins, came through with a tray of kippers. He gave her a disapproving glare that said much on his opinion of a young lady caught eavesdropping on her own family. Eavesdropping was, by rights, a butler's proprietary art form.

"Good morning, Lady Maccon," he said loudly enough for the family to hear even through their chatting and clattering, "you received several messages yesterday." He handed Alexia two folded and sealed letters and then waited pointedly for her to precede him into the breakfast room.

"Yesterday! Yesterday! And why, pray tell, did you not *give* them to me yesterday?"

Swilkins did not reply.

Nasty bit of bother, this new butler. Alexia was finding that little was worse in life than existing in a state of hostility with one's domestic staff.

Entering the breakfast room, Alexia actually flounced slightly in her annoyance and turned her ire upon those seated before her. "Good morning, dearest family."

As she made her way to the only empty chair, four pairs of blue eyes watched her progress with an air of condemnation. Well, three pairs—the Right Honorable Squire Loontwill was entirely taken with the correct cracking of his soft-boiled egg. This involved the application of an ingenious little device, rather like a handheld sideways guillotine, that nipped the tip off the egg in perfect, chipless circularity. Thus happily engrossed, he did not bother to attend to the arrival of his stepdaughter.

Alexia poured herself a glass of barley water and took a piece of toast from the rack, no butter, trying to ignore the smoky smell of breakfast. It had once been her favorite meal; now it invariably curdled her stomach. So far, the infant-inconvenience—as she'd taken to thinking of it—was proving itself far more tiresome than one would have thought possible, considering it was years away from either speech or action.

Mrs. Loontwill looked with manifest approval at her daughter's meager selection. "I shall be comforted," she said to the table at large, "by the fact that our poor dear Alexia is practically wasting away for want of her husband's affection. Such fine feelings of sentimentality." She clearly perceived Alexia's breakfast-starvation tactics as symptoms of a superior bout of wallowing.

Alexia gave her mother an annoyed glance and inflicted minor wrath upon her toast with the butter knife. Since the infant-inconvenience had added a small amount of weight to Alexia's already substantial figure, she was several stone away from "wasting." Nor was she of a personality inclined toward wallowing. In addition, she resented the fact that Lord Maccon might be thought to have anything whatsoever to do with the fact—aside from the obvious, of which her family was as yet unaware—that she was off her food. She opened her mouth to correct her mother in this regard, but Felicity interrupted her.

"Oh, Mama, I hardly think Alexia is the type to die of a broken heart."

"Nor is she the type to be gastronomically challenged," shot back Mrs. Loontwill.

"I, on the other hand," interjected Evylin, helping herself to a plateful of kippers, "may jolly well do both."

"Language, Evy darling, please." Mrs. Loontwill snapped a piece of toast in half in her distress.

The youngest Miss Loontwill rounded on Alexia, pointing a forkful of egg at her accusingly. "Captain Featherstonehaugh has thrown me over! How do you like that? We received a note only this morning."

"Captain Featherstonehaugh?" Alexia muttered to herself. "I thought he was engaged to Ivy Hisselpenny and you were engaged to someone else. How confusing."

"No, no, Evy's engaged to him now. Or was. How long have you been staying with us? Nearly two weeks? Do pay attention, Alexia dear," Mrs. Loontwill admonished.

Evylin sighed dramatically. "And the dress is already bought and everything. I shall have to have it entirely made over."

"He did have very nice eyebrows," consoled Mrs. Loontwill.

"Exactly," crowed Evylin. "Where will I find another pair of eyebrows like that? Devastated, I tell you, Alexia. I am utterly devastated. And it is all *your* fault."

Evylin, it must be noted, did not look nearly so bothered as one rightly ought over the loss of a fiancé, especially one reputed to possess such heights of eyebrow preeminence. She stuffed the egg into her mouth and chewed methodically. She had taken it into her head recently that chewing every bite of food twenty times over would keep her slender. What it did was keep her at the dinner table longer than anyone else.

"He cited philosophical differences, but we all know why he really broke things off." Felicity waved a goldedged note at Alexia—a note that clearly contained the good captain's deepest regrets, a note that, judging from the stains about itself, had received the concerted attention of everyone at the breakfast table, including the kippers.

"I agree." Alexia calmly sipped her barley water. "Philosophical differences? That cannot be true. You don't actually have a philosophy about anything, do you, Evylin dear?"

"So you admit responsibility?" Evylin was moved to swallow early so she could launch the attack once more. She tossed her blond curls, only one or two shades removed from the color of her egg.

"Certainly not. I never even met the man."

"But it is still *your* fault. Abandoning your husband like that, staying with us instead of him. It is outrageous. People. Are. Talking." Evylin emphasized her words by stabbing ruthlessly at a sausage.

"People do tend to talk. I believe it is generally considered one of the better modes of communication."

"Oh, why must you be so impossible? Mama, do something about her." Evylin gave up on the sausage and went on to a second fried egg.

"You hardly seem very cut up about it." Alexia watched as her sister chewed away.

"Oh, I assure you, poor Evy is deeply effected. Shockingly over-wrought," said Mrs. Loontwill.

"Surely you mean *a*ffected?" Alexia was not above a barb or two where her family was concerned.

At the end of the table, Squire Loontwill, the only one likely to understand a literary joke, softly chortled.

"Herbert," his wife reprimanded immediately, "don't encourage her to be pert. Most unattractive quality in a married lady, pertness." She turned back to Alexia. Mrs. Loontwill's face, that of a pretty woman who had aged without realizing it, screwed itself up into a grimace Alexia supposed was meant to simulate motherly concern. Instead she looked like a Pekingese with digestive complaints. "Is that what the estrangement with *him* is over, Alexia? You weren't . . . brainy . . . with *him,* were you, dear?" Mrs. Loontwill had refrained from referring to Lord Maccon by name ever since her daughter's marriage, as if by doing so she might hold on to the fact that Alexia *had* married—a condition believed by most to be highly unlikely right up until the fateful event—without having to remember *what* she had married. A peer of the realm, it was true, and one of Her Majesty's finest, to be certain, but also a werewolf. It hadn't helped that Lord Maccon loathed Mrs. Loontwill and didn't mind who knew it, including Mrs. Loontwill. *Why,* Alexia remembered, *once, he had even*—She stopped herself from further thought of her husband, squashing the memory ruthlessly. Unfortunately, she found that, the agitation of her thoughts had resulted in toast mutilated beyond all hope of consumption. With a sigh, she helped herself to another piece.

"It seems clear to me," interjected Felicity with an air of finality, "that your presence here, Alexia, has somehow overset Evy's engagement. Even you cannot argue your way out of that, sister dear."

Felicity and Evylin were Alexia's younger half-sisters by birth and were entirely unrelated if one took into account any other factors. They were short, blond, and slender, while Alexia was tall, dark, and, quite frankly, not so very slender. Alexia was known throughout London for her intellectual prowess, patronage of the scientific community, and biting wit. Felicity and Evylin were known for their puffed sleeves. The world, as a result, was generally more peaceful when the three were not living under the same roof.

"And we are all aware of how considered and unbiased your opinion is on the matter, Felicity." Alexia's tone was unruffled.

Felicity picked up the scandal section of the *Lady's Daily Chirrup,* clearly indicating she wanted nothing more to do with the conversation.

Mrs. Loontwill dove courageously on. "Surely, Alexia, darling, it is high time you returned home to Woolsey? I mean to say, you've been with us nearly a week, and, of course, we do love having you, but *he* is rumored to be back from Scotland now."

"Bully for *him*."

"Alexia! What a shocking thing to say!"

Evylin interjected. "No one has seen him in town, of course, but they say he returned to Woolsey yesterday."

"Who says?"

Felicity crinkled the gossip section of the paper explanatorily. "Oh, *they*."

"He must be pining for you, my dear," Mrs. Loontwill resumed the attack. "Pining away, miserable for want of your . . ." She flailed.

"For want of my *what*, Mama?"

"Uh, scintillating companionship."

Alexia snorted—at the dining table. Conall may have enjoyed her bluntness on rare occasion, but if he missed anything, she doubted her wit was top of the list. Lord Maccon was a werewolf of hearty appetites, to say the least. What he would miss most about his wife was located substantially lower than her tongue. An image of her husband's face momentarily broke her resolve. That look in his eyes the last time they saw each other—so betrayed. But what he believed of her, the fact that he doubted her in such a way, was inexcusable. How dare he leave her remembering some lost-puppy look simply to toy with her sympathies! Alexia Maccon made herself relive the things he had said to her, right then and there. She was *never* going to go back to that—her mind grappled for a description—that untrusting nitwit!

Lady Alexia Maccon was the type of woman who, if thrown into a briar patch, would start to tidy it up by stripping off all the thorns. Over the past few weeks and throughout the course of an inexcusably foul train journey back from Scotland, she thought she had come to terms with her husband's rejection of both her and their child. She was finding, however, at the oddest and most irregular moments, that she hadn't. She would feel the betrayal, like some writhing ache just under her ribs, and become both incredibly hurt and transcendently angry without warning. It was exactly like an acute attack of indigestion—only with one's finer feelings involved. In her more lucid moments, Alexia reasoned that the cause of this sensation was the unjustness of it all. She was quite accustomed to defending herself for having done something inappropriate, but defending herself when completely innocent made for a dissimilar, and far more frustrating, experience. Not even Bogglington's Best Darjeeling succeeded in soothing her temper.

And if tea wasn't good enough, well, what *was* a lady to do? It was not, certainly not, that she still loved the man. That was entirely illogical. But the fact remained that Alexia's temper was tender about the edges. Her family ought to have recognized the signs.

Felicity snapped the paper closed suddenly, her face an uncharacteristic red color.

"Oh, dear." Mrs. Loontwill fanned herself with a starched doily. "What *now*?"

Squire Loontwill glanced up and then took refuge in close examination of his egg.

"Nothing." Felicity tried to shove the paper under her plate.

Evylin was having none of it. She reached over, snatched it away, and began scanning through it, looking for whatever juicy tittle-tattle had so disturbed her sister.

Felicity nibbled on a scone and looked guiltily at Alexia.

Alexia had a sudden sinking feeling in the pit of her stomach. She finished her barley water with some difficulty and sat back in her chair.

"Oh, golly!" Evylin seemed to have found the troublesome passage. She read it out for all to hear. "'London was flabbergasted last week when news reached this reporter's ears that Lady Maccon, previously Alexia Tarabotti, daughter of Mrs. Loontwill, sister to Felicity and Evylin, and stepdaughter to the Honorable Squire Loontwill, had quit her husband's house, after returning from Scotland without said husband. Speculation as to the reason has been ample, ranging from suspicions as to Lady Maccon's intimate relationship with the rove vampire Lord Akeldama, to suspected family differences hinted at by the Misses Loontwill'—oh look, Felicity, they mentioned us twice!— 'and certain lower-class social acquaintances. Lady Maccon cut quite a fashionable swath through London society after her marriage'—la, la, la . . . Ah! Here it picks up again—'but it has been revealed by sources intimately connected to the noble couple that Lady Maccon is, in fact, in a most delicate condition. Given Lord Maccon's age, supernatural inclination, and legally recognized postnecrosis status, it must be assumed that Lady Maccon has been *indiscreet*. While we await physical confirmation, all signs point to The Scandal of the Century.'"

Everyone looked at Alexia and began talking at once.

Evylin snapped the paper closed, the crisp noise silencing her family. "Well, that explains *that*! Captain Featherstonehaugh must have read this. Which is why he broke off our engagement this morning. Felicity was right! This really is your fault! How could you be so thoughtless, Alexia?"

"No wonder she's been off her feed," commented Squire Loontwill unhelpfully.

Mrs. Loontwill rose to the occasion. "This is simply too much for a mother to endure. Too much! Alexia, how did you manage to bungle matters so completely? Didn't I raise you to be a good, respectful girl? Oh, I don't know what to say!" Words failed Mrs. Loontwill. Luckily, she did not try to strike her daughter. She had done that once, and it hadn't worked out well for anyone. Alexia had ended up married as a result.

Alexia stood. Angry again. *I spend a considerable time out of temper these days,* she reflected. Only four people had known of her unseemly condition. Three of them would never even consider talking to the press. Which left only one option, an option that was currently wearing the most reprehensible blue lace dress, sporting a suspiciously red face, and sitting across from her at the breakfast table.

"Felicity, I should have realized you wouldn't be able to keep your trap shut!"

"It wasn't me!" Felicity instantly leaped to the defensive. "It must have been Madame Lefoux. You know how these Frenchwomen are! They'll say anything for a modicum of fame and money."

"Felicity, you knew about Alexia's condition and did not inform me?" Mrs. Loontwill recovered from her shock just in time to be shocked again. That Alexia would keep a secret from her own mother was to be expected, but Felicity was supposed to be on Mrs. Loontwill's side. The chit had been bribed with enough pairs of shoes over the years.

Lady Alexia Maccon slammed one hand down on the tabletop, causing teacups to rattle ominously, and leaned forward toward her sister. It was an unconscious application of intimidation tactics learned during several months spent living with a werewolf pack. She was nowhere near as hairy as was generally required for the maneuver, but she still managed to execute it flawlessly. "Madame Lefoux would do *no such thing.* I happen to know for a fact she is the soul of discretion. Only one person would talk, and that person is not French. You promised me, Felicity. I gave you my favorite amethyst necklace to keep silent."

"Is that how you got it?" Evylin was envious.

"Who is the father, then?" asked Squire Loontwill, apparently feeling he ought to try and steer the conversation in a more productive direction. The ladies, fluttering agitatedly all around the table, entirely ignored him. This was a state comfortable to them all. The squire sucked his teeth in resignation and went back to his breakfast.

Felicity went from defensive to sulky. "It was only Miss Wibbley and Miss Twittergaddle. How was I to know they would go running off to the press?"

"Miss Twittergaddle's father owns the *Chirrup*. As you are very well aware!" But then Alexia's anger simmered off slightly. The fact that Felicity had held her tongue for several weeks was practically a miracle of the third age of mankind. Undoubtedly, Felicity had told the young ladies in order to garner attention, but she probably also knew such gossip would effectively dissolve Evylin's engagement and ruin Alexia's life. Sometime after Alexia's wedding, Felicity had evolved from frivolous to outright spiteful, which, combined with a gooseberry-sized brain, resulted in her being an acutely disastrous human being.

"After all this family has done for you, Alexia!" Mrs. Loontwill continued to heap recriminations on her daughter. "After Herbert permitted you back into the safety of his bosom!" Squire Loontwill looked up at that turn of phrase, then down at his portly frame with disbelief. "After the pains I went through to see you safely married. To go outside of all standards of decency like a common strumpet. It is simply intolerable."

"Exactly my point all along," stated Felicity smugly.

Driven to heights of exasperation, Alexia reached for the plate of kippers and, after due consideration of about three seconds, upended it over her sister's head.

Felicity shrieked something fierce.

"But," Alexia muttered under the resulting pandemonium, "it is *his child*."

"What was that?" Squire Loontwill brought a hand down sharply on the tabletop this time.

"It is his bloody child. I have not *been* with anyone else." Alexia yelled it over Felicity's whimpering.

"Alexia! Don't be crass. There is no need for specifics. Everyone is well aware that is not possible. Your husband is basically dead, or was basically dead and is mostly dead now." Mrs. Loontwill appeared to be confusing herself. She shook her head like a wet poodle and sallied stoically on with her diatribe. "Regardless, a werewolf fathering a child is like a vampire or a ghost producing offspring—patently ridiculous."

"Well, so is this family, but you all appear to exist in accordance with the natural order."

"What was that?"

"In this case, 'ridiculous' would seem to require a redefinition." *Blast this child to all four corners of hell, anyway*, thought Alexia.

"You see how she is?" interjected Felicity, picking kipper off herself and glowering murderously. "She just keeps talking like that. Won't admit to doing a single thing wrong. He has chucked her over—are you aware of that? She is not returning to Woolsey because she cannot return. Lord Maccon cast her out. That is why we left Scotland."

"Oh, my goodness. Herbert! Herbert, did you hear that?" Mrs. Loontwill looked about ready to have the vapors.

Alexia wasn't certain if this was manufactured distress at Conall publicly booting Alexia or if it was genuine horror at the prospect of having to board her eldest for the foreseeable future.

"Herbert, do something!" Mrs. Loontwill wailed.

"I have died and gone to the land of bad novels," was Squire Loontwill's response. "I am ill-equipped to cope with such an occurrence. Leticia, my dear, I leave it entirely in your capable hands."

A more inappropriate phrase had never yet been applied to his wife, whose hands were capable of nothing more complex than the occasional, highly stressful, bout of embroidery. Mrs. Loontwill cast said hands heavenward and sagged back into her chair in a partial faint.

"Oh, no, you don't, Papa." An edge of steel entered Felicity's tone. "Forgive me for being autocratic, but you must understand Alexia's continued presence under our roof is entirely untenable. Such a scandal as this will substantially hinder our chances of matrimony, even without her actual attendance. You must send her away and forbid her further contact with the family. I recommend we quit London immediately. Perhaps for a European tour?"

Evylin clapped her hands, and Alexia was left wondering how much planning Felicity had put into this little betrayal. She looked hard into her sister's unexpectedly pitiless face. *Deceitful little plonker! I should have hit her with something harder than kippers.*

Squire Loontwill was taken aback by Felicity's forthright talk, but always a man to take the path of least resistance, he took stock of his collapsed wife and fierce-faced daughter and rang the bell for the butler.

"Swilkins, go upstairs immediately and pack Lady Maccon's things."

Swilkins remained motionless, impassive in his surprise.

"Now, man!" snapped Felicity.

Swilkins retreated.

Alexia made a little huffing noise of exasperation. Just wait until she told Conall about this latest familial absurdity. Why he'd . . . *Ah, yes, never mind.* Her anger once again died, buckling under the ache of a werewolf-sized hole. Attempting to fill up the void with something, she helped herself to a dollop of marmalade and, because she had nothing left to lose, ate it directly off the spoon.

At that, Mrs. Loontwill actually did faint.

Squire Loontwill gave his wife's limp form a long look and then, with due consideration, left her there for the time being and retreated to the smoking room.

Alexia remembered her mail, and since she needed a distraction and would rather do anything other than converse further with her sisters, she picked up the first letter and broke the seal. Until that moment, she had actually thought things couldn't get any worse.

The seal on the letter was unmistakable—a lion and a unicorn with a crown in between. The message on the interior was equally forthright. Lady Maccon's presence was no longer welcome at Buckingham Palace. The Queen of England would henceforth be unable to receive her. Lady Maccon's duties as a member of the Shadow Council were suspended until further notice. She no longer carried Her Majesty's confidence or authority. The position of muhjah was once more vacant. She was thanked kindly for her previous services and wished a pleasant day.

Alexia Maccon stood up very decidedly, left the breakfast room, and walked directly into the kitchen, ignoring the startled servants. With barely a pause, she marched over and stuffed the official missive into the huge iron range that dominated the room. It caught fire and immolated instantly. Craving solitude, she went from the kitchen into the back parlor, rather than back to the breakfast room. She wanted to retire to her room and crawl back under the bed covers in a tiny—well, not that tiny—ball. But she was already dressed, and principles must be maintained even in the direst of times.

She should not have been surprised. For all her progressive politics, Queen Victoria was morally conservative. She still wore mourning for her husband, dead, ghosted, and gone for over a decade. And if any woman didn't look good in black, it was Queen Victoria. There was no way that the queen would allow Lady Maccon to continue in her clandestine role of preternatural advisor and field agent, even if it remained an entirely secret and classified position. Lady Maccon could not possibly have even a hint of an association with the queen, not now that she had become a social pariah. The morning's news was probably already common knowledge.

Alexia sighed. The potentate and the dewan, fellow members of the Shadow Council, would be delighted to see her gone. She hadn't exactly made life easy for them. That, too, had been part of the job requirements. She experienced a shiver of apprehension. Without Conall and the Woolsey Pack to protect her, there were probably quite a number of individuals who would count her as better off deceased. She rang the bell for one of the maids and sent her to retrieve her parasol-cum-weapon before the butler packed it away. The maid returned shortly, and Alexia felt slightly comforted by having her favorite accessory on hand.

Her thoughts, unbidden, returned once more to her husband, who had so thoughtfully gifted her with the deadly ornament. *Damn and blast Conall.* Why didn't he believe her? So what if all known history contradicted her? History wasn't precisely revered for its accuracy at the best of times. Nor was it overflowing with female preternaturals. Scientifically, no one understood how she was what she was or did what she did even now, with all England's vaunted technology. So what if he was mostly dead? Her touch turned him mortal, didn't it? Why couldn't it also turn him human enough to be able to give her a child? Was that so impossible to believe? *Horrible man.* So like a werewolf to get overly emotional and fluff up the duster like that.

Just thinking about him and Alexia became overcome with senti-ment. Annoyed at her own weakness, she dabbed the tears away and looked to her other note, expecting more bad news. However, the writ-ing on this one, bold and entirely too flowery, made her give a watery smile. She'd sent a card 'round shortly after she returned to London. She wouldn't be so rude as to ask, but she had hinted at her uncomfort-able domestic situation, and he, of course, would know what had hap-pened. *He* always knew what was happening.

"My *darling* Chamomile Button!" he wrote. "I received your card, and given certain recent intelligence, it has occurred to me that you may be in ever-increasing need of accommodation but were far too polite to request it openly. Let me tender my most humble offer, to the *only person* in *all* of England currently thought *more* outrageous than myself. You would be welcome to share my *unworthy* domicile and hospitality, such as they are. Yours, et cetera, Lord Akeldama."

Alexia grinned. She had been hoping he would read the appeal be-hind her formal social nicety. Even though his card had been written before her condition had become public knowledge, she suspected her vampire friend would still be amenable to an extended visit and had probably already known about the pregnancy. Lord Akeldama was a rove of such consistently shocking dress and manner that his reputa-tion could only be amplified by taking in the now-ruined Lady Mac-con. In addition, he would have her at his mercy and disposal, thus able to extract all truths from her ad nauseam. Of course, she intended to accept his offer, hoping that, as the invitation had been made yesterday— damn the irascible Swilkins—she was not too late. She was rather look-ing forward to the prospect. Lord Akeldama's abode and table were quite the opposite of humble, and he kept the companionship of a large

collective of such shining paragons of foppishness as to make any so-
journ in his company one of unending visual delight. Relieved that she
was no longer homeless, Lady Maccon sent a note to that effect. She
took pains to ensure that the missive was carried by the Loontwills'
most attractive footman.

Maybe Lord Akeldama would know something that would explain
the presence of a child parasiting about inside her. He was a very old
vampire; perhaps he could help prove to Conall her upstanding virtue.
The ludicrousness of that thought—Lord Akeldama and virtue in the
same sentence—made her smile.

Her luggage packed and her hat and cape in place, Alexia was preparing to quit her family's house, probably for the last time, when yet
more mail arrived addressed to her. It was in the form of a suspicious
package accompanied by a message. This time she intercepted it before
Swilkins could get his mitts on it.

The package contained a hat of such unparalleled biliousness that
Alexia had no doubt as to its origin. It was a felt toque, bright yellow in
color and trimmed with fake black currants, velvet ribbon, and a pair of
green feathers that looked like the feelers from some unfortunate sea
creature. The accompanying note boasted remarkably exclamatory grammar and, if possible, attained new heights of flowery penmanship above
and beyond that of Lord Akeldama. It was, admittedly, a tad harrowing
to read.

"Alexia Tarabotti Maccon, how could you behave so *wickedly*! I
just read the morning paper. You had my heart in my chest, you really
did! Of course, I should never have believed such a thing in all my born
days! Never! In fact, I do not believe a word of it now. You understand
that we—Tunny and I—would *love* to have you to stay, but circumstances being, as they say, indefensible—or it is indefatigable?—we
cannot possibly tender the offer. You understand? I'm certain you do.
Don't you? But I thought you might require some consoling, and I
remembered how much attention you paid this adorable hat last time
we were out shopping together—ah, these many months ago, in our
careless youth, or do I mean carefree youth?—so I picked this out for
you at Chapeau de Poupe. I had intended it to be a Christmas gift, but
such an emotional crisis as you must be suffering clearly indicates that
now is obviously a far more *important time for hats*. Wouldn't you say?
Love, love, love, Ivy."

Alexia perfectly understood all the things Ivy hadn't written, if
such a thing was to be believed possible given the length of the missive.
Ivy and her new husband were committed theatricals and, quite frankly,
could not afford to lose patronage through association with the now-

besmirched Lady Maccon. Alexia was relieved she would not have to turn them down. The couple lived in the most horrible little set of apartments imaginable, down in the West End. They had, for example, only one parlor. Lady Maccon shuddered delicately.

Tucking the repulsive hat under her arm and grabbing her trusty parasol, Alexia made her way down to the waiting carriage. She gave Swilkins a haughty sniff as he handed her up and directed the driver on to Lord Akeldama's town house.

CHAPTER TWO

In Which Lord Maccon Is Likened
to a Small Cucumber

Lord Akeldama's house was located in one of the most fashionable parts of London. A part that had probably become fashionable because it was fortunate enough to host said town house. Lord Akeldama did *everything* fashionably, sometimes to the exclusion of all else, including common sense. If Lord Akeldama were to take up wrestling in vats of jellied eels, it would probably become fashionable within a fortnight. The exterior of his house had been recently redecorated to the height of modern taste and the worshipful approval of the ton. It was painted pale lavender with gold trim swirling and flouncing around every window and aperture. An herbaceous border of lilac bushes, sunflowers, and pansies had been planted as a complement, forming a pleasing three-level effect as visitors wandered up to the front steps, even in winter. The house stood as a solo bastion of cheer, battling valiantly against the London sky, which had undertaken its customary stance halfway between an indifferent gray and a malnourished drizzle.

No one responded to Lady Maccon's knock, nor to her tug on the bell rope, but the gilded front door had been left unlocked. Waving at the driver to wait, Alexia made her way cautiously inside, parasol up and at the ready. The rooms lay in unabashed splendor—fluffy carpets depicting romantically inclined shepherds, paired with arched ceilings playing host to equally amorous cherubs painted *a la Roma*.

"Halloo. Anybody home?"

The place was completely and utterly deserted, obviously in exceptional haste. Not only was there no Lord Akeldama, but there was no Biffy, nor any other drone. Lord Akeldama's abode was normally a carnival of delights: discarded top hats and piles of playbills, the scent of expensive cigars and French cologne, and it boasted a background hum of chatter and hilarity. The silence and stillness were all the more noticeable by comparison.

Alexia made her way slowly through the empty rooms, as though she were an archaeologist visiting an abandoned tomb. All she found was evidence of departure, certain items of importance taken down from places of honor. The gold pipe was missing, the one that normally sat atop the mantelpiece in the drawing room like some revered item of plumbing but that—Alexia knew from personal experience—hid two curved blades. The fact that Lord Akeldama saw fit to take *that* particular item with him did not bode well for the reason behind his departure.

The only living thing on the premises, aside from Alexia, appeared to be the resident cat. The feline in question was a fat calico that possessed the disposition of a placid narcoleptic and that roused only periodically to enact potent and vicious revenge upon the nearest tasseled throw pillow. Currently, the animal lay sprawled across a puffy hassock, the remains of three decapitated tassels nestled near her chin. Cats, as a general rule, were the only creatures that tolerated vampires. Most other animals had what the scientists termed a well-developed prey response behavior pattern. Felines, apparently, didn't consider themselves vampire prey. This one, however, was so utterly indifferent to any non-tassel-related creature, she could probably have tolerated residency among a pack of werewolves.

"Where has your master disappeared to, Fatty?" Alexia inquired of the creature.

The cat had no definitive answer but graciously allowed herself to be scratched under the chin. She was sporting a most peculiar metal collar, and Lady Maccon was just bending down to examine it closer when she heard muffled footsteps in the hallway behind her.

Lord Conall Maccon was drunk.

He was not drunk in the halfhearted manner of most supernatural creatures, wherein twelve pints of bitter had finally turned the world slightly fuzzy. No, Lord Maccon was rip-roaring, tumble down, without a doubt, pickled beyond the gherkin.

It took an enormous quantity of alcohol to get a werewolf that inebriated. And, reflected Professor Lyall as he steered his Alpha around the side of an inconvenient potshed, it was almost as miraculous a feat to attain such quantities as it was to ingest them. How had Lord Maccon finagled such an arrangement? Not only that, how had he managed to acquire said booze so consistently over the past three days without visiting London or tapping into Woolsey Castle's well-stocked cellar? *Really,* thought the Beta in annoyance, *such powers of alcoholism could almost be thought supernatural.*

Lord Maccon lurched heavily into the side of the potshed. The meat of his left shoulder and upper arm crashed against the oak siding. The entire building swayed on its foundation.

"Pardon," apologized the earl with a small hiccough, "didna see ya there."

"For Pete's sake, Conall," said his Beta in tones of the deeply put-upon, "how did you manage to get so corned?" He tugged his Alpha away from the abused shed.

"Na drunk," insisted his lordship, throwing one substantial arm across his Beta's shoulders and leaning heavily upon it. "Jush a tiny little slightly small bit'a squiffy." His lordship's accent got distinctly more Scottish in times of great stress, strong emotion, or, apparently, under the influence of vast amounts of liquid intoxicants.

They left the safety of the potshed.

The earl pitched forward suddenly, his grip on his Beta the only thing that managed to keep him upright. "Whoa! Watch that bit'o ground there, would ya? Tricky, tricky, jumps right up at a man."

"Where did you acquire the alcohol?" Professor Lyall asked again as he tried valiantly to get his Alpha back on track across the wide lawn of Woolsey's extensive grounds, toward the castle proper. It was like trying to steer a steamboat through a tub of turbulent molasses. A normal human would have buckled under the strain, but Lyall was lucky enough to have supernatural strength to call upon at times of great difficulty. Lord Maccon wasn't simply big; he was also tremendously solid, like a walking, talking Roman fortification.

"And how did you get all the way out here? I distinctly remember tucking you into bed before leaving your room last night." Professor Lyall spoke very clearly and precisely, not entirely sure how much was seeping into his Alpha's thick skull.

Lord Maccon's head bobbed slightly as he attempted to follow Professor Lyall's words.

"Went for a wee nightly run. Needed peace and quiet. Needed air in my fur. Needed fields under my paws. Needed, oh I canna—*hic*—explain . . . needed the company of hedgehogs."

"And did you find it?"

"Find what? No hedgehogs. Stupid hedgehogs." Lord Maccon tripped over a daphne bush, one of the many that lined the pathway leading up to a side entrance of the house. "Who bloody well put that there?"

"Peace, did you find peace?"

Lord Maccon stopped and drew himself upright, straightening his spine and throwing his shoulders back. It was an action driven by memory of military service. It caused him to positively tower over his second. Despite his ramrod-straight back, the Alpha managed to sway side to side, as if the aforementioned molasses-bound steamboat was now weathering a violent storm.

"Do I," he enunciated very carefully, "*look* like I have found peace?"

Professor Lyall had nothing to say in response to that.

"Exactly!" Lord Maccon made a wide and flailing gesture. "She is wedged"—he pointed two thick fingers at his head as though they formed a pistol—"here." Then rammed them at his chest. "And here. Canna shake her. Stickier than"—his powers of metaphor failed him—"stickier than . . . cold porridge getting all gloopy on the side of a bowl," he finally came up with triumphantly.

Professor Lyall wondered what Lady Alexia Maccon would say to being compared to such a pedestrian foodstuff. She would probably compare her husband to something even less agreeable, like haggis.

Lord Maccon looked at his Beta with wide, soulful eyes, the color of which changed with his mood. Currently they were a watered-down caramel and highly unfocused. "Why'd she have ta go an do a thing like that?"

"I don't think she did." Professor Lyall had been meaning to have this out with his Alpha for some time. He had simply hoped the discussion would occur during one of Lord Maccon's rare moments of sobriety.

"Well, then, why'd she lie about it?"

"No. I mean to say, I do not believe she was lying." Lyall stood his ground. A Beta's main function within the werewolf pack was to support his Alpha in all things—publicly, and to question him as much as possible—privately.

Lord Maccon cleared his throat and looked at his Beta in myopic seriousness from under fierce eyebrows. "Randolph, this may come as a shock, but I *am* a werewolf."

"Yes, my lord."

"Two hundred and one years of age."

"Yes, my lord."

"Pregnancy, under such circumstances, you must understand, is not possible."

"Certainly not for *you*, my lord."

"Thank you, Randolph, that is verra helpful."

Professor Lyall had thought it rather funny, but he'd never been much good at humor. "But, sir, we understand so very little about the preternatural state. And the vampires never did like the idea of you marrying her. Could it be they knew something?"

"Vampires always know *something*."

"About what might happen. About the possibility of a child, I mean."

"Poppycock! The howlers would have said somewhat to me at the outset."

"Howlers do not always remember everything, do they? They cannot remember what happened to Egypt, for one."

"God-Breaker Plague? You saying Alexia is pregnant with the God-Breaker Plague?"

Lyall didn't even dignify that with an answer. The God-Breaker Plague was the werewolf moniker for the fact that in Egypt supernatural abilities were rendered negligible. It could not, by any stretch of the imagination, act as a paternal agent.

They finally made it to the castle, and Lord Maccon was momentarily distracted by the Herculean task of trying to climb steps.

"You know," continued the earl in outraged hurt once he'd attained the small landing, "I groveled for that woman. Me!" He glared at Professor Lyall. "An' *you* told me to!"

Professor Lyall puffed out his cheeks in exasperation. It was like trying to have a conversation with a distracted and very soggy scone. Every time he pushed in one direction the earl either oozed or crumbled. If he could simply get Lord Maccon off the sauce he might be able to talk some sense into him. The Alpha was notoriously emotional and heavy-handed in these matters, prone to flying off the cogs, but he could usually be brought around to reason eventually. He wasn't all *that* dim.

Professor Lyall knew Lady Maccon's character; she might be capable of betraying her husband, but if she had done so, she would admit to it openly. Thus, logic dictated she was telling the truth. Lyall was enough of a scientist to conclude from this that the currently accepted gospel truth, that supernatural creatures could not impregnate mortal women, was flawed. Even Lord Maccon, pigheaded and hurt, could be convinced of this line of reasoning eventually. After all, the earl could not possibly *want* to believe Alexia capable of infidelity. At this point, he was simply wallowing.

"Don't you think it's about time you sobered up?"

"Wait, lemme ponder that." Lord Maccon paused, as though giving the matter deep consideration. "Nope."

They made their way inside Woolsey Castle, which was no castle at all but more a manor with delusions of dignity. There were stories about the previous owner that no one entirely believed, but one thing was for certain: the man had an unhealthy passion for flying buttresses.

Lyall was grateful to be out of the sun. He was old enough and strong enough not to be bothered by direct sunlight for short lengths of time, but that didn't mean he enjoyed the sensation. It felt like a tingling buzz just underneath the skin, highly unpleasant. Lord Maccon, of course, never seemed to notice sunlight at all, even when he was sober— *Alphas*!

"So where *are* you acquiring the alcohol, my lord?"

"Didna drink—*hic*—any alcohol." Lord Maccon winked at his Beta and patted him on the shoulder affectionately, as though they were sharing some great secret.

Lyall was having none of that. "Well, my lord, I think perhaps you would have had to."

"Nope."

A tall, striking blond, with a perennially curled lip and hair in a military queue, rounded a corner of the hall and halted upon seeing them. "Is he soused again?"

"If you mean, 'is he drunk *still*?' then, yes."

"Where, in all that is holy, is he getting the plonk?"

"Do you think I haven't tried to figure that out? Don't just stand there gawping. Make yourself useful."

Major Channing Channing of the Chesterfield Channings slouched reluctantly over to brace his pack leader from the other side. Together the Beta and the Gamma steered their Alpha down the hall to the central staircase, up several floors, over, and up the final steps to the earl's tower sleeping chamber. They managed this with only three casualties: Lord Maccon's dignity (which hadn't very far to fall at that point), Major Channing's elbow (which met a mahogany finial), and an innocent Etruscan vase (which died so that Lord Maccon could lurch with sufficient exaggeration).

During the course of the proceedings, Lord Maccon started to sing. It was some obscure Scottish ballad, or perhaps some newer, more modern piece about cats dying—it was difficult to tell with Lord Maccon. Before his metamorphosis, he had been a rather well-thought-of opera singer, or so the rumors went, but all remnants of pitch were shredded beyond hope of salvation during his change to supernatural state. His skill as a singer had fled along with the bulk of his soul, leaving behind a man who could inflict real pain with the slightest ditty. *Metamorphosis,* reflected Lyall, wincing, *was kinder to some than to others.*

"Dinna wanna," objected his lordship at the entrance to his sleeping chamber. "Reminds me."

There was no trace of Alexia left in the room. She'd cleared out all of her personal possessions as soon as she returned from Scotland. But the three men in the doorway were werewolves; they merely needed to sniff the air and her scent was there—vanilla with a trace of cinnamon.

"This is going to be a long week," said Channing in exasperation.

"Just help me get him into bed."

The two werewolves managed, through dint of cajoling and brute force, to get Lord Maccon into his large fourposter bed. Once there, he flopped facedown, and almost immediately began snoring.

"Something simply must be done about him." Channing's accent was that of the privileged elite. It irritated Professor Lyall that the Gamma had never bothered to modify it over the decades. In the modern age, only elderly dowagers with too many teeth still spoke English that way.

Lyall refrained from comment.

"What if we have a challenger or a bid for metamorphosis? We should be getting more of both now that he has successfully changed a *female* into a werewolf. You cannot keep Lady Kingair a secret in Scotland forever." Channing's tone was full of both pride and annoyance. "Claviger petitions have already escalated; our *Alpha* should be handling those, not spending his days falling down drunk. This behavior is weakening the pack."

"I can hold the challengers off," said Professor Lyall with no shame, no modesty, and no boasting. Randolph Lyall might not be as large, nor as overtly masculine, as most werewolves but he had earned the right to be Beta in London's strongest pack. Earned it so many times over and in so many ways that few questioned his right anymore.

"But you have no Anubis Form. You cannot cover for our Alpha in *every* way."

"Just you mind your Gamma responsibilities, Channing, and leave me to see to the rest."

Major Channing gave both Lord Maccon and Professor Lyall disgusted looks and then strode from the room, the tail of his long, blond hair swaying in annoyance.

Professor Lyall had intended to do the same, minus the long, blond hair, but he heard a whispered, "Randolph," come from the wide bed. He made his way along the side of the big feather mattress to where the earl's tawny eyes were once more open and unfocused.

"Yes, my lord?"

"If"—the earl swallowed nervously—"if I *am* wrong, and I'm na saying I am, but if I am, well, I'll have to grovel again, won't I?"

Professor Lyall had seen Lady Maccon's face when she returned home to pack up her clothing and quit Woolsey Castle. She wasn't big on crying—practical minded, tough, and unemotional even at the worst of times, like most preternaturals—but that didn't mean she wasn't utterly gutted by her husband's rejection. Professor Lyall had seen a number of things in his lifetime he hoped never to see again; that look of hopelessness in Alexia's dark eyes was definitely one of them.

"I am not convinced groveling will be quite sufficient in this instance, my lord." He was not disposed to allow his Alpha any quarter.

"Ah. Well, bollocks," said his lordship eloquently.

"That is the least of it. If my deductions are correct, she is also in very grave danger, my lord. Very grave."

But Lord Maccon had already gone back to sleep.

Professor Lyall went off to hunt down the earl's source of inebriation. Much to his distress, he found it. Lord Maccon hadn't lied. It was, in fact, not alcohol at all.

Alexia Maccon's parasol had been designed at prodigious expense, with considerable imagination and much attention to detail. It could emit a dart equipped with a numbing agent, a wooden spike for vampires, a silver spike for werewolves, a magnetic disruption field, and two kinds of toxic mist, and, of course, it possessed a plethora of hidden pockets. It had recently been entirely overhauled and refurbished with new ammunition, which, unfortunately, did little to improve its appearance. It was not a very prepossessing accessory, for all its serviceability, being both outlandish in design and indifferent in shape. It was a drab slate-gray color with cream ruffle trim, and it had a shaft in the new ancient Egyptian style that looked rather like an elongated pineapple.

Despite its many advanced attributes, Lady Maccon's most common application of the parasol was through brute force enacted directly upon the cranium of an opponent. It was a crude and perhaps undignified modus operandi to be certain, but it had worked so well for her in the past that she was loath to rely too heavily upon any of the newfangled aspects of her parasol's character.

Thus she left Lord Akeldama's chubby calico reclining in untroubled indolence and dashed to the side of the door, parasol at the ready. It was an odd set of coincidences, but every time she visited Lord Akeldama's drawing room something untoward happened. Perhaps this was not quite so surprising if one knew Lord Akeldama intimately.

A top hat, with attached head, peeked into the room and was soon followed by a dashing figure sporting a forest-green velvet frock coat and leather spats. For a moment, Alexia almost pulled back on her swing, thinking the intruder was Biffy. Biffy was Lord Akeldama's favorite, and prone to wearing things like velvet frock coats. But then the young man glanced toward her hiding spot—a round face sporting muttonchops and a surprised expression. Not Biffy, for Biffy abhorred muttonchops. The parasol hurtled in the unfortunate gentleman's direction.

Thwack!

The young man shielded his head with a forearm, which took the brunt of the blow, and then twisted to the side and out of the parasol's reach.

"Good gracious me," he exclaimed, backing away warily and rubbing at his arm. "I say there, *do* hold your horses! Pretty poor showing, walloping a gent with that accessory of yours without even a by-your-leave."

Alexia would have none of it. "Who are you?" she demanded, changing tactics and pressing one of the lotus petals on the shaft of her parasol, arming the tip with a numbing dart. This new stance did not look quite so threatening, as she now appeared to be about to issue a prod instead of a thwack.

The young gentleman, however, remained respectfully wary. He cleared his throat. "Boots, Lady Maccon. Emmet Wilberforce Bootbottle-Fipps, but everyone calls me Boots. How do you do?"

Well, there was no excuse for rudeness. "How do you do, Mr. Bootbottle-Fipps?"

The self-titled Boots continued. "All apologies for not being someone more important, but there's no need to take on so vigorously." He eyed the parasol with deep suspicion.

Alexia lowered it.

"*What* are you, then?"

"Oh, no one of significance, my lady. Just one of Lord Akeldama's"—a hand waved about, indicating the general splendor of the house—"newer boys." The young gentleman paused, frowning in concentration and stroking one of his muttonchops. "He left me behind to tell you something. A sort of secret message." He winked conspiratorially and then seemed to think better of the flirtation when the parasol was raised against him once more. "I think it is in code." He laced his hands behind his back and stood up straight as though about to recite some long Byronic poem. "Now what was it? You were expected sooner, and my memory is not so . . . Ah, yes, *check the cat.*"

"That was all he had to tell me?"

Green-clad shoulders shrugged. " 'Fraid so."

They spent several moments staring at each other in silence.

Finally, Boots cleared his throat delicately. "Very good, Lady Maccon. If you do not require anything further?" And without waiting for her to reply, he turned to leave the room. "Pip pip. Must, you understand, press on. Top of the morning to you."

Alexia trailed him out of the room. "But where have they all gone?"

"Can't tell you that, I'm afraid, Lady Maccon. I understand it's not safe. Not safe at all."

Alexia's confusion turned to worry.

"Not safe for whom? You, me, or Lord Akeldama?" She noticed he hadn't actually admitted to knowing his master's new location.

Boots paused at the door and looked back. "Now, don't you worry, Lady Maccon; it'll be all right in the end. Lord Akeldama will see to it. He always does."

"Where is he?"

"Why, with the others, of course. Where else would he be? Off and about, you know how it goes. A goodly numbered hunting party has gone afield, you understand, *tracking,* as it were. Gone to find . . ." He trailed off. "Oops. Never you mind, Lady Maccon. Just attend to what his lordship said about the cat. Toodles." And, with that, he gave her a funny little half bow and let himself out of the house.

Alexia, mystified, returned to the drawing room where the calico still held court. The only thing odd about the animal, apart from the creature's murderous tendencies toward tassels, was the metal collar about her neck. Alexia unclipped it and took it over to the window to examine it in the sunlight. It was thin enough to unroll into a flat ribbon and had been punched all along in an apparently random pattern of dots. It reminded Alexia of something. She ran one glove-covered fingertip along the indentations, trying to remember.

Ah, yes. It was very like the loops that fed through music machines, making those little chiming repetitive tunes that so delighted children and so annoyed adults. If this ribbon also made some kind of sound, she would need a means of listening to it. Rather than search Lord Akeldama's entire house without knowing what exact device she was looking for, and figuring the vampire in question would not be so irresponsible as to leave it on the premises, anyway, she could think of but one person who could help her at this juncture—Madame Lefoux. She headed back out to her carriage.

CHAPTER THREE

Alexia Engages in Entomology

Someone was trying to kill Lady Alexia Maccon. It was most inconvenient, as she was in a dreadful hurry.

Given her previous familiarity with near-death experiences and their comparative frequency with regards to her good self, Alexia should probably have allowed extra time for such a predictable happenstance. Except that in this particular instance, the unpleasant event was occurring in broad daylight, while she was driving down Oxford Street—not, as a general rule, the expected time or location for such an event.

She wasn't even in a rented hackney. She'd grown to anticipate regular attacks when hired transport was involved, but this time she was riding in a private conveyance. She had pinched Squire Loontwill's carriage. As her dear stepfather was giving her the royal heave-ho, she figured he wouldn't mind if she loaded his personal mode of transport with all her worldly goods and stole it for the day. As it turned out, he did mind, but she wasn't there to witness his annoyance. He had ended up borrowing his wife's pony and trap, a contraption decked in yellow tulle and pink rosettes, which was vastly ill suited to both his dignity and girth.

Her attackers didn't appear willing to follow previously established patterns in the murder arena. For one thing, they weren't supernatural. For another, they were ticking—quite loudly, in fact. Lastly, they were also *skittering*. They were undertaking the ticking because, so far as Alexia could determine, and she rather preferred not to get too close, they were clockwork, or some variety of windup mechanical. And they were undertaking the skittering because they were beetles—large, shiny red beetles with black spots and multifaceted crystal eyes, boasting nasty-looking syringes that poked upward in place of antennae.

Ladybugs were invading her carriage, a whole herd of them.

Each ladybug was about the size of Alexia's hand. They were crawling all over the conveyance, trying to break inside. Unfortunately, this did not require much diligence, as the window above the door was open wide enough for any old killer ladybug to sneak right in.

Alexia lurched up, crushing her poor hat against the ceiling of the cab, and tried to slam the sash closed, but she was far too slow. They were remarkably fast for such tubby creatures. A closer view of those antennae revealed tiny beads of moisture oozing from the tips—probably some brand of poison. She reworked her assessment of her attackers: homicidal mechanical dripping ladybugs—*ugh*.

She grabbed for her trusty parasol and bashed the first one that she could with the heavy handle. The bug crashed into the opposite wall, fell onto the back-facing seat, and scuttled once more in her general direction. Another mechanical beetle crawled up the wall toward her, and a third pushed itself off of the window sash at her shoulder.

Alexia squealed, half in fear, half in irritation, and began hitting at the creatures as hard and as fast as she could within the confines of the carriage, at the same time trying to think of some part of her parasol's armament that might help her in this particular situation. For some reason, Madame Lefoux had never specified ladybug protective measures in its anthroscopy. The toxic mist wouldn't cover enough territory to catch them all, and there was no guarantee either the lapis solaris or the lapis lunearis solutions would have any effect on the creatures. Those liquids were designed to eliminate organics, not metals, and the red and black shell looked to be some kind of shielding enamel or lacquer.

She struck out and whacked at three more of the bugs crawling across the cabin floor, holding the parasol by its tip and wielding it as though it were a croquet mallet. The carriage seemed to be positively swarming with the creatures, all attempting to stick those dripping antennae into some part of Alexia's anatomy. One of them got perilously close to her arm before she punched it away. Another climbed all the way to her stomach and struck, only to be thwarted by the leather belt of her traveling dress.

She yelled for help, hoping all the banging and clattering she was making would convince the driver to stop and come to her rescue, but he seemed oblivious. She continued to catalog her parasol options. The numbing dart was useless, and the metal and wooden stakes equally so. It was then that she remembered the parasol was equipped with a magnetic disruption field emitter. Desperately, she flipped the accessory around to its normal position and groped along the handle for the one carved lotus petal that protruded slightly more than the others. Catching it with her thumbnail, she pulled it back, activating the emitter.

It appeared that the deadly ladybugs had iron parts, for the disruption field did as designed and seized up their magnetic components. The beetles, in deference to their nature, all stopped in their tracks and turned upside-down, little mechanical legs drawn up against their undersides just as ordinary dead beetles might. Alexia sent a grateful thank-you to Madame Lefoux for her forethought in including the emitter, and began hurriedly scooping up and throwing the ladybugs out the carriage window before the disruption field wore off, careful not to touch those sticky, dripping antennae. Her skin shivered in disgust.

The driver, finally discerning that something was not quite right with his passenger, drew up the carriage, jumped down from the box, and came around to the door, just in time to get bonked on the head with a discarded ladybug.

"All right there, Lady Maccon?" he asked, giving her a pained look and rubbing his forehead.

"Don't just stand there waffling!" instructed her ladyship, as though she wasn't bumping about the interior of the carriage, pausing only to throw enormous red bugs out of its windows. "Drive on, you cretin! Drive on!"

Best get myself into a public place, thought Alexia, *until I'm certain I'm out of danger. And I need a moment to calm my nerves.*

The driver turned to do her bidding, only to be forestalled by a "Wait! I've changed my mind. Take me to the nearest teahouse."

The man returned to his post with an expression that spoke volumes on his feelings over how low the aristocracy had fallen. He clicked the horses into a trot and pulled the carriage back out into London traffic.

Showing worthy forethought, Alexia felt, under such trying circumstances, she trapped one of the bugs in a large pink hatbox, drawing the cords tight. In her agitation, she accidentally dumped the box's previous occupant (a rather nice velvet riding topper with burgundy ribbon) out the window. Her precautionary measures were undertaken none too soon, for the disruption field wore off and the hatbox began to shake violently. The bug wasn't sophisticated enough to escape, but it would keep skittering about inside its new prison.

Just to be certain, Lady Maccon stuck her head out the window to look behind and see if the other ladybugs continued their pursuit. They were trundling in confused circles in the middle of the street. So was her velvet hat, burgundy ribbons trailing behind. It must have landed on top of one of the bugs. With a sigh of relief, Alexia sat back, placing one hand firmly on top of the hatbox.

The Lottapiggle Tea Shop on Cavendish Square was a popular watering hole among ladies of quality, and mid-morning was a popular time to be seen there. Alexia alighted at the curb, instructed the driver to meet her at Chapeau de Poupe in two hours' time, and then dashed inside. The streets were not yet busy, so she would have to wait out the quietest part of the day until the real shopping began.

The inside of Lottapiggle was, however, quite as crowded as Alexia might want. No one would dare attack her further there. Unfortunately, while she had momentarily forgotten her ruined reputation, no one else in London had, and ladybugs weren't the only kinds of ladies with vicious tendencies.

Lady Maccon was allowed in, seated, and served, but the twitching hats and excited chattering of the women assembled abruptly ceased upon sight of her. The hats craned about eagerly, and the chattering evolved into whispered commentary and very pointed looks. One or two matrons, accompanied by impressionable young daughters, stood and left in a rustle of deeply offended dignity. Most, however, were far too curious to see Lady Maccon and were quite giddy at being in her disgraced presence. They basked in the delectable shock of the latest and greatest scandal calmly sipping tea and eating dry toast among them!

Of course, such marked attention might be attributed to the fact that said lady was carrying with her a ticking, quivering hatbox, which she proceeded to place carefully on the seat next to her and then tie to the seat back with the strap of her reticule for security. As though the hatbox might try to escape. At that, all expressions indicated that the tea-swilling ladies felt Lady Maccon had lost her sense along with her reputation.

Alexia ignored them all and took a moment to put her finer feelings back in order and soothe her ladybug-addled nerves with the necessary application of a hot beverage. Feeling more the thing, she made several forthright decisions that resulted in her requesting pen and paper from the hostess. She dashed off three quick notes and then settled in to wait out the lazy part of the morning. Several hours passed thus agreeably, with nothing but an occasional lurch from the hatbox to disturb her reverie.

Upon entering Chapeau de Poupe, Professor Lyall thought that the proprietress was looking a little tired and substantially older than when he'd seen her last. This was peculiar, as on all their previous encounters, the lady inventor had possessed that indefatigably French air of agelessness. Of the kind, of course, that did not come from actually being ageless. She was dressed in her usual odd attire—that is to say, masculine clothing. Most of them considered this shockingly inappropriate, but some were coming to expect such eccentricities from artists, authors, and now milliners. That said, Madame Lefoux may have been dressed as a man, but that did not stop her from being stylish about it, employing perfect tailoring and pleasing subtle grays and blues. Professor Lyall approved.

Madame Lefoux glanced up from an emerald-green silk bonnet she was trimming with satin roses. "Ah, she wanted to see you as well? Very good. Sensible of her."

The establishment was devoid of customers despite the excellent selection of headgear, probably because a polite little sign on the door indicated it was currently closed to visitors. The hats were beautifully arranged, displayed not on stands but dangling at the ends of gold chains attached to the arched ceiling far above. They fell to different heights so that one had to brush through them to cross the shop. The hats swayed slightly as Professor Lyall did so, simulating a pleasing undersea forest.

Professor Lyall took off his hat and bowed. "Sent a note a few hours ago. She has her moments, does our Lady Maccon."

"And you brought Woolsey's librarian with you?" Madame Lefoux's perfectly tended eyebrows arched in surprise. "That is unexpected."

Floote, having followed Professor Lyall in from the street, tipped his hat to the Frenchwoman in such a way as to indicate mild censure, which Lyall supposed stemmed from the fact that he did not approve of her choice of attire and never had.

"Lady Maccon's missive indicated his presence might be acceptable." Lyall set his hat carefully down on the edge of the sales counter, where it would not look as though it were part of the stock. It was a favorite hat. "You are aware that he was valet to Lady Maccon's father? If we are going to discuss what I believe we are going to discuss, his input might prove invaluable."

"Was he really? Of course, I knew he was butler to the Loontwills before Alexia's marriage. I don't recall her revealing anything further." Madame Lefoux looked with renewed interest at Floote, who remained stoic under her pointed scrutiny.

"Everything that has happened, up to a point, probably has something to do with Alessandro Tarabotti." Professor Lyall drew her attention back to himself.

"You believe so, do you? Including this impromptu clandestine meeting of Alexia's?"

"Isn't that always the way of things with preternaturals? Should we go somewhere more private?" The open airiness of the hat shop with its long front windows made the Beta feel uncomfortably exposed. He would feel more relaxed below the shop in Madame Lefoux's secret underground contrivance chamber.

Madame Lefoux put down her work. "Yes, Alexia will know where to find us. If you would like to—"

She was cut off by a knock sounding at the shop door. Bells jingled charmingly as it was pushed open. A cheerful-looking ginger-haired young blunt entered the room wearing a tan top hat, slightly too-tight red plaid breeches, gaiters, and a wide smile that had the unmistakable air of the theater about it.

"Ah, Tunstell, of course." Professor Lyall was not surprised at this addition to Lady Maccon's little gathering.

Floote gave Lord Maccon's former claviger a nod. Then he slipped past him to shut the shop door and check the CLOSED sign. He'd only lately been made Alexia's personal secretary and librarian; before that he'd been a *very* good butler. Sometimes it was hard to take the butlering out of a fellow, especially where doors were concerned.

"What ho, Professor? Lady Maccon's note didn't say you'd be here. What a pleasure, indeed. How's the old wolf?" Tunstell doffed his hat and gave the assembly a sweeping bow and an even wider grin.

"Floppy."

"You don't say? I should think, from what I read in the paper this morning, he'd be rampaging about the countryside, threatening to tear folk limb from limb. Why—" Tunstell was warming to his topic, striding around the room in the sentimental style, arms waving, crashing into hats. He had recently earned himself a reputation as an actor of some note, but even before his fame, his mannerisms had leaned markedly in the dramatic direction.

A humorless little smile crossed Madame Lefoux's lips, and she cut the former claviger off midgesticulation. "Not taking the marital separation well, your Alpha? I am very glad to hear it." It wasn't exactly rude of her to interrupt Tunstell. The redhead was a well-meaning fellow, with a perpetually jovial disposition and an undeniable stage presence, but, it must be admitted, he was prone to hyperbole.

Professor Lyall sighed heavily. "He has been *intoxicated* these last three days."

"Good gracious me! I wasn't even aware of the fact that werewolves could *become* intoxicated." The Frenchwoman's scientific interest was piqued.

"It takes some considerable effort and real allocation of resources."

"What was he drinking?"

"Formaldehyde, as it turns out. Just this morning I deduced his source. It is most wearisome. He worked his way through all of my reserves and then demolished half my specimen collection before I realized what he was up to. I keep a laboratory, you see, on Woolsey Castle grounds in a converted gamekeeper's hut."

"Are you saying that you actually *are* a legitimate professor?" Madame Lefoux tilted her head, her eyes narrowing in newfound respect.

"Not as such. Amateur ruminantologist, to be precise."

"Oh."

Professor Lyall looked modestly proud. "I am considered a bit of an expert on the procreative practices of *Ovis orientalis aries*."

"Sheep?"

"Sheep."

"Sheep!" Madame Lefoux's voice came over suddenly high, as though she were suppressing an inclination to giggle.

"Yes, as in *baaaa*." Professor Lyall frowned. Sheep were a serious business, and he failed to see the source of Madame Lefoux's amusement.

"Let me understand this correctly. You are a *werewolf* with a keen interest in *sheep breeding*?" A little bit of a French accent trickled into Madame Lefoux's speech in her glee.

Professor Lyall continued bravely on, ignoring her flippancy. "I preserve the nonviable embryo in formaldehyde for future study. Lord Maccon has been drinking my samples. When confronted, he admitted to enjoying both the refreshing beverage and the 'crunchy pickled snack' as well. I was not pleased." At which, Professor Lyall felt that nothing more was required of him on this particular topic. "Shall we proceed?"

Taking the hint, Madame Lefoux made her way to the back of the shop. In the farthest corner was a pretty marble-topped stand with an attractive display of gloves spread atop it. Lifting one of the many glove boxes, the Frenchwoman revealed a lever. She pressed it sharply down and a door swung open from the wall before her.

"Oh, I say!" Tunstell was impressed, never having visited Madame Lefoux's laboratory before. Floote, on the other hand, was untroubled by the almost magical appearance of the doorway. Very little ever seemed to ruffle the feathers of the unflappable Floote.

The hidden doorway led into neither a room nor a passageway, but instead a large cagelike contraption. They entered, Tunstell with much highly vocalized trepidation.

"I'm not certain about this, gents. Looks like one of those animal-collecting thingamabobs, used by my friend Yardley. You know Winston Yardley? Explorer of some renown. He was off down this engorged river, the Burhidihing I think it was, and came back with a ruddy great ship packed with cages just like this, full of the most messy kinds of animals. Not certain I approve of getting into one myself."

"It is an ascension room," explained Madame Lefoux to the worried redhead.

Floote pushed a lever, which closed the door to the shop, and then he pulled the small metal safety grate closed across the open side of the cage.

"Cables and guide rails allow the chamber to move up and down between levels, like so." Madame Lefoux pulled a cord on one side of the cage. She continued explaining to Tunstell as the contraption dropped downward, raising her voice above the din that accompanied movement. "Above us is a steam-powered windlass. Do not worry; it is perfectly capable of sustaining our weight and lowering us at a respectable speed."

So it proved to be the case as, with many ominous puffs of steam floating into the cage and some creaking and groaning that made Tunstell jump, they moved down. Madame Lefoux's definition of a respectable speed might be questioned, however, as the contraption plummeted quickly, bumping when it hit the ground, causing everyone to stumble violently up against one side.

"At some point, I suppose I shall have to get around to fixing that." The Frenchwoman gave an embarrassed little smile, showing small dimples. Straightening her cravat and top hat, she led the three men out. The passageway they walked into was lit by neither gas lamps nor candles, but instead by an orange-tinted gas that glowed faintly as it traveled through glass tubing set in one side of the ceiling. It was carried by an air current of some kind. The gas swirled constantly, resulting in patchy illumination and a shifting orange glow.

"Oooh," commented Tunstell, and then, rather unguardedly, "What's that?"

"Aetheromagnetic currents with a gaseous electromagnetic illuminatory crystalline particulate in suspension. I was interested, until recently, in devising a portable version, but, if not precisely regulated, the gas has a tendency to, well, explode."

Tunstell didn't miss a beat. "Ah, some questions are best left unasked, I take it?" He gave the tubing a wary look and moved to walk on the opposite side of the passageway.

"Probably wise," agreed Professor Lyall.

Madame Lefoux gave a half shrug. "You *did* ask, no?" She led them through a door at the end of the passage and into her contrivance chamber.

Professor Lyall sensed that there was something different about the place. He could not determine exactly what it was. He was familiar with the laboratory, having visited it in order to acquire various necessary instruments, gadgets, and devices for the pack, for the Bureau of Unnatural Registry (BUR), and sometimes for his own personal use. Madame Lefoux was generally thought to be one of the better young members of the mad-scientist set. She had a reputation for good, hard work and fair prices, her only idiosyncrasy of consequence, so far, being her mode of dress. All members of the Order of the Brass Octopus were notorious for their eccentricities, and Madame Lefoux stood comparatively low on the peculiarity scale. Of course, there was always the possibility she would go on to develop more offensive inclinations later. There were rumors, but, to date, Lyall had had no cause to complain. Her laboratory was everything that was to be expected from an inventor of her character and reputation—very large, very messy, and very, very interesting.

"Where is your son?" inquired Professor Lyall politely, looking around for Quesnel Lefoux's mercurial little face.

"Boarding school." The inventor dismissed her child with a faint headshake of disappointment. "He was becoming a liability, and then the muddle with Angelique last month made school the most logical choice. I anticipate his imminent expulsion."

Professor Lyall nodded his understanding. Angelique, Quesnel's biological mother and Alexia's former lady's maid, had been working undercover for a vampire hive when she fell to her death out of the window of an obscure castle in Scotland. Not that such information was common knowledge, nor likely to become so, but the hives were not above recrimination. Angelique had failed her masters, and Madame Lefoux had involved herself unnecessarily in the matter. It was probably safer for Quesnel to be out of town and away from society, but Professor Lyall had a soft spot for the little ragamuffin, and would miss seeing him around the place.

"Formerly Lefoux must be missing him."

Madame Lefoux dimpled at that. "Oh, I doubt that. My aunt never did like children very much, even when she was a child."

The ghost in question, Madame Lefoux's dead aunt and fellow

inventor, resided in the contrivance chamber and had been, until recently, responsible for Quesnel's education—although, of course, not during the daytime.

Floote stood quietly while Professor Lyall and Madame Lefoux exchanged pleasantries. Tunstell did not. He began poking about the vast muddle, picking up containers and shaking them, examining the contents of large glass vials and winding up sets of gears. There were cords and wire coils draped over hat stands to investigate, vacuum tubes propped in umbrella stands to tip over, and large pieces of machinery to rap on experimentally.

"Do you think I should warn him off? Some of those are volatile." Madame Lefoux crossed her arms, not particularly concerned.

Professor Lyall rolled his eyes. "Impossible pup."

Floote went trailing after the curious Tunstell and began relieving him of his more dangerous distractions.

"I see there is a reason Lord Maccon never decided to bite him into metamorphosis." Madame Lefoux watched the exchange with amusement.

"Aside from the fact that he ran away, got married, and left the pack?"

"Yes, aside from that."

Tunstell paused to scoop up and put on a pair of glassicals as he walked. Since Madame Lefoux had entered the London market, the vision assistors were becoming ubiquitous. They were worn like spectacles but looked like the malformed offspring of a pair of binoculars and a set of opera glasses. More properly called "monocular cross-magnification lenses with spectra modifier attachments," Alexia called them "glassicals," and Professor Lyall was ashamed to admit even he had taken to referring to them as such. Tunstell blinked at them, one eyeball hideously magnified by the instrument.

"Very stylish," commented Professor Lyall, who owned several pairs himself and was often to be seen wearing them in public.

Floote gave Professor Lyall a dirty look, removed the glassicals from Tunstell, and prodded him back to where Madame Lefoux leaned against a wall, arms and ankles crossed. Large diagrams drawn in black pencil on stiff yellow paper were haphazardly pinned behind her.

Professor Lyall finally realized what it was about the contrivance chamber that was so different from his last visit: it was quiet. Usually the laboratory was dominated by the hum of mechanicals in motion, steam puffing out of various orifices in little gasps and whistles, gears clanking, metal chains clicking, and valves squealing. Today everything was silent. Also, for all its messiness, the place had an air of being put away.

"Are you planning a trip, Madame Lefoux?"

The Frenchwoman looked at the Woolsey Beta. "That rather depends on what Alexia has summoned us together to discuss."

"But it is a possibility?"

She nodded. "A probability at this juncture, if I know anything about Alexia."

"Another reason to send Quesnel away to boarding school."

"Just so."

"You understand much of Lady Maccon's character, for such a comparatively short acquaintance."

"You were not with us in Scotland, Professor; it encouraged intimacy. In addition, I have made her a bit of a pet research venture."

"Oh, have you, indeed?"

"Before Alexia arrives, I take it you all read the morning papers?" Madame Lefoux switched the subject, levered herself upright from the wall, and took up a peculiarly masculine stance: legs spread, like a boxer at White's awaiting the first blow.

The men around her all nodded their affirmation.

"I am afraid they do not lie, for once. Alexia shows every sign of increasing, and we must presume that a physician has corroborated my initial diagnosis. Otherwise, Alexia would likely be back at Woolsey Castle, chewing Lord Maccon's head off."

"I never noticed any of the aforementioned signs," protested Tunstell, who had also traveled to the north with Madame Lefoux and Lady Maccon.

"Do you think said signs are generally something you're likely to observe?"

Tunstell blushed red at that. "No. You are perfectly correct, of course; most assuredly not."

"So are we agreed that the child is Lord Maccon's?" Madame Lefoux clearly wanted to find out where everyone stood on the matter.

No one said anything. The inventor looked from one man to the next. First Floote, then Tunstell, and then Lyall nodded their assent.

"I assumed as much, or none of you would have acquiesced to her request for this clandestine meeting, however desperate her circumstances. Still, it is curious that none of you challenges Alexia's veracity." The Frenchwoman gave Professor Lyall a sharp look. "I am aware of my own reasons, but you, Professor Lyall, are Lord Maccon's Beta. Yet you believe it is possible for a werewolf to father a child?"

Professor Lyall had known this moment would come. "It is not that I know the answer as to how. It is simply that I know someone else who believes that this is possible. Several someones, in fact. And they are usually correct in these matters."

"They? They who?"

"The vampires." Never comfortable being the center of attention, he nevertheless attempted to explain himself further as all eyes turned to him. "Before she left for Scotland, two vampires tried to kidnap Lady Maccon. While she was on board the dirigible, her journal was stolen and someone tried to poison her. Most of the other incidents up north after that can be placed in Angelique's hands." Professor Lyall nodded to Madame Lefoux. "But those three episodes could not have been the maid. I believe the Westminster Hive was responsible for the attempted kidnapping and the theft of the journal, probably under Lord Ambrose's orders. It seems like Ambrose; he always was ham-handed with his espionage. The kidnappers, whom I intercepted, said they were under orders not to harm Lady Maccon, but simply intended to *test* her—probably for signs of pregnancy. I believe they stole the journal for the same reason—they wanted to see if she was recording anything about her condition. Of course, she herself had not yet realized, so they wouldn't have learned anything. The poisoning, on the other hand . . ."

Lyall looked at Tunstell, who'd been the inadvertent victim of that bungled attempt at murder. Then he continued. "Westminster would wait for confirmation before taking any action so final, especially against the wife of an Alpha werewolf. But those who are outside hive bonds are not so reticent."

"There are very few rove vampires with the kind of social irreverence and political clout needed to risk killing an Alpha werewolf's wife." Madame Lefoux spoke softly, frowning worriedly.

"One of them is Lord Akeldama," said Lyall.

"He wouldn't! Would he?" Tunstell was looking less like an actor and more like the semiresponsible claviger he'd once been.

Professor Lyall tipped his head noncommittally. "Do you remember? Formal complaints were filed with the Crown when Miss Alexia Tarabotti's engagement to Lord Maccon was first printed in the papers. We brushed them off at the time as a matter of vampire etiquette, but I am beginning to think some vampire suspected something like this might occur."

"And with the morning gossip rags printing what they did . . ." Tunstell looked even more worried.

"Precisely," said Professor Lyall. "The vampires have had all their worst fears confirmed—Lady Maccon *is* pregnant. And while the rest of the world sees this as proof of an infidelity, the bloodsuckers would appear to believe her."

Madame Lefoux's forehead creased with worry. "So the hives, originally inclined toward nonviolence, have had their fears confirmed, and Alexia has lost the protection of the Woolsey Pack."

Floote's normally dispassionate face showed concern.

Professor Lyall nodded. "All the vampires now want her dead."

CHAPTER FOUR

Tea and Insults

Lady Maccon was on her third piece of toast and her fourth pot of tea, entertaining herself by glaring at some young lady or another simply to evaluate the color of the blush that resulted. She was no closer to determining who might want her dead—there were just too many possibilities—but she had made some concrete decisions about her more immediate future. Not the least of these being that, without Lord Akeldama, her safest course of action was to leave London. The question was where? And did she have the necessary finances?

"Lady Maccon?"

Alexia blinked. Was someone actually talking to her? She looked up.

Lady Blingchester, a mannish-faced matron of the stout and square variety with curly gray hair and too-large teeth, stood frowning down at her. She was accompanied by her daughter, who shared much the same expression and teeth. Both of them were known for having decided opinions on matters of morality.

"Lady Maccon, how dare you show your face here? Taking tea in such an obvious manner with"—she paused—"an agitated hatbox for company. In a respectable establishment, frequented by honest, decent women of good character and social standing. Why, you should be ashamed! Ashamed to even walk among us."

Alexia looked down at herself. "I believe I am sitting among you."

"You should be at home, groveling at the feet of your husband, begging him to take you back."

"Why, Lady Blingchester, what would you know about my husband's feet?"

Lady Blingchester was not to be forestalled. "Or you should have hidden your shame from the world. Imagine dragging your poor family into the mire with you. Those lovely Loontwill girls. So sensible, with so much promise, so many prospects, and now your behavior has ruined them as well as yourself!"

"You couldn't possibly be talking about my sisters, could you? They have been accused of many things, but never sense. I think they might find that rather insulting."

Lady Blingchester leaned in close and lowered her voice to a hiss. "Why, you might have done them a favor by casting yourself into the Thames."

Alexia whispered back, as if it were a dire secret, "I can swim, Lady Blingchester. Rather well, actually."

This latest revelation apparently too shocking to tolerate, Lady Blingchester began to sputter in profound indignation.

Alexia nibbled her toast. "Oh, do shove off, Lady Bling. I was thinking some rather important thoughts before you interrupted me."

The hatbox, rattling mildly against its confining cords throughout this conversation, gave a sudden enthusiastic upward lunge. Lady Blingchester squawked in alarm and seemed to feel this the last straw. She flounced away, followed by her daughter, but she paused and had some sharp words with the hostess before leaving.

"Blast," said Alexia to the hatbox when the proprietress, looking determined, headed in her direction.

The hatbox ticked at her unhelpfully.

"Lady Maccon?"

Alexia sighed.

"You understand I must ask you to leave?"

"Yes. But tell me, is there a pawnshop in the vicinity?"

The woman blushed. "Yes, my lady, just down off Oxford Circus past Marlborough Bank."

"Ah, good." Lady Maccon stood, untied the hatbox, and gathered it up along with her reticule and parasol. All conversation quieted as she once again held everyone's attention.

"Ladies," said Alexia to the assembled faces. Then she made her way, with as much gravity as possible for a woman clutching an epileptic pink hatbox to her bosom, to the counter, where she paid her account. The door behind her did not close fast enough to cut off the excited squeals and babble that heralded her departure.

The road was now crowded enough for safety, but still Lady Maccon walked with unseemly haste down Regent Street and into a small pawnshop. There she sold all the jewelry she was currently wearing at a shockingly devalued rate, which nevertheless resulted in quite an obscene amount of money. Conall might be an untrusting muttonhead, a Scotsman, and a werewolf, but the man knew a thing or two about feminine fripperies. Mindful of her circumstances alone in the city, Alexia secreted the resulting pecuniary return in several of the hidden pockets of her parasol and proceeded furtively onward.

Professor Lyall looked at the French inventor with a cutting eye. "Why is Lady Maccon involving you in this matter, Madame Lefoux?"

"Alexia is my friend."

"That does not explain *your* eagerness to be of assistance."

"You haven't had many friends, have you, Professor Lyall?"

The werewolf's upper lip curled. "Are you certain friendship is all you want from her?"

Madame Lefoux bristled slightly. "That is a low blow, Professor. I hardly think it your business to question my motives."

Professor Lyall did something quite unusual for him. He colored slightly. "I did not intend to imply . . . that is, I had not meant to insinuate . . ." He trailed off and then cleared his throat. "I planned to hint at your involvement with the Order of the Brass Octopus."

Madame Lefoux rubbed the back of her neck in an unconscious gesture. Hidden under her short dark hair, just there, was a small octopus tattoo. "Ah. The Order has no direct involvement, so far as I can tell."

Professor Lyall did not miss the implication of that phrasing. Madame Lefoux might literally be unable to tell of the OBO's interests if she had been instructed to remain silent.

"But it is undoubtedly scientifically intrigued by Lady Maccon?" Professor Lyall pressed her.

"Of course! She is the only female preternatural to enter our sphere since the Order's inception."

"But the Hypocras Club—"

"The Hypocras Club was only one small branch, and their actions became sadly public. Quite the embarrassment, in the end."

"So why are you such an eager friend?"

"I cannot deny a certain fascination with Alexia as a scientific curiosity, but my research, as you well know, tends to be more theoretical than biological."

"So I was inadvertently closer to the mark initially?" Professor Lyall regarded Madame Lefoux with a wealth of understanding.

Madame Lefoux pursed her lips but did not deny the romantic insinuation. "So you will allow my motives to be, if not pure, at least in Alexia's best interest? Certainly, I care more for her well-being than that rubbish husband of hers."

Professor Lyall nodded. "For now." He paused and then said, "We must convince her to leave London."

At which Lady Alexia Maccon herself bustled into the laboratory. "Oh, no convincing needed, I assure you, my dears. The ladybugs did that. In fact, that was why I summoned you. Well, not because of the ladybugs—because of the leaving." She was clearly a little flustered. Still, all efficiency, she stripped off her gloves and dropped them, her reticule, her parasol, and a gyrating pink hatbox on a nearby worktable. "It is about time I visited the Continent, don't you feel? I thought, perhaps, one or two of you might like to accompany me." She gave them all a timid smile and then remembered her manners. "How do you do, Tunstell? Good day, Genevieve. Floote. Professor Lyall. Thank you all for coming. I do apologize for being late. There were the ladybugs, you see, and then I simply had to take tea."

"Alexia." Madame Lefoux was all concern. Lady Maccon's hair was mussed, and it looked as though there might be a rip or two at the hem of her dress. The inventor took one of Alexia's hands in both of hers. "Are you quite all right?"

At the same time, Professor Lyall said, "Ladybugs? What do you mean, ladybugs?"

"Ah, halloo, Lady Maccon." Tunstell grinned and bowed. "Do you really intend to leave? How unfortunate. My wife will be most upset."

Floote said nothing.

Professor Lyall looked at the Frenchwoman's intimate clasp on Lady Maccon's hand. "You intend to volunteer yourself as companion, Madame Lefoux?" He was thinking about the fact that all the machines in the contrivance chamber had been shut down and tidied away.

Lady Maccon approved. "Excellent. I was hoping you would agree to accompany me, Genevieve. You have the necessary contacts in Europe, do you not?"

The inventor nodded. "I have already put some thought into possible escape routes." She shifted her attention back to Lyall. "Did you think you could leave the Woolsey Pack for that long?"

"Woolsey is used to being split. We are one of the few packs that do it regularly, in order to satisfy both military and BUR obligations. But, no, you are right. I cannot leave at this juncture. The situation is most delicate."

Madame Lefoux brought a hand to her face hurriedly and pretended to cough but could not quite hide the snicker. "Obviously, you cannot abandon Lord Maccon in his current . . . state."

"State? My repulsive husband is in a 'state'? Good! He jolly well should be."

Professor Lyall felt like he might be betraying his Alpha somewhat but couldn't help admitting, "He is practically inhaling formaldehyde in an effort to stay inebriated."

Lady Maccon's smug expression became suddenly alarmed.

"Don't concern yourself," Lyall hastened to reassure her. "It cannot harm him, not seriously, but it is certainly doing a bang-up job of keeping him utterly incapacitated in the meantime."

"Concerned." Lady Maccon turned away to fiddle with the hatbox, which had been working its way toward the edge of the table. "Who's concerned?"

Professor Lyall moved hurriedly on. "He is, simply put, not acting the Alpha. Woolsey is a tough pack to hold steady at the best of times, restless members, and too much political clout not to be a tempting prospect for opportunistic loners. I shall need to stay here and safeguard the earl's interests."

Lady Maccon nodded. "Of course you must stay. I'm certain Genevieve and I can manage."

The inventor looked hopefully at Professor Lyall. "I'd be obliged if you could find the time to look after my lab while I am away."

The Beta was pleased to be asked. "I would be honored."

"If you could stop by of an evening to check for intruders and ensure a couple of the more delicate machines remain oiled and maintained? I'll provide you with a list."

Tunstell perked up at this point in the conversation. "I'm convinced my wife would be thrilled to oversee the day-to-day operations of your hat shop, if you would like, Madame Lefoux."

The Frenchwoman looked utterly horrified at the very idea.

Professor Lyall could just imagine it: Ivy, in charge of a whole roomful of hats. Such a thing could only bring about disaster and mayhem, like putting a cat in charge of a cage full of pigeons—a turquoise brocade cat with very unusual ideas about the coloration and arrangement of pigeon feathers.

Lady Maccon rubbed her hands together. "That was one of the reasons I invited you here, Tunstell."

Madame Lefoux gave Alexia a very appraising look. "I suppose it would be better if some semblance of normal business operations continued while I was away. It would be best if the vampires did not know exactly *who* your friends are." She turned to Tunstell. "Do you think your wife equal to the task?"

"She'd be unconditionally thrilled." The redhead's broad grin was back in place.

"I was half afraid you would say that." Madame Lefoux gave a rueful little smile.

Poor Madame Lefoux, thought Professor Lyall. There was a distinct possibility she would end up with no hat shop to return to.

"Vampires? Did you say vampires?" Lady Maccon's brain suddenly caught up with the second part of the conversation.

Lyall nodded. "We believe that, now that your delicate condition is public information, the vampires are going to try and—not to put too fine a point on it—kill you."

Lady Maccon arched her eyebrows. "Through the judicious application of malicious ladybugs, perhaps?"

"Come again?"

"Ladybugs?" Tunstell perked up. "I am rather fond of ladybugs. They are so delightfully hemispherical."

"Not of these you wouldn't be." Lady Maccon detailed her recent ladybug encounter and the fact that she had only just narrowly escaped being pronged with an antennae. "This has not been a very pleasant day so far," she concluded, "all things considered."

"Did you manage to capture one for closer examination?" asked Madame Lefoux.

"What do you think is in the hatbox?"

Madame Lefoux's eyes began to sparkle. *"Fantastique!"* She dashed off and fussed about her contrivance chamber for a moment, emerging wearing a pair of glassicals and massive leather gloves sewn with chain mail.

Professor Lyall, being the only immortal present, took it upon himself to actually open the hatbox.

The Frenchwoman reached inside and lifted out the large ticking bug, its little legs wiggling in protest. She examined it with interest through the magnification lens. "Very fine craftsmanship! Very fine, indeed. I wonder if there is a maker's mark." She flipped the mechanical over.

The creature emitted a very high-pitched whirring noise.

"Merde!" said Madame Lefoux, and threw the ladybug hard up into the air.

It exploded with a loud bang, showering them with bits of red lacquer and clockwork parts.

Alexia jumped slightly, but recovered quickly enough. After the type of morning she'd had, what was one little explosion added to the mix? She sneered at the resulting mess.

Professor Lyall sneezed as a cloud of greasy particulates tickled his sensitive werewolf nose. "That is vampires for you. What they cannot suck dry they explode."

Floote began cleaning up the disarray.

"Pity," said Madame Lefoux.

Professor Lyall gave the Frenchwoman a suspicious look.

The inventor raised both of her hands defensively. "Not my crafts-manship, I assure you. I do not deal in"—a sudden dimpled grin spread over her face—"coccinellids."

"I think you had better explain why you're blaming the vampires, Professor." Alexia brought the matter back to hand and gave her husband's Beta a very hard look.

Professor Lyall did explain, starting with his deductions about the poisoning, the missing journal, and the kidnapping attempt, and moving on to his belief that now that Lady Maccon's pregnancy was in print, and she was no longer officially under the Woolsey Pack's protection, such incidents were only likely to increase in both frequency and ferocity.

Enchanting. What do I expect next? Hordes of barbaric brass bumblebees? "Why do they want me dead? I mean, aside from the customary reasons."

"We think it has something to do with the child." Madame Lefoux took Alexia's elbow softly in hand, trying to steer her in the direction of the overturned barrel.

Alexia resisted, instead turning to Professor Lyall, her throat tight with pent-up emotion. "So you believe me? You believe that this infant-inconvenience is Conall's?"

He nodded.

" 'Infant-inconvenience'?" whispered Tunstell to Floote.

Floote remained impassive.

"Do you know something Conall does not?" Alexia's heart leapt with the possibility of exoneration.

Sadly, the Beta shook his head.

Hope dissipated. "Funny that you should trust me more than my own husband." Alexia sat down heavily on the barrel and scrubbed at her eyes with her knuckles.

"He has never acted reasonably where you are concerned."

Lady Maccon nodded, her mouth tight. "That does not excuse his behavior." Her face felt stiff, as though it were made of wax. An image that brought back some very uncomfortable memories.

"No, it does not," Professor Lyall agreed with her.

Alexia wished he wouldn't be so nice—it drove her pathetically close to actual wallowing. "And the only vampire likely to be on my side in this is Lord Akeldama. And he has disappeared."

"He has?" Madame Lefoux and Professor Lyall said it at the same time.

Alexia nodded. "I was at his house earlier this morning. Abandoned. And that after he asked me to stay with him."

"Coincidence?" Tunstell looked like he already knew the answer to such an idea.

"That reminds me of an old saying of Mr. Tarabotti's," offered Floote, speaking for the first time. " 'Floote,' he used to say to me, 'there's no such thing as fate—there's just werewolves, and there's no such thing as coincidence—there's just vampires. Everything else is open to interpretation.' "

Alexia looked at him hard. "Speaking of my father . . ."

Floote shook his head, glanced at Lyall, and then said, "Classified information, madam. Apologies."

"I didn't know you were an agent, Mr. Floote." Madame Lefoux was intrigued.

Floote looked away. "Not as such, madam."

Alexia knew Floote of old; he would not budge on the subject of her father. It was maddening behavior from the otherwise exemplary family retainer. "To the Continent, then." Alexia had given this some thought while in the tea shop. America was out of the question, and vampires were much more vulnerable in Europe—where few countries had followed King Henry's example and integrated the supernatural set. Perhaps they would not be quite so deadly. Or, at least, have access to fewer ladybugs.

"I do not mean to be rude," said Professor Lyall, employing the phrase most often used by those who are about to be very rude indeed, "but such travel should commence quickly. It would be no bad thing for you to leave London before the next full moon, Lady Maccon."

Madame Lefoux consulted a lunar calendar posted on the wall alongside various diagrams. "Three nights from now?"

Professor Lyall nodded. "Preferably sooner. I can use BUR agents to protect you until then, Lady Maccon, but at full moon all of my werewolves are out of commission and my secondary resources are tapped, for I cannot rely on the vampire agents. They will go against BUR orders if under the influence of a queen."

"You can store your possessions here while we are away," offered Madame Lefoux.

"Well, that is something. At least my clothing will be safe." Alexia threw her hands up in exasperation. "I knew it was a terrible idea to get out of bed this morning."

"And Ivy, I am certain, would be happy to write you regularly with all the latest news from London." Tunstell offered up his form of encouragement, accompanied by the expected flash of persuasive white teeth. Alexia reflected that it was a good thing her husband hadn't turned Tunstell into a werewolf. The redhead smiled too often. Most werewolves did not do smiling very adeptly; it came off as sinister.

Neither Lady Maccon nor Madame Lefoux saw fit to explain how unlikely it was that any missive would actually reach them.

"So where are we going?" Madame Lefoux looked at her friend with interest.

Alexia had also given this due consideration over her tea and toast. If she had to leave, she was going in pursuit of information. If she had to flee, she might as well flee toward the possibility of proving her innocence. Only one country knew anything substantial about preternaturals.

"I hear that Italy is lovely at this time of year."

CHAPTER FIVE

In Which Ivy Hisselpenny and Professor Lyall Are Given Too Much Responsibility

Italy?"

"The hotbed of antisupernatural sentiment," spat Professor Lyall.

"The cesspit of religious fanaticism," added Tunstell.

"The Templars." That last was from Floote, and he whispered it.

"I think it's a perfectly topping idea," said Alexia, expressionless.

Madame Lefoux examined Alexia's face sympathetically. "You think the Templars can explain how Lord Maccon managed to get you with child?"

"Why don't you tell me? You once said you managed to read a portion of the Templars' Amended Rule."

"You did *what*?" Professor Lyall was impressed.

Floote looked at the Frenchwoman with renewed suspicion.

"They must know *something* about this thing." Alexia poked an accusatory finger at her still-flat stomach.

Madame Lefoux looked thoughtful but clearly did not want to tempt Alexia with false hope. "I think they might be so intrigued at meeting a female preternatural that they will be unguarded in their approach. Especially if they find out you are pregnant. But they are warriors, not intellectuals. I'm not convinced they can furnish you with what you *actually* desire."

"Oh, and what's that?"

"The return of your husband's regard."

Alexia glared daggers at the Frenchwoman. *The very idea!* She didn't want that disloyal fuzz-ball back in love with her. She simply wanted to prove him wrong.

"I think," said Professor Lyall before Alexia could commence a diatribe, "that you are entering a wasp hive."

"So long as it is not a ladybug hive, I shall be fine."

"I think," said Floote, "that I should come with you ladies."

Neither of the ladies in question objected.

Alexia raised a finger in the air. "Might I recommend we arrange a regular aethographic transmission date, Professor Lyall? Although that presupposes the fact that we will be able to find a public transmitter."

"They have become more popular recently." Madame Lefoux clearly approved of the idea.

The Beta nodded. "Keeping a time slot open at BUR headquarters is an excellent notion. I shall give you a list of all the names and locations of transmitters for whom we have crystalline valve frequensors, and with whom we can thus transmit. From what I recall, Florence has a good one. You understand, our apparatus is not as sophisticated as Lord Akeldama's?"

Alexia nodded. Lord Akeldama had recently purchased the latest and greatest in aethographic transmitters, but BUR's was old and clunky. "I shall need a valve for your transmitter as well, for the Italian end of the business."

"Of course. I will send an agent 'round directly. Shall we set the appointment for just after sunset? I will have my men set ours to receive from Florence and hope something comes through from you at some point on that frequency. If only so that I know you are alive."

"Oh, that is terribly optimistic of you," said Alexia in mock umbrage.

Professor Lyall did not apologize.

"So, Italy it is?" Madame Lefoux rubbed her hands together in the manner of one about to embark on an adventure.

Lady Maccon glanced about at the four standing around her. "One should always visit one's roots once in one's lifetime, don't you feel? I expect the carriage with my things has arrived by now." She turned to leave. The others followed. "I shall have to repack. Better do it quickly, before anything else goes wrong today."

Madame Lefoux touched her arm before she could dash off. "What else happened to you this morning?"

"Aside from the announcement of my rather embarrassing condition in the public papers and an attack of virulent ladybugs? Well, Queen Victoria fired me from the Shadow Council, my family ejected me from their house, and Lord Akeldama vanished, leaving me a very terse message about a cat. Which reminds me." Lady Maccon took the mysterious metal cat collar out of her reticule and waved it at Madame Lefoux. "What do you make of this?"

"Magnetic auditory resonance tape."

"I thought it might be something like."

Professor Lyall looked on with interest. "Do you have a resonance decoding cavity?"

Madame Lefoux nodded. "Of course, over here somewhere." She disappeared behind a vast pile of parts that looked to be the dismembered components of a dirigible's steam engine combined with half a dozen enormous spoons. She returned carrying an object that gave every indication of being a very tall stovepipe-style top hat, with no brim, mounted on a teapot stand with a crank attachment and a trumpet coming out its underside.

Lady Maccon had nothing to say upon seeing such a bizarre-looking contraption. She handed over the metal tape in mystified silence.

The inventor fed the tape in through a slit in the underside of the hat, turning the crank to run it through the device. As she did so, a pinging sound began to emerge, akin to the noise a piano might make after inhaling helium. She cranked faster and faster. The pings began meshing together, and eventually a high voice came into existence.

"Leave England," it said in a tinny, mechanical tone. "And beware Italians who embroider."

"Useful," was Madame Lefoux's only comment.

"How on earth did he know I would choose Italy?" Sometimes Lord Akeldama still managed to surprise Alexia. She pursed her lips. "Embroidery?" Lord Akeldama was never one to prioritize one vital factor, such as murder, over another, such as fashion. "I'm worried about him. Is it safe for him to be away from his house? I mean to say, I understand his being a rove detaches him from the hive, but I was under the impression roves also became part of a place. Tethered, a little like ghosts."

Professor Lyall tugged on one earlobe thoughtfully. "I wouldn't concern yourself overly, my lady. Roves have a much larger roaming ability than hive-bound vampires. It takes considerable strength of soul to break the queen dependency to begin with, and the older the rove, the more mobile. It is their very capacity for movement that keeps most roves in favor with a local hive. They are untrustworthy but useful. And since the rove needs the queen to convert his drones, they are vested in each other's survival. Have you seen Lord Akeldama's BUR file?"

Lady Maccon shrugged noncommittally. She was not above poking about her husband's office, but she did not think Lyall needed to be made aware of that little fact.

"Well, it is quite substantial. We've no record of his original hive, which suggests he has been a rove some considerable time. I should think he could easily travel outside London city limits, perhaps even as far as Oxford, with very few psychological or physiological consequences. He is probably not mobile enough to handle floating the aether or crossing the water out of England, but he is certainly capable of making himself difficult to find."

"Difficult to find? We are talking about the same Lord Akeldama?" The vampire in question had many sterling qualities—admirable taste in waistcoats and an acerbic wit to name but a few—but subtlety was not among them.

Professor Lyall grinned. "I should rest easy if I were you, Lady Maccon. Lord Akeldama can take care of himself."

"Somehow I do not find a werewolf's reassurances on behalf of a vampire all that heartening."

"Shouldn't you be worrying about your own problems?"

"What enjoyment is there in that? Other people's are always far more entertaining."

With that, Lady Maccon led the way back into the hallway, up in the ascension room, through the hat shop, and out into the street. There she supervised the removal of her luggage and sent the waiting coachman off. He was clearly pleased to be heading back toward the comparative sanity of the Loontwill household, where excitable members of the aristocracy did not hurl mechanical beetles at him.

Professor Lyall hailed a hansom and directed it to BUR headquarters to continue on with what looked to be a most demanding day. Floote used the Woolsey carriage to return to the castle and collect his own meager belongings. He arranged to meet the ladies back at the Chapeau de Poupe in under four hours. They agreed that they should depart as quickly as possible, thus traveling under the comparative protection of daylight. Madame Lefoux, of course, was already packed.

Lady Maccon immediately began upending her many suitcases, with Tunstell's assistance, right there in the midst of the forest of hats. The bags had been hastily and rather upsettingly packed by the petulant Swilkins, and Alexia couldn't seem to find anything she might require for a trip to Italy. Mindful of Lord Akeldama's message, she eliminated all articles of clothing afflicted by the presence of embroidery.

Madame Lefoux contented herself with puttering about with her hats, putting them in order in anticipation of their abandonment. They were all thus agreeably occupied when an enthusiastic rat-tat-tatting at the door interrupted them. Alexia looked up to see Ivy Tunstell, black curls bouncing in her eagerness, waving madly from the other side of the glass.

Madame Lefoux went to let her in.

Ivy had taken to both married life and a considerable fall in social station with unexpected gusto. She seemed to genuinely enjoy her new role as wife to an actor of middling reputation and denizen of—gasp— *rented* apartments in Soho. She spoke with pride of entertaining poets on a regular basis. Poets, of all things! She even made murmurs about treading the boards herself. Alexia thought this might be a good plan, for Ivy had just the right kind of pleasant, animated face and inordinately melodramatic temperament to suit life as a thespian. She certainly needed little help in the wardrobe department. Always one for the outrageous hat in her unmarried state, her taste, cut free of her mother's apron strings, now extended to the rest of her attire. Today's offering was a bright apple green, pink, and white striped visiting gown, with a matching hat that boasted feathers of such epic proportions that Ivy actually had to duck slightly upon entering the shop.

"There you are, you wretched man," she said affectionately to her husband.

"Hello, magpie," was his equally warm response.

"In my favorite hat shop." Ivy tapped Tunstell coquettishly on the arm with her fan. "I wonder what could ever have brought you *here.*"

Tunstell looked desperately at Lady Maccon, who flashed him an unhelpful smirk.

"Well"—he cleared his throat—"I thought you might want to pick out some new frippery or another, on the occasion of our"—he scrabbled wildly—"month anniversary?" Alexia gave him a slight nod, and he let out a sigh of relief.

Trust Ivy to see nothing but the hats and not notice Lady Maccon's copious luggage strewn about the place, or, for a few moments, Lady Maccon herself. When Ivy finally did, she was quite forward in her questioning.

"Alexia, good gracious me! What are you doing *here*?"

Alexia looked up. "Oh, hello, Ivy. How are you? Thank you kindly for the hat you sent over this morning. It was very, um, uplifting."

"Yes, well, never mind that now. Pray tell, what are you about?"

"I should think that was perfectly obvious, even to you, my dear. I am packing."

Ivy shook her head, plumage swaying back and forth. "In the middle of a hat shop? There is something amiss with such a situation."

"Needs must, Ivy. Needs must."

"Yes, I can see *that,* but what one must need to know at this juncture is, not to put too fine a point on it, *why?*"

"I should think that, too, would be perfectly obvious. I am in imminent danger of traveling."

"Not because of this upsetting business with the morning papers?"

"Precisely so." Alexia figured it was as good an excuse as any. It went against her nature to be seen fleeing London because she was thought adulterous, but it was better than having the real reason known to the general public. Just imagine what the gossipmongers would say if they knew vampires were intent on assassinating her—so embarrassing. *Look at her*, they would say. *Oh, la, multiple assassination attempts, indeed! Who does she think she is, the Queen of Sheba?*

And really, wasn't that what all disreputable ladies did in the end—escape to Europe?

Ivy knew nothing of Alexia's soulless state. She did not even know what *preternatural* meant. Lady Maccon's affliction was a not-very-well-kept secret, what with BUR and all the local werewolves, ghosts, and vampires in on it, but the majority of the daylight folk were ignorant of the fact that there was a preternatural in residence in London. It was generally felt, by Alexia and those intimate with her, that if Ivy knew of this, all attempts at anonymity would be null and void within several hours. Ivy was a dear friend, loyal and entertaining, but circumspection could not be listed among her more sterling qualities. Even Tunstell acknowledged this flaw in his wife's nature and had refrained from informing the new Mrs. Tunstell of her old friend's real eccentricity.

"Yes, well, I suppose I can understand the need to absent yourself from town. But where are you going, Alexia? To the country?"

"Madame Lefoux and I are traveling to Italy, for my low spirits, you understand."

"Oh, dear, but, Alexia, you do realize"—Ivy lowered her voice to a whisper—"that Italy is where they keep *Italians*. Are you quite certain you are adequately prepared to cope?"

Lady Maccon suppressed a smile. "I think I might just be able to muddle along."

"I am certain I heard the most horrible thing about Italy recently. I am failing to recall quite what it was, but it cannot possibly be a healthy place to visit, Alexia. I understand that Italy is the place vegetables come from—all that weather. Terribly bad for the digestion—vegetables."

Lady Maccon could think of nothing to say in response to that, so she continued packing.

Ivy returned to perusing the hats, finally settling on a flowerpot style covered in striped purple and black tweed, with large purple rosettes, gray ostrich plumes, and a small feathered pouf at the end of a long piece of wire that stuck straight out of the crown. It looked, when Ivy proudly donned said hat, as though she were being stalked by an enraptured jellyfish.

"I shall have a new carriage dress made to match," she announced proudly while poor Tunstell paid for the atrocity.

Lady Maccon remarked, under her breath, "Wouldn't it be more sensible to, for example, simply throw yourself off a dirigible?"

Ivy pretended not to hear, but Tunstell shot his wife's friend a wide smile.

Madame Lefoux cleared her throat, looking up from the transaction.

"I was wondering, Mrs. Tunstell, if you might do me a very great favor."

Ivy was never one to let down a friend in need. "Delighted, Madame Lefoux. How may I be of assistance?"

"Well, as you may have surmised"—never a good phrase when applied to Ivy—"I will be accompanying Lady Maccon to Italy."

"Oh, really? How noble of you. But I suppose you *are* French, which can't possibly be all *that* different from Italian."

Madame Lefoux paused in stunned silence before recovering her powers of speech. She cleared her throat. "Yes, well, I was wondering if you might consider overseeing the day-to-day running of the hat shop while I am away."

"*Me?* Engage in *trade?* Well, I don't know." Ivy looked about at the dangling hats, undeniably tempting in all their feathered and flowered glory. But still, she had not been raised for commerce.

"You could, of course, borrow from the stock at your leisure and discretion."

Mrs. Tunstell's eyes took on a distinctly covetous sheen. "Well, if you put it like that, Madame Lefoux, how can I possibly refuse? I would be absolutely delighted to take on the task. What do I need to know? Oh, wait just a moment, before we start, if you please. Ormond." Ivy summoned her husband with a little flap of her hand.

Dutifully, Tunstell trotted over, and Ivy issued him a complex set of whispered instructions. In a flash, he had doffed his hat to the ladies, let himself out the front door, and was off down the street about some errand at his wife's behest.

Alexia approved. At least Ivy had him well trained.

Madame Lefoux led Mrs. Tunstell behind the small counter and spent the next half hour showing her how to cook the books.

"No need to place any new orders, and no need to open the shop for business all that frequently while I am away. I have listed the important appointments here. I understand you are a busy lady."

Ivy displayed surprising aptitude for the accounting. She always had been good with sums and figures, and she was obviously capable of being serious, at least about hats. Just as they were finishing up, Tunstell reappeared, clutching a small brown paper package.

Alexia joined them to make her good-byes. Directly before leaving, Ivy handed Alexia the package that Tunstell had just acquired.

"For you, my dearest Alexia."

Curiously, Alexia turned it about in her hands before unwrapping it carefully. It turned out to be a whole pound of tea inside a decorative little wooden box.

"I remembered that awful thing I had heard about Italy." Ivy dabbed at the corner of one eye with her handkerchief in an excess of sentiment. "What I heard . . . Oh, I can hardly speak of it . . . I heard that in Italy they drink"—she paused—"*coffee.*" She shuddered delicately. "So horribly bad for the stomach." She pressed Alexia's hand fervently with both of hers and the damp handkerchief. "Good luck."

"Why, thank you, Ivy, Tunstell, very thoughtful and kind of you both."

It was good-quality tea, large-leaf Assam, a particular favorite of Alexia's. She tucked it carefully into her dispatch case to carry with her on board the trans-channel dirigible. As she was no longer muhjah and the dispatch case could not serve its intended purpose of carrying secret and highly significant documents and gadgets belonging to queen and country, it might as well carry an item of equal value and importance.

Ivy might be a tad preposterous at times, but she was a kind and thoughtful friend. Much to both of their surprise, Alexia kissed Ivy on the cheek in gratitude. Ivy's eyes welled with tears.

Tunstell gave them yet another cheerful grin and shepherded his still-emotive spouse from the shop. Madame Lefoux had to dash after them to give Ivy the spare key and a few last instructions.

Professor Lyall had endured a long and trying day. Ordinarily, he was well equipped to cope with such tribulation, being a self-assured gentleman possessed of both mental acumen and physical prowess accompanied by the economy of thought required to choose quickly which best suited any given situation. That afternoon, however, with the full moon rapidly approaching, an Alpha out of commission, and Lady Maccon heading to Italy, it must be admitted that he *nearly,* on two occasions, lost his temper. The vampire drones were being unresponsive, only admitting to the fact that their respective masters "might not be available" for BUR duty that evening. There were three vampires on staff, and BUR was not designed to cope with a sudden loss of these supernatural agents all at once. Especially not when the four BUR-affiliated werewolves were all young enough to already be out of commission on their monthly bone-bender. To compound the staffing issue, certain supplies hadn't arrived as scheduled, two suspicious dirigible accidents needed to be investigated, and there was an exorcism to perform just after sunset. While dealing with all of this, Professor Lyall had to foil no less than eight reporters hoping to interview Lord Maccon, ostensibly about the dirigibles but undoubtedly about Lady Maccon. Needless to say, Lyall was in no mood to find, upon returning home just prior to sunset, his Alpha singing opera—or what might have been considered opera by a tribe of tone-deaf orangutans—in the bathtub.

"You managed to break back into my specimen collection, didn't you? Really, my lord, those were the last of my samples."

"Ish good stuff, fermaldathdie."

"I thought I set Major Channing to keep watch over you. He hasn't gone to sleep, has he? He should be able to hold for one full day. He can take direct sunlight—I have seen him do it—and you are not so difficult to track, not in this condition at least." Professor Lyall looked accusingly around the bathing chamber, as though the Woolsey Gamma's blond head might just pop up from behind the clothing rack.

"He canna poshibly do tha."

"Oh, no, why not?" Professor Lyall tested the water in which Lord Maccon splashed and wallowed like some bewildered water buffalo. It was quite cold. With a sigh, the Beta retrieved his Alpha's robe. "Come on, my lord. Let's get you out of there, shall we?"

Lord Maccon grabbed his washrag and began conducting the opening sequence of *The Grand Duchess of Gerolstein,* flicking water all about the room as he did so. "Maidens, never mind us," sang the earl, "twirling 'round and 'round."

"Where has Major Channing gone off to, then?" Professor Lyall was irritated, but it didn't show in his voice. It seemed he had spent a lifetime being irritated with Channing, and given the day so far, this was nothing more than what was to be expected. "I gave him a direct order. Nothing should have superseded that. I am still Beta of this pack, and Major Channing is under my command."

"Under mine firsh," objected Lord Maccon mildly. Then he warbled out, "For you'll be left behind us, you'll be safe and sound."

Professor Lyall attempted to part pull, part lift his Alpha out of the bathtub. But he lost his grip and Lord Maccon slipped and went falling back into it with a tremendous splash. The massive tub, with its small steam-heating attachment, was extremely well constructed and had been imported from the Americas at great expense because there they *knew* steel. But it still wobbled dangerously on its four clawed feet under Lord Maccon's weight.

"If a bullet's billet, you are doomed to fall," sang out the drenched werewolf, skipping several of the words.

"You gave Channing a direct order? In this state?" Professor Lyall tried once more to extract the earl from the tub. "And he obeyed you?"

For one brief second, Lord Maccon's eyes sharpened and he looked quite sober. "I am still his Alpha; he had *better* obey me."

Professor Lyall finally managed to get his Alpha out of the water and into the robe in a desultory kind of way. The thin material stuck indecently close in places, but the earl, never one to suffer the strain of modesty under any circumstances, clearly didn't give a fig, or a fig leaf.

Professor Lyall was used to it.

Lord Maccon began swaying back and forth in time with his singing. "Take your glass and fill it, laugh and drink with all!"

"Where did you send him?" Professor Lyall, supporting the brunt of his Alpha's weight, blessed his own supernatural strength, which made the massive man merely awkward rather than hopeless to maneuver. Lord Maccon was built like a brick outhouse, with opinions twice as unmoving and often equally full of crap.

"Aha, wouldna you like ta know tha?" The Alpha did not do coy well, and Professor Lyall was not amused at the lack of a direct answer.

"Did you send him after Lord Akeldama?"

Lord Maccon came over slightly sober once more. "That pansy. Missing, is he? Good. He reminds me of limp custard filling, all cream and no crust. Never could understand what Alexia saw in that pointy-toothed ninnyhammer. My wife! Cavorting about with a crustless vampire. Least I know *he* isna the father." The Alpha's yellow eyes squinted, as if he were trying to keep from thinking about that.

Suddenly, he flopped downward with all his weight, slipped out of Professor Lyall's hold, and landed in a cross-legged heap in the middle of the floor. His eyes were starting to go completely yellow, and he was looking altogether too hairy for Professor Lyall's liking. Full moon wasn't for a couple more nights, and Lord Maccon, by Alpha rights and strength, ought to be able to resist the change easily. Apparently, he wasn't bothering to try.

The earl continued to sing even as his slurring from the drink gave way to slurring from his jawbones breaking and re-forming into those of a wolf's muzzle. "Drink and sing a ditty, good-bye to the past, all the more's the pity, if this cup's our last!"

Professor Lyall was Woolsey Pack Beta for many reasons, one of them being that he knew perfectly well when he needed to ask for assistance. A quick run to the door and one loud yell had four of Woolsey's strongest clavigers in to help him navigate his lordship, now a very drunken wolf, down into the cellar lockup. Four legs offered no improvement in the matter of the earl's wobbling, and instead of singing, he merely took to letting forth with a mournful howl or two. An aggravating day was looking to become an equally aggravating night. With Major Channing vanished, Professor Lyall really had only one recourse left to him: he called for a pack meeting.

CHAPTER SIX

Under the Name Tarabotti

It was early evening, the sun just setting, when three unlikely-looking companions boarded the last dirigible for Calais, leaving from its mooring atop the white cliffs of Dover. No reporters managed to capture the departure of the notorious Lady Maccon. This may have had something to do with the swiftness of her response to the publication of her alleged indiscretion, or it may have been the fact that the lady in question was traveling incognito by means of being outrageous in entirely new ways. Instead of her fashionable but severely practical garb, Alexia sported a black floating dress with chiffon ruffles, yellow modesty straps dangling about the skirt, and a hideous yellow hat. She bore, as a result, some passing resemblance to a self-important bumblebee. It was a truly ingenious disguise, for it made the dignified Lady Maccon look and act rather more like an aging opera singer than a societal grande dame. She was accompanied by a well-dressed young gentleman and his valet. Only one conclusion might be drawn from such a party—that it was an impropriety in action.

Madame Lefoux gave herself over to the portrayal of a boy paramour with enthusiasm, affecting many acts of sycophant-like solicitousness. She donned an extraordinarily realistic-looking mustache for the charade—a large black waxed affair that curled up at each side just over her dimples. It managed to disguise much of the femininity of her face through sheer magnitude, but the protuberance had the unfortunate side effect of causing Alexia fits of intermittent giggles whenever she had to look Madame Lefoux directly on. Floote had an easier time of it, sliding comfortably back into his old role of valet, dragging behind him Madame Lefoux's boxes and his own battered portmanteau, which looked about as old as he was and much the worse for wear.

They were greeted with ill-disguised contempt by the float staff and with actively shocked avoidance by the rest of the passengers. Imagine, such a relationship openly flaunted on board! Disgusting. The resulting isolation suited Alexia perfectly. At Floote's suggestion, she had purchased her ticket under her maiden name, Tarabotti, never having gotten around to commissioning new travel papers after her marriage.

Madame Lefoux had initially objected. "Is that wise, do you think, given your father's reputation?"

"Wiser than traveling under the name of Lady Maccon, I suppose. Who wants to be associated with Conall?" Safely ensconced in her apartments, Alexia pulled off the bumblebee hat and flicked it, as though it were a poisonous snake, across the room.

While Floote puttered about seeing to the unpacking, Madame Lefoux came over and stroked Alexia's hair, now freed from its confines, as though Alexia were a skittish animal. "Only among the supernatural set does the name Tarabotti carry much meaning. There are those who will make the connection eventually, of course. I am hoping we will move through France faster than the gossip does."

Alexia did not object to the petting—it was comforting. She assumed Madame Lefoux was simply entering into the spirit of her role. Very enthusiastic about such things, the French.

They ate a private meal in their quarters, declining to join the rest of the passengers. Judging by the rapid appearance and freshness of the foodstuffs, the staff approved of this maneuver. Most of the offerings were cooked over the steam engine—a refreshing, if bland, method of preparation.

After supper they left their quarters and made their way up to the squeak deck for some air. Alexia was amused to find that those already relaxing in the evening aether breezes hurriedly departed as soon as she and her party arrived.

"Snobs."

Madame Lefoux dimpled slightly from behind her preposterous mustache and leaned against Alexia as they both propped their elbows on the railing, looking down at the dark waters of the channel far below.

Floote watched. Alexia wondered if her father's faithful valet mistrusted Madame Lefoux because she was French, because she was a scientist, or because she was so consistently inappropriately dressed. With Floote, all three qualities were likely to engender suspicion.

Alexia herself had no such reservations. Genevieve Lefoux had proved herself a most loyal friend over the past month, perhaps a little guarded in matters of the heart, but she was kind of word and more importantly, intelligent of action.

"You miss him?" The Frenchwoman did not need to specify further.

Alexia stuck out one gloved hand and let it ride the rushing aether currents.

"I don't want to. I'm so blasted angry with him. I've come over all numb. Makes me feel slow and stupid." She glanced sideways at the inventor. Genevieve, too, had experienced loss. "Does it get better?"

Madame Lefoux closed her eyes for a long moment. Probably thinking of Angelique. "It changes."

Alexia looked up at the almost-full moon, not yet high enough in the sky to vanish behind the enormous balloon section of the ship. "It's already changing. Tonight"—she gave a tiny shrug—"hurts differently. Now I'm thinking about full moon. It was the one night we remained close, touching, the entirety of the night. Other times, I tried to refrain from extended contact with him. He never cared, but I didn't feel it worth the risk, to keep him mortal for longer than necessary."

"Were you afraid you would age him?"

"I was afraid some loner wolf with madness in his eyes would savage him before I could let go."

They were silent for a brief while.

Alexia pulled her hand back in and tucked it under her chin. It was numb. *Familiar sensation.* "Yes. I miss him."

"Even after what he did?"

Unconsciously, Alexia slid her other hand down to her stomach. "He was always a bit of a jackass. To be smart, he should never have married me in the first place."

"Well"—Madame Lefoux tried to lighten the mood by changing the subject—"at the very least, Italy should be interesting."

Alexia gave her a suspicious look. "Are you quite certain you entirely understand what that word means? I understand English is not your native tongue, but really."

The inventor's fake mustache was wiggling dangerously in the breezes. She put one elegant finger up to her face to hold it in place. "It is a chance to find out how you got pregnant. Isn't that interesting?"

Alexia widened her dark eyes. "I am perfectly well aware of *how* it happened. What it is, is a chance to force Conall to recant his accusations. Which is more useful than interesting."

"You know what I mean."

Alexia looked up into the night sky. "After marrying Conall, I assumed children were not possible. Now it's like some exotic disease has happened to me. I cannot bring myself around to being pleased. I should like to know how, scientifically, such a pregnancy occurred. But thinking about the infant too much frightens me."

"Perhaps you just do not want to become attached to it."

Alexia frowned. Trying to understand one's own emotions was a grueling business. Genevieve Lefoux had raised another woman's child as her own. She must have lived constantly with the fear that Angelique would come and simply take Quesnel away from her.

"I could be doing it unintentionally. Preternaturals are supposed to be repelled by one another, and we are supposed to breed true. By rights, I ought to be allergic to my own child, unable even to be in the same room with it."

"You believe you are going to miscarry?"

"I believe that, if I do not lose this child, I may be forced to attempt to rid myself of it, or go insane. That, even if, by some miracle, I manage to carry through my confinement, I will never be able to share the same air as my own baby, let alone touch it. And I am so angry that my great lout of a husband has left me to deal with this alone. Couldn't he have, oh, I don't know, *talked* to me about it? But, no, he gets to blunder about acting all put-upon and getting sloshed. While I—" Alexia interrupted herself. "That's a fantastic idea! I should do something equally outrageous."

At which statement Madame Lefoux leaned forward and kissed her, quite softly and gently on the mouth.

It wasn't entirely unpleasant, but it also wasn't quite the done thing in polite society, even among friends. Sometimes, Alexia felt, Madame Lefoux took that regretfully French aspect of her character a little too far.

"That wasn't exactly what I had in mind. Got any cognac?"

The inventor only smiled. "I think, perhaps, it is time for bed."

Alexia felt very worn about the edges, like an old carpet. "This is exhausting, talking about one's feelings. I am not sure I approve."

"Yes, but has it helped?"

"I still loathe Conall and want to prove him wrong. So, no, I don't think it has."

"But you've always felt that way about your husband, my dear."

"True, true. Are you certain you don't have any cognac?"

They set down in France the next morning with surprisingly little incident. Madam Lefoux brightened considerably once they landed. Her step was light and cheerful as they walked the gangplank down from the dirigible, leaving the colorful ship bobbing against its tethers behind them. The French, who, in addition to a marked preference for ridiculous mustaches, had a propensity for highly civilized mechanicals, were prepared for vast amounts of luggage. They loaded La Diva Tarabotti's trunks, Mr. Lefoux's cases, and Floote's portmanteau onto a kind of platform that floated, kept aloft by four aether-inflated balloons and pulled along by a lackadaisical porter. Madame Lefoux engaged in several protracted arguments with various staff, arguments that seemed to be more the general formula of conversation than embodying any genuine vehemence. From what Alexia could follow, which wasn't much given the rapidity of the tongue, there appeared to be some question concerning the bill, the gratuity, and the complexity of hiring transport at this time of the morning.

Madame Lefoux admitted the time of day to be unacceptably early but would brook no delay on their journey. She rousted up a youngish carriage driver, who had a particularly spectacular mustache and who met them rubbing sleepy eyes. With baggage in place and Alexia, Madame Lefoux, and Floote safely ensconced within, they drove some ten miles or so to a station where they caught the mail train on its six-hour journey to Paris, via Amiens. Madame Lefoux promised, in a low voice, there would be sustenance available on board. Sadly, the provisions on the rail turned out to be wretchedly inferior. Alexia was underwhelmed; she had heard such wondrous things about French cuisine.

They arrived in the late afternoon, and Alexia was perturbed to find, never having traveled to foreign climes, that Paris seemed just as dirty and crowded as London, only peopled by buildings more swooped and gentlemen more mustached. They did not go directly into town. Despite a most pressing need for tea, the possibility of pursuit remained uppermost in all their minds. They went to the city's main train station, where Floote pretended to purchase train tickets, and they made a prodigious fuss over catching the next high-boil steamer to Madrid. They went loudly in on one side of the train, with luggage, and then quietly off the other, much to the annoyance of one long-suffering porter who was liberally rewarded for his pains. They then exited at the back end of the station, into a large but seedy carriage. Madame Lefoux directed the driver to a tiny, rickety little clockmaker's shop nestled next to a bakery in what appeared, shockingly enough, to be the tradesmen's quarter of Paris.

Mindful that she was a fugitive and could not afford to be particular, Alexia trailed her friend into the tiny shop. She spotted the small brass octopus above the door and could not quite prevent a lurch of apprehension. Once inside, however, her fears were quickly dissipated by curiosity. The interior was littered with clocks and companion devices of all shapes and sizes. Unfortunately, Madame Lefoux pressed on through rapidly into a back room and up a set of stairs. They arrived thus, with very little pomp or circumstance, in the tiny reception chamber of a set of residential apartments above the shop.

Alexia found herself surrounded and embraced by a room of such unmitigated welcome and personality that it was akin to being yelled at by plum pudding. All the furniture looked comfortable and worn, and the paintings on the walls and side tables were bright and cheerful. Even the wallpaper was equally amiable. Unlike in England, where courtesy to the supernatural set prevailed, resulting in interiors kept dark with heavy curtains, this room was bright and well lit. The windows, overlooking the street below, were thrown open and the sun allowed to stream in. But for Alexia, the most welcoming thing about the place was the myriad of gadgets and mechanical knickknacks strewn about. Unlike Madame Lefoux's contrivance chamber, which had no other purpose but production, this was a home that also happened to be a work space. There were gears piled atop half-finished knitting and cranking mechanisms attached to coal scuttles. It was a marriage of domesticity and technology like none Alexia had witnessed before.

Madame Lefoux gave a funny little holler but did not go looking for the denizen of the abode. With the air of a regular visitor, she settled herself easily into a soft settee. Alexia, finding this familiar behavior highly irregular, resisted joining her at first, but due to the weariness of extended travel was eventually persuaded not to stand on ceremony. Floote, who seemed never to tire, laced his fingers behind his back and took up his favorite butler stance near the door.

"Why, Genevieve, my dear, what an unexpected pleasure!" The gentleman who entered the room matched the house perfectly—soft, friendly, and gadget-riddled. He wore a leather apron with many pockets, a pair of green spectacles rested upon his nose, a pair of brass glassicals perched atop his head, and a monocle hung about his neck. The clockmaker, no doubt. He spoke in French, but fortunately much less rapidly than others Alexia had met so far, allowing her to follow the conversation.

"There is something different about you?" The man adjusted his spectacles and contemplated Madame Lefoux for a moment through them. Apparently not pinpointing the enormous mustache draped atop the inventor's upper lip as the culprit, he added, "Is that a new hat?"

"Gustave, you never do change, do you? I hope you do not mind such an unexpected visit." Madame Lefoux addressed their host in the queen's English, in deference to Alexia and Floote's presence.

The gentleman in question switched smoothly into Alexia's native language as though it were a tongue as familiar to him as his own. In the same instant, he seemed to notice Alexia and Floote for the first time. "Not at all, not at all, I assure you. I adore the company. Always welcome." There was a tone to his voice and a twinkle to his blue-button eyes that suggested real truth to the social niceties. "And you have brought me guests! How marvelous. Delighted, delighted."

Madame Lefoux made introductions. "Monsieur Floote and Madame Tarabotti, this is my dear cousin, Monsieur Trouvé."

The clockmaker gave Floote a measured look and a small bow. Floote returned both in kind, after which Alexia found herself the object of bespectacled scrutiny.

"Not *that* Tarabotti?"

Alexia would not go so far as to describe Monsieur Trouvé as shocked, but he was certainly something more than complacent. It was difficult to see the exact nature of his expression as, in addition to the ubiquitous mustache, the clockmaker also wore a golden-brown beard of such epic proportions as might dwarf a mulberry bush. It was as though his mustache had become overly enthusiastic and, seized with the spirit of adventure, set out to conquer the southern reaches of his face in a take-no-prisoners kind of way.

"His daughter," confirmed Madame Lefoux.

"In truth?" The Frenchman looked to Floote, of all people, for confirmation.

Floote nodded curtly—once.

"Is it so very bad a thing, to be my father's daughter?" Alexia wondered.

Monsieur Trouvé raised both bushy eyebrows and smiled. It was a small, shy smile that barely made it through the shrubbery of his beard. "I take it you never met your father? No, of course, you wouldn't have, would you? Not possible. Not if you *are* his daughter." He looked at Madame Lefoux this time. "Is she really?"

Madame Lefoux dimpled at him. "Without question."

The clockmaker brought his monocle up, peering through both it and his spectacles at Alexia. "Remarkable. A female preternatural. I never thought I would live to see the day. It is a true honor having you to visit, Madame Tarabotti. Genevieve, you always did bring me the most charming surprises. And trouble with them, of course, but we won't talk about that now, will we?"

"Better than that, cousin—she is with child. And the father is a werewolf. How do you like *that*?"

Alexia gave Madame Lefoux a sharp stare. They had not discussed revealing the personal details of her embarrassing condition to a French clockmaker!

"I must sit down." Monsieur Trouvé groped without looking for a nearby chair and collapsed into it. He took a deep breath and then examined Alexia with even more interest. She wondered if he might try to wear the glassicals as well as the spectacles and the monocle.

"You are certain?"

Alexia bristled. She was so very tired of having her word questioned. "I assure you. I am quite certain."

"Amazing," said the clockmaker, seeming to recover some of his equanimity. "No offense meant, no offense. You are, you must realize, a marvel of the modern age." The monocle went back up. "Though, not so very much *like* your dear father."

Alexia glanced tentatively at Floote and then asked Monsieur Trouvé, "Is there anyone who *did not* know my father?"

"Oh, most people didn't. He preferred things that way. But he dabbled in my circle, or I should say, my father's circle. I met him only the once, and I was six at the time. I remember it well, however." The clockmaker smiled again. "He did have quite the habit of making an impression, your father, I must say."

Alexia was unsure as to whether this comment had an underlying unsavory meaning or not. Then she realized it must. Given what little she knew of her father, a better question might be, to which form of unsavory meaning was the Frenchman alluding? Still, she was positively dying of curiosity. "Circle?"

"The Order."

"My father was an *inventor*?" That surprised Alexia. She had never heard *that* about Alessandro Tarabotti. All his journal entries indicated he was more a destroyer than a creator. Besides, by all accounts, preternaturals couldn't really invent anything. They lacked the necessary imagination and soul.

"Oh, no, no." Monsieur Trouvé brushed two fingers through his beard thoughtfully. "More of an irregular customer. He always had the oddest requests. I remember, once, my uncle talking about how he actually asked for a—" The clockmaker looked up at the doorway, apparently noticing something that made him stop. "Ah, yes, never mind."

Alexia glanced over to see what had caused this gregarious fellow to silence himself. But there was nothing there, only Floote, impassive as always, hands laced behind his back.

Alexia looked to Madame Lefoux in mute appeal.

The Frenchwoman was no help. Instead, she excused herself from the discussion. "Cousin, perhaps I could go find Cansuse for some tea?"

"Tea?" Monsieur Trouvé looked taken aback. "Well, if you must. Seems to me you have been in England too long, my dearest Genevieve. I should think such an occasion as this would require wine. Or perhaps brandy." He turned to Alexia. "Should I get out the brandy? You look as though you might need a bit of a pick-me-up, my dear."

"Oh, no, thank you. Tea would be perfectly suitable." In truth, Alexia thought tea a brilliant idea. It had taken well over an hour to conduct their train subterfuge, and while she knew it was worth it, her stomach objected on principle. Ever since the onset of the infant-inconvenience, food was becoming an ever more pressing concern in some form or another. She had always pondered food overmuch for the safety of her waistline, but these days a good deal more of her attention was occupied with where it was, how soon she could get it, and, on the more embarrassing occasions, whether it would remain eaten or not. Yet another thing to blame on Conall. *Who would have thought that anything could affect my eating habits?*

Madame Lefoux vanished from the room. There was an awkward pause while the clockmaker continued to stare at Alexia.

"So," Alexia began tentatively, "through which side of the family are you related to Genevieve?"

"Oh, we aren't actually family. She and I went to school together— École des Arts et Métiers. You've heard of it? Of course you have. Naturally, at the time, *she* was a *he*—always did prefer to play the man, our Genevieve." There was a pause while bushy eyebrows descended in thought. "Aha, that is what is different! She is wearing that ridiculous fake mustache again. It has been a long time. You must be traveling incognito. What fun!"

Alexia looked mildly panicked, unsure as to whether she should tell this affable man about danger of a vampiric persuasion heading in their direction.

"Not to worry, I wouldn't dare to pry. Regardless, I taught Genevieve everything she knows about clockwork mechanisms. And mustache maintenance, come to think on it. And a few other things of note." The clockmaker stroked his own impressive mustache with forefinger and thumb.

Alexia didn't quite follow his meaning. She was saved from having to continue the conversation by the return of Madame Lefoux.

"Where is your wife?" the Frenchwoman demanded of their host.

"Ah, yes, about that. Hortense slightly, well, died last year."

"Oh." Madame Lefoux did not look particularly upset by this news, only surprised. "I am sorry."

The clockmaker gave a small shrug. "Hortense never was one for making a fuss. She caught a tiny cold down the Riviera way, and the next thing I knew, she had just given up and expired."

Alexia wasn't sure what to think of such a blasé attitude.

"She was a bit of a turnip, my wife."

Alexia decided to be mildly amused by his lack of sentiment. "How do you mean, turnip?"

The clockmaker smiled again. Clearly, he had been hoping for that question. "Bland, good as a side dish, but really only palatable when there is nothing better available."

"Gustave, really!" Madame Lefoux pretended shock.

"But enough about me. Tell me more about yourself, Madame Tarabotti." Monsieur Trouvé scooted toward her.

"What more should you like to know?" Alexia wanted to ask him more questions about her father but felt that the opportunity had passed.

"Do you function the same as a male soulless? Your ability to negate the supernatural, is it similar?"

"Having never met any other living preternaturals, I always assumed so."

"So, you would say, physical touch or very near proximity with a rapid reaction time on the part of the victim?"

Alexia didn't like the word "victim," but his description of her abilities was accurate enough, so she nodded. "Do you make a study of us, then, Monsieur Trouvé?" Perhaps he could help with her pregnancy predicament.

The man shook his head, his eyes crinkling up at the edges in amusement. Alexia was finding she did not mind the copious facial hair, because so much of the clockmaker's expressions were centered in his eyes. "Oh, no, no. Far outside of my sphere of particular interest."

Madame Lefoux gave her old school chum an assessing look. "No, Gustave, you never have been one for the aetheric sciences—not enough gadgetry."

"I'm an aetheric science?" Alexia was mystified. In her experience as a bluestocking, such studies focused on the niceties of aetheronautics and supra-oxygenic travel, not preternaturals.

A diminutive maid with a shy demeanor brought in the tea, or what Alexia supposed passed for tea in France. The maid was accompanied by a low tray of foodstuffs on wheels, which seemed to be somehow trailing her about the apartments. It made a familiar tinny skittering noise as it moved. When the maid bent to lift the tray up and place it on a table, Alexia emitted an involuntary squeak of alarm. Quite unaware of her own athletic abilities until that moment, she jumped over and behind the couch.

Acting the part of footman in tonight's French farce, she thought with a bubble of panicked hilarity, *we have a homicidal mechanical ladybug.*

"Good lord, Madame Tarabotti, are you quite well?"

"Ladybug!" Alexia managed to squawk.

"Ah, yes, a prototype for a recent order."

"You mean, it is not trying to kill me?"

"Madame Tarabotti, I assure you, in my own home, I should never be so uncouth as to kill someone with a ladybug."

Alexia came cautiously back out from behind the couch and watched warily as the large mechanical beetle, all unconcerned for her palpitating heart, trundled after the maid and back out into the hall.

"Your artisanship, I take it?"

"Indeed." The Frenchman looked proudly after the retreating bug.

"I have encountered it before."

Madame Lefoux turned accusing eyes onto Monsieur Trouvé. "Cousin, I thought you preferred not to design weapons!"

"I do! And I must say I resent the implication."

"Well, the vampires have turned them into such," Alexia said. "I experienced a whole herd of homicidal ladybugs, sent to poke me in a carriage. Those very antennae that yours was using to carry the tea tray had been replaced with syringes."

"And one exploded when I went to examine it," added Madame Lefoux.

"How perfectly dreadful." The clockmaker frowned. "Ingenious, of course, but not my modifications, I assure you. I must apologize to you, dear lady. These things always seem to happen when dealing with vampires. Although it is hard to refuse such consistent customers with such prompt accounting."

"Can you reveal the name of your client, cousin?"

The clockmaker frowned. "American gentleman. A Mr. Beauregard. Ever heard of him?"

"Sounds like a pseudonym," said Alexia.

Madame Lefoux nodded. "It is rather common to use handlers in this part of the world, I'm afraid. The trail will have gone quite cold by now."

Alexia sighed regretfully. "Ah, well, deadly ladybugs will happen,

Monsieur Trouvé. I understand. You can repair my finer feelings with some tea, perhaps?"

"Of course, Madame Tarabotti. Of course."

To be certain there was tea, of indifferent quality, but Alexia's attention was drawn to the food on offer. There were stacks of raw vegetables—raw!—and some sort of pressed gelatinous meat with tiny nutty-looking digestive biscuits. There was nothing sweet at all. Alexia was deeply suspicious of the whole arrangement. However, upon selection of a small mound of nibbles, she found the fare to be more than passing delicious, with the exception of the tea, which proved itself to be as indifferent in taste as it had appeared initially.

The clockmaker nibbled delicately at some of the foodstuffs but took no libations, commenting that he believed tea would make a superior beverage served cold over ice. Were ice, of course, to become a less expensive commodity. At which statement, Alexia utterly despaired of both him and his moral integrity.

He continued his conversation with Madame Lefoux, as though they had never been interrupted. "On the contrary, my dear Genevieve, I am interested enough in the aetheric phenomena to keep up with the current literature out of Italy. Contrary to the British and the American theories on volatile moral natures, blood derangements, and feverish humors, the Italian investigative societies now hold that souls are connected to the correct dermatological processing of ambient aether."

"Oh, for goodness' sake, how preposterous." Alexia was not impressed. The infant-inconvenience appeared to feel equally unimpressed by raw vegetables. Alexia stopped eating and put a hand to her stomach. Damn and blast the annoying thing. Couldn't it leave her in peace for one meal?

Floote, previously occupied with his own comestibles, immediately moved toward her in concern.

Alexia shook her head at him.

"Ah, you are a reader of scientific literature, Madame Tarabotti?"

Alexia inclined her head.

"Well it may seem absurd to you, but I believe their ideas have merit. Not the least of which being the fact that this particular theory has temporarily halted Templar-sanctioned vivisections of supernatural test subjects."

"You are a progressive?" Alexia was surprised.

"I try to stay out of politics. However, England seems to be doing rather well having openly accepted the supernatural. That is not to say I approve. Making them hide, however, has its disadvantages. I should love to have access to some of the vampires' scientific investigations for one; the things they know about clocks! I also do not believe the supernatural should be hunted down and treated like animals as in the Italian mode."

The little room in which they sat turned a pretty shade of gold as the sun began to set over the Parisian rooftops.

The clockmaker paused upon noticing the change. "Well, well, we have chatted long enough, I suspect. You must be exhausted. You will be staying the night with me, of course?"

"If you don't mind the imposition, cousin."

"It's no trouble at all. So long as you forgive the arrangements, for they will be quite cramped. I am afraid you ladies will have to bunk down together."

Alexia gave Madame Lefoux an assessing look. The Frenchwoman had made her preferences, and her interest, clear. "I suspect my virtue is safe."

Floote looked as though he would like to object.

Alexia gave him a funny look. There was no possible way her father's ex-valet could be a prude in matters of the flesh. Was there? Floote had terribly rigid ideas about sensible dress and public behavior, but he had never batted a single eye at the entirely untoward private doings of Woolsey Castle's rambunctious werewolf pack. On the other hand, he had never particularly liked Lord Akeldama, either. Alexia twitched a small frown in his direction.

Floote gave her a blank stare.

Perhaps he still mistrusted Madame Lefoux for some other reason?

Since puzzling over the matter would certainly yield no results, and talking to Floote—or, more precisely, *at* Floote—never did any good, Alexia swept by him and followed Monsieur Trouvé up the hallway to a tiny bedroom.

Alexia had changed into a claret-colored taffeta visiting dress and was just enjoying a little nap before supper when the most amazing racket awakened her. It seemed to be emanating from the downstairs clock shop.

"Oh, for the love of treacle, what now?"

Grabbing her parasol in one hand and her dispatch case in the other, she charged out into the hallway. It was very dark, as the lights in the apartment were not yet lit. A warm glow emanated up from the shop below.

Alexia bumped into Floote at the top of the stairs.

"Madame Lefoux and Monsieur Trouvé have been consulting on matters clock-related while you rested," he informed her softly.

"*That* cannot possibly account for such a hullabaloo."

Something crashed into the front door. Unlike London, the Paris shops did not stay open late in order to cater to werewolves and vampires. They shut down before sunset, locked firmly against any possible supernatural clientele.

Alexia and Floote bounded down the stairs—as much as a dignified butler-type personage and a pregnant woman of substance can be said to *bound.* There Alexia thought Paris's closed-door policy might well have its merits. For just as she entered the clock shop, four large vampires did the same by way of the now-broken front door. Their fangs were extended, and they did not look in favor of formal introductions.

CHAPTER SEVEN

The Trouble with Vampires

The trouble with vampires, thought Professor Lyall as he cleaned his glassicals with a handkerchief, was that they got hung up on the details. Vampires liked to manipulate things, but when things did not turn out as planned, they lost all capacity for refinement in the resulting chaos. The upshot was that they panicked and resorted to a course of action that never ended as elegantly as they had originally hoped.

"Where is our illustrious Alpha?" asked Hemming, sitting down at the table and helping himself to several slices of ham and a kipper. It was dinnertime for most, but for the werewolves this was breakfast. And since gentlemen were never served at breakfast, the staff merely provided mounds of meat and let the pack and clavigers see to themselves.

"He is in the clink and has been all day, sobering up. He was so drunk last night he went wolf. The dungeon seemed like the best place to stash him."

"Golly."

"Women will do that to a soul. Best avoided, if you ask me." Adelphus Bluebutton wandered in, followed shortly thereafter by Rafe and Phelan, two of the younger pack members.

Ulric, silently chomping on a chop at the other end of the table, glanced up. "No one did ask you. No one has ever been in any doubt as to your preferences."

"Some of us are less narrow-minded than others."

"More opportunistic, you mean to say."

"I get bored easily."

Everyone was grumpy—it was that time of the month.

Professor Lyall, with great deliberation, finished cleaning his glassicals and put them on. He looked around at the pack through the magnified lens. "Gentlemen, might I suggest that a discussion of preference is better suited to your club? It is certainly not the reason I have called a meeting this evening."

"Yes, sir."

"You will note that the clavigers have not been invited?"

Around him, all the immortal gentlemen nodded. They knew that this meant Lyall wanted to discuss a serious matter with the pack alone. Normally, the clavigers were in on everyone's business. Living with several dozen mostly out-of-work actors will do that to a man's private life—that is, make it considerably less private.

All the werewolves seated about the large dining table tilted their heads so that their necks were exposed to the Beta.

Professor Lyall, aware that he now had their full attention, began the meeting. "Given that our Alpha is pursuing a new and glorious career as an imbecilic twit, we must prepare for the worst. I require two of you to take leave of your military duties to help handle the extra BUR workload."

No one questioned Professor Lyall's right to make changes to the status quo. At one point or another, each member of the Woolsey Pack had tested himself against Randolph Lyall. All had discovered the damage inherent in such an undertaking. They had, as a result, settled into the realization that a good Beta was as valuable as a good Alpha, and it was best to be happy that they had both. Except, of course, that now their Alpha had gone quite decidedly off the rails. And their reputation and position as England's premier pack was one that had to be defended constantly.

Professor Lyall continued. "Ulric and Phelan, it had best be you two. You have dealt with BUR paperwork and operational procedure before. Adelphus, you will handle the military negotiations and make all accommodations needed to compensate for Channing's absence."

"Is he drunk, too?" one of the youngsters wanted to know.

"Mmm. No. Missing. I don't suppose he told any of *you* where he was going?"

Silence met that question, broken only by the sound of chewing.

Lyall pressed his glassicals up the bridge of his nose and looked down through them at his cup of tea. "No? I suspected as much. Very well. Adelphus, you will have to liaise with the regiment and persuade them to assign Channing's majority temporarily to the nearest eligible officer. It will probably have to be a mortal." He looked at Adelphus, whose rank was lieutenant and who thought rather too well of his own abilities and rather too meanly of others'. In truth, he had fifty years more experience than most, but military protocol must be followed.

"You will continue to obey his orders as you would any supernatural superior officer. Is that clear? If there is any question of improper use of pack abilities, or excess risk due to immortal prejudice, you are to come directly to me. No dueling, Adelphus, not even under the most trying circumstances. That goes for the rest of you as well."

Professor Lyall took off the glassicals and issued the table of large men a cutting glare.

They all hung their heads and focused on their food.

"Too much dueling gives a pack a reputation. Any questions?"

No one had any. Professor Lyall himself held the rank of lieutenant colonel with the Coldsteam Guards, but had, in the last fifty years, rarely had cause to serve. He was beginning to regret not maintaining a more consistent presence within the regiment by letting his BUR duties supersede his military obligations. But even he, a man of considerable forethought, had not planned for a contingency wherein the regiment would be in residence *and* both Lord Maccon and Major Channing would, essentially, *not* be in residence.

He allowed the pack to continue the rest of their meal untroubled. They were nervous and a little restless. Merely through his presence alone, Lord Maccon kept them tame. Professor Lyall could fight them each individually, but he hadn't the charisma to control them en masse, and if Lord Maccon continued to remain sloshed, problems might well arise from within the pack as easily as from without it. Either that, or England would run out of formaldehyde.

Just as the gentlemen were finishing their meal, a timid knock sounded against the closed door. Professor Lyall frowned; he had left orders they were not to be disturbed.

"Yes?"

The door creaked open and a very nervous-looking Rumpet entered, carrying a brass tray with a single card resting atop it.

"Begging your pardon, Professor Lyall, sir," said the butler. "I know you said only in cases of emergency, but the clavigers don't know what to do, and the staff is in an uproar."

Professor Lyall took the card and read it.

Sandalius Ulf, Barrister. Messrs. Ulf, Ulf, Wrendofflip, & Ulf. Topsham, Devonshire. Underneath that in very small letters was one additional printed word: *Loner.*

The Beta flipped over the card. On the back had been scrawled, in the appropriate medium—blood—the fated phrase, *Name your second.*

"Oh, just wonderful." Professor Lyall rolled his eyes. And he had taken such prodigious care with his dress for the evening. "Bother."

Lyall had spent a good deal of his existence as a werewolf avoiding becoming an Alpha. Not only was his temperament ill-suited to the job, but he had no desire for that kind of physical responsibility, quite apart from the fact that he was unable to affect Anubis Form. Alphas had, he observed over the centuries, remarkably short life spans for immortals. His circumspect attitude toward brawling had served him in good stead. The devil in his current situation was that despite himself, Professor Lyall was rather fond of his current Alpha and was, as yet, unwilling to acquiesce to a regime change. Which meant that when upstart loners came to Woolsey to fight for the right to lead England's most powerful pack because the Alpha was rumored to be incapacitated, there was only one thing poor Lyall could do—fight in Lord Maccon's stead.

"Lieutenant Bluebutton, if you would attend me?"

One of the stronger and more senior pack members objected to that. "Shouldn't *I* be Gamma in Channing's place?"

"Given that the regiment is still here, it had better be a ranking officer."

Professor Lyall had to maintain military support and, with the Gamma gone, this could prove difficult. Major Channing might be a pain in the proverbial posterior as a pack mate, but he was an excellent officer with a reputation as a fire-eater, and he had the respect of both soldiers and fellow officers. Without him standing as second, Lyall needed another officer to act the part so that the pack was seen as united with the regiment, should he need to bring soldiers in to support Woolsey as a last resort. It was a truly horrible idea, using Her Majesty's army to prevent an Alpha coup. Werewolves had served their military contracts with dedication since Queen Elizabeth first integrated them, but they had always strived to keep pack protocol separate. Nevertheless, Lyall was a man of ingenuity, and he would call up the Coldsteam Guards if he had to.

Hemming was no Beta, so he objected further. "Yes, but—"

"My decision is final." Professor Lyall finished his tea in one gulp, stood, summoned Adelphus to follow him, and left for the cloakroom.

There, both gentlemen stripped down to the skin and donned long wool cloaks before exiting through the front door, where an excited milling mass of clavigers and Woolsey staff waited in the cold evening air.

Professor Lyall could smell the loner even before he saw him. His scent was not that of the Woolsey Pack, nor of any distant association. The bloodline was off, making Lyall's nose twitch.

Professor Lyall went forward to greet him. "Mr. Ulf? How do you do?"

The werewolf looked at Lyall suspiciously. "Lord Maccon?"

"Professor Lyall," said Professor Lyall. And then to make matters clear to this upstart, "And this is my second, Lieutenant Bluebutton."

The loner looked offended. Lyall could tell from the man's scent that this was for show. He was neither upset nor nervous at seeing Lyall instead of Lord Maccon. He had not expected the earl to meet his challenge. He had heard the rumors.

Professor Lyall's lip curled. He loathed lawyers.

"The Alpha will not even acknowledge my challenge?" Mr. Ulf's question was a sly one. "I know of you by reputation, of course, Professor, but why is Lord Maccon himself not meeting me?"

Professor Lyall did not dignify that with an answer. "Shall we proceed?"

He led the challenger around the back of the castle, to the wide stone porch where the pack fought most of its practice bouts. Spread out and down the long sloping green of Woolsey's well-tended lawn, a vast number of military-issue white canvas tents had sprouted, clearly visible under the almost full moon. The regiment usually camped around the front of Woolsey, but Alexia had had kittens over their presence and insisted they remove themselves to the back. They were scheduled to depart for winter quarters in a week or so, having squatted at Woolsey merely for the sake of unity with the pack. Conventional niceties having been observed, pretty much everyone was now ready to move on.

The rest of the Woolsey Pack came wandering after the three men, followed by a handful of clavigers. Rafe and Phelan were looking rather haggard. Lyall suspected he would have to insist they confine themselves to the dungeon presently, before the onslaught of moon madness. Curious, a few of the officers left their evening campfires, grabbed lanterns, and meandered over to see what the pack was getting up to.

Lyall and Mr. Ulf both stripped and stood naked for all the world to see. No one commented beyond a hoot and a whistle or two. Military men were used to werewolf changes and the indecency that preceded the affair.

Professor Lyall was older than he cared to admit and had grown, if not comfortable with shape change, at least enough in control of his own finer feelings not to show how much it hurt. And it *always* hurt. The sound of shifting from man to wolf was that of breaking bones, tearing muscle, and oozing flesh, and, unfortunately, that was also what it felt like. Werewolves called their particular brand of immortality a curse. Every time he shifted, Lyall wondered if this weren't true and if the vampires might not have made a better choice. Certainly they could be killed by the sunlight, and they had to run around drinking people's blood, but they could do both in comfort and style. At its root, being a werewolf, what with the nudity and the tyranny of the moon, was essentially undignified. And Professor Lyall was rather fond of his dignity.

If asked, the surrounding men would have admitted that if anyone could be said to change from man to wolf with dignity, it was Professor Lyall. He did the regiment proud and they all knew it. They had seen their attachment of Woolsey werewolves change both on and off the battlefield, but none were as fast and quiet about it as Lyall. Spontaneously, they gave him a round of polite applause when he had finished.

The smallish, sandy, almost foxlike wolf now standing where Professor Lyall had been gave a little nod of embarrassed gratitude at the clapping.

The challenger's change was not nearly so elegant. It was accomplished with much groaning and whimpers of pain, but when complete, the black wolf that resulted was a good deal larger than Professor Lyall. The Woolsey Pack Beta was not perturbed by this discrepancy in size. *Most* werewolves were a good deal larger than he.

The challenger attacked, but Lyall was already in motion, twisting out of the way and darting in for the other's throat. There was so much to do back at BUR and he wanted to end the bout quickly.

But the loner was a crafty fighter, nimble and adept. He avoided Lyall's counterattack, and the two circled each other warily, both coming to the realization that they might have underestimated their opponent.

The men around them closed in, forming a circle of bodies around the pair. The soldiers called insults at the challenger, the officers catcalled, and the pack stood in silent wide-eyed attention.

The loner charged at Professor Lyall, snapping. Lyall dodged. The challenger skidded slightly on the smooth paving stones, his claws making an awful scraping noise as he scrabbled for purchase. Taking advantage of the skid, Lyall dove at him, hitting him broadside with enough force to knock him onto his side. The two wolves rolled over and over together, bumping into the shins of those who goaded them on. Professor Lyall could feel the claws of the other wolf tearing against his soft underbelly as he bit viciously into the creature's neck.

This was what he disliked most about fighting. It was so embarrassingly untidy. He didn't mind the pain; he would heal fast enough. But he was bleeding all over his own pristine coat, and blood from the challenger was dripping down over his muzzle, matting the fur of his white ruff. Even as a wolf, Professor Lyall did not like to be unkempt.

Still the blood flowed, bits of fur flew about the challenger's scrabbling back legs in white puffs, and the sound of growling rent the air.

The wet, rich smell of flowing blood caused the noses of the other pack members to wrinkle with interest. Professor Lyall wasn't one to play dirty, but things being as they were, he thought he might have to go in for an eyeball. Then he realized something was disturbing the crowd.

The tight circle of bodies began rippling, and then two pack members were thrust violently aside and Lord Maccon entered the ring.

He was naked, had been all day, but under the moonlight, he was once more looking scruffy and feral. From his mild weaving back and forth, either a day in dry dock hadn't sufficiently eliminated the formaldehyde from his system or he'd managed to acquire more. Professor Lyall would have to have words with the claviger who'd been persuaded to let Lord Maccon out of the dungeon.

Despite the presence of his lord and master, Lyall was in the middle of a fight and did not allow himself to be distracted.

"Randolph!" roared his Alpha. "What are you about? You hate fighting. Stop it immediately."

Professor Lyall ignored him.

Until Lord Maccon changed.

The earl was a big man, and in wolf form, he was large even for a werewolf, and he changed loudly. Not with any vocal indication of pain—he was too proud for that—it was simply that his bones were so massive that when they broke, they did so with a real will to crunch. He emerged from the transformation a huge brindled wolf, dark brown with gold, black, and cream markings and pale yellow eyes. He bounced over to where Lyall still scrabbled with the challenger, wrapped his massive jaws about his Beta's neck, and hauled him off, tossing him aside with a contemptuous flick.

Professor Lyall knew what was good for him and stepped away into the crowd, flopping down onto his bloody stomach, tongue lolling out as he panted for breath. If his Alpha wanted to make a fool of himself, there came a point when even the best Beta couldn't stop him. But he did stay in wolf form, just in case. Surreptitiously, he licked at his white ruff like a cat to get the blood off.

Lord Maccon barreled into the loner, massive jaws snapping down.

The challenger dodged to one side, a glint of panic in his yellow gaze. He had banked on not having to fight the earl; this was not in his plan.

Lyall could smell the wolf's fear.

Lord Maccon swiveled about and went after the challenger again, but then tripped over his own feet, lurched to the side, and came down hard on one shoulder.

Definitely still drunk, thought Professor Lyall, resigned.

The challenger seized the opportunity and dove for Lord Maccon's neck. At the same moment, the earl shook his head violently as though to clear it. Two large wolf skulls cracked together.

The challenger fell back, dazed.

Lord Maccon, already in a state of confusion, did not register the encounter, instead lurching after his enemy with single-minded focus. Normally a quick and efficient fighter, he ambled after his bemused opponent and took one long second to look down at him, as if trying to remember what, exactly, was going on. Then he surged forward and bit down on the other wolf's muzzle.

The fallen wolf squealed in pain.

Lord Maccon let go in befuddled surprise, as if shocked that his meal should yell back. The challenger stumbled to his feet.

The earl wove his head back and forth, an action his opponent found disconcerting. The loner crouched back onto his haunches, forelegs splayed out before him. Lyall wasn't certain if he was bowing or preparing to spring. He had no chance to do either, for Lord Maccon, much to his own astonishment, stumbled again, and in an effort to regain his balance, jumped forward, coming down solidly on top of the loner with a loud thud.

Almost as an afterthought, he craned his neck around and sank all of his very long and very deadly teeth into the upper portion of the other wolf's head—conveniently spearing one eye and both ears.

Because werewolves were immortal and very hard to kill, challenge fights could go on for days. But a bite to the eyes was generally considered a no-contest win. It would take a good forty-eight hours to heal properly, and a blind wolf, immortal or no, *could* be killed during the interim merely because he was at such a grave disadvantage.

As soon as the teeth struck home, the challenger, whimpering in agony, wriggled onto his back, presenting his belly to Lord Maccon in surrender. The earl, still lying half on top of the unfortunate fellow, lurched off of him, spitting and sneezing over the flavor of eye goo and ear wax. Werewolves enjoyed fresh meat—they needed it, in fact, to survive—but other werewolves did not taste fresh. They tasted perhaps not quite so putrefied as vampires, but still old and slightly spoiled.

Professor Lyall stood and stretched—tail tip quivering. Perhaps, he thought as he trotted back to the cloakroom, this battle might be a good thing: to have it publicly known that Lord Maccon could still defeat a challenger, even when drunk. The rest of the pack could take care of cleaning up the mess. Now that the matter was settled, Professor Lyall had business to attend to. He paused in the cloakroom. He might as well run to London in wolf form, as he was already wearing his fur and his evening attire was now hopelessly wrinkled. He really *must* get his Alpha back on the straight and narrow—the man's behavior was affecting his clothing. Lyall understood a broken heart, but it could not be allowed to rumple perfectly good shirtwaists.

The trouble with vampires, thought Alexia Tarabotti, was that they were quick as well as strong. Not as strong as werewolves, but in this particular instance Alexia didn't have any werewolves fighting on her side—*blast Conall to all three atmospheres*—so the vampires had a distinct advantage.

"Because," she grumbled, "my husband is a first-rate git. I wouldn't even be in this situation if it weren't for him."

Floote gave her a look of annoyance that suggested he felt that now was not the time for connubial recriminations.

Alexia took his meaning perfectly.

Monsieur Trouvé and Madame Lefoux, having been disturbed from some detailed consultation on the nature of spring-loaded cuckoo clocks, were making their way around from behind a little workman's table. Madame Lefoux pulled out a sharp-looking wooden pin from her cravat with one hand and pointed her other wrist at the intruders. Upon that wrist she wore a large wristwatch that was probably no wristwatch at all. The clockmaker, for lack of any better weapon, grasped the mahogany and pearl case of a cuckoo clock and brandished it in a threatening manner.

"Quoo?" said the clock. Alexia was amazed that even a tiny mechanical device could sound inexplicably French in this country.

Alexia pressed the appropriate lotus leaf, and the tip of her parasol opened to reveal a dart emitter. Unfortunately, Madame Lefoux had designed the emitter to fire only three shots, and there were four vampires. In addition, Alexia could not recall if the inventor had told her whether or not the numbing agent even worked on the supernatural. But it was the only projectile in her armament, and she figured all great battles began with an airborne offensive.

Madame Lefoux and Monsieur Trouvé joined Alexia and Floote at the bottom of the stairs, facing off against the vampires, who had slowed their hectic charge and were moving forward in a menacing manner, as cats will stalk string.

"How did they find me so quickly?" Alexia took aim.

"So they are after *you*, are they? Well, I suppose that is hardly a surprise." The clockmaker glanced in Alexia's direction.

"Yes. Terribly inconvenient of them."

Monsieur Trouvé let out a rolling bark of deep laughter. "I did say you always brought me charming surprises, and trouble with them, didn't I, Genevieve? *What* have you gotten me into this time?"

Madame Lefoux explained. "I am sorry, Gustave. We should have told you sooner. The London vampires want Alexia dead, and they appear to have passed the desire on to the Parisian hives."

"Well, fancy that. How jolly." The clockmaker did not seem upset, behaving more like a man on the brink of some grand lark.

The vampires pressed closer.

"Now, see here, couldn't we discuss this like civilized beings?" Alexia, ever one for form and courtesy, was in favor of negotiations whenever possible.

None of the vampires responded to her request.

Madame Lefoux tried the same question in French.

Still nothing.

Alexia thought this dreadfully boorish. The least they could do was answer with a "No, killing is all we are interested in at the moment, but thank you kindly for the offer all the same." Alexia had, in part, compensated for a lack of soul through the liberal application of manners. This was rather like donning an outfit consisting entirely of accessories, but Alexia maintained that proper conduct was never a bad thing. These vampires were behaving *most* improperly.

There were plenty of tables and display cabinets in the little shop that currently stood between the vampires and Alexia's small band of defenders. Most of the surfaces of these were covered in disassembled clocks of one style or another. It was, therefore, not unexpected that one of the vampires, probably intentionally—given the general grace and elegance of the species—knocked a pile of mechanicals to the floor.

What was unexpected was Monsieur Trouvé's reaction to this event.

He growled in anger and threw the cuckoo clock he was holding at the vampire.

"Quoo?" questioned the clock as it flew.

Then the clockmaker began to yell. "*That* was a prototype atmos clock with a dual regulatory aether conductor! A groundbreaking invention and utterly irreplaceable."

The cuckoo clock hit the vampire broadside, startling him considerably. It did minimal damage, landing with a sad little "Quooooo?"

Alexia decided it was probably a good time to start shooting. So she shot.

The poisoned dart hissed slightly as it flew, struck one of the vampires dead center to the chest, and stuck there. He looked down at it, up at Alexia with an expression of deep offense, and then crumpled limply to the floor like an overcooked noodle.

"Nicely shot, but it won't hold him for long," said Madame Lefoux, who should know. "Supernaturals can process the numbing agent faster than daylight folk."

Alexia armed her parasol and shot a second dart. Another vampire collapsed, but the first was already beginning to struggle groggily to his feet.

Then the remaining two were upon them.

Madame Lefoux shot at one with a wooden dart from her wrist-watch, missing his chest and hitting the meaty part of his left arm. *Hah,* thought Alexia. *I knew it wasn't an ordinary watch!* The Frenchwoman then slashed at that same vampire with her wooden cravat pin. The vampire began to bleed from two spots, arm and cheek, and backed away warily.

"We are not interested in you, little scientist. Give us the soul-sucker and we'll be away."

"*Now* you want to engage in conversation?" Alexia was annoyed.

The last of the vampires lunged for her, clearly planning to drag her off. He had one hand wrapped around her wrist when he realized his miscalculation.

Upon contact with her, his fangs disappeared, as did all of his extraordinary strength. His pale, smooth skin turned fleshy peach with freckles—freckles! He was no longer capable of dragging her off, yet no matter how hard Alexia pulled, she could not break his grip. He must have been a strong man before he changed. She began bashing at the no-longer-supernatural creature with her parasol, but he did not let go, even as she inflicted real injury upon him. He seemed to be recovering his powers of deduction and realized he would have to fall back on leverage for this task. So he shifted about, preparing to haul Alexia up and over one shoulder.

A gunshot rattled throughout the shop, and before he could do anything further, the vampire collapsed backward, letting go of Alexia in order to clutch at his own side. Alexia glanced to her left, astounded to see the unflappable Floote pocketing a still-smoking, single-shot derringer with an ivory handle. It was undoubtedly the tiniest pistol Alexia had ever seen. From the same pocket, he pulled a second slightly bigger gun. Both were horribly antiquated, thirty years or more out of date, but still effective. The vampire Floote had shot stayed down, writhing in agony on the floor. Unless Alexia missed her guess, that bullet was made of a reinforced wood of some kind, for it seemed to continue to cause him harm. There was a good chance, Alexia realized with a sick kind of dread, that a vampire could actually die from a shot like that. She could hardly countenance it, the very idea of killing an immortal. All that knowledge, gone just like that.

Monsieur Trouvé seemed momentarily captivated. "That's a sundowner's weapon you have there, isn't it, Mr. Floote?"

Floote did not respond. There was accusation inherent in the term, for "sundowner" implied official sanction from Her Majesty's government to terminate the supernatural. No British gentleman without such authorization ought to carry such a weapon.

"Since when would you know anything about munitions, Gustave?" Madame Lefoux issued her friend an imperiously quirked brow.

"I've developed a keen interest in gunpowder recently. Terribly messy stuff, but awfully useful for a directed mechanical force."

"I should say so," said Alexia, readjusting her parasol and shooting her last dart.

"Now you've wasted them all," accused Madame Lefoux, letting fly with her own, more effective wooden dart at the groggy vampire just after Alexia's projectile struck home. It hit him in the eye. Sluggish black blood oozed out from around it. Alexia felt ill.

"Really, Genevieve, must you go for the eye? It's so unsightly." Monsieur Trouvé appeared to agree with Alexia's disgust.

"Only if you promise never to use a pun like that again."

Thus two of the vampires were now incapacitated. The other two had retreated out of range to regroup, clearly not having anticipated such resistance.

Madame Lefoux glared at Alexia. "Stop stalling and use the lapis solaris."

"Are you certain that is strictly necessary, Genevieve? It seems so discourteous. I could accidentally kill one of them with such a substance. We've already had a little too much of that kind of tomfoolery." She nodded with her chin at the vampire Floote had shot, who now lay ominously still. Vampires were scarce, and generally rather old. Murdering one even in self-defense was like thoughtlessly destroying a rare aged cheese. True, a fanged and murderous rare aged cheese, but . . .

The lady inventor gave the preternatural woman an incredulous look. "Yes, final death was the idea when I designed it."

One of the vampires lurched forward again, intent on Alexia. He held a wicked-looking knife. Clearly he was adapting better to her preternatural ability than his now-inert cohorts.

Floote shot his other gun.

This time the bullet hit the man's chest. The vampire fell backward, crashed into a loaded display cabinet, and landed on the floor, making exactly the same sound a carpet makes when whacked to get the dust out.

The remaining vampire was looking both annoyed and confused. He had brought no projectile weapons. The vampire Madame Lefoux had spiked in the eye yanked out the offending optical impairment and lurched to his feet, the socket oozing blackened, sluggish blood. The two joined forces to charge once more.

Madame Lefoux slashed, and Monsieur Trouvé, finally understanding the gravity of the situation, reached around and pulled a long, wicked-looking spring-adjuster from its cradle on the wall. It was brass, so it was unlikely to do any serious damage, but it might slow even a vampire if applied properly. A sharp wooden knife had now appeared in Floote's hand—both guns being of the single-shot variety and thus out of ammunition. *Such a competent man, Floote,* thought Alexia with pride.

"Well, if I must, fine. I'll guard the retreat," said Alexia. "Buy us some time."

"What, in a clock shop?" Madame Lefoux clearly couldn't resist.

Alexia gave her a withering look. Then she opened and flipped her parasol over in a practiced motion so that she held it backward by the tip instead of the handle. There was a tiny dial just above the magnetic disruption emitter, set into a nodule. She stepped slightly forward, mindful that she could harm her friends as well as the vampires with this particular weapon. Then she clicked the dial round two times, and three ribs of the parasol began to spew forth a fine mist of lapis solaris diluted in sulfuric acid.

At first the stampeding vampires didn't quite understand what was happening, but when the mixture began to burn them severely, they backed out of range.

"Up the stairs, now!" yelled Alexia.

They all began to retreat up the tiny staircase, Alexia bringing up the rear, brandishing the misting parasol. The smell of acid burning through carpet and wood permeated the air. A few drops landed on Alexia's claret-colored skirts. *Well,* she thought, resigned, *there is one gown I won't ever be able to wear again.*

The vampires stayed just far enough out of range. By the time Alexia had reached the top of the stairs—going backward and up with both hands occupied was no mean feat in long skirts and a bustle—the others had gathered together a quantity of large, heavy objects with which to barricade the top. Alexia's parasol sputtered once, then emitted a sad little hissing noise and stopped misting, having used up its store of the lapis solaris.

The vampires renewed their attack. Alexia was alone at the top of the stairs. But Madame Lefoux was ready for them and began hurling various interesting-looking gadgets down, until, at the last possible minute, Alexia managed to sneak behind the rapidly growing pile of furniture and trunks that Floote and Monsieur Trouvé had piled at the head of the staircase.

While Alexia recovered her breath and equanimity, they built up the improvised rampart, wedging and tilting a mountain of furniture downward, relying on gravity and weight as assistants.

"Anyone have a plan?" Alexia looked around hopefully.

The Frenchwoman gave her a fierce grin. "Gustave and I were talking earlier. He says he still has the ornithopter we designed at university."

Monsieur Trouvé frowned. "Well, yes, but it isn't certified by the Ministry of Aethernautics to fly within Parisian aetherspace. I did not think you actually intended to use it. I'm not sure if the stabilizers are working properly."

"Never you mind that. Is it on the roof?"

"Of course, but—"

Madame Lefoux grabbed Alexia by the arm and began dragging her down the hall toward the back of the apartment.

Alexia made a face but allowed herself to be tugged along. "Well, then, to the roof with us! Ooof, wait, my dispatch case."

Floote dove to one side to retrieve her precious luggage.

"No time, no time!" insisted Madame Lefoux as the vampires, having attained the top of the stairway, were apparently engaged in trying to bash their way through to the landing by application of pure physical force. *How vulgar!*

"It has tea in it," Alexia explained gratefully when Floote reappeared with her case.

Then they heard a horrible noise, a rumbling, growling sound and the crunch of flesh between large, unforgiving jaws. The banging on the barricade stopped as something sharp-toothed and vicious distracted the vampires. A new sound of fighting commenced as the vampires engaged whatever it was that was hunting *them*.

The little group of refugees reached the end of the hallway. Madame Lefoux leaped up, grabbing at what looked to be a gas lamp fixture but what turned out to be a pull lever that activated a small hydraulic pump. A section of the ceiling flipped down at them, and a rickety ladder, clearly spring loaded, shot down, hitting the hallway floor with an audible thump.

Madame Lefoux scampered up. With considerable difficulty, hampered by dress and parasol, Alexia climbed after her, emerging into a crowded attic richly carpeted in dust and dead spiders. The gentlemen followed and Floote helped Monsieur Trouvé winch the ladder back up, disguising their retreat. With any luck, the vampires would be stalled trying to determine where and how their quarry had attained roof access.

Alexia wondered what had attacked the vampires on the stair: a savior, a protector, or some new form of monster that wanted her for itself? She didn't have time to contemplate for long. The two inventors were fussing about a machine of some kind, running around loosening tether ropes, checking safety features, tightening screws, and lubricating cogs. This seemed to involve a phenomenal quantity of banging and cursing.

The ornithopter, for that is what it must be, looked like a most incommodious mode of transport. Passengers—there was room for three in addition to the pilot—were suspended in nappylike leather seats the top of which strapped about the waist.

Alexia dashed over, stumbling against an inappropriately placed gargoyle.

Monsieur Trouvé ignited a small steam engine. The craft lurched upward and then tilted to one side, sputtering and coughing.

"I told you: stabilizers!" he said to Madame Lefoux.

"I cannot believe you don't have strapping wire on hand, Gustave. What kind of inventor are you?"

"Did you miss the sign above the shop door, my dear? Clocks! Clocks are my specialty. No stabilizers needed!"

Alexia intervened. "Wire, is that all you require?"

Madame Lefoux held her fingers a short width apart. "Yes, about so thick."

Alexia, before she could be shocked by her own audacity, lifted her overskirts and undid the tapes to her bustle. The undergarment dropped to the ground, and she kicked it in Madame Lefoux's direction. "That do?"

"Perfect!" the Frenchwoman crowed, attacking the canvas and extracting the metal boning, which she passed to Monsieur Trouvé.

While the clockmaker went to work threading the wire through some kind of piping about the contraption's nose, Alexia climbed inside. Only to discover, to her abject embarrassment, that the nappy-seat design caused one's skirts to hike up into one's armpits and one's legs to dangle below the enormous wings of the aircraft with bloomers exposed for all the world to see. They were her best bloomers, thank goodness, red flannel with three layers of lace at the hem, but still not a garment a lady ought to show to anyone except her maid or her husband, a pox on him, anyway.

Floote settled comfortably in behind her, and Madame Lefoux slid into the pilot's nappy. Monsieur Trouvé returned to the engine, situated behind Floote and under the tail of the craft, and cranked it up once more. The ornithopter wiggled, but then held steady and stabilized. *Victory to the bustle,* thought Alexia.

The clockmaker stepped back, looking pleased with himself.

"Are you not coming with us?" Alexia felt a strange kind of panic.

Gustave Trouvé shook his head. "Glide as much as you can, Genevieve, and you should be able to make it to Nice." He had to yell in order to be heard over the grumbling engine. He passed Madame Lefoux a pair of magnification goggles and a long scarf, which she used to wrap about her face, neck, and top hat.

Alexia, clutching parasol and dispatch case firmly to her ample chest, prepared for the worst.

"That far?" Madame Lefoux did not raise her head, busy checking on an array of dials and bobbing valves. "You have made modifications, Gustave."

The clockmaker winked.

Madame Lefoux looked at him suspiciously and then gave a curt nod.

Monsieur Trouvé marched back around to the rear of the ornithopter and spun up a guidance propeller attached to the steam engine.

Madame Lefoux pressed some kind of button and, with a massive whoosh, the wings of the craft began flapping up and down with amazing strength. "You *have* made modifications!"

The ornithopter jerked into the air with a burst of power.

"Didn't I tell you?" Monsieur Trouvé was grinning like a little boy. He had a good pair of lungs in that wide chest of his, so he continued to yell after them. "I replaced our original model with one of Eugène's bourdon tubes, activated by gunpowder charges. I did say I had taken a keen interest recently."

"What? Gunpowder!"

The clockmaker waved at them cheerfully as they flapped upward and forward, now a good few yards above the rooftop. Alexia could see much of Paris laid out below her wildly waving kid-boots.

Monsieur Trouvé bracketed his mouth with his hands. "I'll send your things on to the Florence dirigible station."

A great crash sounded, and two of the vampires burst out onto the roof.

Monsieur Trouvé's grin vanished into the depths of his impressive beard, and he turned to face the supernatural threat.

One of the vampires leapt up after them, hands stretched to grab.

He got close enough for Alexia to see that he had an impressive collection of jagged bite marks now about his head and neck. His hand just missed Alexia's ankle. A huge white beast appeared behind him. Limping and bleeding, the creature charged the airborne vampire, hamstringing him and bringing him back to the rooftop with a crash.

The clockmaker yelled in fear.

Madame Lefoux did something to the controls, and the ornithopter flapped two mighty strokes and surged up. Then it shifted suddenly sideways in a gust of wind, tilting precariously. Alexia lost sight of the action on the rooftop behind one massive wing. It was presently to become irrelevant, for the ornithopter reached ever-greater heights, and Paris became lost under a layer of cloud.

"Magnifique!" yelled Madame Lefoux into the wind.

Sooner than Alexia would have believed possible, they attained the first of the aether atmospheres, the breezes there cool and slightly tingly against Alexia's inexcusably indecent legs. The ornithopter caught one of the southeasterly currents and began to ride it with, blessedly, a long smooth glide and much less flapping.

Professor Lyall had plenty he ought to be doing that night: BUR investigations, pack business, and Madame Lefoux's contrivance chamber to check up on. Naturally, he ended up doing none of those things. Because what he really wanted to find out was the current location of one Lord Akeldama—vampire, fashion icon, and very stylish thorn in everyone's side.

The thing about Lord Akeldama was—and in Lyall's experience, there was always a *thing*—that where he himself was not a fixture, his drones were. Despite supernatural speed and flawless taste in neckwear, Lord Akeldama could not, in fact, attend every social event of note every single evening. But he did seem to have a collection of drones and associates of drones who could and did. The *thing* that was bothering Lyall at the moment was that they weren't. Not only was the vampire himself missing, but so were all of his drones, assorted sycophants, and poodle-fakers. Usually, any major social event in London could be relied upon to temporarily house some young dandy whose collar points were too high, mannerisms too elegant, and interest too keen to adequately complement his otherwise frivolous appearance. These ubiquitous young men, regardless of how silly they might act, how much gambling they might engage in, and how much fine champagne they might swill, reported back to their master with such an immense amount of information as to put any of Her Majesty's espionage operations to shame.

And they had all vanished.

Professor Lyall couldn't identify most of them by face or name, but as he made the rounds of London's various routs, card parties, and gentleman's clubs that evening, he became painfully aware of their collective absence. He himself was welcome at most establishments but was not expected, for he was thought to be rather shy. Yet he was familiar enough with high society to mark the difference one vampire's disappearance had wrought. His carefully polite inquiries yielded up neither destination nor explanation. So it was that, in the end, he left the drawing rooms of the wealthy and headed down toward dockside and the blood brothels.

"You new, gov'na? Like a li'le sip, would ya? Only cost ya a penny." The young man propping up the shadows of a scummy brick wall was pale and drawn. The dirty scarf wrapped around his neck no doubt already covered a goodly number of bite marks.

"Looks like you've given enough already."

"Not a chance of it." The blood-whore's dirty face split with a sudden smile, brown with rotting teeth. He was of the type vampires rather crudely referred to as snacky-bites.

Professor Lyall bared his own teeth at the youngster, showing the boy that he did not, in fact, have the requisite fangs for the job.

"Ah, right you are, gov. No offense meant."

"None taken. There is a penny for you, however, if you provide me with some information."

The young man's pale face became still and drawn. "I don't grass, gov."

"I do not require the names of your clientele. I am looking for a man, a vampire. Name of Akeldama."

The blood-whore straightened away from the wall. "Won't find 'im 'ere, gov; 'e's got enough of 'is own ta slurp from."

"Yes, I am well aware of that fact. But I am wondering if you might know his current whereabouts."

The man bit his lip.

Professor Lyall handed him a penny. There weren't a lot of vampires in London, and blood-whores, who made it their livelihood to service them, tended to know a good deal about the local hives and loners as a matter of survival.

The lip was nibbled on slightly more.

Professor Lyall handed him another penny.

"Word on the street is 'e's left town."

"Go on."

"An' how. Didn't suss a master could be mobile like that."

Professor Lyall frowned. "Any idea as to where?"

A shake of the head was all Lyall got in answer.

"Or why?"

Another shake.

"One more penny if you can direct me to someone who does."

"Ya ain't gunna like me answer, gov."

Professor Lyall handed him another copper.

The blood-whore shrugged. "You'd be wantin' the other queen, then."

Professor Lyall groaned inwardly. Of course it would turn out to be a matter of internal vampire politics. "Countess Nadasdy?"

The young man nodded.

Professor Lyall thanked the blood-whore for his help and flagged down a seedy-looking hansom, directing the driver toward Westminster. About halfway there, he changed his mind. It wouldn't do for the vampires to know so soon that Lord Akeldama's absence was of interest to either BUR or the Woolsey Pack. Banging on the box with his fist, he redirected the driver toward Soho, intending to call upon a certain redhead.

Professor Lyall alighted from the hansom at Piccadilly Circus, paid the driver, and walked a block north. Even at midnight, it was a pleasant little corner of the city, swimming in young people of artistic propensities, if perhaps a bit dingy and lowbrow. Professor Lyall had a good memory, and he recalled the cholera outbreak of twenty years earlier as though it had happened only yesterday. Sometimes he thought he could still smell the sickness in the air. As a result, Soho always caused him to sneeze.

The apartment, when he knocked and was duly admitted by a very young maid, proved to be neat and tidy if a tad gleefully decorated. Ivy Tunstell bustled forward to greet him in the hallway, her dark curls bobbing out from under a large lace cap. The cap had blue silk roses clustered above her left ear, which gave her an oddly rakish appearance. She was wearing a pink walking dress, and Lyall was pleased to see he had not disturbed her at rest.

"Mrs. Tunstell, how do you do? I do apologize for calling at such a late hour."

"Professor Lyall, welcome. Delighted to see you. Not at all. We keep to a sunset schedule. After he left your service, my dear Tunny never could manage to break the habit, and it does suit his chosen profession."

"Ah, yes. How is Tunstell?"

"Auditioning as we speak." Ivy led her guest into an absolutely tiny receiving room, with barely enough space to house a settee, two chairs, and a tea table. The decor seemed to have been chosen with only one theme in mind—pastel. It was a resplendent collection of pink, pale yellow, sky blue, and lilac.

Professor Lyall hung his hat and coat on a spindly hat stand crowded behind the door and took one of the chairs. It was like sitting inside a bowl of Easter candy. Ivy settled herself onto the settee. The young maid, having followed them in, gave the mistress of the house a quizzical look.

"Tea, Professor Lyall, or would you prefer something, uh, bloodier?"

"Tea would be lovely, Mrs. Tunstell."

"You are certain? I have some delightful kidney set aside for a pie tomorrow, and it *is* getting on to full moon."

Professor Lyall smiled. "Your husband has been telling you things about living with werewolves, hasn't he?"

Ivy blushed slightly. "Perhaps a little. I am afraid I have been terribly nosy. I find your culture fascinating. I do hope you do not think me impertinent."

"Not at all. But, really, just tea would be perfectly fine."

Ivy nodded to her maid, and the young girl scuttled off, clearly excited.

"We don't get many visitors of your caliber," lamented Ivy.

Professor Lyall was too much a gentleman to remark that Miss Hisselpenny's elopement, and consequent loss of what little status she'd had, made her a less than desirable acquaintance for most. Only a high-ranking original, as Lady Maccon had been, could afford to continue such an association. Now that Alexia herself had fallen from grace, Ivy must be a veritable social pariah.

"How is the hat shop coming on?"

Mrs. Tunstell's big hazel eyes lit up with pleasure. "Well, I have only had it under my charge for the one day. Of course, I kept it open this evening as well. I know Madame Lefoux caters to the supernatural set, but you would not believe the things one overhears in a hat shop. Only this afternoon, I learned Miss Wibbley was engaged."

Prior to Ivy's marriage, Professor Lyall knew she had relied upon Alexia, who was at best disinterested and at worst obtuse, for all her society gossip. As a result, Ivy had been in a constant state of frustration.

"So you are enjoying yourself?"

"Immeasurably. I never thought *trade* could be so very entertaining. Why, this evening, Miss Mabel Dair paid us a call. The actress, you've heard of her?" Ivy looked to Professor Lyall inquiringly.

The werewolf nodded.

"Well, she came by to pick up a special order for Countess Nadasdy herself. I had no idea the countess even wore hats. I mean to say"—Ivy looked to Lyall in confusion—"she does not actually leave her house, does she?"

Professor Lyall highly doubted that a special order from Madame Lefoux for a vampire queen bore any resemblance whatsoever to a hat, aside from being transported inside a hatbox. But he perked up with interest. He had thought to ask Tunstell for information as to Lord Akeldama's disappearance, given the vampire's affection for the theater and Tunstell's previous investigative training under Lyall's tutelage, but perhaps Ivy might unwittingly have some information to impart. Mabel Dair, after all, was Countess Nadasdy's favorite drone.

"And how did Miss Dair seem?" he asked carefully.

The maid returned and Ivy fussed with the tea trolley. "Oh, not *at all* the thing. Dear Miss Dair and I have become almost friendly since my marriage. She and Tunny have appeared onstage together. She was clearly most upset about something. And I said to her, I did, I said, 'My dear Miss Dair,' I said, 'you do not look *at all* the thing! Would you like to sit, take a little tea?' And I think she might have." Ivy paused and studied Professor Lyall's carefully impassive face. "You are aware, she is a bit of a, well, I hardly like to say it to a gentleman of your persuasion, but a, um, vampire drone." Ivy whispered this as if she could not quite believe her own daring at being even a nodding acquaintance with such a person.

Professor Lyall smiled slightly. "Mrs. Tunstell, do you forget I work for the Bureau of Unnatural Registry? I am well aware of her status."

"Oh, of course you are. How silly of me." Ivy covered her embarrassment by pouring the tea. "Milk?"

"Please. And do go on. Did Miss Dair relay the nature of her distress?"

"Well, I do not think she intended me to overhear. She was discussing something with her companion. That tall, good-looking gentleman I met at Alexia's wedding—Lord Ambrittle, I believe it was."

"Lord Ambrose?"

"Yes, that! Such a nice man."

Professor Lyall forbore to mention that Lord Ambrose was, in fact, a not very nice vampire.

"Well, apparently, dear Miss Dair caught the countess and some gentleman or another arguing. A potent gentleman, she kept saying, whatever that means. And she said she thought the countess was accusing this gentleman of having taken something from Lord Akeldama.

Quite astonishing. Why would a potent man want to steal from Lord Akeldama?"

"Mrs. Tunstell," Professor Lyall said very precisely and unhurriedly, "did Lord Ambrose notice that you had overheard this?"

"Why? Is it a matter of significance?" Ivy popped a sugared rose petal into her mouth and blinked at her guest.

"It is certainly intriguing." Lyall took a cautious drink of his tea. It was excellent.

"I hate to speak ill of such a nice man, but I believe he did not recognize me. He may even have thought I was a genuine *shopgirl*. Shocking, I know, but I *was* standing behind a sales counter at the time." She paused and sipped her tea. "I thought you might find the information useful."

At that, Professor Lyall gave Mrs. Tunstell a sharp look. He wondered for the first time how much of Ivy was, in fact, comprised of dark curls and big eyes and ridiculous hats and how much of that was for show.

Ivy returned his direct gaze with a particularly innocent smile. "The great advantage," she said, "of being thought silly, is that people forget and begin to think one might also be foolish. I may, Professor Lyall, be a trifle enthusiastic in my manner and dress, but I am no fool."

"No, Mrs. Tunstell, I can see that." *And Lady Maccon*, thought Lyall, *would not be so friendly with you if you were.*

"I believe Miss Dair was overset, or she would not have been so indiscreet in public."

"Ah, and what is your excuse?"

Ivy laughed. "I am well aware, Professor, that my dearest Alexia does not tell me much about certain aspects of her life. Her friendship with Lord Akeldama, for example, has always remained a mystery to me. I mean really, he is *too* outrageous. But her judgment is sound. I should have told her what I heard, were she still in town. As it stands, I judge you will make an adequate substitute. You stand very high in my husband's regard. Besides which, I simply do not believe it is right. Potent gentlemen should not go around stealing things from Lord Akeldama."

Professor Lyall knew perfectly well the identity of Ivy's "potent gentleman." It meant that this was rapidly becoming an ever more serious and ever more vampire-riddled conundrum. The potentate was the premier rove in all of England, Queen Victoria's chief strategist and her most treasured supernatural advisor. He sat on the Shadow Council with the dewan, werewolf loner and commander in chief of the Royal Lupine Guard. Until recently, Alexia had been their third. The potentate was one of the oldest vampires on the island. And he had stolen something from Lord Akeldama. Professor Lyall would wager good money on the fact that it was in pursuit of that very object that had caused Lord Akeldama, and all of his drones, to leave London.

What a fine kettle of fangs this is becoming, he thought.

Mostly unaware of the exploding steam engine she had just landed her guest in, Ivy Tunstell bobbed her curls at Professor Lyall and offered him another cup of tea. Lyall decided that his best possible course of action was to head home to Woolsey Castle and go to sleep. Often vampires were better understood after a good day's rest.

Consequently, he declined the tea.

CHAPTER EIGHT

Trial by Snuff, Kumquat, and Exorcism

Alexia's legs were stiff from the cold, but at least they were decently covered by her skirts once more, even if those skirts were now coated in mud as well as burned by acid. She sighed. She must look like a veritable gypsy with her spattered dispatch case and wild hair. Madame Lefoux also looked the worse for wear, speckled with mud, her goggles dangling about her neck. Her top hat was still secured to her head by the long scarf, but her mustache was decidedly askew. Only Floote somehow managed to look entirely unruffled as they skulked—there really was no other word for it—through the side alleys of Nice in the wee hours of the morning.

Nice proved itself smaller than Paris, characterized by a casual seaside attitude. Madame Lefoux, however, hinted darkly that the city's "Italian troubles" of ten years ago remained, hidden but unabated, and that this upsetting situation gave Nice a restless undertone not always sensed by strangers.

"Imagine! Trying to contend that Nice is really Italian. Pah." Madame Lefoux flicked one hand dismissively and glared at Alexia, as though Alexia might side with the Italians in this matter.

Alexia tried to think of something reassuring to say. "I am certain there is hardly any pasta in the whole city," was the best rejoinder she could come up with on such short notice.

Madame Lefoux only increased the pace of their skulking, leading them around a pile of discarded rags into a dingy little alleyway.

"I do hope the ornithopter will be safe where we left it." Alexia tried to change the subject as she followed her friend, lifting her skirts away from the rags. There was hardly any point in the effort at this juncture, but instinct dictated one's skirts be lifted.

"Should be. It's out of gunpowder charges, and very few, apart from Gustave and myself, know how to fly it. I shall send him a note as to its location. I do apologize for that unfortunate landing."

"You mean that unfortunate *crash*?"

"At least I chose a soft bit of ground."

"Duck ponds usually are soft. You do realize, ornithopter only *means* bird? You don't actually have to treat it as such."

"At least it didn't explode."

Alexia paused in her skulking. "Oh, do you believe it ought to have done so?"

Madame Lefoux gave one of her annoying little French shrugs.

"Well I think your ornithopter has earned its name."

"Oh, yes?" The inventor looked resigned.

"Yes. The Muddy Duck."

"*Le Canard Boueux*? Very funny."

Floote gave a tiny snort of amusement. Alexia glared at him. How had he managed to entirely avoid the mud?

Madame Lefoux led them to a small door that once might have been colored blue, and then yellow, and then green, a history it displayed proudly in crumbling strips of paint all down the front. The Frenchwoman knocked softly at first, and then more and more loudly until she was banging quite violently on the poor door.

The only reaction the racket caused was the immediate commencement of an unending bout of hysterical barking from some species of diminutive canine in possession of the other side of the door.

Floote gestured with his head at the doorknob. Alexia looked closely at it under the flickering torchlight; Nice apparently was not sophisticated enough for gas streetlamps. It was brass, and mostly unassuming, except that there was a very faint etched symbol on its surface, almost smoothed away by hundreds of hands—a chubby little octopus.

After a good deal more banging and barking, the door cautiously opened a crack to reveal a mercurial little man wearing a red and white striped nightshirt and cap, and a half-frightened, half-sleepy expression. A dirty feather duster on four legs bounced feverishly about his bare ankles. Much to Alexia's surprise, given her recent experience with Frenchmen, the man had no mustache. The feather duster did. Perhaps in Nice mustaches were more common on canines?

Her surprise was abated, however, when the little man spoke, not in French, but in German.

When his staccato sentence was met only by three blank expressions, he evaluated their manners and dress and switched to heavily accented English.

"Ya?"

The duster ejected itself through the partly opened door and attacked Madame Lefoux, gnawing at the hem of her trouser leg. What Madame Lefoux's excellent woolen trousers had done to insult the creature, Alexia could not begin to fathom.

"Monsieur Lange-Wilsdorf?" Madame Lefoux tried tactfully to shake off the animal with her foot.

"Who would be wishing to know?"

"I am Lefoux. We have been in correspondence these last few months. Mr. Algonquin Shrimpdittle recommended the introduction."

"I thought you were of the, uh, persuasion of the feminine." The gentleman squinted at Madame Lefoux suspiciously.

Madame Lefoux winked at him and doffed her top hat. "I am."

"Leave off, Poche!" barked the German at the tiny dog. "Monsieur Lange-Wilsdorf," Madame Lefoux explained to Alexia and Floote, "is a biological analytical technician of some note. He has a particular expertise that you may find rather interesting, Alexia."

The German opened his door farther and craned his neck to see around Madame Lefoux to where Alexia stood shivering.

"Alexia?" He scanned her face in the faint light of the street torch. "Not *the* Alexia Tarabotti, the Female Specimen?"

"Would it be good or bad if I were?" The lady in question was a little distressed to be engaging in a protracted doorstep conversation in the nighttime cold with a man garbed in red and white striped flannel.

Madame Lefoux said, with a flourish, "Yes, *the* Alexia Tarabotti."

"I cannot believe it! The Female Specimen, at *my* door? Really?" The little man thrust said door wide and nipped out and around Madame Lefoux to grab Alexia warmly by the hand, pumping it up and down enthusiastically in the American style of greeting. The dog, perceiving a new threat, let go of Madame Lefoux's trouser and began yipping again, heading in Alexia's direction.

Alexia wasn't really sure she enjoyed being referred to as a specimen. And the way the German looked at her was almost hungry.

Alexia prepared her parasol with her free hand. "I would not, young sir, if I were you," she said to the dog. "My skirts have been through quite enough for one evening." The dog appeared to think better of his attack and began jumping up and down in place, all four legs oddly straight.

"Come in, come in! The greatest marvel of the age, here, on my very doorstep. This is—how do you say?—fantastic, ya, fantastic!" The little man paused in his enthusiasm upon noticing Floote for the first time, silent and still to one side of the stoop.

"And who is this?"

"Uh, this is Mr. Floote, my personal secretary." Alexia stopped staring ominously down at the dog in time to answer so Floote didn't have to.

Mr. Lange-Wilsdorf let go of Alexia and went to walk a slow turn around Floote. The German gentleman was still in his nightshirt, in the street, but he didn't seem to notice the faux pas. Alexia figured that as she had just shown her bloomers to half of France, she didn't have the right to be scandalized by this behavior.

"Is he, is he *really*? Nothing more evil than that? No? Are you certain?" Mr. Lange-Wilsdorf reached out a crooked finger and yanked down Floote's cravat and shirt, checking the neck area for marks.

Growling, the dog glommed onto Floote's boot.

"Do you *mind*, sir?" Floote looked decidedly put-upon. Alexia couldn't tell if it was the man or his dog that irritated most; Floote could abide neither a wrinkled collar nor damp shoes.

Seeing nothing incriminating, the German left off torturing Floote with his vulgar behavior. Once again he grabbed Alexia by the hand and positively dragged her into his tiny house. He gestured for the other two to follow, giving Floote yet another dubious once-over. The dog escorted them inside.

"Well, you realize, under ordinary circumstances, I wouldn't. Not a man, not so late at night. Never can tell with the English. But I suppose, just this once. Though, I did hear some of the terrible, terrible rumors about *you*, young miss." The German raised his chin and attempted to look down on Alexia, as though he were some kind of disapproving maiden aunt. It was a particularly unsuccessful look, as, aside from not being her aunt, he was a good head shorter than Alexia.

"Heard you had married a *werewolf*. Ya? What a thing for a preternatural to go and be doing. A most unfortunate choice for the Female Specimen."

"Is it?" Alexia managed to get just those two words in before Mr. Lange-Wilsdorf continued on without apparent pause or need for breath, shepherding them into a messy little parlor.

"Yes, well, we all make the mistakes."

"You have no idea," muttered Alexia, feeling a strange aching pain of loss.

Madame Lefoux began poking about the room with interest. Floote took up his customary station by the door.

The dog, exhausted by his own frenzy, went and curled in front of the cold fireplace, a posture that made him look, if possible, even more like a common household cleaning device.

There was a bell rope near the door, which the little man began to tug on, at first gently and then with such enthusiasm he was practically swinging from it. "You will be wanting tea, I am certain. English are always with the wanting of tea. Sit down, sit down."

Madame Lefoux and Alexia sat. Floote did not.

Their host bustled over to a little side table and took a small box out of a drawer. "Snuff?" He flipped the lid and offered the leaf about.

Everyone declined. But the German seemed unwilling to accept Floote's refusal. "No, no, I insist."

"I do not partake, sir," objected Floote.

"Really, I *insist*." A sudden hardness entered Mr. Lange-Wilsdorf's eyes.

Floote shrugged, took a small portion, and inhaled delicately.

The German watched him closely the entire time. When Floote showed no abnormal reaction, the little man nodded to himself and put the snuffbox away.

A disheveled manservant entered the room.

The dog awoke and, despite a clearly extensive association with the domestic staff, launched himself at the boy as though he posed a grave threat to the safety of the world.

"Mignon, we have the guests. Bring up a pot of Earl Grey and some croissants at once. *Earl Grey*, mind you, and that basket of kumquats. Thank God for the kumquats." He narrowed his eyes at Floote once more, in an "I'm not finished with you, young man" kind of way.

Floote, who was a good deal older than the German gentleman, remained utterly impassive.

"Well, this is delightful, ya, delightful. Alexia Tarabotti, here in *my* home." He took off his nightcap to enact a twitchy little bow in Alexia's direction. The action revealed a set of precariously large ears, which looked as though they rightly belonged to someone else.

"Never met your father, but I have studied much over his stock. First to breed a female soulless in seven generations, ya. It is a miracle, some have claimed, the Female Specimen." He nodded to himself. "I have the theory, of course, to do with brood female mixing outside of Italy. Brilliant choice of your father's, ya? A little of the fresh blood of English."

Alexia could hardly believe the statement. As though she were the result of some kind of horse-breeding program. "Now, I say—!"

Madame Lefoux interjected at this juncture, "Mr. Lange-Wilsdorf here has been studying the preternatural state for many years now."

"It has been difficult, most difficult, indeed, ya, to find a live specimen. My little trouble with the church, you understand."

"Come again?" Alexia checked her rage in favor of curiosity. Here was a scientist who might really know something.

The German blushed and worried his sleeping cap about with both hands. "A little—how do you say?—spot of bother. Had to move to France and leave much of my research behind. A travesty."

Alexia looked to Madame Lefoux for an explanation.

"He was excommunicated," said the inventor in a grave, hushed voice.

The little man blushed even redder. "Ah, you heard of it?"

Madame Lefoux shrugged. "You know how the Order gossips."

A sigh met this statement. "Well, regardless, you have brought me this fine visitor. A living, breathing female preternatural. You will allow me to ask you questions, young lady, ya? Perhaps, a test or two?"

A tap came at the door, and the manservant entered bearing a tea tray.

Mr. Lange-Wilsdorf accepted the tray and then waved the man away. He poured the tea, strong and redolent of the scent of bergamot. Alexia didn't much like Earl Grey; it was well out of fashion in London and was never served in any of the establishments she frequented. Vampires were not fond of citrus. Which, she realized, must be why the little man was now pressing the tea and a small pile of kumquats on the austere Floote.

"The snuff!"

Everyone looked at her.

"Ah, you decided you wanted to try some, ya, Female Specimen?"

"Oh, no. I simply realized. You made Floote take snuff as a werewolf check. They hate snuff. And now you're using the Earl Grey and the kumquats to see if he's a vampire."

Floote arched one eyebrow, took a kumquat, and popped it whole into his mouth, chewing methodically.

"You do realize, Mr. Lange-Wilsdorf, that vampires are perfectly capable of consuming citrus? They just don't like it."

"Yes, of course, I'm well aware. But it is a good—how do you say?—initial check, until sun comes up."

Floote sighed. "I assure you, sir, I am not of a supernatural inclination."

Alexia snickered. Poor Floote looked extremely put-upon.

The little German did not seem convinced by mere verbal guarantees. He kept a jaundiced eye on Floote and maintained proprietary control of the bowl of kumquats. For future use as projectile weaponry, perhaps?

"Of course, you could still be a claviger or drone-type person."

Floote huffed out a small puff of annoyed breath.

"You already checked him for bite marks," pointed out Alexia.

"Absence of the marks is not absolute proof, especially as he may be a claviger. You *did* marry a werewolf, after all."

Floote looked as though he had never been more insulted in his life. Alexia, still smarting over the "Female Specimen" moniker, sympathized.

In a lightning change of mood that seemed to characterize the little man's paranoia, the German looked with sudden new suspicion at Alexia. "The verification." He muttered to himself. "You understand, ya? Of course you do. Must verify you as well. Ah, if only I had my counter. Have this little poltergeist problem. Perhaps you could see your way to an exorcism? Should not be hard for the Female Specimen." He glanced at a small window to one side of the room, curtains thrown wide to let in the rapidly brightening dawn. "Before sunrise?"

Alexia sighed. "This could not possibly wait until tomorrow evening? I have been traveling most of the night. I suppose you could call it traveling."

The little man grimaced at her but did not take the hint, as any good host would have.

"Really, Mr. Lange-Wilsdorf, we have only just arrived," Madame Lefoux protested.

"Oh, very well." Alexia put down her tea, which wasn't very good, anyway, and half a croissant, which was buttery and delicious. If it was necessary for this odd little man to trust them in order to get some answers out of him, she was equal to the task. Alexia sighed, angry once more at her husband's rejection. She wasn't entirely certain how just yet, but she intended to blame this latest nuisance on Lord Conall Maccon as well as everything else.

The dog, Poche, led the way down several flights of stairs and into a tiny cellar, barking with unwarranted enthusiasm the entire time. Mr. Lange-Wilsdorf apparently did not notice the racket. Alexia resigned herself to the fact that it was the creature's normal mode of operation— when its eyes were open, so, too, was its mouth.

"You must think me the terrible host, ya." The German said this with an air of one attending to the requirements of society rather than one experiencing actual remorse.

Alexia could think of nothing to say in response, as, so far as it went, it was perfectly true. Any host worth his blood would have seen them decently abed by now, supernatural or not. No gentleman would insist his guest perform an exorcism without providing accommodations first, let alone a decent meal. So Alexia simply clutched her parasol and followed the German and his frenzied canine down into the bowels of his cramped and dirty house. Madame Lefoux and Floote seemed to feel their presence was not required on this jaunt and remained upstairs in the parlor, sipping at the vile tea and consuming, very probably, all of the excellent croissants. *Traitors.*

The cellar was gloomy in all the ways cellars ought to be and included, just as the man had said, a ghost in the final throes of poltergeist phase.

Above the little dog's barking came the intermittent keening wail of second-death. As if that were not bad enough, the poltergeist had gone to pieces. Alexia could not abide clutter, and, having lost almost all of its capacity for cohesion, this ghost was very messy, indeed. It was flitting about the dark musty interior as pale wisps of body parts, entirely dismembered—an elbow here, an eyebrow there. Alexia started and let out a little squeak upon encountering a single eyeball, all intelligence gone from its depths, staring at her from the top of a wine rack. The cellar also smelled badly of formaldehyde and rotten flesh.

"Really, Mr. Lange-Wilsdorf." Alexia's voice was cold with disapproval. "You ought to have seen to the unfortunate soul weeks ago and never let it get this bad."

The man rolled his eyes dismissively. "On the contrary, Female Specimen, I rented this house because of the ghost. I have long been interested in recording exact stages of *homo animus* disanimation. And since my trouble with the Vatican, I switched the focus of my studies onto ghosts. I have managed three papers on this one alone. Now, I must admit, she has become much less. The staff refuses to come down here. I keep having to fetch wine myself."

Alexia narrowly avoided walking through a floating ear. "Which must be very vexing."

"But it has been useful. I theorize that remnant animus is carried on aether eddies as weakening of tether commences. I believe my work here has proved this hypothesis."

"You mean to say that the soul rides the aether air, and as the body decomposes, its hold on the soul disintegrates? Like a sugar lump in tea?"

"Ya. What else could explain random floating of noncorporeal body parts? I have excavated the corpse, just there."

Sure enough, a hole had been dug into one corner of the cellar floor, inside of which lay the mostly decomposed skeleton of a dead girl.

"What happened to the poor thing?"

"Nothing significant. I got much needed information out of her before she went mad. The parents could not afford graveyard fees." He tut-tutted and shook his head at the shame of it. "When she turned out to have excess soul and went ghost, the family enjoyed still having her around. Unfortunately, they all then died of cholera and left her here for the next occupants to enjoy. Been that way until I came along."

Alexia looked about at the floating wisps. A toenail bobbed in her direction. In fact, all of the remnant body parts were floating softly toward her, as water will go down a drain. It was both eerie and unsettling. Still she hesitated. Her stomach, and its nearby problematic companion, objected to both the smell of death and the certain knowledge of what she must do next. Holding her breath, Alexia crouched down near the gravesite. The hole for the body had been dug directly into the dirt of the cellar floor with no attempt made to preserve the corpse for supernatural longevity until the German came along. The child would not have had long to be a proper ghost before the madness of decomposing flesh began taking her away. It was a cruel business.

What was left was a sad crumpled little skeleton, mostly defleshed by maggots and mold. Alexia carefully removed one glove and reached down. She chose what looked to be the least decomposed part of the child's head and touched her there once. The flesh was incredibly squishy under her fingertip and compressed easily like wet sponge cake.

"Ugh." Alexia drew her hand back with a jerk of disgust.

The faintly luminescent wisps of body parts floating around the cellar vanished instantly, dispersing into the musty air as preternatural touch severed the last of the soul's tether to its body.

The German looked around, mouth slightly open. The little dog, for once, stopped barking. "Is that all?"

Alexia nodded, brushing her fingertip against her skirt several times. She stood.

"But I did not even have my notebook out yet! What a—how do you say?—wasted opportunity."

"It is done."

"Extraordinary. I have not observed a preternatural end a ghost before now. Quite extraordinary. Well, that confirms that you are in truth, what you say you are, Female Specimen. Congratulations."

As if I have won some sort of prize. Alexia raised her eyebrows at that, but the little man didn't seem to notice. So she made her way firmly back up the stairs.

The German trotted after. "Truly, truly extraordinary. Perfect exorcism. Only a preternatural can accomplish such a thing with one touch. I had read of it, certainly, but to see it, right there, in front of me.

Do you find the effects more rapid for you, than for the males of your species?"

"I would not know, never having met one."

"Of course, of course. Ya. Cannot share the same air, preternaturals."

Alexia made her way back to the parlor, where Madame Lefoux and Floote had left her one of the croissants. *Thank goodness.*

"How was it?" asked the Frenchwoman politely, if a little coldly. The last ghost Alexia had exorcised had been a very dear friend of Madame Lefoux's.

"Squishy."

Madame Lefoux wrinkled her pert little nose. "One imagines it must be."

The German went to look out the window, clearly awaiting full sunrise. The sun was beginning to show just over the rooftops, and Alexia was pleased to see that Nice might, just possibly, be slightly less dirty than Paris. The dog vibrated its way around the room yipping at each visitor in turn, as though it had not remembered their presence, which might be the case given its apparent lack of a brain, before collapsing in an exhausted pouf under the settee.

Alexia finished her croissant using only her untainted hand and then waited patiently, hoping against hope that sometime soon they might be offered beds. It felt like a very long time since she'd slept. She was beginning to feel numb with tiredness. Madame Lefoux seemed to feel much the same, for she had nodded off. Her chin dipped down into the bow of her cravat. Her top hat, still partially wrapped with Monsieur Trouvé's scarf, tipped forward on her head. Even Floote's shoulders were sagging ever so slightly.

The first rays of the sun crept in over the windowsill and speared into the room. Mr. Lange-Wilsdorf watched avidly as the light touched Floote's trouser leg. When Floote did not immediately burst into flames or run screaming from the room, the little German relaxed for what Alexia suspected was the first time since they had knocked on his door.

With still no offer of a sleeping chamber forthcoming, Alexia took a deep breath and faced her host squarely. "Mr. Lange-Wilsdorf, why all this bother and testing? Are you a true believer? I would have thought that odd in a member of the Order of the Brass Octopus."

Madame Lefoux cracked her eyelids at her friend's direct speech and tipped her top hat back on her head with one elegant finger. She regarded the little German with interest.

"Perhaps, perhaps. My research is delicate, dangerous, even. If I am to trust you, or help you, it is important, vital, that none of you are— how do I put this?—*undead*."

Alexia winced. Madame Lefoux straightened out of her slouch, abruptly much less drowsy. "Undead" was not a word one used openly in polite society. The werewolves, vampires, and even newly minted ghosts found it understandably distasteful to be referred to as such. Much in the same way that Alexia objected when the vampires called her a soul-sucker. It was, simply put, vulgar.

"That is a rather crude word, Mr. Lange-Wilsdorf, wouldn't you say?"

"Is it? Ah, you English and your semantics."

"But 'undead,' certainly, is not apt."

The man's eyes went hard and flinty. "I suspect that depends on what you define as living. Ya? Given my current studies, 'undead' suits very well."

The French inventor grinned. Her dimples showed. Alexia wasn't certain how they did it, but those dimples managed to look quite crafty. "Not for long it won't."

Mr. Lange-Wilsdorf tilted his head, intrigued. "You know something of relevance to my research, do you, Madame Lefoux?"

"You are aware that Lady Maccon here married a werewolf?"

A nod.

"I think you should tell him what has happened, Alexia."

Alexia grimaced. "He might be helpful?"

"He is the closest thing to an expert on the preternatural the Order of the Brass Octopus has. Templars might know more, but it's difficult to say."

Alexia nodded. She weighed her options and finally decided the risk was worth it. "I am pregnant, Mr. Lange-Wilsdorf."

The German looked at Alexia with a distinct air of covetousness. "Felicitations and condolences. You will not, of course, be able to—how do you say?—carry to term. No preternatural female has in recorded history. A great sadness to the Templars and their breeding program, of course, but . . ." He trailed off at Madame Lefoux's continued grin.

"You are implying? No, it cannot be. She is pregnant *by* the werewolf?"

Alexia and Madame Lefoux both nodded.

The German turned away from the window and came to sit close to Alexia. Too close. His eyes were hard and greedy on her face.

"You would not be covering up for, how you English might say, a little indiscretion?"

Alexia was tired of all the games. She gave him a look that suggested the next person to even hint she was unfaithful would be receiving the worst her parasol had to offer. She had hoped he would know something that might result in a different reaction.

"How about," she suggested in clipped tones, "you assume I am telling the truth in this matter and we leave you to theorize on the subject while we attend to some much-needed rest?"

"Of course, of course! You are with child; you must sleep. Imagine such a thing, a preternatural pregnant by a supernatural. I must do research. Has it ever been tried before? The Templars would not think to breed the werewolf with soulless. The very idea. Ya, amazing. You are, after all, scientific opposites, each other's end. With rarity of females of either species, I can see a basis for absence of proper documentation. But if you speak truth, why, what a miracle, what a fabulous abomination!"

Alexia cleared her throat loudly, placing one hand to her stomach and the other on her parasol. She might think of this baby as inconvenient, even hate it sometimes, but far be it for some diminutive German with bad taste in pets to describe it as an *abomination*. "I do beg your pardon!"

Madame Lefoux recognized *that tone* in Alexia's voice and jumped to her feet. Grabbing Alexia by the hand, she attempted to pull her friend up and out of the room.

Mr. Lange-Wilsdorf had whipped out a notepad and, oblivious to Alexia's anger, began scribbling away, all the while muttering to himself.

"We shall find guest rooms on our own, shall we?" suggested the Frenchwoman over Alexia's angry sputtering.

Mr. Lange-Wilsdorf made a dismissive movement with his stylographic pen, not looking up from his ruminations.

Alexia found her voice. "Couldn't I just whack him once? Just a little one, over the head? He would hardly notice."

Floote raised one eyebrow and took hold of Alexia's elbow, helping Madame Lefoux to remove her bodily from the room. "Bed, I think, madam."

"Oh, very well," conceded Alexia, "if you insist." She glared at Madame Lefoux. "But you had better be right about this character's character."

"Oh"—the dimples were back—"I believe he may surprise you."

"Like being served wet toad on toast?"

"He could prove you're right. That Lord Maccon fathered your child."

"That's the only possible way this could be worth it. 'Female Specimen,' indeed! Sounds like he plans to dissect me with a clinkering-spud."

* * *

When Alexia finally came down to breakfast the next morning, it was, in fact, no longer morning at all, but early afternoon. Madame Lefoux and Floote were already seated at the small dining table, as was the little German scientist. He was entirely absorbed in some research while eating—*deplorable behavior*! He was positively vibrating in excitement, almost as much as his feather duster of a dog.

As it was now daytime, both the German and his dog were a tad more formally attired. Alexia was a little surprised. She'd half expected Mr. Lange-Wilsdorf to still be wearing his striped nightshirt. Instead, he looked perfectly respectable in a tweed coat and brown trousers. He wore no cravat, to Floote's obvious dismay. Alexia was, perhaps, less shocked by the missing cravat than she should have been. After all, eccentricity of dress was to be expected in foreigners for whom neckwear and cravats were regarded with suspicion, as they made it difficult to identify drones. Poche also wore tweed; a length of it was tied in a waterfall knot about the dog's neck. *Aha,* thought Alexia, *the missing cravat!* The creature greeted Alexia's arrival with the expected volley of frenzied barking.

Alexia arranged herself at the table without direction from her host and, as he did not appear to care one way or the other, she began helping herself to the repast. Today the infant-inconvenience wasn't objecting to food. Buggery thing couldn't make up its mind. Madame Lefoux greeted her with a fond smile and Floote with a little nod.

"Sir," said Alexia to their host.

"Good afternoon, Female Specimen." Mr. Lange-Wilsdorf did not look up from the open book and companion notepad upon which he was scribbling some complex formula.

Alexia scowled.

Whatever else might be said about Mr. Lange-Wilsdorf—and after his use of the term "abomination," Alexia could certainly think of a good deal that *she* might say about him—he provided a decent spread. The food laid out for luncheon was light but tasty: roasted winter vegetables, cold poultry, bread that managed to be both crispy and fluffy, and a selection of flaky pastries. Alexia had extracted from the depths of her dispatch case some of the precious tea that Ivy had given her. It had survived the journey far better than anything else. She had also, after a moment's consideration, transferred a small emergency amount into one of the pockets of her parasol, just in case. Fortunately, milk remained a cross-cultural universal, and the tea managed to taste just as delicious as it might have back in England. This resulted in a pang of homesickness so acute that Alexia actually did not speak for a good few minutes after the initial sip.

Madame Lefoux noticed her uncharacteristic silence.

"Are you feeling well, my dear?" The inventor placed a soft hand on Alexia's upper arm.

Alexia started slightly and experienced an unacceptable welling of tears. Really, at her age! It seemed to have been a very long while since anyone touched her with genuine fondness. Air kisses and three-fingered pats on the head comprised the bulk of affectionate action in the Loontwill household, and had done since she was a child. It wasn't until Conall had come into her life that Alexia became accustomed to physical intimacy. He enjoyed it immensely and had engaged in it with her at every possible opportunity. Madame Lefoux was not quite so aggressive, but she was French, and seemed to feel that verbal comfort ought to be companioned by a soothing caress. Alexia leaned into the embrace. The hand around her shoulder was not large and calloused, and Madame Lefoux smelled of vanilla and engine oil, not open fields, but beggars couldn't be choosers.

"Oh, it is nothing. I was reminded of home there for one moment." Alexia took another sip of the tea.

The German looked up at her curiously. "He did not treat you well? The werewolf husband?"

"Not as such in the end," Alexia prevaricated, never one to talk about personal matters with strange little Germans.

"Werewolves, ya. Difficult creatures. What is left of the soul is all violence and emotion. It is a wonder you English have managed to integrate them into society."

Alexia shrugged. "I am under the impression the vampires are more difficult to handle."

"Really?"

Alexia, feeling she may have been traitorously indiscreet, grappled for the right way of phrasing it. "You know how vampires get, all high-up-mucky-mucky and I'm-older-than-thou." She paused. "No, I suppose you do not know how they get, do you?"

"Mmm. I should have thought werewolves more an issue. With the running about in armies and the marrying of normal humans."

"Well *my* particular werewolf did turn out a bit difficult. But, to be fair, he was perfectly suitable right up until the end." Alexia was painfully conscious that "perfectly suitable" was a rather understated way of putting it. Conall had been a model husband in his massive grumpy way: tender, except when it wasn't necessary, and then rough until gentleness was called for once more. She shivered slightly at the memories. He had also been loud and gruff and overprotective, but he had adored her. It had taken her a good deal of time before she believed that she was worth all that fierce affection he lavished upon her. To have it stolen away unjustly was that much more cruel.

"Isn't the end result what counts?" Madame Lefoux cocked her head. She had taken against Conall most decidedly when he kicked Alexia out.

Alexia grimaced. "Spoken like a true scientist."

"You cannot possibly forgive him for what he did?" Madame Lefoux seemed ready to reprimand Alexia.

Mr. Lange-Wilsdorf glanced up from his meal. "Cast you out, did he? Does he not think the child is his?"

"Howlers have never sung of a werewolf child." Alexia couldn't believe it, but she was actually defending her husband. "And loving me apparently wasn't enough to get him over that fact. He didn't even give me a chance."

The German shook his head. "Werewolves. Emotion and violence, ya?" Then he put down his stylographic pen decidedly and leaned forward over book and notepad. "I spent all morning with research. My records would seem to substantiate his assessment. Although, lack of corroborative cases or other information does not make for real evidence. There are older records."

"Records kept by vampires?" Alexia theorized, thinking of the Vampire Edicts.

"Records kept by Templars."

Floote gave a little wince. Alexia glanced at him. He chewed his food impassively.

"So you think the Templars might have some hint as to how *this* is possible?" Alexia gestured delicately at her midsection.

"Ya. If this has happened before, they will have records of it."

Alexia had grand romantic visions of marching into Conall's office and slamming down proof of her innocence—of making him eat his words.

"And what of your theories, Monsieur Lange-Wilsdorf?" asked Madame Lefoux.

"I believe, if I abandon the concept of undead but maintain my aetheric analysis of the composition of the soul, I might be able to explain this pregnancy."

"Will you be able to maintain the principles of epidermal contact?"

The German looked impressed. "You are indeed familiar with my work, madame. I thought you were an engineer by training?"

Madame Lefoux flashed her dimples. "My aunt is a ghost and so was my grandmother. I have a keen interest in understanding excess soul."

The horrible little dog came over to yap at Alexia's ankle, and then, to add insult to injury, began to chew on one of her bootlaces. Alexia picked the serviette up off of her lap and surreptitiously dropped it on Poche's head. The animal attempted to back out from under it, with little success.

"You believe you may have excess soul?" The German was apparently unaware of his dog's predicament.

The Frenchwoman nodded. "It seems likely."

Alexia wondered what that might feel like, knowing one was likely to end life as a poltergeist. She herself would die with no possibility of salvation or immortality. Preternaturals had no soul to save for either God or ghost.

"Then why not seek immortality, now that you live in England where such atrocities are openly encouraged?" Mr. Lange-Wilsdorf curled his lip.

Madame Lefoux shrugged. "Despite my preferred mode of dress, I am still a woman, and I know my chances of surviving a werewolf bite, not to mention vampire blooding, are extremely slim. Besides, I do not wish to lose what little skill I have as an inventor alongside the bulk of my soul. To become entirely dependent upon the goodwill of a pack or a hive? No thank you. And simply because my relatives were ghosts does not necessarily mean I, too, have excess soul. In the end, I am not that much of a risk taker."

The little dog had managed to circumnavigate the entire table without shaking off the offending serviette. Alexia coughed and rattled her dinnerware to disguise the sound of the animal bumping into various objects about the room. Floote, now within reach, bent down and removed the cloth from the dog's head, issuing Alexia a reproving look.

Alexia had never thought to ask, but come to think of it, it was indeed odd that an inventor of Madame Lefoux's particularly high creative skill level should have no supernatural patron. The Frenchwoman maintained good working relationships with the Westminster Hive and the Woolsey Pack, but she also dealt with loners, roves, and daylight folk. Alexia had thought the inventor's avoidance of metamorphosis and supernatural patronage stemmed from personal objections, not practical ones. Now she was forced to consider, had she herself been born with Madame Lefoux's options, would she choose the same path?

The German was not impressed. "I should prefer if you were a religious protester rather than an ethical objector, Madame Lefoux."

"It is better, then, Monsieur Lange-Wilsdorf, that I act to suit myself and not you. Is it not?"

"So long as the end result is one less supernatural."

"Oh, really. Must we talk politics while eating?" Alexia interjected at this juncture.

"By all means, Female Specimen, let us turn the conversation back to you." The little man's eyes were quite hard as he focused them upon her, and Alexia had a sudden sense of alarm.

"It is quite remarkable, you understand, your pregnancy. Until last night, I would have sworn that vampires and werewolves could only breed through metamorphosis. Ya? Your preternatural touch, it does not cancel out the fact that the supernatural person has, already, mostly died. It turns them mortal, ya, but not *human*, certainly not sufficient to procreate naturally."

Alexia nibbled a piece of fruit. "Obviously this is an incorrect statement you make, sir."

"Obviously, Female Specimen. So I have—how do you say?—rethought the situation. There is one line of scientific evidence to support your claim. That line is the fact that both vampires and werewolves still engage in"—the little man paused, a bright flush suffusing his pale features—"well, bedroom activities."

"Of an extensive and rather experimental nature, if the rumors are to be believed." Madame Lefoux waggled her eyebrows suggestively. Trust the only French person at the table to be at ease with this topic of conversation. Alexia, Floote, and Mr. Lange-Wilsdorf all looked painfully uncomfortable and shared a moment of awkward solidarity. Then the little German soldiered bravely on.

"There has to be a reason the procreative urges aren't eliminated postmetamorphosis. Yet, none of my books could adequately address this concern. If they really were undead, werewolves should no longer have need of that particular *biological* function."

"So how, exactly, does this pertain to my situation?" Alexia stopped eating to listen with renewed interest.

"It seems clear that your husband's capacity to continue to, er, perform, even as a werewolf, must be linked to an instinctual need to produce offspring the old-fashioned way. Modern science tells us that, thus, offspring must be a possibility, however infinitesimal. You, it would appear, are that infinitesimal possibility. The problem is, of course, the inevitable miscarriage."

Alexia blanched.

"I am sorry to say there is no way around that fact. If the Templar preternatural breeding program proved nothing else, it proved that

preternaturals always breed true. And similarly that they cannot occupy the same air space. Essentially, Female Specimen, you have an
intolerance for your own child."

Alexia had shared a room with a preternatural mummy once; she
knew the feeling of discomfort and repulsion that would be her fate
should she ever encounter another preternatural. But she had not yet
felt that feeling from the embryo inside her.

"The child and I are not sharing any air," she objected.

"We are aware that preternatural abilities are a matter of physical
contact. In this, the Templar records are clear, and I recall them well.
All Female Specimens experimented upon over the centuries were barren or unable to carry a child. It is not a matter of *if* you will lose this
embryo—it is a matter of *when*."

Alexia sucked in her breath. Unexpectedly, it hurt. Quite apart
from the loss of the child, this would mean that Conall's rejection and
abuse had all been for naught. It was stupid, and hopeless, and . . .

Madame Lefoux came to her rescue. "Except that this may not be
an ordinary preternatural child. You said it yourself—they are usually
the result of daylight and preternatural crossings. Alexia's baby has a
werewolf father, and as mortal as her touch would have made him at
the time of conception, he was still not human. Not entirely, for he had
already lost much of his soul. This child is something *different*. It must
be." She turned to look at her friend. "It is a safe bet that the vampires
aren't trying to kill you simply because you are about to miscarry a
soulless. Particularly not the English vampires."

Alexia sighed. "It is at times like this I wish I could talk to my
mother."

"Good gracious, what good would that do, madam?" Floote was
moved to speak by the outrageousness of Alexia's statement.

"Well, whatever she said, I could simply take the opposite point of
view."

Mr. Lange-Wilsdorf was not to be distracted by family history.
"You have felt no queasiness or revulsion for the specimen inside?"

Alexia shook her head.

The German began muttering to himself. "Something must be off
in my calculations. Perhaps the aetheric exchange conduction between
mother and child is limited by partial soul retention. But why, then,
wouldn't a child retain part of the soul of a daylight father? Different
kind of soul, perhaps?" He scratched out his careful notes with a sweeping motion of the stylographic pen, flipped to a new page, and began
scribbling again.

They all watched him in silence, Alexia having mostly lost her appetite, until he stopped midnotation.

He looked up, his eyes popping wide as the second half of Madame Lefoux's statement finally worked its way into his brain. "Vampires trying to kill her? Did you say they were trying to kill her? That *thing*, sitting there at *my* table, in *my* house!"

Madame Lefoux shrugged. "Well, yes. Who else would they want to kill?"

"But that means they will be coming. They will be following her. *Here*! Vampires. I *hate* vampires!" Mr. Lange-Wilsdorf spat noisily on the floor. "Nasty, bloodsucking tools of the devil. You must get out. You must all leave, now! I am terribly sorry, but I cannot have you here under such circumstances. Not even for the sake of scientific research."

"But, Mr. Lange-Wilsdorf, what a way to treat a fellow member of the Order of the Brass Octopus. Be reasonable; it is the middle of the day!"

"Not even for the Order!" The little man stood, looking as though he were about to get just as hysterical as his dog. "You must leave! I shall give you provisions, money, contacts in Italy, but you must quit my house now. Get to the Templars. They will take care of you, if only because the vampires want you dead. I am not equipped. I am not able to handle this."

Alexia stood to find that Floote, being Floote, had at some point during the conversation sensed impending doom and vanished to their rooms. There he had obviously packed up her dispatch case, retrieved her parasol and their outerwear, and was waiting patiently in the doorway. He, at least, did not seem at all reluctant to leave.

CHAPTER NINE

How Not to Cross an Alpine Pass

Upon reflection, Alexia decided it was perhaps safer to press on toward Italy during daylight, anyway. It was becoming painfully obvious that should she expect any answers as to her current condition and situation, she would have to extract said answers from either the Templars or the vampires. And of the two, only one was likely to talk to her *before* they tried to kill her.

Another thing had also become apparent. As driven as she might be to prove Conall wrong, the fate of the infant-inconvenience was now at stake. Alexia might be frustrated with the tiny parasite, but she decided, after contemplation, that she did not, exactly, wish it dead. They'd been through a lot together so far. *Just you allow me to eat regularly,* she told it silently, *and I'll think about trying to grow a mothering instinct. Won't be easy, mind you. I wasn't ever expecting to have one. But I'll try.*

On the run from the murderous hordes, cashiered by an eccentric German, Alexia was nonplussed to find they did what anyone might have done under more mundane circumstances—they caught a cab. Hired transport, as it turned out, was much the same in France as it was in England, only more limited. Madame Lefoux had a brief but intense conversation with the driver of a fly, after which a good deal of money exchanged hands. Then the inventor sat down next to Floote, and the handsom took off at a terrific pace, heading for the coast through the streets of Nice, which were crowded with invalids and wet-weather refugees. Alexia supposed it was a sensible mode of transport when one was on the run, but the fly was a tight fit for three passengers.

The driver, up high and behind them, encouraged the horse into a fast trot with a long whip. The creature surged forward, taking turns and racketing down alleyways at quite the breakneck velocity.

In no time whatsoever, they had left Nice behind and were headed along the dirt road that wound along the cliffs and beaches of the Riviera. It was a drive Alexia might ordinarily have enjoyed. It was a crisp winter day, the Mediterranean a sparkling turquoise blue to their right. There was very little traffic, and their driver cut loose along the long slow turns and straight stretches, allowing his horse a distance-covering canter.

"He said he would take us all the way to the border," Madame Lefoux spoke into the rushing wind. "Standing me up a pretty penny for the favor, but he *is* making very good time."

"I should say so! Will we reach Italy before dark, do you think?" Alexia tucked her dispatch case more firmly beneath her legs and skirts, and placed her parasol across her lap, trying to get comfortable while wedged tightly between Madame Lefoux and Floote. The seat really was only meant for two, and while none of them was overly large, Alexia had cause to be grateful she was currently without her ubiquitous bustle. It was by no means an ideal arrangement.

The driver slowed.

Taking advantage of the more relaxed pace, Alexia stood, turning precariously backward so she could look over the roof and the driver's box to the road behind them. When she sat back down again, she was frowning.

"What is it?" Madame Lefoux demanded.

"I do not mean to concern you, but I do believe we are being followed."

Madame Lefoux stood in her turn, holding her top hat firmly to her head with one hand and grasping the edge of the hansom's roof with the other. When she sat back down, she, too, sported a crease between her perfectly arched eyebrows.

Alexia looked to her valet. "Floote, how are you fixed for projectiles?"

Floote reached into his inner jacket pocket and presented the two tiny guns. He cracked each open in turn. They were both loaded. He'd obviously taken the time to reload the single shots after their spot of vampire bother. He fished about further in his coat and produced a small quantity of gunpowder in a twist of paper and eight more bullets.

Madame Lefoux reached across Alexia and picked up one of the bullets, examining it with interest. Alexia looked on as well. They were made of some kind of hard wood, tipped in silver and filled with lead.

"Old-style sundowner bullets. Not that we will need such as these at this time of day. Any followers would have to be drones. Still, Mr. Floote, what are you doing with such things? You cannot possibly be certified to terminate supernaturals."

"Ah." Floote put the bullets back in his jacket pocket. "Let us say I inherited them, madam."

"Mr. Tarabotti?" Madame Lefoux nodded. "That explains the age of the guns. You want to get yourself one of those newfangled Colt revolvers, Mr. Floote, much more efficient."

Floote looked with a certain degree of fondness down at the two tiny guns before tucking them back out of sight. "Perhaps."

Alexia was intrigued. "Father was an official sundowner, was he?"

"Not as such, my lady." Floote was always cagey, but he seemed to reach new heights of tight-lippedness whenever the subject of Alessandro Tarabotti came up. Half the time Alexia felt he did it out of obstinacy; the other half of the time she felt he might be trying to shield her from something. Although with vampire drones on their tail, she could hardly imagine what she might still need protection from.

Madame Lefoux pushed back the sleeve of her jacket and checked her own little wrist-emitter device. "I have only three shots left. Alexia?"

Alexia shook her head. "I used up all my darts in the clock shop, remember? And I haven't anything else left in the parasol but the lapis lunearis mist for werewolves and the magnetic disruption emitter."

Madam Lefoux sucked her teeth in frustration. "I knew I should have given it a greater carrying capacity."

"You cannot very well have done much more," consoled Alexia. "The darn thing already weighs twice as much as any ordinary parasol."

Floote stood and checked behind them.

"Will they catch us before we cross the border?" Alexia had no clear grasp on the distance from Nice to the Italian frontier.

"Most likely." Madame Lefoux, however, did.

Floote sat back down, looking quite worried.

They clattered through a small fishing town and out the other side, improved paving on the road allowing them a fresh burst of speed.

"We will have to try to lose them in Monaco." Madame Lefoux stood, leaned across the roof, and engaged in a protracted conversation with the driver. Rapid-fire French scattered on the wind.

Guessing the gist of it, Alexia unclipped the ruby and gold brooch from the neck of her traveling gown and pressed it into the inventor's small hand. "See if that will encourage him."

The brooch vanished across the roof of the hansom. The whip flashed. The horse surged forward. Bribery, apparently, worked no matter what the language.

They kept a good pace and steady distance from their pursuers right up and into the town of Monaco, a decent-sized vacation destination of some questionable repute.

The driver undertook the most impressive series of twists and turns, breaking off from the main road and dodging through some truly tiny alleys. They ran pell-mell into a line of laundry stretched across the street, taking a pair of trousers and a gentleman's shirtfront with them, in addition to a string of French curses. They ended their obstacle run, clattering out of an upper section of the town away from the ocean, heading toward the Alpine Mountains. The horse tossed off the pair of scarlet bloomers he had been wearing about his ears with a snort of disgust.

"Will we be able to cross through the mountains at this time of year?" Alexia was dubious. It was winter, and while the Italian Alps hadn't the reputation of their larger, more inland brethren, they were still respectably mountainous, with white-capped peaks.

"I think so. Regardless, it is better to stay off the main road."

The road narrowed as they began to climb upward. The horse slowed to a walk, his sides heaving. It was a good thing, too, for soon enough the track became lined with trees and a steep embankment to one side and a treacherous drop to the other. They clattered through a herd of unimpressed brown goats, complete with large bells and irate goat girl, and seemed to have shaken off pursuit.

Out the left side window of the hansom, Alexia caught sight of a peculiar-looking contraption above the embankment and trees. She tugged Madame Lefoux's arm. "What's that, Genevieve?"

The inventor cocked her head. "Ah, good. The sky-rail system. I had hoped it was operational."

"Well?"

"Oh, yes. It is a novelty freight and passenger transport. I had a small hand in designing the control mechanisms. We should be able to see it in full presently, just there."

They rounded a bend in the road and began climbing ever more steeply. Before and above them stood the contraption in all its glory. To Alexia it looked like two massive laundry lines strung parallel across the tops of pylons. It became clear, however, that the lines were more like sky-high train tracks. Straddled atop them, crawling along in a rhythmic, lurching, buglike manner on large wheels threaded with moving treads, marched a series of cabins, similar in size and shape to stagecoaches. Each cabin emitted billowing gouts of white steam from underneath. Hanging from the cabin, down below the cables, each supported a swaying metal net on long cords, loaded with lumber. Like a spider with an egg sac or a trapeze train trolley.

"Goodness!" Alexia was impressed. "Are they unidirectional?"

"Well, most are going downhill with freight, but they are designed to go up as well. Unlike trains, those cable rails require no switchbacks. One car can simply climb over the other, so long as it is not carrying a net, of course. See the way the cabling goes over each side of the cabin roof?"

Alexia was enough impressed by the invention to be distracted from her current predicament. She'd never seen or heard of anything like it—a railway in the sky!

Floote kept popping up and looking back over the cab roof like a jack-in-the-box. Alexia became quite sensitive to the pattern of his movements and so noticed when his legs became suddenly tense and he spent longer than usual standing. Madame Lefoux did as well and bounced up to lean next to him, much to the driver's annoyance. Scared of further upsetting the fly's center of balance, Alexia stayed seated, her view filled with trouser-clad legs.

She heard a faint yelling behind them and could only imagine that there were drones following. On the next switchback, she caught sight of their enemy. Out the right side window of the cab, she could see a four-in-hand coach loaded down with intense-looking young men in hot pursuit. There was some kind of firearm equipage mounted atop the carriage roof.

Just wonderful, thought Alexia. *They have a ruddy great gun.*

She heard the pop of Floote firing off one of the tiny derringers and the sharp hiss of Madame Lefoux doing the same with one of her darts.

Floote popped back down to change guns and reload. "Madam, I regret to inform you, they have a Nordenfelt."

"A what?"

Madame Lefoux sat down to reload while Floote stood back up and fired again.

"I have no doubt we shall witness it in action shortly."

They reached the snow line.

A whole fleet of bullets of ridiculously large size hissed by the cab and embedded themselves in an unsuspecting tree. A gun that could fire multiple bullets at once, imagine that!

Floote hurriedly sat back down.

"The Nordenfelt, madam."

The horse squealed in fear, the driver swore, and they came to an abrupt halt.

Madame Lefoux didn't even try to argue their case. She jumped down from the fly, followed by Floote and Alexia. Floote grabbed Alexia's dispatch case. Alexia grabbed her parasol. Without waiting to see if they would follow, Alexia charged up the embankment, stabilizing herself with the parasol, and began slogging through the snow toward the cable lines.

Another burst of bullets churned up the snow just behind them. Alexia let out a most undignified squeak of alarm. What would Conall do? This kind of gunfire action was not exactly her cup of tea. Her husband was the trained soldier, not she. Nevertheless, she recovered enough to yell, "Perhaps we should spread out and make for that support pole."

"Agreed," said Madame Lefoux.

The next round of fire was not nearly so close.

Soon they were too high up to be seen from the road below, even by that deadly swiveling gun. Also, the four-in-hand was even less able than the fly to handle off-road terrain. There came a good deal of shouting, probably the drones and the cab driver yelling at each other, but Alexia knew it was only a matter of time before the young men left their precious Nordenfelt behind and took to the ground in pursuit. At which point, she was at a distinct disadvantage with her heavy unbustled skirts dragging through the snow.

As they neared the cable rail, one of the laden cars came heading downward toward them. Of course the darn thing was going in the wrong direction, back into France, but it still might provide some limited refuge. The three made it, finally, to the support pole. It was furnished with flimsy-looking metal rungs, intended to be used for emergency evacuation or repair.

Floote seemed to be taking stock of their situation like some extremely dapper Roman general. "Madame Lefoux's dart emitter is the fastest weapon we have, madam."

"Good point, Floote. Genevieve, please guard the base while Floote and I climb."

The Frenchwoman nodded, looking fierce.

Alexia hated to leave her alone, but there was no other option. She hoisted her muddy skirts over one arm. Well, Paris had already seen them; she might as well show the rest of France her bloomers.

Floote and she climbed the post.

Floote paused on the small platform at the top, put down the dispatch case, and crouched to fire downward with a derringer, reloading and firing each gun in turn until he was out of ammunition, while Madame Lefoux climbed up behind them. Meanwhile, Alexia aimed her parasol at the approaching rail cabin. She could see the startled face of a driver in the window. She fully understood his confusion. She must present quite the lunatic picture—a statuesque Italian woman dressed English-style in a gown gone well beyond grubby, hair wild, and hat askew, pointing an ugly parasol at his large mechanical transport in a threatening manner.

Just as the front of the cabin drew level with the platform, Alexia pulled back on a protruding carved lotus petal in the handle of her parasol. The magnetic disruption emitter sent off its silent but deadly signal and the rail car jerked to a halt.

Inside the cable compartment, Alexia could see the engineer yelling at her in confusion. Behind her on the platform, she heard Madame Lefoux screaming obscenities in French, and the drones, now climbing up the support pole after them, were also shouting.

She turned to see if she could help her companions in any way. The infant-inconvenience kicked an objection to all her recent exertions, but Alexia disregarded it with an internal, *Pack it in, proto-nuisance. Time for that later.*

One of the drones now had Madame Lefoux by the boot. She was kicking at him while simultaneously attempting to climb the last handbreadth up onto the platform. Floote, finally out of bullets, was pulling at the Frenchwoman's shoulders in an attempt to assist.

Alexia, thinking quickly, opened and flipped her parasol. As swiftly as possible, she turned the special inset dial in the parasol's tip around to its alternate setting. Holding the parasol far out over the edge of the platform, Alexia rained a mixture of lapis lunearis and water down onto the young men climbing after them.

Dilute silver nitrate was designed for werewolves, not humans, and usually had no more disturbing a result on daylight folk than skin discoloration. But since the gentlemen in question were looking up, it had the beneficial effect of hitting the eyeballs and causing all to let go in startlement. The resulting screams may have been because they were falling, or perhaps they were the result of the chemical sting, but, as it ended with the drones writhing in the snow far below, Alexia considered the maneuver an unqualified success. Included among the writhers was the man who had had hold of Madame Lefoux's boot. He still had her boot, but Madame Lefoux was able to attain the top of the platform with a look of profound relief on her pretty face.

The three of them dashed to the rail cabin. Floote overrode the driver's objection to their presence by smashing in the front window with Alexia's dispatch case, climbing inside, and punching the poor man hard in the jaw. He fell like a stone, and his stoker, a slight, reedy boy with wide, anxious eyes, meekly acquiesced to their demands.

No one else was on board.

Alexia ripped off her bustle fall, tore the length into strips, and handed them to Floote. He showed remarkable dexterity and mastery of knot work, trussing up the boy and his unconscious supervisor with ease.

"You do that quite efficiently, don't you, Floote?" commented Alexia.

"Well, madam, being valet to Mr. Tarabotti had its advantages."

"Genevieve, can you drive this contraption?" Alexia asked.

"I only worked on the initial schematics, but if you can stoke the boiler, I will figure it out."

"Done!" Alexia thought stoking couldn't be that difficult.

Soon enough, the effects of the magnetic disruption emitter wore off, and the massive steam engine in the center of the cabin rumbled back to life. The cabin was designed with a windowed steering area at either end so that the car did not itself turn around. Instead, the engineer merely shifted position in order to drive in the opposite direction.

Madame Lefoux, after a quick review of the controls, pulled down on a massive lever at one end of the lurching cabin and then dashed to the other end, pulling a similar lever up.

An alarmingly loud horn sounded, and the contraption, cabin, and massive hanging net of lumber down below began moving backward in the direction it had come, up the mountain once again.

Alexia let out a little cheer of encouragement.

Floote finished trussing up their two prisoners. "I do apologize, sirs," he said to them in English, which they probably didn't understand.

Alexia smiled to herself and kept stoking. Poor Floote, this whole escape was rather beneath his dignity.

Stoking was hot work, and Alexia was beginning to feel the strain of having dashed across rough terrain and then climbed a pylon. She was, as Ivy had once scornfully pointed out, a bit of a sporting young lady. But one would have to be positively Olympian to survive the past three days without some physical taxation. She supposed the infant-inconvenience might also have something to do with her exhaustion. But never having run while pregnant, she did not know quite who to blame—embryo or vampires.

Madame Lefoux was leaping about the end of the cable cabin, pulling levers and twisting dials maniacally, and the rail contraption lurched forward in response to her ministrations, moving from a sedate step-by-step crawl to a kind of swaying shambling run.

"Are you certain this thing can take this kind of speed with a load?" Alexia yelled from her self-prescribed stoker's post.

"No!" Madame Lefoux hollered cheerfully back. "I am attempting to deduce how to set loose the cargo straps and net, but there seems to be a safety override preventing a drop while in motion. Give me a moment."

Floote pointed out the front window. "I do not think we have that long, madam."

Alexia and Madame Lefoux both looked up from what they were doing.

Madame Lefoux swore.

Another loaded cart was coming down the cables toward them. It was crawling along at a sedate pace, but it seemed to be looming very fast. While one cabin could climb over another, they were not designed to do so while still lugging a net full of lumber.

"Now would be a very good time to figure out a drop," suggested Alexia.

Madame Lefoux looked frantically underneath the control board.

Alexia thought of a different tactic. She ran over to the other end of the cabin.

"How do I cut the cargo free?" she spoke in French and leaned close in to the frightened young stoker boy. "Quickly!"

The boy pointed in silent fear at a lever off to one side of the steam engine, separated from both sets of steering controls.

"I think I have it!" Alexia dove for the knob.

At the same time, Madame Lefoux began an even more frantic dance about the steering area, employing a complex series of dial-cycling and handle-pulling that Alexia could only assume would allow their cabin to climb over the other heading toward them.

They were close enough now that they could see the frightened gesticulations of the driver through the window of the other cable cabin.

Alexia pulled down on the freight-release lever with all her might.

The overrides screamed in protest.

Floote came over to help her, and together they managed to muscle it down.

Their rail car shuddered once, and seconds later they heard a loud crash and multiple thuds as the load of lumber fell down to the mountain below. Mere moments after that, there was a lurch as their cabin climbed its buglike way over the oncoming coach, swaying in a most alarming fashion from side to side, ending with one additional shudder as it settled back onto the rails on the other side.

They did not have much time to appreciate their victory, for the pinging sound of bullets on metal heralded the return of their pursuers.

Floote ran to look out a side window. "Revolvers, madam. They're pacing us by foot."

"Doesn't this thing go any faster?" Alexia asked Madame Lefoux.

"Not that I can make it." The Frenchwoman issued Alexia a demonic dimpled grin. "We shall just have to take the cable as far as it goes and then run for the border."

"You make it sound so simple."

The grin only widened. Alexia was beginning to suspect Madame Lefoux of being a rather reckless young woman.

"Italy makes for a strange refuge, madam." Floote sounded almost philosophical. He began a stately tour of the interior of the carrier, looking for any loose objects that might serve as projectile weaponry.

"You do not like Italy, do you, Floote?"

"Beautiful country, madam."

"Oh?"

"It took Mr. Tarabotti quite a bit of bother to extract himself. He had to marry an Englishwoman in the end."

"My mother? I can't think of a worse fate."

"Precisely, madam." Floote used a large wrench to break one of the side windows and stuck his head out. He received a near miss from a bullet for his pains.

"What exactly was he extracting himself from, Floote?"

"The past." Hoisting some kind of large metal tool, Floote chucked it hopefully out the window. There was a cry of alarm from below, and the young men drew slightly back, out of detritus range.

"Shame we did not eliminate any of them when we dropped the lumber."

"Indeed, madam."

"What past, Floote?" Alexia pressed.

"A not very nice one, madam."

Alexia huffed in frustration. "Did anyone ever tell you, you are entirely insufferable?" Alexia went to shove more coal into the stoke hole.

"Frequently, madam." Floote waited for the men to gain courage and catch up again, and then threw a few more items out the window.

Floote and the drones proceeded in this vein for about a half hour while the sun set slowly, turning the trees to long shadows and the snow to gray. A full moon rose up above the mountaintops.

"End of the cable just ahead." Madame Lefoux gestured briefly with one hand before returning it to the controls.

Alexia left off stoking and went to the front to see what their dismount looked like.

The ending area was a wide U of platforms atop multiple poles, with cables running down to the ground, presumably used for the lumber. There was also some kind of passenger-unloading arrangement, built to accommodate the anticipated tourists. It was a basic pulley system with a couple of windlass machines.

"Think those will work to get us down?"

Madame Lefoux glanced over. "We had better hope so."

Alexia nodded and went to devise a means of strapping her dispatch case and her parasol on to her body; she'd need both hands free.

The rail cabin came to a bumpy halt, and Alexia, Floote, and Madame Lefoux climbed out the broken window as fast as possible. Madame Lefoux went first, grabbing one of the pulley straps and dropping with it over to the edge of the platform without a second thought. *Definitely reckless.*

The pulley emitted a loud ticking noise but carried her down the cable at a pace only mildly dangerous. The inventor landed at the bottom in a graceful forward roll, bouncing out of it onto her stockinged feet with a shout of well-being.

With a deep breath of resignation, Alexia followed. She clutched the heavy leather strap in both hands and eased off the edge of the platform, zipping down the line far faster than the lean Frenchwoman. She landed at the bottom with a terrific jolt, ankles screaming, and collapsed into a graceless heap, taking a wicked hit to the shoulder from the corner of her dispatch case. She rolled to her side and looked down; the parasol seemed to have survived better than she.

Madame Lefoux helped her up and out of the way just as Floote let go of a strap and landed gracefully, stopping his own forward momentum by bending one knee, managing to make his dismount look like a bow. *Show-off.*

They heard shouts behind them from the oncoming drones.

It was getting dark but they could still make out a track heading farther up the mountain toward what they could only hope was a customhouse and the Italian border.

They took off running again.

Alexia figured she might be getting enough exercise to last a lifetime in the space of one afternoon. She was actually sweating—so very improper.

Something whizzed by her shoulder. The drones were firing their guns once more. Their aim was, of course, affected detrimentally by their pace and the rough terrain, but they were gaining ground.

Up ahead, Alexia could make out a square structure among the dark trees to one side of the road—a shed, really—but there was a large sign on the other side of the road that appeared to have something threatening written on it in Italian. There was no other gate or barrier, nothing on the track to mark that they were about to go from one country to another, just a little mounded hillock of dirt.

So it was that they crossed the border into Italy.

The drones were still following them.

"Wonderful. Now what do we do?" panted Alexia. Somehow she had thought once they entered Italy, everything would change.

"Keep running," advised Madame Lefoux unhelpfully.

As if in answer to her question, the deserted pass, now heading down the other side of the mountain, suddenly was not quite so deserted after all.

Out of the shadows of the trees to either side materialized a whole host of men. Alexia only had time to register the utter absurdity of their dress before she, Madame Lefoux, and Floote found themselves surrounded. A single, rapidly lyrical utterance revealed that these were, in fact, Italians.

Each man wore what appeared to be entirely pedestrian country dress—bowler, jacket, and knickerbockers—but over this, each had also donned what looked like female sleeping attire with a massive red cross embroidered across the front. It greatly resembled an expensive silk nightgown Conall had purchased for Alexia shortly after their marriage. The comedic effect of this outfit was moderated by the fact that each man also wore a belt that housed a large sword with medieval inclinations and carried a chubby revolver. Alexia had seen that type of gun before—a Galand Tue Tue—probably the sundowner model. *It is a strange world,* she ruminated, *wherein one finds oneself surrounded by Italians in nightgowns carrying French guns modified by the English to kill supernaturals.*

The outlandishly garbed group seemed unflustered by Alexia's party, closing in around them in a manner that managed to be both protective and threatening. They then turned to face down the panting gaggle of drones who drew to a surprised stop just on the other side of the border.

One of the white-clad men spoke in French. "I would not cross into our territory if I were you. In Italy, drones are considered vampires by choice and are treated as such."

"And how would you prove we are drones?" yelled one of the young men.

"Did I say we needed proof?" Several of the swords *shinked* out of their sheaths.

Alexia peeked around the side of the Italian hulking in front of her. The drones, silhouetted against the rising moon, were stalled in confusion. Finally they turned, perhaps calculating the better part of valor, shoulders hunched in disappointment, and began walking away back down the French side of the mountain.

The lead nightgowner turned inward to face the three refugees. Dismissing Madame Lefoux and Floote with a contemptuous glance, he turned his hook-nosed gaze onto Alexia. Who could see quite unsatisfactorily far up his nostrils.

Alexia spared a small frown for Floote. He was pinch-faced and white-lipped, looking more upset by their current stationary position than he had been when they were running around under gunfire.

"What is it, Floote?" she hissed at him.

Floote shook his head slightly.

Alexia sighed and turned big bland innocent eyes on the Italians.

The leader spoke, his English impossibly perfect. "Alexia Maccon, daughter of Alessandro Tarabotti, how wonderful. We have been waiting a very long time for you to return to us." With that, he gave a little nod and Alexia felt a prick on the side of her neck.

Return?

She heard Floote shout something, but he was yelling from a very long way away, and then the moon and the shadowed trees all swirled together and she collapsed backward into the waiting arms of the Pope's holiest of holy antisupernatural elite, the Knights Templars.

Professor Randolph Lyall generally kept to a nighttime schedule, but he had spent the afternoon prior to full moon awake in order to conduct some last-minute research. Unfortunately, Ivy Tunstell's revelation had served only to complicate matters. The preponderance of mysteries was beginning to aggravate. Despite a day spent tapping all his various sources and investigating every possible related document BUR might have, Lord Akeldama and his drones were still missing, Alexia's pregnancy remained theoretically impossible, and Lord Conall Maccon was still out of commission. The Alpha was, most likely, no longer drunk, but, given the impending full moon, Professor Lyall had seen him safely back behind bars with strict instructions that this time *no one* was to let him out or there would be uncomfortable consequences.

He himself was so involved in his inquiries as to be quite behind schedule for his own lunar confinement. His personal clavigers—his valet and one of the footmen—awaited him in the Woolsey vestibule wearing expressions of mild panic. They were accustomed to Woolsey's Beta, tamest and most cultured of all the pack, arriving several hours ahead of moonrise.

"I do apologize, boys."

"Very good, sir, but you understand we must take the proper precautions."

Professor Lyall, who could already feel the strain of the moon even though it had not yet peeked above the horizon, held out his wrists obediently.

His valet clapped silver manacles about them with an air of embarrassment. Never during all his years of service had he had to bind Professor Lyall.

The Beta gave him a little half smile. "Not to worry, dear boy. It happens to the best of us." Then he followed both young men docilely down the staircase and into the pack dungeon, where the others were already behind bars. He gave absolutely no hint of the discipline it took for him to remain calm. Simply out of obstinacy and pride, he fought the change as long as possible. Long after his two clavigers had reached through the bars and unlocked his manacles, and he had stripped himself of all his carefully tailored clothing, he continued to fight it. He did it for their sake, as they went to stand with the first shift of watchers against the far wall. Poor young things, compelled to witness powerful men become slaves to bestial urges, forced to understand what their desire for immortality would require them to become. Lyall was never entirely certain whom he pitied more at this time of the month, them or him. It was the age-old question: who suffers more, the gentleman in the badly tied cravat or those who must look upon him?

Which was Professor Lyall's last thought before the pain and noise and madness of full moon took him away.

He awoke to the sound of Lord Maccon yelling. For Professor Lyall, this was so commonplace as to be almost restful. It had the pleasant singsong of regularity and custom about it.

"And who, might I ask, is Alpha of this bloody pack?" The roar carried even through the thick stone of the dungeon walls.

"You, sir," said a timid voice.

"And who is currently giving you a direct order to be released from this damned prison?"

"That would be you, sir."

"And yet, who is still locked away?"

"That would still be you, sir."

"Yet somehow you do not see my difficulty."

"Professor Lyall said—"

"Professor Lyall, my ruddy arse!"

"Very good, sir."

Lyall yawned and stretched. Full moon always left a man slightly stiff, all that running about the cell and crashing into things and howling. No permanent damage, of course, but there was a certain muscle memory of deeds done and humiliating acts performed that even a full day of sleep could not erase. It was not unlike waking after a long night of being very, very drunk.

His clavigers noticed he was awake and immediately unlocked his cell and came inside. The footman carried a nice cup of hot tea with milk and a dish of raw fish with chopped mint on top. Professor Lyall was unusual in his preference for fish, but the staff had quickly learned to accommodate this eccentricity. The mint, of course, was to help deal with recalcitrant wolf breath. He snacked while his valet dressed him: nice soft tweed trousers, sip of tea, crisp white shirt, nibble of fish, chocolate brocade waistcoat, more tea, and so on.

By the time Lyall had finished his ablutions, Lord Maccon had almost, but not quite, convinced his own clavigers to let him out. The young men were looking harassed, and had, apparently, deemed it safe to pass some clothing through to Lord Maccon, if nothing else. What the Alpha had done with said clothing only faintly resembled dressing, but at least he wasn't striding around hollering at them naked anymore.

Professor Lyall wandered over to his lordship's cell, fixing the cuffs of his shirt and looking unruffled.

"Randolph," barked the earl, "let me out this instant."

Professor Lyall ignored him. He took the key and sent the clavigers off to see to the rest of the pack, who were all now starting to awaken.

"Do you remember, my lord, what the Woolsey Pack was like when you first came to challenge for it?"

Lord Maccon paused in his yelling and his pacing to look up in surprise. "Of course I do. It was not so long ago as all that."

"Not a nice piece of work, the previous Earl of Woolsey, was he? Excellent fighter, of course, but he had gone a little funny about the head—one too many live snacks. 'Crackers' some called him." Professor Lyall shook his head. He loathed talking about his previous Alpha.

"An embarrassing thing for a carnivore to be compared to a biscuit, wouldn't you say, my lord?"

"Your point, Randolph." Lord Maccon could only be surprised out of his impatience for a brief length of time.

"You are becoming, shall we say, of the biscuit inclination, my lord."

Lord Maccon took a deep breath and then sucked on his teeth. "Gone loopy, have I?"

"Perhaps just a little bit noodled."

Lord Maccon looked shamefacedly down at the floor of his cell.

"It is time for you to face up to your responsibilities, my lord. Three weeks is enough time to wallow in your own colossal mistake."

"Pardon me?"

Professor Lyall had had more than enough of his Alpha's nonsensical behavior, and he was a master of perfect timing. Unless he was wrong, and Professor Lyall was rarely wrong about an Alpha, Lord Maccon was ready to admit the truth. And even if Lyall was, by some stretch of the imagination, incorrect in his assessment, the earl could not be allowed to continue to be ridiculous out of mere stubbornness.

"You aren't fooling any of us."

Lord Maccon resisted admission of guilt even as he crumbled like the metaphorical cracker. "But I turned her out."

"Yes, you did, and wasn't that an idiotic thing to do?"

"Possibly."

"Because?" Professor Lyall crossed his arms and dangled the key to his Alpha's cell temptingly from one fingertip.

"Because there is no way she would have canoodled with another man, not *my* Alexia."

"And?"

"And the child must be mine." The earl paused. "Good gracious me, can you imagine that, becoming a father at my age?" This was followed by another much longer pause. "She is never going to forgive me for this, is she?"

Professor Lyall had no mercy. "I wouldn't. But then I have never precisely been in her situation before."

"I should hope not, or there's a prodigious deal regarding your personage about which I was previously unaware."

"Now is not the time for jocularity, my lord."

Lord Maccon sobered. "Insufferable woman. Couldn't she have at least stayed around and argued with me more on the subject? Did she have to cut and run like that?"

"You do recall what you said to her? What you called her?"

Lord Maccon's wide, pleasant face became painfully white and drawn as he went mentally back to a certain castle in Scotland. "I'd just as soon not remember, thank you."

"Are you going to behave yourself now?" Professor Lyall continued to wave the key. "Stay off the formaldehyde?"

"I suppose I must. I've drunk it all, anyway."

Professor Lyall let his Alpha out of the cell and then spent a few minutes fussing about the earl's shirt and cravat, tidying up the mauling Lord Maccon had inflicted while attempting to clothe himself.

The earl withstood the grooming manfully, knowing it for what it was: Lyall's unspoken sympathy. Then he batted his Beta away. Lord Maccon was, when all was said and done, a wolf of action.

"So, what do I have to do to win her back? How do I convince her to come home?"

"You are forgetting that, given your treatment of her, she may not *want* to come home."

"Then I shall make her forgive me!" Lord Maccon's voice, while commanding, was also anguished.

"I do not believe that is quite how forgiveness works, my lord."

"Well?"

"You remember that groveling business we once discussed during your initial courtship of the young lady?"

"Not that again."

"Oh, no, not precisely. I was thinking, given her flight from London and the generally slanderous gossip that has resulted and permeated the society papers ever since, that *public* groveling is called for under such circumstances."

"What? No, I absolutely refuse."

"Oh, I don't believe you have a choice, my lord. A letter to the *Morning Post* would be best, a retraction of sorts. In it you should explain that this was all a horrible misunderstanding. Hail the child as a modern miracle. Claim you had the help of some scientist or other in its conception. How about using that MacDougall fellow? He owes us a favor, doesn't he, from that incident with the automaton? And he is an American; he won't protest the resulting attention."

"You have given this much thought, haven't you, Randolph?"

"Someone had to. You, apparently, were not putting thought very high up on your list of priorities for the past few weeks."

"Enough. I still outrank you."

Professor Lyall reflected he may have, just possibly, pushed his Alpha a little much with that last statement, but he held his ground.

"Now, where is my greatcoat? And where is Rumpet?" Lord Maccon threw his head back. "Rumpet!" he roared, bounding up the steps.

"Sir?" The butler met him at the top of the staircase. "You yelled?"

"Send a man into town to book passage on the next possible channel crossing. It's probably first thing in the morning. And from there a French train to the Italian border." He turned to look at Lyall, who made his own more sedate way up the stairs from the dungeon. "That *is* where she has gone, isn't it?"

"Yes, but how did you—?"

"Because that is where I would have gone." He turned back to the butler. "Should take me a little over a day to cross France. I shall run the border tomorrow night in wolf skin and hang the consequences. Oh, and—"

This time it was Professor Lyall's turn to interrupt. "Belay that order, Rumpet."

Lord Maccon turned around to growl at his Beta. "Now what? I shall go by the *Post* on my way out of town, get them to print a public apology. She is very likely in danger, Randolph, not to mention pregnant. I cannot possibly win her back by dawdling around London."

Professor Lyall took a deep breath. He should have known having Lord Maccon in full possession of his faculties might result in rash action. "It is more than just the regular papers. The vampires have been mudslinging and slandering your wife's character in the popular press, accusing her of all manner of indiscretions, and unless I miss my guess, it all has to do with Alexia's pregnancy. The vampires are not happy about it, my lord, not happy at all."

"Nasty little bloodsuckers. I shall set them to rights. Why haven't Lord Akeldama and his boys been able to counteract the gossip? And why hasn't Lord Akeldama explained away my wife's pregnancy, for that matter? I bet he knows. He is quite the little know-it-all. May even be Edict Keeper, unless I miss my guess."

"That is the other problem: he has disappeared along with all of his drones. Apparently, they are off searching for something the potentate stole. I have been trying to find out what and why and where, but it has been a tad hectic recently. Both BUR and the pack keep interfering. Not to mention the fact that the vampires really aren't saying anything of interest. Why, if it weren't for Mrs. Tunstell and the hat shop, I might not even know the little I do."

"Hat shop? Mrs. Tunstell?" Lord Maccon blinked at this diatribe from his normally quietly competent Beta. "You mean Ivy Hisselpenny? *That* Mrs. Tunstell? What hat shop?"

But his Beta was on a verbal flyaway and unwilling to pause. "What with you constantly sloshed and Channing gone, I am at my wit's end. I really am. You, my lord, cannot simply dash off to Italy. You have responsibilities *here*."

Lord Maccon frowned. "Ah, yes, Channing. I forgot about him."

"Oh, yes? I didn't think that was possible. Some people have all the luck."

Lord Maccon caved. Truth be told he was rather worried to see his unflappable Randolph so, well, flapped. "Oh, very well, I shall give you three nights help sorting out this mess *you* have gotten us into, and then I'm off."

Professor Lyall emitted the sigh of the long-suffering but knew it was the closest he was likely to get to victory with Lord Maccon and counted his blessings. Then he gently but firmly put his Alpha to work.

"Rumpet," he addressed the frozen and confused butler, "call the carriage. We are going into the city for the night."

Lord Maccon turned to Professor Lyall as the two made their way through the hallway, collecting their greatcoats on the way.

"Any other news I should be made aware of, Randolph?"

Professor Lyall frowned. "Only that Miss Wibbley has become engaged."

"Should that information mean something to me?"

"I believe you were once fond of Miss Wibbley, my lord."

"I was?" A frown. "How astonishing of me. Ah, yes, skinny little thing? You misconstrued—I was simply using her to needle Alexia at the time. Engaged, did you say? Who's the unfortunate fellow?"

"Captain Featherstonehaugh."

"Ah, now that name does sound familiar. Didn't we serve with a Captain Featherstonehaugh on our last tour in India?"

"Ah, no, sir, I believe that was this one's grandfather."

"Really? How time flies. Poor man. Not much to hold on to with that chit. That's what I like about my lass—she's got a bit of meat on her bones."

Professor Lyall could do nothing but say, "Yes, my lord." Although he did shake his head over the obtuseness of his Alpha. Who, having decided all would once more be blissful in his marriage, already referred to Alexia as his again. Unless Lyall was wrong, and circumstances had already proved how improbable that outcome, Lady Maccon was unlikely to see the situation in the same light.

They swung themselves up easily into the grand crested coach and four that served as Woolsey's main mode of transport when the wolves weren't running.

"Now, what is this about Mrs. Tunstell and a hat shop?" Lord Maccon wanted to know, adding before Professor Lyall could answer, "Sorry about drinking your specimen collection, by the way, Randolph. I wasn't quite myself."

Lyall grunted softly. "I shall hide it better next time."

"See that you do."

CHAPTER TEN

In Which Alexia Meddles
with Silent Italians

Lady Alexia Maccon did not, of course, realize that they were Templars until she awoke, and even then there was a lengthy adjustment period. It took her several long moments to discover that she was, in fact, not exactly a prisoner but relaxing in the guest quarters of a lavish residence located in, if the view from the window was to be believed, some equally lavish Italian city. The room had a delightful southern aspect, and a cheerful spray of sunlight danced over plush furnishing and frescoed walls.

Alexia tumbled out of bed, only to find she had been stripped and redressed in a nightgown of such frilliness as might have given her husband conniption fits under other circumstances. She wasn't comfortable with either the notion of a stranger seeing her in the buff nor the copious frills, but she supposed a silly nightgown was better than nothing at all. She soon discovered she had also been provided with a dressing gown of velvet-lined brocade and a pair of fluffy bed slippers. Her dispatch case and parasol, apparently unmolested, sat on a large pink pouf to one side of her bed. Figuring that any person of refined sensibility would have burned her unfortunate claret-colored gown by now and finding no more respectable attire anywhere in the room, Alexia donned the robe, grabbed her parasol, and stuck her head cautiously out into the hallway.

The hall proved itself to be more of a large vestibule, covered in thick carpets and lined with a number of religious effigies. The humble cross appeared to be a particularly popular motif. Alexia spotted a massive gold statue of a pious-looking saint sporting jade flowers in his hair and ruby sandals. She began to wonder if she was inside some kind of church or museum. *Did churches have guest bedrooms?* She had no idea. Having no soul to save, Alexia had always considered religious matters outside her particular sphere of influence and therefore interest.

All unbidden, her stomach registered its utter emptiness and the infant-inconvenience sloshed about sympathetically. Alexia sniffed the air. A delicious smell emanated from somewhere close by. Alexia had decent eyesight and adequate hearing—although she had been remarkably capable of tuning out her husband's voice—but it was her sense of smell that set her apart from ordinary mankind. She attributed this to her oversized nose. Whatever the case, it stood her in good stead this particular day, for it led her unerringly down a side hallway, through a wide reception chamber, and out into a massive courtyard where a multitude of men were gathered about long tables to eat. *Imagine that, eating outside and not for a picnic!*

Alexia paused on the threshold, unsure. An assembly of masculinity, and her in only a dressing gown. Such a danger as this she had never before had to face. She braced herself against the horror of it all. *Here's hoping my mother never gets wind of this.*

The seated masses made for a bizarrely silent assembly. Hand gestures were the main method of communication. Seated at the head of one of the tables, a single somberly dressed monk read unintelligible Latin out of a Bible in a monotonous tone. To a man, the silent eaters were darkly tan and dressed respectably but not expensively in the kind of tweed-heavy country garb young men about the hunt might favor— knickerbockers, vests, and boots. They were also armed to the teeth. At breakfast. It was disconcerting to say the least.

Alexia swallowed nervously and stepped out into the courtyard.

Strangely enough, none of the men seemed to notice her. In fact, none of them registered her existence at all. There were one or two very subtle sideways glances, but, by and large, Alexia Maccon was entirely and utterly ignored by everyone there, and there were at least a hundred assembled. She hesitated.

"Uh, hallo?"

Silence.

True, prior familial experiences had prepared Alexia for a life of omission, but this was ridiculous.

"Over here!" A hand waved her over to one of the tables. In among the gentlemen sat Madame Lefoux and Floote, who, Alexia saw with a profound feeling of relief, also wore robes. She had never seen Floote in anything less than professional attire, and he seemed, poor man, even more embarrassed than she by the informality of the dress.

Alexia wended her way over to them.

Madame Lefoux appeared comfortable enough, although startlingly feminine in her dressing gown. It was strange to see her without the customary top hat and other masculine garb. She was softer and prettier. Alexia liked it.

Floote looked drawn and kept darting little glances at the silent men around them.

"I see they absconded with your clothing as well." Madame Lefoux spoke in a low voice so as not to interfere with the biblical recitation. Her green eyes glittered in evident approval of Alexia's informal attire.

"Well, did you see the hem on my gown—mud, acid, dog drool? I cannot say I blame them. Are these the famous Templars, then? Well, Floote, I can see why you do not like them. Highly dangerous, mute clothing thieves. Ruthless providers of a decent night's sleep." She spoke in English but had no doubt that at least some of the men around them could entirely understand her language, and could speak it, too, if they ever did speak.

Madame Lefoux went to make room for Alexia, but Floote said firmly, "Madam, you had best sit next to me."

Alexia went to do so, only to find that the continued complete disregard for her presence extended to offering her a seat on the long bench.

Floote solved this problem by pushing hard against one of his neighbors until the man shifted over.

Alexia squeezed into the space provided to find, once she had settled, that the gentleman nearest her had suddenly found himself needed elsewhere. In an organic manner, and without any obvious movement, her immediate area became entirely vacant of all personnel save Floote and Madame Lefoux. *Odd.*

No one brought her a plate of any kind, nor, indeed, any other means by which she could partake of the food currently being passed about the tables.

Floote, who had already completed his meal, shyly offered her his dirty trencher. "Apologies, madam, it is the best you'll get."

Alexia raised both eyebrows but took it. What an odd thing to have to do. Were all Italians this rude?

Madame Lefoux offered Alexia the platter of sliced melon. "Three nights of decent sleep. That's how long you've been out."

"What!"

Floote intercepted the melon when Alexia would have served herself. "Let me do that for you, madam."

"Why, thank you, Floote, but that is not necessary."

"Oh, yes, madam, it is." After which he proceeded to serve her anything she wished. It was as though he was trying to keep her from touching any of the utensils. Peculiar behavior, even for Floote.

Madame Lefoux continued with her explanation. "Don't ask me what they drugged us with. My guess is a concentrated opiate of some kind. But we were all asleep for three full nights."

"No wonder I am so hungry." This was rather worrying. Alexia glanced again at the silent, weapon-riddled men around her. Then shrugged. Food first, ominous Italians second. Alexia tucked in. The fare was simple but delicious, although entirely lacking in any meat. In addition to the melon, chunks of crunchy, salted bread, white with flour, were on offer, as well as a hard, sharp yellow cheese, apples, and a pitcher of some dark liquid that smelled like heaven. Floote poured a portion for her into his cup.

Alexia took a tentative sip and was quite overwhelmed by an acute sense of betrayal. It was absolutely vile tasting, a mixture of quinine and burnt dandelion leaves.

"That, I am to assume, is the infamous coffee?"

Madame Lefoux nodded, pouring herself a splash and then adding a good deal of honey and milk. Alexia could not believe a whole hive of honey capable of rescuing the foul drink. Imagine preferring *that* to tea!

A bell sounded and, in a shifting rustle, most of the gentlemen departed and a new crowd entered. These men were slightly less well dressed and a little less refined in their movements, although they, too, ate in complete silence to the sound of the Bible being read aloud. And they, too, were covered in weaponry. Alexia noticed with annoyance that clean utensils were set before *them* without bother. But the staff, milling about with platters of food and additional coffee, ignored Alexia with as much thoroughness as the men seated around her. Really, it was beginning to make her feel quite invisible. She attempted a subtle sniff of her arm. Did she stink?

Just to test a theory, and because she was never one to take anything sitting down—even when she was, in fact, sitting down—Alexia scooted along the bench toward her nearest Italian neighbor, stretching out a hand in his direction, pretending to reach for the bread. In a flash, he was up off the bench and backing away, still not exactly looking at her but warily watching her movements out of the corner of his eye. So it wasn't just that they were ignoring her; they were actively avoiding her as well.

"Floote, what *is* going on? Do they think I am contagious? Should I assure them I was born with a nose this size?"

Floote frowned. "Templars." He intercepted another platter that would have bypassed Alexia and offered her some steamed greens.

Madame Lefoux frowned. "I did not know their reaction to a soulless would be quite so extreme. This is bizarre, but I suppose given their beliefs . . ." She trailed off, looking at Alexia thoughtfully.

"What? What did I do?"

"Something highly offensive, apparently."

Floote snorted in a most un-Floote-like manner. "She was born."

For the moment, Alexia decided to follow the Templars' lead and so ignored them in turn, eating her meal with gusto. The infant-inconvenience and she appeared to have reached an agreement. She was now allowed to eat in the mornings. In return, Alexia was beginning to think upon the little being if not with affection, then at least with tolerance.

At the sound of a second bell, all of the men rose and began filing out of the courtyard, going off about their business without a by-your-leave. Even the Bible reader departed, leaving Alexia, Floote, and Madame Lefoux alone in the massive courtyard. Although Alexia managed to complete her meal before the staff were done cleaning up, no servant took her now-twice-dirty trencher. At a loss, Alexia began to gather up her eating utensils herself, thinking she would take them into the kitchen, but Floote shook his head.

"Allow me." He picked up the trencher, stood, took three quick steps, and hurled it over the courtyard wall, where it shattered loudly in the city street beyond. Then he did the same with Alexia's cup.

Alexia stared at him with her mouth open. Had he gone completely mad? Why destroy perfectly good pottery?

"Floote, what *are* you doing? What has the crockery done to offend?"

Floote sighed. "You are an anathema to the Templars, madam."

Madame Lefoux nodded her understanding. "Like being one of the untouchables in India?"

"Very like, madam. Anything in contact with a preternatural's mouth must be destroyed or ritually cleansed."

"Oh, for goodness' sake. Then why bring me here?" Alexia frowned. "And one of them must have carried me down the Alpine pass and then put me into bed."

"A professional handler," answered Floote curtly, as though that were explanation enough.

Madame Lefoux gave Floote a very long look. "And how long *did* Alessandro Tarabotti work for the Templars?"

"Long enough."

Alexia gave Floote a stern look. "And how long did you?"

Floote came over all inscrutable at that. Alexia was familiar with that attitude; he got it when he was about to clam up and become his most cagey. She faintly recalled from her nightmare time locked away in the Hypocras Club, some scientist saying something to the effect of Templars using soulless as agents. Had her father really been so bad as that? To work for a people who would have regarded him as not human. *No. Could he really?*

Alexia did not have an opportunity, however, to try and crack Floote's hard, curmudgeonly shell, for someone came out into the courtyard and began walking purposefully toward them. A Templar, but this one seemed perfectly capable of looking Alexia full in the face.

The man wore practical middle-class dress twisted into absurdity through the presence of a white sleeveless smock with a red cross embroidered on the front. This absurdity was somewhat mitigated by the sinister presence of a particularly large sword. At his approach, Alexia and Madame Lefoux extracted themselves from the bench seats. Alexia's nightgown ruffles got caught on the rough wood in a most annoying manner. She tugged them away and drew the robe closed more securely.

Looking down at her attire and then back up at the man approaching, Alexia grinned. *We are all dressed for bed.*

This Templar also wore a hat of such unsightliness as to rival one of Ivy's more favored investments. It was white and peaked, boasting yet another red cross emblazoned on the front and gold brocade about the edge.

Floote stood at Alexia's side. Leaning over, he whispered in her ear, "Whatever you do, madam, please do not tell him about the child." Then he straightened to his stiffest and most butlerlike pose.

The man bared his teeth when he reached them, bowing slightly. It could not possibly be a smile, could it? He had very straight white teeth, and a lot of them. "Welcome to Italy, daughter of the Tarabotti stock."

"You are *speaking* to me?" Alexia said dumbly.

"I am preceptor of the temple here in Florence. You are considered a small risk to *my* eternal soul. Of course, there will be five days' cleansing and a confessional after I have terminated contact with you, but until then, yes, I may speak with you."

His English was simply too good. "You are not an Italian, are you?"

"I am a Templar."

At a loss over what to do next, Alexia resorted to politeness and proper etiquette. Trying to hide the fuzzy slippers under the frilly hem of her nightgown, she curtsied. "How do you do? Allow me to introduce my companions, Madame Lefoux and Mr. Floote."

The preceptor bowed a second time. "Madame Lefoux, I am familiar with your work, of course. I found your recent paper on the aerodynamic adjustments needed to compensate for aether currents quite intriguing."

Madame Lefoux looked neither flattered nor inclined to make small talk. "Are you a man of God or a man of science?"

"Sometimes I am both. And, Mr. Floote, how do you do? I believe I am familiar with your name as well. You are in our records, yes? You have maintained an unwavering connection to the Tarabotti stock. An intriguing display of loyalty not normally engendered by preternaturals."

Floote said nothing.

"If you would all please follow me?"

Alexia looked at her companions. Madame Lefoux shrugged and Floote appeared only slightly more stiff than usual, but he was blinking apprehensively.

Alexia figured there was nothing for it but to play along.

"With pleasure," she said.

The preceptor led them through the temple, all the while talking to Alexia in a mild, silky voice.

"And how do you like Italy, My Soulless One?"

Alexia did not like his use of the possessive, but nevertheless tried to answer this question. Since she had not, as yet, seen very much of the country, it was difficult. Still, from what she had glimpsed out of her window that morning, she had formulated one ready opinion. "It is very orange. Is it not?"

The preceptor gave a little chuckle. "I had forgotten how extremely prosaic the soulless are. Here we sit in Florence, the most romantic city on God's earth, queen of the artistic world, and she finds it *orange*."

"Well, it is." Alexia gave him an inquisitive look. Why should she be the only one on the defensive? "I read somewhere that the Templars have an initiation ritual involving a dead cat and a duck made from a rubber tree. Is that true?"

"We do not discuss the secrets of the brotherhood with outsiders. Certainly not with a soulless."

"Well, certainly, you *would* like to keep that a secret." He looked dismayed but did not rise to the bait. Apparently, he was unable to. He could not refute her statements without discussing the very secrets he hoped to hide. Alexia relished her small victory.

The rest of the temple, as it turned out, was just as richly furnished and religiously decorated as the parts Alexia had already observed. There was a certain sparseness to the design and a complete absence of personal items that gave the place the unmistakable aura of a monastery despite its luxuriousness. This feeling of piety was helped along by the general hush and quiet all about.

"Where have all the other gentlemen gone?" Alexia asked, surprised not to have encountered any of the many men they had seen in the dining courtyard.

"The brothers are practicing, of course."

"Oh?" Alexia had no idea what their host was talking about, but he clearly believed that she ought to. "Um, practicing what, exactly?"

"The fighting arts."

"Oh." Alexia tried a new tactic after that, asking about some of the artifacts on display in an effort to get him to reveal more about his agenda.

The preceptor explained one or two with the same smooth calmness. "Salvaged from the treasury at Outremer," he said of an entirely unremarkable piece of rock raised in glory atop a marble column, and, "The letter written by Preceptor Terric of Jerusalem to Henry II" of a papyrus scroll yellowed with age.

Madame Lefoux paid attention with the interest of a bluestocking. Alexia was intrigued by the history but mostly mystified; she found religious relics rather dull, so the meaning was generally lost on her. The preceptor failed to reveal any useful secrets despite her cross-examination. Floote strode stoically behind, disregarding the artifacts being described and focusing on the Templar leading them.

Eventually, they ended their tour in a massive library, which Alexia supposed must pass for the relaxation area. The Templars didn't seem like the type of men to boast a card room. Not that she minded; Alexia had always preferred libraries herself.

The preceptor rang a little hand bell, like those Alexia had seen worn by cows, and within moments a liveried servant appeared. Alexia narrowed her eyes and drummed her fingers. After a rapid conversation in Italian, in which the preceptor did most of the talking, the servant left.

"Did you catch that?" Alexia asked Madame Lefoux in a whispered tone.

The Frenchwoman shook her head. "I do not speak Italian. You?"

"Apparently not well enough."

"Really? Italian *and* French?"

"And a little Spanish and some Latin." Alexia grinned. She was proud of her academic achievements. "We had this fantastic governess for a while. Unfortunately, Mama found out that she was filling my head with useful information and dismissed her in favor of a dance instructor."

The servant reappeared with a tray covered in a white linen cloth. The preceptor lifted this with a flourish to reveal not tea but a piece of mechanical gadgetry.

Madame Lefoux was immediately intrigued. She apparently preferred such things to tea. There was no accounting for taste.

The preceptor allowed the inventor to examine the device at length. Alexia thought it looked . . . uncomfortable.

"Some sort of analog transducer? It bears a passing resemblance to a galvanometer but it isn't, is it? Is it a magnetometer of some kind?"

The Templar shook his head, face stiff. Alexia realized what it was that bothered her so excessively about this man—his eyes were flat and expressionless.

"You are clearly an expert in your field, Madame Lefoux, but no. Not a magnetometer. You will not have seen one of these before. Not even in one of England's famed Royal Society reports. Although, you may know of its inventor, a German: Mr. Lange-Wilsdorf?"

"Really?" Alexia perked up at *that* name.

Both Floote and Madame Lefoux shot her dirty looks.

Alexia backed hurriedly away from any show of enthusiasm. "I may have read one or two of his papers."

The preceptor gave her a sharp glance out of his dead eyes but seemed to accept her statement. "Of course you would have. He is an expert in your field; that is"—the man flashed her another nonsmile of perfect teeth—"in the field of *you*, as it were. A remarkable mind, Mr. Lange-Wilsdorf. Unfortunately, we found his faith"—he paused meaningfully—"inconsistent. Still, he did devise this wonderful little tool for us."

"And what is it designed to detect?" Madame Lefoux was still troubled by her own inability to understand the gadget.

The Templar answered her with action. He cranked a handle vigorously, and the machine whirred to life, humming softly. A little wand was attached to it by means of a long cord. There was a rubber stopper at the wand's base, which corked up a glass jar in which the end of the wand resided. The preceptor pulled off the glass, exposing the wand to the air. Immediately, the small contraption began to emit a metallic pinging noise.

Madame Lefoux crossed her arms skeptically. "It is an oxygen detector?"

The Templar shook his head.

"A methane detector?"

Yet another shake met that guess.

"It cannot possibly be aether. Can it?"

"Can't it?"

Madame Lefoux was impressed. "A miraculous invention, indeed. Does it resonate to alpha or beta particles?" Madame Lefoux was a follower of the latest theory out of Germany that divided up the lower atmosphere into various breathable gases and divided the upper atmosphere and its travel currents into oxygen and two types of aetheric particles.

"Unfortunately, it is not that precise. Or, I should say, we do not know."

"Still, any mechanism for measuring aether ought rightly to be considered a major scientific breakthrough." Madame Lefoux bent once more over the contraption, enraptured.

"Ah, not quite so important as all that." The preceptor reined in Madame Lefoux's enthusiasm. "It is more a device for registering the *absence* of aetheric particles, rather than measuring their presence and quantity."

Madame Lefoux looked disappointed.

The Templar elaborated further. "Mr. Lange-Wilsdorf referred to it as an aether absorption counter. Would you allow me to demonstrate its application?"

"Please do!"

Without further ado, the man placed the wand into his mouth, closing his lips about the rubber stopper. No change occurred. The machine continued to emit the same metallic clicking noise.

"It is still registering."

The preceptor removed the wand. "Exactly!" He carefully wiped the wand down with a small piece of cloth soaked in some kind of yellow alcohol. "Now, My Soulless One, if you would be so kind?"

Eyebrows arched with interest, Alexia took the wand and did as he had done, closing her lips about the end. The wand tasted pleasantly of some sweetened lemony liquor. Whatever the preceptor had used to clean it was mighty tasty. Distracted by the taste, it took Alexia a moment to notice that the clicking noise had entirely stopped.

"Bless my soul!" exclaimed Madame Lefoux, perhaps not so wary as she should have been over her use of religious language in the house of Christ's most devout warriors.

"Merph!" said Alexia with feeling.

"Well, then, it cannot possibly be registering aether. Aether is around and inside of everything, perhaps in more minor quantities groundside than it is up in the aether-atmospheric layer, but it is here. To silence it like that, Alexia would have to be dead."

"Merph," agreed Alexia.

"So we have previously thought."

Alexia was moved by a need to speak and so removed the wand from her mouth. The device began ticking again. "Are you saying the soul is composed of aether? That is practically a sacrilegious concept." She cleaned the end as the preceptor had done, with more of the yellow alcohol, and passed it to Madame Lefoux.

Madame Lefoux turned the wand about, examining it with interest before popping it into her own mouth. It continued ticking. "Merfeaux" was her considered opinion.

The preceptor's flat, blank eyes did not stop staring at Alexia. "Not exactly. More that the lack of a soul is characterized by increased absorption of ambient aetheric particles into the skin, much in the way that a vacuum sucks air in to fill its void. Mr. Lange-Wilsdorf has theorized for years that preternatural abilities are the result of a lack of internally produced aether, and to compensate, the preternatural body seeks to absorb ambient aether from the outside. He invented this machine to test the theory."

Floote shifted slightly from his customary stance near the door, then stilled.

"When it is in my mouth, it detects nothing because I have nothing to detect? Because I am absorbing it all through my skin instead?"

"Precisely."

Madame Lefoux asked brightly, "So could this device detect excess soul?"

"Sadly, no. Only the absence of soul. And since most preternaturals are registered with the local government, or are at least known, such an instrument is mainly useless except to confirm identity. As I have just done with you, My Soulless One. I must say, your presence presents me with a bit of a conundrum." He took the wand back from Madame Lefoux, cleaned it once more, and switched the machine off. It let out one little wheeze and then the metallic clicking noise stopped.

Alexia stared at it while the preceptor capped the wand with the little glass jar and then covered the machine with the white linen cloth. It was odd to encounter an instrument that existed solely for one purpose—to tell the world that she was different.

"What do you Templars call that little device?" Alexia was curious, for he had specified that "aether absorption counter" was Mr. Lange-Wilsdorf's name for it.

The preceptor did not flinch. "A daemon detector, of course."

Alexia was decidedly taken aback. "Is that what I am?" She turned to look accusingly at Madame Lefoux. "You would tell me if I suddenly developed a forked red tail, wouldn't you?"

Madame Lefoux pursed her lips provocatively. "Would you like me to check under your skirts?"

Alexia backpedaled hurriedly. "On second thought, I think I should notice such a protuberance myself."

Floote wrinkled one corner of his nose in a remarkably understated sneer. "You are a daemon to them, madam."

"Now, gentlemen." Madame Lefoux leaned back, crossed her arms, and dimpled at them all. "Be fair. The last I heard was that the church was referring to preternaturals as devil spawn."

Alexia was confused. "But you gave me a bed . . . and this rather excitable nightgown . . . and a robe. That is hardly the way to treat devil spawn."

"Yes, but you can see why none of the brothers would talk to you." Madame Lefoux was clearly finding this part of the conversation amusing.

"And you understand the nature of our difficulty with your presence among us?" The preceptor seemed to think this fact obvious.

Floote interjected, his tone gruff. "You have found good use for her kind before, sir."

"In the past," the preceptor said to Floote, "we rarely had to deal with *females*, and we had the daemons controlled and isolated from the rest of the Order."

Floote acted as though the Templar had inadvertently given up some vital piece of information. "In the past, sir? Have you given up your breeding program?"

The man looked thoughtfully at Alessandro Tarabotti's former valet and bit his lip as if wishing he could retract the information. "You have been gone from Italy a long time, Mr. Floote. I am under the impression that England's Sir Francis Galton has some interest in expanding our initial research. 'Eugenics,' he is calling it. Presumably, he would need a method of measuring the soul first."

Madame Lefoux sucked in her breath. "Galton is a purist? I thought he was a progressive."

The Templar only blinked disdainfully at that. "Perhaps we should pause at this juncture. Would you like to see the city? Florence is very beautiful even at this time of year, if a trifle"—he glanced at Alexia—"orange. A little walk along the Arno, perhaps? Or would you prefer a nap? Tomorrow I have a small jaunt planned for your entertainment. I think you will enjoy it."

Apparently their audience with the preceptor had ended.

Alexia and Madame Lefoux took the hint.

The Templar looked at Floote. "I trust you can find your way back to your rooms? You will understand, it is impossible for me to ask a sanctified servant or brother to escort you."

"Oh, I understand perfectly, sir." Floote led the way from the room in what might have been, for him, a huff.

They began the long trek back to their quarters. The Florentine Temple was indeed vast. Alexia would have gotten hopelessly lost, but Floote appeared to know where to go.

"Well, he was certainly very chatty."

Floote glanced at his mistress. "Too chatty, madam." Floote's walk was stiff—well, stiffer than normal—which meant he was upset about something.

"And what does *that* mean?" Madame Lefoux, who had been distracted by a crude black onyx statue of a pig, trotted to catch up.

"He does not intend to let us go, madam."

"But he just offered to allow us to explore Florence on our own." Alexia was getting ever more confused by the highly contrary nature of these Templars and by Floote's opinion of them. "We would be followed, you believe?"

"Without question, madam."

"But why would they have anything to do with me? If they see me as some kind of soul-sucking daemon of spiritual annihilation?"

"The Templars couple war with faith. They see you as incapable of salvation but still useful to them. You are a weapon, madam."

It was becoming evident that Floote had had far more exposure to the Templars than Alexia had previously thought. She had read many of her father's journals, but clearly he had not written down *everything*.

"If it is dangerous for me here, why did you agree to the jaunt?"

Floote looked mildly disappointed with her. "Aside from not having a choice? You did insist on Italy. There are different kinds of danger, madam. After all, good warriors take particular care of their weapons. And the Templars are very good warriors."

Alexia nodded. "Oh, I see. To stay alive, I must ensure they continue to think of me as such? I am beginning to wonder if proving to my bloody-minded husband that he is an imbecile is worth all this bother."

They arrived at their rooms and paused in the hallway before dispersing.

"I do not mean to be callous, but I am finding I do not at all like this preceptor fellow," declared Alexia firmly.

"Apart from the obvious, why is that?" Madame Lefoux asked.

"His eyes are peculiar. There is nothing in them, like an éclair without the cream filling. It's wrong, lack of cream."

"It is as good a reason as any not to like a person," replied Madame

Lefoux. "Are you quite certain you do not wish me to check for that tail?"

Alexia demurred. "Quite." Sometimes she found the Frenchwoman's flirtations unsettling.

"Spoilsport," said the inventor wryly before retreating into her room. Before Alexia could go into her own, she heard a cry of anger emerge from her friend.

"Well, this is unconscionable!"

Alexia and Floote exchanged startled looks.

A tirade of French outrage flowed out the still partly open door.

Alexia knocked timidly. "Are you quite all right, Genevieve?"

"No, I am not! Imbeciles! Look what they have given me to wear!"

Alexia nosed her way in to find Madame Lefoux, a look of abject horror on her face, holding up a dress of pink gingham so covered in ruffles as to put Alexia's nightgown to shame.

"It is an insult!"

Alexia decided her best move at this juncture was a retreat. "You'll let me know," she said with a grin, pausing on the threshold, "if you need, perhaps, assistance with—oh, I don't know—the bustle?"

Madame Lefoux gave her a dirty look, and Alexia departed in possession of the field, only to find, across her own bed, a dress of equally layered outrageousness. *Really,* she thought with a sigh as she pulled it on, *is this what they are wearing in Italy these days?*

Her dress was orange.

Professor Randolph Lyall had been three nights and two days hunting with very little sleep. The only thing he'd gotten was a lead as to the whereabouts of Lord Akeldama's stolen item, from a ghost agent in good standing assigned to tail the potentate—if one could use the word "tail" when referring to a vampire.

Professor Lyall had sent Lord Maccon off to explore the lead further, arranging it so that the Alpha thought it was his own idea, of course.

The Beta rubbed at his eyes and looked up from his desk. He wouldn't be able to keep the earl in England much longer. He'd managed a series of investigative distractions and manipulations, but Alpha was Alpha, and Lord Maccon was restless knowing Alexia was out in the world being disappointed in him.

Keeping the earl active meant that Professor Lyall was stuck with the stationary work. He checked every day after sunset for a possible aethograph from Lady Maccon and spent much of the rest of his time reading through the oldest of BUR's records. He'd had them extracted with much tribulation from the deep stacks, needing six forms signed in triplicate, a box of Turkish delights to bribe the clerk, and a direct order from Lord Maccon. The accounts stretched back to when Queen Elizabeth first formed BUR, but he'd been scanning through them most of the night, and there were few references to preternaturals, even less about any female examples of such, and nothing at all about their progeny.

He sighed and looked up, resting his eyes. Dawn was imminent, and if Lord Maccon didn't arrive back presently, he'd be arriving back naked.

The door to the office creaked open, as though activated by that thought, but the man who walked in wasn't Lord Maccon. He was almost as big as the Woolsey Alpha and walked with the same air of self-assurance, but he was fully clothed and clearly in disguise. However, when Lyall sniffed the air, there was no doubt as to his identity—werewolves had an excellent sense of smell.

"Good morning, Lord Slaughter. How do you do?"

The Earl of Upper Slaughter—commander in chief of the Royal Lupine Guard, also known as Her Majesty's Growlers; sometime field marshal; holder of a seat on Queen Victoria's Shadow Council and most commonly known as the dewan—pushed his hood back and glared at Professor Lyall.

"Not so loudly, little Beta. No need to broadcast my presence here."

"Ah, not an official visit, is it? You haven't come to challenge for Woolsey, have you? Lord Maccon is currently out." The dewan was one of the few werewolves in England who could give Lord Maccon a fight for his fur and had reputedly done so, over a game of bridge.

"Why would I want to do a thing like that?"

Professor Lyall gave an elegant little shrug.

"The trouble with you pack types is you always assume us loners want what you've got."

"Tell that to the challengers."

"Yes, well, the last thing I need is the additional responsibility of a pack." The dewan fussed with the hood about his neck, arranging it to suit his taste.

The dewan was a man who had taken the curse later in life, resulting in a permanently jowly face, lined about the nose and mouth, with bags under the eyes. He sported a full head of dark hair, with a touch of gray at the temple, and fiercely bushy brows over deep-set eyes. He was handsome enough to have broken hearts in his day, but Lyall had always found the man's mouth a little full and his mustache and mutton-chops quite beyond the limits of acceptable bushiness.

"To what, then, do I owe the honor of your visit at such an early hour?"

"I have something for you, little Beta. It is a delicate matter, and it goes without saying that it cannot be known that I am involved."

"Oh, it does, does it?" But Lyall nodded.

The werewolf pulled forth a rolled piece of metal from his cloak. Professor Lyall recognized it at once—a slate for the aethographic transmitter. He reached into his desk for a special little cranking device and used it to carefully unroll the metal. What was revealed was the fact that a message had been burned through—already transmitted. The note was short and to the point, each letter printed neatly in its segment of the grid, and, rather indiscreetly, it had been signed.

"A vampire extermination mandate. Ordering a death bite on Lady Maccon's neck. Amusing, considering she cannot be bitten, but I suppose it is the thought that counts."

"I understand it is just their turn of phrase."

"As you say. A death order is a death order, and it is signed by the *potentate*, no less." Professor Lyall let out a deep sigh, placed the metal down with a tinny sound on the top of his desk, and pinched the bridge of his nose above his spectacles.

"So you understand the nature of my difficulty?" The dewan looked equally resigned.

"Was he acting under the authority of Queen Victoria?"

"Oh, no, no. But he did use the Crown's aethographor to send the order to Paris."

"How remarkably sloppy of him. And you caught him in the act?"

"Let us say, I have a friend on the transmitter-operating team. He swapped out the slates so that our sender there destroyed the wrong one."

"Why bring it to BUR's attention?"

The dewan looked a little offended by the question. "I am not bringing it to BUR; I am bringing it to the Woolsey Pack. Lady Maccon, regardless of the gossip, is still married to a werewolf. And I am still the dewan. The vampires simply cannot be allowed to indiscriminately kill one of our own. It's not on. Why, that is practically as bad as poaching clavigers and cannot be allowed, or all standards of supernatural decency will be lost."

"And it cannot be known that the information came from you, my lord?"

"Well, I do have to still work with the man."

"Ah, yes, of course." Professor Lyall was a tad surprised; it was rare for the dewan to involve himself in pack business. He and Lord

Maccon had never exactly liked each other ever since that fateful game of bridge. Lord Maccon had, in fact, given up cards as a result.

With his usual inappropriate timing, Lord Maccon returned from his jaunt at that very moment. He marched in, clad only in a cloak, which he removed in a sweeping motion and flung carelessly in the vicinity of a nearby hat stand, clearly intent on striding on to the small changing room to don his clothes.

He stilled, naked, sniffing the air. "Oh, hello, Fluffy. What are you doing out of your Buckingham penitentiary?"

"Oh, for goodness' sake," said Professor Lyall, frustrated. "Do hush up, my lord."

"Lord Maccon, indecent as always, I see," snapped the dewan, ignoring the earl's pet name for him.

Now, bound and determined to remain nude, the earl marched around Lyall's desk to see what he was reading, as it clearly had some connection with the unexpected presence of the second most powerful werewolf in all of Britain.

The dewan, showing considerable self-restraint, ignored Lord Maccon and continued his conversation with Professor Lyall as though the earl had not interrupted them. "I am under the impression the gentleman in question may have also managed to persuade the Westminster Hive to his line of thinking, or he would not have sent that order."

Professor Lyall frowned. "Ah, well, given—"

"Official extermination mandate! On *my wife*!"

One would think, after twenty-odd years, Professor Lyall would be used to his Alpha's yelling, but he still winced when it was conducted with such vigor so close to his ear.

"That lily-livered, bloodsucking sack of rotten meat! I shall drag his sorry carcass out at high noon—you see if I don't!"

The dewan and Professor Lyall continued their conversation as if Lord Maccon weren't boiling over next to them like a particularly maltreated porridge.

"Really, by rights, preternaturals," Lyall spoke coldly, "are BUR's jurisdiction."

The dewan tilted his head from side to side in mild agreement. "Yes, well, the fact remains that the vampires seem to think they have a right to take matters onto their own fangs. Clearly, so far as the potentate is concerned, what that woman is carrying is *not* preternatural and thus no longer BUR's jurisdiction."

"*That woman* is my wife! And they are trying to kill her!" A sudden deep suspicion and sense of betrayal caused the Alpha to turn upon his Beta in accusation. "Randolph Lyall, were you aware of this and yet didna tell me?" He clearly didn't require an answer. "That's it; I'm leaving."

"Yes, yes, well, never mind that." Professor Lyall tried unsuccessfully to calm his Alpha down. "The question is, what do they think she *is* carrying?"

The dewan shrugged and pulled his cloak back up over his head, preparing to leave. "I rather think that is your problem. I've risked enough bringing this to your attention."

Professor Lyall stood, reaching over his desk to grasp the other werewolf's hand. "We appreciate you giving us this information."

"Just keep my name out of it. This is a domestic matter between Woolsey and the vampires. I wash my fur of the entire debacle. I told you not to marry that woman, Conall. I said no good could possibly come of it. Imagine contracting to a soulless." He sniffed. "You youngsters, so brash."

Lord Maccon began to protest at that, but Professor Lyall shook the dewan's hand firmly in the manner of pack brothers, not challengers. "Understood, and thank you again."

With one last mildly offended look at the naked, red-faced, sputtering Alpha, the dewan left the office.

Professor Lyall, drawing on long years of practice, said, "We have got to find Lord Akeldama."

Lord Maccon sobered slightly at that abrupt change in subject. "Why is that vampire never around when you need him, but always around when you don't?"

"It is an art form."

Lord Maccon sighed. "Well, I canna help you find the vampire, Randolph, but I do know where the potentate has his object stashed."

Professor Lyall perked up. "Our ghost overheard something significant?"

"Better, our ghost *saw* something. A map. I thought we might just go steal the object back, before I leave to fetch my wife."

"And you still haven't told me where you sent Channing."

"It's possible I was too drunk to remember."

"It's possible, but I think not."

Lord Maccon took that as an opportunity to get dressed, leaving Professor Lyall in possession of the field but not the information.

"So, about this theft?" Lyall was always one to cut his losses and move on when necessary.

"It should be fun." Lord Maccon's voice emerged from the little changing closet.

When the Alpha reemerged, Professor Lyall wondered, not for the first time, if gentlemen's garb was not made complex through vampire influence as a dig at werewolves who, by their very nature, were often in a tearing hurry to get dressed. He himself had mastered the art, but Lord Maccon never would. He stood to go around his desk and help his Alpha rebutton a lopsided waistcoat.

"It should be fun, you said, this reacquisition operation, my lord?"

"Especially if you like swimming."

CHAPTER ELEVEN

Wherein Alexia Encounters Both Pesto and a Mysterious Jar

H adn't we better go to the local dirigible station? Didn't Monsieur Trouvé say he would send our luggage there?" Alexia looked down in disgust at the orange frilly dress she was wearing. "I could very much use the comfort of my own wardrobe."

"I could not agree with you more." Madame Lefoux's feelings of maltreatment were equally evident, as she was clearly uncomfortable in her pink frilly version of the same gown. "I should like to pick up some supplies as well." The inventor looked meaningfully at Alexia's parasol. "You understand, for a reconstitution of the necessary emissions."

"Of course."

There was no one around them in the temple hallway, but Madame Lefoux's use of euphemisms seemed to indicate that she felt they were in danger of being overheard.

They made their way to the front entrance of the temple and out into the cobbled streets of Florence.

Despite its generally orange overtones—Alexia's dress fit right in—Florence was indeed an attractive metropolis. It had a soft, rich quality about it that Alexia felt was the visual equivalent of consuming a warm scone heaped with marmalade and clotted cream. There was a pleasantness to the air and a spirit about the town that did not come from its color, but from some inner, tasty citrus quality. It made Alexia wonder fancifully if cities could have souls. Florence, she felt, under those circumstances, probably had extra. There were even little bitter bits of rind scattered about the place: the dense clouds of tobacco smoke emanating from various cafes and an overabundance of unfortunates begging from the church steps.

There were no hansoms, nor any other ready form of public transportation. Indeed, the entire city was apparently possessed of only one means of locomotion: walking. Alexia was a profuse walker. Even though she was a little sore from her mountaintop peril, she was equal to further exercise. After all, she had been asleep for three days. Floote valiantly headed their expedition. He was suspiciously familiar with the city, leading them unerringly through a wide open plaza called the Piazza Santa Maria Novella, which Alexia thought sounded like an assembly of sainted literary pundits; down the Via dei Fossi, which sounded like a fascinating geological discovery; across a bridge; and down into Piazza Pitti, which sounded like a pasta dish. It was a long walk, and Alexia had reason to be grateful for her parasol, for Italy did not appear to notice that it was November and poured sun down upon them with unremitting cheerfulness.

As it turned out, the Italians beyond the walls of the temple were a friendly, excitable bunch. Several of them waved to Alexia and her party. Alexia was mildly put out; after all, these were people to whom she had not been introduced and had no particular interest in knowing, yet they *waved* as she passed. It was most disconcerting. Also, it became quickly evident that Alexia's capable governess had been remiss in the matter of the Italian tongue. She had never taught Alexia that a great majority of communication was achieved through hand gesticulations. Although sentiments were often expressed a tad too loudly for Alexia's refined sensibilities, it was indeed as lovely to watch as it was to hear.

Even with such distractions as shirtless men kicking rubber balls around the bank of the Arno and a language that danced, Alexia noticed something amiss.

"We are being followed, are we not?"

Madame Lefoux nodded.

Alexia paused in the middle of the bridge and looked casually back over her shoulder, using her parasol to disguise the movement.

"Really, if they wanted to hide, they ought not to wear those ridiculous white nightgowns. Imagine going out in public in such a state."

Floote corrected his mistress. "Holy Tunics of Piety and Faith, madam."

"Nightgowns," insisted Alexia firmly.

They walked on.

"I counted six. Do you concur?" Alexia spoke in a low voice, although their followers were still a considerable distance behind and well out of earshot.

Madame Lefoux pursed her lips. "Yes, about that many."

"Nothing to be done, I suppose."

"No, nothing."

Florence's dirigible landing green was part of Boboli Gardens, a robust and extensive terraced park that lay in resplendent glory behind the most imposing castle Alexia had ever seen. In truth, Pitti Palace looked more like a prison of unusually fine proportions. They had to walk around the side of the massive edifice to get to the garden gate, where they were checked by a uniformed customs official.

The grounds were quite lovely, teeming with lush vegetation. The landing green was located directly behind the palace and on the same level. In its center stood an Egyptian obelisk, used as a tethering station, although no dirigibles were currently at rest. The luggage depot and waiting area took the form of a rebuilt ancient Roman gazebo. The official in charge was delighted to show them to the baggage storage area, where Alexia found her trunks, Madame Lefoux's modest assortment of carpetbags, and Floote's scruffy portmanteau, courtesy of Monsieur Trouvé.

As they began gathering up their possessions, Alexia thought she saw Madame Lefoux snatch at some small item sitting atop her hatbox but could not be certain what it was. She was about to ask when the station clerk approached to have her sign a chit for their belongings.

Once she had done so, the clerk glanced down and made a sudden face as he read Alexia's name. "La Diva Tarabotti?"

"Yes."

"Ah. I 'ave ze"—he waved his hand in the air, apparently incapable of recalling the appropriate English vocabulary—"thing, para you."

At which he bustled off, returning a moment later to hand Alexia something that amazed the entire party.

It was a *letter* directed to La Diva Alexia Tarabotti in round, sprawling script. And it was not, as any person of sense might have surmised, from Monsieur Trouvé. Oh, no, this missive was from Mrs. Tunstell.

Alexia twisted the heavy folded paper about in her hand for a moment in surprise. "Well, doesn't that just go to show that no matter where you go, Ivy will always find you?"

"Perish the thought, madam," replied Floote with feeling before bustling off to hire a cart.

The clerk kindly handed Alexia a letter opener, and she cut through the seal.

"My dearest, darlingest of Alexias," it began in flamboyant style, and went on from there with no hope of sobriety. "Well, it is all go around London with you gone. All go, I tell you!" The missive employed Ivy's preferred abuse of punctuation and reliance upon malapropisms.

"Tunstell, my brilliant pip, has gotten himself the lead role in the Winter Season of Forthwimsey-Near-Ham's operatic production of the *HMS Pennyfarthing*! Can you envisage that?" Alexia tried desperately not to. "I am lathe to admit it"—Alexia imagined Ivy spinning round and round like a top—"but I am adapting quite comfortably to life in trade, rather too comfortably for my mother's peace of mind. Please tell Madame Lefoux that her hat shop is doing *extremely* well, and I have even made one or two improvements." Alexia relayed this information to the Frenchwoman, who blanched.

"It has been less than a week. How much damage can she possibly have done in such a short time?" Madame Lefoux sounded as though she were trying to convince herself.

Alexia read on. " 'I have even, I blush to admit it here in print, inadvertently precipitated a wildly popular new craze in earmuffs for dirigible travel. I had the notion to affix fake hair falls from Paris to the exterior of the muffs so that the Young Lady Traveler might look as though she had an elaborate hairstyle while still staying warm. Such *hairmuffs,* as I call them, have the added benefit of bearing the brunt of the aether breezes' mussing. Well, I don't mind telling you, Alexia, they are selling by the baker's dozen! They have been heralded, only this morning, as the very *latest* in vital travel wardrobe accoutrements by no less than three leading fashion journals! Have enclosed clipping for your perusal.' " Alexia read this bit of the letter out for Madame Lefoux's continued edification and then handed her the newspaper clipping.

" 'In other shocking news, the dashing Captain Featherstonehaugh has announced his engagement to Miss Wibbley, who really is only *just* out of finishing school! This has had the unfortunate side effect of putting about the rumor that your younger sister was thrown over for a schoolroom chit, quite the persona au gratin, if you take my meaning. You will hardly be surprised when I tell you, London is all in uproars over the impending nuptials! I do hope this letter finds you well. As always, your dearest friend, Ivy.' "

Alexia folded the letter up, smiling. It was nice to be reminded of the mundanities of everyday life where there were no Templars stalking one through the streets of Florence, no drones in armed pursuit, and nothing was more worrisome than Miss Wibbley and her "au gratin" antics. "Well, what do you make of that?"

Madame Lefoux gave Alexia a particularly droll look. "Just out of finishing school, indeed."

"I know. Shocking. Most girls recently out of finishing school are like soufflés: puffed up, not very substantial inside, and prone to collapsing at the slightest provocation."

Madame Lefoux laughed. "And earmuffs with hair attached. How is it you English put it? *I say!*"

Floote returned with a pony and trap for their bags.

Alexia smiled, but she was, she hated to admit it, a little disappointed. She could not help noticing that there had been no mention of Lord Maccon, nor the Woolsey Pack, in Ivy's letter. Either Ivy was being circumspect—which was about as likely as Floote suddenly dancing an Irish jig—or the London werewolves were staying well out of the social limelight.

"You may find yourself the exclusive owner of a highly profitable hairmuff business instead."

Madame Lefoux flipped the newspaper clipping over and then stilled, face drawn.

"What is it? Genevieve, are you unwell?"

Mutely, the inventor passed the bit of paper back to Alexia.

It wasn't the whole of the article, just a section of it, but it was enough.

". . . surprised us all with a printed apology to his wife in the *Morning Post*. He has claimed that all previous rumors and accusations were not only false, but his fault, and that the child is not only his, but a miracle of modern science. Speculation is rampant as to the earl's purpose in issuing this retraction. No one has seen Lady Maccon since . . ."

Alexia's knees, previously quite reliable support structures, failed her, and she sat suddenly straight down onto the stone floor of the customs depot.

"Oh," she said, because it was all she could think to say, followed by, "Blast."

Then, surprising everyone, including herself, she started to cry. And not in the elegant, slow-dripping manner of true ladies of quality, but in loud embarrassing sobs like a little child.

Madame Lefoux and Floote stared down at her in stunned silence.

Alexia simply went on crying. Hard as she tried, she couldn't stop.

Madame Lefoux finally reacted, crouching down to wrap her friend in a bony but comforting embrace. "Alexia, my dear, what is wrong? Isn't this a good thing?"

"B-b-b-bastard," blubbered Alexia.

Madame Lefoux was clearly at a loss.

Alexia, taking pity on her, tried desperately to control herself and explain. "I was doing so well, being angry at him."

"So you are crying because you cannot be angry at him anymore?"

"No. Yes!" Alexia wailed.

Floote handed over a large handkerchief. "It is relief, madam," he explained to the Frenchwoman.

"Ah." Madame Lefoux applied said square of cotton to Alexia's blotchy face with tender care.

Alexia realized she was making a spectacle of herself and tried to stand. Too many things were going on in her head at once, and it was causing her eyes to leak. She took a deep, shaky breath and blew her nose loudly into Floote's handkerchief.

Madame Lefoux patted her back, still looking at her in concern, but Floote's attention had shifted.

Alexia followed his gaze. Four robust-looking young men were heading purposefully in their direction across the garden.

"Those are definitely *not* Templars," said Madame Lefoux with conviction.

"No nightgowns," agreed Alexia, sniffing.

"Drones?"

"Drones." Alexia stuffed the handkerchief up one sleeve and got shakily to her feet.

This time the drones looked to be taking no chances: each man held a wicked-looking knife and walked with decided purpose.

Alexia heard a faint shout and thought she could see, some way across the green, their group of Templar shadows running in their direction. They would in no way be fast enough.

Alexia raised her parasol in one hand and the clerk's letter opener in the other. Madame Lefoux reached for her cravat pins. Finding she wore no cravat, she swore and groped blindly for the nearest heavy object, coming up with her stealth hatbox, the heavy one that contained her tools, from the stack of luggage in the cart behind them. Floote relaxed into a kind of loose-limbed fighting stance that Alexia had seen before: in a battle to defend the location of tents between two werewolves on her front porch. What was Floote doing fighting like a werewolf?

The drones attacked. Alexia's parasol whipped out to deliver a crushing blow, only to be deflected by a knife. Out of the corner of her eye, she saw Madame Lefoux swing the hatbox, cracking the wood casing against the side of a drone's skull. Floote balled up his fist and, fast as any boxer—not that Alexia knew much of pugilism, being a lady of good breeding—dodged the knife slicing down toward him and made two quick hits to his opponent's stomach.

Around them, waiting dirigible passengers gasped in shock, but no one did anything to either help or hinder. Italians were reputed to be a people of violent emotions; perhaps they thought this was a lover's spat of some multifaceted variety. Or perhaps they thought the battle was over a ball sport. Alexia seemed to recall hearing one matron complain that the Italians were very passionate in their support of balls.

They could have used some assistance, for Alexia was no formally trained fighter, and Madame Lefoux, whether she was or not, was considerably hampered by her floofy dress. Quicker than Alexia would have thought possible, the drones had her disarmed, parasol rolling away across the stone floor of the gazebo. Madame Lefoux was thrust to the ground. Alexia thought she heard the Frenchwoman's head hit the side of the cart on the way down. She certainly didn't look to be moving anytime soon. Floote struggled on, but he was not quite so young as he once was, and certainly a good deal older than his opponent.

Two of the drones held Alexia fast between them, while the third, having determined Madame Lefoux was no longer a threat, brandished his knife with the clear intention of slitting Alexia's throat. This time they were brooking no delay. They would simply eliminate the preternatural right there in broad daylight and in front of witnesses.

Alexia writhed in the grip of her two captors, kicking out and wiggling as much as possible, making it difficult for them to steady her for the knife. Floote, seeing her imminent peril, fought all the harder, but death seemed embarrassingly inevitable.

And then a very odd thing happened.

A tall masked man, hooded like some parody of a religious pilgrim, leapt into the fray, and he appeared to be on *their* side.

The unexpected champion was a big man—not so big as Conall, Alexia noticed, but then few were—and clearly quite strong. He carried a long sword in one hand, British military issue, and had a mean left punch, which was also, Alexia guessed, British military issue. The masked man certainly was liberal and enthusiastic with his use of both sword and fist.

Finding her captors distracted, Alexia jerked a knee into one in the vicinity of one's nether regions at the same time twisting violently, trying to shake off the others' grip. The one she'd kneed backhanded her across the mouth, and Alexia felt a starburst of pain before tasting blood.

The masked man reacted swiftly at that, slicing out with his sword and catching the offender behind one knee. The drone crumpled.

The drones regrouped, leaving only one still holding Alexia while two went back on the defensive, facing off against the new threat.

Alexia liked these odds considerably better and did what any proper young lady ought to do: she pretended to faint, collapsing in a sudden dead weight against her captor. The man shifted to hold her with one hand, no doubt reaching for his own knife to slit her throat with the other. Sensing the opportunity, Alexia braced both feet and thrust sharply backward with all her might, knocking both herself and the drone to the floor. Once there, they proceeded to roll about gracelessly on the stone. Alexia had reason to be grateful for her husband's fondness for rolling among the bedsheets, for it had given her some practice wrestling with a man twice this drone's size.

Then, like the knights they had once been of old, the Templars were upon them. *White nightgowns to the rescue,* thought Alexia happily. The drones were forced, once more, to flee from the papal enforcers. Alexia had to admit Templar attire looked much less silly behind flashing, naked blades.

Alexia struggled to her feet in time to see their masked defender, clutching his bloody sword and dashing across the dirigible green in the opposite direction from the drones. In a whirl of dark cloak, he leapt over a row of topiary deer and disappeared into the gardens beyond. Clearly he liked being mysterious, or disliked the Templars, or both.

Alexia checked on Floote, who had not a hair out of place. He, in turn, wanted reassurances that neither she nor the infant-inconvenience had suffered any ill effects from the ordeal. Alexia did a quick internal assessment and discovered that they were both hungry, of which she informed Floote, and then bent to examine Madame Lefoux. The back of the inventor's head was bloody, but her eyes were already blinking open.

"What happened?"

"We were saved by a masked gentleman."

"Pull the other one." Sometimes Madame Lefoux could be surprisingly British in her verbal mannerisms.

Alexia helped her to sit up. "No, really. We were." While she explained what had occurred, she helped the inventor into the cart, and then they both watched with interest as the Templars dealt with the results of the altercation. It was almost like watching BUR at work cleaning up one of Alexia's messes, only faster and with less paperwork. And, of course, there was no Conall marching around waving his massive hands in exasperation and growling at her.

Alexia found herself grinning foolishly. *Conall had apologized!*

The dirigible passengers were clearly uncomfortable with having to deal directly with the Templars and were willing to do anything they were told so long as the men in white left quickly.

Floote disappeared mysteriously and then returned only to offer Alexia a sandwich of what appeared to be some kind of ham on what appeared to be some kind of roll and that turned out to be quite delicious. Alexia had no earthly idea where he had acquired the foodstuff but would not put it past him to have managed to make it during the fight. Having delivered the expected daily miracle, Floote stood in his usual stance and warily watched the Templars work.

"The locals, they are terrified of them, aren't they?" Alexia spoke softly, but she was reasonably certain that no one was paying them any mind. "And they must wield a considerable amount of clout for things to go so smoothly. No one has summoned the local constabulary, even though our little battle occurred in a public arena, in front of witnesses."

"One country under God, madam."

"It happens." Alexia wrinkled her nose and looked about for a scrap of fabric for Madame Lefoux to press against the back of her head. Finding nothing of use, she shrugged and ripped one of the ruffles off her orange dress. The inventor took it gratefully.

"One cannot be too careful with a head wound. Are you certain you are quite the thing?" Alexia watched her with concern.

"Everything is fine, I assure you. Except, of course, for my pride. I tripped, you know. He didn't overpower me. Really, I do not know how you ladies do it, run around dressed in long skirts all day every day."

"Generally, not a whole lot of running is involved. Is that why you dress as a man, then, pure practicality?"

Madame Lefoux looked as though she would like to twirl her fake mustache in thought, although, of course, she wasn't wearing it at the moment. "Partly."

"You like to shock people—admit it."

Madame Lefoux gave her an arch look. "As if you do not."

"Touché. Although we approach the endeavor differently."

The Templars, having concluded their activities, disappeared back into the foliage of Boboli Gardens with an air of hauteur. Even though violent action had been undertaken on Alexia's behalf, they had neither addressed her, nor looked in her direction. Alexia was disgusted to find, once the Templars had gone, that the ordinary Italian folk, including the once affable clerk, now regarded her with suspicion and disdain.

"Persona non grata once more." Alexia sighed. "Beautiful country, as you say, Floote, but the locals. The locals." She climbed into the cart.

"Exactly so, madam." With that, Floote took the driver's seat and, with a steady hand to the reins, guided the pony and trap through Boboli Gardens and out into the city streets. He took the bumpy course slow and gentle in deference to Madame Lefoux's head.

Floote stopped along the way at a small public eatery where, despite the presence of even more of the vile coffee and far too much tobacco, Alexia's opinion of the Italians was greatly improved through the application of the best victuals she had ever eaten in her entire life.

"These little chubby puddings with the green sauce," she declaimed, "must represent the food of the gods. I declare, the Templars may do what they like; I love this country."

Madame Lefoux grinned. "So easily swayed?"

"Did you taste that green sauce? How did they refer to it? Pets-something-or-other. Sheer culinary genius."

"Pesto, madam."

"Yes, Floote, that! Brilliant. Full of garlic." To illustrate her point, she took another mouthful before continuing. "Seems they put garlic in positively everything here. Absolutely fantastic."

Floote shook his head faintly. "I beg to differ, madam. It is, in fact, the result of practicality. Vampires are allergic to garlic."

"No wonder it is so rare back home."

"Terrible sneezing fits, madam. Much in the manner that young Miss Evylin used to come over when faced with a feline."

"And werewolves?"

"The basil, madam."

"No? How intriguing. Same sort of sneezing?"

"I believe it makes the insides of the mouth and nose itch, madam."

"So this pesto I enjoy so much is really an infamous Italian antisupernatural weapon?" Alexia turned accusing dark eyes on Madame Lefoux. "Yet there is no pesto in my parasol armament. I think we ought to rectify that immediately."

Madame Lefoux did not point out that Alexia could hardly go traipsing around toting a parasol that smelled strongly of garlic and basil. She did not have to, as Alexia was distracted by the arrival of some variety of orange fruit—of course it was *orange*—wrapped in a thinly cut piece of pig meat that was almost, but not quite, bacon. Alexia was transported.

"I don't suppose this is a weapon?"

"Not unless you have suddenly taken against the Jews, madam."

It was fortunate that they ate, for no food awaited them upon their return. After a lengthy stop at the alchemist's, which in Italy also stocked pharmaceuticals and fishing equipment, to purchase what Madame Lefoux referred to as "necessary supplies," they returned to the temple. There they found that, despite the early hour—it was not yet six—the Templars were already retired for the evening, undertaking some form of extended silent prayer.

While Madame Lefoux fussed with refilling the parasol and Floote went to do mysterious butler-type duties, Alexia hunted down the library. When no one stopped her, she began reading various books and records with interest. She had Ivy's little clipping with her and paused to reread it now and again. *A printed admission of guilt, imagine that?* She found herself humming from time to time. *You see, infant-inconvenience, it's not so bad.*

She did not find the information she was chiefly interested in: anything pertaining to the preternatural breeding program or concerning Templar use of soulless agents. However, she did find enough entertaining reading matter to keep her occupied well into the night. It was far later than she thought when she finally looked up to find the temple utterly silent around her, and not in the way of an edifice filled with prayer and soft movements. No, this was the silence of sleeping brains that only ghosts were comfortable experiencing.

Alexia padded toward her room, but then, sensing a presence she was not quite certain she could name, she shifted in her purposeful tread and veered down a small hallway. It was undecorated: there were no crosses nor any other religious effigies, and it ended in a tight stairwell that she might have thought only used by servants, except that it was arched and mossy and had the feel of immense age about it.

Alexia decided to explore.

This was, it must be admitted, probably not the most intelligent decision of her life. But how often is one given the opportunity to investigate an ancient passageway in a sacred temple in Italy?

The stairs down were indeed steep and slightly wet, as the back ends of caves will get no matter the climate. Alexia steadied herself with one hand against the damp wall, trying not to think about whether said wall had been cleaned recently. The stairs seemed to go down a very, very long way, ejecting her at the end into another undecorated hallway that in turn ended in what was possibly the most disappointing little room imaginable.

She could see that it was a room because, and this was peculiar, the door to the room was glass. She walked up and peeked through.

A small chamber lay before her, walls and floors of dingy limestone, with no paint nor other form of decoration. The only piece of furniture was a small pedestal in the center of the room, on top of which stood a jar.

The door was locked, and Alexia, resourceful as she was, had not yet learned to pick locks, though she mentally added it to her list of useful skills she needed to acquire, along with hand-to-hand combat and the recipe for pesto. If her life were to continue on its present track, which, after twenty-six years of obscurity now seemed to mainly involve people trying to kill her, it would appear that acquiring a less savory skill set might be necessary. Although, she supposed, pesto-making ought to be termed *more savory*.

She squinted through the door. It was paned with small squares of old leaded glass that were warping and sagging in their frames. This meant that the room within shifted and wiggled, and she squirmed around trying to see. She just couldn't quite make out what was inside the jar, and then finally she got the correct angle and was abruptly rather queasy to her stomach.

The jar held a severed human hand. It was floating in some liquid, probably formaldehyde.

A tactful little cough sounded behind her, just soft enough not to startle.

Alexia still jumped practically out of her frilly orange dress in surprise. Upon landing, she whirled around.

"Floote!"

"Good evening, madam."

"Come look at this, Floote. They have a human hand in a jar in the middle of an empty room. Aren't the Italians strange?"

"Yes, madam." Floote didn't come over, only nodded as though every house in Italy had such a thing. Alexia supposed this might be possible. Gruesome, but possible.

"But don't you think, madam, it may be time for bed? It would not do for anyone to find us in the Inner Sanctum."

"Oh, is that where we are?"

Floote nodded and extended a gracious arm for Alexia to precede him back up the tiny staircase.

Alexia took his advice, as there was apparently nothing else to see besides the random human body part. "Is it very common, in Italy, to keep a jar full of hand, just lying about?"

"For the Templars, madam."

"Uh, why?"

"It is a relic, madam. Should the temple come under serious threat from the supernatural, the preceptor will break the jar and use the relic to defend the brotherhood."

Alexia thought she might understand. She had heard of holy relics in connection with some Catholic cults. "Is it the body part of some saint?"

"They have those, too, of course, but in this case, it is an *unholy* relic, a weapon. The body part of a preternatural."

Alexia shut her mouth on her next question with a snap. She was surprised she hadn't been physically repulsed by the hand as she had been by the mummy. Then she remembered the daemon detector. She and the disembodied hand hadn't been sharing the same air. She supposed that was why the jar had to be broken in case of emergency.

They proceeded the rest of the way to their rooms in silence, Alexia mulling over the implications of that hand and becoming more and more worried as a result.

Floote stopped Alexia before she retired. "Your father, madam, was fully cremated. I made absolutely certain."

Alexia swallowed silently and then said fervently, "Thank you, Floote."

He nodded once—his face, as always, impassive.

CHAPTER TWELVE

The Great Scotch Egg Under the Thames

M uch to Lord Maccon's annoyance, the acquisition operation, as Professor Lyall had termed it, was taking far longer than intended. Impatient to be off after his errant wife, the Alpha was instead stalking back and forth in the drawing room of Buckingham Palace awaiting an audience with Queen Victoria.

He was still unsure as to how Lyall had, in fact, managed to keep him in London all these days. Betas, in the end, were mysterious creatures with strange powers. Powers that, when all was said and done, seemed to involve nothing more than a continued battery of civilized behavior and an excess of manners. Effective, blast him.

Professor Lyall sat on an uncomfortable couch, one stylishly clad leg crossed over the other, and watched his Alpha pace.

"I still don't see why we had to come here, of all places."

The Beta pushed at his spectacles. It was nearing the afternoon of his third day awake in a row, and he was beginning to experience the effects of prolonged daylight exposure. He felt drawn and tired, and all he wanted to do in the world was return to his tiny bed at Woolsey Castle and sleep the afternoon away. Instead, he was stuck dealing with an increasingly edgy Alpha. "I have said it before, and I shall say it again—you will need sundowner authorization for this, my lord."

"Yes, but couldn't you have come and gotten it for me afterward?"

"No, I couldn't, and you know it. This is too complicated. Stop complaining."

Lord Maccon stopped for the simple reason that, as usual, Lyall was correct. It *had* gotten very complicated. Once they'd discovered the location of the stolen object, they'd sent a river rat in to assess the place. The poor lad had come back soaking wet and in an absolute panic, justly earned, as it turned out. Their quick theft and retrieval operation had turned into something far more problematic.

Professor Lyall was a wolf who liked to look on the practical side of any given situation. "At least now we know why Lord Akeldama went into such a tizzy, pulled in all his drones, and ran."

"I didn't realize roves could swarm, but I suppose they have the same protective instincts as hives."

"And Lord Akeldama is a particularly old vampire with a peculiarly large number of drones. He is liable to be overprotective when one is stolen."

"I cannot believe I'm stuck here involving myself in vampiric tomfoolery. I should be hunting my wife, not one of Lord Akeldama's drones."

"The potentate wanted Lord Akeldama panicked for a reason. Your wife is that reason. So, essentially, this *is* your problem, and you have to deal with it before you leave."

"Vampires."

"Exactly so, my lord, exactly so." Professor Lyall's calmness covered his genuine worry. He had met Biffy only once or twice, but he liked the lad. Generally acknowledged as Lord Akeldama's favorite, Biffy was a pretty young thing, calm and capable. He genuinely loved and was loved by his outrageous master. For the potentate to dronenap him was the height of bad taste. The greatest unwritten law of the supernatural set was that one simply didn't steal someone else's human. Werewolves did not poach clavigers, for the key-keepers were vital to the safety of the greater population. And vampires did not take each other's drones, because, quite frankly, one doesn't interfere with another's food source. The very idea! And yet, they were now in possession of eyewitness testimony to the fact that this was exactly what the potentate had done to Lord Akeldama. Poor Biffy.

"Her Majesty will see you now, Lord Maccon."

The earl straightened his spine. "Righty'o."

Professor Lyall checked his Alpha's appearance. "Now *be polite.*"

Lord Maccon gave him a dour look. "I have met the queen before, you know."

"Oh, *I know.* That is why I am reminding you."

Lord Maccon ignored his Beta and followed the footman into Queen Victoria's illustrious presence.

In the end, Queen Victoria granted Lord Maccon sanction in his attempt to rescue Biffy. She refused to believe the potentate was involved, but if, in fact, a drone *had* been kidnapped, she thought it only right that the earl, in his capacity as head of the London BUR offices and chief sundowner, rectify the situation. It was untenable, she claimed, given her experience with vampire loyalty and trust, even among roves, that any vampire would steal another's drone.

"But supposing, Your Majesty, just this once, it has accidentally occurred? And that Lord Akeldama has swarmed as a result."

"Why, then you should carry on, Lord Maccon, carry on."

"I always forget how short she is," the earl commented to Professor Lyall as they readied themselves to "carry on" later that evening. Lord Maccon took the queen's tacit permission to mean he could use his Galand Tue Tue, which he was busy cleaning and loading. It was a graceless little revolver, portly with a square grip and hardwood bullets caged and capped with silver—the Sundowner model designed to kill mortals, vampires, or werewolves. Lord Maccon had designed a watertight, oiled leather case for the gun, which he wore about his neck so that it might be with him whether he was in wolf or human form. Since they would be traveling fast, wolf seemed the most sensible way to get through London.

Biffy, they had learned, was imprisoned inside a rather fantastic contraption. Lord Maccon was still upset that the installation of this device had escaped BUR's notice. It was, according to the trusty river rat, a man-sized sphere made of glass and brass with one large tube coming out its top. The tube was to conduct breathable air, because the sphere had been sunk into the middle of the Thames just under the Charing Cross Rail Bridge near Buckingham Palace. Not unsurprisingly, it had sunk not just into the water, but some way down into the thick mud and garbage at the bottom of the river as well.

When they arrived at the spot, Lord Maccon dove with alacrity off the newly completed Victoria Embankment and into the filthy water. Professor Lyall was more fastidious and thus more reticent. Nothing the Thames could throw at him could damage him permanently, but that didn't prevent his shuddering at the inevitability of the smell he was destined to produce: wet dog mixed with Thames river water.

Lord Maccon's brindled head appeared, fur slicked back like a seal, and he barked at his Beta imperiously. Professor Lyall locked his jaw and leapt stiffly into the water, all four legs extended in disgust. Together, looking like nothing so much as two stray dogs after a stick, the two made their way under the bridge.

Since they knew what they were looking for, they managed to

find the breathing tube affixed to one of the piers. It was stretched upward well out of the high-tide mark. It looked as though it could have also been used as a drop for food and water bags. At least the potentate had no intention of actually killing poor Biffy. Still, it was carelessly done. Should the tube fall, some misguided boat crash into it, or one curious animal climb up and stopper it over, Biffy would suffocate to death.

Lord Maccon dove down to investigate the contraption. This was hard to do in wolf form, and it was hard to see much in the blackness of the river. But he had supernatural strength and wolf night vision helping him. He surfaced looking pleased with himself, tongue lolling.

Professor Lyall winced at the very idea of tongue having any proximity to the Thames.

Lord Maccon, being Lord Maccon and good at such things, then changed, right there in the Thames, from dog-paddling wolf to large man treading water. He did so flawlessly, so that his head never went under the water. Professor Lyall suspected him of practicing such maneuvers in the bathtub.

"That is one interesting little contraption he has down there, like some species of mechanical Scotch egg. Biffy's still alive, but I have absolutely no idea how to get him out, short of simply muscling the blasted thing open and dragging him up through the water. Do you think a human could survive such an experience? There seems to be no means of attaching a crank or pulley to the sphere, nor of getting a net underneath, even if we had ready access to such things."

Professor Lyall sacrificed his meticulousness to the winds and changed form. He was not so good as Lord Maccon, sinking down slowly in the process so that he bobbled up, sputtering and disgruntled, to his Alpha's amused gaze.

"We could raid Madame Lefoux's contrivance chamber, but I think time is of the essence. We are werewolves, my lord. Muscling things is our specialty. If we can open it fast enough, we should be able to get him out with relatively little harm."

"Good, because if I do damage him, my wife will never let me hear the end of it. Once she decides to speak to me again, that is. She is awfully fond of Biffy."

"Yes, I recall. He helped with the wedding."

"Did he really? Well, what do you know? So, on the count of three? One, two, three."

Both men inhaled deeply and dove down to crack open the sphere.

It was constructed in two halves, joined by means of large metal ribs, screwed tightly together. From these stretched a cagelike lattice with glass in between, each square far too small for a man to squeeze through. Each werewolf grabbed at one bolt and began to unscrew it as fast as possible. Soon enough, the pressure of the air within caused the upper half of the sphere to separate from the bottom. Air began to escape and water rushed in to fill the vacancy.

Professor Lyall caught sight of Biffy's panicked expression, his blue eyes wide in a face bushy with weeks' worth of beard. He could do nothing to help free himself. Instead he fought the inrushing water, trying to keep his head afloat and tilted toward the air tube as long as possible.

With two bolts gone, the two werewolves wedged their bodies into the opening and began to physically push, muscles screaming, tearing the sphere apart bodily. The metal buckled, glass broke, and water filled the small compartment.

Even in all the chaos, Professor Lyall heard several out-of-context noises and, moments later, saw from the corner of his eye as the earl popped out of the sphere and began wildly thrashing about. But Lyall maintained his focus on Biffy. Pushing forward with both legs off the edge of the sphere, he dove for the drone, grabbed him around the waist, and with another tremendous push, shot upward toward the surface.

He emerged, panting, Biffy clutched against him. The young man was suspiciously limp, and Professor Lyall could think of nothing but the need to get him to shore as quickly as possible. Drawing on every last iota of his werewolf strength to give him the necessary speed, he plowed through the water, reaching the Westminster side of the Thames in record time and dragging the drone out onto the bottom of a filthy set of stone steps.

Professor Lyall was no medical doctor, but he could say with confidence that the best thing for Biffy at that moment would be to get the water out and the air into his lungs. So the werewolf stood, lifting the young man up by his feet. Lyall had to dangle him off the side of the steps; Biffy was taller than he. Then the Beta proceeded to shake the limp drone vigorously.

As he was shaking, Professor Lyall looked over at the midpoint of the river. The moon was only a few days past full, and it had risen enough for his werewolf eyes to see everything clearly. His Alpha was engaged in a splashy battle with three assailants. Much frothing of the water, yelling, and growling was involved. Lord Maccon was in his

Anubis Form, his head that of a wolf but his body still human. This allowed him to tread water but still apply the trademark werewolf savaging. It seemed to be working. His opponents were human, and, while they were armed with silver knives, they were not so adept at striking and swimming as Lord Maccon.

Professor Lyall returned to his task. As the shaking was proving to be ineffective, he positioned the young man carefully on a higher step and bent over him.

He was at a loss. Werewolves breathed, but not so deeply, nor so frequently as mortals. He wasn't convinced his next idea would even work. But, blushing furiously—after all, he and Biffy had only met casually a few times; they were hardly on terms of any intimacy—he bent forward and sealed the young man's mouth with his. Breathing out in a powerful blast, he attempted to physically force air into the drone's lungs. Nothing happened. So he did it again. And again.

A loud cry caused him to look up, although not stop in his attentions to young Biffy's survival. The figure of a man, a gentleman by his top hat and tails, ran along the rail bridge, faster than was humanly possible. The figure stopped and, in one impossibly quick and smooth movement, drew a gun and fired down into the churning mass of combatants.

Professor Lyall's protective instincts reared up. He had no doubt that the vampire, for that is what the newcomer must be, was firing silver bullets at *his* Alpha. Desperately, he breathed harder, hoping against hope that Biffy would revive so that he could go to his Alpha's aid.

Behind him, Lord Maccon behaved in an unexpectedly sensible manner. Abandoning his roughhousing, the Alpha dove under the surface of the Thames and began swimming toward the steps and his Beta. He stuck his muzzle up for air only once and briefly.

Unfortunately, with his first target underwater, the vampire simply moved on to the second best option. He fired at Professor Lyall and his charge as they hunched unprotected against the embankment. The bullet whizzed by perilously close to Lyall's head and struck the stone wall, causing fragments of rock to pellet downward. Lyall curled himself over the drone's body, shielding it with his own.

Then Biffy began to cough and sputter, spewing out Thames river water in a manner that Professor Lyall felt, while inelegant, was most prudent of him. The drone's eyes opened, and he stared up into the werewolf's sympathetic face.

"Do I know you?" Biffy asked between coughs.

Lord Maccon reached the steps at that point and hauled himself up, still in Anubis Form. He reached for his neck, unclasping the leather case safely fastened there, and pulled out his gun. The case had served its purpose, for the Tue Tue was still dry. He took aim at the vampire silhouetted against the moon and fired.

He missed.

"I'm Professor Lyall. We have met before. Remember the aethographor and the tea? How do you do?"

"Where's—?" But Biffy did not get to finish his thought, for the vampire's return shot scooted right past both Lord Maccon and his Beta, striking the poor drone in the stomach. Biffy's sentence stopped midquestion with a cry, as his body, emaciated from weeks in confinement, convulsed and writhed.

Lord Maccon's second shot back at the vampire did not miss. It was a lucky one, for at such a distance, even his trusty Tue Tue was unreliable. Nevertheless, the bullet struck home.

The vampire fell from the bridge with a shout, hitting the Thames with a loud splash. Immediately his agents—or were they drones?—ceased paddling about, recovering from their altercation with the earl, and swam over to him. From the resulting cries of distress, what they discovered was not to their liking.

Lord Maccon's attention remained fixed on the tableau in the water, but Professor Lyall was once more focused on Biffy. The blood leaking from the young man's injury smelled divine, of course, but Lyall was no pup to be diverted by the scent of fresh meat. The drone was dying. No doctor in Britain could patch up a damaged gut like that. There was really only one solution and no one, in the end, was going to be happy with it.

Taking a deep breath, the Beta reached into the wound, fishing about for the bullet with no care for Biffy's finer feelings. The young man conveniently fainted from the pain.

Lord Maccon came to kneel on the step below them.

He gave a confused whine, unable to talk, as his head was still that of a wolf.

"I'm trying to get out the bullet," Professor Lyall explained.

Another whine.

"It's *silver*. It must come out."

The earl began violently shaking his shaggy brindled head and backing slightly away.

"He is dying, my lord. You have no other choice. You're already in Anubis Form. You might as well make the attempt."

Lord Maccon continued to shake his wolf head. Professor Lyall fished out the offensive bullet, hissing in pain as the vile silver thing burned his fingertips.

"Don't you think Lord Akeldama would rather have him still alive, or at least partly alive, than dead? I am aware that it is not done. Unheard of, even, for a werewolf to poach a drone, but what else can we do? You have to at least try."

The Alpha cocked his head to one side, ears drooping. Professor Lyall knew what he was thinking. If this failed, Biffy would be found dead, savaged by a werewolf. How could they possibly explain that to anyone?

"You metamorphosed a female recently. You can do this, my lord."

With a small shrug that said as clearly as any words that if this didn't work, he would never forgive himself, the Alpha bent over the boy's neck and bit.

Normally, metamorphosis was a violent savaging of flesh, an infliction of a curse as much as a conversion to immortality, but Biffy was so very weak and had lost so much blood already that Lord Maccon took it slowly. He was able to. Conall Maccon had more self-control than any other Alpha Lyall had ever met, for all his Scottish heritage and grumpy temper. Lyall could only imagine how sweet the boy's blood must taste. In answer to that thought, Lord Maccon stopped biting and bent to lap at the bullet wound. Then he went back to biting. The idea of metamorphosis, most scientists believed, was to get the werewolf saliva, carrier of the curse, into the petitioner and to get sufficient human blood out. This would break mortal ties and tether the remnant soul. Supposing there was, of course, excess soul present.

It seemed to take a very long time. But Biffy kept breathing, and so long as Biffy kept breathing, Lord Maccon resolutely continued his repetitive action: bite, lick, bite, lick. He was not to be distracted even by the sloshing arrival of their opponents.

Professor Lyall stood to defend their position, prepared to change form if needed, the moon well overhead and the smell of human blood giving him added strength. But the three young men emerging from the water were obviously uninterested in any further hostility. They hauled themselves out onto the bottom step and held up empty hands at Professor Lyall's threatening stance. Their faces were lined with distress—one was crying openly, and another was keening softly at the limp form cradled in his arms. The third, a grim-faced boy holding one mostly gnawed hand against his chest, spoke.

"We've no reason to fight you further, werewolf. Our master is dead."

Drones, then, and not hired muscle.

Professor Lyall sniffed, trying to catch the scent of the vampire over the smell of human blood and putrid water. The horror of it hit him broadside, and he stumbled back against the stone of the embankment. It was there, the faint odor of old blood and decay that meant vampire, mixed with almost alcoholic overtones that, like the subtle difference between fine wines, indicated lineage. And Lyall smelled an old lineage, with a film of pine resin to the wine, and no ties to the modern hives. It was a scent long since lost and no longer emitted except by this one man. Lyall could have guessed the identity of the vampire from that scent, even were he not already familiar with its owner—the potentate. Or, as the vampire was dead and no longer a denizen of the Shadow Council, Lyall supposed he must be remembered now under his old name, Sir Francis Walsingham.

"Queen Victoria," he said to his Alpha, "is *not* going to be happy about this. Why the hell didn't he send someone else to do his dirty work?"

Lord Maccon did not look up from his self-prescribed penance: bite, lick, bite, lick.

Together, the three drones hefted their dead master and made their way slowly up the stairs around the earl and Biffy's still form. Even in their grief, they winced away from the sight of an Anubis feeding. As they passed, Professor Lyall noticed that Lord Maccon's bullet had hit Walsingham directly in the heart—a lucky shot, indeed.

A vampire was dead. There weren't enough of them around to forgive a transgression like that, even from BUR's chief sundowner. The potentate was a rove, with no major hive connections, and for that Professor Lyall was grateful. But there would be blood payment due to the greater community regardless, and it was the potentate's relationship with Buckingham Palace that was the real stickler. Even if, by his actions, this vampire had shown himself a traitor to his own kind, kidnapping another's drone, his absence left a gap Queen Victoria would find hard to fill. He had served as advisor to the throne since Queen Elizabeth's day. It was his knowledge of Roman strategy and supply management that drove the expansion of the British Empire. For someone like that to die because he had made a mistake, because Alexia Maccon, soulless, had become pregnant by a werewolf and he panicked, was a loss to every British citizen. Even the werewolves would mourn him, in their way.

Professor Lyall, who was cultured and not given to profanity, watched the drones cart the disanimated potentate away and said curtly, "What a bloody awful mess."

After which he stood, silent and waiting, wary and alert, for five long hours while Lord Maccon, stubborn to the last, held Anubis Form and worked over the dying drone.

The earl's stubbornness was rewarded when, just before dawn, before all his labor would be lost to the sun, Biffy's eyes opened, as yellow as buttercups. He howled out his pain and confusion and fear as his form shifted, and he lay there, shuddering but whole, a lovely chocolate-brown wolf with oxblood-red stomach fur.

Lord Maccon changed out of Anubis Form and grinned hugely at his Beta. "And there's another one for the howlers to sing about."

"What is it with you, my lord? Can you only metamorphose the difficult cases?" Professor Lyall was impressed despite himself.

"Yes, well, he is your charge now." Lord Maccon stood and stretched, his spine popping as it realigned. His tawny eyes turned with surprise toward the rapidly lightening sky.

"Best get him indoors right quick."

Professor Lyall nodded and bent to pick up the newly made wolf. Biffy struggled halfheartedly before sagging weakly into the Beta's strong arms. Metamorphosis took even the best of them like that.

Lyall made his way silently up the steps to the top of the embankment, thinking hard. They would have to find shelter nearby. A new pup couldn't take direct sunlight without considerable damage, and poor Biffy had been through more than enough for one night. Just as he figured out a destination and headed purposefully north toward Charing Cross Station, he noticed his Alpha wasn't following him.

"Now where are you going, my lord?" he hollered after Lord Maccon's rapidly retreating back.

The earl yelled over his shoulder without breaking stride. "I have a boat to catch and a wife to find. You can carry on from here."

Lyall would have rubbed his face with his hands, except his arms were full. "Oh, yes, certainly, feel free to depart. And me with a drone changed into a werewolf and a dead potentate. I am certain I have had Alphas leave me with worse messes to tidy up, but I cannot recall them at the moment."

"I am sure you will do very well."

"Wonderful, my lord. Thank you for your confidence."

"Toodles." And with that, Lord Maccon wiggled his fingers in the air in the most insulting way and disappeared around the side of a building. Presumably, he was heading for a busier part of London where he might stand a better chance of hailing a hackney posthaste for Dover.

Professor Lyall decided not to remind him that he was completely naked.

CHAPTER THIRTEEN

Picnicking with Templars

Alexia took a moment before breakfast to drag Floote into a secluded corner.

"We must get a message to the queen on this relic business. Or at least to BUR. I cannot believe you knew about it and never told anyone. Then again, I suppose, you never tell anyone anything, do you, Floote? Even me. Still, I know now and so should the British government. Imagine using preternatural body parts as weapons. Just think what they could do if they knew how to mummify."

"You are no longer muhjah, madam. The supernatural security of the empire is not your concern."

Alexia shrugged. "What can I say? I cannot help myself. I meddle."

"Yes, madam. And on a grand scale."

"Well, my mama always said, one should do what one is best at on as large a scale as possible. Of course, she was referring to shopping at the time, but I have always felt it was the only sensible sentence she ever uttered in her life."

"Madam?"

"We have managed to keep the mummy business mum, even from Madame Lefoux. The point being, we cannot let anyone know that mummies are useful as a weapon. There would be a terrible run on Egypt. If the Templars are using dead preternatural body parts and they figure out the mummification process, I am in real trouble. Right now it is only natural decomposition, and the fact that they have to preserve tissue in formaldehyde, that keeps preternatural-as-weapon limited to special use." Alexia wrinkled her nose. "This is a matter of supernatural security. Italy and the other conservative countries must be kept from excavating in Egypt at all costs. We cannot risk them figuring out the truth behind the God-Breaker Plague."

"I see your reasoning, madam."

"You will need to develop a sudden malaise that prevents you from attending this picnic the preceptor is dragging me on. Get to the Florentine aethographic transmitter by sunset and send a message to Professor Lyall. He will know what to do with the information." Alexia rummaged about in the ruffle of her parasol until she located the secret pocket and extracted the crystalline valve, which she handed to Floote.

"But, madam, the danger of you traveling about Italy without me."

"Oh, fiddlesticks. Madame Lefoux has entirely refitted my parasol with the necessary armaments. I shall have the preceptor and a cadre of Templars with me, and they're bound to protect me even if they cannot look at me. I even purchased this." Alexia exhibited a clove of garlic dangling from a long ribbon about her neck. "I shall be perfectly fine."

Floote did not look convinced.

"If it will help allay your fears, give me one of your guns and some of the spare bullets you purchased yesterday."

Floote did not seem at all mollified. "Madam, you do not know how to shoot."

"How difficult can it be?"

Floote ought to have known after a quarter century of association with Alexia that he could not hope to win any argument, especially as a gentleman of few words and even less inclination to use them. With a faint sigh of disapproval, he accepted the responsibility of sending the transmission and left the room, without giving Alexia one of his guns.

Professor Lyall spent the last hour before dawn coping with the consequences of Biffy's sudden change into a werewolf and the potentate's sudden change into a corpse. He began by seeking out the closest safe house, where no one else would think to look for him and his new charge. And since Charing Cross Station was just south of Soho, he headed north toward the Tunstells' apartments, in all their pastel glory.

While midnight was considered quite an acceptable hour for calling among members of the supernatural set and among the younger, more dashing mortal crowd—drivers of phaetons and the like—dawn was *not*. In fact, dawn might be considered the rudest time for anyone to call upon anyone else, with the possible exception of groups of hardy fishermen in the backwaters of Portsmouth.

But Lyall felt he had no choice. As it was, he had to bang on the door a good five minutes or so before a bleary young maid opened it cautiously.

"Yes?"

Beyond the maid, Lyall saw a head stick out of a bedroom far down the hall—Mrs. Tunstell in an outrageous sleeping cap that resembled nothing so much as a frothy lace-covered mushroom. "What has happened? Are we on fire? Has someone died?"

Professor Lyall, still carrying Biffy in wolf form, muscled his way past the astonished maid and into the house. "You might put it like that, Mrs. Tunstell."

"My goodness, Professor Lyall! What do you have there?" The head disappeared. "Tunny! Tunny! Wake up. Professor Lyall is here with a dead dog. Arise at once. Tunny!" She came bustling down the hallway wrapped in a voluminous robe of eye-searing pink satin. "Oh, the poor lamb, bring him in here."

"Please do forgive me for the presumption, Mrs. Tunstell, but yours was the nearest house." He lay Biffy down on the small lavender couch and quickly reached behind it to draw the curtains over the window, just as the sun's first rays peeked above the horizon. Biffy's previously still form stiffened and then began to shudder and convulse.

Throwing all decorum to the winds, Professor Lyall rushed at Ivy, got one arm firmly about her waist, and hustled her to the door. "Best you not be here for this, Mrs. Tunstell. Send in your husband, would you, once he awakens?"

Ivy opened and closed her mouth a couple of times like an affronted poodle, and then whirled to do as he had bidden. There was a woman, Lyall thought, forced into efficiency through prolonged exposure to Alexia Tarabotti.

"Tunny!" she called, trotting back down the hallway, and then with far greater sharpness, "Ormond Tunstell, wake up. Do!"

Professor Lyall closed the door and turned back to his charge. He reached into his waistcoat for one of his trusty handkerchiefs, only then remembering he was wearing no more than a greatcoat, retrieved from the shore, having dressed for change, not company. Wincing at his own temerity, he grabbed one of Ivy's pastel throw pillows and wedged a corner of it into the new werewolf's mouth, giving Biffy something to bite down upon and also muffling his whimpering. Then Lyall bent low, bracing the shuddering form of the wolf with his own body, curling about him tenderly. It was partly Beta instinct, to protect a new member of the pack, but it was also sympathy. The first time was always the worst, not because it got any better, but because it was so unfamiliar an experience.

Tunstell let himself into the room.

"God's teeth, Professor, what is going on?"

"Too much to explain fully right now, I'm afraid. Can that wait until later? I've got a new pup on my hands and no Alpha to handle him. Do you have any raw meat in the house?"

"The wife ordered steak, delivered only yesterday." Tunstell left without needing to be pressed further.

Lyall smiled. The redhead fell so easily back into his old role of claviger, doing what needed to be done for the werewolves around him.

Biffy's chocolate fur was beginning to retreat up to the top of his head, showing skin now pale with immortality. His eyes were losing their yellow hue in favor of blue. Clutching that writhing form, Lyall could feel as well as hear Biffy's bones breaking and re-forming. It was a long and agonizing shift. It would take the young man decades to master any level of competency. Rapidity and smoothness were markers of both dominance and age.

Lyall held Biffy the entire time. Held him while Tunstell returned with a large raw steak and fussed about with varying degrees of helpfulness. Held him until, eventually, he was left with an armful of nothing but naked Biffy, shivering and looking most forlorn.

"What? Where?" The young dandy pushed weakly against the Beta's arms. His nose was twitching as though he needed to sneeze. "What is going on?"

Professor Lyall relaxed his embrace and sat back on his heels next to the couch. Tunstell came over with a blanket and a concerned expression. Just before he covered the young man over, Lyall was pleased to notice that Biffy appeared to be entirely healed from the bullet wound, a true supernatural, indeed.

"Who are *you*?" Biffy focused fuzzily on Tunstell's bright red hair.

"I'm Tunstell. Used to be a claviger to Lord Maccon. Now I'm mostly just an actor."

"He is our host and a friend. We will be safe here for the day." Professor Lyall kept his voice low and calm, tucking the blanket about the still-shivering young man.

"Is there some reason we need to be? Safe, I mean."

"How much do you remember?" Lyall swept a lock of brown hair back behind Biffy's ear in a motherly fashion. Despite all his transformations, his nudity, and his beard, the young man still looked every inch the dandy. He would make an odd addition to the gruff soldiering masculinity of the Woolsey Pack.

Biffy jerked and fear flooded into his eyes. "Extermination mandate! I found out that there is a . . . Oh, dear God, I was supposed to report in! I missed the appointment with my lord." He made as if to try and rise.

Lyall held him back easily.

Biffy turned on him frantically. "You don't understand—he'll swarm if I don't make it back. He knew I was going after the potentate. How could I have gotten caught? I'm such an imbecile. I know better than that. Why, he'll . . ." He trailed off. "How long was I down there?"

Lyall sighed. "He did swarm."

"Oh, no." Biffy's face fell. "All that work, all those agents pulled out of covert placement. It'll take years to reintegrate them. He's going to be so very disappointed in me."

Lyall tried to distract him. "So, what do you remember?"

"I remember being trapped under the Thames and thinking I would never escape." Biffy brushed one hand over his face. "And that I really needed a shave. Then I remember water flooding in and waking in the darkness to shouting and gunshots. And then I remember a lot of pain."

"You were dying." Lyall paused, searching for the right words. Here he was, hundreds of years old, and he could not explain to one boy why he had been changed against his will.

"Was I? Well, good thing that didn't take. My lord would never forgive me if I up and died without asking permission first." Biffy sniffed, suddenly distracted. "Something smells amazing."

Professor Lyall gestured to the plate of raw steak sitting nearby.

Biffy tilted his head to see, then looked back at Lyall in confusion. "But it's not cooked. Why does it smell so good?"

Lyall cleared his throat. As a Beta, he'd never had to perform this particular task. It was the Alpha's job to acclimatize the newly turned, the Alpha's job to explain and be there and be strong and be, well, Alphaish for a new pup. But Lord Maccon was halfway to Dover by now, and Lyall was left to deal with this mess without him.

"You know that dying issue I just mentioned? Well, it did take, in its way."

At which juncture, Professor Lyall had to watch those beautiful blue eyes turn from dazed confusion to horrified realization. It was one of the saddest things he had ever seen in all his long life.

At a loss, Lyall handed Biffy the plate of raw steak.

Unable to control himself, the young dandy tore into the meat, gulping it down in elegant, but very rapid, bites.

For the sake of his dignity, both Professor Lyall and Tunstell pretended not to notice that Biffy was crying the entire time. Tears dribbled down his nose and onto the steak while he chewed, and swallowed, and chewed, and sobbed.

The preceptor's picnic, as it turned out, was a little more elaborate than Alexia and Madame Lefoux had been led to believe. They trundled a sizable distance into the countryside, away from Florence in the direction of Borgo San Lorenzo, arriving eventually at an archaeological excavation. While the antiquated carriage attempted to park on a hillock, their Templar host announced with much pride that they would be engaging in an Etruscan tomb picnic.

The site was lovely, shaded with trees of various bushy Mediterranean inclinations that took being leafy and green quite seriously. Alexia stood up while the carriage maneuvered around, the better to take in her surroundings.

"Do sit down, Alexia! You shall fall, and then how will I explain to Floote that you had—" Madame Lefoux stopped herself before she inadvertently mentioned Alexia's unfortunate condition in front of the preceptor, but it was clear her worry was largely for the child's safety.

Alexia ignored her.

They were surrounded by a series of tombs: low, circular, and grass covered, almost organic in appearance, quite unlike anything Alexia had ever seen or read about. Never having visited anything more stimulating than a Roman bathhouse, Alexia was practically bouncing with excitement—if a lady once more corseted and trussed up to the height of proper British fashion and encumbered by both parasol and pregnancy could be described as "bouncing." She sat down abruptly when their carriage went over a bump.

Alexia refused, on principle, to admit that her new high spirits were on account of Conall's printed apology, but the world certainly seemed a far more fascinating place today than it had yesterday.

"Do you know anything of these *Etruscans*?" she whispered to Madame Lefoux.

"Only that they came before the Romans."

"Were they supernaturally based or a daylight exclusive society?" Alexia asked the next most important question.

The preceptor overheard her.

"Ah, My Soulless One, you ask one of the most troublesome questions of the great Etruscan mystery. Our historians, they continue to investigate this matter. I did think, however, that given your peculiar skill set, you might . . ." He trailed off meaningfully as though intentionally leaving the thought unfinished.

"Well, my dear Mr. Templar, I fail to see how I could possibly be of assistance. I am no trained antiquarian. The only thing I can identify with any consistency is my own kind. I—" It was Alexia's turn to leave a thought unfinished, as she realized the implications of his statement. "You believe there might be a preternatural focus to this culture? How remarkable."

The Templar only shrugged. "We have seen the rise and fall of many great empires in the past, some run by vampires, others by were-wolves."

"And some that have been founded upon the persecution of both." Alexia was thinking of the Catholic Inquisition, an expurgation movement the Templars were rumored to have taken a keen and active interest in promoting.

"But never yet have we found evidence of a civilization built to incorporate your kind."

"As difficult as that kind of proximity might be?" Alexia was puzzled.

"Why do you think the Etruscans might be the exception?" Madame Lefoux asked.

The coach stopped and the preceptor stepped down. He did not offer Alexia a hand, allowing Madame Lefoux to jump out and take over that dubious honor. Some distance away, the Templar cavalry dismounted as well and stood about as though waiting for orders. The preceptor gave them one of those hand signals, and the men relaxed into a casual milling group. The silent efficiency was unsettling, to say the least.

"Don't say much, do they?"

The preceptor turned his emotionless eyes on Alexia. "Would you ladies prefer to explore or eat first?"

"Explore," said Alexia promptly. She was wildly curious to see the inside of the strange round tombs.

The preceptor led them down into the dry, dim interior of the already cracked tomb. The underground walls were lined with limestone. Steps led into a single chamber, not much bigger than Alexia's drawing room back at Woolsey Castle. The limestone was elaborately carved to look like the inside of a house, with nooks, stone columns, and even ceiling beams picked out in the sandy, porous rock. It was the interior of a home, frozen in stone. Alexia was reminded of the elaborate jelly sculptures she had eaten at fancy dinner parties, made of aspic and formed with the aid of a mold.

There was no furniture, nor any other artifacts inside the tomb, the sole object being an extremely large sarcophagus in the center of the room. On the top lay two full-sized clay figures: a man lounging on his side and leaning up on one elbow behind a woman doing the same, his free arm draped affectionately over her shoulder.

It was a lovely sculpture, but despite what the preceptor had said, Alexia experienced no sense of repulsion, no feeling about the place that she would have expected when in the presence of a preserved pre-ternatural body. Either there was none present, or the remains had long since decomposed beyond effectiveness. The Templar was staring at her, monitoring her reactions closely. Face impassive, she walked about, self-conscious under his dead-eyed scrutiny, examining some painted images on the walls.

The place smelled musty, in the same way that old books do, only with an overlay of dirt and cold stone. But there was nothing there that engendered any adverse reaction in Alexia. In fact, she found the an-cient abode quite comforting and restful. She was glad of this. She would hate to have to hide her instinct to run if there *had* been some kind of preternatural mummy in residence.

"I am sorry to say, Mr. Templar, I do not think I can be of any help. I do not even see why one might associate this culture with my kind."

The preceptor looked disappointed.

Madame Lefoux, who had been watching him while he watched her friend, turned sharply to stare down at the sarcophagus.

"What were they holding?" she asked.

Alexia wandered over to see what Madame Lefoux was on about. She was struck by the pleasantness in the almond-shaped eyes of the statues, but upon looking closer, she realized what it was that had drawn Madame Lefoux's attention. The man was leaning on the elbow of one arm, the hand of which was up and flat as though offering a car-rot to a horse. His other hand, behind the woman's neck, had thumb and forefinger curved in the act of holding some small object. The woman had both hands curved in such a way as one might pour liba-tions or offer up a flask of wine.

"Good question."

Both ladies turned to look at the preceptor inquiringly.

"The woman held an empty ceramic flask, its contents long since dried and evaporated into aether. The man was offering a piece of meat on his open palm. The archaeologists found an animal bone resting there. He was holding something very strange in his other hand."

"What was that?"

The Templar shrugged and fished about his high collar with one finger, finally pulling out a chain that was around his neck. Carefully he lifted it out from underneath nightgown, jacket, waistcoat, and shirt. All three of them moved toward the light streaming down from the entrance. A small gold charm dangled from the end of the chain. Alexia and Madame Lefoux bent to examine it.

"An ankh?" Alexia blinked in amusement.

"From Ancient Egypt?" Madame Lefoux arched one perfect black eyebrow.

"Were the two cultures chronologically comparable?" Alexia scrabbled to remember the dates of Egyptian expansion.

"It is possible they had some form of contact, but it is more likely that this little object came into Etruscan hands through trade with the Greeks."

Alexia studied the small piece of gold closely but, uncharacteristically, pursed her lips and said nothing. She found it odd that an Etruscan statue would offer up the Egyptian symbol for eternal life, and while, to be sure, she had many theories on the subject, she was unwilling to share them with a Templar.

The preceptor tucked his charm away when neither lady had anything further to say and led the way back up the limestone stairs and out onto the sun-dappled hillside. The other tombs were much the same, only in not quite such good repair.

The picnic that followed was an uncomfortably silent affair. Alexia, Madame Lefoux, and the preceptor were seated on a square of quilted gingham spread atop the tomb while the other Templars enjoyed their own meal a short distance away. One of the Templars did not eat, but instead read from the Bible in lugubrious tones. The preceptor seemed to feel this was an excuse not to engage in any conversation with his two companions.

Alexia ate an apple, two rolls of crunchy bread spread with some kind of tomato sauce, and three hard-boiled eggs dipped in more of the green stuff that had so delighted her the day before.

With meal finished and Bible put away, the party prepared to leave. There was one benefit to picnicking, Alexia realized. As she had used no utensils, nothing needed to be destroyed because of contamination.

"It is not a bad life we lead here, is it, My Soulless One?" The preceptor spoke to her at last.

Alexia was forced to admit that it didn't appear so. "Italy *is* a lovely country. And I cannot fault your cuisine or climate."

"You are—how do I say this politely—unwelcome back in England?"

Alexia was going to correct him and boast of Conall's public apology but then thought better of it. Instead she said, "That is a very diplomatic way of putting it, Mr. Templar."

The preceptor smiled his horrible cheerless grimace. "Perhaps, My Soulless One, you might consider staying here with us, then? It has been a long time since we of the temple at Florence had a preternatural in residence, let alone a female of the species. We would make sure of your every comfort while we studied you. Provide for you your own, more isolated quarters."

Alexia's face soured as she thought back to her unfortunate encounter with Dr. Siemons and the Hypocras Club. "I have entertained such an offer before."

The Templar tilted his head, watching her.

Since he seemed, once more, to be in a chatty frame of mind, Alexia asked, "You would put up with devil spawn permanently in your midst?"

"We have done so before. We of the brotherhood are God's best weapon against the supernatural threat. We were made to do what needed to be done no matter what the cost or personal risk. You could be very useful to our cause."

"Goodness gracious, I had no idea I was that appealing." Alexia waggled her eyebrows suggestively.

Madame Lefoux joined the conversation. "If that is the case, why are you not equally welcoming to werewolves and vampires?"

"Because they are not born daemons. To be born with the eternal sin is not much more than to be born with original sin. The soulless suffer, as we all do, under the metaphorical cross, only for them there is no salvation. The vampires and werewolves, on the other hand, have chosen their path voluntarily. It is a matter of *intention*. They have turned their backs on salvation in a way far more reprehensible, because they once had excess soul. *They* could have ascended into heaven had they only resisted Satan's temptation. Instead, they traded the bulk of their soul to the devil and became monsters. They are offensive to God, for only he and his angels are allowed immortality." He spoke calmly, with no emotion, no inflection, and no doubt.

Alexia felt chilled. "Which is why you wish to see all supernatural folk dead?"

"It is our eternal crusade."

Alexia did some calculations. "Over four hundred years or so. Commendably committed of you all."

"A God-sanctioned purpose, to hunt and kill." Madame Lefoux's tone was full of censure, not unsurprising given her choices in life—she was a creator, an engineer, and a builder.

The preceptor looked from the Frenchwoman to Alexia. "And what do you think *her* God-given purpose is, Scientist Lefoux—a soulless creature whose only skill is in neutralizing the supernatural? Do you think she was not placed on this earth as a tool? We can give her purpose, even if she is only a female."

"Now, wait just a minute there!" Alexia remembered once complaining to Conall, before their marriage, that she wanted something useful to do with her life. Queen Victoria had made her muhjah, but even with that gone, killing vampires and werewolves for a sect of religious fanatics was not precisely what she had been hoping for.

"Have you any idea how rare you are, a female of the species?"

"I am beginning to get the impression that I am more rare than I had thought." Alexia looked about suddenly, feigning physical discomfort. "Do you think I might visit a convenient bush, before we depart for the long drive back?"

The Templar looked equally discomforted. "If you insist."

Alexia tugged at Madame Lefoux's sleeve and dragged her off behind the tomb and down the side of the hill a little ways to a small copse of trees.

"It took Angelique this way," commented Madame Lefoux, referring to her former lover. "During her pregnancy, she always had to . . . well . . . you know."

"Oh, no, that was merely a ruse. I wanted to discuss something with you. That ankh around his neck, did you notice that it had been repaired?"

Madame Lefoux shook her head. "Is that significant, do you think?"

Alexia had never told Madame Lefoux about the mummy nor the broken ankh symbol. But in her experience, it was the hieroglyphic sign of a preternatural.

So she quickly moved on. "I think the terra-cotta man in the tomb was a preternatural, and the woman was a vampire, and the offering of meat was for the werewolves."

"A harmonious culture? Is that possible?"

"It would be terribly arrogant of us British to think England was the first and only progressive society." Alexia was worried. If the Templars comprehended the significance of the ankh, she was in more danger than she had thought. They would find a way to turn her into a tool, living or dead.

"I do hope Floote managed to send that message to BUR."

"Love note to your werewolf?" Madame Lefoux sounded wistful. Then she looked about the empty hillside, suddenly nervous. "I think, my dear Alexia, we should head back to the carriage."

Alexia, enjoying the countryside and the intellectual advantages afforded by their ancient surroundings, had not registered the lateness of the hour. "Ah, yes, you may be correct."

It was, unfortunately, well into nighttime before they were even halfway back to Florence. Alexia felt awfully exposed in the open-topped carriage. She kept her parasol close and began to wonder if this whole excursion was not an attempt by the Templars to use her as some kind of bait. After all, they fancied themselves great supernatural hunters and might very well risk her safety simply to draw local vampires out. Especially if the Templars had enough foolish pride in their own abilities to believe there was little true peril. The moon was just rising, no longer entirely full but still quite bright. In its silvery light, Alexia could make out a gleam of anticipation in the preceptor's normally emotionless eyes. *You rotten sod, this was all a setup,* she was about to say, but too late.

The vampire appeared out of nowhere, leaping with exceptional speed from the dirt road into the carriage. He was single-minded in his attack, heading straight for Alexia, the only apparent female of the group. Madame Lefoux gave a yell of warning, but Alexia had already thrown herself forward onto the open seat opposite her own, next to the preceptor. The vampire ended up where she had just been sitting. Alexia fumbled with her parasol, twisting the handle so that the two sharp spikes, one wood and one silver, sprang out from its tip.

The preceptor, suddenly brandishing a long, evil-looking wooden knife, gave a yell of pleasure and attacked. Madame Lefoux had her trusty cravat pin already out and in play. Alexia swung her parasol, but all were merely normal humans pitted against superhuman strength, and even fighting off multiple bodies in the awkwardly tiny venue of an open-topped carriage, the vampire was holding his own.

The preceptor dove forward. He was grinning—a real smile for the first time. Maniacal, but real.

Alexia took a firm grip on her parasol with both hands and used a hacking blow to stab with the wooden spike at any part of the vampire that emerged from the wrestling match long enough for her to pin it down. It was a little like trying to hit the heads of ground moles as they appeared out of their holes. But soon enough, Alexia was getting quite into the game of it.

"Touch it!" yelled the preceptor at Alexia. "Touch it so I can kill it."

The preceptor was an excellent fighter, for he was single-minded in his attempt to drive his wooden weapon into the creature's heart or some other vital organ. But he was simply not fast enough, even when Madame Lefoux came to his aid. Madame Lefoux got in a couple of wicked strikes to the vampire's face with her cravat pin, but the cuts began to heal almost as soon as she had delivered them. With the air of one swatting at an irritating bug, the vampire casually backhanded the inventor with a closed fist. She fell hard against the inside of the carriage and then slumped inelegantly to the floor, eyes closed, mouth slack, and mustache fallen entirely off.

Before Alexia had a chance to react, the vampire managed to heave the Templar up and forward. He hurled the preceptor against the driver so that both fell out of the carriage into the country lane below.

The horses, spooked into screams of panic, took off in a crazed gallop, surging forward, straining against their traces in a most alarming manner. Alexia tried to maintain her footing in the wildly pitching carriage. The four cavalry Templars, who had almost caught up to the ruckus, were left behind in a cloud of swirling dust kicked up by frantic hooves.

The vampire lunged toward Alexia again. Alexia took a firm grip on her parasol and gritted her teeth. Really, she was getting very tired of these constant bouts of fisticuffs. One would think she was a boxer down at Whites! The vampire lunged. Alexia swung. But he batted the parasol away and was upon her, hands wrapped around her neck.

He sneezed. *Aha,* thought Alexia, *the garlic!*

When he touched her, his fangs vanished and his strength became that of an ordinary human. She saw in his beautiful brown eyes a look of surprise. He may have known what she was intellectually but had clearly not experienced the sensation of preternatural touch before. Yet his fingers tightened inexorably around Alexia's throat. He might be mortal but he was still strong enough to strangle her, no matter how she kicked and struggled.

I'm not ready to die, thought Alexia. *I haven't yelled at Conall yet.* And then she thought about the baby really as a baby and not an inconvenience for the very first time. We're *not ready to die.*

She heaved upward, pushing the vampire up and off.

And just then, something white hit the vampire crosswise so hard that Alexia heard bones breaking—after all, the vampire *was* currently quite mortal and lacking any supernatural defenses. The vampire screamed in surprise and pain.

The hit broke his hold around her neck, and Alexia stumbled back, panting hard, eyes fixed on her former attacker.

The white thing resolved itself into the frenzied figure of a massive wolf, growling and thrashing against the vampire in a whirlwind of teeth and claws and blood. The two supernatural creatures scrabbled together, werewolf strength against vampire speed, while Alexia pushed herself and her parasol back into one corner of the seat, protectively shielding Madame Lefoux's fallen form from claws, teeth, and fangs.

The wolf had the advantage, having attacked while the vampire was rendered vulnerable through preternatural contact, and he never lost it. In very short order, he wrapped his powerful jaws about the vampire's neck, sinking his teeth into the man's throat. The vampire gave a gurgling howl, and the smell of rotten blood filled the fresh country air.

Alexia caught a flash of ice-blue eyes as the wolf gave her one meaningful look before he hurled both himself and the vampire out of the moving carriage, hitting the ground with a tremendous thud. The sound of their battle continued but was rapidly lost in the clattering of hooves as the horses raced onward.

Alexia realized it must have been the scent of the wolf that initially panicked the horses. It was now up to her to slow them down before the terrified creatures broke their traces or overturned the carriage, or worse.

She scrambled up onto the driver's box, only to find that the reins had fallen forward and were hanging down near the shackle, perilously close to the kicking hind legs of the horses. She lay, belly down over the box, holding on with one hand and desperately reaching with the other. No luck. Seized with an inspiration, she retrieved her parasol. It still had the two spikes sticking out from its tip, and she managed to use those to catch the dangling reins and pull them sufficiently close to grasp. Victorious, she only then remembered she had never actually driven a carriage before. Figuring it couldn't be too difficult, she tried a gentle tug backward on the reins.

Absolutely nothing changed. The horses continued their mad dash.

Alexia took a firmer grip with both hands and yanked backward, leaning back and applying all her weight. She was not as strong as a gentleman of the Corinthian set might be, but she probably weighed about the same. The sudden pressure caused the animals to slow, first to a canter and then to trot, sides heaving and flanks lathered with sweat.

Alexia decided there was no point in stopping entirely and kept the horses headed back into the city. It was probably better to attain the relative safety of the temple as quickly as possible in case the rest of that vampire's hive were also after her.

Two of the mounted Templars, white nightgowns floating becomingly in the breeze about them, finally caught up. They took up position, one to either side of the carriage, and without acknowledging or even looking at her, proceeded to act as escort.

"Do you think we might just pause and check on Madame Lefoux?" Alexia asked, but no verbal response was garnered. One of the men actually looked at her, but then he turned aside and spat as if his mouth had been filled with something distasteful. Fear for her friend's well-being notwithstanding, Alexia decided that getting to safety was probably most important. She glanced at her two stony-faced escorts once more. Nothing. So she shrugged and clucked the horses into a more enthusiastic trot. There had been four Templars on horseback originally. She assumed that of the other two, one went back for the fallen preceptor and the other was off hunting the vampire and the werewolf.

With nothing else to occupy her but idle speculation, Alexia wondered if this white werewolf was the same as the white creature she had seen from the ornithopter, the one that had attacked the vampires on Monsieur Trouvé's roof. There was something awfully familiar about those icy-blue eyes. With a start, she realized that the werewolf, the white beast, and the man in the mask at the customs station in Boboli Gardens were all the same person and that she knew him. Knew him and was, at the best of times, not particularly fond of him: her husband's arrogant third in command, Woolsey Pack's Gamma, Major Channing Channing of the Chesterfield Channings. She decided she'd been living too long with a werewolf pack if she could recognize him as a wolf in the middle of a battle when earlier, as the masked gentlemen, she had not been able to place him at all.

"He must have been following and protecting me since Paris!" She said out loud to the uninterested Templars, her voice cutting into the night.

They ignored her.

"And, of course, he couldn't help us that night on the Alpine pass because it was *full moon!*" Alexia wondered why her husband's third, whom neither she nor Conall particularly liked, was risking his life inside the borders of Italy to protect her. No werewolf with half a brain would voluntarily enter the stronghold of antisupernatural sentiment. Then again, there was some question, so far as Alexia was concerned, as to the extent of Channing's brains. There was really only one good explanation: Channing would be guarding her only if Lord Conall Maccon had ordered it.

Of course, her husband was an unfeeling prat who should have come after her himself. And, of course, he was also an annoying git for meddling in her business when he had taken such pains to separate it from his own. But the timing meant he still cared enough to bark out an order to see her safe, even before he had printed that apology.

He must still love her. *I think he might actually want us back,* she told the infant-inconvenience with a giddy sense of elation.

CHAPTER FOURTEEN

In Which the Infant-Inconvenience Becomes Considerably More Inconvenient

E ventually Biffy slept and Professor Lyall could afford to do the same. They were safe under the watchful eye of Tunstell, and then Mrs. Tunstell, if such a thing was to be imagined. The two werewolves dozed throughout the day and well into early evening. Eventually, Ivy went off to check on the hat shop, and Tunstell, who had rehearsals to attend, felt it safe enough to wake Lyall.

"I went to the butcher for more meat," he explained as the Beta sawed off a chunk of raw steak and popped it into his mouth.

Professor Lyall chewed. "So I taste. What's the word on the street, then?"

"It's very simple and baldly put, and everyone is talking about it. And I do mean *everyone*."

"Go on."

"The potentate is dead. You and the old wolf had a busy night last night, didn't you, Professor?"

Lyall put down his utensils and rubbed at his eyes. "Oh, my giddy aunt. What a mess he has left me with."

"One of Lord Maccon's defining characteristics, as I recall—messiness."

"Are the vampires very upset?"

"Why, Professor, are you trying to be sarcastic? That's sweet."

"Answer the question, Tunstell."

"None of them are out yet. Nor their drones. But the rumor is they find the situation not ideal, sir. Not ideal at all."

Professor Lyall stretched his neck to each side. "Well, I have been hiding out here long enough, I suppose. Time to face the fangs."

Tunstell struck a Shakespearean pose. "The fangs and canines of outrageous fortune!"

Professor Lyall gave him a dour look. "Something like."

The Beta stood and stretched, looking down at Biffy. The rest was doing him good. He looked if not healthier, at least less emaciated. His hair was matted with muck from the Thames, and his face was streaked with dirt and tears, but he still managed an air of dandified gentility. Lyall respected that in a man. Lord Akeldama had done his work well. Lyall respected that, too.

Without further ado, he swung the blanket-wrapped Biffy up into his arms and headed out into the busy London streets.

Floote was still out when Alexia pulled her panting horses to a stop at the door of the temple. Madame Lefoux was immediately whisked away to the infirmary, which left Alexia to make her way alone through the luxurious building. And, because she was Alexia, she made her way to the calm sanity of the library. Only in a library did she feel completely capable of collecting her finer feelings and recuperating from such a wearying day. It was also the only room she could remember how to get to.

In a desperate bid to cope with the violence of the attack, her discovery of Channing's presence in Italy, and her own unanticipated affection for the infant-inconvenience, Alexia extracted some of Ivy's precious tea. Quite resourcefully, she felt, she managed to boil water over the hearth fire using an empty metal snuffbox. She had to do without milk, but it was a small price to pay under the circumstances. She had no idea if the preceptor had yet returned, or even if he had survived, for as usual, no one spoke to her. With nothing else to do for the moment, Alexia sat in the library and sipped.

It was foolish of her not to realize that the all-pervading silence was not one of prayer but one of impending disaster. Her first warning came in the form of a volatile four-legged duster that hurtled into the library, breaking the calm quiet with a bout of such crazed yipping that a lesser dog would have become ill at the effort.

"Poche? What are you doing here, you vile animal?" Alexia fiddled with her snuffbox of tea.

Apparently, Poche's current and sole desire in life was to launch a vicious attack on Alexia's chair leg, which he got his little teeth around and was gnawing on passionately.

Alexia contemplated whether she should attempt to shake him off, kick him with her foot, or simply disregard him entirely.

"Good evening, Female Specimen."

"Why, Mr. German Specimen, what an unexpected surprise. I thought you had been excommunicated. They let you back into Italy?"

Mr. Lange-Wilsdorf walked into the room, stroking his chin with the air of one who has suddenly acquired the upper hand and was reveling in the state of affairs. "I found myself in the possession of some, shall we call it, negotiating power, ya?"

"Ya?" Alexia was irritated enough to mimic him.

Mr. Lange-Wilsdorf came to stand near her, looking down. Which must be a particularly unusual experience for him given his diminutive stature, Alexia thought nastily.

"The Templars will, with the information I provided, convince His Holiness Pope Blessed Pius IX to repeal my excommunication and accept me back into the fold."

"Will they, indeed? I had no notion they possessed such influence."

"They possess many things, Female Specimen, many things."

"Well"—Alexia was suddenly quite nervous—"felicitations on your reintegration."

"I have my laboratory back," he continued proudly.

"Good, perhaps you can figure out how—"

The preceptor came into the library. Alexia stopped midsentence and looked him over, noticing bandages about his limbs and scrapes across his face. He was clearly a little worse for his encounter with the vampire and subsequent fall from the carriage.

"Ah, how are you feeling, Mr. Templar?"

Not bothering to answer, the preceptor came over, crossed his arms, and looked down at her as well. Eventually he spoke to her as though she were a recalcitrant child. "I am confused, My Soulless One."

"Oh, yes?"

"Yes. Why is it you chose not to inform us of your delicate condition? We would have taken far greater care of your person had we known of it."

Oh, mercy me. Alexia shifted, wary. She put down the snuffbox and grabbed her parasol. "Would you, indeed? Do you imply that you would not have, for example, used me as bait in a vampire trap?"

The preceptor ignored her barb. "Mr. Lange-Wilsdorf informs us that not only are you with child, but that the child's father is a werewolf. Is this—"

Alexia held up a commanding hand. "Do not even begin that line of questioning with me. My husband *is* a werewolf, and despite any and all accusations to the contrary, he is undoubtedly the father. I will neither argue nor tolerate any insinuations against my integrity. I may be soulless, gentlemen, but I assure you I am faithful. Even Conall, blast him, has finally admitted that."

The Templar snapped his mouth shut and nodded. She wasn't convinced that he believed her, but frankly she didn't care.

Mr. Lange-Wilsdorf rubbed his hands together. "Indeed, in conjunction with your insistence, I have devised a new theory as to the nature of soul that I believe not only supports but indeed *relies* upon your avowal that the child has a supernatural father."

"Are you saying the only way I could still be pregnant is if I were telling the truth?" Alexia felt her breath quicken in anticipation. *Vindication at last!*

"Well, ya, Female Specimen, precisely."

"Would you care to elaborate?"

The little German seemed a tad taken aback by her calm acceptance. He did not notice how one of Alexia's hands was now delicately fiddling with the handle of her parasol. She was also watching the Templar almost as closely as she watched him.

"You are not angry with me for the telling to the Templars of your little secret?"

Alexia was, but she pretended to be blasé. "Well, it was all over the London papers. I suppose they would have found out eventually. Still, you are a bit of a repulsive weasel, aren't you?"

"Perhaps. But if this theory is correct, I will also be a most famous weasel."

The Templar had taken a fascinated interest in Alexia's snuffbox full of tea and was examining it. Alexia gave him a narrow look, daring him to comment on her idiosyncratic solution to the fact that none of the temple staff would respond to any of her requests. He said nothing.

"Very well, tell me of this theory of yours. And would you mind, terribly, removing your dog from my chair?"

Mr. Lange-Wilsdorf swooped down and scooped up his energetic little animal. The creature immediately relaxed into a floppy, partly comatose state in his master's arms. Draping the dog over one arm as a footman would a dishtowel, Mr. Lange-Wilsdorf proceeded to use the beastie as a teaching tool for his explanation.

"Let us assume that there are certain particles in the human body that bond to ambient aether." He prodded at the dog with one finger unhelpfully. "I shall call these particles 'pneuma.'" He raised his poking finger into the air dramatically. "Supernaturals have broken this bond, losing most of their pneuma. They become immortal by reconfiguring what trace amounts of pneuma they have left into a *flexible* bond with ambient aetheric particles."

"You are saying that the soul is not a measurable substance after all, but is in fact the type and rigidity of this bond?" Alexia was intrigued despite herself, and she switched the bulk of her attention to the German.

Mr. Lange-Wilsdorf shook Poche at Alexia in his enthusiasm. "Ya! It is a brilliant theory, ya? It explains why we had no luck over the years measuring soul. There is nothing to measure—there is instead only type and strength of bond." He swooped the dog about the room as though flying. "You, Female Specimen, as a preternatural, are born with the pneuma but no bonded aether at all, thus you are always sucking the aetheric particles out of the air. What you do when you touch the supernatural creature is break their flexible bond and suck all the aether out of them, turning them mortal." He made a grasping motion with his hand over the dog's head, as though scooping out the little beast's brains.

"So, when the vampires called me a soul-sucker, they were not so far from the truth of it. But how does this explain the child?" Alexia attempted to refocus the little man on the most important part of his explanation.

"Well, the problem with two preternaturals is that they are both trying to suck aetheric particles at the same time. Thus they cannot share the same air space. But"—and in a triumphant crescendo, Mr. Lange-Wilsdorf held his little white dog over his head in victory—"if the other parent is a *supernatural,* the child can inherit the flexible bond, or as we might think of it, a bit of the leftover excess soul."

Poche gave a funny little howl as though to punctuate his owner's final statement. Realizing he was waving about his pet in a most indiscriminate manner, the German put his dog back down on the floor. Immediately, Poche began barking and bouncing about, eventually deciding to launch a full-blown attack on a small golden throw pillow that was now not long for this world.

Alexia hated to admit it, but Mr. Lange-Wilsdorf's theory was a sound one. It explained many things, not the least of which was why such children as the infant-inconvenience might be so very rare. Firstly, they required a supernatural to preternatural pairing, and the two species had hunted each other for most of recorded history. Secondly, they required either a female soulless, a female vampire, or a female werewolf. Preternaturals were rarely allowed near hive queens, and female werewolves were almost as rare as female preternaturals. There simply wouldn't have been much of an opportunity for interbreeding.

"So, the question is, what kind of child am I going to produce, given Conall's, uh, *flexible bond*?" Said in conjunction with her husband's

name, and considering his carnal preferences, Alexia found the terminology salacious. She cleared her throat, embarrassed. "I mean to say,
will it be born preternatural or supernatural?"

"Ah, ya, well, difficult to predict. But I am thinking, perhaps, in
my theory, that is to say, neither. The child, it could be simply normal.
Perhaps possessing less soul than most."

"But I will not lose it as you had previously thought?"

"No, no, you will not. If you are sensible with your own well-
being."

Alexia smiled. True, she was still not quite settled into the idea of
being a mother, but she and the infant-inconvenience did seem to be
arriving at some kind of arrangement.

"Why, that is superb news! I must go tell Genevieve immediately."
She stood, with every intention of dashing off to the infirmary, regardless of how this might upset any Templars she barreled into along the
way.

The preceptor stood up from his crouch, where he had been trying,
unsuccessfully, to wrestle the pillow away from Poche, and spoke.
Alexia had almost forgotten his presence. "I am afraid that will not be
possible, My Soulless One."

"Why not?"

"The French female was treated for her injuries and released into
the care of the Florentine Hospitallers."

"Were her injuries that serious?" Alexia felt a sudden pang of guilt.
Had she been enjoying snuffbox-scented tea and good news while her
friend lay dying?

"Oh, no, quite superficial. We simply found we could no longer offer her our hospitality. Mr. Floote as well was not invited to return and
stay with us."

Alexia felt her heart sink low into her chest, where it commenced a
particular variety of rapid thumping. The sudden reversal from what,
seconds before, might have been elation caused her to come over almost
dizzy. She breathed in sharply through her nose.

Almost without thought, she opened her parasol, prepared to use
even the sulfuric acid, undoubtedly the vilest of its armaments, if need
be. Madame Lefoux had managed to find some replacement fluids. But
before she had a chance to flip it around to the appropriate position, the
library door opened.

Summoned by some unseen signal, a ridiculously large number of
Templars clattered into the room. And they were *clattering,* for they
were fully armored like the knights of the crusades they had been hundreds of years ago—heads covered in helms and bodies in silver-washed

chain mail and plate under the obligatory nightgowns. Each had on a pair of heavy leather gloves, no doubt so they could touch Alexia without fear for their heavenly souls. Poche went absolutely crazy, barking at the top of his lungs and gyrating about the room in a succession of crazed leaps. Alexia thought it the most intelligent thing the creature had done in all its useless little life. The Templars, showing great reserves of dignity, entirely ignored him.

Alexia's parasol was good, but it wasn't good enough to take out that many people all at once. She closed it with a snap. "Why, Mr. Templar," she said to the preceptor, "I am honored. All this for me? So very thoughtful. You really shouldn't have."

The preceptor gave Alexia one hard, long look and then, taking Mr. Lange-Wilsdorf firmly by the arm, left the library without responding to her sarcasm. Poche circled the room twice more and then bounced out after them like a fierce feather duster ejected at high pressure from a steam engine. *My last defender, gone,* thought Alexia grimly.

She looked to her opponents. "Very well, then. Take me to your dungeon!" Might as well give a command she was reasonably confident would be obeyed.

Professor Lyall set his precious cargo down upon the sofa in his office at BUR headquarters. Still unconscious, Biffy was as limp as overcooked broccoli. The couch was already covered in various piles of paperwork, aethographor slates, a stack of books, and several newspapers and scientific pamphlets, but Biffy didn't seem to mind overly much. He curled onto one side like a little child, hugging an exceptionally uncomfortable-looking metal scroll affectionately to his chest.

Professor Lyall got to work preparing formal statements for the press, calling in various operatives and agents and then sending them back out again on important information-gathering missions, diplomatic interventions, and secret biscuit-acquisition operations (BUR's kitchen was running low). He also sent a runner to the remaining members of the Woolsey Pack, instructing them to stay alert and stay armed. Who knew how the vampires might choose to retaliate? Usually, they were refined in their reactions, but killing one of them was, as a rule, not considered polite, and they might behave unfavorably. After that, Lyall managed one productive hour of activity before he was interrupted by the first in what he had no doubt would be a long line of offended dignitaries. It was not, however, a member of one of the hives come to complain about the potentate's death. Rather unexpectedly, his first caller was a werewolf.

"Good evening, Lord Slaughter."

The dewan hadn't bothered with a cloak this time. With no disguise and no attempt made to hide his displeasure, either, Lyall had no doubt the dewan was officially representing Queen Victoria's interests.

"Well, you made a dog's bollocks of that, didn't you, little Beta? Couldn't have done worse with it when all's said and done."

"How do you do, my lord? Please, sit down."

The dewan gave a disgusted look at the slumbering Biffy. "Looks like you already have company. What is he—drunk?" He sniffed the air. "Oh, for goodness' sake, have you both been swimming in the Thames?"

"I assure you it was entirely involuntary."

The dewan looked as though he was about to continue his reprimanding tone, but then he sniffed the air again and stopped in his tracks. Twirling about, he lumbered over to the couch and bent over the comatose young dandy.

"Now, that is an unfamiliar face. I know most of the Woolsey Pack has been overseas with the regiment, but I think I remember them all. I am not *that* old."

"Ah, yes." Professor Lyall sat up straight and cleared his throat. "We are to be congratulated. Woolsey has a new pack member."

The dewan grunted, half pleased but trying to hide it with annoyance. "I thought he stank of Lord Maccon. Well, well, well, a metamorphosis and a dead vampire all in one night. My, my, Woolsey has been busy."

Professor Lyall put down his quill and took off his spectacles. "The one is, in fact, tied intimately to the other."

"Since when has killing vampires resulted in new werewolves?"

"Since vampires stole other vampire's drones, imprisoned them under the Thames, and then shot at them."

The dewan looked less like a gruff loner wolf and more like a politician at that statement. He drew up a chair on the other side of the desk from Lyall. "I think you had better start explaining what happened, little Beta."

When Lyall finished his account, the dewan was left looking a mite stunned.

"Of course, such a story will have to be corroborated. With the potentate's illegal kill order out on Lady Maccon's head, you must see that Lord Maccon's motives for killing the man are highly suspicious. Still, if all you say is true, he was within his rights as chief sundowner. Such shenanigans cannot be allowed. Imagine, stealing someone else's drone! So rude."

"You must understand I have other difficulties to deal with?"

"Went off hunting that stray wife of his, did he?"

Professor Lyall curled his lip and nodded.

"Alphas are so very difficult."

"My feeling exactly."

"Well, I shall leave you to it." The dewan stood but walked once more over to look down at Biffy before he left.

"Two successful metamorphoses in as many months. Woolsey may be in political trouble, but you are to be congratulated on the potency of your Alpha's Anubis Form. Pretty young pup, isn't he? He is going to bring down a whole mess of trouble on your head. How much worse will it be to have the vampires think werewolves stole a drone away?"

Professor Lyall sighed. "Lord Akeldama's favorite, no less."

The dewan shook his head. "Mess of trouble, mark my words. Best of luck, little Beta. You are going to need it."

Just as the dewan was leaving, one of Lord Maccon's best BUR agents appeared.

The agent bowed to the dewan in the doorway before coming in to stand in front of Professor Lyall, with his hands laced behind his back.

"Report, Mr. Haverbink."

" 'S'not pretty out there, sir. The Teeth are a'stirring up all kinds of toss about you Tails. Them's saying Lord M had a grudge against the potentate. Saying he took him down out'a anger, not duty."

Haverbink was a good solid chap in both looks and spirit. And no one would bet a ha'penny on his having excess soul, but he listened well and got around to places more aristocratic types couldn't. He looked a bit like a farmhand, and people didn't give a man of his brawn much credit in the way of brain. It was a mistake.

"How unsettled?"

"Couple of pub brawls so far, mostly just clavigers giving fist to drones with big mouths. Could get ugly if the conservatives weigh in. You're knowing how they can get: 'none of this would've happened if we hadn't integrated. England deserves it for acting unnatural. Against God's law.' Whine, whine."

"Any word on the vampires themselves?"

"Westminster queen's been dead silent—'scuse the pun—since word on the potentate's death broke. You better believe if she thought she were in the right, she'd be squawking official statements to the press like a hen laying eggs."

"Yes, I would tend to agree with you. Her silence is a good thing for us werewolves. How about BUR's reputation?"

"We're taking the fallout. Lord M was working, not werewolfing, or that's the claim. He should've had more self-restraint." Haverbink turned his wide, friendly face on his commander questioningly.

Lyall nodded.

Haverbink continued. "Those that like BUR are claiming he was within his rights as sundowner. Those that don't like it, don't like him, and don't like wolves—they're going to complain regardless. Not a whole lot would change that."

Lyall rubbed at his neck. "Well, that's about what I thought. Keep talking the truth as much as possible while you are out there. Let people know the potentate stole Lord Akeldama's drone. We cannot allow the vampires or the Crown to cover that up, and we have got to hope both Biffy and Lord Akeldama corroborate the official story or we really will be in the thick of it."

Haverbink looked skeptically over at Biffy's sleeping form. "Does he remember any of it?"

"Probably not."

"Is Lord Akeldama likely to be amenable?"

"Probably not."

"Right'o, sir. I wouldn't want to be in your spats right now."

"Don't get personal, Haverbink."

" 'Course not, sir."

"Speaking of which, still no word on Lord Akeldama's return or whereabouts?"

"Not a single sausage, sir."

"Well, that's something. Very well, carry on, Mr. Haverbink."

"Jolly good, sir."

Haverbink went out, and the next agent, waiting patiently in the hallway, came in.

"Message for you, sir."

"Ah, Mr. Phinkerlington."

Phinkerlington, a round, bespectacled metal burner, managed a slight bow before continuing hesitatingly into the room. He had the manners of a clerk, the demeanor of a constipated mole, and some minor aristocratic connection that temperament compelled him to regard as an embarrassing character flaw. "Something finally came through on that Italian channel you had me monitoring sunset these past few days." He was also very, very good at his job, which consisted mainly of sitting and listening, and then writing down what he heard without thought or comment.

Professor Lyall sat up. "Took you long enough to get it to me."

"Sorry, sir. You've been so busy this evening; I didn't want to disturb."

"Yes, well." Professor Lyall made an impatient gesture with his left hand.

Phinkerlington handed Professor Lyall a scrap of parchment paper, on which had been inked a message. It was not, as Lyall had hoped, from Alexia but was from, of all people, Floote.

It was also so entirely off topic and unhelpful to the situation in hand as to give Lyall a brief but intense feeling of exasperation with Lady Maccon. This was a feeling that had, heretofore, been reserved solely for his Alpha.

"Get queen to stop Italians excavating in Egypt. Can't find soulless mummies, bad things result. Lady Maccon with Florentine Templars. Not good. Send help. Floote."

Professor Lyall, cursing his Alpha for departing so precipitously, balled up the piece of paper and, after minor consideration for the delicacy of the information it contained, ate it.

He dismissed Phinkerlington, stood, and went to check on Biffy, finding the young man still sleeping. *Good,* he thought, *best and most sensible thing for him to be doing at the moment.* Just as he was tucking the blanket a little more firmly about the new werewolf, yet another person entered his office.

He straightened up and turned to face the door. "Yes?"

He caught the man's scent: very expensive French perfume coupled with a hint of Bond Street's best hair pomade and under that the slow richness of the unpalatable—old blood.

"Ah. Welcome back to London, Lord Akeldama."

Lady Alexia Maccon, sometimes called La Diva Tarabotti, was quite comfortable with being abducted. Or, as it might better be phrased, she was growing accustomed to the predicament. She had led, up until a little over a year ago, quite an exemplary spinsterish existence. Her world had been plagued only by the presence of two nonsensical sisters and one even sillier mama. Her concerns, it must be acknowledged, were a tad mundane, and her daily routine as banal as that of any other young lady of sufficient income and insufficient liberty. But she *had* managed to avoid abductions.

This, as matters would have it, was turning out to be one of the worst.

Alexia found the experience of being blindfolded and carried over someone's armor-clad shoulder like a sack of potatoes unconscionably undignified. She was hauled down a seemingly endless series of stairs and passageways, musty as only the deep underground can be. She gave a few experimental kicks and a wiggle, only to have her legs clamped down by a metal-covered arm.

Eventually, they arrived at their final destination, which, she discovered once the blindfold had been removed, was some kind of Roman catacomb. She blinked, eyes adjusting to the dimness, and found herself in an underground ancient ruin dug into the bedrock, lit with oil lamps and candles. The small cell she now occupied was barred over on one side with modern-looking reinforcements.

"Well, this is a much inferior living situation," she objected to no one in particular.

The preceptor appeared in the doorway, leaning up against the metal doorjamb, regarding her with lifeless eyes.

"We found we could no longer adequately ensure your safety in your other location."

"I wasn't safe in a temple surrounded by several hundred of the Knights Templars, the most powerful holy warriors ever to walk this earth?"

He made no answer to that. "We shall see to your every comfort here."

Alexia looked around. The room was slightly smaller than her husband's dressing chamber back at Woolsey Castle. There was a tiny bed in one corner covered in a faded quilt, a single side table with an oil lamp, a chamber pot, and a washstand. It looked neglected and sad.

"Who will? No one has so far."

Wordlessly the Templar signaled and, out of nowhere, a bread bowl full of pasta appeared, and a carrot carved to resemble a spoon was handed over by some unseen companion. The preceptor gave them to Alexia.

Alexia tried not to be pleased by the presence of the ubiquitous green sauce. "Pesto will keep you in my good graces for only so long, you understand?"

"Oh, and then what will you do, devil spawn?"

"Ah, I am no longer your 'Soulless One,' am I?" Alexia pursed her lips in deep thought. She was without her parasol, and most of her best threats involved its application. "I shall be *very* discourteous, indeed."

The preceptor did not look at all threatened. He closed the door firmly behind him and left her locked in the silent darkness.

"Could I at least get something to read?" she yelled after, but he ignored her.

Alexia began to think all those horrible stories she had heard about the Templars might actually be true, even the one with the rubber duck and the dead cat that Lord Akeldama had once relayed. She hoped fervently that Madame Lefoux and Floote were unharmed.

There was something eerie about being so utterly separated from them.

Giving in to her frustration, Alexia marched over and kicked at the bars of her prison.

This only served to cause her foot to smart most egregiously.

"Oh, brother," said Lady Maccon into the dark silence.

Alexia's isolation did not last long, for a certain German scientist came to visit her.

"I have been relocated, Mr. Lange-Wilsdorf." Alexia was so distressed by her change in circumstances that she was moved to state the obvious.

"Ya, Female Specimen, I am well aware of the fact. It is most inconvenient, ya? I have had to move my laboratory as well, and Poche will not follow me down here. He does not like Roman architecture."

"No? Well, who does? But, I say, couldn't you persuade them to move me back? If one must be imprisoned, a nice room with a view is far preferable."

The little man shook his head. "No longer possible. Give me your arm."

Alexia narrowed her eyes suspiciously and then, curious, acquiesced to his request.

He wrapped a tube of oiled cloth about her arm and then proceeded to pump it full of air using a set of bellows via a mini spigot. The tube expanded and became quite tight. Pinching these bellows off, the scientist transferred a glass ball filled with little bits of paper to the spigot and let go. The air escaped with a *whoosh,* causing all the bits of paper to flutter about wildly inside the ball.

"What *are* you doing?"

"I am to determine what kind of the child you may produce, ya. There is much speculation."

"I fail to see how those little bits of paper can reveal anything of import." They seemed about as useful as tea leaves in the bottom of a cup. Which made her think yearningly of tea.

"Well, you had better hope they do. There has been some talk of handling this child . . . differently."

"What?"

"Ya. And using you for—how to say?—spare parts."

Bile, sour and unwelcome, rose in Alexia's throat.

"What?"

"Hush now, Female Specimen, let me work."

The German watched with frowning attention as the papers finally settled completely at the base of the ball, which, Alexia now realized, was marked with lines. Then he began making notes and diagrams of their location. She tried to think calming thoughts but was beginning to get angry as well as scared. She was finished with being thought of as a specimen.

"You know, they gave to me complete access to the records of their preternatural breeding program? They tried for nearly a hundred years to determine how to successfully breed your species."

"Humans? Well that couldn't have been too difficult. I am still *human*, remember?"

Mr. Lange-Wilsdorf ignored this and continued his previous line of reasoning. "You always breed true, but low birth rate and rare female specimens were never explained. Also the program was plagued with the difficulty of the space allotment. Templars could not, for example, keep the babies in the same room or even the same house."

"So what happened?" Alexia couldn't help her curiosity.

"The program was stopped, ya. Your father was one of the last, you know?"

Alexia's eyebrows made an inadvertent bid for the sky. "He was?" *Hear that, infant-inconvenience, your grandfather was bred by religious zealots as a kind of biological experiment. So much for your family tree.*

"Did the Templars raise him?"

Mr. Lange-Wilsdorf gave her a peculiar look. "I am not familiar with the specifics."

Alexia knew absolutely nothing about her father's childhood; his journals didn't commence until his university years in Britain and were, she suspected, originally intended as a vehicle for practicing English grammar.

The little scientist appeared to decide that he ought to say no more. Turning back to his bellows and sphere device, he finished his notations and then began a complex series of calculations. When he had finished, he set down his stylographic pen with a pronounced movement.

"Remarkable, ya."

"What is?"

"There is only one explanation for such results. That you have trace intrinsic aether affixed to the—how to say?—middle zone, but it is behaving wrong, as though it were bonded but also not, as if it were in the state of flux."

"Well, good for me." Then Alexia frowned, remembering their

previous discussion. "But, according to your theory, I should have no intrinsic aether at all."

"Exactly."

"So your theory is wrong."

"Or the flux reaction is coming from the embryo." Mr. Lange-Wilsdorf was quite triumphant in this proclamation, as though he was near to explaining everything.

"Are you implying that you understand the nature of my child?" Alexia was prepared to get equally excited. *Finally!*

"No, but I can say with the absolute confidence that I am very, very close."

"Funny, but I do not find that at all reassuring."

Lord Akeldama stood in the doorway of Professor Lyall's office, dressed for riding. It was hard to read his face at the best of times and, under such circumstances as these, nigh on impossible.

"How do you do this evening, my lord?"

"La, my dear, tolerably well. Tolerably well. And you?"

They had, of course, met on more than one occasion in the past. Lyall had spent centuries nibbling about the great layer cake that was polite society while Lord Akeldama acted the part of the frosting on its top. Lyall knew a man was smart who kept a weather eye on the state of the frosting, even if most of his time was spent cleaning up crumbs. The supernatural set was small enough to keep track of most members, whether they skulked about BUR offices and the soldier's barracks or the best drawing rooms the ton had to offer.

"I must admit to having had better evenings. Welcome to BUR headquarters, Lord Akeldama. Do come in."

The vampire paused for a moment on the threshold, catching sight of Biffy's sleeping form. He made a slight gesture with one hand. "May I?"

Professor Lyall nodded. The question was a veiled insult, reminding them both of what had been taken from the vampire unjustly. That he must now ask to look upon what had once been his. Lyall let him get away with it. Currently the vampire held all the cards, but Professor Lyall was reasonably convinced that if he just gave Lord Akeldama enough cravat material, he might be able to fashion it into a bow pleasing enough for all parties. Of course, the vampire might also turn it into a noose; it depended entirely on the outcome of this conversation.

Professor Lyall knew that vampires had a limited sense of smell and no clear method of sensing right away that Biffy was now a werewolf. But Lord Akeldama seemed to realize it, anyway. He did not try to touch the young man.

"That is quite the quantity of facial hair. I didn't know he had it in him. I suppose that fuzzy is more appropriate given the current situation." Lord Akeldama raised one long, slim white hand to the base of his own throat, pinching at the skin there. He closed his eyes for a moment before opening them and looking down on his former drone once more. "He looks so young when he is sleeping. I have always thought so." He swallowed audibly. Then he turned and came back to stand in front of Lyall.

"You have been riding, my lord?"

Lord Akeldama looked down at his clothing and winced. "Necessity sometimes demands a sacrifice, young Randolph. Can I call you Randy? Or would you prefer, Dolphy? Dolly, perhaps?" Professor Lyall flinched noticeably. "Anyway, as I was saying, *Dolly*, I cannot *abide* riding—the horses are never happy to seat a vampire, and it plays havoc with one's hair. The only thing more vulgar is an open carriage."

Professor Lyall decided on a more direct approach. "Where have you been this past week, my lord?"

Lord Akeldama looked once more down at himself. "Chasing ghosts while pursued by daemons, as it were, Dolly *darling*. I am convinced *you* must be aware of how it goes."

Professor Lyall decided on a push, just to see if he might elicit a more genuine reaction. "How could you disappear like that, just when Lady Maccon needed you most?"

Lord Akeldama's lip curled slightly, and then he gave a humorless little laugh. "Interesting query, coming from Lord Maccon's Beta. You will forgive me if I am inclined to see it as my right to ask the questions under such circumstances." He gestured with his head in Biffy's direction, just a little jerk of controlled displeasure.

Lord Akeldama was a man who hid his real feelings, not with an absence of emotions but with an excess of false ones. However, Professor Lyall was pretty certain that there, lurking under the clipped civility, was real, deeply rooted, and undeniably justified anger.

Lord Akeldama took a seat, lounging back into it, for all the world as relaxed and untroubled as a man at his club. "So, I take it, Lord Maccon has gone after *my* dear Alexia?"

Lyall nodded.

"Then he *knows*?"

"That she is in grave danger and the potentate responsible? Yes."

"Ah, was that Wally's game? No wonder he wanted me swarming out of London. No, I mean to ask, Dolly *dear*, if the *estimable* earl knows what kind of child he has sired."

"No. But he has accepted that it is his. I think he always knew

Lady Maccon would not play him false. He was just being ridiculous about it."

"Normally, I am all in favor of the ridiculous, but under such circumstances, you must understand, I believe it quite a *pity* he could not have come to that realization sooner. Lady Maccon would never have lost the protection of the pack, and none of *this* would have happened."

"You think not? Yet your kind tried to kill her on the way to Scotland when she was still very much under Woolsey's protection. Admittedly, that was done more discreetly and, I now believe, without the support of the hives. But they would all still have wanted her dead the moment they knew of her condition. The interesting thing is that you, apparently, do not want her dead."

"Alexia Maccon is my friend."

"Are your friends so infrequent, my lord, that you betray the clearly unanimous wishes of your own kind?"

Lord Akeldama lost some slight element of his composure at that. "Listen to me carefully, Beta. I am a rove so that I might make my own decisions: who to love, who to watch, and, most importantly, what to wear."

"So, Lord Akeldama, what is Lady Maccon's child going to be?"

"No. You will explain *this* first." The vampire gestured at Biffy. "I am forced to swarm because my most precious little drone-y-poo is *ruthlessly* stolen from me—betrayed, as it turns out, by my own kind—only to return and find him stolen by your kind instead. I believe *even* Lord Maccon would acknowledge I am entitled to an explanation."

Professor Lyall fully agreed with him in this, so he told the vampire the whole truth, every detail of it.

"So it was death or the curse of a werewolf?"

Professor Lyall nodded. "It was something to see, my lord. No metamorphosis I have ever witnessed took so long, nor was conducted with so much gentleness. To do what Lord Maccon did and not savage the boy in the heat of the need for blood, it was extraordinary. There are not many werewolves who possess such self-control. Biffy was very lucky."

"Lucky?" Lord Akeldama fairly spat the word, jumping to his feet. "Lucky! To be cursed by the moon into a slathering beast? You would have done better to let him die. My poor boy." Lord Akeldama was not a big man, certainly not by werewolf standards, but he moved so quickly that he was around Professor Lyall's desk, slim hands about the werewolf's throat, faster than Lyall's eyes could follow. There was the anger Professor Lyall had been waiting for and, with it, a degree of pain and hurt he would never have expected from a vampire. Perhaps

he had pushed a little harder than was strictly necessary. Lyall sat still
and passive under the choking hold. A vampire could probably rip a
werewolf's head clean off, but Lord Akeldama was not the kind of man
to do such a thing, even in the heat of anger. He was too controlled by
age and etiquette to make more than a show of it.

"Master, stop. Please. It was not their fault."

Biffy sat up slightly on the couch, eyes fixed in horror at the sight
before him.

Lord Akeldama immediately let go of Professor Lyall and dashed
over to kneel by the young man's side.

Biffy spoke in a jumble of words and guilt. "I should not have allowed myself to be captured. I was careless. I did not suspect the potentate of such extremes of action. I was not playing the game as you
taught me. I did not think he would use me like that to get to you."

"Ah, my little cherry blossom, we were all playing blind. This is
not your fault."

"Do you really find me cursed and disgusting now?" Biffy's voice
was very small.

Driven beyond his instincts, the vampire pulled the newly made
werewolf against him—one predator consoling another, as unnatural
as a snake attempting to comfort a house cat.

Biffy rested his dark head on Lord Akeldama's shoulder. The vampire twisted his perfect lips together and looked up at the ceiling,
blinked, and then looked away. Through the fall of the vampire's blond
hair, Professor Lyall caught a glimpse of his face.

Ah, oh dear, he really did love him. The Beta pressed two fingers
against his own eyes as though he might stopper up the tears in theirs.
Curses.

Love, of all eccentricities among the supernatural set, was the most
embarrassing and the least talked about or expected. But Lord Akeldama's face, for all its icy beauty, was drawn with genuine loss into a
kind of carved marble agony.

Professor Lyall was an immortal; he knew what it was to lose a
loved one. He could not leave the room, not with so many important
BUR documents scattered about, but he did turn away and put on a
show of busily organizing stacks of paperwork, attempting to provide
the two men some modicum of privacy.

He heard a rustle—Lord Akeldama sitting down upon the couch
next to his former drone.

"My dearest boy, *of course* I do not find you disgusting—although,
we must really have a serious discussion about this beard of yours.
That was only a little turn of phrase, perhaps a bit of an exaggeration.

You see, I did so look forward to the possibility of having you by my side as one of us. Joined to the old fang-and-swill club and all that."

A sniff from Biffy.

"If anything, this is *my* fault. I should have kept a better watch. I should not have fallen for his tricks or sent you in against him. I should not have allowed your disappearance to cause me to panic and swarm. I ought to have recognized the signs of a game in play against me and mine. But who would have believed my own kind—another vampire, another *rove*—would steal from me? *Me*! My *sweet* citron, I did not see the pattern. I did not see how desperate he was. I forgot that sometimes the information I carry in my own head is more valuable than the daily wonders you *lovely* boys unearth for me."

At which point, when Professor Lyall really felt things couldn't possibly get any worse, a bang came on the office door, which then opened without his bidding.

"What—?"

It was Professor Lyall's turn to look up at the ceiling in an excess of emotion.

"Her most Royal Majesty, Queen Victoria, to see Lord Maccon."

Queen Victoria marched through the door and spoke to Professor Lyall without breaking stride. "He is not here, is he? Wretched man."

"Your Majesty!" Professor Lyall hurried from behind his desk and performed his lowest and best bow.

The Queen of England, a deceptively squat and brown personage, swept the room with an autocratic eye as though Lord Maccon, sizable specimen that he was, might manage to hide in a corner somewhere or under the rug. What her eye rested upon was the tableau of a tear-stained Biffy, clearly naked under his blanket, caught up in the arms of a peer of the realm.

"What is this? *Sentiment!* Who is that there? Lord Akeldama? Really, this will not do at all. Compose yourself this instant."

Lord Akeldama lifted his head from where it rested, cheek pressed against Biffy's, and narrowed his eyes at the queen. He gently let his former drone go, stood, and bowed, exactly as deeply as he ought and not one jot more.

Biffy, for his part, was at a loss. He could not get up without exposing some part of himself, and he could not perform the appropriate obedience from a supine position. He looked with desperate eyes at the queen.

Professor Lyall came to his rescue. "You will have to forgive, uh," he floundered, for he had never learned Biffy's real name, "our young friend here. He has had a bit of a trying night."

"So we have been given to understand. Is this, then, the drone in question?" The queen raised a quizzing glass and examined Biffy through it. "The dewan has said you were kidnapped, young man, and by our very own potentate. These are grave charges, indeed. Are they true?"

Biffy, mouth slightly open in awe, managed only a mute nod.

The queen's face expressed both relief and chagrin in equal measure. "Well, at least Lord Maccon hasn't bungled that." She turned her sharp eye on Lord Akeldama.

The vampire, with a studied, casual air, fixed the cuffs of his shirtsleeves so they lay perfectly underneath his jacket. He did not meet her gaze.

"Would you say, Lord Akeldama, that death was an appropriate punishment for the theft of another vampire's drone?" she inquired casually.

"I would say it is a bit extreme, Your Majesty, but in the heat of the moment, I am given to understand, accidents will happen. It was not intentional."

Professor Lyall couldn't believe his ears. Was Lord Akeldama *defending* Lord Maccon?

"Very well. No charges will be brought against the earl."

Lord Akeldama started. "I did not say . . . that is, he also metamorphosed Biffy."

"Yes, yes. Excellent, another werewolf is always welcome." The queen bestowed a beneficent smile on the still-bemused Biffy.

"But he is *mine*!"

The queen frowned at the vampire's tone. "We hardly see the need for such fuss, Lord Akeldama. You have plenty more just like him, do you not?"

Lord Akeldama stood for a moment, stunned, just long enough for the queen to continue on with her conversation, entirely ignoring his bemusement.

"We must suppose Lord Maccon has gone in pursuit of his wife?" A nod from Professor Lyall. "Good, good. We are reinstating her as muhjah, of course, in absentia. We were acting under the potentate's advice when we dismissed her, and now we see he must have been furthering his own hidden agenda. For centuries, Walsingham has advised the Crown unerringly. What could have driven such a man to such lengths?"

All around her, silence descended.

"That, gentlemen, was *not* a rhetorical question."

Professor Lyall cleared his throat. "I believe it may have to do with Lady Maccon's forthcoming child."

"Yes?"

Professor Lyall turned and looked pointedly at Lord Akeldama.

Following his lead, the Queen of England did the same.

No one would ever accuse Lord Akeldama of fidgeting, but under such direct scrutiny, he did appear slightly flustered.

"Well, Lord Akeldama? You do know, don't you? Otherwise none of this would have happened."

"You must understand, Your Majesty, that vampire records go back to Roman times, and there is mention of only one similar child."

"Go on."

"And, of course, in this case she was the child of a soul-sucker and a vampire—not a werewolf."

Professor Lyall chewed his lip. How could the howlers not have known of this? They were the keepers of history; they were supposed to know about everything.

"Go *on*!"

"The kindest word we had for that creature was soul-stealer."

CHAPTER FIFTEEN

Ladybugs to the Rescue

Alexia fought hard. It took some substantial negotiating to convince the German scientist, but in the end all she needed was the right kind of logic.

"I am bored."

"This does not trouble me, Female Specimen."

"This is my heritage we are dealing with, you realize?"

"Ya, so?"

"I believe it may be possible for me to uncover something you and the Templars have missed."

No response.

"I can read Latin."

He pressed down on her stomach.

"Can you? My, my, you *are* well educated."

"For a female?"

"For a soulless. Templar records hold that the devil spawn are not men of philosophy."

"You see, I am different. I might spot something."

The little German pulled out an ear tube from his case and listened to her belly attentively.

"I am telling you, I have excellent research skills."

"Will it keep you quiet?"

Alexia nodded enthusiastically.

"I shall see what I can do, ya?"

Later that day, two nervous young Templars came in carrying some ancient-looking scrolls and a bucket of lead tablets. They must have been under orders to oversee the security of these items, for instead of leaving, they locked the cell door and then sat—on the floor, much to Alexia's shock—crossed their legs, and proceeded to embroider red crosses onto handkerchiefs while she read. Alexia wondered if this were some kind of punishment, or if embroidery was what the Templars did for fun. It would explain the general prevalence of embroidered red crosses everywhere. Lord Akeldama, of course, had warned her. Silly to realize it now that it was far too late.

She bypassed the scrolls in favor of the more intriguing lead squares. They had Latin incised into them and were, she believed, curse tablets. Her Latin was rather rusty, and she could have used a vocabulary reference book of some kind, but she managed to decipher the first tablet after some time and the others came much easier after that. Most of them concerned ghosts and were designed to either curse someone into suffering after death as a ghost or exorcize a poltergeist that was already haunting a house. Alexia surmised that the tablets, in either case, would be entirely ineffective, but there certainly were a large number of them.

She looked up when Mr. Lange-Wilsdorf entered her cell with a new battery of tests. "Ah," she said, "Good afternoon. Thank you for arranging for me to look at this remarkable collection. I did not realize curse tablets were so focused on the supernatural. I had read that they called upon the wrath of imaginary daemons and gods, but not the *real* supernatural. Very interesting, indeed."

"Anything useful, Female Specimen?"

"Ow!" He poked at her arm with a syringe. "So far, they all have to do with hauntings. Very concerned with ghosts, the Romans."

"Mmm. Ya. I had read of this in my own research."

Alexia went back to translating the next tablet.

Having collected a sample of her blood, the German abandoned her once more to the tender mercies of the embroidering Templars.

The moment she started reading the next tablet, Alexia knew she wasn't going to tell Mr. Lange-Wilsdorf about it. It was a small one, and the boxy Latin letters were exceptionally tiny and painfully neat, covering both sides. Where all the previous tablets had been dedicated to daemons or to the spirits of the netherworld, this one was markedly different.

"I call upon you, Stalker of Skins and Stealer of Souls, child of a Breaker of Curses, whoever you are, and ask that from this hour, from this night, from this moment, you steal from and weaken the vampire Primulus of Carisius. I hand over to you, if you have any power, this Sucker of Blood, for only you may take what he values most. Stealer of Souls, I consecrate to you his complexion, his strength, his healing, his speed, his breath, his fangs, his grip, his power, his soul. Stealer of Souls, if I see him mortal, sleeping when he should wake, wasting away in his human skin, I swear I will offer a sacrifice to you every year."

Alexia surmised that the term "Breaker of Curses" must correlate to the werewolf moniker for a preternatural, "curse-breaker," which meant that the curse tablet was calling upon the child of a preternatural for aid. It was the first mention she had yet run across, however minor, of either soulless or a child of a soulless. She placed a hand upon her stomach and looked down at it. "Well, hello there, little Stalker of Skins." She felt a brief fluttering inside her womb. "Ah, would we prefer Stealer of Souls?" The fluttering stilled. "I see, more dignified, is it?"

She went back to the tablet, reading it over again, wishing it might give her more of a clue as to what such a creature could do and how it came into existence. She supposed it was possible that this being was just as nonexistent as the gods of the netherworld that the other tablets called upon. Then again, it could be as real as the ghosts or vampires they were asked to fight against. It must have been such an odd age to have lived in, so full of superstition and mythology, to be ruled by the Caesar's empire hives and a bickering line of incestuous vampires.

Alexia glanced under her eyelashes at the two embroidering men and, in a not-very-subtle movement, tucked the tablet down the front of her dress. Luckily for her, the Templars seemed to find their embroidery most absorbing.

She went on, scanning for the two key Latin phrases "Stalker of Skins" and "Stealer of Souls," but there seemed to be no further mention of either. She weighed her options, wondering if she should mention the phrase to Mr. Lange-Wilsdorf. As it turned out, the preceptor brought her meal that evening, so she figured she might as well go straight to the source.

She took her time working around to the subject. First she asked him politely about his day and listened to the recitation of his routine—really, who would want to attend matins six times?—as she ate her pasta in its obligatory bright green sauce. The preceptor had called the long skinny pasta "spa-giggle-tee" or some such silliness. Alexia didn't rightly care, so long as there was pesto on top of it.

Finally, she said, "I found an interesting tidbit in your records to-day."

"Oh, yes? I had heard Mr. Lange-Wilsdorf brought them to you. Which one?"

She gestured airily. "Oh, you know, one of the scrolls. It said something about a soul-stealer."

That got a reaction. The preceptor stood so fast that he knocked over the little stool he had been sitting on.

"What did you say?"

"I believe the other term used in the document was 'skin-stalker.' I see you have heard of these creatures before. Perhaps you would care to tell me where?"

Clearly in shock, the preceptor spoke as though his mouth were moving while his mind still coped with the revelation. "Soul-stealers are known to us only as legendary creatures, more dangerous than you soulless. They are greatly feared by the supernatural for their ability to be both mortal and immortal at the same time. The brotherhood has been warned to watch for them, although we have not yet encountered one in our recorded history. You believe that is what your child is?"

"What would you do with one if you caught it?"

"That would depend on whether or not we could control it. They cannot be allowed to roam free, not with that kind of power."

"What kind of power?" Alexia tried to sound innocent as she inched her free hand down the side of her small stool, preparing to grab it out from under her to use as a weapon if need be.

"I only know what is written into our Amended Rule."

"Oh, yes?"

He began to quote, " 'Above all this, whosoever would be a brother, you and your profession and faith must deal out death in the name of holy justice against those creatures that stand against God and lead a man unto hellfire, the vampire and the werewolf. For those that walk not under the sun and those that crawl under the moon have sold their souls for the taste of blood and flesh. Moreover, let no brother relax in his holy duty of pure watchfulness and firm perseverance against those unfortunates born to sin and damnation, the devil spawn in soulless state. And finally, the brothers are hereby commanded to fraternize only with the untainted and hunt down the sickness of spirit within those that can both walk and crawl, and who ride the soul as a knight will ride his steed.' "

As he spoke, the preceptor backed away from Alexia and toward the prison door. She was taken by his expression, almost hypnotized by it. As had happened during the battle in the carriage, his eyes were no longer dead.

Alexia Tarabotti, Lady Maccon, had engendered many emotions in people over the years—mostly, she admitted ruefully to herself, exasperation—but never before had she been the cause of such abject revulsion. She looked down, embarrassed. *Guess it is not such a good thing, infant, to be a soul-stealer. Well, never you mind. Templars don't seem to like anyone.*

As she glanced away, her eye was caught by a flash of red coming along the passageway toward her cell—low to the ground. The two young Templars seemed to have noticed whatever it was as well and were looking in fascination at the object trundling toward them.

Then she heard the ticking noise and the tinny sound of multiple tiny metal legs on stone.

"What is going on?" demanded the preceptor, turning away from Alexia.

Alexia seized the opportunity, stood up, and in one smooth movement, yanked the stool out from under herself and struck the back of the preceptor's head with it.

There was a dreadful crunching noise and Alexia grimaced.

"I do beg your pardon," she said perfunctorily, leaping over his fallen form. "Needs must and all that."

The two embroidering guards leapt to their feet, but before they had a chance to lock the door to Alexia's cell, a large shiny bug, lacquered red with black spots, scuttled directly at them.

Alexia, still brandishing the stool, charged out into the hall.

Queen Victoria had been neither as impressed nor as shocked as she should have been upon hearing the term "soul-stealer" spoken in Lord Akeldama's most salubrious tones. "Oh, is that all?" seemed to be her reaction. Her solution fit the standards of all monarchs everywhere. She made up her mind and then made it someone else's problem. In this case, however, Professor Lyall was pleased to find she had not made it his problem.

No, instead, the queen had pursed her lips and delivered an unsavory verbal package into the elegant alabaster hands of Lord Akeldama. "A soul-stealer you say, Lord Akeldama? That sounds most unpleasant. Not to say inconvenient, considering Lady Maccon will be returned to active service as my muhjah as soon as she can be fetched home. We expect Lord Maccon to have that particular task well under way. It goes without saying, the Crown simply will not tolerate vampires trying to kill its muhjah, however pregnant she may be and whatever she may be pregnant with. You must put a stop to it."

"I, Your Majesty?" Lord Akeldama was clearly flustered by this direct instruction.

"Of course, we require a new potentate. You are hereby granted the position. You possess the necessary qualifications, for you are a vampire and you are a rove."

"I beg to differ, Your Majesty. It must be put to the hive vote, any new candidate to the potentate position."

"You think they will not approve your appointment?"

"I have many enemies, Your Majesty, even among my own kind."

"Then you will be in good company, potentate: so does Lady Maccon and so did Walsingham. We shall expect you at Thursday's meeting of the Shadow Council."

With that, Queen Victoria sailed out of the room, adrift on a sea of self-righteousness.

Lord Akeldama raised himself out of his bow, looking flabbergasted.

"Congratulations, my lord," said Biffy timidly, attempting to stand shakily from the couch and approach his former master.

Professor Lyall hurried over to him. "Not yet, pup. You won't have your legs back for a while longer." He spoke the truth for, despite the fact that Biffy obviously wanted to walk on two legs, his brain seemed set on four, and he pitched forward with a surprised little cry.

Lyall caught him up and deposited him back on the couch. "It will take some time for your mind to catch up to your metamorphosis."

"Ah." Biffy's voice caught in his throat. "How silly of me not to realize."

Lord Akeldama came over as well, watching with hooded eyes as Lyall smoothed the blanket over the young man. "*She* has placed me in a most insufferable position."

"Now you know how I feel most of the time," said Professor Lyall under his breath.

"You are more than equal to the task, my lord." Biffy's eyes were shining and full of faith as they looked upon his former master.

Wonderful, thought Lyall, *a newly made werewolf in love with a vampire, and more apt to do his bidding than the pack's.* Would even Lord Maccon be able to break such a connection?

"I rather think the queen is getting the better end of the deal," added Professor Lyall, intimating, but not actually mentioning, Lord Akeldama's fashionable yet efficient espionage regime.

Poor Lord Akeldama was not having a good night. He had lost his lover and his comparative anonymity in one fell swoop. "The pathetic reality is, my *darlings,* I am not even convinced the child of a preternatural and a werewolf will *be* a soul-stealer. And if it is, will it be the same kind of soul-stealer as it was when the sire was a vampire?"

"Is that why you remain unafraid of this creature?"

"As I said before, Lady Maccon is my friend. Any child of hers will be no more or less hostile to vampires than she is. Although the way we are currently behaving may sour her against us. Aside from that, it is not in my nature to anticipate trouble with violence; I prefer to be in possession of all the necessary facts first. I should like to meet this child once it has emerged and then render my judgment. So much better that way."

"And your other reason?" The vampire was still hiding something; Lyall's well-honed BUR senses told him so.

"Must you hound him, Professor Lyall?" Biffy looked worriedly from his former master to his new Beta.

"I think it best. It is, after all, in *my* nature."

"Touché." The vampire sat down once more next to Biffy on the settee and placed a passive hand casually on the young man's leg, as if out of habit.

Lyall stood up and looked down at them both from over his spectacles; he'd had enough of mysteries for one evening. "Well?"

"That soul-stealer, the one the Edict Keepers warn us of? The reason for all this twaddle? Her name was Al-Zabba and she was a relative of sorts." Lord Akeldama tipped his head from side to side casually.

Professor Lyall started. Of all the things, he had not expected that. "A relative of *yours*?"

"You might know her better as Zenobia."

Professor Lyall knew about as much as any educated man on the Roman Empire, but he had never read that the Queen of the Palmyrene had anything more or less than the requisite amount of soul. Which led to another question.

"This soul-stealer condition, how exactly does it manifest?"

"I don't know."

"And that makes even you uneasy. Doesn't it, Lord Akeldama?"

Biffy touched his former master's hand where it rested on his blanket-covered thigh and squeezed as though offering reassurance.

Definitely going to be a problem.

"The daylight folk, back then, the ones who feared her, they called her a skin-thief."

That name meant something to Professor Lyall, where soul-stealer had not. It tickled memories at the back of his head. Legends about a creature who could not only steal werewolf powers but become, for the space of one night, a werewolf in his stead. "Are you telling me we will have a *flayer* on our hands?"

"Exactly! So, you *see* how difficult it will be to keep everyone from killing Alexia?"

"As to that problem"—Professor Lyall gave a sudden grin—"I may have a solution. Lord and Lady Maccon will not like it, but I am thinking you, Lord Akeldama and young Biffy, might find it acceptable."

Lord Akeldama smiled back, showing off his deadly fangs. Professor Lyall thought them just long enough to be threatening without being ostentatious, like the perfect dress sword. They were quite subtle fangs for a man of Lord Akeldama's reputation.

"Why, Dolly *darling*, do speak further; you interest me most ardently."

The Templars seemed, if possible, less prepared to battle ticking ladybugs than Alexia had been when accosted in a carriage not so very long ago. They were so surprised by their unexpected visitors and were torn between squashing them and handling the now-free Alexia. It wasn't until one of the ladybugs stuck a sharp needlelike antennae into one of the young Templars, who then collapsed, that the brothers took violently against them. Once pricked into action, however, their retribution was swift and effective.

The remaining young Templar drew his sword and dispatched Alexia's noble scuttling rescuers with remarkable efficiency. He then whirled to face Alexia.

She raised her stool.

Behind them, in the cell, the preceptor groaned. "What is going on?"

Since the ladybugs might have been sent either by the vampires to kill her or by Monsieur Trouvé to help her, Alexia could not rightly answer that question. "It would appear you are under attack by ladybugs, Mr. Templar. What else can I say?"

At which moment they all heard the growl. It was the kind of growl Alexia was definitely familiar with—low and loud and full of intention. It was the kind of growl that said, clearly as anything, "You are food."

"Ah, and now, I suspect, werewolves."

And so it proved to be the case.

Of course, Alexia's traitorous little heart hoped for a certain brindled coat, chocolate brown with hints of black and gold. She craned her neck over her brandished stool to see if the growling, slavering beast charging down the stone hallway would have pale yellow eyes and a familiar humor crinkling them just so.

But the creature that bounded into view was pure white, and his lupine face was humorless. He launched himself upon the young Templar, without apparent care for the naked blade, which was, Alexia had no doubt, silver. He was a beautiful specimen of *Homo lupis*, or would have been beautiful had he not been bent on mauling and mayhem. Alexia knew those eyes were icy blue without having to look. She couldn't really follow, anyway, as man and wolf met in the hallway. With a vociferous battle cry, the preceptor charged out of the cell and joined the fray.

Never one to sit back and dither, Alexia grabbed the stool more firmly, and when the younger Templar fell back toward her, she clouted him with the stool on top of the head as hard as she possibly could. Really, she was getting terribly good at bashing skulls in her old age—rather unseemly of her.

The boy collapsed.

Now it was just the werewolf against the preceptor.

Alexia figured that Channing could take care of himself and that she'd better break for freedom while the preceptor was preoccupied. So she dropped the stool, hiked her skirts, and took off pell-mell down what looked to be the most promising passageway. She ran smack-dab into Madame Lefoux, Floote, and Monsieur Trouvé.

Ah, right passageway! "Well, hello, you lot. How are you?"

"No time for pleasantries, Alexia, my dear. Isn't it just like you, to be already escaped before we had the opportunity to rescue you?" Madame Lefoux flashed her dimples.

"Ah, yes. Well, I am resourceful."

Madame Lefoux tossed something at her, and Alexia caught it with the hand not holding up her skirts. "My parasol! How marvelous."

Floote, she noticed, was carrying her dispatch case in one hand, and he had one of those tiny guns in his other.

Monsieur Trouvé offered Alexia his arm.

"My lady?"

"Why, thank you, monsieur, very kind." Alexia managed to grasp it and her parasol and her skirts without too much difficulty. "I am rather grateful for the ladybugs, by the way; very nice of you to send them on."

The clockmaker began hustling her down the hallway. It wasn't until that moment that Alexia realized how large the catacombs were, and how far she had been stashed underground.

"Ah, yes, I borrowed the adaptation from the vampires. I put a doping agent in the antennae instead of poison. It proved an effective alternative."

"Very. Until the swords came out, of course. I am afraid your three minions are no more."

"Ah. Poor little things. They aren't exactly battle-hardy."

They ascended a steep flight of stairs and then dashed down another long hallway, one that seemed to go backward above the one they'd just run up.

"If you don't find it impertinent of me to ask," Alexia panted, "what are you doing here, monsieur?"

The Frenchman answered between puffs. "Ah, I came with your

luggage. Left a marker so Genevieve would know I was here. I didn't want to miss all the fun."

"You and I clearly do not share a definition of the word."

The Frenchman looked her up and down, his eyes positively twinkling. "Oh, come now, my lady, I think we may."

Alexia grinned, it must be admitted, a tad more ferociously than genteelly.

"Watch out!" came Floote's shout. He was leading the charge, closely followed by Madame Lefoux, but he had stopped suddenly ahead of them and, after taking aim, fired one of his tiny guns.

A group of about a dozen or so Templars was coming down the passageway toward them, preceded by the tweed-covered, dwarflike form of a certain German scientist. Adding to the generally threatening overtones of the party, Poche led the charge, yapping and prancing about like an overly excited bit of dandelion fluff wearing a yellow bow.

Floote reached for his second gun and fired again, but there was no time to get the first reloaded before the Templars were upon them. Floote seemed to have missed, anyway, for the enemy advanced undaunted. The only member troubled by the shot was the dog, who went into highly vocalized histrionics.

"I would surrender now, ya, if I were you, Female Specimen."

Alexia gave Mr. Lange-Wilsdorf an innocent look from behind her little group of protectors; after all, it hadn't been her idea to be rescued. She also hefted her parasol. Alexia had faced down vampires. A handful of highly trained mortals would be easy by comparison. Or so she hoped.

The little German looked pointedly at Madame Lefoux and Monsieur Trouvé. "I am surprised at you both. Members in good standing with the Order of the Brass Octopus reduced to this, running and fighting. And for what? Protection of a soulless? You do not even intend to properly study her."

"And that is, of course, all you wish to do?"

"Of course."

Madame Lefoux was not to be outmaneuvered by a *German*. "You forget, Mr. Lange-Wilsdorf, that I have read your research. All of your research—even the vivisections. You were always inclined toward questionable methodology."

"And you have no ulterior motive, Madame Lefoux? I heard you had received instructions from within the highest levels of the Order to follow and learn as much as possible about Lady Maccon and her child."

"I am attracted to Alexia for many reasons," replied the French-woman.

Alexia felt a token protest was called for at this juncture. "I mean to say, really, I am near to developing a neurosis—is there anyone around who doesn't want to study or kill me?"

Floote raised a tentative hand.

"Ah, yes, thank you, Floote."

"There is also Mrs. Tunstell, madam," he offered hopefully, as if Ivy were some kind of consolation prize.

"I notice you don't mention my fair-weather husband."

"I suspect, at this moment, madam, he probably wants to kill you."

Alexia couldn't help smiling. "Good point."

The Templars had been standing in still and, unsurprisingly, silent vigil over this conversation. Quite unexpectedly, one of those at the back gave a little cry. This was followed by the unmistakable sound of fighting. Poche began barking his head off even more loudly and vigorously than before. Apparently less eager to attack when faced with real violence, the dog also cowered behind his master's tweed-covered legs.

At a signal from the Templar who appeared to be the leader—the cross on his nightgown being bigger than the others—most of the rest whirled about to confront this new threat from the rear. This left only three Templars and the German scientist facing Alexia and her small party—much better odds.

Floote went about busily reloading his two little pistols with new bullets.

"What—?" Alexia was mystified into inarticulateness.

"Vampires," explained Madame Lefoux. "We knew they'd come. They have been on our tail these last few days."

"Which was why you waited until nightfall to rescue me?"

"Precisely." Monsieur Trouvé twinkled at her.

"We wouldn't want to be so boorish," added Madame Lefoux, "as to arrive unexpectedly for a visit without a gift. So we brought plenty to go around."

"Very courteous of you."

Alexia craned her neck to try and make out what was going on. It was appropriately dark and gloomy in the catacombs, and hard to see around the men standing before her, but she thought she might just be able to see six vampires. *Goodness, six is practically an entire local hive!* They really and truly must want her dead.

Despite being armed with wicked-looking wooden knives, the Templars seemed to be getting the worst of the encounter. Supernatural strength and speed came in rather handy during close-quarters fighting. The three Templars still facing them turned away, eager to join the fight. That helped even the odds a bit, putting them in a two-to-one ratio. The battle was proving to be peculiarly silent. The Templars made little noise beyond the occasional grunt of pain or small cry of surprise. The vampires were much the same, silent, swift, and lethal.

Unfortunately, the broiling mess of fangs and fists was still blocking Alexia's only means of escape. "What do you say—think we can worm our way through?"

Madame Lefoux tilted her head to one side thoughtfully.

Alexia dropped her skirts and lifted her free hand suggestively. "With my particular skill set, such an endeavor could be quite entertaining. Monsieur Trouvé, let me just show you how this parasol works. I think I may need both my hands free."

Alexia gave the clockmaker some quick tips on those armaments that might be used under their present circumstances.

"Beautiful work, Cousin Geneviève." Monsieur Trouvé looked genuinely impressed.

Madame Lefoux blushed and then busied herself with her cravat pins, pulling out both of them: the wooden one for the vampires, and the silver, for lack of anything better, for the Templars. Floote cocked his pistol. Alexia took off her gloves.

They had all forgotten about Mr. Lange-Wilsdorf—an amazing achievement considering that his absurd excuse for a dog was still yapping away at the top of its lungs.

"But you cannot possibly leave, Female Specimen! I have not completed my tests. I did so want to cut the child out for dissection. I could have determined its nature. I could—" He left off speaking, for he was interrupted by a loud growling noise.

Channing came dashing up. The werewolf was looking a tad worse for wear. His beautiful white fur was streaked with blood, many of his wounds still bleeding, for they were slower to heal when administered by a silver blade. Luckily, none of the injuries appeared to be fatal. Alexia didn't want to think about how the preceptor might look right about now. It was a safe bet that one or more of his injuries *were* fatal.

Channing lolled a tongue out and then tilted his head in the direction of the pitched battle going on just ahead of them.

"I know," said Alexia, "you brought the cavalry with you. Really, you shouldn't have."

The werewolf barked at her, as if to say, *This is no time for levity.*

"Very well, then, after you."

Channing trotted purposefully toward the broiling mass of vampires and Templars.

The German scientist, cowering away from the werewolf, yelled at them from his position, flattened against the side wall of the passageway, "No, Female Specimen, you cannot go! I will not allow it." Alexia glanced over at him, only to find he had pulled out an extraordinary weapon. It looked like a set of studded leather bagpipes melded to a blunderbuss. It was pointed in her direction, but Mr. Lange-Wilsdorf's hand was by no means steady on the trigger. Before anyone had a chance to react to the weapon, Poche, seized with a sudden bout of unwarranted bravery, charged at Channing.

Without breaking stride, the werewolf swiveled his head down and around, opened his prodigious jaws, and swallowed the little dog whole.

"No!" cried the scientist, instantly switching targets and firing the bagpipe blunderbuss at the werewolf instead of Alexia. It made a loud splattering pop sound and ejected a fist-sized ball of some kind of jellied red organic matter that hit the werewolf with a splat. Whatever it was must not have been designed to damage werewolves, for Channing merely shook it off like a wet dog and gave the little man a disgusted look.

Floote fired in the same instant, hitting the German in one shoulder and then pocketing his gun, once more out of ammunition. Alexia thought she would have to get Floote a better, more modern gun, a revolver, perhaps.

Mr. Lange-Wilsdorf cried out in pain, clutched at his shoulder, and fell back.

Madame Lefoux marched over to him and grabbed the peculiar weapon out of his limp hand. "You know the truth of the matter, sir? Your ideas may be sound, but your research methods and your moral code are both highly questionable. You, sir, are a *bad scientist*!" With that, she clocked him in the temple with the muzzle of his own bagpipe gun. He fell like a stone.

"Really, Channing," remonstrated Alexia, "did you have to eat the man's dog? I am convinced you will experience terrible indigestion."

The werewolf ignored them all and continued on toward the pitched hallway battle, which showed no signs of being firmly decided in either direction. Two to one were clearly good odds when the two were highly trained warrior monks and the one was a vampire.

Alexia ran after Channing to stir things up a bit.

While the werewolf proceeded to clear them a path via the simple expedient of eating his way through the fighters, Alexia, gloves off, tried to touch any and all that she could. The vampires were changed by her touch and the Templars repulsed; either way, she had the advantage.

Vampires dropped their opponents as they suddenly lost supernatural strength or found themselves viciously nibbling someone's neck, having entirely lost their fangs. The Templars were quick to follow up any advantage, but they were distracted by the presence of a new and equally feared enemy—a werewolf. They were also startled to find their quarry, supposedly a complacent Englishwoman of somber means and minimal intelligence, busily plying her art and touching them. Instinct took over, for they had been trained for generations to avoid a preternatural as they would avoid the devil himself, as a grave risk to their sacred souls. They flinched and stumbled away from her.

Following Alexia came Monsieur Trouvé, who, having utilized some of the parasol's armament, had reverted to swinging the heavy bronze accessory about like a club, bludgeoning all who got in his way. Alexia could understand his approach; it was her preferred method as well. Could that technique, she wondered, be legitimately referred to as a "parassault"? Following him was Madame Lefoux, bagpipe blunderbuss in one hand, cravat pin in the other, slashing and bashing away merrily. After her came Floote, bringing up the rear in dignified elegance, using the dispatch case as a kind of shield and poking at people with Madame Lefoux's other cravat pin, borrowed for the occasion.

Thus, undercover of an uncommon amount of pandemonium and bedlam, Alexia and her little band of gallant rescuers made their way through the battle and out the other side. Then there was nothing for it but to run, bruised and bloody as they were. Channing led them first through the Roman catacombs, then through a long modern tunnel that housed, if the steel tracks were any indication, a rail trolley of some kind. Finally, they found themselves clambering up damp wooden stairs and tumbling out onto the wide soft bank of the Arno. The town obviously observed a supernatural curfew after nightfall, for there was absolutely no one to witness their panting exit.

They climbed up to street level and dashed a good long way through the city. Alexia developed a stitch in her side and a feeling that, should her future permit it, she would spend the rest of her days relaxed in an armchair in a library somewhere. Adventuring was highly overrated.

Having reached one of the bridges over the Arno, she called a stop halfway across. It was a good defensible position; they could afford a short rest. "Are they following us?"

Channing raised his muzzle to the sky and sniffed. Then he shook his shaggy head.

"I cannot believe we escaped so easily." Alexia looked about at her companions, taking stock of their condition. Channing had sustained only a few additional injuries, but all were healing even as she watched. Of the others, Madame Lefoux was sporting a nasty gash on one wrist, which Floote was bandaging with a handkerchief, and Monsieur Trouvé was rubbing at a lump on his forehead. She herself ached terribly in one shoulder but would rather not look just yet. Otherwise, they all were in sufficient form and spirits. Channing appeared to have reached the same conclusion and decided to shift form.

His body began that strange, uncomfortable-looking writhing, and the sound of flesh and bone re-forming itself rent the air for a few moments, and then he rose to stand before them. Alexia gave a squeak and turned her back hurriedly on his endowments, which were ample and well proportioned.

Monsieur Trouvé took off his frock coat. It was far too wide for the werewolf, but he handed it over for modesty's sake. With a nod of thanks, Channing put it on. It covered the necessaries, but was far too short and, coupled with his long, loose hair, made him look disturbingly like an oversized French schoolgirl.

Alexia was perfectly well aware of what she was required to do at this juncture. Courtesy demanded gratitude, but she could wish it was someone other than Channing Channing of the Chesterfield Channings who was to receive it. "Well, Major Channing, I suppose I must thank you for the timely intervention. I am confused, however. Shouldn't you be off somewhere killing things?"

"My lady, I rather thought that was what I just did."

"I mean officially, for queen and country, with the regiment and everything."

"Ah, no, deployment was delayed after you left. Technical difficulties."

"Oh?"

"Yes, it was technically difficult to leave a heartbroken Alpha. And it is a good thing for you I wasn't overseas. Someone had to extract you from the Templars." He entirely ignored the rest of Alexia's rescue party.

"I should have managed perfectly well on my own. But thank you, anyway. You are always terribly impressed with yourself, aren't you?"

He leered. "Aren't you?"

"So why *have* you been tracking me this entire time?"

"Ah, you knew it was me?"

"There aren't a great number of white wolves roaming around safeguarding my interests. I figured it had to be you after the vampire and the carriage incident. So, why were you?"

A new voice, deep and gravelly, came from behind them. "Because I sent him."

Floote stopped attending to Madame Lefoux and whirled to face this new threat, the Frenchwoman was already reaching once more for her trusty cravat pins, and Monsieur Trouvé raised the bagpipe blunderbuss, which he'd been examining with scientific interest. Only Major Channing remained unperturbed.

Lord Conall Maccon, Earl of Woolsey, stepped out of the shadows of the bridge tower.

"You! You are *late*," pointed out his errant wife with every sign of extreme annoyance.

CHAPTER SIXTEEN

On a Bridge over the Arno and Other Romantic Misnomers

Late! Of course I'm late. You do realize, wife, I've been hunting all over Italy for you? You havna been exactly easy to find."

"Well, of course you wouldn't find me if you took that tactic. I haven't *been* all over Italy. I have been stuck in Florence the entire time. I was even trapped in some horrible Roman catacombs, thanks to you."

"Thanks to me? How could that possibly have been my fault, woman?" Lord Maccon came forward and loomed over his wife, both of them having entirely forgotten about their companions, who formed a semicircle of rapt interest about them. Their voices carried far over the water and through the vacant streets of Florence—no doubt providing entertainment for many.

"You rejected me!" Even as she said it, Alexia experienced once more that glorious sense of profound relief. Although this time, thankfully, it was not coupled with the need to break down and cry. Conall had come after her! Of course, she was still mad at him.

Floote bravely interjected at this juncture. "Please, madam, lower your voice. We are not yet out of danger."

"You sent me away!" Alexia hissed, low and fierce.

"No, I didna—that is, not really. I didna intend it that way. You should have known I didna mean it. You should have realized I needed time to recover from being an idiot."

"Oh, really? How was I to know idiocy was only a temporary condition, especially in your case? It never has been before! Besides which, vampires were trying to kill me."

"And they didna try to kill you here as well as back home? 'Tis a good thing I had enough sobriety left to send Channing after you."

"Oh, I like that . . . Wait, what did you say? Sobriety? You mean while I've been running across Europe pregnant, escaping ladybugs, flying in ornithopters, landing in mud, and drinking *coffee,* you have been *inebriated*?"

"I was depressed."

"You were depressed? *You!*" Alexia actually started to sputter, she was so angry. She looked up at her husband, which was always a strange experience, for she was a tall woman used to looking down on people. Lord Maccon could loom all he liked; so far as she was concerned, she was not impressed.

She poked him in the center of his chest with two fingers to punctuate her words. "*You* are an unfeeling"—poke—"traitorous"—poke—"mistrusting"—poke—"rude"—poke—"*booby*!" Every poke turned him mortal, but Lord Maccon didn't seem to mind it in the least.

Instead he grabbed the hand that poked him and brought it to his lips. "You put it very well, my love."

"Oh, don't get smarmy with me, husband. I am nowhere near finished with you yet." She started poking him with the other hand. Lord Maccon grinned hugely, probably, Alexia realized, because she had slipped up and called him "husband."

"You kicked me out without a fair trial. Do stop kissing me. And you didn't even consider that the child might be yours. Stop that! Oh, no, you had to leap to the worst possible assumption. You know my character. I could never betray you like that. Just because history says it is not possible doesn't mean there aren't exceptions. There are always exceptions. Look at Lord Akeldama—he is practically an exception to everything. Why, it took only a little research in the Templar records and I figured it out. Stop kissing my neck, Conall, I mean it. Templars should have practiced more of the scholarly arts and stopped whacking about at everything willy-nilly." She reached into her cleavage and produced the small, now-garlic-scented Roman curse tablet, which she waved at her husband. "Look right here! *Evidence.* But not you, oh no. You had to act first. And I was stuck running around without a pack."

Lord Maccon managed to get a word in at this point, but only because Lady Maccon had run out of breath. "It looks like you managed to build your own pack, anyway, my dear. A parasol protectorate, perhaps one might say."

"Oh, ha-ha, very funny."

Lord Maccon leaned forward and, before she could resume her tirade, kissed her full on the mouth. It was one of his deep, possessive kisses. It was the kind of embrace that made Alexia feel that somewhere in there, even though her touch had stolen all the werewolf out of him, he might still want to gobble her right up. She continued poking him absently even as she curled into his embrace.

Just as swiftly as he had started, he stopped. *"Ew!"*

"Ew? You kiss me when I haven't even finished yelling at you and then you say *'ew'!"* Alexia jerked out of her husband's grasp.

Conall stopped her with a question. "Alexia, darling, have you been eating *pesto* recently?" He started rubbing at his nose as though it were itching. His eyes began to water.

Alexia laughed. "That's right—werewolves are allergic to basil. You see the full force of my revenge?" She could touch him and the allergic reaction would probably stop immediately, but she stood back and watched him suffer. Funny that even as a mortal, he had reacted badly to the taste of her supper. She resigned herself to a life without pesto, and with that thought realized she was going to forgive her husband.

Eventually.

The werewolf in question approached her cautiously once more, as if he was afraid if he moved too fast she would panic and bolt. "It's been a long time since I tasted that flavor, and I never liked it, even as a human. I'll put up with it, though, if you really like it."

"Will you put up with the child, too?"

He pulled her into his arms again. "If you really like it."

"Don't be difficult. You are going to have to like it, too, you realize."

Nuzzling against her neck, he let out a sigh of satisfaction. "Mine," he said happily.

Alexia was resigned to her fate. "Unfortunately, both of us are."

"Well, that's all right, then."

"So you think." She pulled away, punching him in the arm, just to make her position perfectly clear. "The fact remains that you also belong to me! And you had the temerity to behave as though you didn't."

Lord Maccon nodded. It was true. "I shall make it up to you." Adding unguardedly, "What can I do?"

Alexia thought. "I want my own aethographic transmitter. One of the new ones that doesn't require crystalline valves."

He nodded.

"And a set of ladybugs from Monsieur Trouvé."

"A what?"

She glared at him.

He nodded again. Meekly.

"And a new gun for Floote. A good-quality revolver or some such that shoots more than one bullet."

"For Floote? Why?"

His wife crossed her arms.

"Whatever you say, dear."

Alexia considered asking for a Nordenfelt but thought that might be pushing it a bit, so she downgraded. "And I want you to teach me how to shoot."

"Now, Alexia, do you think that's quite the best thing for a woman in your condition?"

Another glare.

He sighed. "Verra well. Anything else?"

Alexia frowned in thought. "That will do for now, but I might still come up with something."

He tucked her in close against him once more, running his hands over her back in wide circular motions and burying his nose in her hair. "So, what do you think, my dear, will it be a girl or a boy?"

"It will be a soul-stealer, apparently."

"*What!*" The earl reared away from his wife and looked down at her suspiciously.

Channing interrupted them. "Best be getting a move on, I'm afraid." He head was cocked to one side, as though he were still in wolf form, ears alert for signs of pursuit.

Lord Maccon turned instantly from indulgent husband to Alpha werewolf. "We'll split up. Channing, you, Madame Lefoux, and Floote act as decoy. Madame, I'm afraid you may have to don female dress."

"Sometimes these things are necessary."

Alexia grinned, both at Madame Lefoux's discomfort and the very idea someone might confuse the two of them. "I recommend padding as well," she suggested, puffing out her chest slightly, "and a hair fall."

The inventor gave her a dour look. "I am aware of our differences of appearance, I assure you."

Alexia hid a grin and turned back to her husband. "You'll send them over land?"

Lord Maccon nodded. Then he looked to the clockmaker. "Monsieur?"

"Trouvé," interjected his wife helpfully.

The clockmaker twinkled at them both. "I shall head home, I think. Perhaps the others would care to accompany me in that general direction?"

Channing and Madame Lefoux nodded. Floote, as ever, had very little reaction to this turn of events. But Alexia thought she detected a gleam of pleasure in his eyes.

Monsieur Trouvé turned back to Alexia, took her hand, and kissed the back of it gallantly. His whiskers tickled. "It has been a pleasure to make your acquaintance, Lady Maccon. Most enjoyable, indeed."

Lord Maccon looked on in shock. "You are referring to my wife, are you not?"

The Frenchman ignored him, which only endeared him further to Alexia.

"And you as well, Monsieur Trouvé. We must continue our acquaintance sometime in the not too distant future."

"I wholeheartedly agree."

Alexia turned back to her faintly sputtering husband. "And we shall go by sea?"

He nodded again.

"Good." His wife grinned. "I will have you all to myself. I still have a lot to yell at you about."

"And here I thought we were due for a honeymoon."

"Does that mean quite the same thing to werewolves?"

"Very droll, wife."

It wasn't until much later that Lord and Lady Maccon returned to the topic of a certain infant-inconvenience. They had had to make their formal good-byes and escape out of Florence first. Morning found them secluded in the safety of an abandoned old barn of the large and drafty variety, at which point things had settled enough for them to undertake what passed, for Lord and Lady Maccon, as serious conversation.

Conall, being supernatural and mostly inured against the cold, spread his cloak gallantly upon a mound of moldy straw and lounged back upon it entirely bare and looking expectantly up at his wife.

"Very romantic, my dear," was Alexia's unhelpful comment.

His face fell slightly at that, but Lady Maccon was not so immune to her husband's charms that she could resist the tempting combination of big-muscled nudity and bashful expression.

She divested herself of her overdress and skirts.

He made the most delicious huffing noise when she cast herself, swanlike, on top of him. Well, perhaps more beached-sea-mammal-like than swanlike, but it had the desirous upshot of plastering most of the length of her body against most of the length of his. It took him a moment to recover from several stone of wife suddenly settled atop him, but only a moment, for then he began a diligent quest to rid her of all her remaining layers of clothing in as little time as possible. He unlaced the back and popped open the front of her corset, and stripped off her chemise with all the consummate skill of a lady's maid.

"Steady on there," protested Alexia mildly, though she was flattered by his haste.

As though influenced by her comment, which she highly doubted, he suddenly switched tactics and jerked her against him tightly. Burying his face in the side of her neck, he took a deep, shuddering breath. The movement lifted her upward as his wide chest expanded. She felt almost as though she were floating.

Then he rolled her slightly off him and, incredibly gently, pulled off her bloomers and began stroking over her slightly rounded belly.

"So, a soul-stealer, is that what we're getting?"

Alexia wriggled slightly, trying to get him back into his customary, rather more forceful handling. She would never admit it out loud, of course, but she enjoyed it when he became enthusiastically rough. "One of the Roman tablets called it a Stalker of Skins."

He paused, glowering thoughtfully. "Na, still never heard of it. But, then, I'm na all that old."

"It certainly has the vampires in a tizzy."

"Following in its mother's footsteps already, the little pup. How verra charming." His big hands began moving optimistically in a northward direction.

"Now what are you about?" wondered his wife.

"I have some further reacquainting to do. Must evaluate size differentials," he insisted.

"I hardly see how you could tell the difference," pointed out his wife, "considering their oversubstantial nature to start with."

"Oh, I believe I am more than equal to the task."

"We all must have goals in life," agreed his wife, a slight tremor in her voice.

"And to determine all the new particulars, I must apply all the available tools in my repertoire." This comment apparently indicated Conall intended to switch and use his mouth rather than his hands.

Alexia, it must be admitted, was running out of both token protests and the ability to breathe regularly. And since her husband's mouth was occupied, and even a werewolf shouldn't talk with his mouth full, she determined that was the end of their conversation.

So it proved to be the case, for some time at least.

extras

Meet the Author

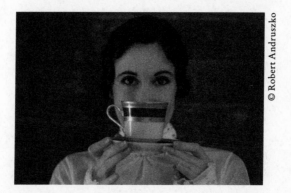

Ms. Carriger began writing in order to cope with being raised in obscurity by an expatriate Brit and an incurable curmudgeon. She escaped small-town life and inadvertently acquired several degrees in higher learning. Ms. Carriger then traveled the historic cities of Europe, subsisting entirely on biscuits secreted in her handbag. She now resides in the Colonies, surrounded by fantastic shoes, where she insists on tea imported directly from London. She is fond of teeny-tiny hats and tropical fruit. Find out more about Ms. Carriger at www.gailcarriger.com.

interview

Have you always known that you wanted to be a writer?

Actually, I'm still not entirely convinced I am one. I seem to have stumbled upon authordom inadvertently. I'm not complaining—never that—just startled.

When you aren't writing, what do you like to do in your spare time?

Drink tea. Although, come to think on it, I do that while I'm writing as well. Truth be told, eating, reading, sleeping, and breathing occupy a considerable amount of my time (generally in that order and often all at the same time).

Who/what would you consider to be your influences?

Jane Austen, P. G. Wodehouse, Gerald Durrell, a tea obsessed expatriate British mum, years of historical study, and a lifetime of BBC costume dramas have all played pivotal roles in Alexia's inception.

Soulless has such a clever melding of alternate history, romance, and the supernatural. How did you derive the idea for this novel?

I knew I wanted to write urban fantasy, and there's one thing I've never been able to understand in the genre: if immortals were mucking about, wouldn't they have been mucking about for a very long time? A speculation arose: what if all those strange and unexplainable bends in history were the result of supernatural interference? At which point I asked myself, what's the weirdest most eccentric historical phenomenon of them all? Answer: the Great British Empire. Clearly, one tiny little island could only conquer half the known world with supernatural aid. Those absurd Victorian manners and ridiculous fashions were obviously dictated by vampires. And, without a doubt, the British army regimental system functioned on werewolf pack dynamics. Of course, as soon as I started scribbling away about a land of bustles and top hats, romance and comedy had to enter the fray. I mean to say, bustles! Then I tossed nineteenth-century science into the mix and realized that if the Victorians were studying vampires and werewolves (which they would do, if they knew about them), not to mention developing weapons against them, technology would have evolved differently. Enter a sprinkling of steampunk, and suddenly, I was juggling more subgenres than Ivy has ugly hats! But then again, you can never have too many hats.

Do you have a favorite character? If so, why?

I'm torn between Professor Lyall and Floote. I have a little bit of a thing for capable and efficient gentlemen with quiet humors and calm dispositions.

What adventures can we look forward to seeing Alexia in next?

I shall say only that Alexia has always wanted to travel by dirigible . . .

Finally, if you had the opportunity to have tea with Lord Maccon, Alexia, or Lord Akeldama, who would you choose and why?

Oh, Lord Akeldama without a doubt. Alexia and I should never get along—we are far too much alike—and Lord Maccon hasn't any manners to speak of. Now, Lord Akeldama may be outrageous, but he's a charming conversationalist, and he knows such fascinating things.